BACK BAY METROPOLITAN HOSPITAL— WHERE NOT ONLY THE PATIENTS WERE SICK

The hospital was dying. The staff knew it, the patients sensed it—and no one knew how to save it.

The hospital doctors decided that only radical action would do—the unthinkable action of a strike.

And now only one group of dedicated professionals— nurses—stood between those in desperate need of the healing arts and the awesome array of afflictions threatening them at every hour of the day and night.

This would be these professionals' ultimate time of testing, of decision, of truth—as each had to meet challenges that meant the difference between life and death, and dealt with desires from which none were immune. . . .

THE NURSES

"Admirers of the author's *The Interns* will find themselves on familiar ground . . . unflagging interest . . . lightning speed."—*Publishers W~~~~*

THE NURSES

Richard Frede

AN ONYX BOOK

NEW AMERICAN LIBRARY

PUBLISHER'S NOTE

This novel is a work of fiction. Names, characters, places, and incidents
either are the product of the author's imagination or are used fictitiously,
and any resemblance to actual persons, living or dead, events, or locales
is entirely coincidental.

To two of the very caring
Emily Chandler and Kay Slyne
and with love to my mother
Helene
and my sons
Ari and Dov
all three of whom did such a good job
of caring for me while I was writing this novel

Acknowledgments

In the course of my research for *The Nurses*, I have been fortunate to enjoy the specialized knowledge, cooperation, and friendship of a number of people, all of whom deserve my considerable thanks:

Marsha Adams; RN; Tina Addison, RN, BS; Marge Andrews, RN; Robin Barnes, MD; Lisa Bean, RN; Jeffrey Boxer, MD; Bruce Brodkin, MD; Victoria Brownstone, RN, BS; Jane Burke, RN, BSN; Paul Carey; Irving E. Chase, MD; Jennifer Chau, *Boston Globe;* Mary Connaughton, RN, MS; Carole Connor, RN, CEN; Lieutenant Ronald Conway, BCPD; Robert Cronin, *Boston Herald;* Janet Crimlisk, RN, MS; Peggy D'Angelo, RN, BS; Lynn Davis, RN, MS; Gerald DeBonis, MD; Meg Doherty, RN, MS; John Van N. Dorr III; Merton Dyer; Luise M. Erdmann; Warren Geier; M. Patricia Gibbons, RN, MS; Robert Grassi, MD; Allan Green, MD; Janet Green, RN; Sheila Levenseler, RN, MS; Tony Lloyd; Anne Mahoney, RN, MS; Nicholas N. Marshall; James Meath, MD; Deputy Superintendent Martin Mulkern, BCPD; Douglas A. McIninch; Argyle McIntyre, MD; Loretta McLaughlin, *Boston Globe;* Nancy Neble, RN, MS; Pat Newcomb, RN; Jeff Paster, RN, BS; Jean Petrallia, RN, BS; David Scott Phillips; Jan Pubiello, RN, BS; Francis X. Quinlan; David Rosenbloom; Jean Rosenthal, MD; Charles J. Seigel, MD; Flo Singer, RN, BS; Eileen Taft, RN; Edward B. Twitchell, MD; Janice Usinger, RN; Don Vincola; and Tania Wilcke.

I owe special thanks to Anne G. Hargreaves, RN, MS, CNAA, FAAN; Elaine Aresty, RNC, MSN, ANP; Julian Aroesty, MD; and Emily Chandler, RN, MS, MDiv; and to Gerard Van der Leun, my editor, and Mitch Douglas, my agent.

And most especially I wish to thank Kay Slyne, RN, BS, who was with me from the beginning of my research and who counseled me during the four years of writing.

R.F.

Contents

Characters

Jamaal
Walker
Miller Woods

Intensive Care Unit

Staff: Tim Holbrook—Head Nurse; NSA Executive
        Committee
      Nan Lassitter—Nurse
      Aaron Silver—Senior Resident
Patients: Mr. Emerson
      Mr. Improta

Medical Floor Three

Staff: Marilyn Barnitska—Nurse
      Debby Fluelling—Nurse
      Audrey Rosenfeld—Head Nurse
      Lucius Schoonoler—Doctor
      Coralee Wafford—Nurse
      Ned Willard—Resident
Patients: Mrs. Armstrong
      Betty Bowen
      Chanda
      Mr. Emerson
      Jan Fox (Mrs. Quimbley)
      Mrs. Gehl
      Mr. Hines
      Mr. Improta
      Ralph Malamet
      Mrs. Parker
      Mrs. Pretty
      Percy Stevens
      Mr. Toby
      Dom Volante
      Mr. Wu
      Russell Younker

Medical Floor Seven

Staff: Nan Lassitter—Nurse
      Selma Pushkin—Head Nurse
      Liz Swanzey—Nurse

Patients: Mr. Larkin
          Mrs. Shaughnessy

Administrative Nurses & House Officers

Molly Chang—Assistant Director of Psychiatry; NSA
  Executive Committee
Norman Childs—Resident
Trevor Davis—Surgical Resident
Sheila Farhm—Intern
Midge Kelly—Surgical Supervisor, Nursing
Elin Maki—Adult Nurse Practitioner, NSA Executive
  Committee
Day O'Meara—Medical Supervisor, Nursing
Selma Pushkin—President, NSA; Head Nurse, Med Seven
Judd—Psychiatric Resident
Scotty McGettigan—Chief Resident; President, ARI
Anita Rounds—ARI Executive Committee; Cardiology
  Resident
Aaron Silver—Senior Resident, Med ICU Five
Diana Vezzina—Acting Head Nurse, Med Four
Ned Willard—Resident
Mozard Wills—Intern, ARI Executive Committee

Administrative & Senior Physician Staff

Bennett Chessoff—Hospital Director
Merton Geier—Chief of Staff
Mildred Isaacs—MD, OBGYN
Donald Kay—Public Relations Director
Dorothea Kullgren—Director of Nursing Services
Dr. Quinlan—MD, New Wing Five
Lucius Schoonoler—MD, New Wing Five, Med Three
Howard Sylvus—Chief Counsel

Other Patients

Mr. Forster, Jessy Gladdens, Mr. Herman, Miss McDonough

Security

Jerry Cleveland, Reynold, Ginny Shiffland

Others

Maurice Allen—Harlem Wiseapples Captain
Jackie Bader—Missy's mother
Mrs. Bradely—Mr. Emerson's sister
Mr. & Mrs. Briggs—Natalie's parents
Ron Casey—stockbroker and friend of Trevor Davis
Donna—friend of Trevor Davis
Nell Dudley—SWAT negotiator
Lionel Emerson—Mr. Emerson's son
Mrs. Emerson—Mr. Emerson's wife
Flynn—Valerie Holbrook's attorney
Warren Gates—Tim Holbrook's attorney
Andrew Harrelson—Suffolk Superior Court Judge
Robert Higby—accused rapist of Jessy Gladdens
Jason Holbrook—Tim Holbrook's son
Valerie Holbrook—Tim Holbrook's ex-wife
Archie Johnson—Boston Red Sox fielder
Josie—friend of Trevor Davis
Lynn Keating—*Boston Eagle* columnist
Lieutenant Kincaid—SWAT commander
Sergeant Kinney—Boston police officer
Hal Levy—third-year medical student
Charles Maki—Elin Maki's ex-husband
Michelle McCabe—*Boston Post* medical editor
Monk McGuire—Baltimore Orioles pitcher
Gardner McIninch—Massachusetts Supreme Judicial Court
    Judge
Jorge Olivera—BBMH laundry worker and translator
Jimbo O'Meara—Day O'Meara's husband
Penny—friend of Ralph Malamet
Nicholas Prudhomme—assistant district attorney
Quentin—Jamaal's brother
Mr. Shaughnessy—Mrs. Shaughnessy's husband
Shawn—mayor of Boston
Arlene Sherk—pediatrics social worker
John Shiffland—Ginny's brother
Paul Squires—DJ and friend of Trevor Davis
Dr. Start—psychoanalyst
Oren Tolman—friend of Nan Lassitter
Dr. Arthur Truell—friend of Audrey Rosenfeld

Preface

The troubles did not appear suddenly. The troubles were there all along. They were inherited from year to year by the residents and interns. They were inherited from shift to shift by the nurses.

The nurses were compelled to treat the hospital as both adversary and patient.

For that reason the nurses had never struck. A nurse does not walk away from a patient.

Even in death the nurse remains with the patient. She cleans and tags and wraps the patient before walking away.

But both as professionals and as women (generally), the graduate nurses of the previous decade or so no longer saw themselves as handmaidens to the all-knowing male (generally) physician, but as colleagues with common determinations and interacting roles and sometimes even identical tasks.

And so when the patient was the hospital itself, the nurses administering to it would have to go through yet another reassessment of themselves and of their relationship to the patient.

Meanwhile, the patient was dying.

ONE

Time Out

1

IT WAS A FEW MINUTES after nine in the evening, late for the day nurses celebrating a birthday at one of the tables in Fritz Moriarty's Piano Bar, but early, Molly Chang decided, for the two baseball players appraising her and the other ladies from their high seats at the tap. Early, Molly thought, in what would be the gents' evening-long campaign to get laid.

Behind the ballplayers, a low mirror ran the length of the bar, reflecting the glasses and bottles standing against it and fragments of customers facing it. Dark wood paneling completed the wall above the mirror, where other faces looked out from framed photographs. Most of the faces were recognizable and all had been photographed with Fritz in this room—actors and actresses, professional athletes, musicians, local and national politicians, presidential aspirants and one who had become president. All had enjoyed Fritz and his music and bar, a watering hole that was socially inclusive. Everyone could come, everyone was welcome. The decor was Boston traditional—borrowed from both the Irish neighborhood bar and the gentlemen's private club.

Fritz was only into his first set, but even though it was a weeknight the room was already crowded. Reservations at Fritz's Piano Bar were not accepted. But a favored table had been kept free for the six nurses from Back Bay Metropolitan Hospital until they had come upstairs from dinner. Fritz had been nearly killed two years before when he had been mugged walking home from his restaurant and bar and a trauma team at Back Bay Met had saved his life.

One of the nurses on that team had been Nan Lassitter. Molly looked over at her, inspired by the licentious intensity focused on her by Monk McGuire, the Baltimore Oriole pitcher

19

seated at the bar. The home team, the Red Sox, was represented by Archie Johnson, the noted hitter. Both gents were All-Stars. But whatever McGuire was throwing at her from across the room, Nan was not catching. She was oblivious to his attention and to Molly's glance and to everything outside herself. She was even oblivious to Selma Pushkin's narration of the day's events on Med Seven—an All-Star accomplishment in itself.

Molly was thirty-two years old and had two titles, psychiatric nurse clinician and assistant supervisor of nursing, Psychiatric Services. In the latter role she helped oversee Back Bay Met's psychiatric nurses in all their roles throughout the hospital. In the former role she provided psychiatric liaison and support for the regular RNs throughout the hospital. She did not see patients herself, but she helped the nurses with problems they had in dealing with patients or patients' families or with their own professional attitudes and relationships. In that capacity she probably knew more about her colleagues at the table—both personally and professionally—than any one of them knew about the others. But Nan Lassitter's sporadic preoccupation through dinner and then her withdrawal once they'd come up to the bar had left Molly without a clue. Not that the staff didn't have private lives and personal problems of which Molly would be entirely ignorant, it was just that this sort of behavior was uncharacteristic of Nan. When she had a problem she fought it and made no secret of the battle.

Nan had spent two years on the ER as a surgical nurse but had transferred to a medical intensive care unit so that her responsibilities and duties would be much more hers alone and of much more significance to the patient. She had been on the unit for two years now. She was twenty-five and single. She smiled easily and with such warmth that women trusted her and men immediately adored her, imagining all kinds of wanton intimacies—such as, Molly observed, McGuire was so nakedly doing at the bar.

Nan Lassitter was thinking about death. She was up on the ICU and she was trapped there with death, an invisible, odorless presence, an invasive presence that she had suddenly this morning found she could no longer tolerate.

She had been adjusting Mr. Emerson's monitor lines. He was not, strictly speaking, her responsibility. He was not her patient. He had been her patient during a previous stay on the unit and she had come to have a warm feeling for him and for his family, but when, several days before, he had come back on the unit, she had refused him as a patient.

This particular morning she had noticed that Mr. Emerson's monitor lines had gotten caught beneath his body, and as she had stopped to free them, her fingers began to tremble.

By afternoon Nan had become preoccupied with feelings of grief and an anxiety for which she could find no source or focus.

Molly Chang was ordering a cognac.

Nan had been drinking white wine, and not very much of that, but she said, "I'll have one of those, too."

She had had little experience with hard liquor and she did not like its taste or its effects. It tasted and felt like liquid anesthesia. And that was why she had suddenly decided to order one.

When it came, the drink's effect was swift and liberating.

Molly saw Nan smile.

Nan felt released from all the anguish of the day. She had had a sudden objectivity, a sudden clarity, about what was happening to her and why and how she could deal with it.

She would resign, leave nursing.

After five years as a professional she would get away from all the terrible things, away from her helplessness.

Molly saw Nan become spirited and leave her cognac unfinished.

Elin Maki, birthday girl and nurse practitioner, was celebrating the beginning of her thirty-fourth year. She was laughing and happy and that astonished her. Something special was going on inside her. And it wasn't the drinks. It had been going on all day.

Molly nodded at Elin. "You see, there *is* life after divorce. It just takes awhile to rediscover."

"And how long did it take you?"

"About ten minutes," Molly said. "But then, I was the one who *wanted* the divorce."

Elin had not wanted hers. "Yours was a long time ago."

"Oh yes." Molly thought about it. "Eight years. I'm very practiced at being divorced."

"How long were you married?" Elin had been married for almost seven years.

"Also about ten minutes. It was more of a brief phenomenon than a marriage. Or it was a cliché. I was the young nurse who fell in love with the doctor. A shrink," she said to Nan, who would not know. "It was because of him I got into psychiatric work. After about three months together, I figured anyone married to him was probably crazy and needed help. So I went to another shrink for some objectivity. I ended up in psychotherapy. As the patient. Then I went on to graduate studies. As a nurse."

Another nurse, a pal of Selma Pushkin's from Massachusetts General, came over from another table and pushed a chair in by Selma. Molly observed that finally the party was going well. Conversation was rampant. Five or six conversations, Molly thought, and there were only seven at the table. There was a general cheerfulness at being in each other's company. At first, predictably, Elin had held back. Elin hadn't wanted the party at all. And then Nan had been silent and away.

Elin leaned over to Molly and said, "Thanks. I'm really enjoying this."

"Had to do it. You were becoming a shut-in, you know."

Elin nodded. "It was scary. Anything but being at work. Or in my own apartment. Was scary. It was just safer to sit there alone, not go out."

"What were you afraid of?"

Elin grinned. "Let up, Moll, huh? It's after hours."

"Just curious. My line of work, I'm always curious. That's why I've gotten so far in my profession."

The nurse from the General, who was a little high, said, "If you're at Back Bay Met, how can you figure you've gotten far in your profession?"

"Lady," Molly said, "you're going to have to defend yourself."

"With boxing gloves," Day O'Meara said. She was the nursing supervisor and coordinator responsible for staffing on all of Back Bay Met's medical floors. She was also thirty-five years old and, in her estimation, several years pregnant. She put down a cigarette she was about to light. The number of nurses, including herself, who still smoked continued to shock and surprise her. She was down to four today. Four too many. She finished her liqueur and stood. Her dress ballooned out over her pregnancy. "Got to split, ladies. Before the fisticuffs commence. My condition, you know."

It was also Jimbo, her husband, the computer whiz, out in their comfy house in Dedham, where he would be waiting angrily until she got home safe with her passenger. He didn't want her working at all at this time, much less gallivanting around Boston in the wee hours of the morning.

She looked at her watch. Twenty after nine. Jimbo was right. Much too late for her.

Fritz was playing standards, setting them in a Bach-like style. In spite of the music and conversation Elin, nodding as if she heard and understood what was being said to her, was listening to herself as, diagnostically, she took her own recent history and tried to figure out the mystery that was going on inside her: to wit, she felt so good today after feeling so lousy for so long. Since Charles had left her and divorced her. A year of that, the divorce now two months old.

She found herself hearing the words to the romantic songs Fritz was playing. She found herself looking around the room, looking at faces, men's faces, as she went through an emotional search of herself and then realized: *I feel free to be loved. All this time, even divorced, I must have been thinking I wasn't free, I still belonged to Charles. Even though he left me. Even though I haven't been with anyone for a year.*

Elin smiled at herself and tried to remember who it was, somewhere in mythology, who had been condemned to fall in love with the first person she encountered.

She felt quite that ready for love.

Molly settled into her second and last cognac. It was a treat. Nan was driving tonight and tomorrow morning. And Nan, happily, wasn't imbibing to any extent. Though that couldn't be said of the rest of the table.

Elin was glowing—from drink or from laughter or both. She was smiling as Selma Pushkin, the senior member among them by age and position, told a story. Selma was forty-two years old, head nurse on Med Seven, president of Back Bay Met's NSA (Nursing Services Alliance), the nurses' union, and wife of one and mother of two.

"So, well," Selma was saying, "Mrs. Shaughnessy, God should love her, was with us again. And last night she starts actively DTing and gets sent down to Psych for the duration. This morning Mr. Shaughnessy comes in with his Polaroid."

"Mr. Shaughnessy is a photographer?" Elin said.

"Mr. Shaughnessy is not a photographer. Mr. Shaughnessy suffers from that affliction that the police refer to as 'no visible means of support.' Mr. Shaughnessy toils not, neither does he spin. I myself believe Mr. Shaughnessy is a bookie, but that's none of my business."

Molly, in her comprehension of the entire scene, noted that Monk McGuire was still doing a heavy piece of admiration upon the person of Nan Lassitter and that Nan, listening to Selma, was unaware of it. As McGuire, the white pitcher from the Orioles, spent his regard on Nan, Archie Johnson, the black hitter from the Red Sox, was talking in one-way communication to his pal, advising him, Molly decided, somewhat like a corner man before his pugilist stands up again. Interesting, Molly thought. Black hitter, white pitcher.

McGuire looked as though he were ready to make a move on Nan but was restrained just now by Johnson. Restrained in order to benefit from a bit more expertise, a bit more detailed discussion of tactics.

Molly looked at Nan again. Quiet, contemplative, graceful Nan. She had such an abundance of stereotypical feminine traits.

Selma was saying, "So, Mr. Shaughnessy, then, has brought his Polaroid camera to Back Bay Metropolitan Hospital, to my floor, and it is not to photograph a photo finish. No. Mr. Shaughnessy has somehow learned that his wife is DTing. It is his intention to take pictures of her while she is DTing that he may show them to her, at some convenient time, before she takes another drink. That may or may not have proven to be an efficacious stratagem on his part, but I had to dissuade him from the project. On the grounds that it was an invasion of the patient's privacy.

"I had to be forceful to get through to him. He had some booze aboard himself. As a matter of professional assessment, he was looped. I thought he was going to hit me."

"That's because as a nurse you automatically inspire trust," Selma's friend from the General said.

"Then Mr. Shaughnessy said he wanted to show me his favorite photograph of Mrs. Shaughnessy. Fine. That's better than his taking a poke at me. It's a picture of her in their kitchen. Scotch bottles all over the place. You could get wiped out just looking at her, she's so boozed. And that's his favorite picture of her.''

"A touching memento," Molly said.

"Typical Back Bay," the nurse from the General said, commiserating with her less fortunate colleagues.

Molly was noticing that the two heroes at the bar, those large men with young faces and godlike, superphysical stances (I need to get fucked, Molly thought), were downing the large portions of beer that remained in their mugs.

Fucked, yes, Molly thought. Though neither of those two appealed to her as a plower. She needed an emotional relationship, a really *personal* relationship, to get *really* fucked. She believed that every seriously sexual woman needed to *get fucked* once a month, one time when the man just had her— all in physical necessity and selfish passion.

The rest of the time, though, the man should show tenderness, consideration, and as much knowledge as necessary to bring her to one or more orgasms.

Christ, Molly thought, I am *ripe*.

Why doesn't someone love me?

Because I have very high expectations.

Which may be self-protective, Moll, old girl, she said to herself.

She glanced at Monk McGuire and her companions at the table. She looked around the room, thought of other friends and acquaintances. We spend so much time yearning, Molly thought. Both men and women.

It was then that Bennett Chessoff, administrative director of Back Bay Metropolitan Hospital, entered and went to the bar.

Ah, thought Molly with considerable ambivalence, the answer to a maiden's prayer.

Selma's pal from the General was expressing the typical Boston-area nurse's attitude toward the nurses at Back Bay Met—a combination of admiration and disdain.

"You're a committed staff, I know," she was saying. "Up against insurmountable odds. But you don't experience a really *professional* role. You can't. In the jungle you can't reach your potential."

"Lady," Molly said, "in our jungle you reach your potential and exceed it. You have to."

2

A FEW MINUTES after nine in the evening. Hal Levy, a twenty-six-year-old third-year medical student, had just completed transferring some basic belongings from his room at Cambridge Medical School to his cubicle in a building two blocks from Back Bay Metropolitan. The cubicle would be his residence during the next six weeks while he did a double off-campus rotation in Psychiatry and Neurology. The building was of fairly recent construction. He had traveled there by cab and even in the limited illumination afforded by the streetlights he could see that it was, if only by contrast, an affluent presence among its neighbors.

Now two other medical students, a young man and a young woman who were also in temporary residence, joined Hal in his room.

Hal knew nothing of the hospital from personal experience. He had never been in this neighborhood before. What he knew of the hospital was that it was one of Cambridge's several teaching adjuncts and that it was tough and demanding and considered a prize internship and residency everywhere because when a doctor had completed an appointment at Back Bay Met, he or she had learned to deal with or at least recognize an astonishing range of medical problems.

"Most of it under impossible circumstances," Edgar said.

"You wouldn't *believe* the kinds of things that get short-supplied. That malfunction and don't get repaired," Sonia said.

"Or just aren't there," Edgar said.

Hal put on his thick glasses and studied his two colleagues. "Then how does the hospital function?"

"Who knows?" Edgar said.

"I think I'll walk over and have a look at it."

"Not a good idea," Sonia said.

"Why not?"

"She means walking over is not a good idea. Running over is a good idea."

Hal studied them again for some indication of humor or a put-on. "You're trying to scare the new boy, huh?"

Edgar said, "This is the highest crime area in the city. Fact of life."

"So you learn to be fast on your feet," Sonia said. "And fast in your head."

3

THE TELEPHONE IN the ER psych nurses' office rang. A nurse picked it up. The other nurse continued with paperwork—report sheets, assessments, proposed care plans.

"Psychiatry, Trina." She listened for a long time.

The other nurse could hear the caller's voice in harsh anger from time to time.

The office was furnished frugally with two worktables, some high-intensity gooseneck lamps that penetrated the darkness with small cones of light, a desk, a cot, and some file cabinets. The broad, single window, adjacent to the ER ambulance bays, looked out into the cobblestone courtyard of the Old Building. Directly across the courtyard was the Old Building wing that housed the pediatrics walk-in clinic on the first floor, above that two GYN floors, a mixed OBGYN floor, two OB floors (including a Neonatal Special Care Unit), and above those the pediatric floors—Children's Seven, Eight, Nine, and Ten.

When Trina finally spoke her voice was conversational. "Mrs. Quimbley, that is not the case, and you know it. Our arrangement was that I would get here early and I would reserve the time just for you. You and I have had that arrangement three times. Today was the third time I was here at two-thirty and you weren't here at all."

Trina listened for another moment. She was twenty-six years old and had been a psych nurse for almost four years. She was slim, attractive, engaging, compassionate, and tough-

minded and Molly Chang prized her, the best member of her
staff in a crisis, even though one of the youngest.

"Mrs. Quimbley, none of this is a matter for a conversation over the telephone. I want to discuss it with you
personally—"

Again she listened. Then she spoke in a firm voice. Vicki
Green, her partner on the shift, looked over.

Trina said, "Mrs. Quimbley, you have three options and
talking on the phone is not one of them. Talking on the phone
is not useful to you at this point. These are your options:
come in, don't come in, seek help elsewhere."

Trina listened, then said, "I hope you'll do that, Mrs.
Quimbley," and after waiting until Mrs. Quimbley disconnected, she hung up.

Vicki said, "Mrs. Quimbley?"

"The woman's depressed. Agitated. I don't know what
precipitated the condition. She called a few days ago and
asked to speak to a psych nurse. She got me. She's made
three different appointments with me and she hasn't kept one
of them."

"So now you threaten her with breaking off communication?"

"I haven't got an address for her or a telephone number.
I've no way of finding her and sending a social worker out to
her. I haven't gotten very far with her on the phone. She's
very guarded and defensive about herself. The priority now
isn't communication. The priority is to get her out from
wherever she is and to some help somewhere."

"Odd name Quimbley . . . There was a woman in a
novel—"

"Mrs. Quimbley in *The WASP Princess*. Decent, hard-
working, penniless Mrs. Quimbley. I've been thinking a lot
about her. I wonder if *our* Mrs. Quimbley is sending us a
message with the name."

"Such as?"

Trina shrugged. "It *is* an odd name. I can't find it anywhere except in that book. Mrs. Quimbley, always the victim."

"The princess' victim. And she never notices what she
does to Mrs. Quimbley."

"Pain, injury, and destruction to poor, lower-class Mrs.
Quimbley. All from that toxic, rich little bitch."

"*Everything* bad happens to Mrs. Quimbley."

"Yes," Trina said, "that's it, everything."

"Could your Mrs. Quimbley be identifying with the novel's Mrs. Quimbley? Taking her name?"

"Yes. I've been wondering about it, anyway."

"Pretty strong identification."

"Yes."

"The woman who wrote it," Vicki said.

"Jan Fox. I remember seeing her on Carson. Back when I was in high school. The boys were all infatuated with her. Brains and body, a centerfold."

"I'd forgotten about that."

"She was everywhere for a while. In print or pictorials, television . . . An odd thing about Mrs. Quimbley."

"Yes?"

"I mean, an odd thing about the portrait of her in the book. There was no rage. Mrs. Quimbley had no rage at what was happening to her."

4

"TRINA WANTED TO be here," Molly said to Elin, "but she couldn't get anyone to switch with her."

"What about Betty? Was Betty asked?"

Elin had been head nurse on Med Three for two years. Betty Bowen had preceded her in that position for a full twenty-seven years before her retirement, and Elin had been her protégée since she had come on Med Three as a new grad nurse. After two years as head nurse, Elin had taken a two-year leave of absence in order to upgrade herself to nurse practitioner. Now, in Primary Care Clinic, Elin saw patients on her own and had a number of responsibilities formerly restricted to doctors.

"I asked her," Molly said. "She sends you her love and says she'll see you soon enough."

"Mysterious."

"I thought so."

*   *   *

Audrey Rosenfeld, who was twenty-seven years old and had spent almost seven of those years as a nurse and four in college to become one, intercepted a look from one of the customers at the bar and stared back at him coolly. But he smiled and indicated with a gesture that it was not her attention he wanted but that of Nan, seated next to her.

Audrey said, "Nan, Trevor Davis is making signals at you." She nodded toward the bar.

Davis was in the company of two other men also in their late twenties. Nan smiled at Davis, who nodded happily. Nan turned back to her own table.

Audrey said, "There's someone I can't stand to see on the floor."

"Trevor? He's okay. We worked together when I was an OR nurse. He's a good surgeon."

"He's a lousy human being. He upsets patients. I think he gets off on it."

"I've only seen him in the OR with a patient. He's good, relaxed, never seems in a hurry, even in a crisis."

"Yes," Audrey said, "I bet he enjoys his work. For the wrong reasons."

"Ladies." Trevor Davis stood behind them.

"Dr. Davis," Audrey said.

Davis ignored her. "Nan, I'm at the bar with a couple of friends. Paul Squires, the DJ?"

"Oh, yes."

"And my college roommate. Went wrong. Became a stock-broker. Would you like to join us?"

"No, I'm here with friends. Thanks, though."

Davis looked around the table. "What is this, a pickles convention?" He laughed and squeezed Nan's shoulder and walked away.

"Dr. Davis, the eminent cutup," Audrey said.

Nan laughed. "Is it just Trevor or do you feel that way about all surgeons?"

Ouch, Audrey thought, though Nan wouldn't have known she had placed a needle in a nerve, or even that she had placed a needle at all.

Well, Audrey thought, I disliked Trevor Davis a long time before I even met the doc. So the one doesn't have anything to do with the other.

*   *   *

Bennett Chessoff was a presence, both as a man and as a political figure, a Boston personality used to personal media attention and to using that attention for his own ends, and Selma Pushkin was commenting on him for the benefit of her pal from the General.

"He'll charm the pants off you if he wants to," Selma was saying.

"Cold," Elin said. "Brilliant. But cold. I like a little warmth. When I take off my pants."

"I'd say manipulative," Selma said. "Not cold. Manipulative."

"Crafty," Molly said.

"He's a sonofabitch," Elin said.

"I think he's a cat's-paw for City Hall," Selma said.

"He fills a lot of slots," Molly agreed. I wonder if he fills a lot of sluts, too. Or slits, she thought.

"I've had to deal with him a lot as president of NSA," Selma said. "You've got to be wary of him. It took me a long time to learn that. You've got to always be wary of him. He's invisible when he's doing things to you."

Molly glanced over at him. Bennett, as if he were aware that the conversation was about him, nodded to her.

The coolest, most opportunistic man I've ever known, Molly thought. And effective.

She nodded back. She did not mention to her friends that she had, that very afternoon, accepted an invitation to dinner from Bennett Chessoff for the following evening.

Two other men had come in with Bennett and were in conversation with him at the bar.

"Somehow it doesn't look like a social occasion, does it?" Elin said.

"No, it doesn't. Not at all," Selma said.

"Who are the other two?" the nurse from the General said.

"Donald Kay, public relations director," Molly said. "And Howard Sylvus, general counsel to the hospital."

"Odd," Selma said.

"Not so odd," her friend from the General said, "if you have labor problems brewing."

"Labor problems?" Selma said.

"Staff problems. The word around the General is that the

interns and residents at Back Bay Met are unhappy with their
lot.''

"So what's new?"

"They intend to do something about it.''

"Really?"

"Some sort of job action.''

"Oh, that,'' Selma said. "Happens every year this time.''

"Spring comes and the juices rise,'' Molly said.

"The senior house officers are going to be leaving in a few
weeks. To go into private practice. So they figure they'll have
a shot at changing a few things before they go.''

"Oh. I got the idea it was more serious than that.''

"If it is,'' Selma said, "it hasn't come to my attention. I'll
tell you what *is* going on, though. ARI—that's the house
officers' organization, the Association of Residents and
Interns—this time of year every year ARI goes to Bennett with
a list of suggestions and grievances. Bennett says that he and
his Director's Council will give every item careful consideration
and he thanks them. What's going on now is the silent stage.
Administration is just waiting for the senior HOs to go.''

"And then Back Bay Met stays the same way for another
year,'' Molly said.

"No,'' Audrey said, "it gets worse for another year.''

"At any rate,'' Selma said, "ARI and Administration are
just playing games with each other.'' She looked over at the
triumvirate at the bar. Howard Sylvus' presence made her
uneasy. She suspected the three of them had just come from a
meeting—a meeting that had taken place after regular hours—
and that the meeting had to do with her hospital and therefore, in one way or another, with her nurses.

5

HAL LEVY DID not run to the hospital, he jogged—a conces-
sion to the warning he had received. But warnings were not a
part of Hal's life. He came from a small town in Connecticut
where safety was so complete and so profound that it per-

vaded his view of his immediate world even after he had gone away to college and medical school.

The staff referred to the two principal structures of the hospital as the Old Building and the New Wing. They both fronted on the same wide street, Tremaine Avenue, and together rose commandingly above the tenements that surrounded them. The New Wing rose six floors and the Old Building, ten.

Hal stood on the other side of Tremaine and looked at them. The two buildings bothered his sensibilities and his sense of logic. They were built wall to wall, but it was as if the architect of the New Wing had refused to acknowledge the presence of the structure that had preceded his own. The surface of the New Wing was all green and silvery aluminum punctuated by spaces of glass. The Old Building, constructed in the first quarter of the century, presented a facade of slabs of gray stone. Through a large archway, the Old Building's access from Tremaine Avenue, Hal could see part of a cobblestone courtyard. An ambulance, its rooflights flashing, turned from Tremaine and sedately passed through the archway.

Hal crossed the avenue and entered the New Wing through a phalanx of glass doors.

He was in a large and airy lobby. A man on crutches removed them from under his arms and manipulated them so that he could ease himself down on a bench. The benches ran along the walls and were covered with a smooth bright orange plastic material. In places the material had been cut or ripped open and the yellow sponge of the interior extruded.

A house officer in white pants and a brightly striped shirt, a black beeper at his side, walked by Hal. A self-absorbed black nurse, her hands in the pockets of her white dress, walked over to the elevators. There were security guards and city police. The guards carried batons at their side. The police had batons and black revolvers. Hal had never gotten used to guns in hospitals.

An elderly black man walked slowly toward a reception and information counter, his body determinedly upright. A young, white male, wearing a knee-length white coat and jeans and old moccasins, strode by. A young Hispanic woman hurried to the elevators.

A young Hispanic couple stood nearby. They spoke rapid, emotional Spanish. The man kissed the woman and attempted to leave, but she held him and spoke even more rapidly, her head against his chest.

A surprising amount of activity for after nine at night, Hal thought.

An elderly black man, walking as if with a limp, was stopped by another black man a few years his junior. The younger man said, "Allen! What you doin' here?" ˉ

"I goes stroke."

A young woman stopped a few feet away from Hal. She seemed to be looking at him, but her eyes were focused beyond him and her face was vacant. Her hair was curly and dark brown, her skin a light brown. She was slender and motionless. There was a dignity to her face, and the face might have been beautiful as well, Hal thought, were there any expression in it at all.

She came over and sat down next to him. She looked across the room when she said, "You a doctuh?"

"I'm a student. A medical student."

"Fixin' t'be uh doctuh." The young woman nodded. Still looking across the room, she said, "You want to come home with me?"

Hal said nothing. Her voice had surprising strength to it in spite of the lack of expression in her face and body. Hal did not know what to say to undo the situation.

"I speakin' to you, you there fixin-t'be-uh-doctuh. You want to come home with me?"

"Thank you, no," Hal said.

She nodded. "I needs a stickterectomy. My ovaries hurt."

She remained close beside Hal for another few seconds, then she got up and walked away, walked very slowly, still nodding to herself. She went to the glass doors. The one in front of her slid open automatically and she went out onto the street, off toward the darkness.

A young, black father sat down nearby. He was holding and talking to his infant. The baby made excited sounds of pleasure—"*Eee-eeeeee!*"— and the father laughed.

Hal had never been in an environment like this, where most of the people were of other races, other colors, where he was a minority because he was white.

A petite woman in a police uniform, her cap tipped back on her blond hair, was stopped by a man a few feet from Hal. She turned with her back to Hal, the butt of her revolver face-on to him, a blank face like that of the young woman who had just left him.

A cab drew up outside and a man got out. He was immaculately dressed in a tailored suit, his topcoat neatly folded over one arm. His other arm was raised to his head, where his hand pressed a blood-drenched handkerchief to his scalp. The man entered the lobby and spoke with the small, blond police officer and then went to some swinging doors at the other side of the lobby. Hal had a glimpse of the shiny metal and antiseptic white of the ER floor where he would begin work the next afternoon with someone named Trina Frankian, a psych nurse.

There was sudden laughter from within an elevator as its doors opened. And sudden, unrelated laughter from the reception and information counter.

A portly, black female medical technician steered her body across the lobby.

"Maureen Halleran, four-seven-six-one, Maureen Halleran, four-seven-six-one," a metallic voice declared from a speaker.

The police officer, her cap still tipped back, crossed the lobby again, this time with a sandwich and a carton of milk in her hands.

From very near him Hal heard the small, sharp, electronic voice of a radio transmission: "Spanish interpreter, Surgical Unit. Spanish Interpreter, Surgical Unit." A walkie-talkie, its antenna extended, was in the hand of a black police sergeant. He had short, gray hair and wore a leather jacket. His equipment belt hung below the jacket, the heavy revolver pulling it down at his hip.

Hal began to feel a little uneasy about doing psych in the ER, working with the craziness people brought in off the streets rather than working with physical problems.

It was time to hit the books again. He went back outside. It seemed as if the streetlights had been turned down. The darkness seemed darker than before. He paused, hesitant about the two blocks back to the students' building.

6

TRINA FRANKIAN HAD been called to one of the two psych rooms at the back of the ER.

The patient was seated. He was white, about thirty, sinewy, his black hair long and unkempt, though he was otherwise neat, shaven, and clean.

Two cops were with him, one black, one white. "Don't get close," the older cop, the black cop, said. "He does things sudden."

There were two remarkable details about the patient. He sat erect, but his body was moved from within as if it contained ocean-force waves that proceeded from his shoulders through his torso into his legs, finally being kicked out of his body by a convulsion in his ankles.

Then there was the intensity of his gaze. It was fixed somewhere, not in his real surroundings. He was smiling.

A wave rolled down through his body. A stifled cry emerged from him. He hunched his shoulders and jerked upright. Something restrained him.

"You got him cuffed," Trina said.

"He still does things sudden," the white cop said.

"We got him down from the edge of a roof," the black cop said.

"What was he doing at the edge of a roof?"

"He was yelling and screaming."

"What was he yelling and screaming?"

"I don't know," the senior cop said. "I don't speak Portuguese."

"He's Portuguese?"

"What the people work with him say. He works in a restaurant. In the kitchen. Guy's slowed down a lot. Back there, when we got him down from the roof, he was trying to kill us."

"With a weapon?"

"With his bare hands. He don't look like much, but he's strong as hell."

"Quick, too," the younger cop said, touching an inflamed and puffy cheek.

The senior cop went on. "His name's Texeira, Alphonso Texeira. Doesn't speak English. Suddenly flipped out. Workin' at the sink, started screamin' and throwin' dishes at people. Went up on the roof and kept screamin'."

"How did you get him down?"

"It was damn scary, him standin' on the edge there. He wasn't lookin' behind him, and that's how we come to get him."

The younger cop was looking at the marks on the walls, all of them at about the same level, where patients had beaten the walls with their fists or hands. Except for the marks, the room was fresh and clean. It was furnished with a padded table bolted to the floor so that it could not be overturned by the thrashing of a patient restrained to it. There was a cabinet containing leather restraints but nothing else. There was no glass in the room and no water. It was the larger of the two ER psych rooms, the prisoner room when one was necessary, for it could accommodate a patient and two guards. There were two wooden chairs for the guards. Nothing else.

Trina went to the wall phone outside the psych room. The door opened outward so that it could not be barricaded from within and so that no one could hide behind it inside. She got the ER triage nurse who would have seen her patient when he was brought in. "Anything on Alphonso Texeira?"

"No medical history here," the triage nurse said. "No observable Organic symptoms. Vital signs elevated. Not severely. Oriented times zilch. As you can see."

"They speak Portuguese on the Cape Verde Islands, don't they?"

"I think so," the triage nurse said.

"A couple of Cape Verdians work in the laundry, I don't know what shifts. Give 'em a call over there? See if one of them's available for translation? And call me a standby."

"That's one Cape Verdian, one standby guard," the triage nurse said. "Missy no wan anything from Column C?"

"Thanks," Trina said. She hung up and went back into the psych room.

She looked at her patient and then moved close to him.

"Hello. I'm Trina. What is your name?" She waited. "Is your name Alphonso?"

The man's body stopped moving. His lips compressed. His gaze remained far away. Trina repeated her statement and question. The lips remained compressed, the gaze fixed. But tears spilled from his eyes and his body remained still.

Trina's advisory voice said to her, The patient is grossly psychotic.

We'll see, Trina thought.

A potential keg of dynamite, the voice cautioned.

We'll see, Trina thought. He had been in no way violent since he had been with her. He had responded to her voice, and his name, with tears and stillness.

"Take the cuffs off," Trina said.

"If you say. But I don't know."

"I say. No one likes being restrained."

"You're the doctor," the senior cop said.

"The nurse," Trina said.

"Yeah," the senior cop said, getting his keys from his belt. "Well, I try not to make social distinctions. In my line of work you're not supposed to."

The younger cop said to Trina, "Aren't you gonna get a shrink in? I mean, this guy's nuts."

"Shrinks don't come to the ER very often. They see patients in clinic and sometimes on the floors. And on the psych floor, of course. Between you and me, shrinks wouldn't see most of the patients we see on the ER. Us psych nurses. On this floor we do the interventions and we do the evaluations."

"You call for a standby?"

"Hi, Ginny," Trina said.

The woman was thirty years old and had been a security guard for five years. She was strong and intelligent and Trina was glad she had drawn her.

Trina said to the police officers, "Thanks for your work. We'll take it from here."

The senior officer nodded. "Okay." He didn't sound certain. "Good luck." He and his partner left.

Ginny hung back in the doorway, looking at the patient.

"C'mon in," Trina said. "Mr. Texeira's been quiet and well behaved in here."

Trina saw Ginny staring at Texeira. The patient continued

to cry. Oh, Trina thought. Uh-oh. Ginny was still staring at the patient.

"You know him?" Trina said to Ginny.

"No."

"Any connection with him?"

"No." But the security guard had taken a step backward.

Trina made a quick assessment—the patient in a posture of fear, the security guard exhibiting fear. It was as if the patient and the guard recognized each other—or their demons did.

There was a trembling in the sleeves of Ginny's blue uniform shirt.

"The translator will be here soon, I hope," Trina said. "I'll talk with Mr. Texeira then. It ought to relax him a little, hearing someone talk to him in his own language. Ginny?" The patient looked frightened. The guard looked frightened. "Are you all right?"

The guard said, "Unsafe." Staring at the patient she said, "I feel nervous. Unsafe."

"Want me to get someone else?"

"Yes."

Shit, Trina thought. Now I have *two* patients.

7

A NICE, BOOZY evening, Audrey Rosenfeld was thinking, having slipped into the contentment of being with people she enjoyed and having a second glass of wine since dinner after a day in which she had been tired and spent from work. With the music and the wine, spirits and energy had been raised all around the table. It was a belated New Year's Eve for Audrey, and she wanted to stay and have it go on and keep feeling so good, but she knew she ought to go home now; it was after nine and she had to get up at five-thirty.

When, until around New Year's Eve more than four months before, Audrey had been almost out of control inside herself, no one had noticed. She had done her job in a model way and then had gone home to her two-room apartment and cried.

New Year's Eve, it seemed to her that she had cried for months. But it had not been anywhere near that long.

She had spent New Year's Eve alone at home. She had had invitations to parties and from admirers. But after the breakup with the doc, the Prick of Manhattan, early in November, she had felt that going out on New Year's Eve would just require more energy than she was willing to expend. Or perhaps even had. The afternoons alone after work had been so mean and lonely that she had begun accepting every double shift Day O'Meara needed to fill, day after day and week after week of them.

She had decided that a quiet New Year's Eve with herself, listening to music, reading, getting to bed relatively early, would be recuperative.

She had taken a good, warm bath, drenching the water with bath oil, and she had drunk a glass of wine while lying in the tub. Still, settled in her nightgown and robe and slippers, she had realized toward midnight that she had been quite wrong about the recuperative values of being alone on New Year's Eve.

She had written a poem: "To Whom It May Concern."

In doing so she was impelled by her loneliness, her anger at the doc, the two-timing, malignant sonofabitch, and by her anger at the person to whom the poem was addressed.

She had met Dr. Arthur Truell at a wedding in New York early in the summer. He was a thoracic surgeon at a hospital in New York and he had been alone. He had taken her out to dinner after the reception. He was twenty-one years older, and Audrey had been entranced by his mixture of dignity and humor. He had asked if he might call her when he next came to Boston. He came to Boston every so often on consults.

In Boston, a few weeks later, he had taken her to dinner again.

He had been so attentive. Sent her flowers from New York, called her long distance for long conversations, wrote her funny letters. In a matter of weeks they had become lovers.

She had wanted to talk to him often. But his home telephone number was unlisted and he said he gave it to no one, absolutely no one. She had felt a little shut out. But it was the only condition he imposed upon their relationship and she accepted it. He must have good reason. Audrey trusted that. In time he would share the reason with her.

He took her on trips. To Montreal. To Chicago. He would always be there first, on a consult, and she would meet him for the weekend. She paid for her flight, he paid for the hotel and any other expenses. In retrospect she realized he never introduced her to anyone. They spent their time in museums and galleries, in restaurants or nightclubs, and in bed. A great deal of time in bed, though she did not begrudge that time at all. She adored his passion and her own.

On New Year's Eve she said to herself, "Why didn't you figure out he was married?"

And she answered herself, "Because you didn't want to, you dumb-dumb."

One day when she had been feeling particularly alone and had not heard from him for a few days, Audrey thought of calling him at his office. She knew he operated in the mornings and had office hours after two. She obtained the office number from Information. The doc's secretary asked if it was a professional or personal call. Audrey said professional. She had wit enough to identify herself as "a nurse calling from Back Bay Metropolitan Hospital in Boston." Which was true at that moment.

He had called her back at home very early the next morning. Twenty minutes after five. It had been, as Audrey had come to think of it, "a truly rude awakening"—in two senses. The doc had said he had now to be truthful with her. He loved her but he was married. He had children and wouldn't leave his wife. She told him not to call again and unplugged the phone and got up and got ready for work. She did not *want* him to leave his wife. She did not want him to be unfaithful to his wife. But she felt so alone. So chilly. And betrayed.

A part of her mind followed her progress, day after day, through a night forest of emotions, much as if she were a little girl lost in a real forest. Part of her followed herself like a patient and waited for her recovery.

She began doing the double shifts. Hiding out on the floors. Hiding out from herself.

She kept wanting to share things with the doc. She might read a poem or see something on television and want to tell him about it. She had restless nights of sometimes angry and sometimes loving dreams of him, but on New Year's Eve she had confronted that dreamer and asked, "What kind of an idiot goes to bed with a man who won't give her his telephone number?'' And she had answered herself, ''Your kind, you dumb-dumb,'' and there, alone with herself, had burst into laughter.

And then she had written the poem, ''To Whom It May Concern.''

Well, I got through New Year's Eve without you,

    again,
    whoever you are, you sonofabitch,
    who wasn't with me again this year
    when, still alone, I wanted you more than
    maybe any other night
    and God knows I've wanted you so many, many nights
    through so many, many years,
    and never even knew who you are.
    Who are you?

Audrey looked around Fritz's piano bar. Whoever it was wasn't in the room. At least she felt no response to anyone she looked at.

Who are you?

8

TIM HOLBROOK, IN his old U. Mass. warmup suit, stood for a moment looking at the backboard above him. He was alone on the basketball court in the playground across from his apartment building. The night air was warm with spring. It was after nine, but he had noticed from his window that, for the first time since fall, the lights over the courts were on. As usual, he had barely been surviving with the silence in his one-room apartment. After two years, it still oppressed him. That the lights were on was also a piece of luck because he had to start getting himself ready for the exhibition game against the Harlem Wiseapples.

He started out with lay-ups and then moved back progressively until he was taking set shots from a yard outside the key. Then two feet beyond that. His arms began to tire. That felt good. He felt loose.

Holbrook was tall by most standards. But he hadn't been tall enough. Or quick enough. Not for pro ball. Though his accuracy and all-around play had been good enough so that he had been a starting player with Dr. J. both his junior and senior years.

He drove into the basket and made a good lay-up, his body all together with itself. And that was pleasing after so many months of irregular play.

Dribbling slowly, moving slowly, he went back to midcourt. Now he sensed the others around him. Players from high school, players from college. He drove in. Stopped. Turned his back on the man guarding him. Looked to pass. No one open. He spun and completed a turnaround jumper to the basket. He dribbled back, grinning, hearing the crowd, a memory of the crowd. He went in over and over. He made moves and shots he had made in high school and college, some of them moves and shots his mind had forgotten he had ever had. But his body was remembering. He played against people he had *never* played against, players from before his time, players in the NBA now. He was surrounded by the best and he was playing among them. He moved, he jumped, he shot, he rebounded, he dribbled, and when he quit, when he stood with the ball at his side, his breath coming hard, the sweat over all of his body, he was alone, and the silence was with him again, all the louder because he had the memory of the ball slapping the court, the calls and grunts of the players, the sound of the crowd. Memory only. What he heard again was silence. He was always alone.

He went back to his apartment and took a shower—as much for the sound and warmth of it as for his need of one.

The apartment was in a good building, and what with child support, which he did not begrudge, and alimony, which he begrudged a great deal, he could not have afforded it without some kind of break. Tim's break was that he was the building's part-time gardener. He had an affection for gardening. It was a sort of substitute shrink. It released tension and calmed him.

After the shower the silence began tracking him again. There was the one room and bath and kitchen, and that so small a space could contain so much silence and so much absence, and for so long, appalled him.

He turned on a table lamp by the sofa bed, turned off the overhead light, opened the sofa into his bed, and got in. It was only nine-thirty, but late for him. Through his window he could see lights in other buildings. Most people were up.

The telephone beside the bed rang, startling him, sending an uncomfortable fix of adrenaline through him. His hand got the phone on the first ring.

"Hello, Tim."

Valerie. Former wife. Custodial parent of his six-year-old son, Jason.

"You can have Jason tomorrow night if you want," Valerie said. "You can have him overnight."

To have him at all, under the conditions awarded Valerie by the court, was extraordinary, Tim got Jason two weekends a month from Saturday morning till Sunday evening and two Wednesday afternoons a month from four until seven. Three weeks in the summer and alternate Christmas and Thanksgiving vacations. None of the day-by-day time of his growing up, the time Tim would have treasured.

Tim had reason to believe that Valerie had been granted such an award simply because she was the female parent and had sought it. And perhaps because the court, a Judge Harrelson, had not approved of "the calling Mr. Holbrook has seen fit to answer," as the judge had characterized it.

The adrenaline of pain and fear had been replaced by an adrenaline of joy and anticipation.

"Of course," he said to Valerie. "Thank you."

"I have a friend I want to be alone with tomorrow night."

"When can I get Jase?"

"Oh—pick him up here at, say, five. No, don't get here at five. Make it four-thirty. Make sure you're no later than four-thirty."

"All right. I'll make sure."

"I really wouldn't want you . . . I wouldn't want you to have to meet my friend. Dr. Teffler says you must be terribly hurt by all that. Still."

Teffler? A name that rang no bell. Yet another shrink? That would be Valerie's . . . fourth. Fourth in two years. Valerie looking for validation—which she never got.

"I'll be there by four-thirty, Valerie."

"My friend is . . . He's a new friend."

So weren't they all. One of many in sequence and sometimes in parallel. He was over that. Except that they got to
spend more time with Jason than Tim did, even if they didn't
care to.

"He's a ski instructor. Very male."

"Yes. Four-thirty."

"You'll do just about anything for time with Jason, won't
you? Dr. Teffler says you're probably a bad role model for
Jason. A bad gender role model for Jason. But I defend you. I
tell Dr. Teffler a father's a father no matter what sort of work
he does."

"That's kind of you," Tim said. Teffler—whoever he was,
whatever kind of shrink, if he were any good—had said no
such thing, Tim knew. But he kept his mouth shut about it
with Valerie. That was how he managed a little extra time
with Jason. Put up with Valerie's shit. Be ever-obliging to
Valerie, keep mouth shut, be ever-thankful to her.

He heard Jason in the background. "Is that Daddy? Is that
Daddy?" Then all the sound of Valerie's end was covered
from him. When it returned he heard television. He could see
Jason sitting in front of the TV, not watching, head down,
Legos scattered in front of him on the carpet. Tim had seen
that a few times. Jason's unhappy withdrawal at Valerie's.

Tim felt infuriated—and tearful. Jason should not be up at
nine-thirty on a school night. He would not be if he were with
Tim. He would be in bed. Safe. Growing.

"May I speak with Jason?"

"He's in bed, Tim. Asleep. You know what time it is."

Her voice was a little fuzzy, Tim realized. As if she'd been
hitting the grape.

He heard a man's voice in the background. He heard
Valerie giggling, the receiver away from her mouth. Then she
came back on. "Why don't you get him after work? Right
after work. If you can tear yourself away from the other
girls."

9

BY THE TIME the new guard arrived, Ginny had withdrawn to the semidarkness of the corridor outside the psych room. The new guard was male, black and physical. His name was Reynold. Trina saw him assess the patient's physical appearance and then look bored. Ginny had left. Reynold took a chair and moved it against the wall by the door and sat facing the patient.

The triage nurse arrived with a large young man dressed in jeans and faded red, long-sleeved thermal underwear. "Jorge Olivera. From the laundry," she said. Then she left.

"Thank you for coming over, Jorge," Trina said. "This man is from Portugal. His name is Alphonso Texeira. I'd like you to help me talk to him."

"Can do, Nurse, can do."

Trina explained the situation in the kitchen and on the roof. "Ask him what made him so angry in the kitchen."

Jorge asked the question and received a few sharp words in reply.

Trina saw that Jorge was embarrassed. She said, "Tell me *exactly* what he said."

Jorge sighed and looked down at the floor. "H'say the fuckeen water inna sink. Thas wha maygue heem s'angree."

Texeira was smiling broadly now.

"Ask him what he was shouting about up on the roof."

Jorge reported that Texeira said he had been calling out to Jesus, Lord Jesus.

Texeira suddenly became rapidly voluble, but his voice and his eyes were not directed at anyone in the room. The intensity of his smile matched the intensity of his gaze.

The security guard stood up.

"What's he saying?" Trina said.

"Talking to Hayzeus."

"Jesus? About what?"

Jorge took a step away from the patient and said, "The fuckeen water inna sink."

Texeira suddenly stood and screamed at Jorge. Then he was silent.

Jorge had backed to the doorway. "H'say h'damn religious man, talkeen to Hayzeus. H'say if *Hah* want to talkeen to Hayzeus, do it by myself, not by heem."

Trina nodded. She went to the patient, touched him, knowing the importance of touching the patients sometimes, making physical contact, reassuring them, the way of her touch telling them that she didn't mean them harm. "Will you sit down, Mr. Texeira?"

Jorge translated the request.

Texeira sat down. He smiled.

"Will you be all right if I leave you with the guard to take care of you for a while?"

Jorge translated. Texeira smiled.

"That okay, Reynold?" Trina said.

The guard shrugged. "Makes no nevermind by me."

"I need to get some history on him," Trina said, "if I can." She turned to Jorge. "Thank you, Jorge. Would you like me to put you down on our list of translators?"

Jorge smiled and stood as straight as he could.

In the psych office Trina called the restaurant where Texeira had worked. They didn't know anything about him; he'd only been there four days. They did have a telephone number, though.

"Hello," Trina said. She listened. "Is your mother there? . . . Some other grownup? . . . Well, do you have a number where I can get her at work? . . . Gee, I'm sorry I woke you up. How old are you? . . . Thank you. You've been a lot of help. I'll tell your mom. Now you go back to sleep. Good night."

She hung up and shook her head and said to Vicki Green, "Little girl eight years old. Her mother waits tables till midnight." She dialed again and identified herself and asked for Mrs. Texeira. Her conversation with the woman was brief, but she got another telephone number. She hung up and said to Vicki, "The patient's estranged wife wishes him a lousy Easter and don't call her or her kid again."

She dialed again. "Portuguese social worker," she said to

Vicki. Then, to the phone, "Mr. Pereira? I'm sorry to bother
you at this hour," and she explained about Alphonso Texeira.
"I understand you've worked with him."

She listened and made notes and asked some questions and
thanked the social worker and hung up.

She dialed the on-call psychiatrist. "Judd? Trina. I think
you better come down here on this one. Scary immediate
history and a long history of violence . . . I think you're
going to have to decide whether or not to commit on history
. . . All right, my opinion is Mr. Texeira is grossly psychotic
. . . No, I have no idea why he's been wandering around. I
have no idea why a lot of people are wandering around."

She thought of Ginny Shiffland, the security guard. But
Ginny wasn't in that category.

It took Trina several minutes to find Ginny and when she did,
on the nonacute side of the ER, Ginny tried to walk away
from her. Trina stopped her and said, "I want to talk to you.
And you *need* to talk to me."

"I'm not like one of them," Ginny said. "I don't need you
at all."

"One of who?"

"The sickies off the street."

"Pardon me, but you reacted to that particular sicky as if
you saw him in your mirror."

Ginny turned angrily at Trina but then said nothing. Trina
nodded toward an empty examination room and Ginny followed her inside.

Trina said, "Ginny, you ever have an experience like that
before?"

"Never," Ginny said defiantly.

"Anything going on in your personal life that's upsetting
you?"

"Nothing."

"No problems?"

"None."

"Except this one. You're called in as a standby and your
professional reaction is tears and shakes."

"I wasn't crying."

"I saw the tears. When you were in the corridor. I'm
trying to help you, Ginny."

"I don't need your kind of help. I don't want it."

"You've been on this job a long time, haven't you? You're very experienced."

"Yes."

"No trouble before."

Ginny looked away. "No." She was trembling.

"Tell Sergeant Cleveland you're not feeling well tonight."

"I can't do that. I'll lose my job."

"Nonsense."

"Please," Ginny said. "Leave me alone."

"I'm going to have to talk to Sergeant Cleveland myself," Trina said.

"I already spoke to him."

"What did you say?"

Ginny was silent.

"Ginny, I know you're in some kind of misery—"

"I'm *okay*, Trina."

"Sure. Except that you can't handle your job."

"That was just once. For a few minutes."

"All right. But you're not hiding the misery. Like anyone else, you want to get out of the misery."

For an instant Trina thought she was going to get an acceptant response. But then Ginny looked away again.

"I'd like you to talk with one of our shrinks."

"No way."

"How about someone not connected with this hospital?"

"No."

"I want you to think about it. After work, away from here. What your needs are, what your troubles are, where you'd like to be inside yourself. Let's talk about it tomorrow."

Ginny looked at Trina carefully. "That's it? I can go?"

Trina nodded.

Sergeant Cleveland was in the psych office when Trina unlocked the door and entered.

"Lookin' for *you*, Trina," the sergeant said. The nighttime chief of ER security was a gray-haired black man.

Trina said to Vicki, "Sergeant Cleveland appears to be annoyed at me."

"Sergeant Cleveland is mad as hell at you, Trina," he said. "What's wrong, lady? You ain't *liberated?*"

"When the sergeant uses a word like 'ain't,' he's not just mad as hell, he's really pissed. What is it, Sergeant Cleveland?"

"Trina, what the hell is goin' on with you? Can't you accept another woman as a guard?"

"Ginny?"

"Yes, Ginny. You ask for a standby, you get Ginny, and you replace her."

"Yes. I can accept a woman as a guard. You know that, Jerry."

"Ginny says you replaced her because she's a woman."

Interesting, Trina thought.

"She says you have it in for her."

"Bullshit," Trina said mildly. "Ginny's got some problems. I don't know what. But she's patient material."

"Are you telling me to get rid of her?"

"She's upset. Depressed. I'd like her to get some help. I'd like her to take some time off. Sick leave, whatever her contract allows."

"What does Ginny say?"

"She's thinking it over." Trina described the experience with Mr. Texeira.

"Look, Trina, I'm not saying it didn't happen the way you say. And I'm not saying you're right and I'm not saying you're wrong about Ginny. But she's been here as long as I've been in charge. She's always been reliable, she's always hung in. Whatever she decides, I'm not going to let one incident screw her. She gets this one for free."

Trina nodded. "I'm not in agreement, but I'll go along with you. For one incident. And you're right, Ginny didn't quit, she hangs in. But she needs help. Maybe because she hangs in. Beyond her resources. Jerry, I don't want her out. I want her helped."

10

MOLLY WATCHED MONK McGuire peel off from the bar. He apparently took his wingman by surprise, and a fraction of time elapsed before Archie Johnson dove after the Monk and then managed to precede him in the duo's descent upon the nurses' table. Molly turned to Nan. "I think you're going to have visitors."

"Visitors, yes," Selma said. "But I believe it's Mr. McGuire in particular who wishes to pay his respects."

Well, Molly thought, with all her conversation Selma hadn't missed the girding up of the loins at the bar. Probably hadn't missed anything else that had gone on in the room either, including Molly's own nonverbal exchange with Bennett Chessoff. Very little got by Selma. Which was just one of several good reasons her colleagues had drafted her into being chief executive of the Nursing Services Alliance.

Selma went on. "Mr. McGuire looks like a little boy with candy on his mind."

Nan looked embarrassed.

"It's not candy he has on his mind," Molly said.

"Just a manner of speaking, sayeth Selma, wife, and mother of two teenage boys."

Archie Johnson stood by their table, having positioned his pitching associate next to Nan, and said, "Good evening, ladies. May we be permitted to introduce ourselves?"

"It's unnecessary," Molly said, but apparently the introduction was considered an integral part of the act and could not be dropped.

"My name is Archie Johnson and I labor in the center field of Fenway Park. This is my friend Monk McGuire, a gentleman from the city of Baltimore. He is lonely. And because of the rough, masculine vicissitudes of his craft, he is in need of the remedial company of the opposite sex. A lonely visitor from out of town, desirous of a stranger's sympathy."

There was silence. Then Molly said, "That was rather good."

Nan, the object of attention, looked down.

"Sit, stranger," Selma said. "And you, too, Archie. Get yourselves chairs."

The conversation then fragmented. Monk McGuire quietly and immodestly explained his various accomplishments to Nan while trying, Molly observed, to add Nan to them. The pitcher was pitching. The hitter, in support of his friend's endeavors, was politely inquiring after the other ladies at the table.

What a team, Molly thought. I wonder what it's like when the act moves to Baltimore.

Selma said to Molly, "If my husband saw me sitting here with Johnson and McGuire, he'd think I'd died and gone to heaven."

"We bought a microwave oven," Elin was saying. "Because I was spending so much time studying." She was laughing and there were tears at the corners of her eyes. "A microwave oven. Whole dinners in five minutes. It was supposed to save our marriage, but it didn't."

"Microwaves aren't good at listening," Molly said.

Selma immediately said, "I'm glad you're going to see Liz Swanzey right off tomorrow morning. I told her you'd be on the floor at ten."

"What did she say when you told her you'd set up the consult with me?"

"She was noncommittal. She didn't say anything. However, she walked away."

"She said something all right."

"What beats me is, the patient she's been blowing up at! She's been blowing up at him since he came in. She just can't seem to control herself with him."

"Not good for the patient. How is she otherwise? What kind of nurse?"

"Super. One of the best. Very good with alcoholics. Which is why I find this so puzzling. This patient. The patient's problems are all alcohol-related."

"Well, I've got to listen to her, but I know one thing right off."

"Such as?"

"Hostility is a strong indication."

"Of what?"

"A need for self-protection," Molly said. "I've got to find out what Liz Swanzey thinks she needs to protect herself from."

Molly, as she spoke, was also listening to McGuire's inept courtship of Nan. He was curiously unskillful in his attempted seduction. Molly heard him saying, "I'm great on the baseball mound. Girls say I'm greater on other kinds of mounds." And then he didn't leave that alone. "Like the mound of Venus."

Molly thought, Oh shit, McGuire, you need help.

Elin was saying, "I'd like to sleep with someone."

"I would, too," Molly said. She nodded toward Johnson

and McGuire. "I have reason to believe that both of those gentlemen are available."

"I mean someone I care about."

"Of course, men like me," McGuire was saying, "when you're as good as I am at something, like me and pitching, men like me who insist on excellence," he said, looking intently at Nan, "we're not just good at one thing, we're excellent at whatever we decide to do. On the field or off."

Mr. McGuire cannot really think this sort of approach can work on a grown woman, Molly thought. But obviously he does. That's how much I know about Mr. McGuire.

"I've got two things going for me," McGuire told Nan. "Very unusual combination in a pitcher. Strength *and* finesse."

Molly thought about Bennett Chessoff's strength and finesse and wondered if it included his penis and his lovemaking. Does his strength include tenderness? Then she thought, Am I thinking about Bennett's penis because I think he's a prick?

"I've got all kinds of pitches," McGuire was saying.

"No, Mr. McGuire," Nan said, "what you've got is all kinds of balls. And I'm not interested in any of them."

There was a silence around the table.

"Ball four," Molly said.

11

VIOLA CHAMBERS CAME on duty on Children's Seven at eleven o'clock at night. She was twenty-three years old and had been an RN for almost two years. For as long as she could remember she had wanted to be a nurse and for all of that time she had wanted to be a pediatric nurse. She had elected to work the late shift because if a child needed her, she could usually give the child one-to-one attention for as long as the child needed or wanted it through the night. On other shifts that would not be possible.

There were sixteen children on the floor and Viola would be alone with fifteen of them until morning. Jamaal, the sixteenth child, was by himself with his own nurse and required her total attention.

The lights had been dimmed to minimum on the floor except inside Jamaal's windowed cubicle and in the glassed-in nurses' station, where one bright lamp illuminated a work surface.

"What have we got tonight?" Viola said to the charge nurse, who was going off duty.

"Nothing much. The status is quo." She reviewed the children and the orders for each one.

Viola had the charts to refer to, but she also made notes. "Who's covering?"

"Mozart. He's sleeping up on a floor. Here's the number. Okay? You set?"

"All set."

The charge nurse looked around the floor. "Peaceful enough. Good night then."

"Good night," Viola said.

The charge nurse was joined by the other evening RN and the two of them went down a dim corridor to wait for the elevator. Viola left the station to silently visit each of the children.

The first two beds—really a bed and a bassinet—were occupied by a child and an infant whose mothers, for very different reasons, were incapable of caring for them.

The bed was occupied by a six-year-old black boy named Miller Woods whose mother, it was Viola's opinion, was in need of a head transplant. You couldn't reach the mother. The father wasn't around. A psych nurse had tried to talk to the mother. So had a social worker. Miller was on the floor for lead poisoning, the third such admission for him in two years. The family squatted in buildings. When they were discovered and forced out they went and squatted in another building. The mother provided no guidance. So the kids (Miller's older brother had also been in) went right on eating whatever flaked off the walls. Out of hunger. Painful and degenerative, the poisoning was cumulative, and Miller had been brought in this last time in a coma and had been over on the Adult Med ICU, since Pedi did not have a unit of its own, until he had been safely managed through it by the nurses there. Viola and the social worker were attempting to find a legal solution to Miller's and his brother's medical problems.

Viola shone her penlight on Miller. He breathed easily and his face was calm.

The bassinet was occupied by a white female infant nick-named Missy by her mother. In Viola's professional opinion, the mother was in need of a heart transplant. At eight months Missy was in for failure to thrive. When awake, the child had a blank look. The etiology of the baby's failure to grow vigorously was in the mother's personality. It wasn't so much how well the mother could cope (in contrast to Miller's mother) or with what she could cope, but simply how much she *wanted* to cope. On her visits the mother was cheerful and well dressed and assiduously attentive to her daughter for all of about ten or fifteen minutes before she departed. And the visits were not frequent. "The mother is a butterfly," the social worker reported. "Her own pleasure comes first. The self she wishes to present in public comes next. The infant comes last of all after a number of other items that can be simply summarized as narcissistic gratification."

Viola touched the child's cheek. So smooth and cool. Treatment for Missy's failure to thrive was nutrition and stimulation and a lot of demonstration of love and affection. It was amazing to Viola that a physically healthy mother had to bring her child to a hospital so that it might receive nutrition and stimulation and love and affection. This was the second time Missy had been on the floor.

The third child Viola stopped by was awake.

"I heard you, Vi," the little girl said. She spoke with her eyes closed and as if from a great distance.

Viola moved closer to hear her better. "How's it goin', Natalie? How's it goin', baby?"

The little white girl was eight years old and had a special affection for Viola. Natalie was on the floor because of an anaphylactic reaction to medicine that had been ordered for her at home for an infection of the middle ear. She was receiving codeine for the pain from infection, and Viola had noted on the chart that the dosage had been significantly increased.

The little girl lay still, her eyes closed, the covers tucked up under her chin. She did not answer Viola.

"You feel okay, Natalie? Are you comfortable?"

"Doesn't hurt, Vi . . . ."

"Then you sleep, baby." She turned to go.

"Vi?"

"Yes, baby."

"I went down to the playground tonight."

"You did?"

"Yes. The playground. Where I go at night . . . It was lots of fun."

"I bet it was."

"You can't tell my momma, Vi . . .'cause it's a secret . . .' "

"All right. I won't. You sleep."

"Yes . . . G'night, Vi . . .''

"Good night, baby."

Viola continued her rounds, entering each curtain-hung cubicle, shining her penlight on the child, seeing that each one was resting comfortably and that there were no indications that vital signs ought to be taken or medications delivered.

Viola's last visit was to Jamaal. Jamaal had been born at Back Bay Metropolitan eleven months before and he had never been home, never left the hospital, and the unwritten prognosis was that he never would.

"We do what we can for him while he's still with us," Viola explained to others and to herself.

He was sleeping now, his little brown body dressed in a little blue jacket, a white diaper, and white socks. There was a small doll in one partially open hand. A baseball cap, which one of his nurses had brought him, hung at the corner of his raised bed. One of Jamaal's multiple problems was that his muscles were limp. Still, there were times when he was not only alert, but playful.

Jamaal survived simply because he had continuous human, mechanical, and medicinal support. His mother desperately wanted to care for him herself, but she would have had to remain awake twenty-four hours a day seven days a week to keep him alive. In the hospital a vent nurse—a nurse who had had special training in the operation and monitoring of a ventilator—was with him at all times. The ventilator delivered oxygen under a small amount of pressure directly to Jamaal's lungs by way of a tube that entered his body through a tracheotomy.

He was fed solids through a gastrostomy tube and received his medications and other nutrition through an intravenous line into his arm. The continuous liquid IV was monitored by an IVAC, a machine that controlled the drops per minute from a clear plastic bag hung from a bedside pole. The gastrostomy tube had been placed through the baby's abdomen into his stomach. When Jamaal had at one time been fed through his mouth, he had reacted with reflex regurgitation and some of the regurgitated food had entered his lungs. The gastrostomy tube eliminated that problem.

Jamaal was being treated—maintained—but the doctors couldn't establish the underlying syndrome. No bone growth, a floppy baby, though an adorable and handsome one. Cerebral palsy? Birth paralysis?

Viola entered the room. Out of habit from her own vent training, she glanced over at the ventilator's flow meter and other gauges to make sure that Jamaal's pressures were where they should be, that there was no leak around the tracheotomy seal where the supply line entered Jamaal, that his PEEP and PIP indications—the mechanically elevated resting volume and the peak volume of his lungs—were where they should be.

The trach tube also allowed for easier access to Jamaal's lungs so that they might be suctioned—the regular cleaning out of the mucus that, if allowed to accumulate sufficiently, would suffocate him.

Viola said, "Nancy, you look beat."

"I am. This is my second shift."

"You've been here since three?"

"The afternoon nurse called in sick this morning and Day couldn't find anyone else. So she called me."

"Take a break. I'll stay with Jamaal."

"I'd love to sit down for a few minutes and have some coffee."

"Go ahead."

"I was just going to suction him."

"I'll do it."

"Gee, Vi, thanks a lot. I'll be at the station."

Viola nodded. "I like being with Jamaal. I like helping him."

The other nurse left and Viola bent over Jamaal and auscultated his lungs with her stethoscope. She placed the stethoscope over her shoulders behind her neck and then, with an efficiency of motion that appeared leisurely, she instilled Jamaal's lungs through the trach tube with normal saline from a dropper and then clapped his chest, her brown hand sharp against his brown skin. The child awoke, seemed about to cry, saw Viola, recognized what was happening, was reassured, and did not cry.

The saline solution and the claps to the chest combined to loosen the mucus from the inner surfaces of the lungs so that it could be suctioned out.

To make up for the temporary loss of vent-delivered oxygen that was about to occur, Viola disconnected the vent and gave Jamaal 100% oxygen from an ambu bag through the trach tube. One minute of 100% oxygen. Jamaal had shut his eyes again. The chest PT and the other attentions he received and the discomforts he experienced were the only way of life he had ever known. He accepted it all, usually.

Viola removed the small rubber mask and disconnected the vent tube from the trach tube. With a suctioning device she entered the lungs through the trach tube and drew out the creamy white secretions.

In and out in ten seconds.

Ambu with oxygen one minute, suction ten seconds, repeat three times.

She reconnected Jamaal to the vent and bent over him with her stethoscope again and listened to his lungs to see if she had done him any good.

Periodically Jamaal's left lung collapsed, but tonight both were working; Viola was pleased with herself and with Jamaal.

12

TRINA AND VICKI Green stood in the courtyard of the Old Building. The two ambulance bays behind them were brightly lit, the rest of the courtyard in near darkness except for the walk-in entrances to the ER, the Med wing and the Pedi and OBGYN wing.

Vicki said, "What's going on with your rape case?"

"Jessy Gladdens? Nothing much."

"The law's delays?"

"We're not even that far yet. There's a warrant for Higby's

arrest, but no word where he is. So there's no one to prosecute."

"The victim?"

"She's so scared she won't come back and see me. She thinks Higby'll catch up with her at the hospital. So she's staying with someone somewhere in Roxbury. I've got the telephone number, so of course I could find out the address. But I'd just as soon not even know if she doesn't want to volunteer it."

The two women walked to their cars in side-by-side spaces. The parking spaces in the courtyard were privileged.

Trina already had her key out when she stopped beside her old yellow Volkswagen Beetle. She paused, feeling the comfort and reassurance of the new warm air of spring. Some of the windows of the medical floors above her were lit as were some of the windows of the surgical floors above the ER. Other windows were lit on Two, Three, Four, Five, and Six of OBGYN. But there was almost no light to be seen above them on Children's Seven, Eight, Nine, and Ten. The children were asleep. There was no emergency, no midnight crisis. That made Trina feel good. She unlocked her car and got in.

13

AUDREY ROSENFELD'S TELEPHONE rang. In the darkness and silence of her apartment it had the suddenness and loudness of an explosion.

Not fair, Audrey thought. She had been sleeping in such rapturous tranquillity.

"Hello," she said.

"Hi."

The doc. His voice customarily diminished by long distance.

She felt some sort of constriction within herself. Loss? Anger?

"I've been thinking about you. A lot," he said. "Actually, I haven't stopped thinking about you."

She remained silent.

"I'm calling from New York, but—"

"Not calling from home, I imagine."

"Actually, I am. Susan is away."

"And how are the children?" She thought of his courtship of her and how he had deliberately neglected to inform her of his familial ties.

"Cut it out, Audrey."

"I'm only being polite," Audrey said, fully conscious that that was *not* what she was being and that, if she were so quick to be bitchy to him, she must still have reserves of emotional investment in him—reserves she very much regretted. "*You* are not being polite by calling me at this hour. You know what time I have to get up."

She hoped he would react to her voice, apologize, hang up. But he didn't. The doc did not, in Audrey's experience, apologize for anything.

"I'm coming to Boston. I want to see you."

"No."

"I'm going to, Audrey. You can count on it."

"Good night," she said, and hung up.

Then she lay awake and heard, in the silence, the sudden, startling ringing of the telephone again, not the real ringing, but the memory of it. Not only had she been physically awakened, but some feelings about the doc had been re-awakened—highly mixed and ambivalent feelings.

When she slept again she was fitful, pushing off the covers and then drawing them up and then pushing them off again.

14

VIOLA STOOD AT the bedside of Natalie, the little girl with the middle ear infection who earlier, in pretend or in her dreams, had gone down to the playground.

Viola's penlight showed her that Natalie had apparently not moved since she'd said good night to Viola, her little chin still resting just so on the edge of the bedcovers.

Viola moved rapidly.

She turned on the overhead light. The child's face was a very pale blue. Viola tore the covers down. The respiration was so very shallow. She bent with her stethoscope and listened for an obstruction in the throat. There was very little air moving and the child's body showed little effort to move air at all. Her heart rate had slowed considerably. Still, she might be in a very deep sleep, though in a quickness of desolation Viola thought not. Viola shook the child, then pinched her.

She ran to the telephone, the child's body unmoving on the bed.

"Mozart. Vi. *Stat.*"

She ran back to the bed and began mouth-to-mouth resuscitation. She heard Mozart's steps behind her and felt his hand on her shoulder, pulling her away.

"Heart rate's forty," she said as the intern took her place and began to repeat Viola's examination with his stethoscope placed on the child's throat. "Pulse skipped beats. Cyanotic. No prior history. Brain infection from the otitis? Drug error?"

Mozart was now bent right down on the child. There were a few seconds of silence and then, "Shit," Mozart said quietly, "oh shit."

Viola was already moving to the telephone.

"Call the code," Mozart said. *"Respiratory arrest."*

Viola dialed, saw Mozart crouched over in mouth-to-mouth resuscitation.

TWO

The
Time Machine

15

THE DAY WAS gray and peculiarly warm for early spring and for six-thirty in the morning. The two women had the side windows down.

Nan Lassitter had never driven Molly Chang to work before, but Molly had been complaining the night before about her car's being in the garage and the two of them had discovered that they took much the same route in each morning from the same suburban area, so Nan had offered to pick Molly up. Nan shared an apartment in Newton Center with another nurse and Molly lived alone in a house a little farther out.

"It's a pretty street," Nan said as she pulled away from Molly's home. The frame houses were two or three generations old, and there were sidewalks and trees and lawn areas where the earth was tinted over with the yellow-green of springtime regrowth.

"It *is* a pretty street," Molly said. "And it doesn't cost me much more than an apartment downtown. I moved here for the tranquillity. And the space. But it's a family street. I'm out of place. I'll move this summer."

"Where to?"

"Don't know. It depends on what I'm going to be doing in the fall."

"You're leaving Back Bay Met?"

Molly was silent for a time before she said, "It's an option I'm considering. Keep it to yourself, huh?"

In a few minutes they had left the suburban stillness. On the Massachusetts Turnpike, even at that hour, the sounds of trucks and cars crowded them, though the traffic was not heavy and Nan could drive her subcompact sedan without pause or maneuver. Far ahead they could see the buildings of downtown Boston interrupting the horizon.

"You were some cool lady last night," Molly said. "You're likely to be a legend in your own time. Turning down Monk McGuire."

"He was arrogant and egotistical."

"He was an asshole," Molly agreed.

"Also, he didn't turn me on."

"Ahhh. Now we get to the root of the matter."

From the elevation of the Pike, Nan and Molly both saw, in the far distance, the buildings of Back Bay Metropolitan Hospital. They rose up from everything else around them, dominating their section of the city. The several buildings seemed a single gray structure, a structure which, according to that morning's *Boston Eagle* and its columnist, Lynn Keating, ought to be shut down for the well-being of its patients. The newspaper, folded to the front-page article, lay on the drive shaft tunnel between the two nurses.

SHUT DOWN BACK BAY MET

"The city should close Back Bay Metropolitan Hospital."

So stated Dr. Scott McGettigan, Senior Resident in Medicine at BBMH and president of the hospital's Association of Residents and Interns (ARI), to this reporter last evening.

"I'm concerned about the patients' safety and so are the other house officers," McGettigan said as he stood by to receive critical transmissions on the medical communications radio in the hospital's emergency room.

Dr. McGettigan cited nonfunctioning cardiac monitors and EKG equipment, serious understaffing at all levels, and "an administration insensitive to the needs of the patients."

Hospital Director Bennett Chessoff denied these charges and responded with one of his own.

"There have been instances in which house officers tampered with EKG equipment and made it inoperable," Chessoff said.

"That's an outright lie," Dr. McGettigan replied to the allegation.

McGettigan continued, "The director doesn't know the functional status of the equipment in the hospital. He is a poor guardian of the trust placed in him."

Mr. Chessoff declined to reply to Dr. McGettigan's characterization of him.

A technician on the staff of Back Bay Met's Central Logistical Services, which is responsible for the maintenance of medical equipment such as EKG machines, stated that he was personally aware "that house officers did tamper with a couple of EKG machines. But only after the machines had ceased functioning properly and we couldn't get service or replacements on line. Nobody was trying to pull anything that I know of."

Nan patted the newspaper, nodded toward the hospital, and said, "It looks like Scotty and Bennett are going for a head-to-head."

"It appears that way."

"I wonder why."

"Actually, it appears that Scotty wants it that way," Molly said. She thought about her statement. "Though Bennett might want it to appear that way."

"Why?"

"I suppose we shall learn in due course."

"Fascinating man, our director," Nan said.

"I think so." Molly looked over at Nan. "I was a little concerned about you last evening. You looked troubled. Then you perked up."

Nan smiled a little and nodded. That had been when she had decided to leave nursing, had realized that she no longer had any reason to go back to the unit and endure the stress and the pain—either Mr. Emerson's or her own.

Molly, sensing that she was not going to get any voluntary elucidation from Nan, began to think of her day's rounds and in particular of her meeting with Liz Swanzey, the nurse who was blowing up at a particular patient.

Nan was slowing and moving into the exit-ramp lane. She rolled her window up and reached behind herself to check that the rear door was locked. She turned off the Pike at the Tremaine Avenue exit and was stopped by a red light at the end of the ramp. Nan looked over at Molly. With a feeling of self-exposure she said, "Put your window up, huh? Your door locked?"

They could make either a left or a right on Tremaine, a four-lane avenue. A left would take them under the Pike and

over to Beacon Street and Commonwealth Avenue, to neigh-
borhoods of shops and restaurants and comfortable apartment
houses. A right would take them to Back Bay Met, some
twenty blocks away and far from any vestige of affluence.
The light changed and Nan turned right.

The storefronts here were grimy: used furniture, auto parts,
wholesale calendars, a luncheonette, a liquor store. Most of
the doors and windows were covered with black steel grilles.
The light at the corner of the next side street was against them
and Nan stopped. She looked to each side, then in the rearview
mirror. Then she looked to each side again.

The light changed and she moved forward. There were
trees planted at the edge of the sidewalk on every block of
Tremaine. Gaunt and bleak from winter, they had nevertheless just begun to bud. Within six blocks the residential area
began. None of the buildings was more than four stories high.
Some of the windows had curtains. Some of the windows
were boarded up. Nan came to another red light. She slowed,
looked to each side, and drove through the light.

Peripherally she saw Molly watching her. Well, screw you,
Molly Chang, Nan thought.

There was trash and garbage on the street now, cans and
boxes of it. Some of the cans had been tipped and spilled.
Some of the trash appeared to have been dumped without a
container.

Nan came to another red light, glanced each way, and
drove through it.

Most of the windows were curtainless now. There was
nothing to be seen behind them. They were black holes.
Some entire buildings were boarded over wherever they might
be entered. Some buildings had been hollowed by fire, their
windows empty and filled with darkness.

Nan slowed for a red light at a main intersection, slowed to
nearly a stop, and then drove through it.

"It scares the shit out of me," Nan said. "Every day.
Driving in through here. What if I get a flat?"

Molly said nothing. She looked away from the red lights
ahead. Driving this same approach to the hospital every day,
she never had a chance to look at the surroundings closely.
Now she had the opportunity to look behind windows—or try
to. An occupational habit, Molly thought, or perhaps obses-
sion. Most of the windows were empty, broken, or boarded,

but behind some, she was surprised to see, there were pieces of living green, plants that had been tended against all odds of survival through the frightfully low tenement temperatures of the winter. Not unlike the patients at Back Bay, Molly thought.

The lights were green now. They drove under the elevated trolley line that crossed Tremaine two blocks from the hospital.

16

NAN TURNED THE car off Tremaine and in under the great gray arch that led into the large cobblestone courtyard of the Old Building. The security guard inside wearily waved her through. It was not seven o'clock yet and he had been on duty all night. Nan drove across to a parking space in front of the medical wing.

Molly said, "How did you wangle this?"

"I was held up at knifepoint in the garage. I made an appointment with Dorothea and told her either I got in-house parking or I quit."

Molly nodded. Dorothea Kullgren, the director of Nursing Services for the hospital. "What *if* you had a flat?"

"I didn't think you were listening."

"If you were any old white lady, you might run some risk. As a nurse, I think people would take care of you. The black population would. It's the *white* guys in this neighborhood who scare me."

"Why them?"

"Those dudes like violence for its own sake."

"I saw an awful lot of black trauma in the ER. Knife wounds, gunshot, beatings—"

"Personal violence. Check the records. Friend against friend, family member against family member, neighbor against neighbor. Self-directed violence. Not against you, not against me—against themselves mostly."

"Really?"

"Take my word. We analyzed the stats."

"It's hard to believe," Nan said. "I mean, it doesn't sound right, people being violent to each other. I guess I could understand if it was against outsiders."

"Listen, Nan, these people are ghettoed here. Economically and politically, right up the kazoo. They haven't *got* any outlet for their anger except each other. Excuse me. Their *rage.*"

"It still frightens me," Nan said quietly.

Molly shifted in her seat so that she was facing Nan. "Sure it does. You might like to know, I drive with my doors locked and my windows up even on the hottest days. As soon as I get off the Pike. In the mornings, if there's no cop around, I don't stop at red lights either."

Nan sighed and looked off distantly and spoke to the windshield. "In the afternoons, that's scary, too. The traffic has you boxed in. I think someone's going to come over and bust a window and unlock the door and force himself in. I never said that out loud before. I pretend to myself I don't even think it."

"So what's new?" Molly said, surprising her. "You're just entertaining all the garden-variety fantasies around here. My guess is, it's why a lot of nurses leave Back Bay Met— the fear. But they won't admit it, not even to themselves. They can't deal with the fear. So they get out of the environment that stimulates it." Molly paused. "Of course, there're some who get off on it, too."

Nan removed the keys from the ignition. "I'm even scared inside sometimes."

Molly sat back. "Here we are in the highest crime area in the city. All *embraced* by Back Bay Metropolitan Hospital's catchment. And it comes in off the street sometimes, too. You've got grounds to be scared. That's your turf, lady. So let it make you careful . . . You can also take a big load of pride in it too, you know. You're helping folks who don't get much help from anyone else."

"But you're leaving."

"Maybe. I don't know yet."

"Why would you? I mean, after what you just said."

"I think there're ways I can be more effective. If I have the opportunity."

They got out and locked the doors.

"It's depressing and hardening, the violence around here," Molly said. "The staff won't talk to each other about it. Let's all pretend it doesn't exist."

17

SELMA PUSHKIN ALSO made a habit of arriving twenty minutes to half an hour before she was required to, but instead of going directly to her floor this morning, she made an excursion into the ER and found the person she hoped might be there. He looked very tired.

"What the hell do you think you're doing, Dr. McGettigan?" Selma said, holding out the paper quoting him. "You trying to put all our patients into fib?"

"Not my intention, Selma. The director's already in. Whatever you say to me will be an anticlimax. Bennett's really pissed, and that's putting it mildly."

"You look terrible."

"I feel terrible. It's been a long night."

"Social reform is always wearying."

"Fuck off, will you, Selma? We saved some lives in here last night."

"That's what we're supposed to do here, isn't it? Now, about scaring the patients shitless—"

"The newspaper article."

"Lynn Keating, Scotty. What was she doing here? Was she one of the lives you saved last night?"

"What she was doing here late yesterday afternoon was ambulance chasing. She got a tip from an EMT. Man down on the street. Guy was a hero six months ago, a harbor policeman. He jumped into freezing water and saved a child from drowning. A couple of weeks later the city laid him off. Budget cuts. Name of Percy Stevens. The EMTs brought him in and one of them called Keating. Human interest story. Laid-off hero found passed out on the street."

"Alcohol?"

"Some. Not enough to account. He's up on Med Three."

"So you and Lynn Keating just got to chatting and you suggested the hospital ought to be shut down, the patients aren't safe? *Jesus,* Scotty, you want to panic the patients?"

McGettigan stood up. He was twenty-nine years old and chief resident in Medicine and he said, "I'll assume you're addressing me as head of ARI and I'm talking to you as head of NSA."

He did look weary, Selma thought. "Also as professionals who do not wish to terrify their patients."

"ARI is preparing a handout that'll go to all the patients about ten o'clock this morning. It'll reassure everyone. It explains what I did and what I did not say."

Selma looked at her copy of the *Eagle.* "Let's start with Dr. McGettigan saying, 'The city should close Back Bay Metropolitan Hospital'!"

"I was doing a bunch of other things. Yes, I thought we were just chatting. I said, though, if the city isn't prepared to fund the hospital properly, it ought to consider the alternatives— one of which would be closing it down. I said some of the patients would be better off."

"Nobody is ever just chatting to Lynn Keating, Scotty."

"I know. That was a damn fool thing to say."

"Wow. We agree on that."

"We both know it's true."

Selma was silent.

McGettigan picked up the newspaper. "Yeah, I'm concerned about the patients' safety. I said that. The nonfunctioning equipment. The nonexisting equipment. That was at about six. So Keating went over to the New Wing and Bennett was still there and she presented some of my statements, I guess. Bennett reacted, and she brought his reaction back to me."

"And you called him a liar."

"I said the statement was inaccurate. There's a difference."

"And you elaborated. You said he was unfit to be director."

"I have to admit to that. But I said he wasn't paying attention to the communications his medical staff sends him. You know, we sit with Bennett, Selma, we talk to him about what this hospital needs, what it *desperately* needs, and he listens, and nods, and says, 'Thank you for sharing your thoughts with me.' And then nothing. Nothing changes. Except everything gets worse. Slowly. And Bennett can go to

City Hall and tell them everything's cool over here and they clap him on the back and pay him his forty-six thousand per because he's keeping the lid on.''

"He does earn it in that respect, doesn't he?"

"I've been trying for *months* to get Bennett to talk patient issues with ARI. We're looking at the same shit I walked into when I came here as an intern, only worse."

"Scotty, think of the patients next time. When Ms. Keating is looking for a lid to take off."

"All right. I was tired and frustrated, and that was no excuse for talking to Keating and having her do what she did and maybe upsetting the patients, maybe."

"Not maybe."

"I'm not glad about how she turned it. But maybe I was right. We *all* keep the lid on here. Maybe no one *knows* about us."

"I've got to go to work," said Selma.

"Thank you for sharing your thoughts with me," McGettigan said.

18

ARRIVING AT THE hospital at twenty to seven, Audrey Rosenfeld did not take the elevator to Med Three—it was almost always a long wait—but went up the stairwell and out onto the corridor, where she suddenly became head nurse in charge of staff and of patients' lives. She hung up her coat and took summary report from the night charge nurse. She would take a detailed report in a few minutes when her partner on the shift came in.

It had been a quiet night. "No problems," the charge nurse said. "One admission." She explained about Percy Stevens, the former harbor policeman found passed out on the street. "Pneumonic, seems malnourished, disoriented. Medicated and fed by IV. The docs will work him up this morning."

"Disoriented still?" Audrey said.

"Was when he came up. Been sleepin' ever since. Trina

Frankian came up from the ER with him. Says to let him sleep and see if he can make sense when he wakes up. Doesn't, get a shrink, get an evaluation. Malnutrition and pneumonia causing the disorientation, the doc and Trina think.''

"What's his background?"

"Trina did some phonin' around. The patient's a pretty straight dude. Family man, out of work, depressed. Two kids at home. Wife told Trina nothin' significant in his history. Couldn't understand how the malnutrition could be. Food on the table, they still have savings to live off. Some alcohol on board when he was brought into the ER. But not enough to account for the disorientation.''

Audrey began her care of the new patient while still at the nurses, station. She got out a large placard, wiped away some previous entries, and, with a felt marker, entered some new information. She took the placard to Percy Stevens' room and hung it on the wall at the foot of his bed so that he would see it when he awoke.

The skin of the patient's face was ruddy, but beneath the ruddiness it was as if there were another skin, the second one pale.

Audrey glanced at the placard, trying to intuit what the patient might think upon awaking and seeing it.

THIS IS BACK BAY METROPOLITAN HOSPITAL
IN BOSTON, MASSACHUSETTS
TODAY IS *THURSDAY, MAY 16*
THE WEATHER IS *WARM, CLOUDY*
THE NEXT HOLIDAY IS *MEMORIAL DAY*

Audrey went back to the station. Coralee Wafford, the other regular daytime RN on Med Three, was reviewing the overnight paperwork and listening to the night nurse's comments. Coralee's nearly black skin was emphasized by the brilliant white of her uniform pants and tunic. Audrey, though the younger of the two by more than a decade, was strictly old school about uniform. She wore the traditional white dress and white stockings and even the cap, which most nurses no longer wore at all.

In terms of experience and years at work, Coralee ought to have been head nurse on the floor. But she had only recently come back to full-time employment after having spent several

years in the hospital's flexie pool so that she might devote
most of her time to her young children.

The night nurse began her report: "Mrs. Davies was moved
a little while ago. Pain, swelling, right leg. Clot? Medicine
worked her up, doesn't think it's a clot. Transferred her back
to Surgery, see what they think."

The telephone rang. "Medicine Three, Audrey . . . For
what time? . . . All right, we'll be ready to go." She broke
the connection and then dialed a number. "Okay, stretcher to
Medicine Three . . . Thanks." She hung up. "They're putting
Mr. Toby on call. Put him on meds, Valium. Mrs. Karlin?"

"Mrs. Karlin got chemo last night. She got Adriamycin on
the evening shift . . . Cytoxin, two hundred an hour. That's
what's running now, and when that finishes she's to get a unit
of blood."

"Is that it on her? And she's going home?"

"She slept the whole night, no temp."

When they finished taking the report, it was fifteen minutes
after seven and Audrey and Coralee were alone at the station.
There were supposed to be two other members of their team
with them, an LPN and either a nursing assistant or, at least,
a medical worker. Neither of them had arrived on Medicine
Three.

Audrey looked at Coralee and said, "Uh-oh."

Coralee nodded.

They were going to be alone on the floor with the heaviest
part of the patient-care twenty-four hours about to begin.
They had their own work to do and, in addition, the work that
would usually be done by two other people—such as the
making of beds and the delivery of two of the day's meals.

19

BY SEVEN O'CLOCK Day O'Meara was in her office on Medicine Two and at work on what she knew to be the most lethal
issue in the hospital: staffing.

As clinical coordinator for Medicine, she was responsible

for providing the nursing staff for each one of Medicine's ten floors. During the day, when complete patient care was required, the hospital's standard had been set at a ratio of five patients to each staff member on the floor (RN, LPN, nursing assistant, or medical worker), with a minimum of two RNs on each floor. It was commonplace for the ratio of patients to staff to be higher. Med Three had already called in short and Day had no one to substitute.

Evenings and nights, when the workload was lighter, the ratio became seven to one. Often this standard was not met either. At night a single RN might be responsible for an entire floor of more than twenty patients.

Midge Kelly, at the other desk in the glassed-in office, looked up from her set of master sheets of nurses over to Day. Midge was staffing the surgical floors and she said, "I'm sorry. I can't let you have anyone. My floors are running heavy."

The coordinators' clerk came in and spoke to Day. "Barnitska on Med Three called in. She won't be in this afternoon. Her grandmother died."

"I'm going to look it up in the paper," Day said.

"Don't bother," Midge said. "Her grandmother is still in Russia."

Day looked at the set of master sheets in front of her. She did not have enough RNs for the next shift. In particular, she now had no regular Med Three RN—the other nurse scheduled for the afternoon had been hired from an agency for the one shift. In addition, Day needed someone exactly like herself for the next shift, a nursing supervisor who was also qualified for Medicine's cardiac arrest team.

Her telephone rang. She said to Midge, "I'll flip if it's another resignation." She picked up the phone. "Day O'Meara."

A nurse on the Burn Unit said, "We have a twenty-five-year-old burn coming out of the unit having consistent respiratory distress. She's been on Silvadene. She's eating and drinking. Can you put her someplace?

"I have the beds," Day said, "but I haven't got the staff."

"We may need her bed on the unit at any time."

"I understand. But it's no good if we can't give her the care she requires. I'll see what can be done. I'm going on rounds in a while. I'll get back to you."

Med Three had a water bed. Ideal for a burn patient. But Med Three didn't have an RN coming in who knew anything of consequence about the care of a burn patient.

Day's telephone rang again. A house officer getting off duty on the emergency floor was calling to complain about a nurse's behavior toward some recent ER patients, "all of them ETOH," all of them with alcohol aboard when they'd come in. He said, "She's got to be told it's inappropriate, indoctrinating patients into AA meetings when they're bleeding to death."

Day said she would speak to the nurse.

Her back ached. She suspected it was tension. She stood up, and her white dress ballooned out. She looked down at her pregnancy. Pretty soon I'll need a wheelbarrow for it, she thought.

She saw from the papers on her desk that everyone from the flexie pool had already been booked.

There were agency nurses who might be available, nurses whom the hospital contracted for on a quota basis. Day distrusted the agency nurses. They worked for an agency rather than for a hospital. They often did not know where things were. They did not get to know the patients personally, as even the flexies did. The potential for human error in nursing care was thus vastly increased. And the patient's normal anxiety was that much increased when a new nurse suddenly replaced a familiar one.

But she needed RNs for the next shift. She called Dorothea Kullgren's office and was informed that the contractual quota for agency nurses had already been met for the next shift.

Viola Chambers stood in Day's office doorway. Her shift was long since over. She should have gone home long before.

"Do you want to see me?" Day said.

Viola looked at the two nurses at work with their master sheets and she shrugged and went over to a window that faced outside the hospital. There was no secret playground out there now. No Natalie up on Pedi to make one anymore.

Day tried calling some of her flexies direct. She had no success. Maybe, she thought, she would find someone on rounds willing to do a double shift. Nan Lassitter on the ICU would sometimes take a double shift. And Audrey Rosenfeld, who was already on Med Three, had been eager to take double shifts for a while a couple of months back.

In the other slots, Day figured she could always get by with LPNs and nursing assistants so long as she had an experienced RN on the floor. The critical problems remained an RN for Med Three, a supervisor, and an arrest team RN.

She kept pushing aside her awareness that she could fill two of those slots herself. But Jimbo would be upset or angry if she stayed the second shift. He did not want her working at all so close to her delivery date.

On the other hand, people might die if she or someone equally qualified did not work the next shift.

She not only had the next shift to be concerned about, but staffing for the weekend. It was not even eight in the morning and Day felt that she—and the hospital and the patients— were in deep trouble, lethal trouble. Somehow she would wrest them all out of it. She always had. In her mind she laughed at herself, at her sense of self-importance. Supernurse to the rescue.

20

BENNETT CHESSOFF'S OFFICE on the sixth floor of the New Wing was a large corner room. The two outside walls were of glass from waist height to the ceiling, giving him a splendid view of the surrounding slums. It was a view he enjoyed presenting to his visitors, particularly those from City Hall and the legislature.

He had spent part of the afternoon before at City Hall, receiving a short course in fiscal reality from the mayor himself. He was going to have to cut services and close beds. Some of his patients would die—some who didn't have to.

Then there had been the shit with McGettigan, via Keating, when he had gotten back from City Hall. One of his media contacts—a pressroom employee at the *Eagle*— had read him the Keating piece at two o'clock in the morning.

Today he got into his office a few minutes before seven, after stopping off in the ER to suggest to McGettigan his displeasure at McGettigan's statements to the press. Then he went up to his office, the outer office gray and still, the three desks for his secretary and two assistants not to be occupied until eight. His own office was also gray and still.

He turned on the single lamp on his desk and called Howard Sylvus at home. He woke Sylvus' wife. She told Bennett to call Howard on the mobile telephone in his limousine, he was already being driven into the city. Sylvus had agreed to divert to the hospital instead of going to his offices downtown.

Sylvus ignored the view. He had seen it before. "I hate like hell coming here in the limo," he said. "Makes a terrible impression. I always try to come here by cab."

"Your sensitivity is a wonder, Howard."

"This facility enjoys my counsel, and the counsel of the members of my firm, because we bill you as a hardship client. We are indeed sensitive to this neighborhood. Or we would not be your counsel."

Sylvus had read the Keating piece. He saw no particular significance in it. "We can negotiate with ARI. We can, as usual, negotiate till the cows come home."

"I don't think that's advisable," Bennett said.

"Then, of course, before the cows come home, ARI's leadership will disperse to follow individual careers and the situation will be defused. We've only to wait—what—six weeks? You take my point."

"I take your point, Howard. Howard, we have the chance to dispose of this situation, or its recurrence—dispose of it entirely—for years to come.

"Perhaps I haven't represented the situation clearly enough, Bennett. I thought I had last night. ARI has the right to negotiate. They have the right to present their grievances and have them discussed. I am your representative, the hospital's representative in those discussions, and, as I've just outlined, we can get out of them, as usual, free and clear, if—"

"Howard, I want you to be intentionally obnoxious to McGettigan. And to anyone else from ARI you meet with. I want you to be as arrogant and unreasonable as you can be."

"Bennett, I am obligated to take my instructions from you. Still, I have to question whether—

"There will be no questioning of this decision, Howard. None. My decisions are the Director's Council's decisions in this matter as well as my own."

"I see." Sylvus was reduced to plaintive body language. He spread his hands and arms. "It's just beyond me. We have the chance to avoid a real mess and—"

"My instructions to you are: I want you to be as arrogant and as unreasonable as you can be. Howard, I do not want you to come to me with terms of a settlement."

After Sylvus left, Bennett looked up the home telephone number of Michelle McCabe, the medical editor of the *Boston Post*. He called McCabe at her home and then he called Day O'Meara in her office over on Med Two.

21

TRINA FRANKIAN AWOKE because her telephone was ringing. She looked at her clock. The call would not be a trivial one. It was seven-thirty A.M. Anyone who knew her would know this was her sleeping time.

"Hello?"

"This is Jessy. Jessy Gladdens. I'm real, real scared, Trina."

Trina sat up in bed. She had seen the black teenager two nights before on the ER. Jessy had been raped by her ex-boyfriend, a neighborhood delinquent named Robert Higby, and Trina, who among other clinical specialties was a rape victim counselor, had been assigned to her.

Jessy had expressed such desperation and had been possessed by such a pervasive need for her counselor's support that Trina had given the young woman her unlisted number.

"I told you that might happen, Jessy. It's natural."

"I'm so scared. My friend's gone to work. I'm so *frightened*."

"You're alone?"

"Yes."

"Is there anyone you can call to stay with you till your friend gets home? Someone you can go to?"

"I'm scared to call anyone else. I don't want anyone to know where I am."

"What about your mother?"

"She thinks what happened got to be *my* fault." Trina heard the girl cry and then speak through her sobs. "I feel so dirty. I keep goin' to take a shower. But I'm scared to get undressed."

"Jessy, you have reasonable feelings of vulnerability. But scared of what? Anything in particular?"

"That he'll find me. Robert. That he'll get me for telling the police and the district attorney on him."

Trina spent a quarter of an hour reassuring Jessy of the normalcy of her fears and feelings about herself as a result of the violation. "These things can be talked out, Jessy. With me, or your friend, or anyone else you trust."

"I jes want to stay put. I'm too scared to go out."

"You ought to come in for a physical follow-up. That's important."

"He find me, I come to the hospital."

Over the minutes Trina managed to steady Jessy a little, lessen the degree of fear and agitation. Almost immediately after she'd said good-bye the telephone rang again. "Hello?"

She heard breathing, nothing else.

She said, "You can talk to me or I'll hang up and disconnect the phone."

"Gonna get you, bitch," a male voice said. "Gonna cut you bad. Less you stay outa my business."

"What business is that?"

"You been sendin' my lady to the police and a DA, and you been havin' her tell lies 'bout me. Case you don't unnerstan' who this is, that little Jessy twat is who I'm talkin' 'bout. You unnerstan' what I'm sayin' to you, bitch?"

"I understand."

She heard a click. She hung up.

She waited twenty minutes and while she waited she dressed. Once during the twenty minutes the telephone rang just part of a ring, just enough for someone to satisfy himself that her telephone was not in use, that she was not talking to the police. If he had her telephone number, did Robert Higby have her address, too? She lived in a third-floor walkup on Beacon Street just above Kenmore Square.

She placed her hand on the phone, admitting to herself that she was uneasy. She called Jessy. She tried to keep any indication of tension out of her wording. "Feeling any better?"

"Still scared. I almost jumped outa my skin, this phone rang. I was scared it was him, that he'd gone and found me."

Trina offered her another dose of reassurance. Then, "One thing I forgot to ask. Is there anyone you'd like me to talk to? Anyone you'd like to call me?"

"Can't think of no one."

"Anyone you might have given my number to?"

"No, ma'am."

The reply overstressed? "Sometimes a patient will give my number to someone they want to call me. I just want to know in advance."

She hoped Jessy believed her.

She called Sergeant Kinney, the officer assigned to Jessy's case, at District Sixteen, the police station that covered the area where the rape had occurred and that included the hospital as well. She was fortunate and got Kinney at his desk. She told him about the call from Higby. Kinney put her on Hold, which she thought was odd.

Then he got back on. "I just gave 'em a shout over your way at District Four. They're dispatchin' a cruiser to you. They'll have a reconnoiter for Higby and then they'll check out your building and you." They discussed how Higby might have gotten Trina's number. "I mean," the sergeant said, "you don't think the girl herself would give your number to Higby, do you?"

"No, I don't."

"Prob'ly be a good idea if you stay with a friend yourself, next coupla days. Till we pick this jerk up."

"I appreciate your concern, Sergeant. But I'll stay here. I get threats all the time. If I acted on them, I'd never be able to stay in the same place two weeks in a row."

"Yeah, I can see that, your line of work. Mine, too. But you usually get these threats at home onna *un*listed telephone?"

Trina went into the bathroom, put a towel over her shoulders, and began brushing her hair. After a while she made coffee. When the knocking came it was very loud. She stood without moving. The knocking was repeated even more insistently and then a male voice identified himself as a police officer.

When she let them in, the two officers informed her that the basement, stairs, and roof of her building were clean and that they had seen no one of Higby's description around the premises. The district would run twenty-four-hour spot checks in the area. At night, when she was about to leave work and come home, she should call the district and they'd try to have a cruiser meet her, a couple of officers see her safely inside. In any event she should report to the district when she was safely home.

22

VIOLA CHAMBERS HAD remained in the nursing coordinators' outer office. She looked out the window. She did not realize that she had placed the palm of one hand against the glass. The sky was gray and low and still and, in the distance, it seemed to press down like some massive, solid weight. From beyond the hospital's laundry building, the faces of the tenements, she thought, stared back at her with condemnation. She felt herself become angry at the people out there, as if they had chosen to live where they lived, chosen deprivation for their children.

Day O'Meara left the inner office and went over to Viola. She saw tears on the young woman's face. She made a deliberately neutral remark: "Your shift was over awhile back."

"I thought they could use some extra help over there."

"Why?"

Viola shrugged. "Talk to the children."

"About what?"

"Last night."

Day nodded. "Pedi."

"Children's Seven." The tears continued. There was no sound of crying.

Day had seen a report, but it had told her little enough, and nothing at all about the nurse. "What happened?"

"A little girl. A child. Wasn't *supposed* to be that sick. Nothing in her history . . . She just went into respiratory arrest *and there was nothing we could do!*" Her hand on the window glass contracted into a fist.

Day placed her arm around Viola. Viola looked at the older nurse angrily, but Day held on to her. In a moment the rage in Viola's face dissipated and exhaustion succeeded it. She took a handkerchief from her pocket and patted the streaks of tears.

Day said, "Want to talk it over with a psych nurse?"

"I came over to say I'm tired. I'm tired in my mind. I came over to say I can't work tonight, I can't work this weekend." She shrugged. "I guess I'm gonna, though. I guess I will."

"I see where you have one Critical on Children's Seven. Still," Day said.

"Yes."

"It's gotten so that's good news. Every time I see that, I know Jamaal's still alive. He got through another day. And night."

Day thought of the little brown body in the white diaper and tiny white socks. Never been home, never going home.

"Yes," she said. "We still have one Critical on Children's Seven." She turned and left, her head down, her body moving slowly.

From her desk the clerk said, "What numbers you got, Day?"

Day took the two beepers out of her pocket and looked. "Two-four-six and three-two-six."

The clerk wrote the numbers down and Day started to leave for rounds, then she heard the telephone and her clerk saying, "Day, it's the director."

Day took the telephone and said, "Day O'Meara."

"Day, Bennett. You're about to start on rounds?"

"Yes."

"I'd like you to delay and be in my office at nine."

"I can be in your office at nine. But I should go ahead and make my first stop. The ICU."

"Any problems there?"

"How do you mean, Bennett?"

"Did you see the Keating piece this morning?"

"Yes."

"Problems such as McGettigan alleged?"

"No. No problems like those. Not that I know of."

There was silence on the director's end. "Well then, go

ahead and visit the unit.'' There was a pause. ''What do you
think of what McGettigan said?''

''I thought it stank.''

''Nine o'clock,'' the director said and disconnected.

Day did not immediately appreciate that she had never
before been summoned to the director's office.

23

THE INTENSIVE CARE unit was on Medicine Five, an entire floor
that was otherwise closed except for the seven beds in the
unit. Day walked down the empty corridor. On an understaffed Memorial Day weekend—prior to Bennett Chessoff's
arrival four years back—the floor had been consolidated with
Med Four in order to make the most efficient use of beds and
staff. But Med Five had never been reopened, not even when
the funds had become available. Bennett Chessoff had gotten
his precious Gold Coast instead.

At the end of the corridor there were aluminum swinging
doors placarded in English and Spanish against unauthorized
visitation and smoking. Day went through the doors and a
separation corridor and through another set of doors into the
unit.

Six beds faced each other from either side of the unit.
Above each bed was a clock with a single hand pointing to
zero. A seventh bed in an isolation room was reserved for
dangerously infectious patients or patients especially suscepti-
ble to the common infectious agents in the hospital.

Between the two rows of beds was a glassed-in room that
had the appearance of the top floor of an airport control
tower. The resemblance was intensified by the multiscreen
patient-monitoring equipment within. The glass enclosure was
the nurses' station. Two crash carts standing outside it contained the medications and equipment for addressing cardiac
arrest. On the other floors, where there were three and four
times as many patients, there would only be a single crash
cart. But here even simultaneous arrests were not uncommon.

Day entered the station. The head nurse was involved in some paperwork. Outside the station a white male in his fifties was sitting in front of his bed, watching a cartoon on a black-and-white television set. Nearby a black man sat upright in a chair asleep, invasive lines, Day thought, extending into every God-made and man-made orifice in his body. Mr. Emerson. Nan Lassitter, in a green scrub dress, crossed from a bed on one side of the room to a bed on the other. Another nurse was checking a ventilator.

The nurses on this unit cared for the most acute of the hospital's patients, those suffering from multisystem disease and critical trauma. The ratio of patients to nurses was two to one and sometimes was adjusted to one to one. The ICU nurses dealt with the same sort of priorities as the surgeons and often with the same urgency. The equipment with which they tended their patients tapped into the patients' bodies and both supported and monitored them. The equipment was elaborate, sophisticated, and sometimes subject to inexplicable erraticism to which the nurses had to respond immediately and deliberately and without being intimidated by either the equipment or the patient's possible crisis. The nurses on the unit worked in unremitting challenge and at extremely high levels of stress and technical competency.

The head nurse closed a binder and put it aside.

Day said, "How's it goin', Tim?"

The head nurse, as if reassuring himself, glanced at a console of miniature screens that gave him, in line display, the cardiac readouts of the patients on the unit. "Not bad," he said. "Been quiet. I'm having a hassle with the Respiratory Therapy Department. We can get to that later."

He wore a short-sleeved blue scrub shirt. A stethoscope lay across his shoulders and his all-purpose tool, Kelly clamps, was clipped to the shirt. He had a short, evenly trimmed, and intensely black beard. He was thirty-two years old and had been a registered nurse for three years, two of them in the ICU.

Tim Holbrook, Day thought, like the other male nurses she knew, was a great deal more career-oriented than most of his female colleagues. He had *had* to be in order to withstand the severe buffeting he had suffered as a result of his decision to quit an entirely different sort of career and enter nursing. His buffeting came not from within the profession but from the outside community and, most fiercely and painfully, from his wife, Valerie.

"For some reason," Tim said, "I'm not getting any numbers today. No lites, no crits."

"There's probably some reason. God knows what. Some godawful reason. I'll get back to you." She made a note. "Anyone bumpable?"

The figure of speech obscured the life-and-death nature of the question. Patients were triaged to the unit not only on the basis of critical need, but also in competition with each other for the seven beds. If two patients were equally needful and only one bed was available, the patient who was most likely to benefit from the unit got the bed—the patient more likely to live.

"Mr. Kincaid. His crit's been stable for the last two days. He's not even going to DT. A great candidate for the floor. Also, we have a diabetic who could go to the floor. Mr. Lieberman came in with a blood sugar of two thousand—"

"Two thousand? I never heard of that."

"Yup. Two thousand. He got five units and it went from two thousand to four hundred." He noded toward a corner bed. "Mr. Carpenter down there with Nan is a white twenty-five-year-old who overdosed on one of the methanols—automobile antifreeze. His friends brought him into the ER last night. He's not bumpable."

Tim turned toward a sleeping, thirty-five-year-old black woman. "Mrs. Saunders," he said. "Just after suctioning she's always dropping her rate. On the other hand, everything I do today she's yelling at me."

"She's getting better," Day said.

Tim indicated another patient. "Miss Carmona is stabilizing nicely. But she's still critical."

Nan Lassitter came to a doorway of the station. "See you before you go, Day?"

"Sure, Nan."

Tim and Day looked at the only patient on the unit whom they had not yet discussed. "Mr. Emerson," Day said. Tim exhaled deeply.

They were looking at the man who was asleep in his chair. Over his johnnie he was dressed in a vest of silvery material, a wraparound armless jacket that, in the back, secured him to the chair and held him upright. His shoulders slumped in sleep, but his head remained nearly erect. A tube entered his broad nose through a nostril and connected his lungs to a ventilator. Other tubes connected him to medication, nourishment, a gastric suctioning machine, and monitoring equipment. His hands were in mitts to prevent him from harming himself or his tubular environment.

Tim said, "If the HO keeps increasing support, Mr. Emerson's going to die in agony. His mind's functioning. He's going to know what's going on as it happens. It's going to be very bad."

He was a strong, thick, healthy-looking man. His shoulders were broad and supported by a prodigious trunk. But the multisystem diseases that immense trunk encased, Day thought. A big, floppy heart subject to congestive failure. Kidney disease that necessitated twice-weekly peritoneal dialysis. Pulmonary complications. Mr. Emerson could receive maintenance only. Surgery was out of the question. What Tim was talking about was the pulmonary condition, the inevitable course it was taking. Mr. Emerson's chronic obstructive pulmonary disease had been critically complicated by the failure of his blood to clot. He could bleed into any area of his body.

"He's started to bleed from the mucosa of his lungs. There's no response to anything we do for him. We can't break the cycle. He's just going to get much, much worse."

Until he drowns, Day thought. Drowns in his own blood seeping into his lungs. With his mind aware of it as it happens. The mind gasping for breath the lungs cannot take. The process not a swift one.

"I don't know where the fuck the HO's head is," Tim said. He looked back toward Mr. Emerson. "Fifty-nine years old and he's lived in the neighborhood all his life. His wife said they could have moved, he's a postal worker, but he kept every cent he could for his son's education. The son's a third-year law student at Suffolk now. Mrs. Emerson delivered here and they used to bring the son to Pedi. Mrs. Emerson thinks the medicine here is great. She's seen Mr. Emerson here on the unit twice before and, of course, both times he went home. Which makes all this misleading to her. And to the son and to Mr. Emerson's sister. The HO wasn't straight with them. You can look at the chart and you can see we're dealing with rapid deterioration, the coping systems are failing—and the HO just skimmed over that like it was reversible. He told them, 'It's a wait-and-see situation.' Which is bullshit. It's just misrepresenting things to them terribly.''

"Well?" Day said quietly. "The doc's got some emotional investment in the patient, a professional investment. The docs can't stand it when they discover they're not in control."

Tim made deliberate eye contact with Day. "The doc hasn't discussed it with me and I haven't discussed it with him, but I think the doc's orders are going to have to be reevaluated."

Day was looking at Mr. Emerson. Even in sleep he had tremendous male dignity. Tim was talking about a change of orders. A new order the house officer could write. DNR. Do not resuscitate.

So that Mr. Emerson would be spared the singular experience of feeling his own blood fill his lungs while his mind struggled without recourse against the fact.

At the next crisis prior to his drowning here five floors above street level, at some other crisis during which Mr. Emerson was unconscious, neither medication nor mechanical support would be increased. Nothing sustaining Mr. Emerson would be withdrawn. But nothing that might prolong his life would be offered. If the HO wrote the order.

"The family has got to be talked to straight," Tim said. "It ought to be done today."

"Well, clear it with the HO and talk with them yourself."

"Trina's been up a couple of times with them. Maybe she'll help."

Day found herself looking at what she always thought of as *the zero clock* above Mr. Emerson's bed.

In the event of an arrest, the nurse was to call the code and start the clock as she initiated cardiopulmonary resuscitation by means of mouth-to-mouth respiration and, if she had another nurse to assist, chest compressions. If the arrest were successfully countered, the clock would have recorded how much time the patient's brain had been without oxygen. That in turn would indicate how much brain damage had probably been incurred.

Day had never seen a zero clock in motion. When an arrest was in progress, people had too many other things to do than start the clock.

Day looked at her notebook. "Mr. Improta's down on Med Three."

"How's he doing?"

"His respiratory status is fine. He's hardly arrhythmic. He's under control. His problem is, he has a lot of anxiety about the way he acted when he was up here—he remembers some of his psychotic behavior when he was hooked up to the machines."

"I'll stop by and reassure him on my way home—*oh Jesus!*"

"What?"

"I'm supposed to pick up Jason right after work."

"Valerie's letting you have Jason?"

"She's probably got an overnight date and couldn't find an overnight sitter. Not on a school night."

"You could see Mr. Improta tomorrow."

"No, I'll work it in before I get Jason. No use leaving people in pain. Or anxiety."

"There's nothing good on TV," the man who had been watching television called.

Tim went to the open entry and said, "I'll get the sheets on for you in a minute, Mr. Lieberman." He came back to Day and said, "The other thing. The Respiratory Therapy Department thinks it's going to bring medical students onto the unit."

"I haven't heard a thing about it."

"There's no protocol been established, no curriculum. Nothing about what will be taught and in what manner."

"I don't believe it."

"A bunch of students in here. What do they think an ICU is?"

"It must have bypassed committee. I haven't heard a thing about it."

"It's got to be settled."

"We'll settle it with boxing gloves if we have to."

"It's not fair to this patient population," Tim said.

"I agree. It needs to be checked out. It needs to be blocked. Look, I'll just call over there and remind them that Nursing is still responsible for respiratory care on ICUs." She made a note. Then she paused and looked around the unit. "But everything's under control?"

"We're sitting pretty."

"Don't tell anyone."

*   *   *

Tim relieved Nan, and she accompanied Day out into the empty corridor. "I have a simple request, Day, but it's urgent."

"What?"

"I want to get off the unit."

Day nodded. "Is this sudden or—"

"It's Mr. Emerson. And maybe I've been on the unit too long anyway. Almost two years. You can stay on the unit too long."

Day nodded again. "I'm short of staff. *We're* short of staff, all over."

"Then I can be used somewhere else. It's either that or I resign. Last night and this morning I thought I was going to leave nursing entirely."

"Why aren't you?"

"I really don't want to."

"If you had a choice, where would you like to be?"

"I'd like to be with Selma Pushkin on Med Seven."

"There's a lot of geriatric work on that floor."

"I know. I had a lot of geriatric experience. Before I graduated. I'd like to get back to it."

"Sort of like going from the Celts and the NBA . . . to what? The Wiseapples?"

"No, it isn't, Day. Fix it up for me. Today or tomorrow. I don't want to see Mr. Emerson die."

24

DAY GOT TO Bennett Chessoff's office just at nine and the secretary sent her right in. The room was a surprise to Day. There was pebbled gray and white wall-to-wall carpeting. A white couch faced a glass coffee table. Matching armchairs, covered in the same white material, faced each other from either end of the coffee table. At one end of the room was a large conference table. At the other end, Bennett's desk faced inward from in front of a panoramic window. Day thought it was a splendid office. Then she was vaguely irritated by it. It was entirely too cheerful, entirely too expensive and *comfortable* for the institution it both governed and represented.

Bennett, in shirtsleeves with gold cuff links, was seated at one end of the couch talking with a woman seated at the other end. The woman was about forty, her hair pulled back tightly. She wore a tailored dark suit.

"Ah, Day," Bennett said. He and the woman rose. "Do you know Michelle McCabe of the *Post?*"

"Not personally. But I certainly know the byline." The two women shook hands and Bennett indicated that they were all to sit.

"Michelle is interested in perhaps writing a response to the Keating piece."

"Not a response," McCabe said, "an overview."

"She'd like to look at conditions in the hospital. I thought if she accompanied you on rounds she'd see exactly what this hospital is and what it isn't. An objective view because she'll see everything you see. Also objective because you can't be said to be either management or ARI."

"That's not exactly true. I'm a supervisor. That's a managerial position.

"Your contract is that of a nurse."

Several odd things had just happened, Day realized. One of them was that Bennett was so intimate with her contract. Another was that he was going to let a reporter onto the medical floors—the guts, so to speak, along with the surgical floors, of the hospital. Bennett encouraged and even courted media coverage of the hospital, but it was always restricted to the glory exploits of the trauma teams in the ER or to celebrity presences on the Gold Coast.

Day led Michelle McCabe from the bright modernity of the New Wing to the worn interior of Medical One where they waited, at the end of a corridor, for an elevator. A transportation worker was already waiting with a patient on a gurney.

"Been some wait," the transportation worker said. "I sure am glad I ain't got a patient that's really, really bad off."

The patient, an elderly black man, looked up at Day with a passive, silent beseechment. It was a look common to patients who find themselves on gurneys in hospitals. Day did not recognize the man. She said to the transportation worker, "What floor is he going to?"

"Three."

She said to the patient, "You've got good nurses on your floor. Audrey Rosenfeld, Coralee Wafford. I hope they're doing right by you."

"They'se been fine." He continued to look at Day pleadingly.

The elevator door slid open. Day got in and flipped the red emergency switch to its STOP position. She nodded to the transportation worker and he rolled the patient in. Day pressed the emergency switch to its OFF position and then pushed the button for the third floor.

She said to the patient, "I'm glad to hear that. You're Mr. . . . ?"

"Toby."

"Maybe I can look in on you later, Mr. Toby."

"They'se gettin' ready to fix me up with a pacemaker."

The elevator stopped and Mr. Toby was rolled onto Med Three. Then Day pushed the button for Med Ten. She said to McCabe, "We'll start at the top and work our way down floor by floor."

"Does the elevator usually take that long?"

"Often," Day said. "A lot of people have to use it. There's only one at each end of a floor."

When, after stops on the way up for patients and some staff, they got off at Med Ten, Day said, "This is really fast work on your part."

"How do you mean?"

"Catching the Keating article, getting on to Bennett right off—"

"Oh no. Bennett called me. This piece is his idea."

25

TIM HOLBROOK STOOD by the phone in the station. He did not want to make the calls that might result in a DNR order for Mr. Emerson. It was the only humane thing that could be done for Mr. Emerson at this irreversible stage. But now, inside his own self, Tim could understand the HO's refusal to confront this responsibility to his patient.

Tim went out to Mr. Emerson. Through a nasal-gastro tube, a Gomco machine provided intermittent suctioning of Mr. Emerson's stomach. The machine stood on its own cart. A light on it lit up, there was a click, and then a sucking and slurping sound as liquid was suctioned through thick, clear tubing and into a small, heavy, plastic cylinder. Tim unscrewed the suction top and removed the disposable suction bottle from the heavy cylinder. He assessed the gross-looking contents and the discoloration due to the percentage of blood present. He replaced the suction bottle with a new one and screwed the parts together again so that the machine and the lines and the receptacle were once more self-enclosed. He sealed the top of the old suction bottle and disposed of it in a hopper. He washed and then preoxygenated Mr. Emerson and then gave him chest PT, clapping the man's chest hard enough to loosen whatever materials were adhering to the lungs. Mr. Emerson's eyes blinked open and then closed. Tim suctioned the lungs. There was more blood after the chest suctioning—increasing amounts of bright red streaky blood.

When the procedure was done, Mr. Emerson, as if he had been waiting, opened his eyes again and looked at Tim.

"Anything I can do for you, Mr. Emerson?"

Mr. Emerson closed his eyes, but not in sleep or unconsciousness.

After several seconds he opened his eyes again. Tim put his hand on Mr. Emerson's shoulder. "I'll do everything I can for you, Mr. Emerson."

Mr. Emerson nodded slightly. Then he closed his eyes.

His family would be in at two. It was now near ten.

Tim called a hospital extension and when there was no answer he had Dr. Silver, the ICU chief resident, paged. Silver rang back within the minute.

"Nothing wild going on, Aaron. Just want to talk to you for a minute about Mr. Emerson." Tim emphasized the blood content in the suctionings from both stomach and lungs. "It's coming in a lot more quickly, Aaron."

"Well, DIC, they bleed if you look at them. What about irritation from the lines?"

"It's not the lines."

"Yeah."

"The patient shouldn't have to drown."

"It's not as if we could prevent that. There's nothing we can do."

"Yes, there is."

"I haven't ever . . . I couldn't. *I can't.*"

"It's unfair to the patient."

"No."

"It's *cruel* to the patient."

"No. I can't." His voice had a pleading quality to it.

"The family will be here at two. I'm going to get Trina up if I can. She and I will talk to them. Explain what's going on, what the options are. It ought to be you doing that. You should at least be here with us.

"No . . ."

"He's your patient."

"I am not available for that conference. Do you understand?"

"I understand, Aaron. You understand something from my side."

"I'm listening."

"You don't sit up here in the ICU. You visit. For you it's a rotation. A particularly demanding one, but a rotation. We're here all the time. Have I still got your attention?"

"Yes."

"People don't have to die in agony. They may have to die, but there's some choice at the end. There's needless agony on this unit sometimes, Doctor."

Aaron Silver was silent. Then, in a quiet voice, he said, "I'll tell you this, Tim, I wish I was off the damn unit."

"You'll be getting that luxury. So will Mr. Emerson. Of course, you'll leave a little more comfortably than he will."

"That's a shit remark to make, Holbrook."

"I know it is."

There was a silence and Tim thought nothing more was going to be said. Then he heard the resident's voice. "You talk to the family. You and Trina." Another silence. "I'll follow the family's wishes."

26

ELIN MAKI'S SCHEDULED patient had not shown up and in the interim before her next appointment she was catching up on paperwork.

"Mrs. Maki?"

She looked up and decided that the young man standing in the doorway to her office was a medical student. He wore a white jacket over his tie and shirt and he had the subdued look of someone who was both overworked and attentive.

"Mrs. Maki?"

"Sort of."

"My name is Hal Levy. I'm a third-year student over from Cambridge."

Elin found herself engaged by the way the fellow looked out at her from behind his glasses, so studious and vulnerable. He had to be older than he seemed, but he *appeared* to be ten years younger than she.

"Your husband—"

"Ex-husband. Charles."

"I met him at a party a few days ago." He seemed very hesitant, Elin thought. His head tilted down ever so slightly. Then he looked at her fixedly again and if there was something boyish about him, there was also something very grown up and very male. "Some friends of mine invited me to a party of theirs. Computer people.'

"Ah," Elin said. Charles was a program designer.

The young man took out an envelope. "I hardly spoke to him. But anyway, when Charles left, he gave me this." Hal removed some money and two sheets of paper, which he unfolded. Elin recognized Charles' odd handwriting, half cursive, half block. The young man handed her the two sheets of paper.

Elin read:

Dear Dr. Levy, or you soon shall be, at any rate. I wish you every success in your grueling and demanding prep-

*aration. It leaves, I know, precious little time for social
or even home life. My former wife demonstrated that.
But human companionship ought to be a part of a
physician's—or even a nurse clinician's—daily bread,
don't you agree? so that they take their places in their
profession as human beings. When you settle yourself at
Back Bay Metropolitan Hospital, please introduce yourself to Elin Maki of the nursing staff there. Perhaps you
might show her this communication, a brief moment the
three or us may share together, though at a distance, as
tomorrow I fly to California to begin new employment
there.*

Elin was transfixed. It was eerie. She could hear Charles'
voice. She was aware, as well, that Hal Levy was watching
her. She glanced at him. His physician's look, she decided,
the assessing look. She continued to read:

*The enclosed fifty dollars is in the nature of an invitation
to human companionship. If time permits from your mutual grueling professional demands, please have dinner
together at my expense. Sincerely,*

                                        Charles Maki

"The sonofabitch," Elin said.
"This is an easy rotation," Hal Levy said. Elin saw that he
was deeply flushed, embarrassed. "I'm off Sunday evening."
"Thank you, but I think not."
"I don't mind. I mean, I don't know anybody here. It
could be sort of professional, not like a date."
Elin laughed. Hal looked down and Elin felt like getting up
and hugging him. Instead she said, "Thank you, Hal. It was
kind of you to stop by. I appreciate it. I know Charles does."
Hal held out the money. "Maybe you could take yourself
out to dinner."
"No, you keep it. I'm sure there's someone you'd like to
go out with."
"Not really," he said with his direct, boyish look and the
unnecessary honesty. "We broke up over Christmas. She said
I don't have enough time for her."
Elin laughed. "I'm sorry," she said, "for laughing." She
felt like reaching out her hand to him, but he stood too far

away. "Let's have coffee sometime. What's your schedule like?"

"I start Psychiatry today. Evening shift the next six weeks. And I start Neurology tomorrow. Daytimes."

"We'll get together. Call if you need any help."

He started to put the money down on a table by the door.

"I really don't want it," Elin said.

Her tone was such that Hal nodded. She noticed that he did not put the money in his pocket, but left with it still in his hand, as if he had no idea what to do with it.

Did I really freeze Charles out like that? Did I really shut him out that completely? Her phone rang. Reception had her next patient. Her mind reviewed the history even as she lifted the chart from the stack on her desk.

27

ON MED TEN. Day said hello to a woman who was sitting outside her room in a wheelchair and then went to the station and introduced Michelle McCabe to the head nurse. The head nurse looked fatigued. She said to Day, "One of our patients didn't make it through the night."

"I know. But you're sending three people home today, right?"

The head nurse's face relaxed slightly. "Right."

"I want to check the potassium level on this lady who came in last night."

"It went up to three point one at one A.M. and then to three point zero at three A.M. Where it is now, I don't know. The lab says don't expect anything back till one. I just hope her bloods and her sugar correlate."

"And on this other lady," Day said. She looked at her book. "Mrs. Pine."

"Yeah, she developed focal seizures."

"I want to check the Dilantin level." She said to McCabe, "There's a good chance the medication is causing the vision problems."

"The Dilantin's been DCed," the head nurse said.

"For how long?"

"Since last night."

Day said, "Well then, tell her, cut out the bullshit, no more seizures.

"I did. Didn't work. I'm trying to get the HO now. He's not answering his page."

"Anything else?"

"We're low on laundry."

"So what else is new?"

"We ran out of johnnies last night. A seventy-two-year-old woman, she was incontinent. She got herself out of her johnnie and the night nurse found her on the floor by her bed. Asleep and naked. She got a johnnie from another floor—"

"She left the floor to get it?"

"What do you think? The johnnie walked up here by itself?"

"Terrific. I'll have to speak to her." She made a note.

"I still can't get any johnnies from the laundry."

"I'll check it out."

Neither of the nurses on Med Ten was available for a double shift.

Day took McCabe down a fire-safe stairwell to Med Nine. As soon as they entered the corridor Day said, "Uh-oh."

"What?"

"The HO at the station is Anita Rounds. A cardiologist. Normally she wouldn't be on this floor." She was on the phone.

At the station the head nurse said to Day, "A patient in for a general metabolic workup. But this morning he started complaining of chest pains, nausea, pain in the left arm. I called Anita."

Still holding the phone to her ear, the HO looked at Day angrily and said, "I'm trying to make a diagnosis and the EKG isn't working." She waved at a machine. A handprinted sign on it read: NON-FUNCTIONAL. BIOMED PLEASE FIX.

"Someone in with the patient?"

"Yes," the head nurse said.

"We've got an MI? An incipient arrest? How can I tell without a machine?" the HO said.

The head nurse said, "I reported it yesterday and I reported it again this morning, and no one's been up from BioMed to pick it up or replace it.''

The HO slammed down the receiver. ''They don't have anything to replace the machine. They don't have the staff to work on it. They've got other machines already on the bench.'' She stopped. ''All right. I've got to move the patient to a machine.'' She dialed a number. ''This is Dr. Rounds on Med Nine. I need to move a patient to the ER. I need a gurney or even a wheelchair.'' She listened. She smiled at the head nurse. ''Transportation doesn't have anyone available.'' Then, into the phone, ''Goddamn it, *make* someone available.'' She slammed the receiver down again. ''Have we got a wheelchair on the floor?''

''Yes, but one of the wheels is locked.''

''This is incredible,'' the HO said. ''You've got an incipient arrest situation and what does the cardiology resident do? Has to go looking for a wheelchair.''

Day said to the head nurse, ''Go up to Med Ten. They'll have a wheelchair for you.'' She picked up the phone and dialed.

The head nurse left.

''Beautiful,'' the HO said, and strode away to her patient.

''Jane? Day. I want you to bump that lady in the wheelchair back into bed. We need the chair on Nine real quick.''

After she hung up she said to Michelle McCabe, ''You don't take notes.''

''I'll remember what's significant. The down EKG machine, is that usual around here?''

''It happens.''

''And the wheelchair?''

''That happens too.''

''Is anything done about it?''

''Not much. Not since I've been here.''

''How long have you been here?''

''Fourteen years.''

''And it's been the same all that time?''

''Even before. This patient population has no political clout. There's no money, and a lot of people don't vote. They're dependent on City Hall and the legislature for medicine. So, as a population, they're last in line for whatever they get.''

In a few moments they saw Anita Rounds wheel her patient into an elevator as the head nurse came back to the station.

Day said, "How's the patient?"

"The signs are the same. So're his complaints. It's Anita who's ready to blow a vessel."

Day said to McCabe, "There's a new breed of house officer that doesn't adapt to this place very well."

The head nurse said, "Anita's furious about all the time she already had to spend this morning being a medical secretary. Now she's bitching about having to be a transportation worker. 'Is that the proper way for a physician to spend her time?' she says."

"Nonadaptive breed," Day said. "Wants to change everything. All talk. Like Scotty."

The head nurse said to McCabe, "Anita's vice-president of ARI." And to Day, "Maybe just talk, but it seems to me they've all gotten a lot more vocal the last few days."

"Okay. Back to the floor."

"They're telling me we can't do blood gases on the floor today."

"I don't understand that."

"Neither do I," the head nurse said.

"I'll check it out," Day said, making a note.

"There're lab tests not being returned. There's no excuse for that."

Day sighed. "The HOs are going to have to use their own leverage on that."

"I've had to get johnnies and sheets from other floors. And Med Ten called down asking *us* for johnnies. What are those people *doing* over in the laundry? I work my ass off here and what are they *doing* over there?"

"I suspect what they're doing is being overworked. The lab technicians too. The same as the rest of us."

The nurse bit her upper lip and looked at Day, and Day understood that now she would hear the deepest worry, not just the concerns that were bad enough but recurrent.

"I have a full floor of patients," the head nurse said. "No vent nurse. But I've got a patient on a vent. I almost missed giving a patient his heart medication. *Can you believe that?*"

Day nodded slightly.

No, neither of the floor nurses was available for a double.

The head nurse said, "I'll be working into the next shift just getting my page twos done. And it's my son's birthday."

Day started to leave, then stopped. She said to McCabe, "Something is peculiar. Something is not going on." She turned back to the head nurse. "Any fallout from the Keating article? Patient anxiety?"

"I don't think they know about it."

"How is that?"

"The candy lady doesn't get here till noon."

Day said to McCabe, "The candy lady is the one who brings the newspapers."

28

MOLLY CHANG MET Liz Swanzey in the conference room on Medicine Seven. Molly closed the door and sat at the pink Formica-topped table where house officers wrote up patients and where nurses sometimes found a moment for a hasty sandwich or salad.

"Hello," Molly said. Liz did not respond. She did not sit when Molly sat. Molly reminded herself of her hypothesis that the nurse's outbursts were acts of self-protection. She said, "Tell me about the patient."

Liz remained standing, her stance expressing anger. She was looking out the window and she continued to do so as she said, "Don't bullshit me. It's *me* you want to talk about. What did *I* do?"

"You tell me."

The nurse sat down, but her body remained tense. "His name's Larkin. Fifty-five years old. White. Mild cirrhosis. A drunk. He's been in before. He's being treated for an ulcerated thigh."

"He gives you trouble?"

"He thinks he can run my life."

"Can he?"

"He's constantly ordering me around."

"Like what?"

"Roll me over. Get me a glass of water. Give me a massage."

Molly waited for something more significant, but Liz was silent. "And how do you respond to that?"

Liz looked at Molly steadily and angrily, but she spoke quietly. "I yelled at him. I gave him what he deserved. I told him the truth. That he's a drunk. That he wouldn't be in here if he took care of himself. Elin Maki saw him in Primary Care before the thigh became ulcerated. He just didn't take his meds. Of course it got worse and worse till he finally had to come back and go to a floor. I can't stand the drunks, the self-abusers, come back over and over again. We work so hard for them and they don't do *anything* for themselves."

"They still have their rights."

"What rights?"

"The right to be rolled over in bed. The right to respect from us no matter what we think of them privately." Molly got no reply. "There's something here that mystifies me, Liz."

"What?" Her voice was tentative.

"You're good with alcoholics. Especially good."

"I should be. I've had enough practice. My father's a drunk."

"In the past . . . that experience of yours benefited the patient. What's the difference this time?"

The nurse shrugged, looked out the window.

"Anything about Mr. Larkin remind you of your father?"

Liz's posture became rigid. "He orders me around. He criticizes me."

"Mr. Larkin or your father?"

"Both. No, my father." Then she was silent. She looked down at her hands grasping each other.

"Yeah, it's difficult when we have patients who make us think of someone close." Molly was thinking that she had to be very careful now. Not to let the nurse embarrass herself. Not to get further into something deeply personal. Rearrange the furniture in the living room. Do not attempt to redesign the house.

"He calls me up," Liz said. "These past few weeks he's been on me all the time." She stood up suddenly and just as suddenly became tearful. "What did I *do?* I'm twenty-five years old, I'm not a baby. Why am I still feeling this way?"

"You're disappointed in not having the father you wanted. And angry."

The nurse sat down.

"This has been around forever probably. But now it's kicking up so much shit in you, you can't suppress it."

Liz was looking down at her now-open hands, tears still on her face.

"Would you like some help? A referral? There's no stigma."

Liz spoke hesitantly. "You understand already. Would *you* work with me?"

"I wouldn't want to interfere with the regular relationship. You might have trouble working with me here on the job, looking at me. You might be hurt by what I say. But I'll get you someone good."

Liz dried her face. "I feel like I've gone through something terrible but now I'm okay."

"No, you're not okay." Molly paused. "That's important for you to realize."

"I feel a lot better."

"You feel relief. For temporary relief, see Molly Chang. For something more permanent, see whoever Molly comes up with."

Molly looked at Liz and was not sure whether she would or wouldn't.

Liz's face hardened. "One thing I know. I want off this floor. The sooner the better. I can't work with Selma anymore."

"Why?"

"She turned me in."

"Is that the way you see it?"

"Part of me does, yes. I know she did it for the patient's good. And my own good, too. Though that's hard to accept."

"Give it a few days."

"I've given it a lot of days. I don't really want to deal with patients anymore, Molly."

"Yes . . . Well, it's going to be difficult to find a position in the hospital for you. Where a nurse doesn't have to deal with patients."

"I told you, this isn't new. I've given it a lot of thought. I know where I can go and be useful. I've worked there before."

"Yes?"

"Neonatal Special Care."

"Ah," Molly said. "Perfect. The patients don't talk back to you there, do they?"

29

AUDREY PASSED CORALEE in the corridor of Med Three. It seemed as if they were half a day behind in their responsibilities, though that couldn't be, not yet, the shift wasn't half over yet. But near enough to it and the nine o'clock meds weren't out yet. No help had arrived. As intensively as she and Coralee worked, the undone work and the new demands piled up. It was getting difficult to decide on priorities. Everything was *necessary*. Audrey was trying to balance her time between the routine necessary work and the unanticipated necessary work. Now she found herself simply responding to the strongest and most recent demand.

She entered a patient's room. "Mr. Arcady, did they x-ray your feet yesterday?"

"No. They didn't."

The patient was elderly. Audrey slowed herself. She asked again, speaking slowly, clearly, and loudly, "Did you go anywhere in a wheelchair yesterday?"

"Been right here the whole time."

"The doctor wants you to have your feet x-rayed."

"Why?"

"It will tell us how deep the infection is."

"Then why didn't they *take* the x-ray yesterday?"

"It's a medical mystery, Mr. Arcady. Chin up. I'll give X-ray a little goose on your behalf, okay?"

"Thank you, Nurse."

On the way back to the station she stopped in on another patient. At the bedside she said, "How do you feel, Mrs. Wilks? Does your stomach feel upset?"

". . . Yes."

"That might be the medicine. It can make you a little

queasy. I'll tell the doctor about it. Do you want to rest or what do you want to do?''

"Rest."

Audrey went to the station. A resident named Ned Willard was looking over paperwork and waiting for her. An intern stood by the resident. Audrey looked at the name on the chart the resident was reviewing and said, "She thinks she's going home today. But there's nothing in the chart about her going home."

Willard nodded and flipped pages.

Audrey dialed. "Hello, X-ray, this is Med Three . . . Yes, about Mr. Arcady again . . . No, you *didn't* x-ray him yesterday . . . Then you x-rayed someone with the same name, but not *our* Mr. Arcady, not Dr. Willard's Mr. Arcady . . . All right." She hung up and said to Willard, "This afternoon."

"They *say* this afternoon. They said the same thing yesterday."

Coralee entered the station. She looked at Willard and indicated the chart in his hand. "What do you think about her going home? I guess the attending told her she was going to."

"Bad move. She's fat. We should do a venogram. But she's allergic to the dye."

"I think we can watch her on the outside. I've talked to her about it. I think she'll cooperate."

"Has she got a neighborhood clinic?"

"She came in through Primary Care. Elin Maki."

"Make sure we recheck."

"Okay. I'll get together with Elin on it."

The two HOs left the floor.

Audrey headed back to the medications. An elderly man was setting up a folding chair against the wall partway down the corridor. He wore shiny slacks and an old blue sweater torn at the elbow. He had set a newspaper and a brown sandwich bag on the floor. Back Bay Met was *his* hospital in a most possessive sense. For forty-five years, until retirement, he had been a Back Bay Met transportation worker. Now he returned to the hospital each morning to read his newspaper and to spend the day sitting and watching. The past few days he had been coming to Med Three.

Audrey said, "You're late joining us today, Mr. Hines."

"Didn't feel so good last night. Slept late, I did."

"What was the trouble?"

"Prob'ly somethin' I et."

"How are you today?"

"Doin' better."

"Good. You let me know if you want a doc to have a look at you."

"Sure."

"Promise?"

"Sure."

Audrey went to get the late medications. She looked at each medication three times. When she picked it up, when she placed it in a medicine cup, and when she threw out the package.

Coralee came up to her. "Mrs. Parker. Have you seen her?"

"Not yet today. I looked in on her when she came in yesterday." She threw away a container. "I remember when she was with us before."

"She's in tach, one twenty-nine to one thirty-one."

"What's her blood pressure?"

"One-forty over eighty."

"That's what she always is."

"She just got another point two five of digoxin last night," Coralee said.

"Are you sure? 'Cause the HO said to give it to her this morning."

"Well, that's what I thought."

"Check it out with the HO then," Audrey said.

"Mr. Stevens is awake now. Oriented times four. Want me to take the history?"

"No, I'll do it. Chance to get to know him."

"We're way low on heparin drips."

"I know. I'll call down."

"I tried," Coralee said. They say we've been overloading. Stockpiling."

"Well I know where I can lay my hands on some. If I have to."

Before going in to Mr. Stevens Audrey went back to Mrs. Wilks and her upset stomach. She talked to the patient and got a frightened admission of other symptoms and decided the problem was digitoxicity, a reaction to the digitoxin tablets Mrs. Wilks was being given to decrease her heart rate and put her into a normal sinus rhythm. The dig ought to be discontinued, Audrey thought.

On the phone to the HO Audrey said, "She's nauseated, seeing colors—green and yellow spots—blurred vision."

The HO paused, then said, "Okay, DC the dig and watch her. I'll check back."

Audrey made the entry and then went to Mr. Stevens. On the way she passed Coralee again. Coralee looked sick. "What is it?"

"You don't even want to know," Coralee said, continuing to walk away. "If I can't handle it, I'll get back to you."

Audrey entered Mr. Stevens' room. Again she was struck by his ruddiness, the apparent health from the outdoor life. And struck by the odd pallor beneath the ruddiness.

"Hello, Mr. Stevens. My name is Audrey Rosenfeld. I'm the head nurse on this floor. How're you feeling?"

Mr. Stevens smiled. "I feel all right. Rested. I guess I needed a rest."

"You passed out. On the street. Some EMTs brought you in. EMTs are—"

"I know what EMTs are. And paramedics."

"That's right. You worked with them. What happened last night?"

"I was just walkin' around. Got feelin' queer. Like I couldn't breathe fast enough, y'know? So then . . . I remember keelin' over."

"Remember anything else?"

"It felt good. Like I been workin' too hard, y'know. Felt like I was goin' t'sleep. Peaceful like."

"Anything precede it that you remember?"

"Nothin' special. Just walkin' around."

"How many drinks had you had?"

Mr. Stevens looked embarrassed. "Ohh . . . three or four shots of whiskey. A beer chaser."

"A chaser after each shot? Boilermakers?"

Mr. Stevens grinned. "Naw. The shots. Then a brew before I hit the street."

"Out with some friends? Celebrating? Neighborhood bar?"

"Naw. Jus' out walkin', takin' the evenin' air. Didn't even know the joint.

"How much do you drink, Mr. Stevens? Each day. Take a guess."

"Not much till I got laid off. I got laid off a coupla months ago, you know?"

"Harbor Police. I know. I'm sorry. I remember how you saved that little girl."

"Well, I guess I do like I did last night. Maybe a coupla beers in the afternoon. After I look for work."

"Whiskey your main drink?"

"Naw, beer is. The whiskey, though . . ."

"Yeah?"

"Sometimes I . . ."

He didn't want to say. Audrey nodded. "I understand. It's probably something you don't want to talk about. But we're here to help you, whatever it is. This whole hospital is."

"Well, see, sometimes my chest don't feel right. A coupla shots a whiskey, all's right with the world!" He grinned.

"How does your chest feel when it doesn't feel right?" Audrey displayed no overt reaction when Mr. Stevens reported coughing up blood.

"Not regular," Mr. Stevens said.

"How often?"

"You know, from time to time . . . Out in rough weather sometimes . . . Strainin' myself in zero temperatures sometimes . . . We got to work in *harsh* cold winds sometimes."

"Do others get it, the people who work out there with you?"

He looked down at his hands. "Naw. Not that I know of."

If anything, Audrey established, the discharges had increased in frequency since Mr. Stevens had been laid off. "Do you smoke, Mr. Stevens?"

"Naw. Not since my oldest was born. That's Glen. He's fourteen." The man glowed with a new hue and his face lost the lines of anxiety and concentration. He looked directly at Audrey. "Jeff, he's eleven. I'm forty-eight. Well, you know that. I married late. Used to smoke like a chimney. But when Mary got pregnant, I says to myself, 'That's it, boyo. Cut the crap. Got to live straight now, you want to be 'round for the child, help the child grow up.'"

Audrey nodded. Everyone who came into the hospital had a chest x-ray. Mr. Stevens' showed a mass in one lung—what could be a coin lesion, a disk.

Audrey completed the history.

"Well, whadya think, miss?"

"I think I'll call your doctor. That's Dr. Willard. And tell him you're awake and he can come see you."

"Tell'm I'm hungry, too." And as Audrey grinned, "What's the big smile for, miss?"

"Jewish mothers and Jewish nurses like to see people with appetites."

"Well, I could eat a horse now, m——, I mean, Nurse. Course, a steak would be better."

"We'll see what Dr. Willard says. For now we'll keep you on the drip food, nothing by mouth till the doctor says so."

"Nurse, could I use a telephone somewhere?"

"You're to stay in bed till the docs have a good look at you. But I already called your wife, if that's what you're thinking about."

"Hey, *that's terrific!*"

"I told her the docs'll be seeing you, probably this morning, and she can probably come see you this afternoon. I told her I'd call her."

"The boys, too?"

"Jeff shouldn't. The hospital has a rule. No one under fourteen on the floors. But on this floor some of the rules about visiting get forgotten most of the time."

"Gee . . . thanks . . . Yeah, but . . . I mean, isn't it so Jeff, bein' eleven and all, don't get infected or somethin', come down with somethin' he picks up here?"

"No, Mr. Stevens. I will share a professional secret with you. Most hospital rules about visiting are bullshit. They're designed for the convenience of the staff. Not for the convenience of the visitors. Or the pleasure of the patients. On this floor the patients and their visitors come first. If we can manage."

"Gee. That's great. Nurse, it's been great talkin' with ya. You jus' go on about your business."

The business, Audrey immediately learned from Coralee, was a mess.

"The autoclave," Coralee said. "There wasn't a good seal."

"I told them about the gasket. For *days* I've told them—"

"I've told them, too. But the thing of it is, nothing was done."

They went to the entrance of the autoclave room. A shiny puddle of water extended into the corridor. The floor of the room was covered with water. The two nurses stood outside the doorway looking in.

Audrey was furious.

"There was steam just *pouring* out," Coralee said. "Physical Facilities has *promised* to send someone up. Someone is supposed to come up from Housekeeping to clean up, too. But the thing of it is, nothing's been sterilized, and now we're without—"

"We'll just have to try other floors." Audrey could not understand the feeling of desperation that was taking hold of her. This was not the first time the autoclave had malfunctioned. "See if they'll let us borrow—"

A house officer—a woman—stopped by them and said, "That's it, ladies. Just stand around and admire the view."

30

"ELIN?" THE WOMAN stood in the doorway of Elin Maki's office. She was some thirty years older than Elin and her name was Betty Bowen and she was not on Elin's appointment calendar.

Elin got up and went over and embraced the woman who had been her head nurse on Med Three when she had first joined the staff.

"Dear Elin," Betty said.

"I *missed* you last night. I knew you were invited."

"I stayed home. It was the right thing for me." She broke the embrace and closed the door to Elin's office. "I've got something for you to help see me through." She sat down in the patient's chair next to Elin's desk. "I pulled some strings to see you."

She put down a plastic bag from Paperback Booksmith. Elin saw that the bag had letters and books in it and, on top, a deep blue freeform ceramic ashtray that had been a gift from Betty's husband one Christmas. Elin had been there. With Charles. "I left my suitcase at Reception," Betty said. She looked down at the plastic bag. "The real important stuff I keep with me."

"Are you saying you're here for me to see you professionally?"

"I had one of your patients bumped. To a real doctor."

"Something for me to help see you through, you said."

"Yes. Not exactly through, dear Elin, but to the end of it."

Elin took out her pen and history and examination forms. "I think I'd better start the way you taught me, don't you?"

"No. I don't think so. I'm going to tell you right at the start what you and the rest are going to find. Then you can take your history and do your exam and send me around for tests. But I've had some diagnostic procedures done already. I can put it together for you quite briefly."

"Go ahead."

"The patient, a sixty-seven-year-old white female, a retired nurse, *known* for her uncompromising objectivity—you agree?"

"So far."

"The patient reported a history of shoulder and joint pain over recent months. Physicians were cursory in their pursuit of the complaint. They treated it as if it were arthritis or bursitis. They were, I am deeply embarrassed to say, *encouraged* to do so by the nurse." Betty stopped. "The nurse assisted this misdiagnosis because she was so deeply afraid."

Elin kept herself silent. She insisted to herself that she was, in these minutes, dealing with a patient, not a friend.

"The admitting diagnosis, Elin, is joint pain, weight loss, and lowered blood pressure. The findings will be metastasis of bone from a mastectomy years before." She put her shoulder bag on her lap and reached a hand inside. "I've gone back to smoking. Do you mind if I do? Crummy for your office."

Elin put out her hand. "Give me one, too."

"I don't want to encourage bad habits."

"I quit the bad habit. I'm going to join a friend in a smoke."

"As you wish." Betty took out cigarettes and a lighter and then reached down into the bookstore bag and placed the ceramic ashtray on Elin's desk. She lit their cigarettes. "All right. That's what you're going to find—"

"You can't be that sure."

"I've confirmed it, Elin. To my satisfaction."

"Satisfaction?"

"Dissatisfaction. You'll find I'm right. The next thing is, you're going to have to tell me, 'You're only going to live for a short period of time.' And I'm going to say, 'How long will that be?' Because that is what I don't know. That's what you're going to find out for me. That's why I'm here."

She looked at her cigarette. "Smoking cigarettes. Brings back so many memories. Like the summer I met Kayo. Lying by the lake at night. Letting him feel me up. I can remember the taste of his mouth. The cigarettes." She put out her cigarette. Elin put out her own.

"When you confirm all of this, Elin, you, or some house officer who isn't old enough to be my grandson—"

"They're old enough to be that," Elin said quietly.

"Yes. No disrespect. They're going to have to take care of me. I'm going to have to let them do it. You know, we spend our lives teaching these people? The interns and residents go, but we stay on . . . and we're always teaching them. They go on. And we stay here. Taking care of the people. That's the most important part, taking care of the people . . ." She shook her head, then righted it. "Senility creeps in from time to time. Now, Elin." She waited.

"Yes?"

"What you're going to have to say to me is—because I've done it myself, I know the speech—you're going to have to say, when the diagnosis is confirmed, and it will be, 'We can make you as comfortable as possible for a short period of time. Or we can make you uncomfortable and you'll live longer.'"

Elin was not writing. She held herself steady. She showed no reaction.

"What you are going to do, I hope, is send me up to Med Three. Put me in bed there. Give me pain medication and antinausea medication and let's let it happen."

"It's still speculation on your part," Elin said.

"No, my dear. You wish. But it isn't."

"We don't know yet," Elin said, picking up her pen.

"Don't retreat into writing me up. Do you know how much distance doctors put between themselves and patients *by writ-*

ing things down? They can get lost in that. Nurses can, too.''
She smiled. ''Even nurse practitioners.''

Betty took out another cigarette but did not light it. ''You
know how many nurses have to end up *being family* for a
dying patient. I've been family to so many . . . I decided to
come to my family. To this hospital. To you and the others.''

She got up and took the ceramic ashtray to the stainless
steel sink. She wet the cigarette butts thoroughly and disposed
of them and then washed and dried the ashtray with paper
towels. She returned to her seat and replaced the ashtray
carefully in the plastic bag.

''I brought the ashtray because I'll be staying. I won't be
leaving. The books are some I always meant to read. Now,
dear Elin, get on with the necessities. Then I hope you'll find
me a bed on Med Three. Who's over there now? What sort of
head nurse?''

''Audrey Rosenfeld. She's a young nurse. Very concerned,
very committed.''

31

AUDREY ROSENFELD WAS eavesdropping outside a patient's room.
Her posture was so rigid, her body so self-controlled, that it
seemed as if its motion had been stopped and held in some
filmic frozen action. There was a half-killed pint bottle of
booze in her hand and the smell of whiskey was ripe about
her.

Inside the room, the only doctor in the hospital Audrey
both disliked and distrusted was having a conversation with
one of her patients, a fifty-eight-year-old white woman. Dr.
Trevor Davis had come to Mrs. Armstrong's room without
Audrey's knowledge and was forcing a medical decision upon
Mrs. Armstrong without having first discussed it with Audrey—
that he was going to have the patient make the decision.
Davis was within his privilege but had usurped procedure that
protected the patient.

From within the room Audrey heard the surgical resident's

voice: "All I'm saying is, you'll probably live longer. The amputation will almost certainly eliminate the pain."

"Both legs above the knee," Mrs. Armstrong said. She cried a little. As if she did not have the physical resources to cry more than a little. "Both legs above the knee."

"The way to get rid of the pain is to remove the source of the pain."

"Couldn't you give me something for the pain? More of what I've been getting? Or something else?"

"You're on about as much medication as you can take."

"Try more."

"You can't take more."

"Why not?"

"Because it will knock you for a loop. Now, you just think about what I've said. I'll see you this afternoon. I'd like to schedule this as soon as possible. For tomorrow."

"But I haven't decided yet . . ."

"I'll see you this afternoon."

He came out smiling. He nodded, "Nurse," and started down the corridor.

Audrey followed him, her legs moving in a quick, stomping gait. "Terrific bedside manner, Doctor."

Davis kept moving. He glanced down at Audrey's hand. "Your taste in liquor needs education." He looked at her breastline and then at her face. "I'll see to it when I find the time."

The two of them were moving quickly and running out of corridor. "The way you treated that woman. You sonofabitch."

"I probably didn't hear that," Davis said and left the floor through the door to the stairwell.

Audrey walked back to the station, the smelly bottle of whiskey at her side. A patient in a doorway said, "Some nurses we got here."

"I'm not a nurse," Audrey said, "I'm a city councilman."

"I can *believe* that one," the patient said.

Coralee was at the station involved in paperwork. Audrey set the bottle down in front of her. Coralee said, "No thanks, not my brand." Without looking up she took the bottle and dropped it into the wastebasket beside her. "I know the guy you got it off. The wild Irish rose. I smelled it, but I couldn't find it."

"He had it in his pillow. He cut a hole in his pillow."

Coralee stopped her work. "Sometimes there's more sadness here than I can get used to. It still sneaks up on me."

"I'm going to spend some time with Mrs. Armstrong. I'm going to hold her hand. Don't call me for anything less than an arrest."

"What was that with Dr. Davis?"

"I'll tell you about Dr. Trevor Davis." Audrey looked down the corridor as if challenging Davis to reappear and hear what she had to say. "Dr. Trevor Davis gets off on pain. He likes the emotional kind best.

32

ON MED EIGHT there was also a laundry problem. "I can't keep up with the urine," the head nurse said to Day. "I'm running low on medicine cups. Central Supplies says not till next week."

"Can you get through the weekend?"

"Maybe. With a little help from my friends—if I can find any."

"I'll see what I can do."

The nurse started away, then turned back to Day. "I've only got one nursing assistant and some very sick patients on this floor." She said to Michelle McCabe, "Every day here is like Sunday. The understaffing. We only get done what has to be done."

Day said, "The patients say anything about the Keating article?"

"The candy lady hasn't been here yet, thank God." The head nurse left them at the station.

McCabe said to Day, "I have a feeling a show is being put on for me."

"No. All of this is normal. I don't understand why the director would deny it and then invite you in."

"Normal? *Normal?*"

"We deal with it. Most of the time we deal with it successfully."

"And when you don't?"

Day sighed. "Most of the time we deal with it success-fully. Ninety-nine percent of the time."

On Med Seven Selma Pushkin was on the phone and seemed to be taking grim professional delight in her circumstances. If there was one factor in her circumstances that she could count on, it was frustration with the support given to her by the hospital service departments. "This is Med Seven. Have you got our drugs ready? . . . No? Of course not." She hung up.

"How are ya?" Day said.

"I can't complain. If I do, no one listens. You got two hours?"

"How did things go with Liz Swanzey and Molly Chang?"

"Liz won't be hollering at the patient anymore."

"Who said?"

"Liz said. Molly said Liz has some personal things to sort out, she's going to work at it and it shouldn't interfere with her job. Also, she's resigning from the floor, which I under-stand. We had a talk about it."

"Nan Lassitter would like to work here."

"Just like that?"

"Don't question the Almighty. Compensations are known even here."

"My rabbi's going to hear about this. I've been worried he's losing his faith."

Day looked at her notebook. "Mrs. Spence?"

"She finally voided. After sixteen hours. She says that happens to her from time to time. The HO isn't concerned."

"Mr. Herman?"

"He looks terrific, really good. His trach was plugged. He was standing and showering this morning."

"Showering?"

"Yes, ma'am. We do good work on this floor. Us and God. Of course, God sometimes forgets to lend a hand."

"Mrs. Shaughnessy?"

"She's back with us, praise God, and her husband, the Polaroid fancier, has not yet visited us today, also praise God."

"Mr. Wah?"

"He's coming along fine. He's producing urine. That, however, Day, produces a further problem—"

"You haven't got enough linen and johnnies."

"It's not just Mr. Wah."

"I understand that, Selma."

"Good. Mr. Wah is a nice man. It should be understood, there is not a causal relationship between the linen shortage and Mr. Wah."

"What else?"

"I'm stockpiling heparin for the weekend. Or trying to since I can't get any."

"Have you got enough for the weekend?"

"Maybe. But that's it. I don't know."

"I happen to know OB has laid by a *huge* supply of heparin. You might call over there. Tell them you're going to blow the whistle on them if they don't come across for you."

"I'll do that. Now listen to this, Day. Med Four called to make inquiries about medicine cups. They ran out of medicine cups during nine o'clock meds. Can you believe that?"

"Unfortunately, I can."

"When I looked at our supply, *we're* low. Central Supplies says—"

"Not till next week."

"Day, this hospital is a catastrophe on its way to a disaster."

"It's gone most of the distance already."

33

ELIN MAKI HAD written the orders and cleared the patient through channels and seen Betty Bowen to Radiology for a metastatic bone survey. Elin felt profoundly sorrowful. Betty had convinced her that the diagnosis had already been established.

Once again someone was standing in Elin's doorway. She looked up to see an elderly white man. Albert Cornelius was somewhere in his seventies, Elin remembered from the two or three brief times she had seen him. He was not a regular patient. He offered her a slight bow and a hand-extended flourish of his sporty yellow hat. Then he held the hat against his worn dark suit jacket.

"Albert, didn't you see someone here just yesterday?"

"Somebody took my wallet. Not here." He laughed. "But there weren't no money in it."

"No. You keep your money in your sock, don't you?"

"Yes. Indeed I do. I keep my money in my sock. I'll show you."

"You already showed me, Albert."

The man pulled up a black pants leg and exposed a tall, white athletic sock. The top of the sock had been rolled over twice around paper money.

"Did someone mug you again, Albert?"

"Yestidy."

"Did they hit you or throw you down?"

"Naw. It was onna car. Streetcar."

"Maybe because you're all dressed up."

"Yes. I like to look good. My three ladies like it."

"What about medicines? What about your Medicare card? Have you got it?"

"No. It was in the wallet. My Medicare card was in there."

"You know what to do to get another one, don't you? You've been through this before."

He laughed. "Oh, quite a number of times. Once a month, maybe." He laughed again. "But they never find any money. No sir, never have."

"Are they the same people, Albert?"

"What people?"

"The people who mug you."

"I don't know." Elin noted that he didn't laugh.

"Don't you see their faces?"

"I don't know." He took out a thin cigar. "All I can tell the police is, they're white boys."

"Well. But. Yesterday. They didn't hit you on the head?"

"No."

"Or throw you down?"

"No."

"You keep being careful, Albert. Don't fight them. I don't want them to hit you on the head."

"No, I don't fight them."

"Good. What're your plans for today, Albert?"

"First off, gonna put on the feedbag. Been plannin' all week for this. Sauerkraut, knockwurst, potato salad, dill pickle, milk."

"You're making me sick, Albert. You're also making my mouth water."

"Then I guess I'll just take my ease. Till I get the radio message from my ladies." He lit his cigar with a disposable lighter.

Elin said, "You know you're not supposed to be smoking around here."

"I woulda' left, 'cept you been talkin' to me here." He sighed and walked away.

Constantly getting rolled, Elin thought. Maybe he likes it. Testing them, taunting them. Proving an old man can outsmart a bunch of punk kids. Even if he has to get mugged doing it. Elin made a note to speak to a psych nurse about it. Then she wrote in *Trina Frankian* and underlined it. Trina had seen Albert in the ER. Elin wrote, *Tell Trina it seems like he's inviting these attacks.* She sat back. Reception buzzed with her next patient. She put the phone down and thought, Hal Levy will be on duty with Trina when I get to her. The pervasive sorrow she had been feeling about Betty Bowen was interrupted by the pleasure she had in thinking of Hal. The sorrow, she quickly recognized, was for herself as well as for Betty, the self-sense of mortality.

34

THE ANXIETY ATTACK first showed itself on Med Three in the form of patient irritability and instances of weeping. "What's going to happen to me?" one weeping woman said to Audrey. "Who's going to take care of me?"

Audrey finally sorted it out and said, "I will."

The candy lady had gotten to the floor around quarter of ten. Three *Eagles* had been purchased. It had taken an hour for the word to go from patient to patient on the floor that the doctors were saying the hospital ought to be shut down, that it wasn't safe for the patients. Audrey had gone from patient to patient saying that was not true, think of all the people who came to the hospital sick and went home better or well.

The one patient who was entirely untouched by the proposition that the hospital ought to be shut down was an eighty-one-year-old white woman who was a longtime intermittent patient. She belonged in a hospital for chronic disease and ought to have been already moved to such a facility. But over and over, and without explanation, the paperwork failed to go through. Audrey and Day and Ned Willard, the house officer, had been at work on it for months.

"I don't care if they shut it down," Mrs. Gehl said. "What difference does it make to me?"

"They're not going to shut it down, anyway. But wouldn't you miss having this marvelous resort to come to?"

Mrs. Gehl shrugged.

Audrey said, "You're not looking good today, Mrs. Gehl."

"What do you expect at eighty-one?"

"You haven't fixed yourself up today."

"What for?"

"Why, for me. And the rest of the staff. We like to see people looking pretty. It cheers us up."

Mrs. Gehl looked away.

"I want to see you caring for yourself."

Mrs. Gehl still did not look at Audrey.

She's giving up, Audrey thought. The body would follow quickly enough. Unless we can get her into a chronic facility, they'll just find her dead in her room at home.

On Med Six they were out of Betadine and aqueous penicillin.

"What are you doing about it?" Day asked.

"Pharmacy says they're sending both up."

"Did they give you an ETA? I repeat, what are you doing about it?"

"I've got a medical worker picking up Betadine from Med Nine and there's a team of HOs out stealing pen wherever they can find it."

"Good work," Day said. "That's the realistic approach."

"We're out of towels."

"Jeezum. How's the rest of your linen supply?"

"We're okay for a change. We got extra of everything yesterday for some reason. But no towels."

"Rip up sheets."

"Really?"

"That's what I did when I was on a floor. But don't tell anyone."

There were no takers on Med Six for a double shift.

Day took Michelle McCabe into the Med Six conference room. She looked out the window toward the tenement rooftops as she lit a cigarette. McCabe regarded her. "I know," Day said. "It's amazing how many nurses still smoke. The docs don't. The nurses keep at it." She snuffed the cigarette out. "It's bad for the baby. I'm down to four a day."

McCabe said, "You go through this every day."

"Oh yes, every day. Just about. Some days it's worse. Some days it's not so bad." She pointed to the rooftops. "Sometimes they seem to loom up. Like they've gotten taller. Sometimes I get the idea this hospital is sinking into the very community it's attempting to serve." As if it were not already out, Day ground the cigarette into the ashtray again. "What afflicts this hospital and its patient population is plain hopelessness."

When Day opened the stairwell door to Med Four, she and McCabe immediately heard music from a radio at the nurses' station half a corridor away. The sound was more of a pulsating rhythm than defined melody.

"It's always the same," Day said. "On this floor we are dealing with diddy-boppers. Today the head nurse is out and the other regular nurse is running the floor. Her name is Diana Vezzina and she's twenty-three years old. The head nurse is twenty-four. Which may account for their taste in music."

"In most places, that's young for a head nurse."

"I wouldn't trade her for a head nurse from most places. She's been working in this hospital for five years. She knows how to keep her floor together."

Diana Vezzina wore a T-shirt under a washed-out sleeveless blue denim smock. She was bent over paperwork and the T-shirt motto was visible: ST. THOMAS, V.I.

"The ensemble does not quite meet the hospital's dress code," Day said, "but I've given up remarking on it." Then she said directly to the charge nurse, "I can't believe everyone on the floor wants to hear rock and disco all day long."

She received no reply. Diana continued writing. When she finished she said, "I would like to see in this hospital a clerk on each floor so I could attend to nursing."

"The HOs have the same desire. They'd like to spend more time doctoring and less time filling out forms."

"Most hospitals have clerks to take care of most of this scut."

"Most hospitals have a more affluent patient population."

"I would also like to see in this hospital all the IVs sent up mixed."

"Young nurses spend a great deal of time complaining," Day said to McCabe. To Diana she said, "You know the conversion costs for unidoses are prohibitive."

"I know the conventional wisdom about the costs of unidoses. I also know it's bullshit. The initial outlay is steep. But in six months you're saving time and money."

"How do you know?"

"I researched it. I can prove all that."

"Why don't you write a report?"

"I am."

"That is a pleasant surprise."

The two nurses reviewed the patients. When they finished the younger nurse said, "Now to something *really* important."

"Yes?"

"Medicine cups. Does anyone have them? I ran out during nine—"

"I heard."

"Medicine cups are not life and death. But it's a facility I've come to depend on. Hand-delivering each medication from the bottle is somewhat time-consuming. Central Supplies says they're out. Won't have any before next week."

"I know."

"Can you believe it?"

"Oh, sure."

"It's *incredible*."

"But you came to the right lady. There is a hidden network that extends from this hospital to the more affluent hospitals and I'm part of it. I have a friend who's a unit manager at Beth Israel. I'll call her and get a couple dozen cartons of medicine cups."

"*Fantastic*."

"If I do, will you go over after work and pick them up?"

"*Absolutely*. That's *fantastic*."

"Make sure you drop some off on Med Eight. They're getting low."

"Free?" the younger nurse said. "They'll just give them to me free?"

"Did you know that salesmen give *this* hospital as much as they can free?"

"No, I didn't."

Day said to McCabe, "Everyone gets sucked into the system here."

35

DAY AND MCCABE got down to Medicine Three at eleven twenty-five. Neither Audrey Rosenfeld nor Coralee Wafford was to be seen. The corridor was silent and, except for a man seated on a folding chair, vacant of human presence. The man held a newspaper at arm's length. His obtruding paunch reminded Day of her own figure.

"He's a mascot," Day explained to McCabe. "You'll find them almost anywhere in the hospital. Retired workers. Usually they hang out where they used to work. This one was a floater till a few days ago. Never in the same place twice. Because he was a transportation worker, I figure. But now he seems to have settled on Med Three. A widower. Lives alone nearby somewhere."

Day took McCabe over to the man and said, "You settling in here, Mr. Hines?"

"The nurses are nice to me here. And pretty. And there's always somethin' goin' on on Med Three, there is."

"Seems quiet now."

"I guess the nurses went and give everyone Demerol or somethin'."

McCabe said, "I see you're reading the wrong newspaper."

Mr. Hines looked down at the *Eagle*, then back at McCabe. "It's got a good story 'bout shuttin' down this hospital."

"How would you feel about that, Mr. Hines?" McCabe said.

"Never happen. People always talkin' 'bout it, long as I can remember. But it'll never happen."

"Why not?"

"Where'd the poor go? Course, we'd all like to see this place fixed up some. But no one's goin' t'do anythin' 'bout it. Talk, talk, talk, is all anyone ever does." And he belched.

"Catch you later," Day said.

"Sure. Right here. My wanderin' days are over."

Day and McCabe had to wait a few minutes before Audrey and Coralee separately got back to the station. Audrey's lips were, as usual, smiling, but her eyes, Day noted, looked as if the smile could abruptly turn to tears.

"Hi," Day said. "How y'doin'?"

"Hangin' in there," Audrey said.

"Sounds like you're hanging by a thread."

"Two threads."

"One more than me. Okay then, I won't ask you to do a double."

"On this floor?"

"Yes. Barnitska won't be in and I've already got an agency nurse booked into the other slot. I'm short-staffed all over."

"We've got more sick calls on this floor. There's just Coralee and me today. What about tomorrow?"

"You'll have at least an aide and a worker tomorrow."

"What about tomorrow afternoon?"

"Barnitska will be back—"

"Don't count on that."

"Why?"

"I don't think she likes nursing much anymore."

Day looked at Audrey to assess the solemnity of her statement. "I see." Day made a note for herself. "Anyway, Dorothea's got a new nurse coming on the floor tomorrow afternoon. Some young thing who's been working in a private hospital in the suburbs. Decided she wanted to come here because there wasn't much going on where she was."

"Has she had a mental status exam?" Coralee said.

"What about you, Coralee? A double?"

"I can't do it, Day. I've got a wedding at five. My brother."

"It's nice to see that life goes on," Day said. She introduced Michelle McCabe. Coralee nodded and went into a patient's room next door. Day asked Audrey, "How's your morning been?"

"Well, we had an awful morning, starting right off. We just finished nine o'clock meds a few minutes ago. For one thing, I had to bail out the autoclave."

"A nice start to the morning."

A tone sounded and a patient call light went on as well as a corresponding light above a door down the corridor.

"That's Mrs. Nelson," Audrey said. "A nice old lady. What she wants is company, just someone to talk to her for a few minutes. I pass her door and I say, 'I'll be with you soon, Mrs. Nelson,' but there just hasn't been time." Audrey smiled and said, "Goddamn." She picked up the phone. "I've got to get someone to go down to Pharmacy for a pickup. Who's got a worker or an aide?"

"Try Med Ten. It was quiet up there a little while ago."

Coralee's voice carried from the next room. "My dear, much as you hate to take medication, you lie in bed like a millionairess on the loose, your blood tends to clot. You have to take medicine to prevent that from happening. I'm afraid it goes in a rather unpleasant spot at noon and midnight. Just be patient with me."

Audrey disconnected by depressing the plungers with one hand while she kept the receiver in the other. "Well, at least something's accomplished. I've got two discharge rooms to get done up and I called Housekeeping at eight and *still* no one's been up. I just keep calling." She looked at the receiver in her hand. "Why waste my breath?" she said, returning the receiver to the cradle.

"One of those rooms wouldn't be the water bed room, would it?"

"What water bed?" Audrey said.

"Say again?"

"What water bed?"

"What happened?"

"They came and took it away."

"Who?"

"The people we bought it from. The supplier who never got paid."

"When did this happen?"

"Yesterday afternoon."

"I hope there was no one on it," Day said.

"No, no one was on it."

"Could you handle a burn patient? Just coming out of the unit?"

"If we had to. But, Day, you've got to get us some help if—"

"Look, I'll try Med Ten. They were sending some people home. But I wanted to check out the water bed before I tried another floor."

"Day, that water bed was here for months. The hospital just didn't pay for it. The supplier said when he talked to Purchasing about it, they couldn't give him a date when it would be paid for. He was terribly apologetic about taking it. He gave me a sort of sales talk. How the bed is so good for burn patients and pressure sores and MS patients and how it frees the nurses. I think the poor man would have let me keep it if I'd just asked him."

"Why didn't you? That's how we survive here."

"I don't know. I started figuring out if I could pay for it myself, and then I thought, *Screw it*. Does that answer you?"

"Absolutely." Day looked at her notebook.

"Before you start, I've got to talk to you about Mrs. Gehl and Mrs. Armstrong."

"Okay."

"Trevor Davis is pushing Mrs. Armstrong for bilateral amputation."

"We knew that was in the cards."

"He's such a sonofabitch the way he's going about it."

"Trevor Davis is a sonofabitch. On the other hand, he's one of the best we've got in Surgery. I'd rather have him than a couple of others I could name."

"Spend a couple of minutes with Mrs. Armstrong. Reassure her."

"You mean undo old Trev's bedside handiwork?" Day said.

"Yes. It'll back me up. Mrs. Armstrong needs both of us."

"Will do. Mrs. Gehl?"

"Are you and Ned Willard ever going to get Mrs. Gehl into a chronic facility—"

'The HO and I have been working on it for a long time—"

"—because if you don't real, real soon, Mrs. Gehl is going to pass on for the lack of a suitable environment."

"Ned and I are being persistent. There's a paper foul-up somewhere."

Audrey said, "She's going to pass on for the lack of anything better to do. She as much as said so this morning. She wasn't even threatening."

Day sighed. "I don't know what else I can do, but I'll find something."

"Okay. Your turn."

Day looked at her notebook again. "Mrs. Parker?"

"Atrial flutter. She's been BID two days. She was one twenty-nine to one thirty-one the whole night. Up in the one-fifties before. Still tached, taching away. One-forty over eighty, same as it was all day yesterday."

Audrey reviewed other patients at Day's request and then abruptly interrupted herself. *"Hello."*

A young black man in a tan uniform stood in front of the station. "You send f'Housekeepin'?"

"Yes. I have two discharge rooms to be done up."

"Scrub down beds? Clean the rooms?"

"Yes."

"I do precautions. I don't scrub beds and clean rooms. It's not in my job description."

"That's *incredible,*" Audrey said.

"He's right," Day said. "The union now has it split up in the contract. He can bomb a room. He can't scrub a bed or clean a room. Fumigation only."

Audrey repeated herself: "Incredible." The young man walked away. "Guess what? My Thorazine tolerance has just risen acutely. A monster dose wouldn't affect my mood at all."

"What can you tell me about the patients' mood? Regarding Dr. McGettigan's pronouncement."

"It was an asshole thing for Scotty to say."

"If he said it."

Audrey saw the attentive but blank-faced McCabe suddenly smile. Audrey said, "A scare went through here. There's no doubt. Coralee and I talked it down. I don't know how much anxiety is left. Day, is Scotty serious?"

"Like I said, we don't even know if he said it. But the word is, there's more fire here than smoke. Between ARI and Bennett." Day glanced at her notebook. "You had a discharge. Mr. Ornstein?"

"Yes. Mr. Ornstein. He's still talking to himself, but he's talking to everyone else, too . . ." Audrey was looking down the corridor. "Oh, Jesus. Here it comes again. *Damn it.*"

Dr. Trevor Davis had returned to the floor. He smiled as he passed the nurses. "Ladies," he said, as if he were tipping his hat.

"Anything we can do?" Audrey said.

He stopped. "Well, not at the moment." He assessed Audrey's body. "But keep in touch." He walked away.

Audrey followed him. "Excuse me."

"Yes?"

"My patient is upset. She needs some time to herself."

Davis smiled. "I have a new lab report I want to share with her."

He walked away. "Oh shit," Audrey said quietly.

She returned to the station. Her fingers drummed on the countertop. "The nurse being calm keeps everyone else calm, right?" She looked down the corridor again, her attention turned by some noise. A tray truck was being wheeled onto the floor from an elevator. "Wow," she said, "lunch is here. *Terrific.*"

Day said, "Guess someone saw you standing still and figured *idle hands*, better get her something to do. Like serve trays."

Coralee was looking at Day's pregnancy. She patted her own rear and said to Day, "Mine's back here. Yours is up front."

"You've got to be careful," Day said. "When it shifts, that's the problem." She looked down at herself again. "Little while, I'll deliver a full-term elephant." Then she looked at the two nurses. "Any problems, give me a scream. I hope things slow down for you. You look tired."

Audrey said, "I was alone on this floor last June when we had new interns coming in and I still didn't quit."

36

DAY COMPLETED HER rounds and got back to her office with
Michelle McCabe at twenty-five past one. She said to her
clerk, "Any takers for coordinator for the next shift?"

The clerk shook her head. "No takers."

"Great."

McCabe followed Day into the office and said, "Was that
really bad news out there?"

"Why?"

"You turned *grim*."

"It just means I'm going to have to make a call that's
going to be very uncomfortable for me. To my husband."

"Well, if that's the tour, I'll be going. Unless I can hook
up with Dr. McGettigan."

"I'll see if I can get him for you." In a moment McCabe
was on Day's phone and arranging to meet McGettigan in the
ER. When she hung up, Day said, "I'll be looking forward to
the article."

"I don't think there'll be one."

"That is . . . That surprises me."

"There's nothing to write here. It's gone on for years. I
could do a piece on survival—like you going to the BI for
medicine cups. But that's more a Sunday feature piece. Things
are just no better and no worse than they ever were here.
There's no news. Unless Scotty McGettigan has something."

After McCabe left, Day looked at her notes. Shit, she
thought, I forgot Mr. Toby—that patient from Med Three
who'd been waiting for the elevator, the one I said I'd look in
on. Maybe this after.

She called the Respiration Therapy Department and spoke
to the director and got him to call off their medical student
program in the ICU until it had been properly planned and
cleared through committee.

She called the lab and was assured that, though short-
handed, results were going back to the floors regularly now.

She called Tim Holbrook. He said thanks, he was getting results already. She reassured him about respiratory care. He thanked her again and told her he had the meeting with Mr. Emerson's family and Trina coming up in a few minutes.

She called Molly Chang about Mrs. Gehl, the woman who was giving up. Molly said she would consult with Audrey.

She caught Anita Rounds, the cardiologist with the suspected heart patient from Med Nine, down in the ER sitting with Scotty McGettigan and Michelle McCabe. The heart patient had been monitored, medicated, and sent up to the Med Five unit. In a change of subject, Anita, who was first executive officer of ARI, suddenly said, "We're pumping the press full of background information."

"Background for what?"

"For whatever has to be done." She hung up.

Day went down her list of patients and nurses and floors and predicaments and absurdities and called the appropriate respondents.

She suddenly thought, Is this nursing? Yes, she decided. And the patient is the hospital.

She made direct and indirect inquiries about the laundry situation. She was unable to establish anything that satisfied her inquiries.

She called her friend at Beth Israel and arranged for the gift of two dozen cartons of medicine cups. She called Diana Vezzina and explained how to pick them up.

She wanted to eat her veggie grinder, but she had to make the hard call first. Her stomach was already feeling uncomfortable about the call. Tension. Lousy emotional atmosphere for the baby.

She called her husband at his office. When he answered, she rushed in. "Jimbo, I've got to do a double shift. There's no one else to take my place." Her husband was silent and Day's stomach knotted a little more. She had to remember she had made this call before. Too many times before. And now that she was so far into the third trimester, Jimbo wanted her to leave work altogether till after the delivery. Where there had been forbearance Day was now confronted with anger, Jimbo's overlay to his fear for Day and the child-to-be. "Jimbo? It's got to be done."

"Who says, Day? You're the only one I ever hear talking."

"Take my word."

"What's the hospital going to do when you're home with the baby?"

"That'll be someone else's problem. Whoever takes my place."

"Really? I have the funny picture in my mind of the hospital calling up and you taking the baby into work with you. Because there's no one else."

"Sometimes there *is* no one else."

He was silent again. Then he said, "You better stay there tonight."

"Yeah. Sure." Usually she was the one who suggested it. Then he would say, "Give me a call at home tonight when you're off, huh?"

She said, "I'll give you a call at home tonight."

"Yeah. Sure. I've got to go. I've got other calls waiting, Day."

After Jimbo hung up, Day thought about the suburban neighborhood where they lived. Where there was no violence and children played without their parents being in fear for them. Going back there each afternoon was like leaving a submarine that had been under the surface for months. Today she would stay down and she felt down.

She started to eat the veggie. For her blood, for the baby. When the telephone rang immediately after, she was up and then down again when it was not Jimbo, nor was it any of the return calls she had been expecting.

"Hi. This is Audrey on Med Three."

"How's it going now?" Day had a premonition that Audrey was calling to say she had had it, she was packing it in.

"You still need someone for the next shift?"

"Yes."

"Okay. I'm your gal."

"I don't want any heroines."

"I thought that's how this hospital functioned."

37

IT WAS JESSY Gladdens whom Robert Higby *really* wanted to cut—for getting the police on him, for telling the people she never did want him to fuck her spite of how she came on to him, rolling her tits and her ass at him. What'd she 'spect?

But he didn't know where Jessy Gladdens was and he did know where Trina Frankian was, the other cunt who had the police and the DA out for him.

When he was about eight, Robert Higby discovered that he could scare people with a knife; that a sharp, pointed blade produced fear and fear gave him power. Twice he himself had gotten cut. But only twice.

He had decided he was going to talk to this nurse cunt with his knife. Then she could change her mind about Jessy Gladdens and this rape shit, maybe change her mind 'bout a lot of things, learn what a *man* Robert Higby was.

But first he needed to be alone with her. Someplace where no one was goin' t'go bustin' in on them. He knew just the place, her own personal place, which made it better the more he thought of it. He'd get alone with her in her car. Jes him and his blade and the cunt.

What he had now was a good place to watch where she lived. Looked like he was some dude waitin' on a trolley up the block, same as other folks. He jes never got on.

Long about one o'clock he was pretty sure it was her. White pants, white shirt, two cops comin' out with her, cop car waitin'. Gonna drive off in *that?*

The cops walked the little bitch over to a beat-up yellow Volkswagen Beetle. She got in, and Robert Higby climbed aboard the MBTA trolley that halted in front of him seconds later.

38

TIM HAD ESTABLISHED a harmony on the ICU that, with the other two nurses' attention and barring any crisis, ought to free him for the meeting with the Emersons for a half hour or so. That fucking little time allotted to discuss a man's death.

Tim looked at his watch. Ten minutes till the meeting. Ten minutes till he would argue for Mr. Emerson's death. Killing wasn't what it was. His mind knew that. But his emotions didn't. His prickly skin didn't know it. Most particularly, his *guts* didn't know it. They wanted to heave themselves out.

Tim thought about the evening, this very evening he would have with Jason. He laughed. Such a quick, fine, direct association. Father. Son. Life. Death. Watching the monitors, alert to the nuances of the unit, he succumbed to the pleasant waves of expectation at having so much time with his son—some games and dinner and the evening and an overnight together and getting to take him to school in the morning—the night charge covering for him till he got in—being part of that, the boy's growing time. And the pain renewed itself. It forever renewed itself. That he could never get this time back, forever lost to him, the days of his son's growing up, of discovery and wonder.

The telephone gave its quiet signal.

"ICU, Med Five. Tim."

"I'm sorry, Tim, but I've decided to keep Jason with me tonight after all."

"Valerie, you, you can't just—"

"I've had a change of plans, Tim. That's all."

"Valerie, *for chrissake*—"

"You'll see him at your usual times. Have a nice day, Tim." She hung up.

In court, arguing the issues of the divorce, Valerie's attorney had made a number of allusions to the fact that *Mr.* Holbrook was a *nurse*. He was hardly any longer part of his son's life. There was a great irony, Tim thought, in the award of sole custody to Valerie because Tim was a nurse, a man who cared.

When Jason was born, Tim had abruptly discovered that he deeply loved being with and taking care of this new infant. That was fine with Valerie. She liked to spend as much time away from her baby as she could. As his devotion to his child grew—and his awareness of emotional interests and capabilities within himself—he found a concurrent diminishment of interest in his work. Pushing computer buttons and being fascinated by what he could accomplish with them no longer compelled him. His nearly $40,000 a year no longer compelled him, either. He recalled having worked in a camp for handicapped children one summer. He recalled how much he had liked the feeling of helping people. He resigned from his job and became a candidate at Cambridge University for a degree in Nursing.

Valerie was furious. The loss of income. "The utter disregard of responsibility to your family." All of that was smoke, Tim saw, as confusing to Valerie as it was obvious to him. Her deepest complaint—indeed, her outrage—expressed itself clearly enough. "Why not a doctor? I can see you quitting a good job and all of us sacrificing so you can be a doctor, but a *nurse?* What kind of a man are you."

"You know what kind of man I am."

"A nurse. What will people think?"

"I don't know. I always thought nursing was an honorable profession."

"For a woman!"

There had been a considerable silence after that. Then, very quietly, Valerie had said again, "Why not a doctor?"

"I don't want to be a doctor. I considered that. I would like to help people. I would also like it to be an eight-hour job. I would like to be with you and Jason and have a garden."

"Have a garden? What's that got to do with it?"

Tim was suddenly aware of differences between them, vast empty spaces, that he had never acknowledged or measured or attempted to traverse. The character of that dialogue was representative of much of the dialogue that was to occur between them during a good part of the next two years, though, to Tim, there were thoroughly misleading interludes of lovemaking and periods of calm and seeming affection.

Valerie did not leave him until a few days before graduation, though, unknown to Tim, she had taken up with another
man months before. Her leaving had actually surprised him.
Why go through all the difficulties of having a husband who
was a student and then walk out when the reward was about
to be achieved?

He had thought about that. Because the reward was what
she couldn't stand. That he was going to be a nurse.

"What do you think that makes me?" she had said, with
no understanding of her statement of doubt about her own
femininity.

39

TRINA FRANKIAN HAD come in an hour earlier than necessary in
order to meet with Mr. Emerson's family. She parked the
yellow Volkswagen in a reserved space in the courtyard of the
Old Building and went up to the ICU on Med Five. With Tim
she looked over the recent report sheets again.

"It's happening awfully fast," she said.

"Awfully fast. And all the HO can write is *Prognosis
uncertain. Prognosis uncertain.*"

"There's a denial of death on Aaron's part, that's for sure.
He still unavailable for the meeting?"

"That's what he says."

Trina nodded.

Mrs. Emerson, her son Lionel, and Mrs. Bradely, who was
Mr. Emerson's sister, were already in the outside corridor
when Tim and Trina appeared.

Mrs. Emerson looked at Trina fearfully and Trina took her
arm. It was trembling beneath the sleeve of her dress.

"We have a room where we can sit and talk," Trina said.
Mrs. Emerson was silent, but she let Trina take her into the
room, and Lionel and Mrs. Bradely followed.

Mrs. Emerson sat at the table in the room and then looked
at each of the others as they took seats. She finally said, "It's
so lonely without him at night." Silent tears ran down her face.

"It's all right to cry," Trina said.

"I know, I know . . ." Mrs. Emerson said, her sobs distorting the sound of her words. Lionel got up and put his arms around his mother. "Ma . . . Ma . . ." he said. Mrs. Bradely sat completely still, watching.

Tim said, "Would you like some coffee, Mrs. Emerson?"

Through her tears she said, "Yes. That would be a kindness."

Tim left and came back with hot water, a jar of coffee, creamer, sugar, picnic cups, and plastic spoons. He made Mrs. Emerson's coffee for her and then the others made their own. Finally he made a cup of black coffee for himself.

He said, "Mr. Emerson . . ." But that didn't sound right. He looked at each member of the family. "Your husband . . . your father . . . your brother . . . my patient . . . is in for needless suffering. That's what Trina and I want to talk to you about."

"Where's the doctor?" Lionel said.

"He couldn't be here," Tim said.

"No doctor," Lionel said. "How are we going to know it's true? What you're going to tell us?"

"It is."

Lionel looked down at the table. "Hey, we got to keep Pop. He's my *man*. I *need* him."

Trina said, "Your father's dying. We can't keep him from dying. That's what we have to talk about. Whether he dies . . . in great distress, sometime in the next few days—"

"The next few days," Mrs. Bradely said. "My brother."

"Or whether he dies in as little distress as possible."

"What we're talking about is letting him die in his sleep," Tim said.

"What's he like when he's awake?" Lionel said.

"He hasn't been awake," Tim said. "Not to acknowledge anyone or anything. Almost everything is being done for him by machine or through the lines now."

"Does he know what's happening to him?" Mrs. Bradely said.

"Sometimes he does. That's where the suffering comes in. A great deal of the time he's asleep."

"Can he see?" Lionel said. "I mean now, today. Does he see people when he wakes up?"

"He doesn't really wake up. Not that way. He can't equate

what he's seeing a lot of the time. But he can hear, sometimes. That's the last sense loss."

Aaron Silver entered the room but remained standing, his back against the wall. He nodded. "Mrs. Emerson. Mr. Emerson. Mrs. Bradely. I wish you'd just go on," he said to Tim.

"He can feel pain," Tim said. "Inside. It jars him awake."

"How do you know it's pain?" Lionel said.

"The eyes. The movement then. It's involuntary. The expression on his face. There's considerable pain."

Mrs. Emerson turned and said, "You think so, Doctor?"

The HO pursed his lips and nodded.

Tim summarized Mr. Emerson's deteriorative multisystem diseases. "The only way we can deal with them is through further invasive support the next time there's a crisis. That could be this afternoon. And the next crisis could be an hour after that. All this for a few days at most."

The family members looked at the HO. The HO nodded.

Tim felt his heart rate speed. "I don't want to tell you this. But I have to tell you what finally happens. The artery will bleed into the lung. It bleeds with full pulsation. The patient drowns."

The women cried out at the same time and the HO said, "I have to go" and left the room. The two women held each other and cried.

Lionel said, "You can't let that happen to Pop."

Mrs. Emerson managed to speak through her tears. "Could we talk to him, see what he thinks? Could we talk to him about it?"

Trina said, "If we could, Mrs. Emerson, we wouldn't be talking to you, we wouldn't be asking the family to decide what ought to be done."

"I know, I know," Mrs. Emerson said. "I had to ask it, I just had to."

Trina put her arm around Mrs. Emerson. "I know you had to. You ask anything else you need to. We have as much time as you need."

"Maybe we could think about it overnight," Mrs. Emerson said.

"No," Tim said. "There isn't that much time."

40

MR. HINES, THE mascot, saw the new nurse walk by him. All dressed up, she was—coat and a hat, not a cap. Hadn't ever seen her before, all his years in the hospital. It was gettin' on to time to go home and watch afternoon TV, almost three, almost quittin' time. Brown paper bag next to his chair, still hadn't eaten lunch, didn't know why his stomach felt ornery, how come the rheumatism had got in his collarbone. What did he eat last night that made him feel sick today? He couldn't remember. Age gettin' hold of my mind, he thought.

The agency nurse reported to Audrey and asked for a safe place for her hat and coat and bag. "I had to take a cab to get here. Terribly costly. But prudent, don't you think?"

"I ride the T," Audrey said.

"How terribly brave of you. Actually, I've never worked in a place like this. But the agency said you were desperate here, so I said to myself, All right, give the poor dears a hand, it can't be as bad there as I hear, and if it is, they'll need my experience all the more."

Audrey thought she would be better off working the new shift alone and she ought to throttle the woman on the spot. Coralee simply backed away and returned to the patients.

Audrey said, "I'm sure we all appreciate your coming to us. But excuse me, I think we ought to spend a moment discussing this hospital and your attitude."

"Really? I don't think so. You do your work and I'm sure I'll do mine."

The woman was about forty, Audrey thought. Probably spent her professional life specialing private patients who required little attention. Must have screwed even that up, Audrey thought bitterly, for her to end up here.

"Actually," the woman said, "I find wards so depressing, so indiscriminate."

"This is not a ward, it's a floor."

"Yes, dear. Now, before I start work, would you be good enough to direct me to the facilities?"

"The facilities. Oh," Audrey said, "the shithouse." She was astounded when the woman smiled back at her.

"You can't offend me," the woman said. "You offend only yourself with such language."

Audrey directed the agency nurse down the corridor. When she was gone Coralee returned. "God, Audrey, what have you been doing in private to deserve this?"

"I haven't been doing anything privately."

"Maybe that's it. Upstairs you are perceived as wasting your life and your bod."

"I have not had the stimulus to do anything else."

"Well, Lady Macbeth there may not be a stimulus to your private life, but she sure is a kick in the ass. Look, babe, I'll hang around for as long as I can."

"Coralee, you've got your brother's wedding. Get *your* ass out of here."

"I hate to do it."

"Go."

"I can manage half an hour more. While you show her what's needed."

There was a cry from the corridor, a prolonged moan. Coralee and Audrey looked up and then hurried to Mr. Hines. The mascot was in his chair, the newspaper fallen to the floor beside him, his head tipped back. He was sweating profusely. They talked to him quickly as they got his sweater off and his shirt open and a sleeve rolled up, and Audrey began taking signs while Coralee got a blood pressure machine and wound it onto Mr. Hines's arm as Audrey flicked her stethoscope off and went to the station and dialed.

"Med Three," she said. "We have a chest pain that needs evaluation stat. That's right, Med Three." She dialed another number. "Med Three. We need an EKG machine stat. That's right, Med Three." She went back to Coralee and Mr. Hines. "Let's get him on a bed—"

"Hurts. *Hurts,*" Mr. Hines said.

"The discharge beds still aren't—"

"Doesn't matter," Audrey said. "Let's get him on one." They tipped the chair, held Mr. Hines in place, and pulled the chair on its two back legs.

"Can't breathe."

"It's okay, Mr. Hines. I've got a doc coming."

An EKG machine and a portable x-ray arrived along with technicians. Under Anita Rounds's attention, Mr. Hines began to slow his rate and lower his blood pressure. Audrey drew blood and iced it and went out to the station to send it on for blood gases analysis. When she returned to Mr. Hines she was no longer needed. That left her able to introduce the agency nurse to the floor and to become totally exasperated with the woman. She functioned on a mechanical level that allowed for no personal interaction with the patients and no effort beyond the completion of immediate physical tasks. Audrey quickly realized she did not dare give the woman any significant responsibility and ought not, in fact, to leave her unsupervised at all. But the latter was impossible. Audrey would talk to Day about preventing the woman from ever working in the hospital again.

41

As TIM WAS about to leave the ICU to go down to Med Three, the charge nurse called him back to the phone in the station.

Selma Pushkin was calling in her role as president of the Nursing Services Alliance and she was calling Tim in his role as the critical care nurses' representative on NSA's executive council.

Selma said, "Scotty McGettigan has just requested a meeting with as many of our exec as I can get together."

"What about?"

"He wouldn't say. But if you weren't so isolated from the rest of the hospital, you might have heard that ARI and Bennett are displeased with each other."

"So? Situation normal."

"I don't think so," Selma said and rang off when Tim said he could meet her at four in ARI's office in the Old Hospital. He went down to Med Three.

Audrey someone was at the station. Her face startled him. He felt a tension throughout his body that was like the pierce of electric shock, but pleasant. He did not know this woman, yet he was suddenly and exquisitely moved by her eyes, by the expression of her face and body. He had simultaneous feelings of sorrow and rapture. The episode scared *the shit* out of him, he noted.

"You're Audrey—"

"Rosenfeld."

"I'm Tim Holbrook, I'm—"

"Yes. Day said you'd be down. Mr. Improta. Thanks for coming. He's real worried about the way he acted on the unit. He's worried he may have insulted you."

Tim laughed first. Then Audrey.

"Anyone who's worried about insulting a member of the staff can't be all bad. What room's he in?"

"I'll take you."

"Hey," Mr. Improta said when he saw Tim, *"you're* the one who took care of me. Thank you."

"How're you feeling, Mr. Improta?"

"I'm okay. I'm good."

"They treating you okay here?"

"This lady has taken excellent care of me."

"That's good. I like people to take good care of my graduates." Tim found himself glancing at Audrey's left hand, her ring finger. Audrey saw it. He said, "Mr. Improta, Miss Rosenfeld feels you're concerned about how you were up on the ICU."

Mr. Improta nodded quickly and spoke quickly. "What was I like? What did I say?"

"You hung in real good, Mr. Improta. Those are tough times, being on the ICU. You were good."

"I know I wasn't. I said insulting things to you."

"Mr. Improta, if a friend of yours has an illness, do you get angry at him for having it?"

"No."

"Neither do I. I get angry at the illness. Okay, you're up there, you're plugged in every which way, there're psychotic episodes. You've got all this dependence, all the stuff you've got sticking in you, lights on day and night, you want to sleep and things are happening to you. That's scary stuff up there. You wake up and you've got stuff jammed into you and your body wants to expel it all. That's the reality. And it's terrifying. The psychotic behavior helps you get through. It takes you away from the reality. Till you're well enough so that's not your reality.''

Mr. Improta stared at Tim. He looked uncertain and uncomfortable.

Tim smiled. ''You've got beeping machines, burping machines, gurgling machines—all kinds of machines all around you. Mr. Improta, you're an astronaut being flown by *the spacecraft* and you've got no training to prepare you and no control. No wonder patients act a little crazy up there from time to time.'' Now Mr. Improta smiled. ''You were fine.''

Audrey had been watching Tim as he spoke. She found she was watching his eyes. He had good eyes, eyes she trusted. His eyes were open right into his feelings. And she liked the way he spoke to Mr. Improta. And she thought, Damn, let me out of here, I don't have any business feeling so nice about this man.

''Thank you,'' Mr. Improta said quietly.

''It's nice to have the opportunity to get together with you, Mr. Improta. ICU nurses don't get very much personal interaction with the patients. You get moved out as soon as you start getting better.''

He shook hands and he and Audrey left the room.

They stood in the corridor. Audrey thought of the things she had to do. She wanted, though, to reach over and touch Tim's hand with her fingertips. She wanted to say something to let him know she liked him and was interested in him.

Grownup lady, she thought. Can't say a thing. No more socially adept than you were in ninth grade.

Tim looked at her. He seemed incapable of conversation himself. Then he said, ''Call me. If I can be of some more help with Mr. Improta.''

''I will. Thanks for stopping to see him.''

Tim was silent. Then he said, ''Okay.'' He turned and walked back down the corridor.

Goddamn, Audrey thought, watching him walk away.

After Mr. Hines was worked up over the course of two hours—EKGs, blood gases, chest x-ray—Anita Rounds reported to Audrey that he had probably suffered a mild infarction and that, hooked up to a monitor and IV medication, he would best be left right where he was on Med Three for rest and continued observation.

''He should be on a monitor,'' Anita Rounds said, ''but

right now that would mean taking it off someone else I know needs it more. BioMed expects to have one off the bench later. They'll send it up when they do."

The station phone rang. "Audrey, Day. Your discharge rooms made up yet?"

"Finally."

"Good. Because Elin Maki's on her way up with a special patient."

"Special how? And what's Elin doing transporting a patient?"

"She'll explain. Now . . . Mr. Stevens. Has the HO been on to you about him?"

"Not about Mr. Stevens."

"The x-ray showed a mass." But there was that history of coughing blood to worry about. "They're scheduling a bronchoscopy for tomorrow. He's already NPO, isn't he?"

"Right." Nothing by mouth.

"I'm sure they'll get to you soon on the orders. And they've got to get together with Mr. Stevens."

"I think they're doing it now," Audrey said as she saw three house officers going into Mr. Stevens' room. "Ned Willard and a couple of other docs." Then Elin Maki came on the floor from an elevator, pushing a patient in a wheelchair. The patient—a woman in her sixties, Audrey guessed—had a bulging Paperback Booksmith bag in her lap. A transportation worker followed with a suitcase.

Elin introduced Audrey to Betty Bowen. "Betty was head nurse on this floor before me. For twenty-seven years."

"How could you take it that long?" Audrey said. I'm not even twenty-seven years old, she thought.

"Things weren't so bad then," Betty said. "Now you only have beds for the critical, it seems."

Audrey looked at the woman in quick assessment.

"Betty will present her own case," Elin said. "I'll just stand by."

Down the corridor, a woman and two boys stood outside Mr. Stevens' room. The woman showed some distress. She came over to the station. "Nurse, I'm Mary Stevens. They won't let me in my husband's room. Why not?"

"I'm sure they'll let you in in a few minutes, Mrs. Stevens. Are those your boys? There're some chairs down the hall—"

"But why can't I go in? He's my husband."

42

THE INTERIORS OF the nine floors above the ER in the Old
Building were time-worn and scarred, but the suites of rooms
that made up the emergency floor on the street level had been
rebuilt and modernized four years earlier—upon the advent of
Bennett Chessoff as director of the hospital. Chessoff had
appreciated immediately that the ER was the focus of media
interest in the hospital. There were the trauma units where the
docs performed like the Celtics, coming from behind in the
last few seconds of the game. There were the results of the
meetings of the Saturday Night Knife & Gun Club, a regular
feature on which the media relied. Chessoff had given the ER
total cosmetic surgery and had created a respectable visual
background for television. At the same time he had refur-
bished the medical equipment on the floor.

Hal Levy went to a blond counter that enclosed several
desks. A black woman with glasses sat at a small switchboard, a phone to her ear, her other hand resting near a
microphone. A security officer sat at a desk studying entries
in a looseleaf binder. The woman keyed the microphone and
spoke into it, and Hal heard her normal voice in front of him
and a harsh, amplified version from a speaker behind him.
"Triage, line five." She looked at Hal. "Yes?"

"I have a three-thirty appointment with Trina Frankian."

The woman dialed three digits and waited. Then she disconnected. "They don't answer back there." She keyed the
microphone and Hal heard her double voice again. "Psych
nurse to the desk. Psych nurse to the desk." The woman
indicated a large cluster of chairs behind Hal. "You can wait
there. I'll send her over."

Hal went over and sat. A few chairs away a young black
man—twenty or so, Hal thought—sat slumped to the side in
sleep. He wore a team jacket and sneakers. A set of dentures
lay in his lap. A white security officer was looking at the

young man from across the room. Hal had an unaccustomed feeling of sleeping violence. All around him.

From a desk at a nearby doorway Hal heard a black triage nurse taking a history from an aged and unkempt white man. The white security officer was coming over toward Hal. He was about Hal's age but taller and broader. He had red hair and the sort of pink, boyish face that always seemed to be somewhat embarrassed. He leaned over the young man who was asleep and said, "Hey. Hey there. Can you hear me?"

The patch on his uniform sleeve read: DEPT. OF HEALTH AND HOSPITALS. These words circled other words: BACK BAY METROPOLITAN HOSPITAL. Two units of police on the premises, city police and hospital security police.

The young man's head had tipped back and his eyes were partly open.

The guard said, "Now *listen* to me. This is Emergency. Would you like to speak to the nurse about detox? Would you like to sober up?" The young man made no response. "How y'doin'? Are these your teeth? Why don't you put them in?" The young man went back to sleep.

"Hi. I'm Trina."

Hal looked up at a slim, young white woman. She wore a white shirt tucked into white pants. A rectangular red identification tag pinned to her shirt was imprinted in white with her name and below, PSYCHIATRIC CLINICIAN. "Be with you in a minute," she said and went and stood by the guard. "Thornton, isn't it?"

"Yeah, Thornton," the guard said. Thornton's eyes opened. "You want to go home, Thornton?"

"No." His eyes began to close.

Trina said, "You either go to detox or go home."

"Put your teeth back in your head."

"You can't sit here," Trina said.

"I ain't."

"You're not sitting here? Thornton, stand up for me."

The security guard said, "Hey, buddy, grab your choppers. Put 'em in your pocket so you don't lose 'em."

Trina said, "You go to detox or you can leave." Thornton's head nodded to the side. "You been drinking?"

"I don't drink."

"I can't hear you. Speak up. Hey, sit up. When are you planning to leave?"

"Memorial Day."

"You can't stay here till then. So when you planning to leave?"

"When can I leave?"

"You can leave now," Trina said. "Or go to detox."

Thornton looked at Trina and then, with difficulty, got up. Trina and the guard watched him as, lurching, he made his way out of the ER to the main lobby.

"Lost soul," Trina said.

The guard said, "You done your best."

"You have to wonder what will happen to him out there."

The woman at the switchboard said to Trina, "Call for you. You take it here or—"

"I'll take it here," Trina said and went around behind the counter.

After Elin Maki had taken Betty Bowen to Med Three, she returned to her office and recognized in her feelings of lethargy and anxiety and mortality the symptoms of depression. It was the sense of her own mortality and need that prompted her to call Trina, but it was Albert Cornelius who gave her the excuse. She explained to Trina how the man went around getting himself mugged and seemed to be inviting it.

"He's not a primary patient of mine, or anyone's, for that matter," Elin said. "But I see him from time to time. I'd like to steer him to you."

"I think I know him," Trina said. "Is he the one who gets the radio messages from the hookers?"

"You got him. It also occurs to me he may get himself mugged as an excuse to come in."

The two nurses discussed Mr. Cornelius, and Trina said she'd have a look at his records and see him. Then Elin said, "Have you got someone named Hal Levy with you?"

"Yes. Right here."

"Let me talk to him."

"Hello?" Hal said after Trina handed him the phone.

"Hal? Elin Maki. Look, I'd like to go to dinner with you on Sunday."

Hal smiled and put down the telephone, then was startled by a woman who suddenly yelled, "Don't you go tellin' me *nothin'!* I told you, boy, go fuck y'self!"

She was a tall and regal black woman made even taller by a red turban. Improbably—for the warm weather—she wore an ankle-length red cloth coat cut in military fashion. There was a double row of large gold buttons down the front and gold buttons on the sleeves. She was yelling at the red-haired, pink-faced security guard, who continued to appear more embarrassed than insulted. "Or you too dumb to know what I mean when I say *go fuck y'self?*"

Trina went over to her. The black woman was a foot taller than Trina and the turban further exaggerated the discrepancy. Trina seemed to be a child entreating a vastly superior parent as she said, "Dora, you're in a hospital. You're insulting a member of the staff. You're disturbing the work here. You better take yourself home."

"Who you *talkin'* to, girl? You pale little cunt."

The security guard began to smile and then controlled himself.

"You can leave on your own, Dora," Trina said, "or I'll have you escorted off."

Dora pointed at the guard. "Take *five* more like this one to 'scort *me* off. Who you *talkin'* to *anyway?* This here is goddamn fuckin' public property and I has my rights to stand here same as any other human person. I pay the fuckin' taxes—"

"You have no right to stand here and be abusive."

"Asshole!"

A black security guard came over and stood near his colleague.

"Dora, that's enough," Trina said. "Do you want to sign yourself in?"

"So you can get holt of me? Shit, girl, what you take me fo'?"

"Then you'll have to leave."

"You gonna try movin' me, cunt?"

Trina turned to the black guard. She nodded at his walkie-talkie. "Tell Operations, unwanted visitor."

The black woman lunged at her. When the white guard seized one arm before it could strike Trina, Dora tried to claw the guard's face with her free hand. He blocked the attack with his forearm, and the black guard grabbed Dora's free arm and forced it down. With her arms locked on each side, the woman was moved to the courtyard exit and on outside.

As she went, she made loud animal sounds that did not form themselves into words. Trina heard the deep pain and felt it in herself for an instant, then was able to stand back from it and recover. Hal also heard the pain, but the anguish remained with him for a long, distressing moment.

"Dora's one of our regulars," Trina said. "She's a hanger-on. She's made the hospital part of her extended family. She's a psychotic with delusions of grandeur. But she can control her behavior even when she's real crazy. Usually she just comes in, talks, hangs around for a while. But when she's rowdy and abusive like that, we have to put her out."

"Why isn't she institutionalized?"

"She's certainly a candidate. But there's not enough room for the borderlines. Real crazies are put out on the street all the time. It's a matter of money. The hard reality is, *everything* in this hospital is a matter of money. The patients just don't count downtown."

"But isn't she dangerous?"

"She's swung at people a couple of times. When she's ETOH. But if she doesn't sign in to the docs' discretion, there's really nothing we can do. So I try the hard line first, on occasions like this. But you're right. You always worry about someone like that. Someone who's willful going out and doing something severe."

43

THE OLD HOSPITAL was a seven-story gray stone structure built before the turn of the century. It stood, isolated, behind the New Wing, the on-call rooms on its upper floors used as little as possible, only by house officers with no alternative.

Selma Pushkin, Molly Chang, Elin Maki, and Tim Holbrook went up a flight of stone steps at the side of the Old Hospital to the second-floor office of the Association of Residents and Interns.

The room was dreary and made more so by the pale gray light that filled the shadeless window. The beige walls were peeling here and there. The floor was wood gone dark from age and wear. An overhead light turned the air in the room a dull yellow. Beneath the light, Scotty McGettigan and Mozart Wills sat at a scarred wooden table that was otherwise surrounded by empty folding chairs.

"Coffee?" Scotty said. "Soda?"

"Business," Selma said as she and the others took seats.

"You've seen this?" Scotty said. He pushed over copies of an ARI newsletter. It was an agenda of grievances and patient issues that the house officers wished to discuss with the administration. It was weeks old.

"We've all seen it," Selma said.

"Well, look it over again anyway. See if there's anything in there you don't agree with. That NSA doesn't agree with."

The agenda was extensive. An increase in Ancillary Services personnel so that physicians would not have to regularly and recurrently, in violation of their contract, act as ward clerks, laboratory messengers, medical record messengers, blood drawers, transportation workers, and so on. Sufficient nursing aides and medical workers to support the nursing staff. Adequate nurse staffing so that nursing would not be regularly and recurrently understaffed and sometimes skeletal. A seat on the Director's Council. Decent on-call rooms. An increase in house officer salaries. An ICU for Pedi. An across-the-board stop to all hospital job cutbacks. Guarantees of equipment, supplies, and laboratory facilities. A Patient Care Fund to be administered by the house officers to purchase equipment and supplies the house officers knew the patients needed.

Molly did not turn to the second page. She said to Scotty, "You should have done your residency at Mass. General."

"I have that choice. The patients don't."

"We're all here by choice," Selma said.

"Is there anything on there that NSA can't support?"

"There're a whole lot of things you won't get," Selma said, "under any circumstances. Like a seat on the Director's Council. Like a Patient Care Fund. Like—"

"That's not what I asked."

"I know. I don't think NSA could support you on salary. But we're certainly in agreement with you about patient care issues. So what?"

"Salary is a patient care issue. But we don't need you on

that. Dr. Geier has told me privately he agrees with us on that."

"Interesting," Selma said, "Dr. Geier being chief of staff."

"I find that hard to believe," Elin said. "I find it incredible."

"A ten percent raise in salary would bring us up to parity with the other hospitals in this city. Dr. Geier and the other chiefs would like to see that. There are people Geier and the others would like to have recruited. But they lost them to higher salaries."

"Just not dedicated enough," Molly said. "The ones that got away."

Tim said, "The proceeds from the basketball game are earmarked for the Pedi ICU."

"This proposed agenda was drawn up before we knew about the game," Mozart said. "Besides, the director hasn't said anything to us about it."

"He hasn't really said anything to us period. You sit and talk with him and you think he's saying something, and you go away and you realize he hasn't said anything about anything."

"There was a news release about the proceeds going for a unit for Pedi," Tim said. "It was in both papers."

"I don't have time to read papers," Scotty said.

"Except the one this morning," Molly said.

"People forced me to read that."

Tim said to both Scotty and Mozart, "You guys going to make practice today?" The game between the hastily organized Back Bay Mets and the Harlem Wiseapples was only a couple of weeks away. It was a Bennett Chessoff media event. They were even going to play in Boston Garden.

Scotty said, "I've got to get some sleep. I may even sleep here." He meant upstairs.

"You're not that desperate," Selma said.

People had gotten bedbug bites upstairs. The bedding was left unchanged for days, and Housekeeping wouldn't give the HOs bedding so they could change it themselves. Toilets didn't necessarily flush and showers weren't necessarily operative. Windows were stuck open in freezing weather, closed in stifling weather.

Anita Rounds came in and sat down. "I'm sorry. I've got a suspected MI on Med Three. I couldn't even get him a monitor."

Scotty said, "Well, Bennett is refusing to discuss that sort of thing. In fact, he's refusing to discuss anything at all. He's refusing to *listen* to anything at all. The message came down. Bennett is refusing to see me or any representative of ARI. Sylvus won't return my calls and he left word that he has no intention of returning them.''

"Do you think they're giving you a message?" Molly said.

"Yes. They're saying, 'Fuck you.' ''

"Loud and clear.''

There was silence until Selma said, "Did you try other channels?''

"The only other one open to me. Merton Geier.''

"Well?" Anita said.

"Dr. Geier all of a sudden had limited conversation. All he wanted to talk about was the Celts and our game with the Wiseapples.''

Again there was silence until Selma spoke. "Freezeout,'' she said. "Because of the Keating piece you're all bad little boys and girls. Bennett doesn't even have to go through the *appearance* of negotiations now. And in a few weeks the senior leadership of ARI will be gone.''

Scotty looked out the window toward the Old Building. "Couple of days ago, a medical resident, he found himself in an emergency situation and he had to make a cut and there was no suturing thread on the floor.''

"I wish that was hard to believe,'' Selma said. "But it was my floor.''

"I know it was. But you see, you accept it.''

"I don't accept it. I don't like it, but—''

"But you accept it. That's the way things are around here. You and the other nurses make it work. We all do. Maybe it shouldn't work for a while.''

"Meaning?'' Selma said.

"Oh, some sort of job action maybe.''

Molly noted that Scotty said the words entirely too casually and then looked at the nurses entirely too intently.

"Strike?'' Selma said.

"It's in a talking stage. A lot of us feel a job action would draw attention to the conditions here.''

"Splendid,'' Elin said. "What about the patients?''

"I myself have this difficulty,'' Selma said. "I may be chief steward of the nurses' union, but I don't believe in nurses going out on strike. Or house officers, either.''

"It's been a long, hard winter," Molly said.

"What's that supposed to mean?" Scotty said.

"Spring is here. The juices rise."

"Don't be flip."

"I'm not being flip. I'd just like to know how serious the membership of ARI is about this proposed job action."

"Well, we haven't set a date. But we're pretty much in agreement. Ever since we realized Bennett was hardly listening to us, much less negotiating. I did my internship here. I've done all my years of residency here. Nothing's changed since any of us got here. We decided we're going to *see* some change before we go. Not just leave things the same as always, the way everyone else before us has." He stopped a moment. "Lynn Keating misquoted me. But what I said to her was meant to be a kick in the ass to Bennett, get him talking with us, talking *seriously.*"

"It didn't work that way, did it?" Molly said.

Anita said, "What we're interested in is what kind of support we can expect from the nursing staff."

"The nursing staff cannot support a physicians' strike," Selma said without hesitation. She didn't even need to look at the others for confirmation.

44

TRINA WAS SHOWING Hal the two psych rooms off the dark corridor behind the ER.

"See where we are now? The psych rooms are pushed all the way to the back. Just like always. Have a psychiatric problem? Hide it. Put it in the attic. Put it in the basement. If you haven't got an attic or a basement, put it in back somewhere. Some of the doctors—they can look at the bloodiest mess, but the crazies kick up too much shit in them. Things the docs haven't dealt with inside themselves. They meet up with a crazy and they just shut down."

Her voice was quite pleasant as she spoke. It didn't seem to match the content at all, Hal thought. Or else she was entirely at ease with her subject.

"On the other hand," she said, "if I leave you alone with a patient back here, in a psych room, and you get uneasy, get out. Your body is telling you something. Don't be macho. Trust your body. That's the most important beginning lesson I can teach you about working with me."

She turned out the light in the psych room and they walked down the dark corridor toward the illumination from the ER.

"I had a security guard working with me last night who had to get out. But she wasn't alone. There were two cops with the patient as well as me. The guard took one look at the patient and almost freaked out. She saw herself in the patient. She recognized all the violence in herself in the patient. She was scared it was going to come out."

"His or hers?"

"That's a good question. But just now she's in the wrong line of work."

By the time Trina's tour got them to the medical communications center in the ER, Scotty McGettigan was back on the floor. He was talking with a nurse. Part of the wall behind him was stacked with communications equipment, including visual display screens.

"She's bleeding out," the nurse said.

"Have we got a cross yet?"

"No. Not back yet."

"Okay. Let's get some O negative going."

The nurse moved away.

Trina said, "This radio controls half of Boston. The other half is controlled by Boston City Hospital. The police get a call and they dispatch a paramedic or EMT unit. If it's in our catchment area, they ring in here to see what to do and what hospital to take the patient to."

Trina introduced Hal to Scotty. Peripherally she saw Ginny Shiffland, the security guard, on her way over to Scotty. Trina turned toward her and Ginny abruptly stopped, then changed direction.

Trina went after her. "How's it going today, Ginny?"

The guard stopped and faced Trina. "Why don't you mind your fucking business. I'll do my job, you do yours."

"I am, Ginny."

"No you aren't. You're trying to do a job on me. Take my job from me."

"Sergeant Cleveland makes those decisions, not me."

"With you giving him poison about me."

"I'm sorry you see me as a threat, Ginny. I'd like to help you—

"You're getting off on doing a job on me, aren't you, Trina?"

"Let's start again. About doing your job. You were on your way over. On some errand, weren't you? To Dr. McGettigan." Trina paused. "But you didn't do your job. When you saw me you decided not to do your job."

The guard's voice became a whisper. "Leave me alone, Trina. No more mind games."

There was a shrill, insistent signal from one of the communications consoles. Scotty McGettigan glanced at the time. Six twenty-two. Trina came back as he picked up a microphone and depressed the key and said, "C-Med, Scotty McGettigan, chief medical resident, on line."

A Woman's voice replied, "Back Bay Trauma Center, this is Paramedic Two twenty-five. How do you read?"

"Paramedic Two twenty-five, Back Bay Trauma reads loud and clear. Go."

"Forty-two-year-old white female. Found lethargic in bed. Past medical history diabetes. Took insulin this morning. Skipped lunch. Past history of hypertension. Angina meds are nitro and Isordil. Blood pressure eighty over sixty. Heart rate a hundred. Respiration twenty-four and regular. Patient lethargic. Does not respond to verbal stimuli. Rousable to pain. Doesn't appear to have any puncture tracks. No apparent drug abuse."

Trina was picturing it in her mind. The paramedics would be at the woman's bedside. Someone who knew the woman must be with them. The rig would be parked on the street, lights flashing, waiting.

"Paramedic Two twenty-five, Back Bay Trauma. I copy." He repeated the paramedic's summary. "Over."

"Back Bay Trauma, Paramedic Two twenty-five. Affirmative. Over."

"Please start IV with D-five-W to keep open, then administer one hundred milligrams thiamin also intravenous and one amp D-fifty."

The paramedic acknowledged. A minute later she reported, "Paramedic Two twenty-five. Completed IV each."

"Roger that. Give me blood pressure and heart rate."

"Paramedic Two twenty-five. Blood pressure one-twenty over eighty. Heart rate eighty and regular. Patient seems more alert."

"What's your location?" The paramedic gave it. "What's your destination time to Beth Israel?"

"Six minutes."

"To Trauma Center?"

"Three minutes."

"Proceed to Back Bay Trauma Center."

As the paramedic acknowledged, Trina said to Hal, "We'll be seeing her in a little while. After the docs see her. If she's conscious enough I'll talk to her and evaluate her mental status."

"Psych nurse to the desk. Psych nurse to the desk."

When Trina saw the man waiting for her she smiled. She had met him only once, two days before, and she remembered that he kept his pants up with red suspenders. In a society of compulsively modern men, she found that charming and endearing.

He was in his early thirties and looked a little rumpled and a little tired today. He said, "I had to work late anyway, so I thought I'd come by in person. Instead of calling."

Trina realized he was tentative, almost apologetic. "Hal, this is Nicholas Prudhomme. Nick is an assistant DA. He's handling a rape case where I'm the victim's counselor."

They went out to the psych nurses' office and Trina unlocked the door. Inside she sat, Hal leaned against a table, and Prudhomme remained standing.

He said, "I can't get hold of my client."

"Jessy Gladdens? She called me this morning. I've got a number for her. I'll get her on the line for you if you want."

"I hear you got a threatening call, too. I'm concerned about that."

"Thank you. I'm getting some police protection."

"I know that, too. Still, it's distressing. And we can't know how serious this Higby is. About coming after you. Or how crazy."

"Oh, he's serious about coming after me, I think."

Hal was again astounded by her mild tone of voice.

"Why do you think that?" Prudhomme said.

"Because he called me. He wants contact. He wants communication."

"Contact and communication are not necessarily the same thing."

"Presumably he could have come after me without calling first."

"Maybe he was warning you."

"I think he was telling me about himself. What he's capable of. From listening to him and from what Jessy told me about him, I think he's crazy. I think he wants out of his craziness." She smiled. "I think his craziness is bugging him. He didn't call you. He didn't call the investigating officer. He called the psych nurse. People who call the psych nurse usually want help."

"Unless they call for some other reason," Prudhomme said. He had a pleasant smile, Trina saw. The smile went away. "Still, he threatened you. Very specifically. With a knife."

"I'll let you know. If he gives me the opportunity to interview him."

"I certainly hope he doesn't."

Trina liked the way he looked at her after he said that. She suddenly realized that Prudhomme's trip to the hospital to see her was precisely that—a trip *to see her*. She swiftly found herself wishing that Hal weren't there so that Prudhomme would be freer to express himself. Immediately she thought, Is this man married? She did not allow herself to get involved with married men.

She said, "Would you like me to get Jessy on the phone for you?"

"Please."

45

THE AGENCY NURSE said to Audrey, "That Mr. Stevens is just nagging me *unmercifully* to see you."

"I'll see him now."

"He's been asking for *hours*."

And if I hadn't had to do so much of your work as well as my own, I would have seen him, Audrey thought. And it was not *hours*. It was since dinner. Dinner had been served at five-thirty. Mr. Stevens had been asking to see her—but without any medical complaints—for a little over an hour. "I'll see him now."

She entered his room and was again struck by his ruddiness. His hands were shaking. He placed them under the bedcovers. Audrey said, "I'm sorry I couldn't get to you sooner, Mr. Stevens. Something's upsetting you?"

Stevens glanced over at his roommate. "It ain't him, but what I got to say is private."

"Okay if I take a walk?" said the other patient.

"Thank you," Audrey said.

"Yeah, thanks," Stevens said. He waited until the man had gotten into his robe and slippers and left the room. "Nobody's bein' straight wid me."

Okay, Audrey thought. Thanks, Doc. Leave the talking to the nurse. "What's concerning you, Mr. Stevens?" She didn't know how much Mr. Stevens had been told.

"They was gonna give me food this aftanoon. Said so. This mornin'. Then they come in this aftanoon and keep me on this drip stuff. Buncha' doctors inun outa' here, mumblin' t'each other. Wouldn' let my wife and my boys in for a while. Scares a person, y'know?"

"I know—"

"An' this one doctor, Dr. Willard? He says they got me scheduled for a trip to a operatin' room t'morra' mornin'."

"Short trip, Mr. Stevens."

"Short trip or not, I gotta sign a paper that says they're not responsible if I die. Short trip? What difference it make if I die in there?''

"It's not a dangerous procedure, Mr. Stevens.''

"So they tell me. But now, what's got me considerable worried is, what's this all about? Why're they doin' it?''

"They told you what they're going to be doing?''

"They're gonna take some tissue outa my lungs.''

"Right.''

"Why?''

Oh, c'mon, Doc, why leave it to the poor nurse? The thing is, I have no more idea what to tell this man than the docs do. But they didn't do. They left it.

"Mr. Stevens, everyone who comes into this hospital has a chest x-ray. Yours showed a shadow. You reported coughing up blood.''

"Not regular.''

"From time to time.''

"Yes. You know . . . Out in rough weather sometimes. Strainin' myself in zero temperature sometimes. You know . . .'' He took his hands out from beneath the covers and spread them apart.

"What they're going to do is called a bronchoscopy,'' Audrey said. "They'll take you to a minor OR, nothing fancy, and they'll have you in and out in very little time.''

"Now you tell me why, Nurse. And how. As if I didn't know.'' His hands shook again, but he looked straight at Audrey and did not put his hands beneath the covers.

"They'll take a piece of tissue or some mucus with the bronchoscope. If it's tissue, they'll cut it into a very thin section and they'll stain it—''

"To see if it's cancer or not,'' Mr. Stevens said.

"Yes.''

"Thanks. It's Miss Rosenfeld, right?''

"Yes. But I go by Audrey.''

"What do you think?''

"I don't know, Mr. Stevens. That's why they're doing the procedure.''

"Can't give me any odds?''

"I'm sorry. Truly I am.''

Mr. Stevens settled back against his pillow. "Thanks. You're a good lady.''

"Things are slowing up, Mr. Stevens. You want to talk some more, you need anything, just let me know."

"I'm okay now, Nurse."

Audrey returned to the work she had to do at the station. The agency nurse was presumably doing something useful somewhere and there were no calls on the board. She settled into the page twos.

"Excuse me, Nurse." She looked up. Trevor Davis had entered the station and was smiling down at her. "May I interrupt you?" Audrey simply looked back at him. "I came over to thank you for helping with Mrs. Armstrong." Audrey questioned her ears and eyes. This fellow looked like Trevor Davis and his voice sounded like Trevor Davis' but the fellow was obviously not Trevor Davis. "Really. Thank you. You did a good job undoing my . . . well, the way I talked to her."

Mrs. Armstrong had been moved to a surgical floor in midafternoon. "Is she okay over there?"

"As much as she can be, the night before a radical procedure. You helped a lot. Sometimes I'm too blunt. I don't know how to talk to people. I just try to be straight out and objective with them. I don't know how to reassure them at the same time."

You're sure doing a job on me, Audrey thought.

He smiled at her gently. "I'm off tomorrow evening. I can't help but find you very attractive. Not just the way you look, but the way you are. I'd be very pleased if you'd have dinner with me. I'd be *very* pleased to have the opportunity to, uh, give you a different impression of myself."

Audrey lightly bit her lip. He was such a sonofabitch. And here he was, such a little boy, asking for a chance to be different.

A rainy darkness smeared the Wide central window of Tim's apartment. The room itself was dark. Tim sat on the sofa bed and tried to occupy himself with three-man weaves and three-on-two and two-on-one drills—the running, passing, dribbling, shooting, and rebounding drills with which he was attempting to make a basketball team from the former athletes banded together as the Back Bay Mets. Usually practice took him out of himself, but this evening it hadn't happened.

He struggled with strategy. It had to be simple, necessitated by the difference in abilities between the Mets and the Wiseapples and by the nature of the game itself—it had to be entertaining. There would have to be a lot of shooting. Most of it from way out. The Wiseapples would easily control everything in close.

It didn't work. He couldn't get outside himself. He was alone in the dark. He had left the lights in the apartment off. He did not want any light or any music or television or any sort of company he might give himself by throwing a switch. And yet, when he got up and moved about, he felt the silence following him around like something tracking him. He turned on a light.

He thought of calling the woman who had so moved him that afternoon. Audrey Rosenfeld. He started toward the telephone and telephone book and then realized Audrey would not be home, would still be at work where he had left her. He looked her up anyway, just to see where she lived.

He looked at pictures Jason's first-grade art teacher had saved for him. They were taped to the refrigerator and kitchen cabinets and tacked up around the living room-bedroom between reproductions of more recognized art.

He had a letter of Jason's that he had carefully framed. The assignment Jason had been given in class had been to write a friendly letter. Jason had written it the day after he had spent a weekend with Tim.

Dear Dad,
    Thanks for those jokes you told me last night. I'll miss you when I go to my Mom's aftr school. And I'll all wase think of the time I will come back after like I all wase think when I go to Mom's.
                                        Yours Truly,
                                        Jason Holbrook

He went to the refrigerator and got a beer. He wanted Jason here with him, but there was nothing he could do about that. He wanted to be together with Audrey Rosenfeld, and he *ought not* to do anything about that now. Not while she was at work.

His urge to call her, Tim realized, *to do it now*, was on a low level of emotional gratification. Immediate need.

To be comforted.

Who better to call to be comforted by than a nurse?

He laughed and called the hospital and asked for Med Three.

"Med Three, Audrey."

"Audrey, Tim Holbrook. Have you got a minute for the phone?"

"Tim? Oh, sure, from the ICU."

"Things busy, or can you talk for a minute?"

"I can talk for a minute."

"Will you have dinner with me tomorrow night?"

Trevor Davis was listening to Audrey's end of the telephone conversation while he waited to find out whether he was going to get together with her the next evening.

He heard her say to the telephone, "Yes. Call me on the floor tomorrow."

46

MOLLY HAD SUPPOSED that Bennett would take her to dinner at one of the modish downtown restaurants currently favored by the media and their subjects. That was his style. But instead he drove her to an old house in the country that turned out to be a French restaurant.

She had never seen him in anything but tailored suits and cuff links and Italian shoes. She had been disappointed in her own very strong physical attraction to anyone who appeared to be so rigid. But now he wore a somewhat rumpled tweed jacket, a button-down tattersall shirt, and old loafers.

Molly considered her own dress. She had almost worn something gray but had recognized that part of her was timid and wanted to hide out in something neutral. So she had deliberately dressed invitingly.

Both in the car and in the restaurant, Molly was aware of a physical charge from Bennett's nearness. She was not about to dismiss that. She was not about to let it mislead her, either.

As she ordered a glass of wine she thought, Dinner out two nights in a row. Wow, my social life's really improving.

"I understand you're considering a change in your professional life," Bennett said.

Molly was startled. She had discussed it with no one at the hospital. Her allusion this morning to Nan Lassitter had simply been to leaving the hospital, not changing careers. She tried to assess the expression on Bennett's face, but the candlelight made it difficult. Was he amused or did the flickering make him *look* amused? "I am always considering a change in my professional life."

"Ah, the neutral response of the psychiatric nurse." He smiled. "Not the forceful retort of the attorney."

"All right. What's your source?"

"My own office. Cambridge Law School called the office a number of weeks ago to find out if one Molly Chang was employed by the hospital. And if so, in what capacity and for how long. They explained the inquiry was a result of Ms. Chang's having applied for admission this coming fall. I'm curious. Why? You probably would have been director of Psychiatric Nursing in a couple of years."

Molly tasted her wine. "I've been a nurse for twelve years. The more I'm at it, the more aware I am of how unfair the system of health care is. Unfair to patients like ours. All the poor, all the disadvantaged. As a nurse, I help to perpetuate that system. My work helps to support it. As a nurse, there's nothing I can do to change it. As a lawyer, I think I can have some impact on the system."

"You're going to change the system."

"I didn't say that. I said I intend to have some impact on it."

"I'm sure you will. What do you think of Scotty and his troops?"

"Did you invite me out to dinner to find out about NSA and ARI?"

"I know, of course, that you met today. But I invited you to dinner yesterday, didn't I?" He had a Scotch-on-the-rocks in front of him and he drank some of it. "I'd been meaning to invite you to dinner for a long time, Molly. When I finally did it, I wondered why I hadn't done it sooner."

"Why hadn't you?"

"I really don't know."

"Think about it."

"Scotty and ARI, please. Your thoughts."

"A lot of their criticisms are legitimate. There are some dangerous deficiencies in the hospital that ought to have been addressed a long time ago."

To Molly's surprise, he nodded. "We both know that."

Exasperated, Molly said, "Then why won't you talk to ARI?"

He took a sip of his drink and his reply again was mild. "Why are you leaving nursing?"

Why do I always feel as if I'm in some sort of confrontation with this man? Wherever we meet, whatever our roles. "When you think of the hospital, what's the first image that comes to mind?"

"A fortress under siege."

"And you're the knight defending it?"

"No. I'm the hospital."

"Wow!" Molly said.

"Do you find that grandiose?"

"The *energy* you must exhaust in self-protection."

"Not self-protection, protecting other people. That's what a hospital does. I identify with that. Sometimes I allow myself to think that I'm responsible for having kept more people alive than anyone else on the staff."

"No. You assist the rest of us."

"There might or might not be a staff without me. There might or might not be a hospital right now without me."

"You are not the hospital, Bennett."

"Consider the hospital the patient, then. Consider all the disease and malignancy attacking it. Consider me the physician charged with its care, its survival." He sat back and looked at her.

He's assessing me, Molly thought. And it's not my mind he's assessing.

She looked back at him. Another confrontation, she thought. She imagined the comfort of being held by him, the sensual pleasure of being caressed by him.

Candlelight, wine, romance—and I'm overcome by a strong need to urinate, Molly thought. She looked at the glass of wine in front of her. It was a second glass of wine, but it wasn't finished. She simply had not had that much liquid. It wasn't liquid, she realized, it was plain old sexual tension.

"I asked you to try to figure out why you didn't call me before," Molly said.

"Well, yes, I've been giving it some thought," Bennett said, still studying her. "I think it's because I realized I didn't have any casual feelings about you."

47

NORMAN CHILDS, an HO presently on rotation in the ER, said to Trina, "I've got an old geezer out back, resting. A Mr. Cornelius."

"Oh yeah. Wanders in from time to time. Great delusional system. Also gets himself pushed around from time to time. Seems to enjoy it. That's the danger."

"Well, he's refusing to move. I can't see anything medically wrong.

"What does *he* want?"

"He wants to be placed on a medical floor."

"He wants to be taken care of," Trina said.

"He's got some stomach discomfort. He ate at eleven o'clock this morning. Knockwurst. Sauerkraut. Potato salad. Mustard. Pickles. Milk. Started feeling not too good a little while later. He's got a roll of Tums with him. Had four or five of those. He thinks maybe he's having a heart attack. He's confusing stomach discomfort with chest discomfort. His postural signs aren't significantly different from what you'd expect them to be."

"Did you do an EKG?"

"There's nothing to warrant one. The guy's just got a slightly upset stomach and he won't leave. It's a psych problem."

Trina, Hal, and the HO entered a small room where patients rested or were held for further examination. Mr. Cornelius lay on an examination table the back of which had been elevated to a forty-five-degree angle. "Hi, Nurse," he said. "I remember you."

"And I remember you, Mr. Cornelius. Not feeling well?"

"My gut. And my pump. I don't feel well, Nurse."

"What would you like, Mr. Cornelius? What do you want?"

"I want to be in a hospital."

"What kind of hospital do you think you want to be in?"

"Medical hospital."

The HO said, "I'm a medical doctor, Mr. Cornelius, and I can see there's nothing wrong with you."

The man just looked at the doctor. His pallor seemed normal, Trina thought. He wore a clean white short-sleeved shirt, open at the collar, and shiny old dark slacks. But they too were clean. His shoes were recently shined. He took care of himself. Now he belched. "Sometimes I think I want to puke, but then I don't."

"You don't vomit?"

"No, I don't feel like doing it anymore. It comes and it goes."

"What does?"

"Like my head gets fuzzy inside."

"When that happens, how's your vision, Mr. Cornelius? Can you see all right or does something happen?"

"I can see fine."

"Doesn't get blurry?"

"No."

"No spots?"

He smiled. "Naw."

The HO said, "I'll be out on the floor," and he left.

"You were talking about being in a hospital, Mr. Cornelius. Tell me again, what kind of hospital do you want to be in?"

He smiled gently. "One with pretty nurses."

"Do you know the name of this hospital?"

"Back Bay Metropolitan Hospital. My hospital."

"Good. Right. Now let me see, you lost your wife, two years ago?"

"Two years." He nodded. "Two years ago. That's right."

"Is it hard living alone?" Trina said.

"Yeah."

"Do you think you need to go to a rest home for a while?"

"Jeez, I can hardly make it. Only if I live long enough. There's so many elderly ahead of me." He looked at Trina sadly. "Sometimes I think I'm going to start dying."

"But not tonight, okay?"

He smiled. "I'll try to oblige." He belched.

"See you in a few minutes, Mr. Cornelius." In the corridor she said to Hal, "I want to find the HO."

Trina found him at the nurses' station on the nonacute side of the ER. She said, "What Mr. Cornelius is telling me is that he doesn't feel intact physically."

"He may feel that way, but I can't find anything," the HO said.

"There's his nausea, his faintness. I want to rule out anything to do with his heart. Have a look at his cardiac enzymes and—"

"Trina, c'mon. The poor old guy's a little loony and a little sick to his stomach, so he thinks he's going to die. We can't—"

"I grant you, he feels very insecure physiologically. There's that chance there's a physical basis."

The HO sighed. "Trina, I was supposed to be off duty hours ago." He looked at her with annoyance. But when he spoke his voice was pleasant enough. "Okay, I'll get an ER nurse to do an EKG. Okay?"

"Fine."

"Trina, you just don't know how to get along with doctors, do you?"

Trina smiled at him and he walked away.

"Psych nurse to the acute side. Psych nurse to the acute side."

On the acute side, a white male in his early twenties lay on a litter and glared at the nurse attending him. *"Asshole!"* he shouted.

The nurse grinned at Trina. "I gave him extra Narcan. He's mad as hell. It blew his fix."

"And maybe prevented respiratory arrest," Trina said to Hal.

"It's the senior, wants to see you," the nurse said to Trina.

Trina led Hal back to the C-Med center.

"Problem for you," Scotty said. "Fellow passed out on a street corner. Conscious now, won't talk to anyone. White, mid to late thirties. No identification, refuses to say a word." Scotty picked up a chart. "When they picked him up, the EMT reports low blood pressure, dry lips, dry mouth. IV D-fifty push with thiamin initially hydrated him and he responded quickly. CBC back in about two hours. We can't get anything on his mental status. He won't even look at people. ETOH, but not much. Facial muscles are drawn. There's poor skin turgor." He looked at Hal. "You pinch it and it stays up."

"Malnourished," Hal said.

Scotty nodded. "The intern who did the exam puts together dehydration, suspected acidosis, ketosis—"

"Ketosis?" Trina said.

"Dipstick test. Ketone bodies in the urine are elevated. Mild ataxia—"

"How so?"

"Some stumbling."

"Could be alcohol, faintness—"

"Could be lots of things. It's the constellation the intern's getting at. Apathy, listlessness—"

"Confusion?"

"We don't know, do we?"

Trina said, "When he wouldn't look at people, was he active or passive? Was it indifference or inattention or avoidance?"

"That's what we'd like you to find out."

Trina said to Hal, "We need to find out, is the patient rational? consistent? disoriented? psychotic? It's hard to tell when he's not talking. A lot of our work is plain old detective work." She said to Scotty, "Not showing any emotion?"

"None observed. Unless it's avoidance itself."

"Your intern?"

"Sheila Farhm."

"She's building a case for Wernicke's syndrome?"

"It's a reasonable speculation. Among others."

"She's also suggesting Korsakoff's psychosis?"

"She's wondering if the nonresponse is a result of a severe memory defect."

"Wernicke, Korsakoff—the daily double. If she's right about one, she's probably right about the other. Lites and crits—"

"Yes. But in the meantime, see if you can get any history."

"I've got a patient waiting for me. I'll see him and then I'll see this fellow." She started to walk away, then stopped. "Has he had any head trauma?"

"There's no external evidence."

*   *   *

A nurse was wheeling an EKG machine out of Mr. Cornelius' room. "EKG's okay," she said to Trina. "I'll take the paper to the HO, but it looks fine to me."

"Thanks," Trina said. She stopped in the doorway. "Comfortable, Mr. Cornelius?"

"Oh yes."

"Good. Take it easy. I'll check back with you in a few minutes. Your test results look fine."

"That's nice."

She said to Hal, "We'll see Patient X now."

He sat in a wheelchair, his head down, an IV pole behind him. His linen shirt was much too big for him. His slacks were pressed, spotless, and expensive. His ankle boots were of a fine pebbled leather and were polished. They had no scuff marks or any sign of the street.

Trina said to herself, I know this man.

She searched herself for associations and found very personal ones—being with boys, teenage longing, drinking beer, being petted, lying at night on the beach outside the resort hotel where she had worked one summer as a waitress and being touched and touching back until she had had her first orgasm with someone else and caused another person to have an orgasm. Dark rooms at college parties. Music. Always music—and always a sadness and a longing for love . . .

But the man in the wheelchair was no one she knew.

She knelt down in front of him so that if he looked directly ahead they would be in eye contact.

"Hi," she said quietly. "My name is Trina." He closed his eyes. "I'm a psych nurse. Your doctor asked me to speak to you. We're concerned that you won't talk."

Trina saw a change in his breathing. Hearing me, she thought. "I'm Trina. I'm here to help you.'

He kept his head down, his eyes closed.

"I'm Trina. I'm a nurse who helps people who feel real bad inside themselves. Want to tell me your name?"

No response, but the breathing remained elevated.

"I think you want to talk to me. I think you want me to help you. But you're scared, right? Just nod if I'm right."

But the man didn't respond.

"Okay. I think you want to be alone with yourself awhile more. And think about things. This is all new to you here.

My name is Trina and I want to help you and I'll be back in a few minutes. Everyone here wants to help you.

She saw a single tear fall from one eye and run down the man's cheek. He made no effort to wipe it away, to respond to it.

She went to a telephone and dialed Security. "This is Trina. I want a standby for a patient in a wheelchair on the nonacute side." She hung up and said to Hal, "We want a security guard standing by because when people don't talk we get nervous." She was concerned about suicide.

48

"I HAVE AN IDEA about Mr. Cornelius," Trina said to Hal as they walked back to him. "I think he comes to the ER for his problems mainly because he doesn't like waiting around in the Primary Care Clinic for someone to see him. Talk about cost-effectiveness—it costs *ninety* dollars just to pull a chart on the ER."

When they entered the room, Mr. Cornelius was standing. He had put on his jacket and he held his sporty yellow hat in his hand.

Trina said, "You're feeling better, Mr. Cornelius."

"Yes, I am. I think I'll be going home now."

"I'm glad you're feeling better. Is there anyone to see after you at home?"

"Upstairs. I just had a call. The three ladies live upstairs from me. Hookers. They call the police station when they want to have sex with me. Then the police station radios me."

"Do you have a radio receiver?"

"In my head."

"Oh yes," Trina said.

"It was installed quite some time ago."

"Well, Mr. Cornelius, I have an idea for you. I think you ought to be followed regularly for your physical problems."

"I don't think much of the walk-ins. When I go there, everyone gets in ahead of me."

"I'll take care of that, Mr. Cornelius. You need to see the same person every visit. When you come to the ER, you don't see the same doctor each time."

"Not at the walk-ins, either."

"You don't have an appointment there?"

"No. I just go in when I need to."

"You really deserve to have your own primary doctor. Or maybe a nurse practitioner." Yes, Trina thought. Elin Maki. She knew Mr. Cornelius already. "Someone you can visit one day a week. I know what it is to wait. This way you can have a routine appointment."

"That would be good."

"You come in and see me in the afternoon, Mr. Cornelius."

"Yes, ma'am. I'll do that."

"Now, Mr. Cornelius, it's dark out, it's after nine, you know what these streets are like. Why don't you take a cab home? Do you have money for a cab?"

Mr. Cornelius pulled up a pants leg and showed her the sock rolled over the money. He let the pants leg fall. "Public transportation is more fun," he said. "It's more exciting."

"I'd feel better if you took a cab home."

"Public transportation is fine for me. I'll take the elevated." He put his hat on carefully. "Thank you," he said and left.

"He has a pretty extensive delusional system," Trina said. "Maybe his wife kept him sane all those years."

Trina kept thinking about love songs—titles, lyrics, phrases, melodies. I'm obsessing, she thought, but why? Maybe it's my own need. She took Hal back to the psych office so that she could sit with a cup of coffee and try to figure out what she was trying to tell herself about Patient X.

The music went away as soon as she sipped the scalding black coffee and started thinking about the elevated ketone bodies in the patient's urine. When the body doesn't get enough sugar, it starts breaking down muscle mass for food. Hydrochloric acid in the stomach doesn't have food to work on, so it starts working on the stomach itself. She picked up the phone and dialed Scotty McGettigan to make sure that GI bleeding had been ruled out.

Robert Higby waited until the security guard at the archway stepped into his office. He hurried under the arch and walked across the courtyard as if he were going to the ER, but he walked by those doors and by the window of the psych office. He saw a nurse on a telephone, but he didn't know what the office was and he didn't know that the nurse was Trina Frankian. He did know her car, though. The yellow Volkswagen Beetle.

It was dark on the driver's side of the car. He crouched below its roofline and, from beneath his jacket, took out a wire hanger he had cut and bent into a nearly straight tool with a loop on the end. He inserted the loop between the window glass and the gasket of the locked door at the upper right corner and maneuvered the loop down until it engaged the door lock. He pulled and the door opened with a slight snap.

He got in and closed the door and wedged himself down between the front and back seats. It was tight and uncomfortable, but in the darkness he could not be seen.

He did not know what time she would leave work and come out to the car, but he and his knife would wait for her.

Ever since he had begun to feel he had to *fuck* Jessy Gladdens because she wouldn't go with him anymore, he had had this feeling of *craziness* in his head, something that didn't go away and was driving him crazy, didn't go away even after he'd put all the craziness into Jessy's pussy and tried to leave it there. But it was still with him even after he'd fucked her, and sometimes now, more and more often, he remembered that the craziness had been coming after him and trying to climb into his head for as long as he could remember, back to when he was a child. It was nothing that was part of him and he fought it all the time, but sometimes it was easier to let it just run him, be the captain, do whatever it wanted him to do, and sometimes all of a sudden it would be gone, and he'd feel good, and he'd wonder how it had ever gotten into him and then start being scared about how it could come back and when it would come back and start after him again, like a cat following him and trying to jump into his head. Now the cat was in there and the cat had been telling him, get rid of this nurse cunt, no more people trying to be in charge of him. Get rid of her and the cat would leave him alone and Jessy Gladdens wouldn't do anything to get back at him and the cat would be free and he and the cat would be free of each other.

*   *   *

Scotty told Trina that they had no signs of GI bleeding.

She had not even replaced the receiver when she realized who the silent patient in the wheelchair was. No wonder her associations had had to do with yearning and music and loneliness and kissing and touching.

She said to Hal, "I don't think it's Wernicke and I don't think it's Korsakoff: He's clean-shaven, his clothes are in good shape, his boots were polished recently. It's as if he's been hiding somewhere. Just stayed in a room somewhere. Shaved, dressed, did everything as usual. Except eat. Look at how big his shirt is on him. Assuming it's his shirt, he's lost a lot of weight."

"Anorexia nervosa," Hal said.

"It's odd. Carol Carpenter died of that. She was a singer, too."

"He's a singer?"

"That's Dom Volante out there."

Very quietly Hal said, "No shit." He closed his eyes. "I see it. I see the resemblance." He opened his eyes and looked at Trina studiously through his thick glasses. "I must have a dozen records of his at home. Whatever became of him?"

"Exactly."

"If he was hiding, then why did he come out?"

"To get help?" Trina said.

Trina consulted with Scotty on the acute side. "I want to see if I can establish his identity. I want to see if he'll voluntarily admit who he is. That's step one."

"Maybe he just looks like Volante."

"Maybe. But I think it's Volante."

"Step one to what?"

"If he says to us, 'I'm me. I'm Dom Volante,' we have a whole person to work with, including his assistance."

"Anorexia nervosa doesn't quite fit. He's male. That makes it unlikely. There's no scut of sexual difficulties. He had a rep for high-powered sex."

"Whatever we end up calling it, if it's *psychogenic* malnutrition, it's a suicidal tendency."

"Not only is he the wrong sex, but he's way overage for anorexia nervosa. He's got no public history of suicidal tendencies."

"He's got no public history at all the past three or four years," Trina said.

"Okay, Trina. Follow it your own way. When the CBC gets back, we'll know more about the body. In the meantime, you see about the head."

Trina and Hal started through the acute side on the way back to Patient X. "Trina, you put together so much from—" Hal began.

"Trina?"

The woman who had spoken was being helped from a wheelchair onto a gurney. There were tears on her face. She was white, probably in her forties, though the general destruction to her person was such that she might have been younger. Nevertheless, she was beautiful. Trina's associations were specific: *bewitching*, a sorceress.

"Trina?"

Trina went over to her. A nurse and a transport worker settled the woman onto the litter. "I'm Trina."

The woman looked up at her. "I'm Mrs. Quimbley."

The woman who had failed to keep three appointments, the woman Trina had spoken to the night before, the woman whose name was the same as that of the consummate victim in *The WASP Princess*.

"We talked on the phone, Trina. You *know* me. Mrs. Quimbley. *Do you remember?*" Mrs. Quimbley looked carefully at Trina through her tears.

"Yes. Of course I do, Mrs. Quimbley. How are you? What's wrong?" Trina picked up the chart. Mrs. Quimbley cried quietly. "It says here your name is Jan Fox." The woman who had written *The WASP Princess*.

"That's right. Jan Fox." The tears became sobs. "Jan Fucks is more like it." She laughed. "Jan fucks up her life. *Oh.*" She reached out. "Oh, Trina, *help me.*"

49

"IT'S SO LONELY out there, so very, very lonely," Jan Fox
said. She wept as she looked up at Trina from the gurney.
Trina held her hand. She was being medicated intravenously
and had been hooked up to a heart monitor. She paid no
attention to Hal.

"No friends?" Trina said gently.

"No. Not anymore." She closed her eyes and the weeping
abruptly became sobbing.

"That is very lonely."

"*Oh, God, you can't know.*"

"I think I do. Enough to be your friend."

Jan's hand tightened on Trina's and she trembled.

"It's so deep and dark and cold where you are," Trina said.
The trembling slowed. "What can I do? What will happen
to me?"

"First we want to get you physically fit. That's going to
help the way you feel emotionally—"

"*I feel like shit.*"

"You feel hopeless and helpless."

"Oh, yes . . ."

"Do you always feel this way?"

"I . . . I don't know." She shook her head. "I'm so used
to it."

"When was the diabetes diagnosed? How long ago?"

"It's hard to remember . . . I was writing a screenplay . . .
They said I was drunk." She closed her eyes.

Trina waited. Then, "Were you? Were you drunk?"

She opened her eyes. "I could have been. I had a lover.
Who thought I could write a screenplay." She turned her
head away from Trina. But there was Hal Levy. She looked
back at Trina. "No. Not true. I let the man be my lover so he
would let me write the screenplay."

She was waiting for a judgmental reaction, Trina saw.
Trina did not offer any. "And what happened?"

"I think I went to sleep. I had a little office at the studio. They found me in there. Out cold on the floor."

"That's when the diabetes was diagnosed?"

"Yes. The doctor told the man who was my lover, told him diabetes accounted for my periods of bizarre behavior. He was wrong about that. The doctor was. The bizarre behavior went right ahead. Ask anyone. Anyone who was my friend. If you can find one." She laughed and wept.

"How long ago? How long have you been taking insulin, Jan?"

"Three years? Four years?"

"And your alcohol intake today?"

She looked away. "I had two mouthfuls from the bottle. This afternoon."

"Okay, Jan. I'll be coming back to see you in a while."

"You'll be my friend? You will, Trina?"

"Yes I will, Jan. Everybody's looking out for you here."

Jan nodded and closed her eyes, the tears continuing.

Scotty leaned against the radio console and Trina sat with a haunch on a desk and Hal stood watching and listening.

Trina said, "So there's the history of alcoholism. Some drugs a few years back, but nothing since. Two shots of Scotch about three this afternoon."

"Well, I'm very concerned about her cardiac status. Her potassium level is important right now, and we want to follow her urine output carefully. Was she hyperglycemic when she was picked up?"

Trina said to Hal, "We need to know if she's a 'brittle' diabetic. Can't keep her blood sugar steady even with medication. Or are the variations due to carbohydrate intake."

"She wasn't tender," Scotty said.

"No abdominal discomfort from what she told me," Trina said.

"Now the psychiatric aspects—"

"Are you satisfied she was found in diabetic coma?"

"Pretty well."

"Okay. She's agitated. Is that due to the metabolic abnormality or is it chiefly psychological? Or are they connected?"

"She talked to you. She didn't talk to me."

"She's depressed," Trina said. "My impression is she's a depressive."

"Any past treatment?"

"Never been to a shrink, she says."

"Amazing. A woman with her history. In this society. I'd expect her to have run through a few shrinks. But never seen one at all? Amazing."

"You remember her?"

"Sure I do. Intimately. I remember her centerfold. I was interested in literature, you see. I was a teenager, and her photos afforded me a good deal of sexual stimulation."

"How candid of you, Doctor."

"Give the lady her due." He glanced up at the clock. "She seems to be stabilizing since she's been with us. If that's so, I'll send her to a floor in a couple of hours."

"I'd like to see her calmed down now," Trina said.

"Valium IV suit you?"

"Just what the doctor ordered."

A man bumped into Trina and said, "Today is Friday."

Trina said, "Yes. Today is Friday." She waited.

The man said, "If it's Friday, this must be the drunk tank."

"You're in a hospital, you're in—"

" 'Scuse me. I gotta go piss." He walked away.

Hal said, "Don't you do something about someone like that?"

"You give him directions to the men's room. If he'll let you." She smiled. "All we can do here is crisis intervention, nothing long term. My objective is, whatever's going on, to keep something *worse* from happening." Trina indicated Patient X, across the room in the wheelchair. "Sometimes you go on your instincts. I think I have this man's attention. He had a tear for me. I've got an idea about getting to him. If I goof, the best that can be said later is that I got nowhere. The thing is, my goof shouldn't blow the patient's mind." They crossed the room. Trina nodded at the standby and then knelt down before the patient again. "Hi. Remember me? Trina?"

His head stayed down. There was no response.

"I guess you're frightened, huh? It's okay to be frightened. We can talk about it." No response at all. Trina lightened her tone of voice. "On the other hand, maybe you're having a blast here, sitting around and getting all this attention. The man of mystery, people so interested in you. You want to tell me?'' She waited. ''We'll still be interested in you. We'll still take care of you.''

The man was silent. He kept his head down, eyes closed.

''Maybe you need to go to a psychiatric hospital.'' A *zinger*, Trina thought. The man responded with alert eyes and alert body.

''I recognize you. I wonder if your silence is because you don't want people to recognize you.'' The eye contact was being maintained. ''Is it that you can't talk? Don't want to talk?'' She waited a few seconds. ''People who get really angry don't want to talk.''

The man glanced at the standby and then looked at Trina.

Trina said, ''We can go to a private room. You can be angry there if you want. I won't get angry at you. As long as it's talking anger. That might be good for you. I've heard screaming and yelling before.''

She had his attention, Trina saw, but she did not have his trust.

''Don't you believe people need other people?'' She touched the front of his shirt. ''Look how big your shirt is on you. You weighed a lot more—not so long ago. You know, some people, when they get sad, they don't eat.''

He began to cry silently, but Trina saw he was in control.

''What about your friends?''

The man suddenly spoke. ''None anymore.''

''No old friends?''

''None.''

Trina thought of Jan Fox's saying the same thing a few minutes before. ''That's hard to believe, a man like yourself—so famous, so successful, so *admired*—''

''No more.''

''What happened?''

''I don't know. Three years ago everything stopped. I couldn't *give* myself away.'' He closed his eyes and lowered his head. She thought she was losing him.

''What brought you to Boston?'' she said quickly.

He did not look up. ''L.A., New York—all I got was pity. Wasn't worth trying to work anymore.'' Tears streamed down his face, fell onto his lap. ''Not marketable. That's what they say is wrong with me. My voice hasn't changed.''

Trina hoped she had picked the right time to introduce the

man's name. "Mr. Volante, didn't you save any money? Don't you have anything to help yourself with?"

He took out a handkerchief and wiped his face and blew his nose, then looked at Trina. "I wasn't smart enough. I thought it was going to go on forever. The *popularity*. The money." His head bent again, his shoulders shook.

"Boston. There must be some reason you came to Boston."

"I thought I could hide in Boston. No one would know me."

"That must have hurt, though. As much as you wanted it, it must have hurt when no one recognized you."

He nodded at Trina. "But don't tell anyone. Who I was."

"We do have to keep some records—"

He looked at her sharply.

She smiled gently. "Records, not recordings, Mr. Volante. Records for medical purposes. The staff that takes care of you needs to know who you are, what you've been through. We'll be discreet."

His head bent again. There was a slight trembling.

Trina placed her hand on his. "I want you to stay with us until you're well. Will you do that for me?"

Dom Volante nodded without looking up.

"I need to go away for a few minutes to arrange a bed for you—"

Volante looked up, frightened. "Not a psychiatric—"

"No. A bed on a general medicine floor. You need to be taken care of and have a good diet. Hal Levy here is a medical student, and I'm going to have him stay with you till I get back. Okay?"

Volante nodded, his head down again, the tears falling onto his lap again.

50

AUDREY WAS WITH a chronic asthmatic who had suddenly developed acute respiratory distress when, earlier in the evening, around six-thirty, the medical worker had come to her and said, "Mr. Hines say he want to see you."

"Get the other nurse."

"Uh-huh," the worker said. He found the agency nurse monitoring the suction bottle on an elderly lady who had been having trouble clearing chest secretions.

"I've got other patients to see first. He'll have to wait in line. What about Miss Rosenfeld?"

"She send me to get you."

"Yeah. Take advantage of the hired help. What's his trouble?"

"He don't say. He jes say get him a nurse."

"Tell him one of us will get in to see him as soon as we can."

In a little while she looked in on him from the doorway, but he was asleep.

Scotty McGettigan was the senior resident on the cardiac arrest team and Mozart Wills the medical intern when the code was called for Med Three.

Audrey was kneeling on the bed trying to force the heart to move, the lungs to breathe.

"Nothing," she said.

The team arrived quickly, pressed in around the bed, shouted at each other. Day handed out the first round of medications and instruments from the crash cart, her hands rapid and anticipatory. Audrey got the EKG machine plugged in and the four limb leads attached to Mr. Hines. "He's tubed," the anesthesiologist said. A medical student said, "Nothing." He was reporting pulse and blood pressure. "Nothing," Audrey reported on the EKG display. An aide had brought a cart with defibrillator machine to the door and Audrey maneuvered it around the crash cart and into the room by the EKG machine. "Goop the paddles," Scotty said. Day handed Audrey an oversized toothpaste tube and Audrey greased the paddles with a clearish gray jelly. "What do you want it set at?" she said, handing the paddles to the resident.

"One hundred. Unplug the EKG. I'm going to shock him! Get away from the bed!"

"EKG's unplugged."

Scotty placed the disks. *"The paddles are on."* He looked at Audrey. "Go!"

Audrey depressed a red button. The team jammed into the bedside again.

"Nothing," Audrey said.

Scotty said to the medical student, "Intracardiac Epi."

The student inserted a ten-inch needle through the chest wall to the heart—they had to get the heart to fibrillate before they could defibrillate.

"Go to three hundred," Scotty said. Bed cleared, paddles held on, "Go!"

"Nothing."

"Four hundred. Now do it!"

"No, nothing," Audrey said.

They were all dripping sweat.

The EKG lines were flat and had been since the machine was attached.

They tried again.

"Nothing," Audrey said.

The team worked for ten more minutes.

"Nothing," Audrey kept saying. "Nothing." Hearing her own voice and not wanting to hear it.

Scotty looked at his watch and said, "It's nine forty-eight. I'm calling it."

The work did not stop all at once. It took a few seconds for the members of the team to unwind from activity, to give up. Then they stood in place a few seconds more.

It wasn't me, Audrey thought. *It's this damn place that let Mr. Hines die. Why am I here?*

"If I had gone to him when he sent for me," Audrey said.

"If you had gone to Mr. Hines," Scotty said, "your other patient might have gone into respiratory arrest."

The medical worker set containers of coffee on the counter of the station. Scotty opened one. Steam jumped out from the black liquid. As always after an arrest—sooner or later—Scotty began to tremble. "Anita Rounds told me she had a patient on this floor with no monitor this afternoon. Now it's six hours later. And he never got a monitor."

"I called down five or six times," Audrey said.

"I'm sure you did."

"I would have *stolen* one if I knew where one—"

"You would have had to take it off another patient. That was Anita's problem." He tried to pick up the coffee. *"Damn."* His trembling fingers had spilled hot coffee on the back of his hand. "So we have a nurse who's unfamiliar with the hospital, unfamiliar with the floor, unfamiliar with the patients. And no monitor."

"The workload here is impossible," the agency nurse said. "I'll never work here again."

Scotty said to her, "What happened?"

The agency nurse was pale. "I walked in and found him like that."

"When was the last time you saw him?"

"An hour ago . . . maybe two hours ago. I thought he was sleeping. That's what I told Miss Rosenfeld."

"Did you take signs?"

"I was too busy."

"How long was he like this?"

The agency nurse looked down. "I don't have a clue."

Scotty looked directly at Day. "The fucking *unforgivable incompetence* is the hospital's thinking it can staff this way. And no fucking monitor." Scotty's hand squeezed the container of hot coffee. The coffee spilled over and splattered. "That is fucking *it!*" he said, paying no attention to his hand. He said to Mozart, "Get Anita. Get the other members of the exec. Get 'em out of bed, get 'em wherever they are. Unless they're in an emergency." He looked at Audrey. "That man served the hospital all his life. And then the hospital let him die. Not you," he said to Audrey. "And not you," he said to the agency nurse. "The hospital let him die. And he didn't have to."

Audrey went into Mr. Hines's room.

There was one last thing she could do for Mr. Hines.

He was pale, going bluish, rigor mortis taking hold.

The room was a mess. The man's discolor disturbed Audrey. It affronted her.

She felt a compulsion to make her patient look good, not in pain.

She reinserted his dentures with difficulty, but the jaw had not entirely tightened yet.

The johnnie had been ripped off in the procedure. She pulled it away from the body and threw it out.

You're very, very sad, she heard her own voice saying inside herself.

She tightened the bed, made the bed beneath the body.

She wrapped Mr. Hines in a shroud.

She placed a tag around his toe and another around his neck.

51

TRINA CALLED from the psych office and said to Audrey, "I hear you've had a rotten evening."

"Oh yes."

"I'm sorry. I hope this isn't going to make it worse. I've got two patients and I want them on the same floor. Day decided on Med Three."

"Day thinks we're not busy enough on this floor."

"Day thinks the nursing on your floor is superb. That's why patients get sent to you. Not just because there are beds." She explained about Jan Fox and Dom Volante.

"Those guys are *celebrities*," Audrey said. "Just as soon as Bennett Chessoff finds out they're here—"

"I know. He's going to try to transfer them to the Gold Coast. But I want both these folks together on Med Three. They don't get moved off the floor, I don't care what."

"Why?"

"I want them together. They've both been reclusive, hiding. Their worlds overlapped. Maybe they even knew each other. I hope we can get some interaction between them. They've had similar experiences these last years. Maybe they can give each other support."

"They could do that on the Gold Coast."

"Mr. Volante wants to remain incognito. I'm not going to ship him to Bennett's media heaven. That would be the same as introducing him to a press conference. So he goes to Med Three and Jan Fox with him. You just see they stay there. Day will back you."

"We'll do what we can."

"You sound beat."

"Like Day said, we've had a rotten evening."

"I've asked for suicidal precautions for Mr. Volante."

"Trina, we can't give him one-to-one coverage."

"Day is pulling someone from somewhere."

"Off the wall, I imagine."

"No reporters on the floor. Tell your staff keep an eye out. Don't hesitate to call Security." A second line lit up. "Got to go. I'll be up tomorrow." She punched in the other line. "Psychiatry, Trina." She listened and said, "Okay," and said to Hal, "They want us at triage."

The young woman at the triage desk was slender and above average height. Her hair was curly and dark brown, her skin light brown. There was great dignity in her face, but her face was vacant.

Before they got close, Hal said, "She came over to me out in the New Wing last night and asked me to go home with her." He blushed.

"What did you say?"

"I said I couldn't. She asked if I was a doctor first. She had a lot of gynecological concerns."

"She has a look. A little glassy."

"Drugs?"

"I don't think so. Psychotic? Watch her behavior, not her words. Does she focus with eye contact? Look at you directly? Or paranoid, maybe. With paranoid patients you have to take advantage of any inroads they'll let you have."

They went to the triage desk. The nurse said, "Name's Olivia, wants a hysterectomy, and that's all I know."

"Ever see her before?"

"Not to recall."

Trina went over to the young woman a few feet away. Twenty-two or twenty-three, she thought. "My name is Trina. Your name is Olivia?"

Olivia was looking at a wall.

"Are you seeing things?" Trina said.

"Naw." She still looked at the wall.

"You ever been hospitalized, Olivia?"

Olivia looked over Trina's shoulder to something beyond. Trina looked behind herself. Nothing there. When she turned back, Olivia was still looking over Trina's shoulder. "I want a stickterectomy," she said.

"They don't do hysterectomies in the ER."

"I want a stickterectomy. My ovaries hurt."

"Is there something else that's troubling you?"

"You a nurse?" She was still staring at some distant place.

"I'm a psychiatric nurse."

"I'm going crazy," Olivia said in a monotone.

"Do you want to sign in and we'll talk?"

"Can I have a stickterectomy if it hurts enough?"

"I think you're distressed. I think you want to talk."

"Can I get x-rays?"

"Have you been here before?"

"Don't you know me?"

"No."

"Yes, you do," Olivia said, a slight anger in her voice. "Know the Snake Lady."

"Tell me about her." Olivia said nothing. "I want you to sit down with me and we'll talk."

"Don't go tellin' me here and there."

"You're confused, Olivia. What I'm willing to do is talk with you."

"Can I have a stickterectomy?"

"Why can't you look me in the eye?"

"My eyes can kill," Olivia said.

She walked by Trina without looking at her and on past the triage desk out to the New Wing. Trina took a few steps and watched Olivia cross the floor out there and go through the glass doors to the street.

Trina said to Hal, "What we were probably looking at was a paranoid schizophrenic." She shook her head. "I'm a litmus for paranoid schizophrenics. I don't know why, but I seem to recognize them. They don't scare me. And we can talk to each other."

It was nearly midnight, and Trina left the ER through the ambulance bays and walked across the quadrangle courtyard to her yellow Volkswagen, her key in her hand.

She stopped four feet away. The lock button on the driver's door was raised. She remembered locking the door.

She continued to walk as if she were going to another car. Then she made a circuit of the courtyard and went to the security guard under the archway.

"There's either someone in my car or someone broke into my car."

"*Lady,*" the security guard said.

He was white, mid-fifties, could have shaved better, and smelled a little of whiskey.

"I'll check it out with you," he said.

"No, never mind. I don't want to report you. The next

time you're carrying booze on the job, I will." She walked away.

"*I said I'd*—" he yelled after her.

She went back to the reception desk in the ER and got Sergeant Cleveland. He listened to her and said, "There're a coupla city cops just came in on a medicine run." What he meant was, city cops had guns.

The two cops were white. They heard Trina through. They recognized the name Robert Higby from their Want List. "You don't know what he's armed with?" the senior officer said.

"I don't even know if he's in there," Trina said. "What he threatened me with on the phone was a knife."

The two city police drove their cruiser through the archway to directly behind Trina's car. They left the cruiser's headlights on at full beam. With their weapons drawn, they moved up on each side of the Volkswagen. Sergeant Cleveland shone a light in and the three of them moved quickly back to the cruiser.

The senior city cop said, "Okay. We tell him to get out."

Sergeant Cleveland said, "He doesn't—what?"

"We throw you in with a can of Mace."

The two white officers moved up on each side of the car again, keeping the protection of the automobile's construction between them and the interior. The junior officer kicked the car violently with the flat of his shoe. The car shuddered as he said, "Get out, asshole, or we gas you out or blow you out."

There was a moaning from inside and a voice said, "I got nothin'."

"You gotta fuckin' knife, asshole. Open the door, throw it out, come out on your hands and knees."

There was a scream from inside. Higby had stabbed himself, Trina thought. Then she realized it was a scream of rage. And hopelessness.

She stepped in front of the city cop to the driver's door and opened it slightly so that she could be heard without yelling the way the police had had to.

"*Don't be crazy, lady.*"

She ignored the cop. "This is Trina out here, Robert. I'm

the nurse you spoke to on the phone this morning. I'd like to talk to you."

"Lady, *get away—*"

Trina said calmly, "Can you hear me okay, Robert?"

"*Meeoww.*"

Trina didn't know whether it was a scream or an animal sound. "I don't understand, Robert."

"*Meeoww,* hurt! Cat jump inna mah hayed, Trina. Cat's gotiz claws inna mah brayen. It hurt!" And he screamed the pain at her and then cried.

"Robert, let me help you get rid of the cat. Let me help you get rid of the pain. Will you let me help you?"

"*Yes!*"

"Do you have a knife?"

"Yes."

"Anything else?"

"No."

"Drop the knife out the door."

"What you promise me?"

"I don't know. What?"

"Keepa cops from beatin' on me?"

Trina looked at the police officers. The senior city cop shrugged. "Okay," Trina said. "Drop the knife out."

The knife fell from the car, glinted, and struck the cobblestones. Trina kicked it away.

"On his hands and knees," the senior city cop said.

"Robert, they want you to come out on your hands and knees."

"You promise now. No beatin'."

"I promise," Trina said.

Higby came out on his hands and knees. A handgun was immediately placed to his head and he was shoved to the ground and handcuffs placed on his wrists behind his back.

Because he had been shoved into the cobblestones, he was bleeding from his mouth and nose so he was taken into the ER. He struggled but did not speak.

Trina waited until he had been examined and treated before she went in to him. He was not struggling. His posture was rigid. He did not recognize her, Trina saw. Hadn't had time to see her. Was going to take a knife to me, Trina thought, and doesn't even know what I look like. "I'm Trina. I'm the nurse."

He stared at her, his body rigid.

"I didn't lie to you. I didn't know they were going to hurt you." He remained as he was. "I said I'd help you with the pain. With the cat." Trina made a swift association from Robert's cat to Olivia's Snake Lady. "I will."

Robert Higby's entire body relaxed, slumped from its rigidity. The police let him lower himself into a chair.

Trina spent a few more minutes with Higby and then went out and paged the psych resident on call. She apparently got him in an ARI meeting. It was awfully late for that. Awfully, awfully late.

"He raped Jessy Gladdens. He threatened me—he threatened *my life*— he's a danger to the community. But the goddamn sonofabitch wants help. You should have seen him. As soon as I identified myself and offered help. The psych nurse. You should have seen what happened to his body. The *relief* he felt."

52

AUDREY WAS FINALLY ready to go home. She was sweaty, grimy, tired, sad, and angry. So very sad and so very angry.

She decided she was not going to the elevated trolley platform and wait there at this hour. She was going to call a cab. She was about to when she thought, *Oh shit. Mrs. Armstrong.* The woman up for bilateral amputation the following morning. It already was the following morning. Audrey had promised to look in and see her before she went home. Audrey kept promises to patients.

On the surgical floor, Audrey checked in with the charge nurse and then went to the doorway of Mrs. Armstrong's room. Mrs. Armstrong had been sedated, but she opened her eyes. " . . . Miss Rosenfeld."

Audrey sat beside her on the bed. "I had to work late. I didn't know if you'd still be awake."

"Thank you . . . I'm awake . . . Scared . . . That keeps me awake."

"Yes." Audrey massaged Mrs. Armstrong's forehead and then her temples with her fingers.

"I thought you weren't coming. Idle promise. Soothe the patient."

"I know you can't sleep. I'll ask the nurse if she can give you something else."

"That feels good . . . That helps most, the way you rub my head . . . I wish you could stay with me. Tonight. I'd pay you for it."

"Mrs. Armstrong, I have to go home and rest myself. I have patients who're counting on me tomorrow. Tomorrow you'll be in the Surgical Intensive Care Unit. There are good nurses there. When you're awake for visitors, I'll come see you."

"All right . . . My dear . . ." Mrs. Armstrong was silent, her eyes closed, and Audrey thought she might have helped Mrs. Armstrong to fall asleep. But then Mrs. Armstrong said, "My dear . . . Miss Rosenfeld . . . I have a favor to ask of you. I have no right to."

"What?" Audrey said.

"Would you kiss me good night . . . Just a kiss on the forehead?"

Just like when you were a little girl, Audrey thought, and she bent and kissed the woman on the forehead and hugged her.

53

VIOLA CHAMBERS HAD, for the first time, been afraid to report to work on Children's Seven. She had had a vision of the hospital that afternoon. From the window of her apartment she could see the Old Building three or four miles away. That afternoon it had been a gray slab standing upright against the gray sky behind it. *Exactly like a tombstone*, she had thought. The afternoon rain had made beads on the glass and then flowed down it, causing the tombstone to blur and sway.

As she dressed for work she had thought, Would someone else like little Natalie have to be wrapped and tagged this night, some other child die?

But, Viola thought, if she didn't go in, some other child might die because she wasn't there.

When she got to the floor, the charge nurse she was replacing said, ''It's been a nightmare because of Natalie's death. Today was a nightmare and tonight was a nightmare. They're all scared. They're frightened out of their wits. Some got inactive, depressive. Some got hyper. Freeman left the floor entirely. Just went out on the street for three hours.'' The evening nurse looked around the quiet, darkened floor. ''We had shrinks and a psych nurse up here all day. And the play lady. And a priest and a minister and a rabbi. The resident spent more time deciding who was doing some good and who wasn't than anything else. A nightmare. Most everyone's had some sort of sedation or tranquilizer once or twice and then something at bedtime, and there's more orders as needed for the night.''

Viola took full report and then took over responsibility for the floor. She made rounds with her flashlight, briefly afraid as she shone it on each sleeping face, anxious as she checked each child's breathing. The floor was quiet, safe for the time being, the children sleeping—as much from having exhausted themselves emotionally, Viola thought, as from any medicine.

She stopped at the crib of the white infant girl who was in for failure to thrive. Viola felt a sudden spurt of anger at the mother, so self-centered and selfish that she had to bring her child to a hospital so that she might receive the love and affection and stimulation that would change her blank look to one of alertness and responsiveness. When, just a month before, the child had been returned to her mother, Viola and the other nurses had succeeded in nourishing her to a point where she smiled. Now she was back again and blank again and Viola felt unaccustomed fury. Little Natalie had died because there was nothing anyone could do. All this child needed to live and thrive was a little mother love. Viola stood by the child for a moment, touching her tiny back with her fingers.

She went to the door of Jamaal's glassed-in cubicle. ''How's he doing?''

''There's all kinds of new instability,'' the vent nurse said.

Viola recognized that because of Jamaal's change, the vent nurse was working in her own personal distress. "I'm available," Viola said.

"I know," the other nurse said, beginning the child's hourly suctioning procedure.

Viola returned to the station and was about to sit at the desk when she saw a figure move between the beds toward her. It was nine-year-old Edward, on the floor for a long-term and potentially life-threatening orthopedic infection. The child was wiping his eyes and Viola saw the streaks of tears on his cheeks. She went to him, put a hand on his shoulder. "I thought you were asleep."

"Was," the boy said.

"How come you're up?"

"I thought I hear Natalie. I thought I hear her talkin'. Like, you know, how she always talkin' to you at nighttime, when she spose t'be sleepin'."

Viola put her arm around the boy and turned him toward his bed. "You want somethin'? Maybe I can find you some juice and crackers. Or a little ginger ale."

"Unh-unh . . ." The boy looked at her. "You sit with me a couple minutes, Vi?"

Oh God, Viola thought, remembering the night before—sitting with Natalie, listening to Natalie tell her about the secret trip to the secret playground.

"Sure, Edward. But let's be quiet."

They went to his bed between the curtains that separated him from the beds on either side of him. He got under the covers and Viola remade the bed around him. Then she sat beside him.

He folded his nine-year-old brown hands on the white sheet over his chest and looked up into the darkness above his bed, not at Viola. "You know, Vi, somethin' magic come to me, give me one wish?"

"What would you wish for, Edward?"

"I make the wish I wish I had me uh *time* machine."

"If you did, where would you go?"

"Go? Go someplace? You some kinda' fool, girl? I wouldn' *go* no place. I jes sit still an' let that ol' machine make *time* for me. 'Cause I hear them one day, the doctuhs talkin' 'bout me, one doctuh, he say, 'Jes time, what he need the most is time.' So I get me uh time machine, I got sumpin' goin' make me time, jes' alluh time I need.''

And Viola suddenly saw the hospital not as a tombstone but as a great time machine producing time for people in its care. She had a sense of joy and she felt like crying in her joy and she bent and held the little boy against her.

THREE

The
Zero Clock

54

WHEN AUDREY GOT OUT of the elevator on Med Three, an unfamiliar nurse was just leaving the station. Audrey watched her walk down the corridor and into a room at the very end that faced the length of the corridor. Audrey glimpsed another unfamiliar nurse already in the room and vent apparatus that had not been there the night before.

She went to the station, but before she could ask about the new patient, the night nurse said, "It's crazy here, Audrey. The word is, they're fixin' to shut down the hospital."

"Where'd you hear that?"

"Night supervisor on rounds. All because of Mr. Hines."

Coralee had come up beside Audrey. She did not interrupt to ask about Mr. Hines. She listened.

"You don't shut down a hospital," Audrey said. "Not just like that."

"You do if you don't have a staff, no house officers," the night nurse said. "Scotty McGettigan and them. ARI. She said Scotty had a meetin' till two, three, last night. Then they called the director, told him he has to negotiate, satisfy their grievances or else they're pullin' out next Sunday midnight, no two ways about it. What they call a *job action*. *Strike* is more like it."

Audrey shook her head. "Now how did the supervisor know all this?"

"Bennett Chessoff himself. He had her to his office at four A.M. Now he's in a meetin' with Dorothea and Day and Midge and Dr. Geier and the hospital lawyer and I don't know who else."

Audrey looked at Coralee. "I think I'll just wait till I hear more."

"Wait on what?" the night nurse said.

Audrey shrugged. "Making vacation plans." She looked down the hall at the room with the vent apparatus in it. "What's going on?"

"ICU patient bumped to us, 'bout five. Needed his bed. A Mr. Emerson."

"Bumped with a vent?" Audrey listened to her own silence. She had an abrupt moment of understanding and she felt as if she had been physically struck. "Give me his book."

The report sheet gave her Mr. Emerson's status. The order sheet was exquisitely simple. All prior orders for increased support as needed had been DCed. The final order was *DNR*.

Audrey went quickly through the preceding report sheets. Her anger grew. Her anger became a fury. She placed the chart on the desk and spoke quietly and with control. "They sent him down here to die. They sent him to *my* floor to die."

Audrey went to Mr. Emerson's room. The night vent nurse was giving report to the new vent nurse. Audrey listened and looked at Mr. Emerson. The patient's bed had been slightly inclined. He was multiple intubated. A large man, he had a broad *strong* face, Audrey thought. A handsome man with no appearance of death in his face. *I am in the presence of death*, Audrey thought, and was so startled by the reality of *death* in the room that she almost cried out. It lurked in Mr. Emerson's body. It permeated him—having its way with him at its own gross pleasure.

The vent nurse had finished her summary. She said, "Who is this man?"

"I don't know," Audrey said.

At the station, the night nurse held out the phone to Audrey. "Tim Holbrook for you."

Audrey started. It was too early to make plans for the evening—and inappropriate with Mr. Emerson's death to see to. But Tim was not calling about the evening.

"You've got a patient of mine down there. Mr. Emerson."

"I just saw him."

"How's he doing?"

"How'm I supposed to answer that? Clinically?"

"I see."

"I'm sorry. But I'm angry. Very damn angry."

"It was the family's decision. But you should know that I urged it on them. And Nan wanted it. He was her patient, too. If we prolonged his life, you know how he'd die."

"I read the report sheets."

"We care about that man a lot. Let us know how things progress."

"Sure. I'll let you know when he's dead."

She had the night nurse continue report. It was essentially the same report she herself had given the night nurse eight hours before, but she listened carefully.

"Mr. Stevens is on call for seven-thirty."

"Yes. Pre-op—"

"Done."

"Thanks."

"Mr. Toby's going home today . . . Mrs. Collins. All that excitement last night—"

"Did we get—"

"A fib. The HO put her in dig about midnight, trying to knock her rate down. But she still isn't back to normal sinus rhythm."

Down the corridor, a corpulent black woman wheeled a large plastic refuse drum from doorway to doorway. She entered each room and returned with plastic disposal bags that she placed in the drum.

Inside Mr. Emerson's room, the vent nurse was checking the numbers she had just recorded. The numbers were becoming aberrant. Mr. Emerson's appearance remained unchanged. He was still. There was no motion to him at all save that which was inspired by the ventilator. His face was calm.

Audrey looked down the corridor again. Her view of the doorway to Mr. Emerson's room was blocked by a tall, young black man who was listlessly pushing a broom in a side-to-side motion so as to cross every square inch of the floor. Another black man, short and gray, followed a few feet behind with a damp mop and a bucket on wheels.

The night nurse said to Coralee, "Mrs. Pretty got her chemo last night. No nausea or vomiting. Tolerated it very well. Still has an IV up. D-five and a half with ten milligrams Trilafon at a hundred. She's going home today, too—"

"But she's getting another unit," Audrey said, "right?"

"I was going to get to that," the night nurse said. "Yes. Right."

Audrey said, "Do either of you know how she's getting home?"

"No."

"No."

"Does *she* know? I'll have to ask her."

A tone and signal light turned the attention of the three nurses. Mr. Emerson's room.

"I'll go," Audrey said.

The vent nurse said, "The blood pressure's pretty steady at one-thirty over sixty-five. But the pulse has gone from ninety to one-thirty."

Audrey nodded, looking at Mr. Emerson. She could see nothing from exterior observation, but she knew exactly what was happening. Mr. Emerson's heart was pumping hard against no resistance. His blood vessels had become acutely enlarged. He was bleeding out, entering septic shock. His blood would start to pool in his system, his heart unable to move it. He would soon enter bradycardia, a slowing of the heart, and from that into the dying heart rhythm. The blood pressure would fall and fall.

Audrey wanted to be cool. She wanted to say to the vent nurse *The process has started. Let me know when it's over.*

She wanted to run from the room.

She said, "I'll call the HO," and she walked quickly to the station.

Coralee listened to and watched Audrey as she spoke to the resident. She listened to the tone of voice, watched her body language. Mr. Hines and now Mr. Emerson quickly afterward. Coralee knew that Audrey felt closed in and vulnerable. When the night nurse had finished her report, Coralee said to Audrey, "That *the* Jan Fox?"

"From what Trina says. Real unhappy lady."

"I used to see her on Carson. She's got to be the meanest, funniest white bitch around. And I do mean bitch." Coralee paused and grinned. "She's not in to have her staples removed, is she?"

Audrey smiled. "If she is, she's on the wrong floor and in the wrong service."

"I haven't heard of that lady in a long time. *Long*, long time."

"She hasn't been around," Audrey said. "That's for sure."

Coralee smiled. "That lady sure could zing people." She paused. "And Dom Volante, too. Anybody'd think this was the Gold Coast. How come Bennett hasn't transferred them out?"

"I expect he'll try. But he's got other things on his mind right now." She explained about Dom Volante's anonymity and privacy and that both were to be protected.

The night nurse said, "He's got a precaution in with him. A Mr. Taylor working a double shift. Snotty sonofabitch. Rented."

The telephone. "Med Three, Audrey."

Day O'Meara said, "Dorothea has called a meeting of all head nurses at three-thirty this after."

"Day, what—"

"You'll get the howl from Dorothea at three-thirty." Day hung up, and that was unlike her.

In Mr. Emerson's room, Aaron Silver stood waiting as the vent nurse pumped the cuff around Mr. Emerson's arm. Once Mr. Emerson was off the unit Aaron could have left the patient to another resident, but he had elected not to.

Audrey looked toward the urinary drainage bag. Nothing in it. Kidneys were not functioning, profusion down.

Silver said, "C'mon, *what's the pressure?*"

The vent nurse slipped her stethoscope off. "Seventy over twenty."

Aaron stared at his patient. "Well. Well. Well, this is the ballgame." He said to Audrey, "Call me when you need me to pronounce." He left.

Now Audrey stared at Mr. Emerson. The vent nurse went back to tending the apparatus.

"Clergyman?" Audrey said. "Family?"

"No one said anything," the vent nurse said.

In the corridor Audrey caught up with Aaron. "What about the family?"

"Call them. Tell them to come in. Tell them there's been an acute change."

Audrey wheeled a scale into Mrs. Pretty's room. "Hi. How you feelin'? Nauseated at all?"

The gray-haired black lady shook her head.

"No? Good. Don't like it here, huh? Goin' home today."

"That's what they tell me." She glanced at a photograph of her toddler grandson.

"He'll be glad to see you, I bet," Audrey said.

"Whatcha got there?"

"Blood."

"You carryin' on last night? Out with the *dee*mons and the *vaam*-pires?"

"Stayed right here most of the time."

"You fixin' t'put that in me?"

"Just a unit before you go home so you don't get sick. First we'll just pop you on this scale. They want to know what your weight is after chemo." Audrey helped the old lady out of bed and onto the scale. Audrey slid the weights on the arms, then said, "Okay, back in bed. Your weight's up. It's all the fluid you get after chemo." She indicated an IV needle. "Uh-oh. Okay, I'm going to pull this one out. It's clotted. Give you a brand-new one in the other arm."

From the doorway Coralee said, "Audrey, Mr. Emerson's nurse would like you."

"Finish up? I'm switching to Mrs. Pretty's right arm."

The vent nurse said, "It was seventy over twenty and in two minutes it went to sixty palp." The vent nurse could no longer hear blood pressure with her stethoscope, but she could feel it with her fingertip. "I keep suctioning, but the blood's clotting off and blocking the tube." The vent nurse knew it was hopeless, but out of her own need she continued to do what she would do if the situation were not hopeless. But Mr. Emerson's airway was blocking with blood.

He was gray. He had entered the agonal breathing process. Four or five or six erratic breaths in the minute. Wide, bizarre beats of the heart. Audrey touched him with her fingertips. She touched coldness, clamminess. Almost like he's already dead in front of me, she thought.

"Twenty palp," the vent nurse said. "Christ," she said softly. Both nurses were still. "Zero palp," the vent nurse said.

The cardiac monitor alarm was buzzing. The line was flat. Aaron Silver nodded at the monitor. "You can turn that off now."

There was the postmortem care to do. Bathing, shrouding, tagging. It was the vent nurse's duty together with whatever aide Audrey sent to help. But Mr. Emerson was a visitor on Audrey's floor and he had died on it. Mr. Emerson was one of *hers*, Audrey thought, and once again, as little as she had been able to do for him in life, she would at least care for him in death. She said to the vent nurse, "I'll do the PM care with you."

When Audrey returned to the station she called the ICU. Nan Lassitter answered. Audrey reported Mr. Emerson's death.
"How long did it go on?"
"Less than an hour."
Nan was silent. Then she said, "There *is* a just God."

55

AUDREY HAD no more than replaced the receiver than the phone rang. "Med Three. Audrey."
"Please hold for the director."
A click, a silence, and then Bennett Chessoff's voice. "Can you spare me a moment, Audrey?"
"Yes." *Shit.* I know what he's calling about.
"You have two patients, Dom Volante and Jan Fox."
"I have a psych order that both are to remain on this floor."
"When the psych order is discontinued, I'd like to have both patients over here on the New Wing. Especially Dom Volante."
"Over on the Gold Coast."
"I wish we could do away with that characterization."
"Do you think a telephone and color television are going to make Mr. Volante better?"
"Perhaps you're having a bad morning."
"My understanding is that, for the present, Mr. Volante's health will be better served with privacy."
"He will have privacy over here."

"He could. But he won't. As I understand it, Director, the patient's placement in a bed is a nursing decision."

"Let's not get into a jurisdictional confrontation."

"Mr. Volante is a patient on this floor and he will remain on this floor until he's ordered elsewhere. I'm not shipping him out."

"Audrey, I think that you don't . . . *appreciate* the help that these people can lend the hospital."

"I'm concerned about helping them. Not them helping us."

"I take *your* point, Audrey. I wish you'd give some consideration to mine."

"I have. All it deserves."

"I think some other time would be a better time to discuss this."

Day put her telephone down. She felt vaguely faint. The master sheets on the desk in front of her would not quite come into focus without concentration. She closed her eyes. There was an image from a recurrent dream of the night before. She had spent the night in an empty room on Med Five. Over and over she had dreamed of the zero clock. But instead of marking off the time *since* a patient had arrested, the clock was running toward zero. The clock was counting down the very little time left to the hospital.

She opened her eyes. There was nothing she could do about that except get on with her job. She dialed another number.

Viola Chambers braced a bag of groceries against herself with one arm and, with her free hand, unlocked the door to her apartment. She was so tired she decided not to put the groceries away properly but just place the entire bag in the refrigerator. Before she could do so the telephone rang.

Day O'Meara's voice said, "Did I wake you? Are you asleep yet?"

"No, I just got in."

"I hate to ask—"

"Then don't. I'm tired. I'm weak."

Day sighed. "*I* am just deadly tired of pulling people off the walls."

"What is it?"

"Children's Seven."

"My floor. How convenient."

"Afternoon."

"Then pull my own at eleven, too—right?"

"I've tried everyone I could think of, but no takers."

"Do you want me to bitch and moan and—"

"Not particularly."

"—tell you how tired I am—"

"Please, no."

"—before I tell you okay?"

"No, but I'll listen to you now."

"I'm real, real tired, Day. In my head and in my body."

"Still Natalie Briggs?"

"I'm obsessing. I can't make any sense out of that child dyin'."

"But you did say yes?"

"Yes. I'll be in. At three." Viola hung up.

Then, instead of putting the bag of groceries in the refrigerator and going to bed, Viola carefully put each purchase in its proper place. Only then did she go to bed, as if she had ordered the world for the brief few hours available to her for sleep.

"Med Three. Audrey."

"Audrey, Tim. We *hoped* it would be peaceful for Mr. Emerson." Audrey did not reply. "That was the most medicine could do."

"I had nothing to do with it."

"Something else, then. We have this meeting this afternoon."

Audrey was surprised at her own surprise. Yes, of course, Tim was a head nurse, too. They had been to these meetings before. "Yes."

"Word is, this one's extraordinary."

"Demobing the hospital. Yes. I guess that's extraordinary."

"It's liable to be a long meeting. Why don't we just plan on going out afterward?"

Audrey thought herself through. "Tim, I don't know. I'm washed out. I don't think I have the energy."

Tim was silent. Audrey could feel his disappointment. Finally he said, "Let's see how you're feeling after the meeting."

*   *   *

When Molly Chang drove herself to work, as she was able to this morning, she did not have to be in her office until after eight. When she unlocked the door, her telephone was already ringing.

"Liz Swanzey, Molly."

"Oh yes."

"I'm calling about the referral. Starting psychotherapy. I'd like to begin."

"I'll make some calls. I'll get you someone good."

"I hope you can do it soon."

Molly paused. "Any particular reason for saying that?"

There was no reply for several seconds. "I think I've been upset most of my life. I pretended it wasn't so. That it would go away. Anger. Anxiety. I stayed up with myself last night and remembered a lot of it. I can see it's not going to go away by itself. I'm scared of psychotherapy, all right. But I want to get started."

She sounded exhausted, Molly thought. "It may take a couple of days, but I'll get back to you, Liz."

Molly hung up and sorted through the mail she had placed on her desk. She stopped at a business-size envelope from Cambridge University, School of Law, Cambridge, Massachusetts. She took a letter opener from her desk and slit the envelope open with some care. Her telephone rang.

"Molly, Bennett."

"Good morning."

"As I told you, I put off calling you these past weeks."

"I recall there was some discussion about that."

"I don't intend to be reticent now. I'd like you to have dinner with me tomorrow evening."

No beating around the bush, Molly thought. Or that's exactly what he's doing. And it's my bush. "Are you impatient?"

"By reputation, no. I have a reputation for biding my time."

"But not this time."

"My schedule is going to become crowded. I have free time now. I'd like to take advantage of it."

"Dare I ask what's going on with ARI and you?"

"Why, nothing's going on with ARI and me. Absolutely nothing."

Molly felt the pleasant tension of being in contact with

Bennett even at the remove of a telephone line. Out of curiosity about the man and out of curiosity about herself, she again agreed to have dinner with him.

She unfolded the letter and read:

Dear Ms. Chang,

On behalf of the Admissions Committee, it is my pleasure to offer you placement with the law school class that will begin its first term of studies on September 15.

Ginny Shiffland, the security guard, had determined upon a means to peace of mind when she was at work. The means certainly wasn't seeing one of Trina Frankian's shrinks, a course she found as threatening as the work itself had become.

She got up early and went to see her brother before he left for his job as a cashier at Suffolk Downs.

"I want you to get me a gun," she said. "Something small I can strap on under my pants leg."

"No way, Gin. It's one year mandatory, you get caught."

"I've got five years into this job. I'm not gonna give it up, start somewhere else again, lose my retirement—"

"Get y'self a license to carry, you can buy a gun y'self."

"They don't let us have guns. Not in the hospital."

"See? So that's it."

"I just want it to get through for a little while. It's *dangerous* down there, John. Then they say, too, we may be alone in there with the wackos, no docs at all next week."

"I hear somethin' about that. Them rich, educated bastards lookin' for more dough."

"I just want it in case they go out. Okay? Only if they go out."

"Naw, Gin."

"I know you've got unregistered guns right here in this house."

"Yeah. But they don't leave the premises."

"I don't get it from you, John, I get it from someone, I don't know who."

Her brother thought. "You oughta come out to the races. Relax you, y'know? I getcha freebie to the Paddock Club—"

"Thanks for nothin', John. Probly whoever I buy it from's gonna stick me a bundle and tell the wrong person, too."

Her brother nodded slowly. "Okay, Gin. But only if those bastards go out. Only if you're alone in there."

56

JAN FOX HAD BEEN sleeping when Audrey looked in on her during rounds. She had woken while her signs were taken and responded to the HO's questions. The HO had been satisfied to let her go back to sleep. She had immediately curled up like a child, innocent and self-protective. She was still in that position when Audrey looked in on her again. Her face was so calm and her sleep so still that Audrey had the idea that Jan Fox had waited a long, long time for this rest. When Audrey took her blood pressure, the woman lay on her back and covered her eyes with her other arm and continued to sleep. As soon as Audrey unwrapped the cuff she curled up on her side again.

Dom Volante was also lying on his side, but his eyes were open. His back was to the man, an LPN, the precaution, seated at Volante's bedside a by-the-book arm's length away. The elpan wore white pants and a white shirt. The shirt was open at the collar and the sleeves were precisely folded back halfway up his forearms. He wore a gold watch on a heavy gold link band.

"What's with this guy?" the elpan said. "I mean, like I try to talk to him, he tells me to shut up."

Audrey said, "He may simply be telling you he would prefer privacy."

"Helluva place to come to for privacy, Back Bay Met."

"You're not staff here, Mr.——" She had to check his ID. "Mr. Taylor. Are you on the staff here?"

"No way. I'm agency, José. Me and Volante, I guess we both messed up, endin' up here. Right, sport?" He tapped Volante's back and then looked at Audrey again. "That's what I was tryin' to talk to him about. We got a lot in common that way."

"I think you could use a break, Mr. Taylor."

Taylor stood up. "You know, I was one of this guy's fans.

Yeah, I was. But no more, I can tell you that. Sittin' here, him with his back to me and all—"

"Mr. Taylor—"

"What comes to mind is, when he was singin'? He wasn't singin' for chrissake, he was masturbatin' his vocal cords—"

"*Enough*, Mr. Taylor. You've been on a long time. Take a break. *Now*."

"Glad to," the elpan said, glancing at Volante, and left the room.

Audrey said to the patient, "My name's Audrey. I'm the head nurse on this floor. We met last night. I don't know if you remember." Volante said nothing. "May I sit down?" Volante remained silent. "I'd like to spend some time with you, Mr. Volante. But I won't sit down unless you say it's all right . . . Okay. If you want me to keep standing, I will."

"No," Volante said, no strength or resonance in the voice that had possessed both. "If you stay, does the asshole stay out?"

"While I'm here."

"Be my guest."

Audrey sat down. "Thank you."

"What's he here for?"

"The asshole?"

"Yes. You have one for every patient?"

"We try not to."

"Just for me, huh? A precaution."

"What has Mr. Taylor said to you, Mr. Volante?"

"He said he's here to make sure I don't *off myself*. Is that it?"

Audrey hesitated and then said, "It was a consideration. For your protection."

He began to shake slightly. "I wouldn't do it."

"It seemed like it might have been an intention, the way you were treating yourself outside."

"No . . ." He turned over slowly and looked at Audrey. "No."

"I'm glad to hear it."

"Will Trina . . . Will Trina be coming to see me?"

"She said so."

"Today?"

"That's what she said. It'll be sometime after three. That's when she comes on."

"Can we get rid of . . ."

"The asshole? I'll see what can be done."

"I don't want anyone in here at all."

"You talk it over with Trina."

"What's going on with me? What are you all doing?"

"We're running tests to see what shape you're in, Mr. Volante. Then we'll give you diet and medication to get you back to yourself."

"I don't want anyone to know I'm here."

"I understand. We're doing our best about that." Audrey got up. "But there's someone on the floor you might have known personally."

Dom Volante looked at her with what might have been fear.

"Jan Fox." When he said nothing Audrey said, "Jan Fox, the writer?"

"I know who Jan Fox the writer is." He turned his back to Audrey again. "Just the person."

Audrey signaled the elpan back to the room. When he entered, she moved the chair away from the bed and to the wall. "I don't think Mr. Volante requires such close attention anymore, Mr. Taylor."

"Whatever you say."

"And he doesn't require conversation."

"Whatever you say."

Audrey went to the station and called Day. "Thank heaven I caught you."

"Caught me? I haven't left this place for days. Maybe weeks. I've lost count."

"We've got a problem here."

"Where have I heard that before?"

"Mr. Taylor, the elpan who's been assigned to Mr. Volante? He's got to go. He's driving Mr. Volante crazy. The man's bedside manner would drive anyone crazy."

"I haven't got anyone to replace him."

"You've got Taylor in there as a precaution. Instead, what you've got in there is an instigation. You could pull someone, couldn't you? An exchange. Put Taylor in somewhere else. For the rest of the shift."

"See what I can do. Get back to you."

Audrey looked down the empty corridor. Now that there

was this rumor of the house officers' going out and shutting down the hospital, she was acutely conscious of how little time the interns and residents and other doctors actually spent on the floor. They made rounds and individual docs visited individual patients and they were busy every minute of the day teaching and learning and diagnosing and prescribing, but ninety-five percent of the time they were not on the floor and ninety-nine percent of the time they were not needed on the floor. Of course, when they were needed, it was critical. But ninety-nine percent of the time they weren't needed. You could say the docs did so well by the patients they were't needed. Or you could say the nurses did so well by the patients the docs weren't needed. That was a wild idea, Audrey thought. But as she went through the morning and thought of hundreds of days like it, there was a certain truth to the idea. It was amazing how little time the docs were on the floor. Hours could go by without seeing one.

Coralee came back to the station and sent an aide off to other work. She and Audrey consulted about the patients they had seen individually.

Coralee interrupted and said, "Well, look here." Betty Bowen was approaching the station. She wore a blue velvet robe, her own nightgown, and fluffy blue slippers. "Aren't you the vision, Betty?" Coralee said, and Audrey remembered that Coralee had been a young nurse on this floor back when Betty had been head nurse. "You look so fine, Betty, you look like you're in the wrong hospital."

"I'm in the right hospital."

Betty paused and then entered the station. "I'm just restless. I try to talk to my roommate, I try to read. But I just lay there now and calculated, I must have visited that one room alone nearly forty-nine thousand times while I was on this floor. It's hard for me to be a patient on this floor, but I wouldn't be anywhere else."

Coralee put her hand on Betty's arm. "I understand."

"Me too," Audrey said.

"Well. You know the way the kids have the play lady over in Pedi? I wonder if you might have some patients who need company? Maybe even company with some medical knowledge. I could be the talk lady." She looked at Audrey and Coralee with need and uncertainty.

"You're hired," Audrey said.

Betty nodded. "One annoys oneself being useless. Much better to go through this process actively rather than passively. To the extent one is able. I promise not to overdo."

Audrey wrote some names and room numbers on a piece of paper. "Just go in and introduce yourself. Tell them you used to be the head nurse on this floor and you want to visit. They'll be thrilled."

Betty took the piece of paper and smiled, then studied the names as if they made up an unfamiliar set of orders. She walked away and down the corridor and an elevator opened. Mr. Stevens, on a gurney, was being brought back to the floor from his bronchoscopy. Audrey went to him and helped the transport worker settle Mr. Stevens back in his bed.

"How was it?" she said.

"Not my idea of a good time," Mr. Stevens said.

He was fatigued. But he tried to get up. "I gotta pee. 'Scuse me, *urinate*. I got to, *bad*." Audrey brought him a urinal and he sat on the side of the bed and relieved himself. "I don' unnerstan'. I ain't had nothin' t'drink at all. You know that."

Audrey said, "But you had lots of liquid. The IV."

"Oh, yeah. Sure." He held the urinal and said to Audrey apologetically, "What should I do with this?"

"I'll take it," she said and took it. "You want to rest? Anything I can do for you?"

"Just rest."

Outside the room she took his chart from the gurney. Nothing unusual post-op, no new diagnostic entries.

Audrey took a call at the station. It was Trevor Davis. "Mrs. Armstrong's in the SICU. I did a good job. I think she's going to do well."

"Thank you. Thank you for letting me know."

"I thought you'd want to. Now, about our dinner—"

"What dinner?"

"The one you didn't accept last night. I'd like to suggest—"

"Trevor, it's been a bad morning. Let's talk another time, okay?"

He chuckled. "Not okay. I don't let go of a dream when I find one."

"I'm not a dream," Audrey said, and gently placed the receiver in its cradle.

The next call, immediately after, was from Ned Willard,

the floor's current chief resident. "I'm down in Path," he said. "Mr. Stevens. It's not good. Oatcell CA."

"How long a—"

"Two or three months."

That was not how long the condition had been in progress, that was what was left.

Audrey turned to a young black woman in a staff, dress-code green pantsuit. "Day O'Meara sent me. Patient needs a precaution?"

"Not exactly a precaution. Just someone to stay with him. He may not be up to talking."

"He don't talk, I don't talk, that the way he wants it. Day say send the elpan up to Med Eight, that's where she took me."

Audrey took the aide to Dom Volante's room and introduced her and made the change of attendants.

In the corridor Mr. Taylor said, "Thanks a bunch. For kicking my ass out."

"You two just weren't getting along. It happens."

"Right when I was really getting to know the bastard. In all his warmth."

"No one's to know he's here."

"Is that a fact?"

"Just reminding you."

"Terrific getting to work here. See you 'round." Mr. Taylor thought that columnist Lynn Keating would love to know that *Dom Volante* was a patient at Back Bay Met.

57

BEFORE VIOLA COULD go up to Children's Seven, she had to pass through the pedi walk-in clinic on the first floor. It was there that she heard about the unexpected meeting of head nurses called for four o'clock. "Management's going to shut the hospital down," a nurse said to her. That was beyond Viola's ability to believe. Another nurse, a Nursing Services Alliance activist of Viola's age, said angrily, "If the HOs go

out, City Hall's goin' to use it as an excuse to close the
hospital and not reopen it again. Ever.''

"How do you know that?''

"The pols been squeezin' this place out of the city budget
for years. What you think they're goin' to do when they can
cut loose completely?''

Cut loose? Viola thought, getting into the old and unsteady
elevator. The graffiti on the walls had been scratched into the
enamel with objects that were pointed. The graffiti was at
grownups' height, not kids'. It was a few minutes before
three, just about seven hours since she had left the floor.

She got off the elevator and saw a man and a woman with
the pedi psych nurse in the station. Viola had never seen them
before, but she knew they were Natalie Briggs's parents.
They were each holding a toy that had belonged to Natalie.
When Viola was closer she saw that Natalie's other possessions—a little nightgown, toys and books and comics, some
hair ribbons—were spread on the counter in the station.

Viola was filled with grief and anxiety. The anxiety came,
as she knew, from the guilt she felt that she could have
somehow done *something* and saved Natalie's life. She knew
it was not so, but she had no defense against the feeling that it
was so. And if she was responsible for the child's death, she
deserved and had to face the parents' rage at her. The parents'
rage frightened her.

A poor black girl who had let a white child die, Viola
thought.

Crap, Viola thought. You still thinkin' that way, *girl?*

She entered the station. "Mrs. Briggs?'' The woman turned.
"Mr. Briggs.'' She held out her hand. "I'm Viola Chambers.
I'm the nurse who was with Natalie . . . when she died.''

The mother started to extend her own hand, then stopped.
"Why did she die?''

"It was respiratory arrest—''

"We know that,'' the father said. "But *why* did she die?''

"I don't know.''

"You don't know,'' the mother said. "There must have
been *something* you could have done.''

"There wasn't.'' She felt tears in her eyes. "I tried everything. I did everything I knew to do.''

"It wasn't enough, was it? Doing everything *you* knew to
do,'' the mother said. "You let my child *die.*''

The father was staring at Viola.

"I did not *let*—"

The father said, "If it had been some *black* child. . . . You and that black intern, you might've managed something, huh? *This hospital.*"

There, Viola thought. Not so far beneath the surface, was it? She was both angered and relieved that the prejudice and distrust had been expressed.

"Dr. Wills and I did everything that could be done. The arrest team came quickly. They did everything they could do." Viola did not mention that all the members of the team had been white.

Viola remembered Natalie's calling her to her bedside and telling her about the secret trip down to the secret playground. *You can't tell my momma, Vi. 'Cause it's a secret.* Viola felt tears again, tears for Natalie, tears for the parents. These people were just parents, no matter what they said to her, just parents taken apart by the very worst thing that could happen to parents.

Viola said, "Mrs. Briggs, Mr. Briggs, I loved Natalie."

Mrs. Briggs began to cry and then to sob. Mr. Briggs took his wife in his arms. The ambulatory kids had started to come over. The psych nurse closed the door to the station. Outside the station, the head nurse began scattering the kids back to other places on the floor.

Mrs. Briggs allowed herself to be comforted by her husband and her sobbing slowed and then stopped. She stood apart from him and looked at Viola. Then she took a step forward and put her arms around Viola.

Viola returned the embrace and did not know if, indeed, she might be physically supporting Mrs. Briggs.

When Mrs. Briggs released Viola, she looked down at the toys on the counter. "I suppose the children here could use these toys." She looked at her husband. "What do you think, Al? Do we want to take them home?"

He shook his head.

Mrs. Briggs looked at Viola. "The children here would play with them?"

"Yes."

"You won't give them away?"

"They'll stay right here on this floor."

Mrs. Briggs nodded. She picked up Natalie's little night-gown. She held it out from herself and then pressed it against herself, as if it were the child's empty body, and she was silent as tears ran down her face.

58

DONALD KAY, the public relations director of the hospital, received a call from Lynn Keating. Keating, at her desk at the *Eagle*, had had a call from a petulant individual who identi-fied himself as Mr. Taylor and who said that Back Bay Metropolitan Hospital had as a patient none other than *the* Dom Volante and that he was being kept on Medical Three anonymously.

"I can't give patient information to the press," Kay said. "Not without permission of the patient."

"My understanding is that you have Dom Volante there."

"You've just got a rumor. Unconfirmed."

"You have an anonymous patient on Med Three."

"We do have a patient who does not want his identity known."

"Donald, you're going to need favors from me, oh, so very soon. In your position there at the hospital, guiding its public image. It looks like the house officers are going to do a number on the hospital's image—and on its administration's image."

"I'm sorry, it doesn't change what I just told you."

"Bear it in mind. I'll be at this number. Or Metro will know where I am.

Donald Kay called Audrey.

The hour before the head nurses' meeting was crowded. Au-drey had simply wanted to get Debby Fluelling, the new nurse, personally acquainted with the floor. If it had not been for the meeting, she would have stayed on an extra three or so hours to do so.

Audrey smiled spontaneously when she first saw Debby.

The new nurse was a dress traditionalist like herself—white dress, white stockings, cap. She had graduated less than a year before.

"You were at Jordan," Audrey said. "That's a quiet place. Why did you want to come here?"

"*Because* it was quiet. Elective gall bladders. Rich drinkers slowing down—admitted for 'nutritional deficiencies.'"

That was when Audrey got the warning call from Donald Kay. "You want to look out for Keating. She already knows he's on Med Three."

"Move him?"

"He's to stay there. Till he's moved to the New Wing. There's nowhere he can hide."

After Audrey hung up, Debby Fluelling went on. "There was nothing happening at Jordan. And it's *so* old-fashioned. You even have to stand up for the doctors when they come into a room."

"It's true. We don't do that here," Audrey said. "C'mon. I'll show you the floor."

It was like having the new grads around in June, Audrey thought—Debby was so full of enthusiasm. Audrey found her own spirits livened. She took Debby in to meet patients and had her do simple things, like count rates on monitors and review charts and orders.

Jan Fox asked for her bed to be raised and Debby immediately went to do so.

"Don't," Audrey said.

"Why not?"

"You don't know whether that's up to your discretion."

"Raising a bed? It's not interrupting medication. It's not interfering with therapy."

"You don't know that—"

"Gee, even at Jordan—"

"Check to see that there's an order that covers you. You can't change a patient's posture without an order that clears you to do so."

"Even at Jordan we had that discretion."

"At Jordan you didn't have our patients. You didn't have the range of medical concerns we have here."

"That's so reassuring," Jan said to Chanda, her roommate, a young black woman. "We're not patients, we're training facilities."

"I'm glad to see you so alert, Ms. Fox," Audrey said.

"Call me Jan. Yes, I'll keep you on your toes, Nurse." She smiled. "It's my specialty."

Audrey understood immediately. Jan Fox had been alone for a long time. Now she had an audience.

Jan turned to Chanda. "Let me tell you about a conversation I had with Sidney Poitier. We were waiting to go on the *Tonight Show* . . ."

There were forty-two head nurses, and bringing them all together at once was highly unusual. The room in which Dorothea had them meet was intended for small medical lectures. The nurses filled all the seats and several had to stand along the walls. They were all still in hospital dress— whites and scrubs. Tim Holbrook and a fellow from a neurological unit were the only males.

Dorothea began by saying, "There are a lot of rumors around. I'm not here to confirm or deny any of them. What I have to tell you is this. It appears that ARI and the administration of this hospital are going to go head to head. Over irreconcilable differences."

"Why irreconcilable?" Selma said.

"They have to do with money. The hospital doesn't have the money. It appears that ARI will go out a week from tomorrow. Sunday midnight. This hospital will then be staffed almost entirely by its nurses—"

"Dorothea?"

"Selma, be patient, I'm sure I'll cover the point, whatever it is, if you'll just—"

"Pardon, but I have the impression you've already passed over the point."

"Well?"

"When you say *go out,* I take it you mean *strike.*"

Dorothea simply nodded her head.

"I don't see that ARI is in a position to walk out or strike."

"Well, yes, I'm afraid they have a legal position."

"There hasn't been a period of negotiation. They can't just—"

Dorothea looked steadily at Selma. "Yes, they can. They claim they've been calling on the director for months now, presenting issues, grievances, violations, and *asking for negotiations.* Management can't deny that. Neither can management deny that it has been remiss in entering into negotiations with ARI. Now it's late. ARI has a contract date coming up in a few weeks. Their claim is that since negotiations weren't commenced, they have every right to go out.'' Dorothea looked around the room. ''There is no contractual or statutory reason to prevent them from going out.''

Selma said, ''Pardon again. Life-safety protectors are prevented by state statute from—''

''The house officers may be life-safety protectors, but they are not state employees.''

''They're *city* employees, anyway, and—''

''No, they are not.'' There was complete silence. ''They are not state employees and they are not city employees. They are students.''

There was a certain amount of laughter, but not much. Dorothea went on. ''This is a teaching hospital. The interns and residents are here to advance their education. Management's attorney has provided a probable legal scenario. Before the HOs go out, the Department of Health and Hospitals will go to a judge. There will be an informal hearing. H and H will argue that the house officers are life-safety protectors in the employ of the city. ARI will argue that they are students who are brutally overworked and undercompensated for the work they do in conjunction with their education. They will argue that the hours they are required to work are without limit and are at the capricious whim of Management and that *that* is an unfair condition of receiving their education.''

Selma was impatient. ''Yes. But you'll get a restraining order. To protect the public welfare.''

''Very good, Selma. Yes, it would seem likely that Management will be successful in obtaining an injunction or restraining order. On the other hand, a court order may prove to have no legal substance. There's a New York City precedent. A court there ruled that interns and residents, being students, that there is no statute to prevent them from striking, from simply walking away from their education. But that's for a court here to sort out later.

''In the meantime, if ARI fails to comply with the dictates of a restraining order and goes out, as seems likely, there's not much anyone can do. The judge will issue a warning and then find ARI in contempt. So Scotty McGettigan will be arrested and fined and maybe jailed. The next day, the same for some ARI officers. Then individual members.''

Audrey said, "Either way, there's no docs on the floors."

"That's right. There will be no house officers on the floors."

Molly recognized that Dorothea was deliberately leaving the truth incomplete. Get the troops to fear the worst. Then give them a small shot of palliative.

Tim said, "We going to demob the hospital, Dorothea?"

"Absolutely not." Dorothea had a careful look at her silent audience. "There will be no demobing, patients will not be transferred to other facilities. This hospital will stand on its own. Just as it is prepared to do in other emergencies."

Molly thought, Now give them the whole truth, Dorothea.

Dorothea said, "You won't be entirely alone. The staff men will take over."

Elin said, "Dorothea, there's one staff man for every *eight* or *ten* house officers. They haven't worked like house officers in . . . *decades*. They've got their private practices. What they do here is teach. And supervise. They're just not used to—"

"Of course not. But let's look at the house officers. They're here for a certain part of their education. *They come and go*. The bulk of the work done for patients here is nursing care. When the students move out and their teaching seniors move in, it's going to be wonderful."

Molly didn't quite believe it. Selma and Audrey didn't believe it at all. Tim wondered what difference it would make—on the ICU he didn't see that it would make any difference at all.

"Nothing much is going to change," Dorothea said. "This hospital *is* its nursing staff."

Audrey had a private laugh. Of course nothing much was going to change. *More* work for the nurses.

59

DOROTHEA LOOKED at her watch. "I have to leave now. Day will take over for me. I think you ought to know where I'm going. The director and I are meeting with the mayor and H and H at City Hall."

Dorothea left and Day took her place. "Dorothea has asked me to go over contingency plans in case the HOs go out. Frankly, I'm sorry to disagree with Dorothea, but I don't think it's going to be wonderful at all."

There was laughter and then applause.

"As Dorothea said, the hospital will stand on its own. There will be no request for support from other systems."

Elin said, "Day, you talk as if this strike is a certainty."

"We have to plan as if it's a certainty." Service by service and floor by floor, she reviewed what the absence of the house officers would mean. Then she went on. "Midnight, Sunday next, attendings and Management take over. One attending per floor. He or she will make rounds twice daily and be available for telephone consultation—"

Audrey said, "Day, it's not going to be like being able to beep up an HO right off. What if we need to increase medication or take someone off something and we can't get hold—"

"You'll have to use discretion and take some responsibility that may not be yours to take. That's my thinking. It's not official."

Selma said, "That's asking for deep legal trouble."

"What we don't want is people calling an attending every few minutes for authorization of medication changes. There will be group calls to the attending every two or three hours. A lot of that is simply going to have to be confirmation of what you've already done. A lot of orders are going to have to be written PRN during this period. That will cover the legal aspects of the nurse's using her own discretion. Of course, there will be instances that are not clearly defined.

There will be some instances that aren't covered at all. You haven't got a house officer to call every time, and as far as I'm concerned, that's fine. We're capable of making many of these decisions, and the only reason we don't is because the physician staff generally doesn't want us to. You can understand that when you remember that the physician staff is responsible for those decisions no matter who makes them.

"But what I don't want is this. I won't tolerate it and you as head nurses are not to tolerate it. For instance, a nurse suspects that an IV may have infiltrated tissue. She thinks it could have penetrated through the vein and it's feeding medication into tissue. Every time something like that comes up she calls the attending. No. The nurse makes the decision about that. Okay?" She looked around. "Okay. You and your staff can operate at your full abilities."

Molly stood up. "I'm uncomfortable with that. There are lots of things we're able to do, but we're prohibited from doing them without an order. There are lots of things we're competent to do that we're not licensed to do."

"The chiefs of the services understand the situation. The attendings will be flexible. It's understood."

"But it's not in writing," Molly said.

"It's understood."

"Will it be understood if the nurse makes the proper decision but something goes wrong? Will it be understood by the family? Will the attending cover for the nurse? Like hell he will. Whatever goes wrong, the nurse is going to be the sacrificial offering."

"It's a delicate situation, I admit," Day said. "Each of us is going to have to make personal decisions about how much responsibility to assume—and when."

Mozart Wills entered and stood at the back of the room.

Elin said, "We are definitely not going to ship patients out? That seems hard-nosed and unrealistic."

"We are going to stabilize the patient community. Please, what I'm asking you to do is simple. The HOs' absence is not to affect the hospital's care for its bed patients."

"What about other services?" Tim said.

"Support services will be there."

"I still think we ought to move patients," Elin said.

"Emergency or critical patients who would have been moved anyway—they'll be moved. Otherwise, no patient will be moved. We've got full paramedic and EMT support. On the accident floor—the ER will simply send new admissions to another hospital. The really acute will come in for stabilization and then support.''

"Stabilization by *whom?*" Elin said. "One attending on the ER when maybe there're two or three traumas?"

Day nodded toward the back of the room. "Mozart wants to talk to us about that."

The nurses turned to look at him. Slowly, tired, and preoccupied, Mozart Wills came to stand in front of them. "At ARI we thought someone ought to tell you about what's going on as we see it."

There were some hisses and boos.

"Yeah, yeah," Mozart said. "But it's as if Management *wants* us to go out. We'd like an NSA observer to verify—"

Day said, "This is not an NSA meeting and you're talking union stuff, Mozart. This is supposed to be medical informational."

"Yeah. So the information is, staff, it looks like Management is going to shove our butts out the door."

"*Mozart—*"

Tim interrupted. "What about the ICUs?"

"If we have to go out, we'll cover the ICUs as usual. We'll be available to the floors when we're really needed."

Selma said, "Mozart, that doesn't sound like much of a strike."

Mozart was rueful. "It's the best we can do. And still meet our professional responsibilities."

"Why go out at all?"

"It's got to be done sometime."

"Well, good luck, you guys."

"Yeah." He started to leave, then stopped. "I plainly don't know what the fuck is going on. Or why. Everything was simple when ARI wanted to go out. Now we don't seem to want to go out and Management seems hell-bent to see us out. To break us? To break ARI as a bargaining unit? Anyway, strikes turn all kinds of people against each other. Now this hospital is special. Medicine and Nursing are colleagues here. I'd hate to see that split."

There was quiet as he left. Day waited until the door was shut behind him. Her voice was level when she spoke. "You may want to support the HOs, but I hope not at the expense

of Nursing. If you feel supportive, that support should stop
before you get into the argument. You must look at this as
nurses. You are not dependent on anyone else. Look to your
own professionalism first. That's what counts here.

"Back Bay Met is not going to discharge patients. The
nursing staff will stand by its own professional base. Care for
the patient."

Day went into a detailed analysis of the nursing staff's
taking on increased responsibility.

60

AUDREY LEFT THE MEETING without waiting for Tim or even
thinking about him. She wanted to go home and shower
herself clean of a despair that had been clinging to her since
Mr. Emerson's death. And then she wanted to go to bed. She
had been working twenty-four out of the last thirty-two hours.

When he could not find Audrey after the meeting, Tim was
wrenched by a feeling of rejection. He went down to the
street and started walking toward the elevated and then he
saw a white dress and a white cap ahead of him and though
she was facing away from him he *knew* it was Audrey, and
his heart sprang with pleasure as he called to her and she
turned.

Tim looked like something wonderful had happened to
him. It did not occur to Audrey that she was in any way
responsible for his pleasure. "Hi," she said quietly.

She's not glad to see me, Tim thought. But his pleasure
was such that the thought disappeared. "You look like you
need cheering up."

Audrey felt herself smiling. She also felt the despair lessen.
Her sensible mind told her to go home, to withdraw and
protect herself. But something brave and impulsive in her had
her say, "Yes. Okay." Tim had already changed and Audrey
said, "I'd like to put on something else."

"You don't have to."

"I want to." Then the brave, impulsive self put her arm

through his. She was shocked by her own gesture. But she felt relieved and secure on the street, where she was almost always a little afraid.

In Audrey's apartment, Tim was surprised by himself. Surrounded by the effects and privacy of this woman, he had the sensation that he had been suffering from faulty vision and it had suddenly been rectified, that a dimness in the perceived world had suddenly been dispelled. He thought that patients returned to full consciousness and absence of pain after intensive care must have much the same sudden sensation of life.

Alone with Tim in her apartment, Audrey was abruptly uncertain—of herself, of him, of any reason for their being together. She was without bravery or impulsiveness and had forgotten both. She looked around her living room quickly, not to check for order but to find some clue to herself and what she was doing. She found none. "Would you like a glass of wine, a beer?"

"A beer would be great."

She brought him an open bottle and a fluted glass. He held the glass up to the window light and felt unaccountably moved by its clarity and fragility. "This is lovely."

"I collect glass."

He noticed the shelves then. Groups of books were interspersed with pieces of glass—flowers, animals, fish, paperweights, vases. But his eye was finally held by a large and simply-framed crayon drawing: a summer meadow in bright colors and the forest beyond.

"I did that a long time ago," she said.

"How long?"

"A long time . . ." She frowned. "No, not really. Just last year." She shrugged. "I'll just be a few minutes."

She went into her bedroom and closed the door and undressed and went into the bathroom to shower. She smiled when she saw the poem hanging next to the mirror.

Well, I got through New Year's Eve without you,
again,
whoever you are, you sonofabitch,
who wasn't with me again this year

Good idea to take that down, she thought, in case the gentleman has to use the facilities. She took it off the wall and put it in the hamper, then she put on a shower cap and turned on the shower and got in. She thought of Tim out in the living room. Why did I invite him here? Why didn't I just meet him someplace?

Because he's a nice man and because I wanted him to see the rest of me, she thought, thinking of her physical surroundings, and then she caught herself looking down at her body and she smiled.

Tim sipped his beer and looked at the titles of Audrey's books. Medical texts, art collections, and poetry in hardback, novels and nonfiction in paperback. He felt content. Something good has happened to you, he thought. There was the slightest addition of sound from the other room and Tim realized that Audrey was showering. She trusts me, he thought. Well, why shouldn't she? You're a colleague. If you can't trust someone you work with, who *can* you trust? Well, yes, but you're a man and she hardly knows you and she's inside taking a shower. There was something very trusting and tender about that, Tim thought.

Nan Lassitter had a conscious sensation that she was being studied. But since paranoia was not a refuge of hers, she ascribed the feeling to her own self-consciousness since Mr. Emerson's death, a sort of embarrassment, as if she had done something socially unacceptable. Letting Mr. Emerson die. There was pain and guilt underneath the mild discomfort that was on the surface and she had been studying that herself. And so, she decided, taking the MBTA downtown, the sensation was just the sensation of herself studying herself.

She looked over at a recruiting ad for A Supplemental Staffing Service for the Professional Nurse, an agency looking for nurses.

You're Caring For Others.
Who's Caring For YOU?

The car was crowded and people were jostled against each other as the train changed speeds or banked or braked. After work on the unit—her last time there—Nan had gone to Med

Seven, her new assignment, to orient herself, but also out of
eagerness. Selma had spent some minutes with her before
going off to the head nurses' meeting and then Nan had just
read charts and talked with the two afternoon nurses as time
allowed and with patients who came to the station as they
might take a constitutional in the park. Most of the patients
on the floor were elderly. It was what Nan had wanted. Real
nursing.

The train took a curve, and Nan and the other standing
passengers swayed beneath their handholds.

When it comes to taking care of people's needs no one
has a better sense of what's important than a Nurse. And
we know what's important to Nurses.
We are a temporary and permanent nursing placement
service. We offer TOP RATES, vacation and holiday pay,
overtime and more.

There was a rate schedule and Nan studied it. She was
making a little more than $18,000 a year with every other
weekend off and two weeks of vacation. She calculated that if
she joined this outfit—became an *agency* nurse—she could
make an additional $115 a week.

The car swayed and she felt a body against hers, a hand on
her shoulder. A voice close to her ear said, *"We know what's
important to nurses."*

She jerked away and turned her head. It was Trevor Davis,
a house officer with whom she had worked back when he was
a new surgical resident and she was already an experienced
ER trauma nurse.

"Scared you, huh?" he said.

She nodded and then smiled a little. She felt better being
with someone she knew, someone she had worked with.
"Tensions of the day," she said.

The train stopped and the doors opened on a sunny late
afternoon. Warm and fragrant air drifted in. Trevor put his
hand on her shoulder again. "Doesn't it make you feel like
beaches and getting your clothes off?"

"Not yet."

"Those are the tensions. Bad stuff, medically. Let Dr.
Davis get rid of them for you. I've got the evening off"

"I promised to see a movie with a friend."

"Just a friend?"

"Just a friend."

"What a terrible waste," Trevor said.

Nan smiled. It was nice to be flirted with and compli-
mented by a colleague, a senior colleague at that. The fact
that there would be no waste of her at all tonight, that she
would be fully occupied with a man she was beginning to
care for, was none of Dr. Davis' affair, no affair of his at all,
she thought, continuing to smile.

She had come a long way down through the darkness, Nan
thought, getting off the MBTA and stepping into the warmth
of the sunshine. She would not be going back to the unit. It
hardly seemed real to her—that she would not have to go
back and that she was standing in the spring sunshine with her
life to do with what she wanted. She skipped a few steps. She
felt as if she had met up with herself after a long absence, and
in her sudden awareness she said to herself, Where have you
been? She smiled and skipped again as she walked up Newbury
Street. She had a lot of catching up to do.

Nan surprised her date, Oren Tolman, not where they were
to meet but outside an open flower shop, with freshly cut
flowers on display in pots all around him. He was paying for
a bunch of vibrant yellow flowers wrapped in green tissue,
and as he turned toward the street he saw Nan and he grinned
and Nan grinned back at him, and he tossed the bouquet in
the air and Nan watched it twirl slowly in the soft air and
caught it as it fell to her. Then Oren was at her side and put
his hand around her waist, their first physical intimacy, as if
he had always done so, and they walked up Newbury Street
and Nan raised the bouquet to smell it. It was some time
before Nan realized that neither of them had said a word yet
and that she was still grinning.

Audrey had put on a sweater and slacks and carried a jacket.
They walked to the restaurant, the newness and harmony of
the two of them together like that of the spring air.

The restaurant was not crowded. Audrey had a glass of
white wine and Tim a beer. Audrey said, "Tell me about Mr.
Emerson. I've felt rotten all day."

Tim told her about Mr. Emerson and himself and Nan and
the family and Trina. He did not say much about Aaron

Silver's struggle. Then he told her stories about the ICU that made her laugh.

His eyes looked out at her with mischief. And *care*, so much *care* for what he was talking about, Audrey thought. She was so taken by those eyes. He makes me feel so good. It's safe to laugh with him. Can I trust this? Can I trust him? He *feels* so good to be with and—

And wait. Hold up. Aren't we being just a little precipitous, perhaps a wee bit premature, in the sense of *adolescent?*

But she had not felt so good in a long time. Not even with the doc. Not ever with the doc. She told Tim about her floor, her inability to laugh at the absurdities and frustrations he laughed at. Tim listened and Audrey thought, He takes me seriously, he listens to me—and without my asking. The doc never did, not even when I asked him. Not even when I goddamn yelled at him.

This woman is very special, Tim thought, and he was uncomfortable with himself. He ought not to be filled with such warmth so quickly. Was it Audrey or was it his need? He had not realized he was so needful for someone else.

Audrey looked to Tim's eyes again. There was something both childlike and very male there. The wonder and bewilderment of a man searching a woman and her body with his eyes. It made her feel wonderful. She said, "The word on you is that you're divorced and your ex gives you a rotten time with your son." There was an entire change in his face. "I'm sorry. I didn't mean to—"

"That's okay. I want you to know about all that."

"How old is your boy? What's his name?"

The Chinese waiter came over. "Order now?"

"Wait a few minutes?" Tim said to Audrey.

"Sure."

They ordered another glass of wine and a beer. Tim told Audrey about Jason and then about Valerie.

Audrey thought, He's so assured at work. But now he's so tentative and sad. And he was so funny and laughing just a moment ago. Alone together we are so different than we are at work. *We,* she thought, and felt some wonder at the word.

"The judge, Judge Harrelson, was a *shit*. He was sitting up there on the bench and he was deciding *Jason's* life, and *my* life, and he didn't hear a word of the testimony. Not our testimony. It was one of the fastest decisions in judicial history. Oh yes, he paused long enough to question my choice of profession—my lifestyle, as he called it. Inability to provide a proper male role model for Jason, he said. Then he came out for motherhood right down the line. He hadn't listened to one word of the testimony about who had taken care of Jason, nothing about one parent being neglectful and the other parent being nurturing. Then he gave custody to Valerie and gave me the minimum time with Jason he could. I hate that man."

Tim's silence was like a third presence at the table. It was cold and it separated her from him. That was when she began telling him about the doc. She felt uncomfortable telling him, but she felt a compulsion to get it out of the way, out of her own way. As she spoke she realized, I didn't love him. All that pain and I didn't even love him. I was just so *hurt* by him, his duplicity. She said to Tim, "I don't think I had fun with him. That's odd, isn't it?"

The waiter said, "You order now?"

When they left the restaurant it was a little after eight. The night air had remained warm. Their time together at dinner had become again one of ease and attraction. They walked and Audrey wanted Tim to take her hand. She smiled, remembering dates like this in high school, walking down a street at night in warm, spring air and *yearning*, but not then for anything she could identify to herself. Their evening was just about over. They had to be up at five-thirty, she thought, warmed and amused by her thought of their arising from the same bed. At her building she saw that Tim did not know whether to say good night or go up with her. She said, "I have some Cherry Heering if you'd like."

But then, sitting in her living room, each with a glass of liqueur, it was as if they had not had any of the intimacy of their being together earlier. When he finished the little glass, Tim stood. Her bedroom door was open and dark behind him and Audrey imagined him in there, in the darkness. *Just touch me, be tender with me,* she thought. But she felt fragile, like a glass too thin to remain unbroken.

Then, in another act of courage, she stood up and stepped in front of him and looked at his eyes and waited.

He took her in his arms and held her to him, and their bodies met with an intimacy almost unaffected by their clothes.

They kissed and after a moment, or much more than a moment, Audrey put her head against Tim's shoulder and said, "Would you like to sleep here tonight?"

"Yes. I would."

In her bed, after they had touched and whispered, she made her body available to him and they spent a time of gentle stillness, their eyes closed until he began to kiss her and move in her.

Audrey waited for the response within herself to his rhythm and physical presence, but she remembered the doc in this bedroom using her and her response would not catch up with Tim's rhythm and here in this intimacy with Tim that she had yearned for what she needed to do was empty her mind of the doc, and, as if understanding and giving her a chance to catch up with him, Tim slowed and she felt him become less hard in her.

And Tim felt himself losing it, the body passion, the erection.

Valerie had completed her job on him, he thought. Now she had his balls. Other times had been all right—the lust, the driven craving—but other times had not been important. He went limp within Audrey. He felt helpless and afraid. Not a man.

Audrey thought, Oh, Christ, I've done it, the one man I've wanted in all this time, this special, special man, and I've turned him off, my body language, my body talked to his and told him I wasn't with it, and he, *he* is so unlike the doc he couldn't just *use* me. And she felt him withdraw but then he was kissing her and her body began to give her mind-shattering sensations.

Tim was thinking, I'm with Audrey. She is not Valerie. As if to test this he kissed her lips, licked them, put his mouth to her nipples, his hand to her breast, down her body, between her legs, hand, mouth, everywhere found Audrey, lost himself in her gasps, the physical responses, moved his mouth back to her breasts, her lips, his fingers caressing between her legs and then his finger at her clitoris, his penis against her thigh, and Audrey helping him, telling him the pressure and the rhythm, and he found himself erect again and beating with desire and he entered her again and, his body lost to its own pleasure, he felt her moan aloud and he leaped within her and heard himself cry out and felt himself fill her with a flood tide of warmth, of passion, of tenderness, and Audrey heard and felt his cry, startling as if it came from pain, and she held him against her and she felt his rhythm slow and then they lay still for a little while without parting from each other.

When Tim did move and lay beside her, he died into sleep, surrendering himself into unconsciousness as he had not been able to do in months and months of nights, willingly letting control of his mind and its images go. And the last thing Audrey thought after they parted was that they had exhausted each other, they had been so complete in what they were doing, and that she felt weepy in her gratification, and that they were asleep in each other's arms, as they were, and as had never happened to her before.

61

IN THE MORNING, darkness still in the windows of Audrey's bedroom, Tim awoke amazed and pleased. Gently he woke Audrey, fondling her, fairly overwrought with his passion and need for her. She turned her body and put her arms around him without any transition from sleep to wakefulness. She looked at him with care for some seconds and then pressed with her hands to bring him to kiss her.

When again they were calm, they lay still for a little while and then Audrey sat up.

"My God," she said, "look at the time."

Oh shit, Tim thought. He had never been late to work before. "Look."

Tim didn't know where the clock was. Audrey pointed. She was laughing. "Four-thirty. We can sleep for another hour."

On the way into work, Audrey felt so fair and light she might have been returning from a long vacation. She was almost unaffected by the Sunday *Post* headline she saw in the hands of other riders: BBMH STRIKE LOOMS.

"I don't think it will happen," she said to Tim. "It's just about inconceivable."

Tim smiled and took out a tramp wallet and found a newspaper clipping. "If you didn't read the sports page yesterday—"

"I didn't."

"Then you missed this."

For just plain fun and antics, set next Saturday noon aside and plan to be at the Boston Garden for the exhibition basketball game between the always-entertaining Harlem Wiseapples and a team comprised of members of the Back Bay Metropolitan Hospital medical staff.

The Wiseapples are led by Maurice Allen, the former All-American playmaker from UCLA who is rated the best ballhandler of all time. Contacted by telephone, Allen said, "We'll do our thing on the court. But don't expect us to operate in the hospital."

The Back Bay Mets will be piloted by player-coach Tim Holbrook, a varsity teammate at UMass of the fabulous Dr. J. and now head nurse on BBMH's medical intensive care unit. Holbrook assessed the Mets as "highly skilled, articulate and not at a loss for team doctors." Among the Mets' standouts, "Dr. Scotty McGettigan played at Chattanooga and Dr. Mozart Wills played at Yale."

The hospital's director, Bennett Chessoff, earlier announced that proceeds will benefit a children's intensive care unit.

Tim said, "I hope you'll set aside next Saturday for fun and antics."

"I'd love to."

"Valerie agreed to trade weekends with me so I can have Jason at the game."

"Well, I guess she's not entirely a bitch."

Tim said nothing for a few seconds. Then, "You and Jase'll be sitting together. I'd like him to meet you before then. He's coming to dinner with me Wednesday."

The night nurse finished report. "Mr. Stevens had nightmares. Shouting out loud."

"Content?" Audrey said.

"Jeff and Glen. Callin' out for his boys. Wouldn't accept anything to help him sleep. Asked could he see you some this mornin'."

But it was not until midmorning that Audrey was able to get to Mr. Stevens. He was sitting in a chair looking out the window. His roommate left the room. Audrey said, "I heard you had a bad night, Mr. Stevens."

"It keeps goin' 'round and 'round in my head. It's like it won't stop goin' 'round and 'round. But it won't stop for me to think about it."

He was sweating. "Would you like a bed bath, Mr. Stevens?" Making him feel more comfortable, Audrey decided, was her immediate and primary nursing objective.

"Naw."

"We have a wonderful woman named Molly Chang. She's a psychiatric nurse and she'll help you stop that spinning in your head."

"She's like a specialist right? For people who are dying."

Audrey started to speak and then only nodded.

"I've got two boys. Jeff and Glen. Eleven and fourteen."

"I remember. Tell me about them."

"No."

Audrey nodded again. "The other nurses and I have orders that allow us to give you tranquilizing agents and sedatives pretty much when you want. When it's pressing on you hard and you want to get out from under."

"That stuff scares me. On the street they call it *shit.*"

"We're not talking about that kind of drug. Nothing addictive—"

"I haven't got time for addiction, right?"

Audrey thought and said, "I think you might like a room to yourself. So you can talk to your family alone. And your friends. If you want, I'll see if I can arrange that." His reaction was such that Audrey immediately understood that something she had just said made him distrust her.

"You want to separate me from the other patients."

"No."

"So they can't catch what I've got."

"No. We don't know anything about *catching* oatcell carcinoma. A room of your own is for your privacy and comfort. And your family's. You can come and go as you want."

He looked out the window. "Yeah. Sure. Why not."

"Did you talk to your family yet, Mr. Stevens?"

"About me?"

"Yes."

"Naw. Everythin' come on so sudden."

"Would you like me to have one of the doctors talk to them?"

He shook his head. "I got to do it myself . . . But I can't."

I know, Audrey thought, because if you say it yourself, then it really is final. "Would you like me to be with you when you talk to them?"

"I don't know if I can do it."

"When you feel ready. Now, can I just take your blood pressure?" She looked at his bare arm where her fingers touched him. "Is this a rash?"

"Naw. I've had it for a long time."

"How long?"

"Years. Long as I can remember."

"Well, I'll have a doctor check it."

Mr. Stevens laughed loudly and then he continued to laugh. Finally he managed to say "Whatever they find, *what are they going to do?* Cure it?" He stopped laughing. "Yes, that'd be fine, Nurse. That'd be real fine of you. You keep me company when I tell them about me."

"I'll stay on till visiting hours. Listen, Mr. Stevens, you tell your family, I don't keep visiting hours rules on this floor. You tell them to come in whenever they want."

"I guess they got to come in after school is out, anyway. But don't you stay late today. I'm not going to tell them today. I jus' wanna see 'em like always, like there was no trouble. I jus' wanna enjoy them."

Audrey was stopped in the corridor by an aide before she could return to the station. "Mr. Volante's cryin' real bad. Some lady in there with him."

"Who?" Audrey said, turning back.

"Dunno."

Dom Volante was huddled upright on his bed, his arms and hands raised as if to protect his head and face. He was crying in gasps. The woman with him was seated in a chair by the bed. She was saying, "Now, Dom, you owe it to the public.

Where you've been, why you're in this joke of a hospital, how you became a failure."

Audrey said, "Whoever you are, get out of this room."

The woman looked at Audrey and smiled. "Dom's public property."

Dom Volante lifted his head. *"Leave me alone!"*

Audrey said to the aide, "Call Security, unwanted visitor."

The woman smiled at Audrey and said, "Call Security and I guarantee Bennett Chessoff will wrap your ass in barbed wire, cutie."

"Bennett Chessoff does not run this floor. I do."

"I'm the press, cutie. We keep this hospital alive. Or hasn't that ever been explained to you?"

Dom Volante's head was down and he continued to cry. Audrey said to the aide, "Go ahead. Call Security."

"It's your ass," the woman said to Audrey. "Let's get to the core of the story, Dom. So tell me, what's it like when no one wants you anymore?"

Audrey pulled the woman from the chair and forced her into the corridor. Jan Fox was standing just outside. In the corridor the woman stopped struggling. She touched her hair. Calmly she said, "That man is a public figure. You can't deny me access."

"That's bullshit, lady, and you know it."

"I'll have a word with Bennett about it. I'll be back in a while, cutie."

Audrey went in again to Dom Volante. He was still huddled self-protectively. "I don't know who that was, Mr. Volante, but—"

Audrey heard Jan Fox say, "You live in Boston and you don't know Lynn Keating?" Dom Volante looked up. "Hello, Dominic," Jan said. "I was taking a stroll and I heard your unmistakable voice. How *does* it feel to be a zero? We could compare notes."

His tears had stopped. His lips parted, but he said nothing.

"You got a trouble type on the floor?" Audrey turned. There were two men from Security.

"It's okay now. She left."

"Want we stick around? Case she comes back?"

"Thanks. Not necessary. Thanks for your response."

"Any time." The two men left.

Jan said, "Of course, Dominic, you had a lot farther to fall than I did." She laughed at him.

Audrey saw Volante become attentive, a change in his manner. "Well, yes." He spoke slowly. "I guess I understand you now. You like making people zero, don't you? That's what gets you off."

"Sure, Dominic, get at me. Now you can feel good about yourself."

Audrey saw a keenness in Mr. Volante's eyes, the man's missing personality coming back.

"You were a zero already professionally. But I didn't know it. I don't think I would've cared. What are you, Jan—four, five years older than me? But we read *The WASP Princess* in high school. You were a legend." He said to Audrey, "I met this wonderful woman at a party. A heroine of mine." He looked back at Jan. "What a great job of seduction. *I'm wonderful, you're wonderful, take me out to dinner, sex is overwhelming me, let's get something to eat before we make it. And please feel me up here in the restaurant.* So that you could slap me. Humiliate me. Set me up for your fun."

Jan looked at Audrey and smiled at her. "Dominic has a penchant for self-pity." She looked back at him. "But here we are, Dominic, finally together in our nightclothes. We both ended up at zero, didn't we? *Oh, oh, oh!*" The sounds wrenched from her and she went to Dom and clenched him to her.

Dom looked at Audrey and then she saw him raise his arms slowly and place them around Jan gently.

Audrey went back to the station, her anger taking charge of her. She called Bennett Chessoff's number and identified herself. She was told he was in conference. "I don't care if he's in conference with the Queen of England. You get him on." There was a click and silence.

Then, "Yes?" Bennett Chessoff's voice.

"Did you invite the press to visit Dom Volante?"

"Of course not."

"Of course not? Lynn Keating?"

"No. Though I understand she's waiting to see me."

"Did you tell the press he's a patient of ours?"

"I did not. I don't like your attitude, Miss Rosenfeld. There are channels for this sort of—"

"I don't know if I believe a word you've said, Director." She hung up.

"Not smart," Coralee said. "Not smart, honey. Believe me."

"I am *furious*. How did Keating learn about him? You tell me that. Who wanted him on the Gold Coast right away? That sonofabitch *plays games* with people. Like we're pieces on a board."

"Yeah. But it strikes me, Audrey, you're gettin' awful fast with your anger."

Audrey found herself suddenly calm and smiling. A single flower wrapped in green tissue lay on the counter. Dermical tape had been stuck round it and her name written on it. The flower was a yellow rose.

"You have an admirer," Coralee said.

Audrey blushed. She picked up the flower and smiled at it.

62

ELIN DID NOT HAVE to work at all on Sunday. She slept late, washed her hair, and read the paper. Bennett Chessoff was quoted as saying that the house officers' strike "appears to be ineluctible in the present situation of house officer requisites." Though she did not have to work, she had work to do. She put Brahms's Quartets on her stereo and read journal articles that had to do with her work. A little after four she began to dress for her five o'clock date with Hal Levy. Getting into her underpants she thought, Now be sensible and careful about anyone else getting into your pants. The idea had not been quashed nor had it been sufficiently suppressed.

She picked him up at five o'clock and drove him to a country inn where Charles Maki's fifty dollars would be well spent. As soon as they were seated Elin ordered a Scotch-on-the-rocks. It was a warm gray day outside, the kind of day she disliked. Also, she felt quite disagreeable with herself for having gone ahead with this silly tryst. Hal looked so young that Elin was self-conscious about being with him.

It was disturbingly quiet. He drank a Scotch-and-soda as if it were something he had to do rather than wanted to do. They ate crackers with a cheese spread and, in their mutual silence and discomfort, spent a lot of attention getting the spread on the crackers.

"Look," Elin said, "why ever did you go through with this?"

"It sounded reasonable." He looked around. "At the time it sounded reasonable." He looked at Elin with his staring, unblinking eyes—open to his very heart, she thought. "We can go," he said. "Or I can go. You can stay and have dinner. I can get back on my own."

"I'm sure you can. Now that I've got the bitchiness out of the way, I'd like to have dinner with you." Such a serious young man.

"Why did you change your mind and call me?"

Because I'm *attracted* to you, Elin thought. Because it's a way of getting back at Charles. "I don't know. Sorry. There are confusing issues involved here."

"Oh," Hal said, trying, as Trina would say, to *hear* what Elin was saying. She was a good-looking woman—once you got by the small lines in her face. Hal liked her deep eyes and the easiness she had with herself. He thought about being with her in bed.

They had a second drink, and the strain Elin had been feeling dissipated. Conversation became easy.

"They are arrogant and elitist," Bennett said to Molly, talking about the house officers. They were having drinks before dinner. He had chosen the restaurant for its approximate equidistance from where each of them lived.

"They deserve what they're after," Molly said.

"Don't we all?" he appeared to study the shape of her body. Or perhaps the pattern of my dress, Molly thought, and doubted it. "There is a dollar pattern and it would have to be broken. That's what all this pattern bargaining is about." He is studying either the dress or what's in it, Molly thought. His interest is not presently in my facial response. "They have their pattern bargaining with me and I have my pattern bargaining with City Hall." Molly had an intuition that, with typical Bennett Chessoff indirection, he was negotiating bed with her. "It's a ridiculous position," he said. "There's a better way. Give them what they want, but preserve the pattern."

"How do you do that?"

He looked at her face and smiled. "There are ways around the patterns. Monkey around with things outside the pattern." His eyes skimmed over her dress.

Monkey with me outside my pattern? Molly thought. She found the idea entertaining. My place or yours? "They're not just thinking about their own pockets—"

"Sure they are. Everyone does. All the time."

Got me on that one, Molly thought. She could see why negotiating with Bennett could be so frustrating. He sat on both sides of the table and mediated, too. "They want the place fully staffed—"

"Don't we all?"

"—adequately supplied—"

"One wishes to do all one can."

"—and properly equipped."

"Some areas are poorly equipped," Bennett said. He looked down at her breastline again. "Some areas are superbly equipped."

"Bennett, frustration with the system has a real basis."

"Do you share that frustration, Molly?"

"We all share it."

"I never met a nurse who had enough."

Molly smiled. "The nature of modern nursing is insatiable. Still, what the nurse is saying is, I'll make do with what I have, but I'd like to have more. And sometimes I don't have what I really need."

Elin and Hal had dinner and a bottle of wine. They did not talk about the hospital or medicine but about things they liked to do, places they had been, people they had enjoyed. At one point Elin felt so much warmth for this open young man that she wanted to place her hand on his. When the meal was over and they had ordered espresso, there was still wine in the bottle. "You have it," Elin said. "I'm driving." Hal nodded and poured the last of the wine. Elin smiled within herself. Am I lubricating him? Do I want to seduce him? Yes. You know you do. He wore those thick glasses, but she now knew he had an active wrestler's body. It would be lithe and hard. She could think of a lot of things she would like to do with that body and have that body do with hers. No, Elin, she thought. He's too young. Not for bed, he isn't. He's too young to have something *ongoing* with. And you don't fuck around in your own hospital, remember? Not if you're smart. And *you* are *smart*, Elin. She said, "Tell me about the hospital."

"What do you mean?"

"Whatever comes to mind."

"Well, if the HOs go on strike, the third-year students will be assigned to the nurses on the floors. To help out."

"What else?"

"People. Faces. Some that go back to my room with me."

"Which ones?"

"A crazy black lady, must be ten feet tall. Big red turban, long red coat. Looks like a general. Dora. I can hear her shouting. She is just so *outraged*. With life. A white lady named Jan. She screams and sobs. She's just pitiful, she's so sad and angry. A black guy, not much younger than me. Thornton. Just wiped out. All boozed up. Just walks around wiped out. Gave up. That's the way the hospital seems. It gave up. And it's filled with anger."

The warmth had embraced Elin again. It was almost excruciating. She needed to hold Hal against her, have him hold her to himself.

Fucking is an active verb, Elin thought. If I take Hal to bed—and it seems as though I can—who am I fucking? Would I be fucking Charles or fucking *with* Hal?

Hal said, "There's someone else. Never makes a sound. Follows me around in my mind. Won't look at me. Looks just over my head. Or to the side."

Elin found Hal looking at her as if he were expecting a response. If you want to go to bed, she said to him in her mind, you're just going to have to make the move yourself. She looked back at him. But he clearly didn't know what to do. I'm not going to do it, Elin thought. I'm not going to be the one. But why? You *want* . . . Because it's safe not to.

"Olivia," Hal said.

"What?"

"Olivia is the name of the one who follows me around and

won't look at me. She's *always* there. She's the one who's really the hospital for me.''

Molly had insisted they go to her house. She had discovered something surprising about herself: she would be less afraid in her own house. She had not known that she was afraid. She had thought she was needful.

Breathing hard, her hands moving in caresses, her fingers touching lightly and swiftly in encouragement, she felt herself *let* herself slip pleasantly into passivity, the self-imposed passivity of a lady who had not been fucked in a long time and who had wanted to be fucked, let the lovemaking come, so to speak, when it might, and she hoped it would, with tenderness and regularity, but just now the physical confrontation inside her and outside occupied her pleasantly and drivingly, asynchronic signals sparking separately from her clitoris and her vagina, and she really didn't care, as long as the signals kept coming and they *got together* at some point—it would be Bennett's point, she thought—keep it up, there's a penalty for early withdrawal, hoping her expectations were not misplaced, the thrust of her expectations, this strange man doing erotic things to her body and mind rather more rapidly than she would have liked, but *good* things anyway, rapid as they were, and she thought, Where did *getting fucked* ever get a bad reputation? And she felt his tension and rhythm counter each other within her body, some pause where strength and power were isolated within her, a part of herself now, and she almost cried out and then she did, astonished at her body's abrupt provision of so much pleasure.

Without Molly's asking him to do so, Bennett remained in her while she came down, while her body and mind got themselves sorted out again, while she got back to being her day-to-day person, not some spatial explosion . . . with continuing reverberations . . .

He was sitting up beside her. Oh fuck, she thought mildly, he's getting ready to leave. I must have slept. She touched her fingers to his lower back.

He shifted his body so that he faced her. With the most tentative of smiles and with the gravest of voices, he said, ''I'd like to stay overnight with you.''

Molly laughed and sat up and put her arms around him and kissed him. "Yes. Yes, I have a bed all ready for you."

He lay down beside her. "I'll have to get up early. I need to go home and change."

Molly looked down his body. "Of course you do. But where do you work? What do you do? What time do you have to be there? What are your needs in the morning?"

"Tea and an English muffin."

"Every morning?"

"Cereal sometimes, sometimes eggs, bacon. Chinese might be good," he said solemnly.

"Yes. You wouldn't have to send out."

63

ON WEDNESDAY Audrey dressed at the hospital for dinner at Tim's. She had carried the dress, freshly ironed, to work on a hanger in a plastic sheath. She was uneasy. Too much was happening too quickly. Too much was at risk in a little person's opinion of her. The dress was a favorite summer dress, a pale green shirtwaist with flecks of darker green. She smiled, thinking it would be the first time Tim would see her in it.

But what would little Jason think of her? How do you get on with a first-grader? How would she? She thought about that as she brushed her hair—as if she had no experience in relating to people. She put a touch of perfume behind each ear. She felt as if it were some first date of her teen years, but the foolishness of it was that it was young Jason she needed to impress.

Tim picked her up downstairs. With the windows of his elderly Mustang open to the spring sunshine and warm air, they drove to his apartment house, Jason in the bucket seat next to his father, Audrey in back. She sat in the middle so that she could have a little glimpse of each of them and hear what they said. Jason had been very formal in meeting her, very appraising as he studied her with serious eyes. In the car he turned all his attention to his father and became intent upon recounting every moment of his life since he had last seen Tim and hearing from Tim every moment of *his* life. "And then I met Audrey," Tim said. "I count that sort of like making a three-point basket."

Jason peered around from his front seat. He was smiling at what his father had said. He looked at Audrey and the smile remained.

It was also Audrey's first visit to Tim's apartment, the one room with kitchen and bath. It gave her a sense of the man beyond her own experience and it was reassuring. There were plants in every window. Jason's drawings were everywhere. Records and books filled the shelves. Some basketball photographs and trophies occupied a corner.

The father and son were taken up with each other, but Audrey saw that Tim intruded on that relationship in order to draw her into it. She wished he wouldn't. It was too early. She didn't want Jason to resent her.

After a while Tim got up from his place on the floor with Jason where, on some newspaper, they had been making a Snap-Together model of a van and gluing it, as Jason had insisted, "So it will stay together forever."

"Time goes very quickly on these occasions," Tim said. "I made dinner yesterday, but I've got to go heat it and do some other things."

"Can I help?" Audrey said, but he didn't answer. She knew he had heard her question. She stood uncertainly *in a no-woman's land*, she thought, between the boy in the living room carefully putting away the unfinished model and the man making a salad in the kitchen.

Jason stood by some shelves—his special part of the room— and looked at Audrey. "Will you play a game with me?"

Outside Valerie's door, Tim got down and hugged Jason. The boy threw his arms around his father's neck and hugged him tightly and kissed him on the cheek.

The door to the apartment opened. Valerie stood there. "Come in, Jason." She did not acknowledge Tim's presence. Jason moved away from his father slowly, then turned his back and went into the apartment. Valerie closed the door.

* * *

Valerie was not interested in Jason's afternoon. She had to get him out of the way and into bed before her date arrived in an hour. She hoped he would crash early. She hurried him through his preparation for bed, but she slowed down when she learned that someone named Audrey had been with Tim and Jason.

"Who is Audrey?"

"Friend of Dad's. From the hospital. A nurse."

"Another nurse."

"Yeah. Now let me tell you about Saturday and Maur—"

"Pretty?"

"Yeah. Now let me tell you about Maurice Allen. Dad told me all about him. He is *excellent*. Gee, thanks for letting me go see Dad play against him. *Saturday*. That is going to be excellent. I'm going to meet him, Dad said. The greatest basketball player I ever met."

"You haven't met any others."

"Well, there's Dad."

"He was never a great basketball player."

"Well, anyway, Maurice Allen is one of the great basketball players of all time. *Dad said."* He looked at Valerie defiantly.

"What about this other nurse?"

"Audrey?"

"Yes."

"She's nice. She says funny things. She's going to sit with me when Dad plays against the Wiseapples. Thanks for letting me go. Really thanks."

"That isn't decided yet, Jason."

"But Dad *said*—"

"He didn't tell me all the circumstances. What does Dad think about this nurse, Audrey?"

"Dad says she's like making a three-point shot."

"I'll bet she is. More like an easy lay-up, probably."

"But the game with the Wiseapples, Mom. *Please?*"

"There are some circumstances I didn't know about. Some circumstances I don't want you exposed to."

Jason put his head down. He couldn't help it if some tears were getting out of his eyes.

"I'm glad to be here. I'm *very* glad to be here," Audrey said. "But you're down."

"It's simple. It's loss. Whenever I have to leave Jason. I never get used to it."

"This turned out to be such a good day for me. I was afraid of it, but it was wonderful. It was a wonderful time for Jason, too. I think any time he has with you must be a very special time for him. He loves you so much."

"It's terrifying not to be in control of your own life. Terrifying." He got up from beside Audrey. "That asshole judge. He said I was a good father, he could see that."

"Oh, Tim, you're so down. I know it's a bummer. Look, I could go home. If it's better for you to be by yourself."

"No. I just get mad and sad. It's such a feeling of hopelessness. But I pull out. I'm glad you're here."

"We could go to bed?"

Tim smiled. "I'm not totally down. I've been thinking of helping you out of that pretty dress."

"I've been wanting to get out of it badly."

But the telephone rang. Tim stood still. "Valerie."

"How can you—"

"The timing. Jason's told her about you, the afternoon."

"So?" Audrey saw that he was motionless, as if he were holding off time.

"I can tell you what she's calling about. I don't get Jason this weekend."

Audrey saw Tim pick up the telephone as if he had some muscular difficulty in doing so. "Hello?"

"Tim, it's me. Not going to work out this weekend. Forgot I've got to take Jason to my mother's. Sorry."

64

IT WAS NINE-THIRTY in the morning When Day dialed Med Three and asked for Audrey. "Things are really bad. Otherwise I wouldn't be calling."

"You want me to do a double shift again."

"Barnitska resigned. She's not going to call in sick anymore, not going to fake a death in the family. She's just burnt out."

"Burnt out or burnt up?"

"Both, of course. Audrey, I haven't got anyone else to go to."

"If it's that bad now, what's it going to be like if the docs go out?"

"That's it. That's exactly it. The staff is shaking out."

"Bailing out," Audrey said.

"We have some slots to fill. But it's amazing, the core we have here."

"Okay. I'm a sucker for flattery. I'll do two."

"Thanks." Day did not want to get off the phone. She wanted to postpone the next calls she would have to make. "Catch the *Eagle* this morning?"

"No."

"Keating finally got around to Mr. Volante. Doesn't mention him by name. *Popular recording star, whose career took plunge, may have tried to take plunge himself. Being maintained incognito at Back Bay Met under mysterious circumstances. More later. Watch this column.*"

"For what?"

"I have no idea. Keep the lid on, huh? She's promising her readers something."

"All this does is violate the man's privacy."

"She's after the hospital, too, in some way. We're getting to be hot copy."

"I hope to God he doesn't see that. You know what he's being treated for—bottom line? Quote deep and debilitating injury to his self-concept unquote."

"I'd be interested in the orders covering that."

"I can summarize. Nutrition, caring, and psychiatric support."

"Sort of as if he were in for failure to thrive."

Then Day made the call she did not want to make. To Jimbo. To explain why she had to do a double shift again. "I've got no choice. I haven't got anyone else to go to. One supervisor's out of town, one's sick, one just did a double and will have to do two more this weekend and . . . And I haven't got anyone else, Jimbo. I haven't even got anyone to take my place on the arrest team."

"Day, you take care of everyone else."

"But I don't take care of you. I'm sorry."

"I was thinking about the baby. You're not taking care of the baby."

"I know my limits. The baby's all right."

"You going to care for it after It's born? Or you going to go your own way instead?"

"That's terrible. That's *shitty*, Jimbo."

"I think so, too. It's the shitty reality."

Day put her hand on her abdomen and closed her eyes and leaned back in her chair. "Look, I'll call you at home this evening and—"

"Don't bother. I won't be home. Why should I?"

"Now, Jimbo—"

"*You* don't care to be home."

He hung up on her. She couldn't remember his ever having done that before. She tried to soothe her pain by thinking about Jimbo's. He feels sorry for himself, Day thought, and he's angry about the baby and he's got some justice for both. I'll call him after rounds. But she did not dare tell him that she might be needed over the weekend. The emotional pain was like another physical presence in her. She was bloody furious at the docs. Her nurses were saying to her, If we can't count on the docs, why bother at all? Get out now before the docs do. *No*. Most of her nurses were *not* saying that. Most of them were already picking up extra loads in preparation.

65

ON MED THREE Audrey was on the phone, routinely attempting to stockpile supplies. Usually the man she spoke to was pleasant and helpful if he could be, but this morning he yelled at her, "Who the fuck do you think I am, lady, Santa Claus?"

"Hey—"

"I got your records right here. Requisitions—whatya doin' up there? Operatin' a goddamn black market?"

Oh, shit, Audrey thought. Caught. Since the beginning of the week, as the Sunday midnight walkout grew nearer, she had been attempting to prepare the floor for chaos. And that had included a siege-preparation storage of whatever medications and supplies she could get hold of that were likely to run out. Virtually everything. What she was usually able to stockpile on Thursday she had left till Thursday. As coolly as she could, Audrey said, "We're going to run out over the weekend. The floor's going to—"

"Call back on the weekend. I ain't here on the weekend."

"That's why I'm calling now—" But the man had hung up.

Mr. Stevens was signaling. He was now in a room by himself and Audrey went to him. "I think I can do it today," he said. "Tell my family. You still with me, Nurse?"

"Sure."

"Funny thing. It's like you're family now, too."

"You just let me know when you want me."

She would have walked by Dom Volante's room except that she saw a scene developing that she wanted to prevent. Jan Fox was sitting at Dom's bedside and she had a newspaper folded open on the bed. "You made the paper," she was already saying. "Your career is on the rise again, Dom. Look what Lynn Keating wrote about you." Jan watched Dom's face. "I'm sure it's you she's writing about, Dom. Don't you agree?"

Dom handed the paper back and turned away.

"Jan," Audrey said, "you might want to get some rest. They've got a barrage of tests set up for you this afternoon and evening."

"For tomorrow?"

"Yes."

Dom looked back at Jan. "What for?"

Jan said to Audrey, "You can tell him."

"It's pre-op stuff. Jan's going to have a cardiac catheterization tomorrow morning."

"I don't know what that is," Dom said.

"They go into the heart," Jan said. "That's what everyone wants to do."

"Open heart surgery?"

"No," Audrey said. "They run lines in. Catheters. Through veins and arteries. To measure pressures in the heart. They want to see how Jan's heart is doing."

"I can tell them," Jan said. "Pretty stinking."

Audrey's sense of professionalism and respect for the patient prevented her from agreeing.

On Med Seven, Day had finished her floor review with Selma. "How's Nan doing?" Nan Lassitter had been on the floor for three days now.

"She's got a real talent for older people," Selma said. "It's all worked out fine. It was good for Liz to get off this floor, I guess. From geriatrics to the neonatal ICU for Liz and from the ICU to geriatrics for Nan. Does that tell us something?"

"I don't even want to consider the possibilities. Nan is doing well?"

"Like she's been here forever. I was sorry to lose Liz, I am *delighted* to have Nan. She has that way—patients respond to her as if they've known her forever."

When Day got together with her, she found Nan looking younger and fresher than she could remember ever having seen her.

Nan said, "I helped out in a geriatrics wing right after high school. I loved it. It was one of my best experiences. You know, the challenge on the ICU is fantastic. But you can stay too long. It stops being nursing. Sometimes I'd get to thinking I was taking care of the machines instead of the patients. That's a defense mechanism, I know. You're defending yourself from the patient's condition. And there's not much human reward. Not from the patients. If they get better, they get moved to another floor."

"I know," Day said. "I have ICU experience. Two years of it not so long ago. That's how I ended up on the arrest team."

Nan glanced along the corridor. "I love these patients. And I get to love them. They need a lot of physical care. But nothing special. Getting them out of bed, feeding them, bathing them, dressing them, changing dressings, grooming them. Talking. You get to know the people. And they—these people—they have nothing, they come from nothing. But they've done so much living. They know what the important things are. And on the other floors, you know, a lot of the time the patient is expected to conform to the staff. But the elderly can't always do that. They're used to their own ways. They need a lot of care. You get the reward of a smile. Or

recovery if you give them good care. So I love it on this
floor. I'm back to nursing the way I used to think of it.''

Instead of coming from nothing, one patient, Ralph Malamet,
chose to go to Back Bay Metropolitan because he wished to
hold on to everything he had, which to his mind was considerable, and which was being put to risk just now by some
poor behavior on the part of his body, perhaps a viral
condition—a physician had told him of such a thing—or
perhaps something more significant. A cab brought him to the
hospital and he was accompanied by an attractive and much
younger woman who, the triage nurse saw, had a proprietary
attitude toward the man. No ring, the nurse observed, and
very anxious.

The nurse looked at the man fixedly and said, ''What's the
problem?''

''Pain in my chest.''

''Where in your chest?''

''Middle.''

''Touch the area for me, will you, please?'' Malamet did
so. ''How long have you had the pain?''

''Four hours, I think.'' The young white woman looked at
the black nurse and shook her head *no*. The man stared at his
watch, all separate hands and calibrations and stop and start
buttons. Standing behind the man, the woman extended her
arm so that the watch on her wrist faced the nurse, and she
drew her finger around the face of the watch in a full circle.

''When did the symptoms start?''

''Maybe last night.''

''What does it feel like? The pain.''

''Feels like there's a truck on my chest . . . Feels like I
can't breathe . . .''

''Anything else? Stomach?''

''Yeah. I threw up. I'm . . . Right now, I'm nauseous.''

''You're sweating.''

The young woman said, ''He's been sweating.''

The nurse said to him, ''Do you have any medical
problems?''

''None,'' Malamet said clearly.

''Diabetes?''

''No.''

''Do you take any medicine?''

"No."

"Drugs."

"No."

"How old are you?"

"Forty-eight."

"Have you ever been in this hospital before? Do we have any records on you?"

"No."

"Have you ever been told you have any problems with your heart?"

"Hell no. I'm an airline pilot. A captain. I pass physicals four times a year."

66

TIM LEANED AGAINST the counter inside the station on Med Three. He wore a jogging suit and there was an oversized tote bag on the floor by him. He said to Audrey, "You must be a rich lady, doing all these double shifts."

"And you're just a playboy on the loose." She looked at the tote bag. "What's in there, Nurse? Your balls?"

"Exactly. Celtics' pride. Back Bay Mets are finally going to have a full team practice."

"I had a conversation with your trainer earlier. I didn't know she was your trainer. I didn't know you had a trainer."

"Every good team has a trainer. Elin Maki is a great trainer."

"She said you dragooned her."

"Team full of doctors, Audrey, every time there's some sort of injury, nobody leaves it alone. Before they were doctors, these guys walked it off, sat out for a while, and then played. What they do now is speculation, disagreement—they start shoving each other around with status. *Whatta you know, y'only uh secon'-yeah resident. I can remember seein' same thing happen, patient hadda have ligaments removed.* So I got Elin in. They got a nurse player-coach, they got a nurse trainer. She doesn't put up with any shit. Somebody bumps

something, twists something, she says put hot on it, put cold
on it, wrap it, don't wrap it, walk it off, sit down. Then I
can't keep them on the bench and they're not mouthing off at
each other, they're *practicing*. She's terrific.''

"Does she really know that much about sports injuries?"

"No. She says you treat the player, not the injury. She
says hot or cold chicken soup applied externally would be just
as effective in this situation. Ordered with enough authority.''

"You're not down about Jason.''

"I told you. I come back.''

"So do I. Your place tomorrow.'' Audrey looked at Tim
with pleasure. "I thought athletes were supposed to be celi-
bate, immaculate before a game.''

"I subscribe to the Joe Namath theory. Fuck your brains
out the night before. Holbrook's corollary is, then you can
play out of your mind the next day.''

Debby Fluelling came down the corridor to the station. The
new nurse made Audrey smile at her again. She looked as if
she had just graduated from the ocean, with honors, and
instructions to cure all evil and really enjoy herself doing it.
At the station she said, "Mr. Stevens asked me to get you.
He's got his family with him.''

Mrs. Stevens and eleven-year-old Jeff and fourteen-year-old
Glen were seated around the bed.

"How's it goin'?" Audrey said.

"Fine. The boys're jus' tellin' me what's been goin' on at
school." The man looked back at his sons. Jeff continued
talking. Audrey realized that Mr. Stevens was not hearing
what his boy was saying. He was all vision, a sponge soaking
it in. Soaking it in to remember for the time when he was
alone. And maybe thinking he could take the memory with
him for after.

He suddenly looked away from his boys and tears streamed
down his face as he said, "I can't tell them.''

"What?'' his wife said. And then she screamed.

The boys were frightened.

"*You* tell them,'' Mr. Stevens said to Audrey.

Audrey hesitated involuntarily. She did not know what to
say. She had not been trained to be competent at this. She felt
helpless and useless.

She went to the door and closed it. She stood behind Mrs.

Stevens and put her hands on the woman's shoulders. Then she told the Stevens family what had been found in the chest x-ray and what had been found by the follow-up procedure. She omitted medical detail that could be of no use to the younger boy in understanding his father's condition. She explained the treatment and the probable course of the disease.

Mrs. Stevens sat with her hands folded in her lap and looked at her husband and cried. The younger boy began to bawl, and the older boy, silent with tears on his face as he looked at his father, put an arm around his brother.

Mrs. Stevens went to her husband and hugged him, then rocked him back and forth. The younger boy got up on the bed and put his arms around both his mother and father. The older boy remained back, his arms around himself as he looked at the others.

Audrey wanted to flee. Flee Mr. Stevens. Flee the floor. Flee the hospital. As a nurse she had never before experienced so visceral a command to flight. But she waited until Mrs. Stevens asked for privacy and then she went outside and pressed her back against the wall and waited for her mind to get hold and reduce all the terrible emotions tumbling over inside her. She wished she hadn't given up cigarettes.

A weird, really weird association, she thought, for a nurse with a patient with a cancerous growth in his lungs.

Debby Fluelling came by smiling. Audrey moved along with her. Debby said, "It's great here. Just what I wanted. I feel useful. I have work to do."

67

THE NEW PATIENT was pale and groggy. "He's groggy from morphine," Audrey said. "To relieve the chest pain." She and Debby and an intern and a transport worker managed Ralph Malamet into his bed, his IV pole alongside him. "Stay with him a few minutes," Audrey said to Debby.

Audrey went to the station and called down to the responsible HO. *"I will not have this patient without a monitor."*

The HO said, "You can quit or walk, like us."

"I'm staying. But I will not have him here without—"

The HO spoke very slowly. "I have asked everywhere. There isn't one."

Ralph Malamet was raised from grogginess to wakefulness by pain—more chest pain and more terrible in its grip than he had experienced before.

He realized it was potentially serious, but he told himself that it would go away. He was not weak. He was not going to display weakness. He was not going to call for anyone. What was happening would go away.

Audrey was so tired, a peace had begun to settle into her. She had a pleasant passing thought of Tim. Then she called down about a monitor again. She had checked Mr. Malamet a few minutes before and when she reported his condition, she was told he was no longer even number one in line for a monitor. "You're the monitor," she was told.

Audrey explained the continuing situation to Debby. "If we don't have a monitor by eleven, one of us is going to have to work the next shift until we do. We can't leave one nurse alone on the floor."

Debby felt chilly and alone. Nothing familiar. This place was so foreign. There should be a monitor.

The corridor had been dimmed to minimal illumination. At Jordan the corridors would have been much brighter at this hour, and some patients would still be up watching television and socializing. Here there was no television. The entire floor was nearly dark and silent except for the humming fluorescent overhead light at the station.

Debby had been thrilled by the opportunity to work at Back Bay Met. But now she felt shut in and endangered by the responsibility. "I don't like it here," she said.

"I don't much like this place either," Audrey said. "I console myself that it's the ultimate challenge in nursing." She put down her pen. "The nurse recruiter greeted you with open arms, right?" Debby nodded. "Come and help us. We really need you. You'll be appreciated here."

"That's what they told me. They didn't tell me you don't have enough monitors for the cardiac patients."

"That's why you're appreciated here. It's nuts, but you're

never bored. There I am, busting my gut just to keep up, and somebody cardiac arrests.''

Debby looked away. "You get off on that?'' she said quietly.

"I get off on seeing that they live." She picked up her pen. "Now go check Captain Malamet. Check his hep lock drip, too.''

Debby entered the dark room and shone her flashlight on Ralph Malamet. His color was dusky. She touched him. His skin was cold and clammy. She shook his shoulders. "Are you okay?" She shone the flashlight on his chest. It wasn't moving. She put her head down and looked and listened and felt, but there was no rise and fall. She put her ear next to his mouth and nose, but there were no sounds of inspiration or expiration. She placed her cheek next to his mouth and *felt* for expiratory air. There was none.

She struck the emergency call button and gave Malamet four quick mouth-to-mouth ventilations. No response. *How bad? How much time do I have to act? What can I do?* No motion, no carotid pulse.

She felt for the cartilage of the xiphoid process and got up on the bed as she landmarked one hand on the chest and then joined her hands and with her arms straight drove the heel of her hand into the lower part of Malamet's sternum. She grunted aloud with the exertion and the patient in the other bed cried out, *"My God! My God! What's happening?"*

Audrey turned on the room light as she entered. She went to the bedside opposite Debby and on Debby's next upstroke she gave Malamet a single mouth-to-mouth ventilation. Debby was compressing too rapidly and Audrey counted aloud, "One one-thousand, two one-thousand," to slow her down. She interrupted her count to shout at the aide in the doorway, *"Bring the cart! Call the code!* . . . Five one-thousand," and at five she gave Malamet another ventilation.

Audrey felt the sweat on her forehead and saw that Debby was dripping and looked desperate and exhausted. She said, *"Next time switch on three."* She gave the next ventilation and counted through and then switched positions, Audrey delivering compressions and Debby ventilations.

*   *   *

Day was just concluding rounds and going back to her office when the beeper in her pocket sounded. For the eight seconds in which the beeper carried voice transmission, she heard: *"Code Six, Med Three, Room Eleven, Code Six, Med Three, Room Eleven,"* but she was running for the stairwell—the two of her were running—before the code had been called twice.

The cart was just inside the door and Audrey was establishing the airway in the patient's mouth and placing the mask of an ambu bag in position over the airway, the new nurse standing to the side with a Formica-covered particle board, performing but no longer entirely comprehending, a terror-inspired dullness occluding her perception.

"Pulse?" Day said. *"Pulse?"*

"No," the new nurse said, and Day sat the patient up and got her to help manipulate the board under him. Day took the squeeze-operated ambu bag and Audrey delivered compressions—after every five, Day squeezed a combination of room air and pure oxygen into the patient's lungs, Audrey counting, ". . . five one-thousand, breathe . . . *Where the hell is the team?"* Every five seconds seemed like half an hour waiting for the others to get there and Audrey knew that less than ninety seconds had elapsed since Debby had begun countering the arrest.

The aide was assisting the other patient out of the room. Debby was moving back, away from the bed. She heard other people running down the corridor. She heard coins and keys jangling in their pockets, beepers sounding insistently, and then the fizzy voice transmission: *"Code Six, Med Three, Room Eleven,"* and then Debby bumped into the aide and patient behind her. Day looked over and said, *"EKG machine."* Debby started to ask where, but the aide said, "I'll get it." Debby stood very still. As if her stillness would relieve her of any responsibility to act. People pushed by her.

The first one, an anesthesiologist, went to the head of the bed. "How long's he been like this?" he said as he introduced a laryngoscope through the airway and into the passage of the throat, the intern, Mozart, saying, "What's his rhythm?" and to a medical student, "Change with her on three," and the student taking over from Audrey as the anesthesiologist completed the laryngoscope insertion and took over the breathing manipulation from Day and said, "Give me an eight," as Day went directly to the cart.

"Defib machine," Audrey said to Debby and then pushed Debby—out of the way and started to go for it herself as the aide pushed the EKG machine past the cart and into the room. Audrey intercepted it and told the aide, "Defib machine," and Day passed the endotrachial tube to the anesthesiologist with a copper stylette to stiffen it for its passage into the lungs. "I called for an eight. There's only a seven."

Debby was shoved again. It seemed to her the room was contracting and wobbling, like a small boat about to capsize, as more people came in. "Have you drawn a blood gas?" Anita Rounds, the cardiac care unit resident, the senior resident on the team, "Getting one," Mozart said, the anesthesiologist getting rid of the ambu bag and airway and intubating Malamet with the ET tube, the intern preparing to take blood for analysis—the destruction in the patient's system—with a glass syringe he had received from Day. "Do you have a line in? Have you a central line in?" Anita was saying, not quite at bedside yet, and Audrey answering, "No," working to attach the four limb leads to Malamet, the anesthesiologist saying, "He's tubed," Anita saying, "How long? What's his underlying problem?" Day rapidly setting up the premixed meds at the cart, the cardiac kit broken open, a respiratory therapist counting a changeover and getting up on the bed in place of the medical student, who went to Mozart's side, Aaron Silver, the ICU resident, arriving and calling, "What's his rhythm? Drawn a gas?", and Anita saying to Day, "Give me a CVP line, get me a pair of gloves, who is this man? What's wrong with him?", Aaron saying to Day, "I want a sixteen-line," and then yelling at Audrey, "Out of my way, I'm trying to get this IV in" as he worked on the left hand and as, jostled by him, Audrey was trying to get an EKG strap around farther up the arm and reporting to Anita, "Forty-eight-year-old ER admission, midafternoon, chest pain, no cardiac history, sent up here about eight o'clock, to R/O," moving to wrap the BP cuff around the patient's arm, Mozart saying "Goddamn it!" and Audrey continuing, "Morphine on the ER, nothing since up here—" Aaron saying, "I asked for a sixteen, you gave me an eighteen! never mind, I'll use it—" "—no distress till now," the aide pushing in a cart with the defibrillating machine on it, maneuvering around the crash cart, the EKG machine, the people at or moving around the bed, "God-*damn* it!" "Will you stay the fuck out of my way!" "Five one-thousand . . . *Breathe* . . ." "*I need*—" "*Give me*—" All the questions and orders and answers at the same time, everyone shouting at each other, *Chaos*, Debby thought, *Pandemonium*. They don't know what they're doing. It's not my fault if he dies. She had withdrawn to the side of the doorway, completely out of the way, but still in the room, her fingertips holding on to the guidebar of the crash cart, though she did not realize that she was doing so.

Anita, gloved by Day, took large Q-Tips from a foil-wrapped package and dunked them and made quick swipes of dark antiseptic on Malamet's right shoulder in the area of the collarbone in preparation for getting the central venous pressure line in, discarding the swipes to the floor, Day joining syringes and removing air bubbles, Aaron getting the long-line IV in, Anita placing a large needle centrally under the clavicle into the vein until dark blood rushed back and spilled out, saying, "Give me an EKG, we need an EKG," Mozart disconnecting the blood-filled canula from the artery and telling the medical student, "Hold the artery, we need a five-minute compression on the artery," and holding the syringe upright and putting a stopper on it, Audrey saying, "Let me through here, let me get this plug in!" and crawling on the floor with a huge fluorescent extension cord, "Let me get this plug in, *please!*", the aide returning with an IVAC and going to Mozart with a cup filled with ice, Anita completing the insertion of a fine, flexible plastic tube into the subclavian needle, people all around the bed, compressions and bagging continuing, the respiratory therapist dripping and apoplectically red, Mozart handing the glass syringe to the aide, "Okay, ice it, get it to the lab," and to Anita, "Got the blood gas drawn—" "Where the fuck's the EKG?" "Long line's in—" "EKG there *yet?*" Audrey saying, "EKG, defib, both plugged in," and going to the EKG, Day passing an ampule of bicarbonate and Anita injecting it into a rubber arrowhead a few inches above the CVP line's entrance into Malamet's body to counter acidosis, Day passing a syringe of epinephrine to increase heart contraction and a syringe of calcium gluconate to facilitate adequate contraction, glucose and water coming down the line. A zero clock would have

indicated two minutes and seventeen seconds since Debby
had discovered the arrest.

Audrey saw a wiggly line on the EKG. "He's fibrillating.
VF." "He's going to need paddles," Anita said. "Goop the
paddles." Audrey moved to the defibrillator and greased the
paddles with clearish gray jelly. "What do you want it set
at?" she said, passing the paddles to Anita. "Give me one
hundred," and Audrey set the machine for hundred-watt seconds, the entire amount to be given in a single jolt. "I'm
ready to shock him, everybody off the bed," Anita said, the
respiratory therapist clearing Malamet's chest and the bed as
the others moved back, Audrey saying, *"Unplug the EKG,"*
and Aaron disconnected the EKG patient cable to the machine, leaving Malamet still wired and the machine still
plugged in, but the machine and the patient not connected.
"Is everybody off the bed?" Anita said, placing one disk at
the end of an upright handle on Malamet's left side below his
armpit, the skin salty, and the other disk on his sternum so
that the shock would strike directly across the heart. *"Paddles are on—is everybody off?* Can I go ahead?" Aaron
saying, "You're clear," and Anita saying, "Hit it, hit it—
give him the jolt!"

A red button with a steel collar around it to prevent its
being depressed accidentally. Audrey depressed it. All of
Malamet's muscles went into spasm. As his muscles contracted, he seemed to rise off the bed.

"What's his rhythm?" Aaron said, the paddles raised from
the patient, Mozart reconnecting the EKG machine to the
patient. "Still VF," Mozart said, Anita twisting her head and
looking at Audrey to say "Give me two-fifty, two hundred
and fifty," and looking at Malamet and replacing the paddles,
Audrey setting the jolt, Mozart disconnecting the EKG. "Off
the bed . . . *Okay, hit it!"*

Audrey depressed the button. Malamet's body jerked and
spasmed. *"What's he got? What's he got?"* Audrey said.
"What's his rhythm?" Anita said, going to the machine and
watching the paper come out of it. Tentatively she held the
paddles out to Audrey. After some ten seconds Anita let
Audrey take them and she touched the paper coming out of
the machine and said, "Okay, hold on now, we've got a
rhythm, he's in sinus rhythm, but he's kinda slow, give me
some atropine." Day said, "How much?" "Give him a full

milligram IV.'' The respiratory therapist on the bed giving compressions again, the anesthesiologist bagging Malamet every five seconds. Day took out a glass vial. It dropped and she said, ''Oh shit,'' and reached to get another one before the first had hit and broken on the floor. She snapped off the top of the new vial and drew the liquid into a syringe and then injected it into Malamet through the rubber arrowhead in the CVP line. ''Where's he at?'' ''Sixty,'' Anita said.

Mozart drew a new set of blood gases. The aide waited at the doorway. There was silence and except for Mozart and the EKG machine, no motion in the room. Mozart nodded, the medical student applied arterial pressure again, and the aide came in and took the new blood and iced it and left. Anita continued to look down at the paper coming out of the EKG machine. ''All right, his rate's speeding up. He's at seventy-five. What's his blood pressure?'' Audrey took it. ''Seventy over fifty.'' They'd want it up. ''Let's start some dopamine,'' Anita said. ''How much?'' ''Two hundred mics.'' Day mixed it and piggybacked it through the CVP line.

''Hey, you shove real hard there, lady,'' Aaron said to Audrey. ''It's your bod I was interested in.'' ''—the hell did it happen?'' ''—get blood gases back—'' ''—not on critical care unit—'' ''Did real good—'' ''God, am I hungry—'' ''Did you see the look—''

''What's his blood pressure doing now?''

''Eighty over fifty-five,'' Audrey said.

The conversation sounded like that in a locker room after a game or backstage after a school play. People coming down, no one particularly listening to anyone else—except to Audrey as she reported the blood pressure every twenty or thirty seconds. Two minutes after the dopamine she said, ''One-oh-five over seventy.''

People nodded at each other. It was acceptable.

My God, Debby thought, *what if the house officers weren't here?*

68

I DON'T BELONG HERE! Debby thought. I could *kill* someone. I never *learned* anything at all, I don't have the *competence* to be here, *I'll resign tomorrow.*

Audrey looked over at Debby, by the door. Blank, Audrey thought.

Day said, "What's the family's status? Has the patient seen a priest, clergy?"

"He hasn't seen anyone," Audrey said. "Trina said a lady came in with him and then disappeared. Someone's trying to get in touch with the family. In New Hampshire."

Malamet began to wake. Some of the members of the team were in the singular circumstance of having known him dead before they ever knew him alive.

Audrey knew that her patient's sensation, with the tube running into his lungs, was that he was being suffocated, though the tube was what was allowing him to breathe. Audrey placed a hand on his forehead. "It's okay. Lie still. Don't fight it. You're in the hospital, Captain Malamet. You had some trouble with your heart. The doctor's here."

But Malamet began to thrash, and Audrey and Aaron together had to restrain him from pulling the tube out of his lungs.

Anita said to the anesthesiologist, "What do you think? Keep him intubated?"

"We need to keep the tube in for a few hours."

"All right. We'll leave him intubated for a while. You want to sedate or paralyze?"

"Paralyze him. Pavulon."

Audrey took Debby down the darkened corridor, but she would not reply when Audrey spoke to her. On the way to the station, Audrey paused at doorways briefly and reassured the patients who had been awakened and startled by what they had heard of the crisis. "You okay?" she said into the doorways. "I'll be coming back real soon."

At the station Debby spoke in a small voice. "I've got to get out. I can't handle this. I didn't know what to do for him. I couldn't help. He was lucky he had the rest of you. I could have *killed* him."

"I understand, Debby. But I haven't time to deal with it now. The patients need to be checked. You're a nurse, not a patient. You're a nurse and *your* patients need to be taken care of. Got that?" Debby's head was down, but she nodded. "Start at the other end."

"What about . . . the patient?"

"They're deciding in there. They'll stay with him for a while. The crisis is over, not the danger. They'll stay with him thirty-five, forty minutes. Then they'll send him to an ICU."

Audrey found herself trembling quite badly.

She picked up the telephone and called Central Logistical Stores and asked for the crash cart to be restocked immediately. Then she ordered a technician and a portable chest x-ray machine and a portable cardiac monitor.

In Malamet's room, people were still sweating and they had begun trembling. They spoke to each other and disregarded their own and each other's trembling. No one tried to hide or suppress the trembling.

"Pulled another one off," Day said, reestablishing some order in the crash cart. I'm *tired,* Day thought. Her back was painful and there was the pain of Jimbo hanging up on her. I've got to call Jimbo. His secretary had said he was unavailable the three times she'd called and there had been no answer at home the two times she'd called during the evening.

The aide brought in the report on the first blood gases. Acidity too high. "Give him another amp of bicarb," Anita said to Day. Then the cardiology resident studied the full EKG. "He had a mild MI. He came up here and quietly extended it."

"A macho type. Wouldn't call for help," Day said.

"Or too groggy."

"Severe denier, maybe."

When the second blood gases came up, Anita read them aloud and then said, "Okay, we're doing fine."

When Jimbo answered the phone, Day heard the eleven o'clock news in the background. "Jimbo, I'm so glad you're home."

He laughed. "Home is where the comfort is. In this case, home is where the bottle is."

"Well, then, I hope you're having a good time."

"The TV is very warm company, great drinking partner. Very informative this time of night. Great conversationalist. Learned. You know what it just said?"

"No."

"Said the nurses at Back Bay Met gonna keep the hospital open, the house officers go on strike. Gonna do double shifts, sacrifice all over the place, keep the hospital open. My own wife didn't tell me that. I guess TV's better informed than my own wife down atta hospital."

"Nothing's certain, Jimbo. We don't know that the HOs are really going out."

"Not what the TV says."

Day was quiet. "I'm sorry I'm not there, Jimbo."

He was silent then for a few seconds. "Me, too. I worry a lot, Day. About both of you."

"I know you do. Trust me."

"It takes a lot of effort, Day. Don't keep pushing me, Day. Don't keep testing me."

"I hope you sleep well. I love you."

"You, too."

She felt her pregnancy with her fingers and palms. If the strike came, she did not know what to expect of Jimbo. She knew what would be expected of her.

69

"CALL IT a night?" Trina said.

"Sure," Hal said. It was almost midnight. "It's more than a night."

"Always is. Some nights more than others, of course."

Trina had completed a statistical analysis of psych nursing on the ER for Molly Chang and Dorothea Kullgren, seen a physically abused child and begun work on a 51-A procedure on behalf of the child and her helpless mother, talked to an airline pilot with chest pains who wanted to tell her nothing about himself or his family and who told the young woman with him to go away, talked two different drug ODs through critical moments, heard from the attorney Nick Prudhomme (whom she hoped was calling *her* but who was calling Trina the rape victim counselor) that Jessy Gladdens had withdrawn rape charges against Robert Higby and he would like to know why, tried unsuccessfully to get in touch with Jessy, successfully talked a stab wound into providing the police with the circumstances of the stabbing, visited Jan Fox and Dom Volante on Med Three and somewhat lowered Jan's anxiety about her cardiac cath the next day, and applied herself to some walk-ins with varying rages, terrors, inebriations, and psychosomatic complaints. Now the night psych nurse was already at work on the floor.

In the ER waiting area, Trina paused by the rows of empty orange chairs. Two people had caused her to stop: Ginny the guard and Olivia of the gynecological concerns. They faced each other, Olivia just in front of the open doorway to the lobby of the New Wing, and Ginny silent and motionless a few feet away, stopped still on her way out as if Olivia were a poisonous snake barring her way.

Trina said to Ginny, "Someone you know?" Then she rephrased it. "Someone you recognize?"

Ginny continued to look at Olivia. Then she took some steps backward before she turned and hurried to another exit.

"Doesn't need any psychiatric help," Trina said. "Now I'm going to have to talk to Sergeant Cleveland about her a third time." She moved closer to Olivia, Hal beside her. "How y'doin' tonight, Olivia?"

The young woman studied the air above Trina's head. "Jes fine, jes fine, jes fine." She looked at the air a little to the side of Hal's head. "There be Mr. Fixin'-t'be-uh-doctuh."

"Hi," Hal said. "Can we do anything for you?"

"My ovaries hurt. Hurt *real* bad. Can I have me the stickterectomy now?"

Trina said, "I need to sit down and talk with you, Olivia."

"Ain't *talkin'* to *you*. Talkin' to Mr. Fixin'-t'be-uh-doctuh."

"But you're still not looking at me," Hal said.

"I look at you, my eyes kill you. You know that lady with the snakes?" She touched her hair.

"Medusa?" Trina said.

"Don't go sayin' the name!" The eyes focused on Trina for one instant, an instant of rage. Then she looked off again and her face became empty. "The Queen."

"Olivia, I really would like to spend some time with you now. Let's you and me—"

"Got to go," Olivia said and walked out.

Trina watched her. "She's staying within a pattern. Same words, same way of holding herself, same concerns. Except for this business of Medusa. I guess I'll read up on Medusa before I go to bed tonight."

"Great bedtime reading."

"Yeah, but it's appropriate, you know? Medusa's considered to be the personification of nightmare."

"You think *she* knows that?"

"I don't know. Maybe some part of her intuits that."

"Then what's she saying?"

"She's saying a nightmare's running her life. Or that *she's* a nightmare. Maybe both.

70

LATE FRIDAY AFTERNOON, and Molly brought along a suitcase for her first visit to Bennett's apartment. She had a change of clothes for the evening, minimal clothes for the night, and some casual duds for going to the Back Bay Mets game with the Harlem Wiseapples the next noon. She also brought along an *Eagle* folded open to a Lynn Keating interview with Howard Sylvus, the hospital attorney.

"The house officers' demands are irresponsible, unreasonable and ignorant of the hospital's financial situation.

"If these people go out, the courts should find that they have been criminally negligent. I do not need a court to inform me that they will be acting immorally."

Molly said, "You hadn't seen this?"
"No."

"The lady would like a glass of wine and a shower. Later she will tour the premises." But Bennett was reading.

"No, there will be no meetings. No further attempt at negotiation."

But, I asked, isn't it the hospital's moral duty to pursue negotiation right up until the twelfth hour?

"We have been badgered into our position by a one-week warning of a physicians' walkout. We have done our best to see that the patients continue to receive the physician care that is their right and due."

Molly poured herself some sherry at the bar. "I would like to take a shower, the lady said invitingly." She raised her voice. "The lady would like to take a shower, the lady said provocatively."

"I hear you, Molly. Give me a couple of minutes and I'll *drown* with you. But let me finish this."

"I'll find the shower myself—"

"Sylvus should be keeping his goddamn mouth shut."

"You've got the same problem I do. None of the men in my life are doing what they should be doing."

"If, by Friday afternoon, the house officers are not persuaded by their moral obligations to remain at their posts, then we must say to them, 'Gentlemen, and ladies, Doctors, walk out on your Hippocratic oaths, walk out on your moral obligations, walk out on your patients' very lives!' "

That would be Sunday midnight. I asked Mr. Sylvus what he would be doing over the weekend. Keeping the lines open?

"I for one am going fishing."

"What a fucking *dumb* thing to say!" Bennett yelled over the telephone to Sylvus.

"Yes, I agree it was. But honest. I thought it was off the record."

"Nothing is off the record with Keating. *Are* you going fishing?"

"Yes. I need clean air."

"I presume you will be available?"

"For what, Bennett? From what I can see, you don't want anything. From what I can see, this whole strike is your idea."

71

AUDREY SAID, "I could go home."

"I think you said that before," Tim said. "The other night?"

"After you left Jason off. You're brooding again."

"Brooding."

"There's your *despair* about Jason. I wouldn't mind so much if I thought my being here helped at all."

"It helps a lot. A *lot*. It's just her *yanking* him. After she said he could be at the game tomorrow."

"Maybe she did promise to take him to her mother's."

"Sure."

"Will you at least have fun tomorrow? Playing?"

"Yes, I will."

"Even without Jason there?" She looked at him levelly.

He smiled slightly. "Yes, I will."

"Life goes on," Audrey said, glad of his slight smile. "How well will the home team do?"

"We'll do as well as they let us. Or as badly as they force us."

Tim got up and stood over her and slid his hands down and across the front of her dress. "What is this?" Audrey said.

"Sheer animal need."

She placed her hand on the bulge of his erection. "Life goes on," she said.

Tim thought he had been asleep only a few minutes when the telephone rang. He felt his heart startle in its rhythm and his stomach muscles constrict in apprehension. He reached for the phone and read the illuminated face of the clock. Three in the very blackness of early morning.

Tim heard soft sobbing on the phone. *"Jason! What is it, Jason?"*

Audrey sat up and turned on the lamp. Her shoulders were tight, arms pressing to her side, her heavy breasts incongruously free of the tension that held the rest of her body.

"Daddy . . . Daddy . . ." Tim heard.

"Jason, let me help you. I'm here, try to take it easy. Are you all right?"

"I'm scared, Daddy."

"Are you hurt?"

"No. Not that. *Scared,* Daddy."

Tim heard more sobs. But they did not run on as they had at first. "Where are you, Jason? At Mom's?"

"Yes."

"Where's Mom?"

"I don't *know.*" It was a plea.

"Who's with you?"

"Nuh, *nobody.* Nobody's with me."

"Mom left you alone?"

"Yuh . . . *Yes.*" There was more sobbing, stronger again.

"When's Mom coming back?"

"Don't *know.* She said to watch TV. Late as I want. Till I got tired. Then go to bed."

"All right, I'll—"

"But I coont sleep. Then I went to sleep. But I got scary dreams so I woked up. I called Mom, I went to look for her and I called . . . and she's not here and I'm alone and . . . *Daddy, Daddy . . ."*

Tim spoke through his son's sobbing. "Jase . . . You listen. Can you hear what I'm saying?"

"Yuh . . . Yes, Daddy . . ."

"I'm coming to get you. It'll take me about fifteen minutes to get there. Maybe twenty."

"I don't know what that is."

"Look at the clock and I'll—No, never mind. Audrey's here and she's going to get on the telephone with you. She'll explain about the time. She'll keep you company till I get there." Tim felt Audrey's hand on his shoulder. He glanced at her. She was nodding, smiling slightly, the line of a tear on each cheek. "Jase?"

"Yes, Daddy."

"You wait for my secret ring. The one Mom doesn't like me to use. Don't open the door till I ring. Okay?"

"Yes, Daddy. Hurry up. *Please?*"

"Yes, Jase. You stay on the phone with Audrey. Don't hang up when you go to let me in. Okay?"

"Hurry. I'm still scared."

"I'm going to get dressed. Here's Audrey." He handed her the phone.

"I'm sorry you're alone, Jason. But your dad's coming right over to get you. I'll keep you company. What would you like when you get back here? Cocoa? Some treat? Something else? Now you tell me . . ."

Tim pulled on sweatpants and sweatshirt and put sneakers on his bare feet.

"Your dad's on the way right now."

Tim double-parked in front of Valerie's apartment house. The doorman would not unlock the door for him. Tim shouted through the glass doors. "You know me. My son's upstairs alone. He's terrified. You let me in or I'll have the police here. I'll have you in jail if anything's wrong with my boy."

The doorman unlocked the door. A part of Tim's mind was monitoring himself and what he was doing as it would monitor and analyze on the ICU. He said to the doorman, "Come upstairs with me."

"Charlie, my job is—"

"Your job is to protect the tenants. I'm telling you to come upstairs to make sure a tenant, a little boy, is all right. And that he's not being kidnapped."

"Kidnapped?" he said.

They took the elevator up, and the doorman waited nervously as Tim rang the familiar bell at the familiar door under these very unfamiliar circumstances.

"Daddy?"

"Jason, yes, it's me."

The chain was undone, the bolt was undone, the lock unlocked—Tim was overwhelmed by the succession of clicks, his child's expertise.

Jason was dressed in an assortment of clothes pulled on over his pajamas. He wore his Red Sox jacket and his Red Sox hat and a Celtics T-shirt. He jumped into his father's arms and would not let go. His crying was steady but subdued. "I packed my good stuff. I never want to come back here!" A tote bag Tim had given Jason lay on the floor. It was heavy and protuberant and stuffed with possessions that were not clothes. Tim picked it up without putting Jason down. *"My Paddington,"* Jason said. "Please, my *Paddington.* Can I get him?"

"Sure."

Tim went to Valerie's desk in the living room. He found a piece of carbon paper and wrote a note with a copy for himself. *3:26. Jason terrified being left alone. I have taken him to my place. Tim.*

He showed the note to the doorman. He had the doorman watch as he placed the note where it could not be missed or disturbed.

Audrey had dressed. She provided Jason with cold cereal, hot turkey noodle soup, and a chocolate pudding pop.

Tim was on the phone during most of this. First, he called the police station for Valerie's district and explained who he was, where he lived, what his telephone number was, what his domestic situation was, what the court's decree had been, and what he had done about removing his child from a situation that was intolerable, terrifying, and dangerous to the child. The sergeant at the other end asked some questions and said he'd call back, not to use the phone. Five minutes later the phone rang. A Lieutenant O'Leary questioned Tim and then said, "Let me talk to the boy." He talked to Jason and then to Tim again. "I've dispatched a unit from your district. They'll be there shortly. Check on the boy."

"Fine," Tim said. He called Warren Gates, his attorney, hating to do it in front of Jason. He apologized to Gates and explained the circumstances as succinctly as he could.

"Okay. Maybe Valerie's done something the court won't understand so easily. I think you have the prerogative to keep Jason in your protection. You risk contempt of court. That's meaningless, generally. We'll talk in the morning."

"If Valerie calls?"

"You are invoking a parent's implicit right to protect your child from danger."

After Jason had eaten he said he wasn't sleepy at all, but his eyes closed as he said it and Tim carried him to the day bed.

"Your bed. Please, Daddy?" Tim placed him on the foldout bed. "Come in to bed soon, Daddy?"

Tim kissed him and pulled the covers up. "Soon."

"I could go home," Audrey said.

"Lady keeps threatening to go home," Tim said to an already asleep Jason.

Audrey said to the sleeping boy, "Your father's grinning. For the first time today, he's really grinning."

"I've got my team with me," Tim said. "What I really wanted to say is, it feels like a family here right now."

"It's early for that."

"I know. Call it the hour. Sentimental hour."

"It scares me." She went to Tim to be held.

"I'm sorry," he said. "I'm sorry I scared you."

"You did, sort of."

"Do you mind sleeping on the day bed?"

"You're a fucking comedian, Holbrook. Tell a girl she's family, intimate, just so you can get her to sleep in another bed."

There was a buzz from downstairs. The police. They interviewed Tim and Audrey quietly and then spoke to Jason. "Son?" an officer said. "Son?"

Jason awoke partially. "Daddy, why police . . ."

"It's okay," the officer said. "Go back to sleep, son." He flipped back in his notepad. "I'll try the boy's mother." Tim indicated the phone. There was no answer to the officer's call.

At eight, his voice clear and crisp, Warren Gates said, "Whatever you do, don't fight with Valerie. Don't get into accusations, threats. Just state your position."

"What if she brings the police?"

"That's possible. But they're reluctant to get involved in domestic matters of this sort. She'd probably have to charge you with kidnapping. That would require explaining how the child came to be alone. No, I think she'll get all juiced up and scream bloody murder. There's not much she can do right off. For the rest, we'll try to stay ahead of her."

"But what if she shows up with the police?"

"They need a warrant to enter unless they think life is in danger. As long as they see Jason's safe and wants to be with you, they'll probably back off and leave things for a court to straighten out."

The telephone did not ring again until a few minutes before nine, presumably the time Valerie finally got back to her apartment. Jason was still deeply asleep, although Tim had had a strong impulse to get the boy up and out of the apartment before Valerie showed up. Audrey had encouraged him to let Jason sleep and that was his inclination anyway. He and Audrey were dressed and Tim had forced himself to load up on carbohydrates—mostly pasta—for the energy he'd need at noon. His gear was packed and he sat next to it like a traveler in a train station, but also within quick reach of the phone. Waiting for the call he experienced some anxiety and nausea, the nausea not attributable to the pasta. The effect of the ringing, when it came, was the same as that of an emergency signal on the unit: a charge of energy and the other feelings became nonexistent.

Whatever you do, don't fight with her. Just state your position.

Valerie said, "You bring him back here right now."

"No, I—"

"What time are you going to bring him back here?"

"When the court tells me to."

"The court has already told you to. Jason belongs to me."

"I'm keeping him with me. Warren Gates is filing motions on Monday. The court will reevaluate. You have placed Jason in impending danger and there is a demonstrable need for immediate action to protect him."

"Terrific speech, Tim, terrific. You get Jason back here or you won't see him again, period."

The threat was as forceful as a blow. *Don't get in a fight State your position.*

"I'm going to seek a change of custodial arrangement—due to performance damaging to the child."

"I'll have your ass, Tim. Or have you grown a cunt now?"

"Good-bye, Valerie." Tim hung up. Then he went to the wall and unplugged the phone.

"Does that mean I get to stay with you, Daddy?" Jason was sitting up in bed.

"You love your mom, don't you?" Audrey said. Tim looked at her sharply.

"Yeah, I guess. But I'd rather be with Dad."

*   *   *

While Jason was in the bathroom Tim said, "That wasn't exactly the best time for you to stick your nose in."

"So much for family, huh, Tim?" Audrey looked at him steadily. "It's going to be asked him. Over and over. It was the *best* possible time. And I'm the best person to ask. Because he doesn't expect his mother's side from me. Just yours."

Tim looked at the floor and nodded. "You really clobbered me when you said that, you know?"

"I know."

He nodded, looking at the floor. Another woman he couldn't trust. When it got down to who should be taking care of Jason. "*Jesus Christ*, Audrey!"

Audrey waited. The doc had been married and claimed his children as an excuse for excluding Audrey from much of his life. Tim was married. In a way. To being Jason's father. And once again there wasn't a whole lot of room for her in someone's life—someone, God help her, she loved.

Tim stood up. "I don't know whether you should have said that then or not."

Once again Audrey was scared. "I don't either. But I had to know."

Tim laughed in a bust. "There it is. *You* had to know."

"Yes. *I* have to know. If there's room for me to be part of this. You and Jason. Or am I expected to stay on the outside?"

72

THEY WERE INTRODUCED to Maurice Allen inside a players' entrance to the Garden. The other members of the Wiseapples— the exhibition team Allen had created twenty-five years before and had reinvented every year since—were much younger than Allen, the oldest about Tim's age. They were also taller than Tim or Allen and wore their hair in various lengths of Afro. Allen's was short and gray. He was in his mid-fifties, Tim figured, but he was trim and his carriage easy. He had a good look at each of them as he shook hands. Quite as if he's glad to meet us, Tim thought. Likes people.

"Do you play basketball yet, Jason?" Allen said.

"I try to. My dad teaches me."

"I bet he's a good teacher."

"Yeah. He is. But the ball's too big."

"You'll grow up to it. Think of getting him a smaller ball, Tim?"

"I did."

"It's still too big," Jason said.

Allen laughed. "I got to take your dad away with me for a while." He said to his road manager, "Put these people down front where I can find them." He turned and extended his hand. "I'm glad to have met you, Audrey. I expect I'll see you during the game. You, too, Jason."

Tim put a hand on Audrey's shoulder and leaned over and whispered, "I'm sorry there was no room for you in that conversation."

She flared inside and then saw that the poor man was serious. "I suppose it was all those big balls," she said. Jason had taken hold of her hand. She kissed Tim quickly on the cheek. "Have fun out there. Enjoy, okay?"

"Okay. Keep Jason close."

Tim walked with Allen to the Wiseapple dressing room. They were lounging, in no hurry to suit up or warm up for a game twenty-five minutes away. The Mets were already out on the floor. Tim was the only one who wasn't dressed.

Allen introduced him to the Wiseapples. They were perfunctory and uninterested. "Tim started with the Doctor in college."

"No shit," said the Wiseapple who was known as Clown. His voice had no inflection, but he looked at Tim. The other Wiseapples had open interest. They questioned Tim, compared observations. It felt good to Tim. He was with his people again. Clown interrupted. "Hey, Nurse. You're a nurse, right, I didn't misapprehend?"

"You got it."

"Don't you know this is a big boys' game?"

Oh boy, Tim thought. The rest of the time my people are mostly women. Tim saw that Maurice Allen had paused, was about to intrude.

Tim said, "It's a man's game, too."

Clown made a sound of disgust. People began paying attention to changing clothes. Maurice Allen took off his jacket and tie and said, "All you need to know is going to take about two minutes. On offense, you people do whatever you want. Try to score."

"Against these guys?"

The Wiseapples were pleased except for Clown. Allen said, "They're not perfect. They can be scored on. Course, your people haven't played regular in a considerable time. I understand that. But you got some shots coming your way from people like yourself and Mozart Wills and Scotty McGettigan—"

Tim looked at Clown. "And we have another nurse. Named Diana Vezzina. She played at UCLA. She's an insect, a darting insect. And she'll steal the ball, your shorts, and your other balls, and she won't give any of them back."

There was laughter. "Gonna *love* this game." But Clown just stared at Tim.

Tim said, "What's wrong, man? I didn't make it to the NBA either."

"Big deal. Started with Dr. J." ·

Maurice Allen said, "On defense, stay man-to-man. No zone, no switching." He saw Tim frown. "It's how we do our thing. We do the same for you, okay?"

"Okay."

"You tell your people just listen and we'll tell you to do certain things at certain times. Remember, it's a show. Go along with what we tell you to do."

"Like what?"

"Something simple like, 'Follow me.' Or, 'I'm going to throw you the ball. Be surprised. Throw it back to me.' Course, we talk in a whisper. Don't try to steal the ball. Just let us do things around you. Any problem with that?"

"No."

"Remember. In the end we always lose."

There were a lot of empty seats in Boston Garden as the Wiseapples, in splendid warmup suits, took the floor after the raggedly uniformed Mets and put on a stylish exhibition. The Mets looked around at the empty seats and felt they had failed before the game had even begun. "We didn't even raise the money for Pedi," Diana Vezzina said.

Elin Maki, setting out her trainer's kit, said, "There's a certain amount of public reluctance at the moment."

"You mean *resistance*," Scotty said. "Because they think we're pricks, walking out."

"Because they think the *house officers* are pricks for walking out," Diana said. "The rest of us are noble."

"I'd like to win the game," Scotty said.

"It's an exhibition, not a game," Tim said.

"I want to win the fucking exhibition."

"Wiseapple opponents always do."

"I mean *win* it," Scotty said.

"Yeah. And I'd like to be playing in the NBA," Tim said.

"I'm not used to so many empty seats," Mozart said.

"That's because Yale's such a small fucking place," a surgeon said.

"Ease it down, guys," Tim said.

The Mets had a status inconsistency. There were internists, surgeons, psychiatrists—and Tim, one of two nurses. On the floor, though, they deferred to Tim's skill and leadership.

Scotty looked at the spectators. "They want us to lose. I know it."

"You mean today or next week?" Mozart said.

"Let's pay attention to right now, huh?" Tim said. "For one thing, there're 15,320 seats in this joint and almost 6,000 of them are paid for. Plus other donations. Pedi gets its unit."

The surgeon said, "Bennett's got the fucking *mayor* with him."

"Wouldn't you?" Scotty said. "If your medical staff was going to walk out on you?"

When the Mets took the floor to be introduced, there was silence and then some booing. Tim saw Jason and Audrey sitting together on a floor-level bench. Jason was excited and talking and pointing at Tim. Audrey stood up and began applauding for the Mets. She was followed by about half of the audience.

It was hopeless from the beginning—except that the Wiseapples created a great deal of laughter at both teams' expense—and any dreams of glory individual Mets may have allowed themselves were put to rest in the sheer exertion of keeping up.

The Clown was the Wiseapple floor leader. He called the plays, decided on the sequence of events. There were the

276 *Richard Frede*

instructions not to try to steal the ball, but at one point Clown said, "Okay, you turkeys, it's open season on Maurice," and the Wiseapple announcer explained that this was a ball-handling exhibition and the object was for the Mets to try to take the ball away from Maurice Allen. Then, for nearly two minutes, Maurice Allen drove and dribbled on his own, in and out of the Mets, up to the board where he could have taken a lay-up, back out to the key, outside the three-point line and back in again, an athlete in complete command as if he were on a stage and the Mets were part of a set design and he was really alone out there. And he quit, Tim saw, only when his body was played out by the demands he put on it. He lofted a long shot from too far out and it hit the backboard, hit the rim, and bounced off. Clown jumped, got the rebound, hit the floor, faked, twisted, and laid the ball in, and Tim stopped the game and pointed to Maurice Allen and began applauding. The audience followed.

"Okay, Turkey," Clown said to Tim, "you and I go one on one from here on in. Here, Turkey, catch the ball. Look surprised. Throw it back to me." Tim did. A fool for his son to see and Clown making fun of him as well. "Okay, Turkey, follow me, follow me," moving Tim back, and back, Tim not allowed to go for the ball. Then Clown rose up in front of him, both bodies going up, and Clown stuffed the ball, making Tim look stupid. Then he led Tim through it again, reversing his lay-up and finishing with a slam dunk that left Tim beaten and too tired to play. He subbed for himself. "So long, Turkey," Clown said.

Tim sat on the bench and said to Elin, "I can't do the things I used to be able to. Your mind says do it, but your body doesn't let you do it."

With a quarter left, the Wiseapples were up 56 to 26 effortlessly and still providing amusement. When Tim went back in, he was oblivious to everything but the game. And it began to come back to him without thinking. He drove in against Clown, knowing he was outdefensed, clearing the path behind him and dropping the ball back to Mozart, who arced it in with a swish. Tim did it again, faking to Mozart and firing underneath to Scotty as Clown went up and Scotty laid the ball in. Once again, varying the same play, the Wiseapples in a collapsed defense, Tim went up and laid the ball off outside to Diana, who made the longer shot—and Clown came down on Tim's foot.

No one saw it except Maurice Allen. "Go see how the bench feels, Clown."

"Without me, you got no laughs."

Tim said, "Leave him in, Maurice, he and I are one on one—a team, aren't we, Clown?"

When Tim felt no limp he was back, he found, at a level he had forgotten. Peripherally he saw Valerie walking along the floor-level bench toward Jason and Audrey. In college, too, she had come to games very late. Tim realized that he trusted Audrey absolutely. He could play his game. It was a security he had never known with Valerie. He eased back into the rhythm of the game and found his own as well. He was playing with the intensity and concentration and lack of emotion that came from being absolutely one with the game, not thinking but doing. He got a pass in to Scotty and Scotty was defensed and so were the other Mets and the ball came back to him outside the three-point circle. And there Tim stood alone with it, Clown in front of him, the eyes, the face, the entire body studious, not taking Tim for granted at all. Tim drifted the ball floor to palm without thinking, already setting up a little weave in the rhythm, a little misdirection in the bounce. "You can't get this ball, Clown."

"Oh, that's smart, Nurse. Rules say I can't."

"Rule's off. *I* say you can't."

"Maurice, this nurse wants to play with me."

From in by the basket Maurice Allen said, "Go ahead."

"Fuckin' right" and Clown's arm swept in, what Tim wanted, the commitment to a ball fake, but Clown got back and Tim tried a head fake together with the ball fake, knowing Clown was too experienced for that, showing Clown how slow and unskilled he was, and then gave Clown the slightest foot fake, so subtle Clown was helpless not to react to it because it had to be the real thing, and Clown was leaning back a little and Tim jumped and got the long shot off and, just as he remembered it in times he had already forgotten, times when he was having a *great* game, he knew the ball was going in.

The ball reached the apex of the parabola and then fell steeply, made a small thud against the rim and then a swish through the net. The Wiseapples were already in a showoff fast break when Maurice Allen raised his arms and whistled. The Wiseapples stopped moving. There was quiet in the Garden. Allen called for the ball. He took it in his left hand and held out his right hand to Tim. "We all like to see things like that happen." To Tim's surprise, Clown nodded. Allen handed the ball to Tim. "We'll sign it later. Give it to your son."

"Thank you, Maurice. Shit. This may be one of the great moments of my life."

"I hope not."

Tim went to the sideline and subbed for himself and took the ball to Jason. Valerie had squeezed in between Jason and Audrey. The boy grinned, embarrassed and proud, as Tim handed him the ball, and then, one arm around the ball, he put his other arm around his father and hugged him.

After the game, the Wiseapples came over and signed the ball for Jason. There was a lot of picture-taking with Bennett Chessoff and the mayor and Maurice Allen and, to Scotty McGettigan's surprise, all the Back Bay Mets at Bennett's insistence. By then most of the crowd had left and Tim and Jason and Maurice were grouped together for a final photograph. Afterward, Valerie said, "Come, Jason. It's time to go home."

Jason looked from parent to parent.

"You're staying with me, Jason," Tim said.

"Can you do that? Is that okay?" Then he looked at Audrey, as if for an independent opinion.

"Don't you look at *her*, young man. She's not your mother! *I am*. Now you're coming home with me!" Valerie took the boy's hand angrily.

"Do I have to?" Jason said to all three adults.

"You see what you're *doing* to Jason?" Valerie said. "And you call yourself a *nurse*." Some people in the seats behind them had paused to watch. Valerie noted them. She screamed at Tim, "You *like* being the center of attention, *don't you?*" She looked up. "Come on down here, people! See a man try to take a child from its mother."

"*Please*, Mom."

Maurice Allen came back and took the ball and said to Jason, "Let's you and I play a game, let the big folks play theirs."

"That's my son you're . . . you . . ." Jason turned to stare at her and Valerie stopped. She turned to Audrey. "You're . . ."

"A friend of Tim's."

"You're . . . tired-looking. You could probably do something with yourself if you decided to. Still, I suppose you're up to Tim's standards. Whatever they are these days." She stopped. "Your name is Audrey. Audrey Rosenfeld."

"Yes."

"So tell me something, Audrey. You do girl things together or boy-girl things together?"

"Mrs. Holbrook, I'm not understanding you."

"Jewish."

"Again?"

"You're Jewish."

"Yes."

"Please, Mom!" Jason screamed. His tears plomped on the basketball.

"I'm tired, I've been out all night—" Valerie stopped herself. She said to Tim, "You're preventing a little boy from going home with his mother. And the judge said you aren't a fit parent for him." Jason stood still among the four adults. Valerie's voice deepened. "I've been talking to lawyers, too, Tim. We will have a motion for contempt of court. A motion to compel and enforce . . . Jason will be returned to me. And I swear you'll never see him again."

"No!" Jason screamed out.

"It's not going to happen," Tim said and put his arm around Jason.

"All he wants to do is watch television," Valerie said. Oddly, she said it to Audrey.

73

AT THE OTHER END of the bench, her obligation to be photographed completed, Elin Maki was packing up the trainer's kit and trying to ignore the painful scene between Jason's parents. It was not too difficult. She had a pain of her own.

It was, Elin decided, probably the sight of all those sweaty male bodies out there. And, of course, the libidinous Hal Levy fantasy she had allowed herself the past few days. She was simply as sexed up as she had ever known herself to be. She was irritable, she had an irritation, an inflammation that extended from between her legs well up into her mind, which it was successfully dominating. She very nearly put her hand between her legs to rub herself with a little reassurance, but it appeared unseemly for a woman of her professional stature to do so on the floor of Boston Garden, it was not the sort of exhibition, presumably, the fans had come to see.

She wondered if Hal was going to be doing a shift with Trina this evening. She had paperwork to do at the hospital, and it would give her the opportunity to bring herself to Hal's attention in the event she might be able to induce him to fulfill, so to speak, her base expectations. Her body entirely *craved* to grip and be filled by a male body and, whatever reservations she herself might have, it was Hal's body her body had decided upon.

And then Hal Levy presented himself to her. He came down from the seats to the Mets' bench and was just sort of *hanging around*, like a displaced teenager, and for a moment Elin felt a little sorry for him, thought he was a little funny, and then pure lust dispersed all that.

He was making himself available to her. Elin recognized that clearly. But the simpleton clearly did not know what else to do.

He is a *boy*, Elin thought, as inexperienced as a *boy*, though clearly in a man's body, and clearly frightened out of his wits about what to do next.

She proposed to herself various pieces of encouraging dialogue she might offer him.

Not working today?

How'd you like to come back to my place? I've got an interesting bottle of wine I'd like you to crack.

How'd you like to spend the afternoon in bed with me?

Part of the afternoon in bed with me?

The best part of the afternoon in bed with me?

How'd you like to come back to my place and just fuck?

She said to Hal, "Hi."

"Hi."

"Going back to the hospital?"

He shrugged. "I don't think so."

"No?"

"No."

Couple of fucking teenagers, Elin thought. *Non*fucking teenagers. "Enjoy the game?" What the fuck am I talking about? *Which* game?

"Tim Holbrook was terrific. I never thought I'd get to see Maurice Allen play."

"Why?"

"So old, you know. Did you ever see him play?"

"On television. Reruns," Elin said. I am giving this whole fantasy up.

"Well, I don't really know what I'm going to do this afternoon. There's studying to do. But you know what it's like. There's no time for anything for weeks, and then all of a sudden there's a whole afternoon free and you don't know what to do with it."

"You don't."

"No."

"No movie you want to see?" Elin said.

"Well, I guess. A couple. Any movies you want to see?"

"I want to go back to my place and have a glass of wine. Your company would give me a great deal of pleasure."

Hal blushed. "Sure."

The apartment was hot. Elin had forgotten to open all the windows to the spring air before she'd gone out. She changed out of her functional slacks and jersey—for treating fallen warriors on the floor—and put on a light dress.

She went into the kitchen and opened a bottle of wine, and then she and Hal sat together on the couch and talked about the wine and other bottles of wine. She stood up. She looked good in the dress. It fit her well. She went to the bathroom. Goddamn sexual tension. She hoped she hadn't ruined the mood of it all by flushing the toilet. She wasn't sure whether she was ready to rape Hal or throw him out for inactivity.

But he kept looking at her so shyly and studiously from behind his thick lenses that she decided she would stay with him for as much desultory conversation and as many bottles of wine as it took. Unless she went to sleep first. Though that was unlikely, what with the inflammation in her crotch.

She stretched her arms in what she presumed to be a

provocative gesture, emphasizing her breasts. *Look at the lean, long length of my supple body, the lushness of my boobs, you dolt.*

"It's good to relax," Hal said. "Have the day off. Thanks for inviting me."

"You're welcome."

"If ARI goes out—"

"ARI is going to go out."

"Third-year students are going to be doing scullery duty."

"It used to be called being a medical orderly. You'll be desperately needed, and that's true."

"What about you?"

"People are going to be discouraged from coming to Primary Care. That will free me to make rounds on medical floors."

"Being a doctor."

"Being a doctor," Elin said.

She poured wine into his glass and he got up and went to the bathroom. *Sexual tension, sexual tension,* Elin thought. He came back into the room and remained standing, looking at her uncertainly, as if his lenses had gotten out of focus.

"Everyone should have the chance to play doctor, don't you think?" Elin said.

But he didn't respond. The dolt had no sense of humor. The inflammation had spread throughout Elin. She reached behind herself and unhooked her dress and unzipped it as she stood up. Then she pulled it over her head. *"It's goddamn hot in here!"* she said, as if it were all his mismanagement, which it was.

She stood in front of him in her bra and bikini brief and he looked at her, and she wondered if he were really deciding whether she was a psych case or not. He didn't touch an article of his own clothing, but he did come to her and begin touching her, kissing her, making love to her, and she discovered, as she helped him out of his clothes and out of the rest of her own, that he was *adoring* her.

74

"IT'S NICE to have you home," Jimbo said to Day.

"Are you being affectionate or sarcastic?"

"Can't you tell?"

"Just being cautious, my love." She crossed the kitchen to where he was sitting with a cup of coffee and put her hands on his shoulders and kissed him lightly. He reached up and stroked her hair. "You've been having a rough time," Day said. "I know. I'm sorry. I don't do it to hurt you. Lord knows, I don't *want* you to worry."

"I know, I know," Jimbo said. Day sat down on a chair next to him and turned it so she faced him and placed her hand in his. "I know you do your best to take care of the baby, and yourself. But I get scared. For both of you. I get fucking ripshit," he said gently.

"I know," Day said just as gently.

"I love you, Day. I love you so much. Sometimes I think you're not going to give me the chance to love the baby. I trust you, you're a nurse, you know better'n I do how to take care of yourself and the baby. I know that in my head. But my *feelings*, that's something else. I get scared. I get *so* scared."

"We're both going to be fine. The baby and me. You'll see. I'm careful, no matter what your feelings say. The three of us are going to be one terrific family."

Jimbo nodded. "Okay," he said softly. He nodded again. "Okay." He stood and drew Day up against him and kissed her gently. "The three of us are going to be one terrific family. I take your word for it."

75

TO THE CONSIDERABLE SURPRISE of participants and sponsors alike, the next day's big Sunday edition of the *Eagle* carried the Back Bay Mets–Harlem Wiseapples game on its front page. A two-column photograph at the bottom of the page showed the Mets in play—Tim with the ball, Scotty and Mozart nearby, two other Mets in clear focus.

The head ran: WHICH ONE WANTS TO PLAY? The text, immediately below, had Lynn Keating's byline.

> The way it is now, only one member of this medical team is going to play ball Monday morning. The rest are going to walk. Off this court and probably into a court of law. For violating their professional obligations to the patients of Back Bay Metropolitan Hospital. Four members of this medical team are doctors and they've decided not to take care of patients after midnight tonight. They want more money. To support their Guccis and Mercedeses. Who's going to stay on the job and care for desperately needful patients?
>
> The one in the middle. The fellow with the ball. He's a nurse.
>
> *Continued Page 14* STRIKE

Trina, on an early double shift in the ER with some other nurse clinicians, was privy to Scotty McGettigan's reaction once he had withdrawn to a conference room to deliver it. *"What fucking Guccis? What fucking Mercedeses?* I still owe forty thousand dollars on my *medical* education!"

It required a colleague who was a shrink to calm him down.

"I don't *want* to calm down! I am fucking-A *ripped*. Is this the kind of coverage we can expect?"

"Yes," said the shrink. "That's why it's advisable to calm down."

"I don't *know* anyone with Guccis or a Mercedes. Not on the staff."

"Yes, you do," Mozart said. "Turn to page fourteen, strike, like the article says."

Anita Rounds was already doing it. And there was Trevor Davis outside Back Bay Metropolitan Hospital, and he was leaning against his Mercedes convertible, his loafered feet crossed, a faddish logo on his jersey.

Dr. Trevor Davis, a senior resident in surgery, said, "Back Bay Met's mission is to provide training for its doctors and care for its patients. Everyone gets what they need, doctors and patients. You could pay a lot for the training we actually get paid to receive at Back Bay Met. I don't understand this strike. I don't know a doctor on the staff who should need more money."

Scotty was fired again. "Who the fuck pays *his* bills?"

Dr. Davis is "morally shocked" by any consideration of a strike.

Asked about the ability of the nursing staff to maintain patient care in the absence of house officers, Dr. Davis was quick to say "Nurses can't keep this hospital open. If they could, they'd be doctors."

Trina said, "Some of us are in very early today to address that problem. The rest of the contingency plans for the ER if you people go out. Could we get to that now?"

76

IT WAS LATE AFTERNOON, and the more information Tim got from phone calls, the more certain he became that the HOs were going out. He called Warren Gates, his attorney. Jason and Audrey were playing on the floor.

"It's important that you stay with Jason," Warren said. "Take personal time."

"I can't. The strike. I've got to be on the unit.

"I appreciate your dedication, Tim. I appreciate how needed you'll be. But it's going to look lousy in court. What Harrelson'll see is the noncustodial parent snatches the child—and then what? Does the same thing Valerie did? Leaves him alone?"

"I'm in a bind, Warren. Normally he'd be in school while I'm at work. And there's an afterschool program. But if I take him to his school, Valerie'll grab him back."

"I know."

"He'd be alone . . . But it'd be daytime . . . He said it was okay with him . . ."

"Isn't there anyone you can get to come in and stay with him?"

"I haven't been able to find anyone. I've just had a couple of hours at it."

"It will look really bad, Tim, to leave him alone. The first working day you have with him—"

"Christ! Don't I know? I don't want to leave him alone at all. I can't transfer him to the new school till the court—"

"I know—"

"I'd stay home with him for weeks! It's this emergency situation tomorrow. I'm *responsible* for my ICU. I can't just—"

"I know. But you've got to appreciate how *Harrelson's* going to look at it. Valerie's lawyer will have you in shambles. I would. He'll just point out that your profession prevents you from being a responsible parent."

"*Christ!* Valerie isn't even home at night, Warren!"

"I know that. What are you going to do?"

"I'll call you back." He hung up and looked at his son. "I'm sorry, Jason. You shouldn't have to hear all that."

To Tim's surprise the boy smiled at him. "That's okay. I hear a lot about stuff at Mom's."

Tim said to Audrey, "I apologize to you, too. I didn't know the conversation was going to get so intense."

"No, I didn't like the conversation at all. But I rather liked that there was room for me. To be part of it." She paused. "I hope you know that if it wasn't for the HOs going out, I'd stay with Jason myself."

"I know. But if it weren't for the HOs going out, *I'd* stay with him. It would, in fact, be a joy. Odd thing here. We're both nurses. We're both head nurses. How come you'd be the one to stay home?''

Audrey's anger was apparent. "Because I'm lazy. Because I'm generous. Because I'm the female. Because—'' She stopped. "Tim, what if you were a working mother like nearly everyone else in the world—at the hospital, anyway?''

"Jesus,'' Tim said.

"You have a day care center at the hospital. You have a child. For a few days the child will be unable to attend school. You have essential work to do at the hospital. That is one reason why there *is* a day care center at the hospital. For working parents like you.''

"Jesus,'' Tim said. "That's brilliant.''

"Can we go play baseball now, Daddy?''

"Something else,'' Audrey said.

"I'll listen to anything you have to say.''

"After work tomorrow, you and Jason go and see Trina Frankian. She initiates Fifty-one-A referrals. She'll know the social worker you ought to get in touch with.''

"Brilliant. *Brilliant.*'' Tim was physically excited. "I'll call Warren right back.''

Audrey said to Jason, "Believe it or not, I played shortstop on a baseball team. Till I was in fifth grade.''

"With *boys?*''

"Yeah, with boys. And most of 'em couldn't field or hit as well as me.''

"Why'd you quit?''

"I was burnin' up the league, kid. In sixth grade they made me play girls' softball.''

"Those dirty—''

"Yeah. Let's you and me go toss the ball around while Dad makes his call. Then he can join us.''

Tim said, "Are you familiar with a Fifty-one-A?''

Warren's end of the phone was silent for several seconds. "Jesus. Terrific. Back door. Who you been talking with, you got other counsel?''

Tim explained about Audrey.

"My compliments to Miss Rosenfeld. Also tell her that her presence will be useful at the hearing.''

"For what?''

"Bluntly, that she's sleeping with you.''

Tim laughed. "She's playing *baseball* with Jason right now."

"Good for her. She's covering all the bases."

"I mean, all of this is pretty innocent, Warren. No one's doing any of this on purpose."

"Bluntly, I would like to get it on the record, in court, that you and Miss Rosenfeld are fucking together."

"I'll speak to her about it."

"Relay my reluctance. Explain the necessity."

"Do you want photographs?"

"That would offend Judge Harrelson. He'd rather hear it. All right . . . looking at my notes. Fifty-one-A. Expedite hell out of things if you can get it. Juice up the motions with official credibility. DSS, right?"

"Department of Social Services. Investigation of a home for potential child abuse and neglect."

"Can you get it done?"

"I'll know tomorrow. Jason'll go to the hospital's day care center. What do you think?"

"It's not school. It's not his customary environment. But under the circumstances, till the court resolves his disposition, it's a reasonable alternative. A responsible one. You're nearby. You can even have lunch with him."

"Warren, I'm going to have to familiarize you with my work. You don't get lunch breaks on the ICU. Most of the time you don't get lunch."

"You get a Fifty-one-A filed that confirms Friday night, it's going to have weight with the court. It's going to have to be considered. Regardless of your profession."

The house officers began going out at midnight. Tim stayed up and called in to make sure it was actually happening.

FOUR

Stop Time

77

THE HOUSE OFFICERS began the job action—none of them referred to it as a strike—at midnight. Most of them ceased to perform their duties and quit the hospital complex at that hour. Others instituted a twenty-four-hour picket line and informational service in front of the New Wing on Tremaine Avenue. Supplemental police and auxiliary lighting had already been placed on station. Patient requirements did not allow everyone to leave at midnight, but most were home or on the street by two A.M. A very few were still in an OR or in the ER or at a bedside at six A.M.

But even at midnight very little changed. A great number of PRN orders—medication at the nurse's discretion—had been written by the HOs before they went out. By midnight, emergencies were being triaged to other facilities by C-Med radio from Boston City Hospital. Emergencies that nevertheless arrived at Back Bay Metropolitan were treated by trauma units that were always part of the picketing. By morning, when the walkout was entirely established, the EMTs and paramedics out in the rigs actively helped to divert patients from Back Bay Met to other hospitals in the overall catchment area—Beth Israel, Deaconess, Brigham and Women's, Children's—and even across town to BCH, Mass. General, and Tufts–New England Medical Center.

Nevertheless, some patients had to be accepted by Back Bay Met because of the conditions or circumstances in which they arrived. And so some new patients continued to be admitted.

Trina worked a double shift, leaving the ER after her regular shift to go to the medical floors and help reduce patient anxiety.

By five-thirty, when she got up, Day found that the "strike" at Back Bay Metropolitan Hospital was the lead item on television and radio news, and later she found it headlined in both newspapers. As she drove to work, she found it on every newscast. All the stories, in whatever medium, eventually emphasized the same points. That the strike was a source of tremendous danger to the patients. That in the best of times the hospital was understaffed. That the nursing staff, upon which the stress and shock of the strike would mainly fall, would be severely worked, painfully worked, and that the chance of human error, due to both ignorance and overwork, had been escalated to an unacceptably perilous level.

It was scary, Day had to admit. She was therefore astounded by what she learned at her desk. It was the best report rate she could remember. She turned to Midge Kelly, the surgical supervisor at the next desk. Midge had the same sort of report rate for her floors. The nursing staff had come in almost without exception.

78

ON EVERY FLOOR it was like skeletal staffing because of the absence of the house officers.

It was the workload, not the staffing itself. On Med Three Audrey and Coralee had an LPN, an aide, and the third-year medical student Hal Levy to help out. "We're positively overstaffed," Coralee said. Not that the full staff afforded enough time to anyone.

"You begin to appreciate the little things the HOs were always doing," Audrey said.

"That's why they're striking. All the little things they had to do. Instead of doctoring. Just like men, though. Walk out and leave the work to the ladies."

"Coralee. Look at all the women HOs—"

"Look at 'em and count 'em on four hands."

They had a hotline to use for problems short of an emergency that required immediate resolution. The customary procedure remained in the event of an emergency such as an arrest—the HOs on the picket line were all carrying beepers. Med Three had not yet been assigned its visiting physician. The visit would be responsible for the one floor and would provide the nursing staff with the medical orders that he deemed necessary after telephone consultation every two or three hours. He was supposed to visit the floor and make rounds with the head nurse first.

But, at eight-thirty, he was not there when he was needed, Audrey hadn't even been told who he was, and the hotline, Audrey thought, ought not to be burdened with questions about obvious procedure. Day had said that herself. More or less.

Chanda, the young woman in with Jan Fox, had a rapidly rising temperature. It had been elevated when Audrey came in. The night nurse had not wanted to do anything. Chanda was allergic to the aspirin and Tylenol families, and without the familiar structure of the physician consult, the night nurse had decided to wait the little while until her head nurse came in and decided what to do. Audrey had initiated a noninvasive treatment, but it was not covered by a treatment order. In order to lower the temperature, Audrey had simply had the aide give Chanda a tepid water sponge bath.

But her temperature was still rising at eight-thirty. Chanda's diagnosis was mononucleosis and there were no new signs or symptoms which counterindicated that diagnosis. Audrey iced the patient herself. That was a slightly more serious procedure than a simple sponging, but she was now responsible for having twice done something she was not supposed to have done without a physician's order, but she managed to bring the temperature down.

It was simple work, clearly a decision that was not at odds with the patient's history or orders—and it could cost Audrey her license if anyone wanted to go after it. It was that way with the nursing staff throughout the hospital.

Day called just after that. "I'll be bringing your visit, Dr. Schoonoler, endocrinologist. Very good at what he does. Very. But most of it is research and teaching. He's a visit on the Gold Coast. Pleasant, but limited. Doesn't see patients much."

"Well, what's he doing on my floor?"

"He volunteered. You were supposed to get Dr. Auerbach. He's down with something undiagnosed. Dr. Schoonoler of-

fered to fill in. Captain Malamet's being returned to you from
the unit. You've got Mr. Jones, the sickle cell from Deer
Island, somewhere in the building on his way to you—''

"Don't they know—"

"They sent him over anyway. They figure he belongs with
you. He's been with you always. Can you do a double?''

"I wondered when that was likely to come up.''

"A lot now.''

"Sure.''

"Catch you soon. Dr. Schoonoler in tow.''

First the sickle cell patient, a twenty-eight-year-old black
male, was brought on the floor. He was accompanied by a
uniformed guard from the Deer Island House of Correction.
The guard sat on a folding chair outside the patient's room.
Mr. Jones, the patient, thin and warped in posture, was
unaware, drugged against pain and tight in the fetal position
due to abdominal pain.

Then Tim was on the phone for Audrey. "This is a professional call,'' he said. "Captain Malamet's on his way down
to you.''

"Day just said.''

"He's a class-A hardass as a patient. A macho overlord.
Practically had to be tied down in bed. I bet he's this way
anyway. But the heart attack—the sonofabitch is trying to
prove it didn't happen. He'll drive himself into another one.''

"Not on this floor. I won't allow it.''

"Good luck.''

"You're seeing Trina this afternoon about the Fifty-one-A?''

"Yeah.''

"I want to fix dinner for you and Jason, but I'm doing a
double. Tomorrow?''

"Hey. That's great.''

"I've got a Nurse Practice Committee meeting tomorrow
after work. I was going to shop today. Pick up some things
for me tomorrow?''

"Sure.''

"When you get the key I'll give you the list and everything'll
be home when I get there. So dinner can get done in time for
Jason.''

"He's adaptable. Listen, I didn't want to bring this up till I
saw you—''

"What?''

"Friday. Warren got the hearing scheduled for Friday. Warren wants you there."

"I bet I can guess why. As a character witness?"

"So to speak."

"Will I have to testify how good you are in bed? Or just that you're good in bed. With me. A woman."

"I suspect that will depend upon the extent of Judge Harrelson's prurient interest."

"We could be on strike then, did you know that?"

"No."

"It's another damn rumor. But some of our young firebrands want to go out. In support of the HOs if this thing isn't settled."

"It won't happen."

"Which one?"

"Both. The HO situation didn't get this far if there's a chance of settling. And nurses don't strike."

"Sure. Neither do house officers. What time is the hearing on Friday?"

"Nine o'clock."

Audrey was silent. The silence hurt both of them. "Tim, that may be impossible for me."

"I figured. But it might make an important difference. Whether I get to keep Jason or lose him entirely. Isn't there someone who owes you?"

"Not right now. How are you going to—"

"Nan's coming back on the ICU for the one day. She's had charge before."

"I'll see what I can do. Right now I can't think of anyone. I'll try, Tim." Audrey put the reciever down. Coralee was standing in front of her.

"Jan Fox is not on the floor," she said.

"She left the room while I was icing Chanda."

Coralee put her hand on the phone. "She left the floor, too. Shall I call Security?"

"You better." She turned, and there was Day and Dr. Schoonoler.

Ten minutes earlier Jan Fox had gotten to a pay phone in the lobby of the New Wing. There she looked up the number of the *Eagle* and put in a call to Lynn Keating. It took time and waiting, but Keating did get on the line. "Do you recognize my name?" Jan said.

"I had no idea whether it was *the* Jan Fox or not."

"It's *the* Jan Fox. I'm a patient at Back Bay Met. I saw you in passing the other day. As you were being dispatched for being naughty with Dom Volante. There wasn't time for introductions."

"I had to leave hurriedly. Is there something . . . ?"

"Oh, quite a bit, I think. As colleagues. You're out and can't come in, as I understand it. And I'm in."

"What do you want and what can you give for it?"

"Four or five fifths of vodka, to start with. It leaves you breathless, you know."

"You've got a problem right away, Jan. Booze is not allowed—"

"Of course not. But you and I will be outrageously subtle. In return, I will be your little fly on the wall. All-hearing, all-observant. In addition, you may ask me anything you want and I will endeavor to find it out for you. How it *is* inside the hospital. How it really is. With examples."

"Do you have anything hard?"

"Will you get me five fifths of the other kind of hard?"

"I don't see how I can get it to you."

"Suppose I start you out with a juicy Dom Volante bio and go on to a bedside report of his condition, history, and diagnosis."

"I could do it without mentioning his name."

"Of course you could."

"But I could make it plain who I was writing about."

"You're good at that, Lynn."

"You've read my stuff?"

"Constantly."

"How am I going to get the booze to you?"

"Flowers. You're going to send me flowers. In narrow-necked vases. Wide at the base."

"Fill 'em with vodka, right?"

"Right."

"Kill the flowers, Jan. Won't work."

"Paper flowers. Lots of Japanese shops—"

"Ah."

"Lynn, it's been awfully nice chatting with you, but the security police are approaching and I do believe they're coming to take me away."

"If that's the case, no deal. How are you ever going to get back to me?"

"People call out all the time. Patients do. Next time I'll simply make arrangements."

"You'll have flowers from an admirer. Paper flowers."

"Today, Lynn. And, Lynn, make it a good brand."

Dr. Schoonoler was in his sixties, avuncular and easy. After he spoke with Betty Bowen, Audrey was a little pleased that Med Three had drawn him.

Before they visited Betty, Audrey explained that Betty had been head nurse on this floor for more than a quarter of a century. As she did each time before they entered a patient's room, Audrey summarized the patient's chart. Dr. Schoonoler had reviewed all the charts and discussed them with Audrey at the station. "There's gross weight loss. Since she's elected painkilling, her meds are Demerol, Dilaudid, and morphine."

"All by injection?"

"Yes."

They entered the room. Betty was sitting up and in sweats. "I just woke up," she said.

Dr. Schoonoler introduced himself. He and Betty talked and remembered people they had worked with—though not together—twenty and thirty years before. Then he and Betty discussed her condition.

Betty said, "My concern now is that what's going on is going to be metastatic to the brain."

"You have no basis on which—"

"Thirty years of basis." Betty smiled slightly. "And an educated hunch." She turned to Audrey. She did not smile. "Or perhaps it's my worst fear. Audrey?"

"Yes?"

"I want you to remember this. If I lose consciousness, I want no more support. Not after I lose consciousness."

Audrey nodded.

"Say it for me, will you, please?" Betty said. "What I just asked."

"That if you lose consciousness, you don't want support."

"Thank you." She moved about beneath the covers. "Now what I have to deal with is myself and this hospital. I am so eternally *drowsy*. An instant junkie. I do *not* want the pain, but I do not want to be drowsy, either. I want to be able to help." She lay back, exhausted. "While the HOs are out. It's my floor." She lay still for a moment. "Let's cut the shit till the HOs are back."

"It's going to hurt like hell, Betty," Dr. Schoonoler said.

"I know how it hurts."

"Maybe we can reach a compromise medication. Give you a few hours up, the rest pain-free."

Betty nodded and closed her eyes. "Skip the next round, Audrey."

The visit said to Betty, "We don't need those little bastards out on the picket line at all, do we?"

"We need them a lot," Betty said.

"No, the nursing staff here is too good."

Audrey said, "I thought the chiefs and the rest of you were on their side."

"The chiefs are. I am. I just don't like the little bastards' acting on their own. But you'll show them. You and Betty and the rest."

In the corridor Coralee said, "I just tucked Jan Fox in. Security found her on the telephone over in the lobby."

"Okay, we'll see her next." Audrey said to Dr. Schoonoler, "She left the floor on her own. She's the aortic stenosis. Diabetic, maybe brittle. We don't know the extent of her alcohol use. She gets Isordil, nitro and insulin."

Jan was sitting up and she smiled at them. "I know. I was naughty. I'm sorry."

"If you want to use a telephone, Jan, there are pay phones right upstairs on Med Four. Just tell us when you want to leave the floor."

"This room is so *dreary*. I called an old friend. He wanted to send me flowers. I detest live flowers. They die. But I adore good paper flowers, bright, well made. Not plastic." She turned to Chanda. "Our room will be splendid, dear." But Chanda was asleep. That did not seem to concern Jan.

Audrey introduced Dr. Schoonoler. "So," he said, "you had a cardiac cath and they found a valve that's not quite right."

"You sound cheerful about it," Jan said.

"Fix you up with a new one with probably no trouble at all these days."

"It's the '*probably* no trouble' that concerns me."

"Take care of yourself, keep fit, a woman your age shouldn't have any trouble."

"There we go again. *Shouldn't* have any trouble.' Still, it's open heart surgery. Gives one pause."

"Still, it's not imminent."

"A year to five years," Jan said. "That's imminent enough for me. I've had whole decades slip by."

"A woman of your talent and beauty, there must have been many, many days that were amusing."

"Not many."

Audrey woke Chanda to take her temperature and the young woman dozed off again. "One hundred point five. That's down three points. I've ordered an ice blanket, but it hasn't come. I hope the blanket will be all right." Audrey explained about icing Chanda's temperature down. Dr. Schoonoler frowned at her.

In the corridor he said, "Icing a patient is not a procedure a nurse initiates without orders. You should have consulted with me first."

"I didn't even know your name."

"Yes. Well, it seems the procedure was beneficial. I guess it's all right. But I'm responsible for this floor, you see."

"I understand. I'd appreciate an order for the ice blanket."

"Done," Dr. Schoonoler said and smiled.

Outside the next room Audrey said, "Captain Malamet's just back on the floor after three days on the unit. There's been a lot of testing to rule out. The cardiologist has ordered more of the same on the floor. Blood tests, cardiograms. He's getting Inderal and quinidine and he's got a nitro patch."

They went in. "Welcome back, Captain Malamet. I don't know if you remember me. I'm Audrey, the head nurse. This is Dr. Schoonoler."

Malamet ignored the doctor. "I don't remember you exactly, but I know who you are. The head nurse on the ICU told me. That fellow Tim. He said you helped save my life. You and Day O'Meara. I saw her in the ICU." He paused. "I can't express my thanks."

Audrey laughed. "I imagine not. You look well, your reports look good—"

"I feel terrific. Must have been something temporary."

"It looked permanent for a little while there, Captain. I don't want to alarm you. I want it to be a caution to you. Not to push, not to overdo. You're permitted activity and you can do more for yourself than you could on the unit and you've graduated a distance from help, you don't have to be ten or twelve feet from emergency care. But your reputation has preceded you. You are inclined to be overactive. I would appreciate some self-control.''

"Do my best, Audrey."

Dr. Schoonoler said, "Pity this happening when you had so many years of flying still ahead of you."

"Done?" Malamet said flatly. "I haven't faced that quite yet. Done?"

"You couldn't pass a third class medical now."

"Are you a flight surgeon?"

"No. But I got a private ticket a number of years ago. I know the medical side. Haven't had time for flying in years. Pity." He had Malamet talk with him about flying for a few minutes and then asked Malamet some questions bearing on his cardiac history.

When they were again in the corridor and away from the doorway, Dr. Schoonoler stopped and said, "Why did he arrest? If it's not a clearcut MI?"

"We're looking out for arrhythmia and ventricular ectopy right now. They want to do a cath."

He laughed. "Who does? And when?"

"The HO. Anita Rounds. When she comes back and when Captain Malamet is ready. Unless he prefers having it done at another facility. But he's got to have it done."

Dr. Schoonoler nodded in agreement. He smiled just slightly and said, "You know, Audrey, it's been thirty years since I've seen an arrest. Much less dealt with one."

Oh God, Audrey thought, he's got less practical knowledge than a new intern.

"If that's it," he said, "I'll give you some numbers where I can be reached during the day. The medical school, office, lab, outside office, home . . . Someone should know how to find me."

"Don't you have a beeper?"

"Never need to carry one. But my goodness, you're right. They've got those signals way outside the hospital these days."

"Ten miles."

"Oh, that should get me at home."

"I'm sure Dr. Geier can have you fixed up."

"Why yes. I'll see Mert about it. But not now. I've got to get back to Cambridge to give a class. Why, here's one of our students. Hello there, Levy."

"Dr. Schoonoler."

"Helping out, are you?"

"Yes, sir."

"Good for you. Keep your hands off the nurses now."

Audrey saw that Hal had the decency to blush. Her own face changed color also, but with anger.

"Audrey," Coralee said from the station, "telephone."

She took the phone. "Audrey."

"Hello there."

The fucking *doc*. "This is an inconvenient time. I don't want to talk, anyway."

"I'm in Boston. I thought I'd drop in on you."

Oh, the sonofabitch. He *could*. He had never returned the keys to her building and her apartment. "Don't you dare."

"Then meet me."

"No." She thought quickly. "Arthur, I have a good, strong relationship with someone. A very good man. Let's you and I just—"

"I told you, I intend to see you."

"There's a job action going on."

"I know."

"I'm doing a double."

"Maybe tomorrow then. I'll be in touch."

79

MOLLY CHANG HEARD the patient calling as soon as she entered the floor from the stairwell.

"Nurse! Nurse!"

The floor was otherwise silent, the corridor empty, as if the patient had been left entirely alone. Molly went to him. He lay on his back, his body pulling this way and that, trying to pull away from the pain inside. Molly spoke to him for a moment. She did not usually see patients, but she assessed this one as if she were once again a floor nurse. Then she went to the station and got the patient's chart and studied it until the head nurse showed up a couple of moments later.

Molly said, "You have a PRN narcotic order for the patient's pain."

The head nurse shrugged.

"A narcotic order as circumstances require. You haven't delivered the medication."

"I'm busy."

"You haven't delivered the medication. Why not?"

"He's not in pain. Not really."

"Who the fuck *says* he's not in pain? *He* says he's in pain."

The head nurse hesitated. "All right, Molly. I'll take it to him right away."

"What's the problem?"

"I'm not used to handling this stuff out on my own. All my training is against it. Everything I've been told."

But that occurrence of self-protection was an exception. Throughout the hospital, nurses were making decisions and taking actions they were legally prohibited from taking.

Audrey had a deep vein thrombosis patient, a forty-year-old white man named Russell Younker who had a twin brother who worked the night shift somewhere and came in to visit his brother midmornings. Audrey smiled at the brother on his way in. The brother came back to the station almost immediately.

"My brother . . ."

"Yes?" Audrey said, checking a list of medication orders against missing meds for the third time.

"My brother ain't feelin' so well."

"Like what, Mr. Younker?"

"Got a pain in his back."

"Lying in bed all this time."

Mr. Younker was being treated with a heparin drip, IV infusion, to prevent a suspected blood clot from becoming larger or, if it was not actually there, from developing at all.

"He's acting weird, too."

Audrey looked up. "How?"

"Says he doesn't know me."

Audrey hurried to Mr. Younker's room. The patient had a shortness of breath, a fast pulse rate, and an elevated blood pressure.

Treat for the worst, hope for the best. Rule out a pulmonary embolus. The senior resident in radiology would do that, preliminary pulmonary A-gram—except that Radiology had to be called in from outside or the chief summoned from elsewhere. It wasn't as if Audrey could call and have Mr. Younker moved off the floor.

She climbed the decision tree and found herself out on a limb. She knew what the astute nurse would do. Except that under no circumstances will the nurse obstruct therapy that is in progress. Not without orders to do so.

Fuck it. There was no time to get the visit or someone in off the line.

Treat for the worst and hope for the best and here goes your professional career and maybe one hell of a lawsuit and even criminal charges.

The heparin drip was an anticoagulant. Was the blood so thinned out that the patient was bleeding out somewhere inside himself? She knew his hydration was adequate from his intake and output sheet. She immediately did postural signs. Blood pressure and rate lying reclined. Wait fifteen seconds and then blood pressure and rate sitting up. If the patient has lost blood someplace because of interior bleeding out, there will be a marked difference between the readings.

When Audrey sat Mr. Younker up, there was a blood pressure drop of forty millimeters of mercury. Mr. Younker's blood would not flow against gravity: there was a large amount of blood that wasn't moving, a pool, a bleeding out, a—

Audrey turned the heparin off.

She worked the manual control under the bed as if she had the strength of Wonder Woman until she had the patient flat and his head down, using gravity to profuse the brain with blood.

A retroperitoneal bleed would account for the back pain, the heparin for the confusion when he was unable to recognize his brother.

Whatever happened to the patient now, Audrey had stopped the therapy. She had knowingly acted in an illegal manner.

She signaled for Coralee, for the LPN, for the aide—someone to stay with the patient while she went to the phone. She had made a medical diagnosis and acted on it. He needed an umbrella insertion immediately, a cath insertion in a large venous vessel, pop the umbrella open in the vena cava to prevent a clot from getting to the neck and on to the brain or any move to the lung. No one came. Audrey called aloud.

Betty Bowen entered. Audrey explained. Betty said, "He's stable?"

"Yes."

"You'll have to send him to surgery."

"I'm going to make the call now."

"I'm sorry. You knew that. I'll stay with him."

"Thanks . . . Nurse."

The surgical visit was already in the OR. Page said they would beep a surgeon in off the line. Audrey tried two of Dr. Schoonoler's numbers. According to his schedule he should have been at one of them. He was at neither. Fuck it, Audrey thought, just wasting time. She called the blood bank for a type and cross of at least two units so that she could start replacing the loss from the interior bleed. If someone would tell her to do so. She went back to the patient and took a blood pressure. It was not up where she had gotten it.

She went out to the med cabinets. The heparin would need to be blocked. Protamine. The circulating volume of vascular fluid has to be increased—I want to dilate the vasal constrictive group, she thought. Dopamine. She prepared and took the meds back to the patient and took another blood pressure. She went back to the station. A call was waiting from a surgical HO in off the line.

Audrey summarized what had happened. "I think an umbrella insertion is indicated. I ordered a type and cross of at least two units. Baseline blood pressure is beginning to lower, a blood volume ought to be done. I have protamine and dopamine ready to start up."

The HO was silent. Then he said, "Good. Yes to all that."

"I need orders."

"You've got'em. I'll come up and write them after the umbrella."

While she was still at the station, Audrey got a blood gas back on a new arrival on the floor. He was one of a small population of patients throughout the hospital for which regular testing was being maintained. He was on a vent, though he did not require a vent nurse, just frequent observation, and Coralee was taking care of that.

Audrey scanned the report. The partial oxygen pressure

displeased her. At fifty, it was ten points below what was acceptable. Oxygen is a medication, the physician's prerogative. Again the hotline was busy, there was no HO quickly available, and Dr. Schoonoler's numbers did not produce him. Audrey went immediately to the vent.

The fractional inspired oxygen delivered by the vent was set at a normal room air of 21%. Changing the patient's oxygenation was well outside Audrey's legal authority. She made an estimation and changed the vent's settings so that the oxygen delivery was increased to 40%. She told Coralee what she had done.

"Draw a new blood gas in twenty minutes, huh?" she said to Coralee.

"Right."

She went back to the station and received a report that required another medication decision. But before she dealt with it, she called the ICU and got Tim and asked for an exact computation for oxygen increase to her own vent patient. The new delivery was correct. Dr. Schoonoler could sign an order for it, albeit after the fact.

The next decision had to do with a patient on an insulin drip of five units per hour. The patient showed a blood sugar increase from six-forty to seven sixty-three. Audrey checked the report and the patient's chart, tracking sugar and acetones in the urine, the ketone breakdown of protein. The hotline continued to be busy and she didn't even try Dr. Schoonoler. The patient was in trouble, and she could either do nothing or increase the insulin immediately. She increased the drip to six units per hour.

And so it was throughout the hospital that nurses like Audrey were taking actions forbidden to them. But patient anxiety was abating. It had been intense in the early hours of the morning and had continued so even in the daylight hours. By late morning the competence of the nursing staff had become so apparent to the patients that the need for tranquilizers was significantly reduced and PRN orders for Librium and Valium went unfilled.

80

AUDREY'S DVT HEPARIN drip patient stabilized as a result of her intervention. After the umbrella insertion and a period of observation in a recovery room, he was returned to Med Three with new orders. The vent patient's partial oxygen pressure rose to sixty. An HO eventually came up from the line and wrote orders for the parameters within which the nurses could reset the vent until the PO_2 was stabilized at an acceptable level. The insulin patient's blood sugar responded positively to the six units per hour without injury to his signs or production of undesirable consequences.

Elin Maki, making rounds on the three medical floors that had become her responsibility, reviewed the results at noon. "Nice work, chaps," she said to Audrey and Coralee.

Day said, "Twelve hours, and we haven't lost anyone yet." She looked at her notebook. "In fact, we can begin to dismiss here and there."

"With the visit's okay," Audrey said.

"Oh, sure."

"Jan Fox is a good bet," Elin said. "Her blood sugar's pegged. She wouldn't have been in at all except she boozed some and skipped the insulin. She'll need to come into clinic. We'll monitor the blood sugar and the heart."

"I don't think that's all," Audrey said. "Skipping the insulin and taking on some alcohol. She's a very lonely woman. She wants friends and attention. Maybe that's why she skipped the insulin and drank. To get in here."

Day looked at Elin. "It's a consideration."

"Oh, I agree. Trina's got a line on her, let's see what she says. We've got plenty of shrinks who'd be glad to see a Jan Fox. Dom Volante's getting along fine."

Audrey smiled. "Yup. Same thing. Needed to get out and be with people. Only I don't worry about him the way I do about Jan. He's like someone who's been under water and he's swimming on the surface now. He likes it. He's less afraid. And he's eating like crazy."

They reviewed the other patients. Then Audrey said, "How's it going on the street?"

"You wouldn't believe it," Day said. "The support the HOs are getting from the neighborhood. There're neighborhood people down there talking *other* neighborhood people out of coming in."

"Volunteers," Elin said. "Scotty says it wasn't even organized."

Hal Levy came to the station with a small tray of blue plastic syringes of blood.

"How's the help been?" Elin said to Audrey and Coralee.

Coralee looked at the tray with disgust. "They stacks, but they'se gentry. Been good."

Hal said to Audrey, "Take these down myself?"

"Please."

"I'm just leaving," Elin said. "I need someone to protect me on the stairwell."

On a landing halfway between floors Elin stopped Hal and took the tray from him and put it on the floor. She put her arms on his shoulders and said, "I need a great big deep kiss. Really."

When they released each other Elin said, "I'm a very needy lady I find—with you. And you're a very helpful man."

"I do what I can," Hal said, inspired with physical passion. He put his hands across Elin's buttocks and shifted himself to press her genital area against his own and stepped on the tray of blood, popping two of the cannulas and spraying blood on Elin's white shoes.

She looked down—blood on her shoes, blood on the floor. "Oh shit," she said. "The first screwup of the day and it's a doc who did it."

"Not yet a doc. Maybe I need more experience. With nurses."

Elin read Hal's lack of smile. "I'm sorry, I didn't mean that to hurt you. It was meant to be a joke."

"The kind you used to make with Charles?"

Oh Jesus, that hurts, Elin thought. I didn't *know* we were this serious. Already ready to hurt each other. "I'm sorry," she said, "that you're hurt, but no, it's not the kind of joke I used to make with Charles. Charles discouraged my jokes. Are you discouraging my jokes, Hal?"

"No."

Trevor Davis came down the stairwell and looked at the blood on the floor. He glanced at Elin as he went by and said, "Didn't your mother ever teach you about Tampax?"

"Fuck off," Elin said without looking as he went on down the stairs.

"I'd like to, but I don't believe in striking. I'm on call." He stopped and turned around half a flight below. "Give me a call anytime, Elin. As soon as you've dried up."

Elin stopped Hal from going down after Davis. "Shhh, baby, you almost stepped on the blood again. C'mon. It's not going to do to leave blood on the stairway. We'll have to clean it up."

"What about the bloods?"

"Oh shit. Go back. Draw them. I'll clean up. The nurse gets stuck with the shit detail again."

Just after Elin and Day and Hal left the floor, Debby Fluelling got off the elevator, crisp and fresh in her white dress, cap, stockings, and shoes.

"Let's standardize our watches," Coralee said, "it's only twelve-fifteen."

"I figured I could help."

"You can. But you won't get paid for it."

"That's not why I'm here."

"Welcome aboard Back Bay Metropolitan Hospital."

Dr. Schoonoler got back on the floor around three-thirty.

"I tried to get you this morning," Audrey said.

He smiled at her. "Makes for a tight day, this schedule. Doing my own work and being here. Not much chance for the telephone. I'm sure you did splendidly, Audrey."

"I wish you'd get a beeper."

"Absolutely. First chance. Oh. Ran into a friend of yours. Lecturing our way this week. Thoracic surgery. Arthur Truell. From New York. Nice fellow. Said he was going to call you, hoped to look you up."

Audrey took Dr. Schoonoler around to the patients.

When they got to Jan Fox's room he beamed and said, "Well *now*. I see your flowers have arrived. Your admirer is most *certainly* an admirer."

Jan looked at Schoonoler directly. "It was *the kindness of a stranger*, actually."

"But—"

"A woman in my position learns to depend upon that sort of thing."

Audrey was suddenly alerted but she did not know to what, except that Jan was not herself as Audrey had come to know her. She was settled, less intense, her inflections neither hysterical nor pleading. Well, there were a lot of stabilizing factors. Insulin as prescribed, emotional support, diet—

"I have a friend, Miss DuBois, a sort of voice coach—she sometimes helps me with what I want to say."

"A collaborator," Dr. Schoonoler said. "Will she be visiting?"

"Miss DuBois regrets. She's unable to visit at all."

"Oh, I'm sorry."

"That's why she sent the flowers. It's the goddamn rutting, you know." She smiled.

Audrey said, "Jan, maybe I don't understand. I'm not making connections between the things you're saying."

Jan looked at Audrey and assessed her. "Oh, *honey*, I'm *so* sorry, I'm just making little, bitty literary things. Jokes. For my own pleasure." She sat up. "That's it. No more."

Audrey felt rotten. She hadn't seen Jan enjoying herself before. And she'd interrupted it and now she had no idea why. Careful, Audrey thought, you've been interrupting things all day. Stop it. You can't be right all the time.

Dr. Schoonoler said to Jan, "Everything's so gosh darn right with you, we'll have you back in a centerfold next thing." He turned to Audrey. "I think we'll send this young woman home day after tomorrow or—"

"You can't do it. *I haven't got a home.*"

"I'm terribly sorry," Dr. Schoonoler said. "Is it an economic matter? Were you dispossessed?"

"Au contraire, Doctor, I am the possessed." She smiled. "*Please don't send me home.*"

"I don't understand."

"I think Jan's saying she's comfortable here and she'd like to stay."

"I do not require a translator when English is being spoken, Nurse. But she's right," Jan said. "I might sicken at home. I might die. I need protection awhile longer. *Please.*"

"Protection? Protection from what?" Dr. Schoonoler said.

"From myself. Please."

In the corridor he said, "I think that psychiatric interview is definitely in order. Her behavior is quite bizarre. Of course, we might look for an organic basis. If this keeps up, I could have her transferred to New Wing Five on a research protocol, do a complete metabolism."

"Jan would love it on the Gold Coast," Audrey said, thinking, Be careful you're not being manipulated, Doc.

"Also, Nurse, I would appreciate less interference when I'm talking with a patient."

"I wasn't aware that—I'm sorry, Doctor."

"Very good. Let's see the others."

Three of the others caused Dr. Schoonoler observable irritation—the three whose therapy had been altered by Audrey. They returned to the station. Dr. Schoonoler was silent, his face set in anger. The station and the area immediately around it were unusually highly populated. Coralee, Hal, and Debby were in the station, Jan, Chanda, Percy Stevens, and Ralph Malamet were talking nearby, there was the guard outside Mr. Jones's room, Betty Bowen was heading toward the station, and a couple of other patients were walking for exercise.

Just outside the station Dr. Schoonoler suddenly turned to Audrey. His voice was low and harsh and carried to everyone. "You didn't even have orders, you didn't have the *right*, to take postural signs."

"I decided it was necessary."

"That decision is not yours. Everything you did could have been countertherapeutic."

"Everything I did was intentionally beneficial. Everything I did *was* beneficial."

Dr. Schoonoler's voice rose. "*Luckily.*"

"Not luckily, *Doctor*. I have my own base of scientific knowledge—"

"You have not been to medical school, young lady."

"I'm a nurse and don't you—Look, I'm getting hot, you're getting hot. Let's both cool it, huh?"

"*You are not educated or licensed to make these decisions.*"

Audrey spoke softly and angrily. "Would you rather I hadn't done anything?"

Dr. Schoonoler said, "You have no authorization from me to do anything like that," and he walked away.

Audrey remained silent for a few seconds, then shouted, "Why don't you stay on the floor, then, you creep!"

Dr. Schoonoler turned around and came back to Audrey and stood very close to her. "I know what's going on, Nurse. But I won't authorize it. And no one will ever be able to say that I did." He glanced at each of the spectators. Then he walked away.

Jan waited in a phone booth on Med Four until Lynn Keating got on the line. "Thank you for the flowers," she said. "They're delicious."

"I hope you'll repay in kind. Something delicious."

"Oh, I can." Jan paused for effect. "The nurses are doing things they aren't supposed to."

"Well now. That is delicious. Such as?"

"I can't say exactly. I haven't been to medical school."

"I need specific examples."

"I'll get them."

With the patients dispersed from the station, Audrey spoke to Coralee, Debby, and Hal. "The nurses in the ER and ICUs make decisions like I made all the time. It's *expected* of them. This entire hospital is an ER now. I'm going to continue acting just as I have. I'm going to make decisions and act on them. Coralee, I expect the same from you. Just as you have. Debby, I want you to check with me first when you go outside orders. Unless it's an immediate emergency. Hal, you don't have any responsibility in this. I just wanted you to know what's going on."

"All right," Hal said. "The thing is, I'm not supposed to be here now. I'm supposed to be down with Trina."

"You're excused," Audrey said.

81

TRINA WAS ON the phone with Jessy Gladdens. "It's all right, Jessy. I don't blame you. You've had a bad enough time, don't blame yourself. Come in and talk sometime, will you? . . . Or just call. I want to know how you are."

She hung up and dialed Nicholas Prudhomme at the district

attorney's office. Hal sat and listened. "The reason Jessy
Gladdens dropped charges, the reason you can't prosecute
Robert Higby, is the victim's mother. She's old-fashioned.
She thinks any woman who gets raped was asking for it. She
blames her daughter. Jessy can't handle that. It's easier for
her just to ask her mother's forgiveness . . .

"Well, you know, the shrinks will keep Higby as long as
they can. Which now means as long as he'll let them. His
stimulus to get therapy may be considerably reduced. But I
don't know. That could go either way. When I spoke to him,
he was aware that he'd been troubled for a long time. He saw
all of this as an opportunity. To attack his troubledness . . .

"It's tragic how Higby got my telephone number. Jessy
gave it to her mother. She wanted her mother to call me so I
could tell her Jessy had not invited the attack. Instead, the
mother decided to dispose of the situation. Let Higby scare
me off. Her daughter's counselor. The mother gave Higby my
number . . .

"I'd like that, Nick. But I'm working a double . . . It
looks like that's going to happen a lot. For the duration . . ."
She glanced at Hal, then looked away as she spoke into the
phone. "Let me encourage you to ask again."

When she hung up, there was a knock on the door of the
psych office. She pushed aside the curtain at the door's
window to see who was outside and then opened the door.
Tim Holbrook and his son, Jason, entered.

There were introductions and then Trina said, "How did
you like our day care center, Jason?"

"It was okay. But I like my own school better."

"Yeah. Here it's just a lot of *little* kids, right?" Jason
grinned at Trina. "We all want to see you back in your own
school. Quick as possible. That's why we're going to do all
this talking."

"Dad said."

"Okay. I want you to understand I'm not on anyone's side,
not your mom's or your dad's."

Jason looked down. "Darn. I thought you was gonna be on
Dad's side."

"I'm going to be on your side, Jason. How's that?"

"Good."

"I just need to find out what's best to do on your side. You
see, I don't know much about what's going on. So I want to

talk to your dad for a while and then I want to talk to you all alone. Is that okay?''

"I guess."

"You like ice cream, Jason?''

Jason looked at her uncertainly. "Yeah."

"Hal, couple of guys on Tremaine are selling ice cream."

"Jason, let's you and I see if we can find these guys."

"Okay, Dad?"

"Go on. See you in a few minutes."

When Hal and Jason had left, Trina said, "Those ice cream guys are doing a land office business out there, what with the strike. All the spectators and HOs and cops, not to mention the media. I'm going to drop the pretense of a professional relationship. You look like shit, Tim."

"Feel like it. I'm scared."

"Of me?"

"Yeah. You too."

"Who else?"

"Valerie. Her attorney."

"Why?"

"You're all in control. I'm not."

"I control nothing. I'm here to listen and assess and advise."

"Valerie and her attorney. They'll take Jason away from me *completely* if they can, this time."

"Just what makes Valerie and her attorney so fucking all-powerful?"

"The judge does." Trina remained silent. "Being here, it's like going to a doctor with symptoms you know are dangerous."

"Let's just see what's going on, okay, Tim?"

"Okay."

After she interviewed Tim, Trina talked with Jason alone. It only took a few minutes. Then she called Tim back in. "You know Arlene Sherk?"

"Social worker? Over in Pedi?"

"Yeah."

"I know her by sight. Not to talk to."

"You're going to talk to her now."

Arlene Sherk was in her mid-forties and had a grave, warning-off expression. She said to Tim in her office, "I've had a summary from Trina. I'd like to talk to Jason alone."

Tim waited in the hallway outside, the voices within soundless until he suddenly heard Jason cry out in pain, *"Mommy leaves me alone."* He wanted to rush in, call it all off, and take Jason away to someplace safe, where he would be untroubled. But that was what he *was* trying to do.

Father, son, Trina, Mr. Emerson, Arlene Sherk—people controlling other people's lives, hadn't he done the best he could for Mr. Emerson? And now this woman talking to Jason was someone who had more control over the fate of his child than he did.

Then Jason was left with a nurse in the Pedi waiting room, where there were playthings.

Arlene Sherk closed the door to her office and said to Tim, "Why did you take Jason from his mother's apartment?" Her voice was accusatory.

Tim was infuriated. The social structure was trapping him again. "That is not a fair description."

"Tell me a fair description."

When he had finished, the social worker seemed to relax. "Do you know what a Fifty-one-A is?"

"Until this minute I thought I did. I don't know that I do."

"Section Fifty-one-A of Chapter One-nineteen of the General Laws of Massachusetts is an act requiring certain persons to report acts of child abuse or neglect. I am one such person. Form Fifty-one-A is the vehicle by which that information is presented for the consideration of the state. Through the courts, I understand you are to have a hearing Friday morning."

"Yes."

"Neglect. It is clear negligence to leave a child alone overnight. There have been other instances. I suppose you know."

"I didn't know at all till this."

"Children in divorce situations are inclined to protect each parent from the other. Jason has been left alone late on several occasions. This was simply the first all-nighter. That doesn't reduce the danger the child was placed in on the other occasions. Or his distress." She gave Tim a hard look. "What if he got sick? What if there was a fire?"

Tim shook his head, exhausted by the possibilities he had endured for so long.

"The Department of Social Services will make an evaluation. I'll file a Fifty-one-A, alleging neglect of a minor child.

It will have to be assessed. Another DSS social worker, an assessment person, makes the inquiries, does the interviews, puts together the examination, and actually fills out the final Fifty-one-A. That usually takes a week, minimum. Can your lawyer get a continuance, do you think?''

"I know he can't. He was very specific about that. I've got to be in court Friday morning.''

She studied Tim and then said, "All right. I'll see what can be done to expedite.''

"What happens if DSS finds neglect?''

"The court can offer the mother the opportunity to reform.''

"Oh shit. Excuse me.''

"Or it can place the child in your custody for a trial period. If neglect is substantiated, I think the department would recommend the court expedite the child to the father's custody.''

"Oh, Jesus,'' Tim said softly.

"Your judge sounds . . . prejudiced. But the risk to the child is the paramount issue. The risk for the child must be resolved as soon as possible.''

82

MRS. MALAMET WAS in her early forties, tanned, sensibly dressed in a tweed suit, and a little thick around the waist. She stopped at the station on her way out. Audrey was reviewing a chart with Debby. Mrs. Malamet said to Audrey, "I want to leave my telephone number with you. I'll be staying in the city till Ralph is discharged.''

"Glad to have it,'' Audrey said. "But I don't foresee having to use it.''

"I'm concerned about Ralph's being here. Because of the strike.''

"We can get physicians up here very quickly if we need to, Mrs. Malamet. At any rate, Captain Malamet is staying with us for observation. He's been quite stable.''

"Yes. Stable. Since his heart stopped. That's difficult to get used to.'' She was silent for some seconds, withdrawn.

Then she said, "He won't let me move him anyway. He doesn't want anyone else to know."

"His records are as private as he wants here."

"It's foolish. He has flight physicals four times a year. He'd have to lie to the flight surgeons. Assuming they didn't find anything. I can't believe that Ralph would lie. But he loves flying so much. He could always work in Operations. That's what they do with pilots who won't take medical retirement." She looked at Audrey and there was a tear on each cheek. "He's very, very sad. He hides it. But he's very, very sad, and angry." She shrugged, as if dispelling the sadness and anger.

"I understand, Mrs. Malamet."

"Well . . . I'll be back tomorrow."

"Are you leaving because of visiting hours? You don't have to. I don't keep that kind of schedule."

"Oh. I'm glad to know that. I'll take advantage of it. But I think I'll go now anyway. It's been a very long weekend. I'm tired." She went to the elevator.

Debby said to Audrey, "It was a long weekend for me, too, just thinking things over. I was surprised to find myself coming in this afternoon. I was surprised to find myself coming in on Friday."

"I wasn't worried about your coming in on Friday. I knew you'd honor that commitment. It was today I was concerned about. The strike."

"I didn't know whether I could adjust. To the responsibilities here. Even without the strike."

"There's nothing like internship for a nurse, nothing to prepare you for the responsibility of the job. But you do adjust. Sometimes you have to shut your mind. Sometimes you have to do that to be effective. First respond to the physiological needs. You have to be objective. But sometimes you do have to build up a wall to the patient's condition."

"Sometimes you build up a wall to your own condition." Betty Bowen had come up to the station and was looking at Audrey. She looked at Debby. "Sometimes a nurse will deny to herself what the work is costing her. Burnout."

"You look a little ragged, Betty," Audrey said.

"You were right. I was up too long. I didn't start back on the Demerol in time. Let's go to Dilaudid."

"You can elect morphine."

"The Dilaudid can be increased. Let's do that."

"Okay. Go back to bed."

But Betty did not leave. The three of them had been joined by a fourth woman, a stranger in a white dress, white hose, and a white cap. "Excuse me," she said. "I'm sorry to come in after visiting hours, but I just got off work. I'm here to visit Captain Malamet."

Audrey looked at her carefully. "Oh. Well, visiting hours are flexible here. Where do you work? Anyplace nearby?"

"Oh . . . No. Not in a hospital at all. Actually, I'm taking care of someone privately."

"I see. C'mon, I'll take you to Captain Malamet."

The captain was not in bed. He hardly ever was. He was standing up and doing something that looked like pushups against the wall. *"Penny!* Why, look at you!" He took her in his arms and almost kissed her on the lips. But then he held her to him. "You feel wonderful."

The young woman looked at Audrey, who said, "Just wanted to make sure you two knew each other," and went back to the station.

Betty was still there. "That is the strangest nurse I have ever seen. Does Captain Malamet know her?"

"They seem familiar."

"That cap," Debby said. "I've never seen anything like it. It looks like a box. And it doesn't have any markings on it. It doesn't look like it's a presentation from a school."

Betty said, "Back in World War Two they let people work in hospitals before they'd finished training. They had caps like that. Universal caps is what they were called."

"This dame is in her twenties," Debby said. "She wasn't even alive in World War Two. And her dress has long sleeves."

Audrey smiled. "Maybe it's her graduation dress and she's trying to wear it out."

"Then she graduated last spring, when I did. This dress looks brand new. I was taught that long sleeves are a source of infection, they carry stuff from one patient to another."

Betty said, "When was the last time you saw a nurse wearing jewelry?"

"The last time was never," Debby said. "They taught us not to."

"Everyone was taught not to," Audrey said. "However,

the visitor can dress any way she wants. We just want to make sure she's not handing out any medication.''

"She doesn't look the type," Betty said.

Debby said, "I'm just, you know, *concerned*. What if Mrs. Malamet shows up?"

"That's why Florence Nightingale is dressed like a nurse and visiting after hours, isn't it?''

Audrey went to prepare a syringe with a narcotic analgesic for Betty.

83

LATE IN THE afternoon Molly went to Bennett's apartment with him to watch the six o'clock news and have a drink. Along with the drinks he brought out cheeses and crackers and nuts. Molly looked at the abundant provisions in front of them and said, ''Anyone would think we were going to watch a football game.''

The first shot was of the picket line. The second was of Bennett himself approaching the picket line from across Tremaine Avenue, a paper-wrapped grinder in one hand, a cardboard beverage container in the other.

A house officer yelled, *"You know why we're out here, Director?"*

Bennett smiled. *"Yes. You don't want to work."*

Molly said, ''I can't believe you're smiling there.''

Another HO yelled, *"You guys cheated us!"*

"—regular and recurrent and your lousy lawyer won't even talk about it—" Bennett walked on by.

A cut to Bennett facing the camera outside the hospital, the reporter's voice over: *"Director, why did you cut off negotiations?"*

"We determined that further negotiations with the house officers are fruitless. The issue is money. There is no money. There is nothing with which to negotiate."

A cut to Scotty McGettigan, the pickets moving behind him, the reporter's voice over: *"Dr. McGettigan, it's charged that salary is the principal issue."*

"It is not. Patient care is the principal issue."

"Could you give us some examples?"

"Inadequate nursing staff. We don't have enough full-time nurses. We don't have enough support staff for the doctors or the nurses."

A cut back to Bennett and the reporter: *"Director, we have heard that Management has decided to discharge as many patients as possible and transfer as many patients as possible to other hospitals until the house officers return to work."*

A close shot of Bennett looking cool and angry at the same time. *"Back Bay Metropolitan Hospital will not discharge any patient who isn't medically ready for discharge. We have no plans to transfer any patients. Our nursing staff is doing a brilliant job. We have the best nursing staff in the city, perhaps in the country."*

"Hooray for you," Molly said, and kissed him on the cheek.

The reporter, now in shadow, faced the camera. In the background some nurses were leaving the hospital.

"Here come the good guys," Molly said.

The reporter: *"It's late afternoon now. Throughout the day nurses have been coming in early and leaving late."*

A cut to earlier in the day, bright sunlight. Liz Swanzey: *"I'm off today, but I decided I'd come in anyway."*

Nan Lassitter leaving the hospital, emerging into shadow. Reporter: *"How is it in there for the nurses?"*

"It's like a weekend. Nothing unusual."

"The patients are getting taken care of?"

"The patients are getting well taken care of."

"Any emergencies?"

"There are always emergencies."

"Today?"

"Including today. We deal with them."

Another cut. The reporter displays his watch as Day comes out of the hospital. *"It's five-thirty,"* the reporter says to the camera. Then he turns to Day. *"Nurse, did you come on at seven this morning?"*

Day: *"Earlier."*

"It's late to be leaving the hospital."

"Not really."

A cut to an earlier shot, a house officer walking the route in front of the hospital with the other pickets and carrying a sign.

Reporter: *"How's the strike going?"* Holds out microphone.
House officer grins and calls out, *"What strike?"*
Reporter: *"Indeed, some people will tell you there is no strike. This is Mozart Wills, a member of the house officers' executive council."*
A medium shot of Mozart with pickets in the background. *"If the nurses on the floors, if the nurses get overwhelmed, it's understood people will come off the street to help. Everyone is carrying a beeper."*
Cut to Scotty McGettigan. *"No, we are not on strike."*
"What do you call it, then?"
"A job action. A protest on behalf of the patients."
"But not a strike?"
"We're available for anybody who needs us."
Cut to the reporter in late afternoon shadow. *"But the hospital's management claims there is a strike in progress. Tomorrow its counsel, Howard Sylvus, will go before the Massachusetts Labor Relations Commission. He will try to convince the LRC that the house officers here are on strike. If he does that, the LRC may issue orders enjoining the strike. Failing compliance, house officers could begin going to jail."*
"First Sylvus has to demonstrate that it's illegal for the house officers to go out," Bennett said. He fiddled with the television set and the VCR. "They got that story awfully fast. About going to the LRC. But what astounds me is, Lynn Keating had it early enough for her four o'clock edition."
"I heard about it around three."
"You're staff."
"If it could get to staff, it could get to anyone. I don't see that it hurts your position."
"No. The HOs had to be informed through counsel anyway. It's just that the leak from inside to outside was so bloody quick."
"Is it arguments tomorrow or a hearing?"
"It's a full-scale hearing. Witnesses who will say there is a strike and witnesses who will say there isn't a strike." Bennett turned on the simultaneous video recording he had made of another channel's six o'clock report. There was Scotty McGettigan. "Young McGettigan certainly has a way with words."
"Young McGettigan is what—six or seven years younger than you?"

Bennett watched a section on the picket line and then reran it.

"They're a pretty grubby-looking bunch. They look like they dress themselves from Goodwill Industries," he said.

"Maybe it shows they need more money. Anyway, Back Bay Met is not known as a center of fashion."

"Dressed like that, who's going to respect them?"

"You sound disappointed. That's the way they dress at work."

"I know. Look at those picket signs, Molly. They look like they were lettered by children."

"Bennett dear, medical school doesn't train you in the niceties of job actions. You have to learn it on the job, you see."

"It's pitiful, really."

Molly laughed. "Are they reflecting poorly on you, Bennett dear?"

"Yes they are," Bennett said without humor.

A reporter held a microphone and spoke and then extended it to Scotty McGettigan. *"Dr. McGettigan, you say there is no strike. Under what circumstances will you return to work?"*

"We haven't left work."

Reporter, facing the camera: *"There are those who might disagree. The nurses alone on the floors. The patients being discouraged from entering the hospital."*

A house officer in a white jacket, information sheets in her hand, talking to a man who had been headed into the hospital. HO: *"It's a neighborhood thing. We need you to stay away so we can take better care of you later."*

"Yeah, I been on strike, too. Thing of it is, I got no job 'tall now."

"Hang in there with us, okay?"

"Well . . . Where'd I go instead?"

The two walked away and the camera remained focused on them with the reporter's voice over: *"The doctor interviewed the patient and recommended a facility for him to go to."*

A cut to a middle-aged black lady who spoke to the camera. *"No way I'm goin' in there. I s'port them."* She turned to the pickets. *"You're fightin' for better conditions here. For us neighborhood folks."*

The camera was jostled. When it was steadied again it had steadied on a very tall black woman who wore shorts and a turban and who was yelling at a white man who wanted to enter the hospital. The man was a foot short of the woman's chin and he looked terrified. "—*you know what's good for you, you sure the beep won't!*" A cop was maneuvering the woman away from the man. A slim young woman watched vacantly, very still.

"The big lady's one of ours. She's crazy. Name's Dora. No one knows how crazy she is. Or how sane," Molly said. "The other one's a new psych visitor. Olivia, I think her name is. Started coming in recently."

"She looks weird, drugged." He stopped and looked again. "Dangerous?"

"She won't let anyone talk to her much. We don't know." Molly looked at the young woman, too. "I didn't know she came out in the daytime."

An elderly white man in a yellow hat said to the camera, "*Long's they don't want me to, I ain't goin' in. Sure is fun to watch, though. Gonna bring my supper back here, stay up real late. Yes, ma'am. Live action here. It's bein' 'part of history is what I'm doin'.*"

"That's Mr. Cornelius. Deluded all the way from the tippy-top of his head to his toenails. But a sweetie."

"Nice to have the human interest angle on this channel," Bennett said. "Well now, this ought to be interesting."

Reporter's voice: "*Dr. Merton Geier, chief of all services at Back Bay Metropolitan. Dr. Geier, you've just met with the chiefs of services?*"

"*Yes.*"

"*What is the attitude of the chiefs toward the house officers? Is there any common opinion?*"

"*Why yes. The chiefs can't and won't support the strike. But we understand the issues and we can support the issues.*"

"The sonofabitch!" Bennett said. But he was grinning.

"Bennett, you confuse me. You look pleased."

"Wasn't his phraseology marvelous?"

"Ah."

A wide shot of the hospital and pickets, police and spectators, with the reporter's voice over: "*An amazing situation. Is it a strike or not? It depends on who you talk to. But one thing is certain here. The house officers are not on the floors, they are not in the hospital, and by and large they are not performing their duties.*"

Bennett turned off the set. *"Is it a strike or is it not?"* he mimicked. "It's a disaster, that's what it is," he said with no kindness at all in his voice.

He stood over her.

Molly looked up at him. She knew exactly what he wanted. She felt that way herself. But she did not respond. She wanted to see what he would do.

He did nothing for some seconds. Then he bent and kissed her and she rose against his body within his arms.

Molly felt hot, animal. *Rutty,* she thought. She responded to Bennett as if they were in physical conflict rather than maneuvering themselves into an embrace for intercourse, their bodies in a power struggle, each to obtain the maximum physical pleasure from the other. Molly gritted her teeth and allowed Bennett entrance but gave not an inch of her position. She rocked the man atop her with thrusts of her own until she smiled at the success of her body against his and his body within hers, and then wave after wave swept through her and broke. Done, sweating, she would not release him.

After a moment she said, "I think you get off on this, Bennyboy."

"I think you do, too."

"Lots of action stimulated by this job action."

"Job action as erotic stimulus," he said without humor. He cupped her breast with his hand, studied the other breast, took it in his mouth for a few seconds, tongued her nipple. Then he looked at her. "There's an old union song, 'Which Side Are You On?' "

"Is that what these confrontations have been about? Where I'm coming from, so to speak?"

"Let's go out to dinner, then come back here."

Molly ignored the suggestion. "I have an association. I'm good at associations. I play poker. I'm good at that, too."

"I bet you are."

"You remind me this evening of a poker player."

"Why?"

"My question exactly."

"Let's go out to dinner and come back here."

"Let's go out to dinner and go back to my place."

"I have to be available. This place is half an hour closer to the hospital."

"I need to be available too," Molly said.

"You can leave this number."

"I'd rather not. I'd rather be available at my own number."

"Why?"

"I don't want to leave your number. I don't want to be available at your number."

"Isn't that a little hypocritical? Considering our present . . . disposition."

"Dining with Management is one thing. Spending the night with it is another just now."

They dressed on opposite sides of the bed. Molly felt that with each piece of clothing they put on, the farther they withdrew from each other. In a superficially pleasant exchange they decided not to have dinner together.

84

DOWN ON THE street, her evening abruptly without structure, Molly decided to go to a meeting of the young firebrands, an invitation to which she had turned down just a couple of hours earlier. Molly was NSA's legal liaison, and after work, at Selma's request, she had spent some time with NSA's counsel and then returned to the hospital to counsel, in turn, Selma and the leader of the young firebrands.

Diana Vezzina, the leader of the young firebrands (as they had been characterized by Audrey), was twenty-three years old, all of four years younger than Audrey. Day had earlier characterized Diana to Michelle McCabe as a diddy-bopper because of the rock that daytimes emanated from a radio in the station on Med Four, where Diana was currently the charge nurse. She was also the nurse who had just submitted a meticulous report to Bennett Chessoff on the financial feasibility and financial benefits to the hospital of converting medications coming up from the pharmacy to unidoses so that multiple medications for the same patient did not have to be delivered separately at the same time.

The meeting of the firebrands was in Diana's apartment, which was crowded by the twelve nurses already there.

"This is us," Diana said to Molly. "The vanguard of reform and justice. Out of three hundred and eighty-two nurses." She smiled. Then Molly saw that the smile was for irony only.

"You're lucky. Any more high-minded people, you'd have to go downstairs and hold the meeting on the street." She turned down a glass of wine.

"I was just about to read them what Lynn Keating wrote this afternoon."

It was the early edition of the *Eagle* that had incited Diana to call Selma, as chief executive of NSA, and had forced Selma to seek legal counsel through Molly.

"This is the end of the article," Diana said to the other nurses. " *'Whatever their sympathies, the nursing staff is showing no support whatsoever for the house officers' refusal to work.'* " Diana put the newspaper down. "Now look, folks, what she says is true. And that sucks."

"Well, what do we do?" a nurse said. "I thought that's what we're here to find out."

Diana said, "First we have to decide if we want to support the HOs."

Another young nurse said, "They're trying to rectify a lot of shit." She said it adamantly, as if the others were unaware.

"Well, what can we do to support the HOs actively?"

"I'll let Molly tell you what she told me," Diana said.

"I'll tell you what you can do legally. You're all members of NSA and you're all bound by NSA's contract. Whatever you do will be within contractual obligations. Also whatever you do will be as individuals, not as members of NSA. NSA will not approve of or disapprove of any legal support you give the house officers."

"Yeah, great, Molly," another young nurse said. "When I want a load of horseshit, I'll let you know. In the meantime I'd like information. Can we, like, walk on their picket line?"

"If it's not your shift. If they'll have you."

The nurse blushed. The rumor was that several had already. Molly said quickly, "What you can do as individuals is this. Honor our contract. Work entirely according to the rules—"

"That's helping the HOs?"

"—and do nothing more. And nothing less."

"That's a slowdown," the nurse who had blushed said.

A nurse spoke from behind some others, and Molly realized she had remained purposely inconspicuous. "I'm not in this to neglect patients," Liz Swanzey said. It was the first time she had spoken to Molly face to face since Molly had seen her about blowing up at a patient.

"You're not being told what to do. You're being told what you *may* do. Presumably, you will each decide for yourself. I'm here to offer information, period."

Diana said to Liz, "You want to support the HOs?"

"Sure."

"Then you do just what our work agreement says and you do nothing more."

"Like what?"

"No one reports to work until they have to," Diana said.

The oldest woman there other than Molly, a thirty-year-old head nurse from Med Eight, said, "I'll be taking report when I'd normally already be with patients—"

"Yes," Molly said, "that's what you'd be doing. That sort of thing. You give the hospital the time you've contracted to give it and no more."

"The hospital won't function, the patients will—"

Diana said, "The hospital will function. It just won't get the benefit of all the extra time we put in."

"Neither will the patients," Liz said.

"Yes, they will," Diana said. "Eventually. When the HOs win. Then the patients will benefit enormously."

Another nurse said, "Pardon me for being stupid, but this is a pretty abstract proposal. What are the specifics?"

Diana said, "This. Day shift. You get to the hospital fifteen, twenty minutes before seven. Earlier if we can agree on it. Six-thirty would be great. We line up across the street on Tremaine. And we just stay there. Supposed to report at seven? We stay on the other side of Tremaine—all of us together—until five minutes of seven."

After a silence Liz said, "All of us?" She looked around. "We aren't many, Diana."

Diana opened an imitation leather portfolio and took out several sets of duplicates. "This is our roster. The nursing staff roster. With telephone numbers. I photocopied them at the hospital."

Molly grinned. "At the hospital's expense."

Diana turned at her. "My check paid for every copy."

"Apologies," Molly said.

"We want to do this? Not report till seven?" It was agreed. "Everyone take a set. We're going to work out a telephone tree. Then you all go home and start calling. Every nurse off duty and on. What we want to do. Starting tomorrow morning."

"What about the afternoon?"

"If your contract calls for you to stay till three, you stay till three. Not a minute later. Three-thirty? Not a minute later than that." Diana began organizing the telephone tree.

Molly found she had company in the hallway. Liz Swanzey had come out after her. Liz said, "Glad I ran into you."

"How's it going?" Molly said in a neutral voice.

"Not the way I figured it at all."

"How did you figure it?"

"A lot of pain, embarrassment."

"And?"

"There's the pain, the embarrassment. A shitload of relief, too."

"You didn't figure on that?"

"Oh, yeah, I figured on that. I relied on it. I relied on you."

The hallway was lit by a single bulb and the shadows distorted Liz's face. "What was it you didn't figure on?"

"I haven't been too happy with nursing. I didn't like the work I was doing. No burnout, I just didn't like it."

Molly waited.

"But I want to take care of people."

Molly remained listening.

"I think I'm finding out I want to take care of people the way you took care of me."

"And your doctor," Molly said flatly.

Liz smiled a little. The shadows did not distort it. "Oh yes, my doctor—transference and all that. I don't want to be like him and like you. I want to do your kind of work. That's what I discovered right away. That's what I didn't figure on. That getting into therapy would lead me right into the work I most want to do, the work I've really always wanted to do. Helping people feel better when they're upset. The way I've always been." Molly offered no response and Liz felt anxious. "Hey, I'm not saying I can join you or Trina next week. Therapy's going to take time and I'll have to go back to school—I know all that."

She looked helpless, Molly thought, and determined. "From a little craziness, good psych nurses are sometimes born. Trina, for instance. She started out in therapy. Me, for instance. You might say it helps to have been there." She added quietly, "Of course, it doesn't help at all to have been there unless you get out."

Liz nodded. She said, "See you," and turned around and went back into Diana's apartment.

Molly started down the dimly lit stairway. Did I come over here myself as a way of getting back at Bennett? Molly granted it was a good piece of speculation.

85

IT WAS QUIET on the ER, the quietest Trina or Elin could ever remember it. Elin herself had spent a year on the ER as a surgical nurse. Tonight she was in charge of the ER and theoretically on call to Med Three and Four. It was her second shift of the day and had begun after her office in the walk-in clinic closed at five. Her duties on the ER were to examine patients, attend to those within her authority herself, and make the decision when to call in a house officer from the line. But patients were not only being diverted to other facilities, they were staying away.

"It's eerie," Elin said. "It's as if the city's dead out there."

Trina thought about that. "Well, it's not. They bring the dead here first."

They were drinking coffee in the psych office and Hal said, "Really? Why?"

"Just to make sure," Elin said. "If *we* say they're dead, they are absolutely, positively dead."

Trina said, "No one from this hospital ever tried to get into a more comfortable position on a table in a morgue." Her telephone rang. "Psychiatry, Trina."

Diana Vezzina explained about her meeting and the proposed display of support for the HOs. "I'm calling all the nurses on duty. What do you say?"

"Diana, I couldn't do my work if I had to stick to a rigid schedule like that."

"It's just for a few days. Till we bring Management to its knees."

Trina did not like the expression. "I don't see it as practical for my work. My patients don't keep orderly schedules."

"Trina, you're a surprise. And a disappointment, a big one."

"Elin Maki's with me. Would you like to talk to her?" Trina held out the receiver to Elin.

Elin took the phone and listened. Then she said, "My responsibilities right now preclude that sort of thing . . . I'm sorry you feel that way . . . No, I'm not going to express an opinion . . ." She looked over at Trina and then at Hal as she said, "Yes, Diana, I realize I'm an individual and I have that right. But I'm not going to. Good night." She handed the phone to Trina for replacement in the cradle. It rang again immediately.

The man was big and white and drunk, mid-thirties, Trina judged, looking around for security people. The ER waiting room was strangely unoccupied except for the triage nurse, the woman behind the counter at the console, and the man himself, who stood in place but teetered as he looked around, both disoriented and angry. Trina went to him. "My name is Trina. I'm a nurse. Do you want some help?"

The man looked down at her, steadied himself, stared at her, and then yelled, "Don't want no fuckin' *nothin'*!" and swung at Trina and missed when she moved away quickly. Hal tried to get between them, the man knocked him to the floor, and Trina peripherally saw the security guards Reynold and Ginny come in from opposite sides and at the same time heard the woman behind the counter signaling out to the line, "Shrink to the ER, shrink to the ER." Trina said to the man, "Do you want help or not? This is a hospital. I'll help you if you behave yourself." The man lunged at her and Trina stepped away again and saw—or thought she saw, but was not certain—an odd sequence of events.

The man turned toward Ginny, his great fist raised like a

rock he would hurl at her. Ginny dropped into a sort of crouch and her right hand went down to her pants leg and started to raise it, her hand going underneath, and it appeared to Trina that Ginny was responding to an absolutely urgent need to scratch herself. Behind Ginny, Trina saw Olivia, the Medusa child, skitter in and then stand in complete stillness, her attention in their direction, but her face blank and eyes as always focused on some place way far away.

The man turned to face Reynold and a third guard came in from behind Ginny, and while the man got ready for Reynold as Reynold closed on him, the third guard got a partial pinion from behind and Reynold leaped against the man and immobilized his right arm and leg.

The man twisted his head toward Reynold. "Don't put your hands on me, nig!"

"Cool it, man. I'm just doing my job."

Trina stood in front of the man. "I'll talk with you. Now slow down."

Behind the man another guard and the shrink were coming in and Ginny had stopped scratching her ankle and had risen and taken two steps in retreat. The new guard locked onto the drunk, but the man was so huge he was able to sway the three guards, though not break loose. The shrink moved Trina away from the man and said, "We're going to keep our distance. He's a big motherfucker and he could kill one of us."

"I was talking to him—"

"Sure. We don't even talk to him till he's in restraints. Sometimes I think *you're* crazy, Trina." He looked at the man. "Okay, we get him restrained and sedated. Psych Two. Let's do it."

Trina was aware of Olivia following as the three guards and the drunk made their slow, forced progress to the psych room behind the ER. Then the man suddenly tired from exertion and alcohol and the guards were able to move him more easily.

In the psych room Trina got the leather restraints out of the cabinet. The man abruptly freed himself from the guards and grabbed the restraints from Trina and swung them at her head, but she turned and they smashed her across the upper arm instead and flung her back against the wall and she saw

Reynold, against regulations and quite beyond what Trina assessed his physical ability to be, cold-cock the sonofabitch.

The Medusa child was out in the darkness at the far end of the corridor when Elin took Trina and Reynold for examination and x-ray. Trina was going to speak to her, but she seemed to meet Trina's eyes from that long distance away and then disappear. Trina went to the phone outside Psych One and dialed Security and asked them to find Olivia for her.

Then, as they went out to the nonacute side of the ER, Trina became aware that Hal was still with her and had been since he had been knocked to the floor. "You okay?"

"Yeah," he said.

She put a hand on his arm. "Thanks for that. Trying to protect me."

"Yeah."

She turned to Reynold. "And you." She put a hand on his shoulder. "You are a wonder. You're half that man's size."

Reynold smiled at Trina. "Prob'ly couldn'ta done it if he was sober."

86

OUTSIDE, ON TREMAINE Avenue, it was like a street party.

The intense white illumination of the auxiliary lighting gave the area a feeling of carnival. The presence of all the police gave the area uncustomary safety. Neighborhood people came out for strolls. Food vendors had been arriving all day, sensing the area's increasing appetite. The cops, in need of nourishment, did not discourage them. The house officers received regular deliveries of sandwiches donated in their support by Fritz Moriarty from his Public House.

The cops were not having a bad time of it. The methodology of violence had been seen to by both the house officers and Management, the only subject the two sides discussed. The neighborhood people were in good humor and were responsive when asked to be. The individual weirdos attached to the hospital were mostly entertaining. There was, for instance, Mr. Albert Cornelius, a particular delight to the cops once he informed them that it was their own District 16 that relayed radio messages to him in his head from the three hookers who lived upstairs from him.

From time to time there were sudden bursts of light around the picket line—Fourth of July stuff, but really electronic flash: Mr. Shaughnessy and his Polaroid camera taking souvenir pictures for the house officers and their partisans. He took two of Dora in her very short shorts and her very long legs and kept one for himself.

Former patients in particular came by to wish the house officers well. Some stayed to help. Some just stayed. Mr. Improta, who had been on the ICU and then down on Med Three a few days before, brought a folding chair and sat where he could watch the picket line and listen in on the HOs' information center. The police tried to move him several times, but he pleaded a heart condition and the need to be near his physicians and he grinned and one cop finally grinned back and said, "Okay for now, Mr. Improta. But we get any complaints *from anyone,* I'm gonna see you off myself."

"No one complains about me."

The second cop suddenly turned angry. *"What're you, some fuckin' Mafia don ganglord, no one complains about you?"*

"C'mon," the first cop said and moved his partner away. "Whadya want to blow up at that old man for?"

"You havin' fun out here, huh?"

"It's not bad, you know?"

"Yeah? That's all you know. You haven't got the sense to be worried, is your trouble. I lay you odds these *doctors* are attractin' every *weirdo* in the city and the *idea is*—"

"Yeah, man, *tell* me."

"The idea *is,* create the biggest fuckin' disturbance in the city's history." The second cop watched his partner. "Not smilin' now, huh? Every fuckin' weirdo from miles around congregatin' here. Some of 'em think they got *licenses,* for chrissake."

"For what?"

"For anything. Doctors go on strike, it's like cops go on strike. You get to do anything you fuckin' want to do."

"Naw. Not the same."

"Trust me."

87

X-RAYS SHOWED THAT bones in Reynold's hand and wrist had been fractured when he'd struck the drunk. The drunk was all right. Trina's arm was black and blue and painful, but she went back to work. Elin called in an orthopedic resident from the line to attend to Reynold, and while he was on the ER, she took the opportunity to go up and check Med Three and Four. On Med Three she found Audrey at the station taking her own call from Diana Vezzina.

"Well, I *know* things stink, Diana. But I've *got* to get in here a little early. My floor depends on it . . . Oh, look, *I* depend on it. Otherwise I can't keep up . . . I *know* I'm being taken advantage of . . . I have to do my job my way, Diana . . . I understand all that, Diana. But look, it's sort of counterproductive, isn't it? What's the sense in standing across the street till five of seven to slow things down and then doing a double to keep the hospital running? . . . No, Debby's in with a patient. I'll leave a note for her to call you." Audrey hung up. "That was—"

"I know. I already spoke to her."

"It's crazy. All I ever wanted to do was help people. And I've got to struggle to do it. The HOs are right, I guess. Diana's probably right. But that's the way things are. If it gets to be too much for me, I don't think I could slow down on the patients—or strike. I think I'd have to quit."

Then Audrey took Elin to see two patients who were uncomfortable but whom Audrey judged not to require a physician. Elin agreed with Audrey after each examination and then said, "I want to stop in on Betty before I leave the floor."

"She's out cold. She elected morphine this evening."

"Oh shit," Elin said softly.

"I agree."

"Still, I want to look in on her."

As they passed the station, Debby was on the telephone. "I know I'm a new nurse and I should fight. I *know* I should do it before I do all the compromising, I know that. But that's just it. I'm not even a part of this place yet . . ."

Elin took Betty Bowen's blood pressure and rate while she slept and then stood by the bed looking at her for almost a minute. Then she said to Audrey, "The gross weight loss—you can't imagine."

"I never knew her. But it's in the chart."

"Of course."

"It's been pretty bad just since she's been in. You can see it just since she's been in."

There was a tear on Elin's cheek. She turned out the light. Audrey put her arm around Elin's shoulder when they were outside the room.

88

VIOLA CHAMBERS CAME into work on Children's Seven at twenty minutes before eleven. She had agreed to remain there for sixteen hours, pulling her regular solo night duty and then staying on as the second nurse on the day shift. She would be working with Margaret Gaines and she looked forward to that. Margaret was the head nurse for Children's Seven as well as the supervising nurse for the other three pediatric floors. She was in her mid-fifties and had been on one or another of these floors for thirty-two years.

When Viola reported in, Nancy, Jamaal's nighttime vent nurse, was just taking off her coat. The charge nurse said, "Diana Vezzina wants you both to call her as soon as you get in."

"What for?" Viola said.

"Let her put it to you in her own words," the charge nurse said. "First, the two of you look in on Jamaal."

"What is it?" Nancy said hurriedly.

"Go see. And hear."

Jamaal was asleep, but his little body moved in twitches. "Restless?" Viola said, hoping.

"He has a fever again."

The little body moved, adjusted itself, moved again in seeking comfort.

"How much?"

"A hundred and two, five."

Nancy gently placed her fingers on the child's skin. "What does the visit say?"

"She says we'll just have to wait and see what's going on. In the meantime, she ordered pheno to block seizures—he's allergic to Tylenol." She nodded toward the gastrostomy tube that would deliver the medication directly to the stomach.

"Nothing to indicate the cause?" Viola said.

"Everything's the same as it's always been. Except for one thing. There's been a weight gain. He's gained almost an ounce a day for the past five days."

"My God," Viola said. "That's just about normal."

"Just about," the vent nurse said.

Nancy went to the chart. "Is there anything in here about bone growth? I don't remember anything."

"There isn't anything. Make a note about it right now." The vent nurse looked up at Viola and Nancy. "This little fellow is scaring me a lot. More than any time before. But then there's this first positive sign, the weight gain. I never was *scared* like this before for him."

The vent nurse looked at the other two imploringly and Viola said, "You never had reason to hope before." She stared down at Jamaal and felt herself ready to cry. "*We* never had any reason to hope before."

Diana Vezzina's line was busy. Viola put the receiver down and heard a small voice suddenly cry out frantically, a voice Viola did not recognize.

"New on the floor this afternoon," the charge nurse said. She took down a chart. "Eighteen-week-old infant with a ten-day history of neighborhood clinic workup, a really *long* roster of tests, and then additional workup downstairs in the walk-in, and what we finally have is nothing at all—no positive diagnosis and no positive response to trial medication."

"That crying is pathetic."

"It can be worse. Much worse. Try not to touch her."

They went to see her. The infant was covered with tiny red dots, as if she were hemorrhaging through her pores, Viola thought.

"She won't eat," the charge nurse said. "Everything is IV."

She lay with her upper legs against her body and her lower legs extended out. "That's her typical posture," the nurse said.

The infant continued to cry frantically, helplessly, and Viola instinctively reached down to pick her up and comfort her, Viola's mind forbidding her to do so just as she touched the infant, who screamed in agony. *"Oh Lord. I'm sorry,"* she said to the infant.

"Once you hear that you won't do it again. Unless you have to. I think we each did it once. I tell you, Vi, if you're like me, this little one is going to break your heart by tomorrow morning. Every time you have to change her, every time you have to do anything for her that means touching her, it's agony for her, it's like you're torturing the poor little thing. It'll tear your heart out . . . I'm glad I'm going home."

Viola looked in the chart for painkilling medications and dosages and frequency. The charge nurse saw what she was doing and said, "They're only moderately effective in that range. But anything more wouldn't be safe." She looked down at the infant. "I've never seen anything like that before. No one has. Have you?"

"No."

"Any ideas?"

"I thought maybe rickets, but I see that's been ruled out."

"Lots of people thought rickets. It's not rickets."

"Those scratches," Viola said. "Where did they come from? How long have they been bleeding?"

"I understand. I went the same route. She was sent up that way. The mother's not sure when the scratches appeared. The pinpoint bleeding preceded the scratches. The mother is single. This is her second child. She works and there's some assistance, but it's all inadequate. She just struggles. No, there's no history of child abuse. The social worker is convinced there's no child abuse. This is a manifestation of something else."

They returned to the station and Viola called Diana Vezzina again. She realized that the charge nurse was listening as she completed the call. Diana explained to Viola about the slowdown.

Viola laughed. "You're talking to the wrong person, Di-

ana. I can't line up anywhere tomorrow morning. I'll still be
on duty." She listened, then said, "No, I guess not, I don't
think so, not the next day either. See, my patients are all
children—and infants. I can't slow down on them, I really
can't . . . I know, I understand you, it's to get things better
for them later . . . But I can't do it. I really can't. I'm
sorry."

Later, after the other two nurses had left and Viola had
checked the children, she was drawn back to little Alice, the
puzzle patient, asleep in her bassinet, her limbs contorted
even in sleep, so small and brown, this ghetto infant, and
Viola found herself thinking of the South Seas and she asked
herself, Why?

89

WHEN ELIN GOT back to the ER from Med Three, she was
upset and honest enough with herself to admit that it was
deep, she was getting kicked around pretty well inside herself. It was seeing Betty asleep, the face so haggard, so much
of her gone in so very few days—the weight loss, the body
loss, the end-stage process of life loss.

Elin realized she had defensed herself well against Betty's
nearness to death, but the defenses had broken entirely when
she saw Betty lying in bed so still and awful, so close an
approximation of death. Elin felt herself grieving. She was
ready to cry. But she was on duty and she would not allow it.

She looked for Hal. When she found him he was alone and
she said, "What are you doing later? I would really like some
company tonight."

"I need a shower. And food. And I'm tired, tired."

"I'll provide the shower and food. I'll let you sleep. I'm
very needful. I'd just like some company, that's all."

"I said I was tired. I didn't say I was dead."

Trina had left Hal so that she could have a private talk with
Ginny. She said to the security guard, "You okay?"

"Huh?"

"You did a pretty good job of withdrawing when you were needed."

"Stuff it, Trina. I was right here. I stayed right here."

"You were backing away. Ginny, I get the impression you're frightened all the time now."

"I told you, Trina. Don't pull that headfucking with me." She started to walk away. Then she turned angrily. "We coulda got killed by that guy. I heard the shrink *say* it. I don't get paid to get killed."

"You get paid to be there when you're needed."

But Ginny was walking away.

Trina went to Sergeant Cleveland immediately. He said, "I know you got this bug about Ginny, Trina. And you may be right on. But we need all the help we can get just now, the next few days. Ginny knows this place and she knows her job."

"Yeah. But will she do it?"

"I tell you this, Trina. I'm payin' close attention from here on in. I'm lookin' for the kind of behavior you describe. I'll be watchin'."

When Hal got back to Trina again, she was sitting with a young white woman in the ER waiting area, holding her hand. As Hal watched, the woman seemed to undergo a wave of discomfort or aversion and drew away from Trina. Trina continued to speak to her but received no reply. After a moment Trina stood and came over to Hal.

"There was a gang fight. Her boyfriend was killed. They brought him here to pronounce. Her name's Agnes. She's seventeen. She's internalized everything she feels. I'll let her sit alone for a few minutes and then I'll try again."

"Why? Why not just send her home—to her parents or friends, people who know her?"

"Because she's not showing anything. You don't know what may come out, or how. You don't know if it's going to be destructive or not. To herself or someone else."

Sergeant Cleveland came over. "We can't find that Olivia girl, Trina. She prob'ly left the building."

"What about our drunk?"

"The doc got 'im to sign himself in. The nurses got 'im in detox now."

"Okay. Thanks, Sergeant." She said to Hal, "I'll give Agnes another try now. You can come sit nearby, but don't get real close." She went over and stood next to Agnes. "I know you're hurting, Agnes. May I sit next to you again?"

There was no response from Agnes except a slight weaving of her body. Pulling back again? Trina thought. "It's a bad time. The worst, isn't it?" Trina touched her, and another wave of discomfort passed through the girl.

"What are you feeling?"

The girl finally spoke. "I'm not feelin' anything." Her face was blanched. Again a wave of discomfort moved her body and this time her hands went to her abdomen.

Trina quickly reassessed on the basis of physical rather than psychological signs. The waves of discomfort were rhythmic. "Are you bleeding?"

"I don't know."

The girl wore black jeans. Trina gently inserted her hand between the girl's legs near the crotch. The fabric was wet. "Are you pregnant?"

"I don't know."

"Sit with her," Trina said to Hal. "This is my assistant, Agnes. He'll stay with you. I'll be right back."

Trina went to the desk and then Hal heard the PA voice say, "Trauma side, nurse clinician to the waiting room, trauma side, nurse clinician to the waiting room."

When Elin came in, Trina intercepted her and summarized, then said, "I think she's cramping and bleeding. I think she's having a spontaneous abortion."

Elin had the girl moved by wheelchair to a gurney on the trauma side. "She's not giving me any history at all," Elin said.

"I know."

"Keep talking to her, huh, Trina?"

"Sure."

Elin said to a trauma side nurse, "Stat CBC. Type and cross for two units. I'll start an IV."

"Agnes, have you missed a period?" Trina said. Agnes did not reply. "Did you have a pregnancy test done?"

Elin pulled a curtain around the bed and she and Trina removed the girl's jeans and underpants. Elin did a partial pelvic examination against physical resistance as Trina tried to reassure the girl. Finally Elin was able to place a pad for the bleeding.

Trina began to talk to Agnes about her boyfriend. "That hurts like hell, I know. If it was me, I'd want to cry *so* hard. It's the right thing to do. Just cry and cry. That's what your body wants to do. Just let it happen." She placed a hand on the girl's forehead. The girl began to cry, slowly and softly.

Trina said, "Can you tell me now, Agnes? Did you miss a period?"

"Yes."

"Did you have a pregnancy test done?"

"Yes."

"Was it positive?"

"Yes."

"How many weeks or months along are you?"

"I don't know. I don't remember." The crying became a kind of mewing and then abandoned sobbing.

Elin had an HO summoned from the line. Before he went in to Agnes, Elin said, "I'm certain she's miscarrying. She's passing huge clots. There's heavy bleeding—she's saturating pads every ten minutes." Then she and the HO took Agnes away from Trina.

"I just happened to find her here," Sergeant Cleveland said to Trina after he called her to come to Psych Two. "She was in here alone in the dark. I turned the light on." Olivia was staring up at a wall. "I told her to move, but she wouldn't."

"Olivia," Trina said, "do you like it in here? Would you like for us to be alone and talk in here?" There was no verbal reply, no physical response, nothing. "It's safe here."

Olivia smiled. She slowly shook her head no.

"Not safe here?"

"Safe fo' me."

"Not safe for me?"

Olivia smiled.

"Why isn't it safe for me?"

"Snake Lady. Jes safe fo' me."

"The Snake Lady said that?"

"Said wait here for the stickterectomy."

"This isn't an operating room, Olivia. This is a room for talking."

Olivia stopped smiling. "Gonna wait."

"Let's talk while you wait." But Olivia would say nothing more.

Finally Trina said, "We're all going to have to leave this room." No response. "C'mon, Olivia, you've got to talk to me or leave." Olivia remained still and silent. "Sergeant, see her out of the building, please."

But Olivia was already leaving the room.

Elin came to the psych office just as Trina was about to go home. Elin said, "Agnes has had a D and C, the bleeding's stopped. They've got her sedated upstairs. The doc figures it was about twelve to sixteen weeks." She looked at Hal and hesitated, then said to Hal in front of Trina, "You ready to go?"

Hal's face brightened with crimson. "Yeah. I was just going to come look for you."

"Privileged communication," Elin said to Trina.

90

ELIN AND HAL left through the lobby of the New Wing to get Elin's car from the hospital garage. Outside on Tremaine they paused to have a look at the continuing show being staged by the house officers, police, and some lingering neighborhood people. The light was so bright it was like stepping out on a stage. Still as stone, Olivia stood facing them—or the doors of the hospital—a few yards away.

Hal said to Elin, "Remember when you asked me what the hospital was? She's the one."

A week and a day ago, Elin thought. Only that long ago I asked this young man that question just to make conversation and now I've put him in the most intimate places in my mind and my body and, God help me, I want to keep him there.

Olivia came over to them. "Fixin'-to-be-uh-doctuh, what a *fine* lady goes with you at night." She looked beyond them. "You muss be *some* stud."

Elin and Hal moved on. Elin said, "What does Trina say now?"

"Trina's still trying to make contact."

Elin laughed. "I think you just missed the opportunity Trina's been waiting for."

Albert Cornelius came over to them, took off his yellow hat, flourished it, and made a partial bow to Elin. "Good evenin' to my doctor who's not a doctor but beter than a doctor," he said to her.

"Good evening, Albert. Aren't you the night owl."

"My age, you can't sleep. You already seen everythin' on TV. I like watchin' what's goin' down on the streets." He looked over to where four young white men stood across the avenue. "See those dudes?"

"Yes," Elin said.

"Layin' for me."

"How do you know?"

"Street smarts. I may be seventy-five, but I know the streets—and I know these wiseass street punks."

"How about letting me give you a ride home, Albert?"

"Naw. Night's still young. Man my age needs more'n Johnny Carson to get off on."

Hal said, "What do you hear from your three hookers, Mr. Cornelius? Maybe they need you."

"They out hookin'. Playin' tricks. Doin' johns. You know."

Elin placed her hand on Mr. Cornelius' arm. "It would really be a pleasure for me to drive you home, Albert."

"Naw. Many thanks. I'll hang out here. Plenty of cops. Drive those kids crazy waitin' to go after me."

"I'm going to see if I can arrange a safe way home for you, Albert. You wait here." Elin went over to a sergeant and explained about Mr. Cornelius. The sergeant said he'd try to see to it that he rode home in a police car. Elin went back. "Albert, when you're ready to go, you tell that sergeant. Do that for me, a favor. They'll get you home safely. Remember, you've got a regular appointment with me now. I want you to be there."

"I'll be there."

But when the time came for him to be driven home, the sergeant wasn't even aware that Mr. Cornelius wasn't there. He did not tell the sergeant he was going home.

By then it was after one and Albert was listening to the wireless transmissions in his head. A quiet night, his hooker friends were already home and waiting for him up in their fourth-floor apartment—though Albert's house ran only to three floors.

Albert looked over at the four white punks hanging out like sleepy jungle animals—*zoo* animals—on the other side of Tremaine, where the zookeepers let them wander around among their own dungheaps.

Albert didn't need any special transportation to get his ass and his money safely back to his ladies. That was his pride. That he could do it on his own. No matter that the animals were always on the wait to hunt him and bring him down.

For one thing, they didn't know his secret trails. He adjusted the sporty yellow hat on his head and set off.

He walked into the lobby of the New Wing, passed the reception desk and the bank of elevators, took the swinging doors into a corridor beyond, and then he was out of the New Wing and into the empty, barely lit open areas between the laundry and the Old Hospital and he laughed aloud because he was more at home in the dark than the animals themselves. He thought he heard an echo of his own laughter. He was in the darkest place now, the area by the wall of the laundry. He could see the lights of the hospital about a city block behind him and lights in the tenements a city block in front of him, but no light fell here.

He heard laughter again, not his own, single voices mimicking him—a laugher behind him, a laugher in front of him, two voices laughing near him. He was between the nearest laughter and the wall of the laundry. He backed away until the wall prevented him from backing any farther. Something struck his head and his head struck the wall. He stumbled and something hit his face and his head snapped against the wall again, and in that instant there was some play of illumination and Albert saw the four jungle animals surrounding him and he saw his sporty yellow hat spin away from him and lie still on the ground as he was struck again and pitched down after his hat.

91

AUDREY GOT DOWN to the street a little after midnight. The hospital was running shuttle vans to transport the nurses—with their now irregular schedule—to places of relatively safe central transportation where they would not have to wait alone or in twos or threes on empty platforms or at empty corners. On the way home, anxiety increased her heart rate and made her perspire and oppressed her respiratory mechanism so that she felt short of breath. There was just *no reason* for the anxiety, she thought. She became angry at herself, angry at her own mind for doing this to her.

When she got home she showered and thought of calling Tim for some comfort, but it was too late and so, as the hot water streamed against her body and soothed it, she carried on an imaginary conversation with him in which she discussed her odd feelings this past hour and he was helpful and caring, then she discussed her feelings about him and finally said, I love you, Tim.

When she got out of the shower the telephone was ringing. She pulled on a terry robe and dried her hands and face and ears and answered.

The voice was a little unrecognizable at first, its timbre and inflection somewhat altered by alcohol. "Well, finally. I've been trying you all evening." The doc.

"I don't want to talk to you when you're sober, I certainly don't want to talk to you when you're drinking."

"Sorry. It's a difficult period in my life. I've come to you for assistance."

"I'm unavailable."

"Just a few minutes, Audrey."

"I didn't want your daytime call, I most certainly don't want one at this hour."

"First you're at the hospital, then it's too late—"

"Good night, Arthur."

"You've never given me a chance to talk to you, explain, tell you how I feel—"

Audrey replaced the receiver and walked back toward the bathroom. The telephone rang. She answered it only because she hoped it might be Tim. It was the doc. She hung up and unplugged the phone and went to the front door to make sure that both the bolt and chain were in place.

She awoke from the same dream several times, hearing the key in her front door, seeing the doc outside trying to get in. But then she willed herself to think of Tim and being with him and the anxiety began to be reduced and finally she slept without interruption until music from the clock-radio woke her.

92

FOR VIOLA THE night was initially a quiet one. Then, at nearly two, Alice, the puzzle patient, began to cry frantically again. It seemed to Viola that she could not possibly draw breath, her cries were so rapid and without pause, and Viola thought of Natalie's not drawing breath and was frightened.

She went to the bassinet and stood by it, unable to do anything, deliver no additional pain medication, not even pick the little body up and hold it to comfort it, tears wetting the little face, eyes tightly shut, so very much pain locked behind them in that little body. Viola felt a terrible helplessness.

She became aware of Missy, the baby who was in for the second time for failure to thrive, staring at her from the other bassinet. It was Missy's way of asking. Viola picked her up and held her and rubbed her back and returned to stand over Alice, as if by standing there and caressing Missy, Viola might communicate some relief to Alice—the little black infant in so much pain for which nothing could be done and the little white infant for whom everything could be done with so very little—love and attention. Viola found herself in a rage at the white mother, a woman she had never met. The report was that the woman dressed well and brought Missy to Back Bay Met by choice. The social worker also reported that the mother "plays socioeconomic games."

After several minutes Alice's crying stopped as abruptly as

it had begun and Viola saw that she was asleep again, the torso trembling but also moving with inhalation and exhalation. Viola remained beside the bassinet, still holding and caressing Missy. When Alice's crying finally stopped echoing in her mind and she found that the floor was truly silent, Viola turned away and lowered Missy into her own bassinet. Missy looked at Viola and then closed her eyes as soon as Viola put her down.

Viola went back to Alice.

It was a deep hour in the night and, in spite of Nancy in with Jamaal, Viola felt totally alone and so chilly that she got a sweater and put it on. She was scared for Alice—the frantic, breathless crying—and she was obsessing about Natalie's respiratory arrest and death. There was an arrest team down on the picket line, but no doc on the pedi floors as Mozart had been. How much longer would it take a team to come in off the street and get to the floor?

Although she had done a regular check just a few minutes before, she got up and went to each bed and with her penlight studied each child and satisfied herself that the children were all as they ought to be for the night.

When she went again to Alice, the little body still drawn up in its bizarre position, she stood by the bassinet for a considerable length of time, playing with her associations, studying the images in her mind and trying to understand why her mind took her to the South Seas when she wanted it to tell her what was wrong with Alice.

Viola was certain that she already knew the diagnosis, that the informatin was in some misplaced file in her mind, a file that suggested warm breezes, coconut palms, shining sand, pale green seas . . . And there she was, aboard a brig, a wooden ship, the square sails hanging loosely above her, hot sun and silence.

The library in the station consisted only of medical product references, nothing diagnostic. Where could she get a copy of *Principles of Internal Medicine* at four-fifteen in the morning?

She began making calls and found one in the ER. The problem was getting it to her. But an hour later Viola had it and after a few minutes of reading she felt pleasure and excitement. She checked Alice's chart and felt assurance as well.

No wonder everyone had suspected rickets. In infants it had been more than a millennium before Alice's condition had been differentiated from rickets. It had been around in recorded medicine since 1500 B.C., had crippled significant portions of the Crusader armies, and had not been successfully identified with a prophylaxis until 1753, when a ship's surgeon (there, that was where the South Seas had beckoned her, Viola thought), *a ship's surgeon* had written on the subject and described the efficacy of oranges and lemons.

The condition had not been recognized because no one saw it anymore. It could only show up at Back Bay Met, she thought.

Viola was pleased with herself, but much more pleased that with intravenous sodium ascorbate, little Alice would be out of her singular posture and relieved of her misery in a week to ten days. Alice had a vitamin C deficiency, and when Viola checked the history she found that, yes, Alice was on a milk formula but had no supplement to it. Her nutrition was simply incomplete.

In Alice's chart, under Nursing Care Impressions, Viola wrote, "Alice's symptoms are consistent with scurvy."

93

ELIN AWOKE TWENTY minutes before her alarm would have signaled her to do so, her body and mind buoyant with enthusiasm for the day. *Be awake! Get on with life!* she thought. She smiled in the darkness, treasuring the present. She felt as if her bed, this recently airborne flying carpet, were tilting a bit, weighed down on one side by all that compact, muscular presence of the young man who lay asleep next to her. He lay so motionless and still, so deep in his sleep, that Elin had an urge to check to see if he was still alive, still so marvelously companionable to her. Instead, she got up, went into the bathroom, quietly closed the door, and, soundlessly humming Brahms to herself, prepared herself for getting dressed.

When she woke Hal, he responded like a stranger. It did

not bother Elin. He was up, he was moving, but apparently still anesthetized with sleep. She turned on the miniature television on the top of her dresser and hummed aloud until the news anchor's voice said, *"Tragedy early this morning at Back Bay Metropolitan Hospital. Albert Cornelius, seventy-five, was found beaten to death—"*

"Ohhh!" Elin cried out and Hal came back quickly, alert now, and the two of them stood side by side and looked at the tiny black-and-white picture.

"His body was discovered on hospital grounds next to the laundry. Cornelius' assailant or assailants are unknown, but police speculate that he was struck in the head until he was unconscious and then beaten until he was dead. Mr. Cornelius was a retired shipyard worker. Police believe that robbery was the motive."

The news broke for a commercial. Music, gaiety. Elin sat on the bed, her hands on her thighs open in helplessness. When Hal spoke to her she did not reply.

As Elin drove them to work, Hal read aloud from Lynn Keating's commentary, a column that began on the front page of the *Eagle*. " 'If the hospital had been properly functioning,' " he read, " 'no one would have been killed in its shadows. Just prior to his murder, Albert Cornelius had been out in front of the hospital showing his support for the house officers. It is tragically ironic that if these arrogant and elitist young doctors had been on duty where they should have been, Albert Cornelius would not be dead today.' That's horseshit," Hal said.

Elin still did not say anything. Hal watched her, not yet enough familiar with her to begin to decipher her long quiet. "There's more," he said. "She goes on about the nurses."

It was not yet six-thirty and Bennett was waiting in his office for Dorothea Kullgren. He reread the end of the Keating commentary:

> Anyone familiar with BBMH, even on its best days when it is fully staffed, knows that it ought to be shut down. Under the present circumstances it ought to be shut down immediately.
>
> Before there is another death such as Albert Cornelius'.

Before some undereducated and unqualified nurse makes a mistake that costs a life.

BBMH ought to be closed immediately and then the city ought to take the opportunity to close it permanently.

Exactly, Bennett thought. Exactly what a lot of people were thinking at City Hall.

At six-thirty Dorothea arrived for the conference with Bennett about the testimony they would present before the Labor Relations Commission later in the morning—testimony that there was a strike by house officers in effect at Back Bay Metropolitan Hospital. She glanced at the newspaper on his desk and said, "The lady is a snake."

Bennett began talking about the testimony. He walked around with a mug of coffee in his hand, and Dorothea noticed that he kept returning to his window and looking down at the street. Finally, at twenty of seven, he remained at the window and said, "Dorothea, come here. What is that down there?"

Dorothea looked down at twenty or so nurses standing together across the street from the hospital. Dorothea herself had been an officer of NSA and active in nurse advocacy before joining Management. "It's a slowdown, Bennett. They're not coming to work until the last minute. They'll leave at the exact minute. They won't do more than their contract calls for during the day. I heard about it last night. Frankly, I didn't think this many would go along with it."

"Well, there aren't many."

"No, there aren't."

Bennett turned and tapped the copy of the *Eagle* on his desk. "What about this? Nurses doing things they're not qualified to do."

"Everyone's working within bounds."

"At the edge sometimes? One foot out of bounds sometimes?"

"I think both feet are in."

Bennett returned to the evidence he wanted presented to the LRC.

Audrey was already tired when she got on the MBTA to go to the hospital. The dreams and the emotional energy involved had exhausted her before she ever got out of bed. But the dreams had finally wrenched her free of the doc. She knew she was no longer harboring any residue of resentment toward him. It had been expended during the restless night. If he called and wanted to speak with her, even that wouldn't bother her.

As she opened her newspaper on the T, her weariness vanished quickly enough when, in Keating's article, she came across what might be references to Med Three and to herself. The references were general enough at first, but then they became more specific:

> In the absence of house officers, nurses at BBMH are breaking every tenet of and restriction upon their profession.
>
> The nurses are literally taking the lives of the patients in their own hands. They are practicing medicine as if they had the education and authority of a physician.
>
> A frightened BBMH patient informed this reporter by phone that ''the nurses think they have a license to do anything they want.''
>
> The patient cited instances of medications being discontinued, dosages being increased, and even new medicines being administered—all without a doctor's order.

When she walked from the elevated station to the hospital, Audrey unconsciously held the newspaper against herself protectively.

''Hey, lady!''

''Audrey, stop!''

She stopped automatically. The voices were coming from a group of nurses on the other side of the street.

''Audrey, come stand with us!''

She smiled at them and shook her head no and shrugged and started toward the archway into the Old Building.

''Crumb!''

Then there was a word she did not expect at all and it quite shook her. *''Bitch!''*

She stopped and turned toward the nurses on the other side of Tremaine. Then one nurse stepped away from the others and crossed the street toward Audrey.

Nan Lassitter came up to Audrey and said, ''I was uncomfortable over there anyway. I'm glad of the excuse to leave.''

She and Audrey began walking together. "Most of them, their hearts are in the right place."

Audrey smiled again. "But not their feet."

Coralee arrived on the floor immediately after Audrey. "I was right behind you. I heard what they called you."

"I'm not used to being yelled at by friends, colleagues. It hurt."

"Diana Vezzina is a smart young nurse, and good. But right now she's being a young smartass."

"I don't think Diana called me a name."

"No. It's this *activity* of hers I'm referring to." Coralee lay an *Eagle* on the counter. "See this?"

Audrey put her own down beside Coralee's. "With headlines like these, who could resist?"

"Probably no one in the city."

"How did Keating find out all this stuff? I mean, some of these things happened right here on this floor."

"My dear, I assure you, I wasn't the one who ratted."

They began to take report from the night nurse. At ten till seven Hal Levy came in. Coralee glanced at him and then looked more closely. "You don't look well."

He put his index finger on the DEATH DUE HOS headline. "I was with this guy, Albert Cornelius, just a couple of hours before he got killed. We tried to give him a ride home. My friend Elin Maki. She was concerned for his safety. He was a patient of hers. She's real shook up."

Hal did not seem aware that he had given away a relationship with Elin. Report continued.

In a few minutes Diana Vezzina came directly to the station from the stairwell. She said, "You ought to have been over there with us, Audrey. But there's no excuse for anyone's calling you names."

Audrey looked at the clock. It was one minute before seven. Diana was headed back to the stairwell and her duty on Med Four.

Tim got Jason to the hospital day care center at twenty of seven and was on the unit five minutes later. Jason was already complaining about being at the day care center instead of school. "They're all *little* kids," he said again, and Tim felt bad about that and said, "It's only for a few days." He still felt bad about Jason being away from his friends and his own age group even as he took report and figured out the priorities immediately ahead.

A little after eight, he was in the station making an entry on a report sheet when he became aware of someone's entering the unit from the corridor and coming to the station. The man wore dark slacks and a short-sleeved tan and red shirt open at the neck. He was tall and somewhat overweight. He did not belong to any of the patients or to the hospital. He should not have been there. Tim rose to challenge the man.

The man said, "Mr. Holbrook? Timothy Holbrook?"

"Yes."

The man reached toward his back pocket and handed Tim a long envelope. "This is for you. Have a good day," and left the unit.

THE STATE OF MASSACHUSETTS

Suffolk County Superior Court. To Timothy A. Holbrook:
  You are required to appear at Suffolk County Superior Court on the 11th day of May, 1984, at 9 A.M., to testify what you know relating to Holbrook v. Holbrook, then and there to be heard, in which seizure of the minor child Jason T. Holbrook shall be adjudged.
  Hereof fail not, as you will answer your default under the penalties prescribed by law.

It was dated and signed by Andrew C. Harrelson, Presiding Justice, and struck Tim with a cold and numbing fear. He had requested this hearing on Friday himself. Why was he being subpoenaed to it? And the language—*seizure*. Why was the court using that language? It had to be Valerie's lawyer.

When Tim got hold of Warren Gates later in the morning, Warren said, "If it's any solace to you, you sure got Valerie juiced up. She and Flynn were very busy yesterday. The papers were just delivered. It's not just the subpoena. There's a motion for contempt, and that's silly. What's the judge going to do, throw you in jail? What's more serious is a motion to prohibit all visitation between yourself and Jason."

"Would the court do that?"

"It could. There's also another motion to change the wording of the original decree. What it comes down to is, Valerie is asking the court to free her from its jurisdiction."

"Why?"

"So that she can move Jason out of town or out of state or even out of the country without having to notify the court and have the move reviewed. Flynn says she's talking about moving to Europe, to Mexico, all over."

"Could she, and take Jason?"

"Oh yes. One way or another, she intends to take you out of Jason's life." Warren was silent for a few seconds. "Let's get together Thursday afternoon. Are you clear for Friday at nine?"

"Yes. I've got someone to take my place."

"Because you can't afford to be even a few minutes late. Both sides have told Judge Harrelson that this is urgent and he changed his calendar for it."

94

BY ELEVEN IN the morning Viola felt weary and abused. It was one thing to do a double by coming on in the afternoon and working through the evening and then staying on for regular night duty. In the course of those sixteen hours the work slowed and even stilled, and there was the opportunity to recuperate. It was quite another thing to follow her own duty with the day duty. The work sped from the beginning and became more and more demanding. And it was one thing to go from afternoon through the evening and into night. That was natural. It was another thing to go from nightwork into daywork. That was unnatural, and Viola's body rhythms and mind rhythms were out of whack.

Now she was alone on the floor except for a visit, who was temporary for the morning and who was writing a very few orders before leaving. Margaret Gaines was making rounds on the other pedi floors she supervised. Viola was being attended by a solemn ten-year-old boy named Walker, who now stood just outside the station staring in at her. He was a severe asthmatic and he had first been brought in on her shift a few nights before. It was the season for severe asthmatics on Pedi as well as on the adult medical floors. Now he was stabilized and was to go home this afternoon. When he found that Viola was staying on duty, Walker had followed he around all morning.

Viola was in the station so that she could keep an eye on the orders the visit was writing. He was not a pediatrician but, as he explained to the children he examined, a "big people's doctor." Some of the children had been proud, some disappointed.

The telephone rang. "Children's Seven. Viola."

"Yeah, Vi. This is Admitting. You've got an eight-year-old male asthmatic coming up. Do you know where you want to put him?"

"I've got the bed. Send him up." She put down the phone and picked up a chart the visit had just closed. She indicated a medication order and said, "Excuse me, Doctor, do you want to float the kid away?"

The big people's doctor looked at what he had written.

Viola said, "A hundred cc's an hour would be fine for an adult. But you've got a thirty-five-pound patient here. We're more used to, like, twenty-five to thirty cc's an hour." She said it quietly.

The visit looked at her, then reached for the chart. "Thanks." He corrected the order. When he was ready to leave, he said, "That's an interesting diagnosis—scurvy. You ever see scurvy?"

"No."

"Neither have I." Then he left.

The eight-year-old asthmatic was delivered. Slo-Phyllin had been ordered to be administered immediately and Viola had to decide quickly which of her tricks she would use to attempt to get the boy to hold the medicine down. Most kids puked it up as soon as they swallowed it.

She saw the boy placed on his bed and then said, "Hi, Adam. My name is Vi and I'm going to take care of you."

"Take *good* care of you," Walker said.

Viola was not certain what Walker's inflection was meant to imply. "I'm going to give you some medicine," Viola said, removing the top from a one-time plastic delivery cup.

"Throw-up stuff," Walker said solemnly to Adam.

"Walker, that is not helpful."

The little boy stared up at both of them. "Betcha can't keep it down," Walker said.

Viola felt a gentle urge to strangle Walker and then realized that his observation might prove a useful challenge. The boy's eyes were back on Viola, but his concentration was simply on breathing. She said, "This medicine is going to make you feel fine in about two or three days."

"Done me," Walker said.

"But you've got to keep it inside you. Even if it makes you feel bad at first."

Adam nodded. Viola handed him the medicine. He swallowed it. He began to gag. Viola glared at him and yelled, "You will not throw up, Adam! You will not!" The child looked at her, terrified. *"Don't throw up, Adam. Don't do it!"*

Adam looked at her with his mouth open and his eyes wide. But he did not throw up.

"Done the same to me," Walker said solemnly. "You got no choice."

Viola said to Adam, "Good boy," and she smoothed his brow and then got him to bed.

"You gonna get better," Walker said to Adam. "Like me. Breathe jes *fine*."

When Viola turned around, two visitors were entering. One was a nine- or ten-year-old black boy. The other was a white woman, twenty-five or twenty-six or twenty-seven. The boy went toward Jamaal's cubicle. From behind the glass the vent nurse smiled and waved him in. The woman went to Missy's bassinet and picked the baby up. Neither the woman nor the baby displayed any reaction to each other.

Viola had never seen the woman before. She went over.

The woman put Missy down almost without looking and then straightened and smiled at Viola extravagantly and extended her hand. "Hello, I'm Jackie Bader. I'm Missy's mother."

She was an extraordinarily attractive woman, Viola saw, the sort of woman who wore her own beauty as if it were a high rank she had achieved. Her dress was patterned and bright and expensive, and it was cut low enough to expose some breast and cleavage and, when she bent, the white frill around the upper edge of her bra.

"Are you new?" she said to Viola.

"I'm Missy's night nurse."

"Really." She smiled extravagantly again. "What *are* we to do about Missy? She has no sense about taking care of herself."

"That's your job, Mrs. Bader."

"Oh, really? Did I need that pointed out?"

"I'm sorry, Mrs. Bader. I only meant that—"

The smile again. Mrs. Bader patted Viola on the shoulder. "Oh, don't apologize there. I know *you* understand, being a nurse. Missy will just *not* do the things she needs to do to grow up to become a beautiful woman. I *cannot* get her to eat. It's as if she's dieting *already*. There's plenty of time for that, I tell her." Mrs. Bader laughed and poked Missy with a finger, not gently, and without looking at her.

"If you'll excuse me, I'll leave you with Missy."

Again she smiled at Viola. "I'm afraid I haven't much time for Missy today. I've a luncheon engagement. At the Ritz. Life makes so many demands. Now, just as soon as Missy is home again—" She stopped and thought. "Are you fond of Missy?"

"Yes."

"Have you ever considered domestic employment?" The woman was smiling.

Viola thought, She just doesn't understand what she's saying. Or she's an all-out bitch. Viola said, "No," and walked away.

Margaret Gaines was back on the floor. In the station she said, "I see you've met dear Mrs. Bader."

"She took a shine to me immediately. She offered me domestic employment."

"How dear of her. She must like you especially. No one else has gotten that offer from her."

"No one else is black daytimes on this floor."

"I didn't miss the shine reference, Viola."

"Okay."

"Mrs. Bader is a trial to us all. We try not to hit her."

Viola smiled. "Who's the kid in with Jamaal?"

"That's his brother, Quentin. Quentin has permission to

come over at noon recess. Comes over every day for about ten minutes.''

"I didn't know that. Why doesn't he come over after school?''

"He has to be home with his little first-grade sister. To take care of her. Quentin's in third grade. Their mother works till four. That's when she comes in.''

"Oh, I know her. I didn't know about Quentin and visiting.''

"Go on in and say hello.'' But then Margaret stopped her. "Tired, Viola?''

"I'll make it.''

"For a minute there it didn't look like it. Go on now.''

Viola went into Jamaal's cubicle. *Sesame Street* was on Jamaal's television, a color set the nurses had gotten him at Christmas. Quentin was explaining the show to Jamaal. "See, ol' Cookie Monster, he tryin' t'fool Ernie, but Ernie, he *suspicious*.'' Jamaal's eyes were not on the television but on Quentin.

The vent nurse introduced Viola to Quentin, who said, "I'm glad t'meet you, but I got to get back soon, so you don't mind, I talk to my brother some more.'' And he turned back to Jamaal.

Viola remained behind him. The scene was now outside the brownstone and Oscar the Grouch was emerging from his garbage can.

Quentin said, "Our house jes like that One-two-three *Sesame Street* house, Jam. I keep tellin' you. We live there on the second floor. You gonna come home to it, see it, *be* there, one a these days. I keep *tellin'* you, you unnerstan' me, Jam?''

Jamaal kept looking at his brother. Viola left. Margaret had been standing outside the cubicle. "He says almost the same thing every day.''

"Sad,'' Viola said. "It makes me want to cry.''

Margaret nodded. "But it gives a body some faith in human goodness. I think all the children have it. To start with.''

Viola had a sudden thought about her head nurse and supervisor. "Is that why you've spent the whole thirty-two years with children?''

Margaret looked surprised and was silent for several seconds. "Why yes, Viola, I think it is.''

Viola went back to check on Adam. He was still breathing
with labor, but Walker was sitting on his bedside talking to
him and he seemed distracted from his discomfort, so Viola
decided not to interrupt. Returning to the station she was
stopped by Mrs. Bader, who thrust Missy at her. "Oh, Viola,
would you take Missy for me, *please*. She has no manners."
Viola received the baby. "She's dribbling all over my dress
and *me*, for heaven's sake." Mrs. Bader bent the fingers of
one hand to some baby dribble on her exposed chest. Alice,
behind Mrs. Bader, began her pathetic, frantic, breathless
crying, torn with pain. Mrs. Bader removed her baby's dribble with a Kleenex and turned to look at the crying baby
behind her. One of the kids, Viola saw, had placed a doll in
the bassinet with Alice, a doll that had belonged to Natalie
Briggs.

"How *sweet*," Mrs. Bader said, reaching for Natalie's
doll.

Holding Missy, cradling her, Viola cried out at the baby's
mother, "Don't you *dare* touch that!"

Mrs. Bader withdrew her hand.

Viola held Missy to herself, Alice's screaming penetrating
her. "You're Fifty-one-A material, lady."

Mrs. Bader did not even reply, but left Viola holding
Missy and went directly to Margaret Gaines. Viola continued
to hold and soothe Missy as the two of them talked. Then
Mrs. Bader left the floor without returning to her baby. Viola
gently returned Missy to her bassinet.

Margaret signaled Viola to the station. "I'm going to call
Day. I want you to see Molly. This afternoon."

"Why? You know that woman—"

"You were verbally abusive. Publicly. You have no right
to judge her."

"She's a terrible person. You said so yourself."

"Not in those words. And not to her face. Not in an
observed situation."

"You *judged* her yourself. To me."

"But I didn't act on it. You did. Also, *neither* of us has
any right to judge her."

"You saw her with Missy."

"Your problem isn't with what Mrs. Bader did or didn't do,
your problem is with what you did. I'm calling Day, I'll have
her get Molly. I've got to *trust* nurses on these floors."

Viola was silent until she could not be. "Are you getting at Natalie Briggs? Because she died?"

"Not a bit of it. No one faults you there."

"But Mrs. Bader—"

"You lost control. That's what concerns me."

95

CORALEE SAID, "CAPTAIN Malamet's monitor is blank."

Audrey was startled. "Did you check—"

"The monitor has been unplugged. The leads have been detached from the patient. Captain Malamet has flown."

"Call Security—"

"I already have. I'm becoming the floor's authority on missing persons."

"Lost another one, huh?" Day said.

Audrey looked at her silently before speaking. "I can't believe you said that. Your humor is appalling."

"It's pregnancy at my age that probably accounts for it. Was Captain Malamet unhappy here, do you think?"

"No. Day, I'm *concerned*."

"Well, steady on, you're going to lose another."

"Day, I'm getting irritated."

"You're not going to believe this. Mrs. Gehl."

"No."

"But yes. She's got a bed in Long Island."

"How did you do it?"

"Massive paperwork. It finally paid off."

"You're right," Audrey said, "I don't believe it." Day abruptly looked grim. "Swallow something?" Audrey said.

"Yes, I'm swallowing it right now. What would probably happen to Mrs. Gehl if we didn't get this bed for her in a chronic facility?"

"They'd find her dead one day in her room at home," Coralee said.

"Look at all the work and energy and time for something that should have been a routine placement."

"It's a victory," Coralee said.

"It's a battle that shouldn't have to have been fought."

"Like the HOs outside."

"The HOs aren't going to win anything," Day said, "except a lot of public animosity."

"You disapprove," Coralee said.

"I disapprove."

"You and I disagree."

Security brought Captain Malamet back to the floor a few minutes later. He had gotten his street clothes out of the closet, put them on, and gone down to Tremaine Avenue. He had a handful of HO material. "I just wanted to see what those people are doing down there. Sort of like the air traffic controllers. Public employees going on strike. Can't be tolerated."

"Some of those people saved your life."

"Controllers were helpful that way too from time to time. But we all have to live by the rules."

"But not you, huh?" Audrey said.

Malamet looked blank. "I don't understand."

"Disconnecting the monitor. Going downstairs."

"Look. I'm as strong as I ever was. And I'm a strong man."

"Captain Malamet, a *strong* man would remain in bed when he's supposed to. Sometimes passivity requires strength."

"Kind of silly. The way I feel."

"Captain Malamet, aside from your personal care, when you pull a stunt like this you interfere with our taking care of other patients. Now please, limit your activity to the floor. We'll decide when you're on the monitor and when you're off."

"When am I off? I mean completely?"

"If Dr. Schoonoler agrees, this afternoon."

"See?" He grinned at Audrey. "This was no big deal." He went back toward his room, whistling.

Hal, down the corridor, was pulling Jan out of Dom's room. Jan was resisting. Audrey went to the two of them as Hal managed Jan into her own room. He said, "Jan just slapped Dom. She hit him pretty good."

Audrey went to Dom immediately and examined him. The damage was superficial. "What happened?"

"She's crazy. I think she's crazy."

"You're not telling me what happened."

"She was telling me a lot of stories. Things she's done, what she thinks she knows about other people. A lot of bullshit. I'm tired. I get drowsy after lunch here. So I told her I wanted to take a nap. And she hit me."

"I think you're okay."

"Yeah, I think so, too. Maybe you can keep her away from me."

"I'll try. I think she needs you."

Audrey went into Jan's room. Chanda was asleep. Jan was sitting up in bed smiling—glowing, in fact, Audrey thought. Audrey said, "What do you think you're doing?"

"Drinking in my flowers," Jan said. She smiled at the brilliant display on a bureau.

"I mean hitting Dom."

"Did I do that?"

"*Jan.*"

"Silly me, I guess I did. Shall I go kiss and make up?"

"You'll stay right here. Answer my question."

"He made me sad. He made me very angry."

"About what?"

She began to cry. Big, free-flowing sudden tears. "*I don't know.*"

Audrey became a little apprehensive and a little cautious. She was not at all understanding what was going on with Jan. Was it emotional or was there a physiological basis? She went to the station and got a blood pressure machine and came back and said, "Jan, I'm going to take your signs." Jan was smiling again.

Her blood pressure was down slightly and there was an increase in pulse—neither significant. The temp was normal, pupils may be dilated, maybe not. "How do you feel, Jan?"

"Sad." But she was smiling.

"I mean, how do you feel physically?"

"Fine." She grinned.

Jan was on Inderal, a heart medicine that protected the patient from changes in pressure and rate. If Jan's odd behavior had a physiological basis somewhere, the Inderal could be subordinating the signs of it. Audrey decided that in the absence of any significant signs, she'd wait and just have Elin look in on Jan, and even Dr. Schoonoler when he came by, and she'd get Trina up from the ER for a chat with Jan and a psych evaluation.

"Actually," Jan said, "this conversation has been a terribly sobering experience." Audrey smiled at Jan's mock gravity. "I know I shouldn't have slugged Dom. I'm sorry. I'll apologize to him later."

"I don't think he wants any more visits from you, Jan."

"I'll be brief, I promise. Now I think I'll have a little nappy-poo."

"All right, Jan." She went back to the station.

Coralee was hanging up the phone. "It's a strike," she said. "The LRC ruling just came down."

"Does it change anything?"

"It's the first step in sending them to jail if they don't come back."

"Are they coming back?"

"No."

96

MOLLY WENT ACROSS Tremaine and got a grinder from a shop and came back and sat on a cement wall outside the hospital and ate her lunch in the warm sunshine. There was a bigger turnout today of ARI people and they were better organized. There were a lot more neighborhood people out, too. Molly recognized a number of people who had been patients. Some of them were actively assisting the HOs. They had positioned themselves near the entrances to the hospital, but carefully away from the access paths guaranteed by the police, and, neighbor to neighbor, they tried to dissuade walk-in patients.

"Hey, brother, why you headin' in there?"

"See my uncle."

"Peace."

A black woman stopped a white man. " 'Scuse me. You fixin' to go in there?"

"Nonna your black business."

" 'Scuse me. It's neighborhood business. You live in the neighborhood?" The white man tried to step around her. A cop marked them. The lady said, "The doctors. You know about them?"

"Heard some on TV."

"Well, you got family in this neighborhood, you don't want to go hurtin' the actors. They're out here on the street to help all of us, black and white, and that's the truth."

The cop came over. He said to the white man, "You got a problem here?"

The lady said, "Both my babies born here. Bring 'em back when they're sick. Doctors take good care of 'em. *Good* people, these doctors."

The white man said, "I don't believe I'm doing this," and he turned and started to walk away, then he turned again and shouted at the lady, *"Where the fuck do I go instead?"*

"If you talk to one of the doctors, they'll advise you where to go."

"I've got a good idea where you can all go."

"Thank you, sir," the lady said as the man headed toward the HOs' information center.

One of the sympathizers was suddenly not so gentle. She was a physically fantastic woman dressed in platform shoes, shorts, a striped jersey, and a white turban. "Fuckin' strikebreakah!" she yelled at a woman who was going into the New Wing. The would-be patient or visitor stopped. "Stay the fuck outa my hospittle! You leave my doctors alone!"

The police were quick to order Dora away and see that she moved, but Molly also recognized from the expressions on their faces that they regarded Dora as something of a comic diversion. Molly thought that was a mistake.

The woman Dora had stopped went on into the New Wing.

The HOs tried to keep the area where they paraded and handed out literature clear of anyone who was not there for information or medical counseling. But they were not always successful.

97

TRINA WAS CALLED OUT to the line almost as soon as she got to work. A disturbance was developing and it was presumed that Trina would know how to handle it.

Trina understood the presumption when she got outside.

The central character was Dora. She was being restrained by
two city police who looked in need of further assistance. She
slowed down when she saw Trina, and the two cops looked
relieved.

"What's she been doing?" Trina said.

"Doin' what's *gots* to be done!" Dora said.

"Blockin' access to the hospital," one cop said. "Threatnin'
people, callin' names, alla time screamin' at people, refusin'
to desist, refusin' to comply with an officer's request she quit
the premises."

The second officer said, "She was goin' t'hit someone 'cept
we grabbed her in time."

"I was just intendin' to move him along," Dora said.
"Ain't gonna *hit* no one."

The first officer said, "We don't want to jug this lady,
Nurse."

"Ain't got a big enough cell," the second one said
admiringly.

"Coupla docs said you got the way to deal with her when
she's wild."

Trina said, "Can you control yourself, Dora?"

Dora actually bowed her head. "Yes."

"I want to talk to you. You come inside with me."

Trina walked away, Dora beside her, the two cops straight-
ening their uniforms and equipment and watching in some
amazement, the nurse and the wild lady departing as if nothing at all had happened.

The ER waiting area was empty except for three ancillary
staff behind the counter and the boyish-faced, red-haired
security guard, who regarded Dora warily.

"Ain't gonna swing at you," Dora said to him. "Not this
week. Big, handsome man like you."

The guard grinned. "Go on there, jus' tryin' t'get on my
good side."

"Honey, I *always* gets on *everybody's* good side. One way
or 'nother, once I sets my mind. There's so much of me."

"Dora," Trina said, "we can have our talk right here or
we can go to a psych room."

"Talk right here. Ain't disturbin' no one."

"You know what you did out there?"

"I was a bad ass."

"A real bad ass. Is that what you want to be?"

"They needs help out there. Keep the strikebreakahs out. I know 'bout strikebreakahs. My daddy got his haid smashed up byuh asshole honky strikebreakah. Got his haid fixed up right here in this hospittle, too. Put some metal in it."

"You can't go around screaming at people because they want to come in here."

"Jes helpin'." She looked at Trina hostilely. "'Pears like my hospittle needs all the help it can get."

"It's not your hospital, Dora. It's the city's, the neighborhood's."

"It's still my fuckin' hospittle, too. *Mine*."

"Dora, how long we been having this conversation? A year? Two years?"

"It's still *my* hospittle. Much as anyone's. You sayin' *no?*"

"No. I'm not."

"Then I gots the right to be here an' *help*."

"But not the right to be abusive. I always have to say the same things to you. You always say the same things back. Then you tear out of here."

"I don't want to leave this time."

"You want to sign yourself in?"

"No. Nonna *that* shit. I jes don't want to leave."

"Why?"

"Got to whisper. Won't make out I'm crazy? No matter what?"

"I'll listen to you, Dora. And I'll talk to you about it."

"I 'bout *goin'* crazy, what I been thinkin'."

"What's that?"

"This strike. I *gots* to stay here, make sure the hospittle don't go 'way. Now ain't that crazy?"

"You're afraid for the hospital. You want to help."

"My *daddy* got his fuckin' life saved here. When no one else gave a shit. I'm out there on the streets, I gets around this neighborhood *a lot*. Ain't a family out there don't owe a life to this place." She was silent. Then she spoke in a rage. *"You know what's gonna happen this place closes, the doctuhs lose?"*

"The place isn't going to close."

"You know white folks don't care about *us!*"

"This is a temporary situation."

"This hospittle closes, Trina, *ma deah*, this whole fuckin'

neighborhood goes down the fuckin' tube." Dora's cheeks
streamed with tears.

"There'll always be someone here to take care of you,
Dora. And the rest of the neighborhood."

"Girl, you ain't got *no way* promisin' that. *No way*. You
know it."

"All right."

"I gots to go out there and do my thing."

"No!" Dora was shocked by the unfamiliar loudness and
command from Trina. "You are *not* to do your thing. Not out
there."

"I gots to do somethin'."

"I'll find you something you can do. I'll talk to the house
officers and find something useful you can do."

Dora spoke meekly for the first time ever. "I'd be
obliged."

"The amazing thing is," Trina told Hal when he came down
from Med Three, "with all that rage in her, she's trying to
use it for something constructive."

"How long will it last?"

"Ah, Dr. Levy. Cynical already?"

"Realistic?"

"I have no idea how long it will last. They've got her
passing out information releases all through the neighborhood."

"Streetwalking?"

"You know, I've never heard anyone call Dora a whore.
No one. For all I know she's got an independent income.
Everyone in the neighborhood knows her. She can be gentle,
she can be abusive and almost violent. People are careful
around her. But when she's behaving, everyone likes her,
everyone trusts her."

"What sets her off?"

"Her sense of injustice. Clinically, though, you see, her
sense of injustice has a few roots in psychosis."

98

MOLLY SAID TO Viola, "It's a bitch having to come see the psych nurse after sixteen hours on the floor, isn't it?"

Viola shrugged. "I'm too tired to care, I guess."

"Sure. You work your ass off two straight shifts, and instead of someone patting it for you, it gets spanked. Sure you don't care?"

"I don't."

"Are you saying the hell with you, Molly, and the rest of you? Or are you saying the hell with me, Viola?"

"I'm here like I'm supposed to be, that's all I'm saying."

"Tell me what's been going on with you."

"Don't you want to hear about Mrs. Bader and Natalie?"

Molly was silent.

"Well," Viola said, "I've just been working. That's about all." She started with the night of Natalie Briggs's respiratory arrest and went on to her diagnosis of scurvy the night before and her anger at Mrs. Bader about Missy today.

They were in Molly's small office, the door closed. Molly had given Viola a chair in front of her desk and taken another one facing her so that the desk was not between them. Molly listened, a glum expression on her face.

"That's all," Viola said after a couple of minutes. "Can I go? I have to be back on duty in less than eight hours. Unless you're going to suspend me or something. I really don't care. I'm too tired."

Molly said abruptly, "You're going to have to deal with Natalie Briggs. Blowing up at Mrs. Bader isn't dealing with Natalie Briggs."

"The one doesn't have anything to do with the other."

"Of course not. Did I say that? No. You did."

"When?"

"At the very beginning. You asked me didn't I want to hear about Mrs. Bader and Natalie."

"No. I said Missy."

"No, Viola, you said Mrs. Bader and *Natalie*." Viola

looked at Molly with anger. "Pardon, but I am not Mrs. Bader nor am I a fan of hers."

"Can I go now?"

"What am I, a policeman, your mother, you've got to ask permission? How old do you feel right now?"

Viola looked at Molly with real fury. Then she sighed and her face softened. "I feel about three years old and you've caught me out."

"Also, I'm not letting you have your way. Make that four or five years old. They're more sophisticated."

Viola looked at Molly and spoke quietly. "I never lost . . . A child never died on me before. Not while I was working. Not while I was caring for it."

"Natalie's death is your responsibility."

"*It is not!*" Viola stood up.

Molly remained seated. "Certainly it is. That's what you keep telling me. That's what you keep telling yourself. Personally, I don't agree. Now which one of us shall we believe?"

Viola smiled at Molly entirely without humor. "You're a real headfucker, aren't you?"

"Sit down, please, Viola. I never lost a patient yet."

"Well, I did!"

"That's what you keep saying. What was it, negligence on your part?"

"*No!*"

"No. It was a spontaneous cerebral aneurysm and it shut down Natalie's respiration. You saw the Path findings and I read them myself a little while ago. Sit down. You look terrible."

"I'm tired."

"Part of that's a defense."

"Oh fuck, Molly." But Viola sat down.

"I have no doubt that after sixteen hours there's some mental and physical basis for your tiredness. But you're a healthy young woman and at your age, a decade ago, I could do a double and boogie all night, so to speak, and come back and do another shift, and I'm sure you've done the same. So let's cut the crap about how exhausted you are and talk about what's really making you feel terrible."

"All right, Molly. By the way, I'm not a patient."

"Of course you're not. My, my. Did I say that? Silly me. I must have confused you with someone else."

Viola smiled.

Molly responded by saying, "Well, maybe we're getting to it. What happened today. Natalie's death is your responsibility. You're pretty angry at yourself for that. You don't know what to do with that anger. You don't even own that it's there. So in walks this certified bitch Jackie Bader and she's a target of opportunity. Natalie's death is your responsibility just like Missy's well-being is her mother's responsibility. But Mrs. Bader is practicing negligence on a twenty-four-hour basis and you let her have all the anger you felt at yourself."

"There's a *reality* I responded to with anger—"

"Of course there is. There's also a nonreality. Mrs. Bader is not responsible for Natalie's death. No one is. Mrs. Bader is responsible for Missy. But you made a neat crossover. Mrs. Bader's coldness and narcissism helped you disguise the truth of it from yourself."

Viola said, "All right," softly. "All right. But Natalie came in . . ." She smiled slightly. "But Missy came in . . . The prime thing is failure to thrive, but she came in with *dirt* under her fingernails. How do you explain that?"

"I know. Neglect. You're trying to defend a defenseless infant. I understand that. You're a person before you're a nurse. You don't leave that part of you at home. But nurses do not blow up at people. People do. Now, as a matter of fact, there's a valid psychological basis for the way you went at Mrs. Bader. If you'd been a little restrained. Confronting her, seeing how much she'd come back in defense of herself and her baby."

"She cut out."

"You were acting like a mirror. She spends a lot of time with a mirror, I bet. You let her see what she looks like to the staff. That's why she cut out. That could be constructive."

"I doubt it. She'll just take Missy someplace else."

"Maybe she's been to other places already. Maybe that's why she brings her baby here. She thinks she's superior to this place. No one's going to hold the mirror up to her . . . She made those color references, racial references."

"I know."

"You didn't say anything about them."

"I was more angry about—" Viola interrupted herself with a smile. "All right. I think I understand."

"Sleep on it."

"Is something going on my record?"

"As a matter of fact, yes. But not this. You're a local heroine for a few hours. Your scurvy diagnosis was confirmed. You are personally responsible for seeing your tiny patient out of all that pain."

"That feels good. Real, real good."

"I am sorry to say that over on the pedi floors you are also an underground heroine. For telling Mrs. Bader off."

"I want to follow up with a Fifty-one-A. But I don't trust myself now."

"Right on both scores. A Fifty-one-A is indicated. You should get together with the social worker and discuss it. But wait till you've cooled down. Make sure it's for the infant, not in anger at the mother."

99

ON MED THREE Coralee was doing a double and was the evening charge nurse. Her partner was Debby. Audrey was still on the floor and still working until her Nurse Practice Committee meeting at four-thirty. The three were momentarily at the station together when Debby looked up and said, "Uh-oh. Trouble."

Florence Nightingale had appeared down the corridor. She was passing the station and heading for Captain Malamet's room.

"What's the problem?" Audrey said.

"Mrs. Malamet is just now in with the good captain," Coralee said.

"We ought to stop her," Debby said.

"Unh-unh," Coralee said. "We do not interfere with a patient's private life."

"Unless it's a life-threatening situation," Audrey said.

The three of them watched as Florence Nightingale went to Captain Malamet's door, turned as if to enter, paused, and continued down the corridor to a padded bench and sat down. She took a magazine out of a shoulder bag and began to read.

A few minutes later Mrs. Malamet left her husband's room.
She also paused outside the door. She looked at the nurse with
the magazine. The nurse studied the magazine. Mrs. Malamet
studied the nurse. It seemed to go on for a very long time,
Audrey thought, alone now at the station.

Her attention was diverted by Percy Stevens' two boys,
Glen and Jeff, passing to visit their father. "Hey, you guys."

"Hi, Audrey."

"Where's your mom?"

"Gonna come later. Dad wants to see us alone."

Mrs. Malamet walked away from her husband's door and
left the floor. Florence Nightingale remained seated for a
couple of moments, then got up suddenly and went into
Captain Malamet's room.

Her name was Penny. That much Audrey had established
the afternoon before, when she had gone in to take a blood
pressure and Captain Malamet had introduced his visitor.
Audrey had said, "Gee, Penny, where did you train? I don't
recognize your cap." I'm being evil, Audrey had thought.

"Oh, here and there . . . Mostly overseas," Penny said
firmly.

"That's interesting. Fascinating. Where overseas?"

"Amsterdam," Penny said without hesitation.

Audrey knew that prior to his emergency landing at Back
Bay Met, Captain Malamet had been flying the Boston-Gatwick-
Amsterdam run with, one might presume, serious layovers
with this visiting nurse, who Audrey had no doubt was a
flight attendant, a stew.

The telephone rang. "Med Three, Audrey." She listened
and took down the information about a new patient who was
being sent to the floor. As Audrey listened, Mrs. Malamet
came back by the station, went to her husband's room, and
entered.

Coralee returned to the station as Audrey hung up, and
Audrey told her about Mrs. Malamet's reappearance.

"I thought you looked a little nervous," Coralee said.

"It's none of my business what's going on in there. But he
arrested on me once. It just makes me uneasy."

"Since he's off a monitor, why don't you go check his
signs?" Audrey hesitated. "Seriously, I think it would be a
good idea."

                    *   *   *

The two women in the room were standing. Mrs. Malamet was at the foot of the bed, facing her husband and Penny. Penny stood beside the bed, her head a little down, her eyes averted from Mrs. Malamet's.

Audrey said, "Excuse me, ladies, Captain. Time for a pressure check." She got her patient's sleeve up and wrapped the cuff around his arm.

Mrs. Malamet looked as stable as steel and as tense. She ignored Audrey and Penny and spoke to her husband. She was, Audrey thought as she pumped up the cuff, extraordinarily explicit. "Ralph, you've followed your prick wherever it wants to go just one time too often. You know, dear, you are yourself a prick. I didn't realize when I married you that you're just one grand prick. I just thought you were grand. Now I see you're just a prick."

"Excuse me—" Audrey started.

"Of course. You need quiet," Mrs. Malamet said. "Let's all be quiet."

Malamet's pressure and rate were minimally elevated. Physiologically he appeared to be untroubled. She unwrapped the cuff.

"Flyboy," Mrs. Malamet said to Audrey. "Just a little boy who can't remember to keep his fly closed or his prick out of strange pussy. You didn't know I could use language like that, did you, Ralph?"

He shook his head in some awe. He also looked about forty years younger. Just like a little boy caught with his hand in the cookie jar, Audrey thought.

Mrs. Malamet said to Audrey, "This lady-in-white here, is she a member of your staff, Miss Rosenfeld?"

"No."

"A member of the hospital?"

"Not that I know of."

"A visitor, then."

"That's my understanding."

"Okay, Miss Visitor, get your ass out of here."

Penny looked at Malamet. He nodded. She went to the door and stopped just long enough to say "I'll be in touch. Be well."

Mrs. Malamet said to Audrey, "I admire the girl's sentiments—at a time like this, confrontation with the wife, etcetera." She turned. "Yes, Ralph, be well. And as far as being in touch with young Penny, or any part of her body, that's okay, too.''

"I'll be going,'' Audrey said.

"No. Stay on, Miss Rosenfeld. A minute or two more. In case I bring on another attack. Though I don't believe he has the heart for it.'' Then she addressed her husband. "I really am concerned for your health, Ralph. Word traveled to me about your wenching. Over the years. It caused me a great deal of anguish the first few years. But I wanted to remain married to you. My commitment was to marriage as well as to you. And you never brought home any disease, thank God. And you never embarrassed me with people who knew me. Till now. Why did you choose to humiliate me here? With that little bitch.''

Malamet said nothing.

"After the arrest, Ralph. After you'd been through the intensive care unit. After you saw that your life needed some . . . some caring for, I thought maybe you and I could have a go again.

"But then I saw little Miss Muffet out there, sitting on her little tuffet, just waiting for me to leave, and I decided that's exactly what I'm going to do.''

Malamet still said nothing.

Mrs. Malamet motioned Audrey outside. She spoke quietly. "He's all right, isn't he?''

"Yes, Mrs. Malamet.''

"You see, it's just as I said. He doesn't have the heart for it.''

Audrey still had a few minutes before she had to go to the Nurse Practice Committee, where she and some colleagues would review current nursing care standards. She remembered Percy Stevens' boys and found some cookies and juice for them. When she took the tray to Stevens' room she stopped still just inside the doorway, halted by the silence and fixedness of the two boys and the man.

Percy raised a hand, palm up, fingers open, toward his boys. Then the hand fell and Percy appeared helpless. He looked at his boys. He did not look at Audrey. He stared at his boys. They waited. Audrey saw that they were dumb with innocence, or unsure, as when love is so deep that it becomes fearful and tries to hide itself.

Both Percy's hands moved, open, a gesture toward his boys, as if both hands together might do what his voice could not. But the hands stilled in the air and then gently, hopelessly, slipped to the sheet and Percy looked at them as if they were the only presence in the room, his hands open and empty. All of this in only so many seconds, but the stillness in the room was forever, Audrey thought, and she found herself frozen into it, frozen still, not able to release herself from the terrible, oppressive silence.

Audrey thought she was failing Percy and Jeff and Glen in some unforgivable way, and she thought there was something fragile in the silence, something that dare not be broken—certainly not by her. As excruciating as the silence was, it was not hers, it was Percy's, and he must be the one to end it.

Percy finally turned his head toward Audrey and looked at her and the tray she held, then he turned back to his boys and whispered, "Snack time," and he began to weep and chuckle at the same time.

When Audrey spoke, she spoke softly, surprised at the quiet and reticence of her own voice. "I thought Jeff and Glen might like something, Percy. I'll just leave it—"

"Don't go, don't go." Now he looked at her. "I'm glad you're here, Nurse. I am. I couldn't talk there for a minute." The boys stared at their father. Percy's hands rose slightly, open to Audrey. "I couldn't talk there for a minute. I got all uptight." The hands folded on his lap. "It's okay now. I was just sayin' good-bye to my boys." The boys continued to stare at Percy.

"Percy, you've got—"

He smiled at Audrey. "I know what I've got. I computed out the time left." He looked at the boys again and said to them, "There's time for us still to do things, boys. No rush. But I finally got somethin' down to a few words for you. Took me, *Jesus, I can't tell you how long*. Just to figure out what to tell you, what I want to say . . . and it's this. My boys. Glen, Jeff. You been the greatest joy of my life. Along with Mom, acourse. I jes wanted to say to you this one very simple thing. I'm jes so very glad I could be with you this long, see you this far along the way."

Audrey found the empty tray still in her hand as she walked down the corridor, everything visual in strange states, bandy and blurry and moving, and she did not know why she allowed herself to be subjected to this sort of experience as a commonplace of her life. She wanted to fight back, but there was nothing to fight. And in that event, she wanted to quit.

She wiped her nose and her eyes and straightened her face and went to the station, again surprised by the tray still in her hand.

She thought of Tim and she wanted to be in his arms and cry as hard as she could and then go to sleep and maybe never come back to Med Three again.

100

"LOOK WHAT AUDREY left for you," Tim said to Jason.

Jason went over to the card table that Audrey had set for dinner with cutlery and plates on a white linen table cover. Where there would have been a fourth setting there were three comics, a pad and colored pencils, and a book of mazes. Jason sat down with the comics right away. Tim saw himself in the same chair listening to Audrey shower just a few days before. He went into the little kitchen and began unpacking the bag of groceries and refrigerating what needed to be.

When he heard the key in the lock he thought it must be much later than he realized or that Audrey's meeting had been called off. He went into the living room.

The man in the doorway was surprised to see the little boy and then surprised by Tim. "I'm Dr. Truell," the man said. "I'm a friend of Audrey's." He removed the key from the lock and shut the door. He carried a box of flowers. He set the box down where Jason's comics had been.

"Is she expecting you?"

"I told her she might expect me."

"My son and I have a dinner engagement with her. Perhaps she wasn't expecting you just now."

"It was an open sort of appointment. I'll wait." He placed his keys in his pocket and then, as if to emphasize his intimacy with the surroundings, he went into Audrey's bedroom and then to her bathroom and urinated loudly without shutting the door.

The sonofabitch! Tim thought.

101

TRINA WAS ALONE with Jan in her room. Chanda had gone to visit Dom, and Trina saw that Jan did not like that at all. But it left Trina alone with Jan and Trina needed that.

"Why did you hit Dom, Jan?"

"Because I felt like it."

"That's not a reason, Jan."

"It'll do."

"You had some reason. You're not crazy, Jan. Why did you hit Dom?"

"He stopped paying attention."

"Why should you hit him for that?"

Jan was silent.

"Can't Dom stop paying attention? Maybe he was tired."

"He was ignoring me."

"Maybe he was tired of listening to you. Also, patients need rest."

"I don't."

"You need company."

"Terrific observation. So who do I get for a roommate? Sleeping Beauty."

"Chanda has mono. She needs lots of sleep. Why did you—"

"Oh, Christ, you're all trying to make me die!"

Trina listened for more and then listened to the words again in her own mind. "How are we trying to make you die?"

But Jan would not say anything.

"What happened when Dom got tired, when he wanted you to leave?"

Jan shook her head and smiled. "That would be telling."

"I think it would be a good idea to tell it."

Tears appeared in Jan's eyes. "Why? So you can send me away? You are, anyway."

"How did you feel when Dom asked you to leave?"

"I got fucking *furious*."

"Why did you get furious?"

"You know."

"I'm not a mind reader, Jan."

"*He was making me disappear!* He was *killing* me!"

"He was tired and he asked you to leave."

"He turned away from me! Like everyone!"

"Everyone?"

"Yes, yes, yes—for years. And even here." The tears ran down her cheeks.

"I think you're getting a lot of attention, Jan. I think you're getting just what you want."

"Bullshit!" She wiped her eyes and face with the turnover of the sheet. "You all want me dead."

"Jan, I don't think you're paranoid, I don't think you're crazy. I think you know perfectly well what you're saying. Now why are you saying it?"

"Because you're *killing* me. You all are, making me go home tomorrow. I'll just be alone again and die." She cried in heaving sobs.

"First of all, Jan, it's not tomorrow, it's the day after, and even that isn't certain. It depends on whether you remain stable. Second, once you're home, you can come see me and we can talk together *anytime*. I hope you'll do that. I care about what happens to you, Jan. Third, I'd like to fix you up with a psychiatrist, someone who can really help take the pain away."

"*See?* First you say you'll be my friend and I can come see you and *right away* you're handing me off to some shrink."

"I'm offering you my care and concern and I'm offering you a shrink's help as well. You think about it."

"Are you going now?"

"I'm not abandoning you, Jan. I have work down on the ER."

But Jan began to cry again.

"I know it feels like abandonment, but it's not."

Jan looked at her flowers. "I'll be okay."

"They're beautiful," Trina said.

"Yes, they are. You don't know how much they help."

Trina paused and looked at the flowers for a few seconds as she thought and decided whether or not to tell Jan what she wanted to tell her. Then she did. "I don't know if I ever mentioned this, Jan, but I'm a fan of yours. I'd like to see another book."

"That would make two."

"Two what?"

"Two books. Two fans." Jan looked from the flowers to Trina. "Two of us who would like to see another book."

102

THE CHANGES OF the nursing shifts were no longer clearly defined.

Before the HOs went out, Tremaine Avenue had had, between three-fifteen and quarter of four in the afternoon, a conspicuous population of women in white dresses and white pants and even scrub smocks.

Now the shift change was not so evident. Afternoon nurses came in early. Morning nurses continued working past contractual hours so that the new shift had as little extraordinary duty to cope with on its own as possible. Later in the evening, the afternoon nurses stayed beyond contractual hours as well.

Out on the line at five o'clock a few nurses had, on their own, joined the house officers to do informational picketing. Liz Swanzey was one. She did not expect to find her *alter* father, Mr. Larkin, the drunk who had brought together her conflicts, present in zealous support of the house officers.

He stood at the edge of the curb and delivered a meandering lecture about physician sacrifice and the nobility of life. He got in the way of both pedestrian and vehicular traffic and was yelled at and warned away by the police. He saw Liz and called out to her, "Why ain't you yellin' at me, too, like always? Dontcha love me anymore?"

"Sure I do, Mr. Larkin. But I have someone else to yell at now."

"Thank God, Jesus and Mary. A body can get some water and a backrub now, hey?"

"Usually."

"Who ya yellin' at? Yer boyfriend?"

"No, a professional. I pay him to listen."

"You *pay* him? And I done it for free!" Mr. Larkin was outraged.

"Take care of yourself, huh, Mr. Larkin? Watch out you
don't get hit by a car."

Mr. Larkin wandered away.

"It's sort of like alumni weekend," an HO said to Liz.
Someone handed the HO an envelope.

The picket line had stopped. Envelopes were being pressed
on all the HOs by members of Management. Scotty McGettigan,
who had been targeted to receive the first envelope, followed
by Mozart Wills and Anita Rounds, read the contents and
shouted, "Hey! Don't accept these things!" but by then it
was too late.

"What is it?" Liz said to the HO.

"Pursuant to the investigative hearing held by the Massachusetts Labor Relations Commission this morning . . . Back
Bay Metropolitan Hospital and the LRC . . . require the
Association of Residents and Interns and all members thereof
. . . as herein named . . . to desist from the collective strike
against Back Bay Metropolitan Hospital and return to work
immediately. Failure to comply will result in fines or impris-
onment or both."

Mr. Toby, the pacemaker recipient who had been sent
home the week before, took his afterdinner stroll among the
neighborhood people around the pickets and told strangers
how good the doctors were and how they ought to get what
they said was needed.

Generally, the neighbors supported the house officers. But
they were also becoming uneasy and even frightened. The
rumor was growing more persistent that City Hall was going
to use the strike to close down the hospital. A number of the
neighbors had begun to perceive that as a life-and-death threat
to themselves and their children, as indeed it was. It was the
single socially cohesive element in the neighborhood, the major
life-promoting facility in the neighborhood. Without it people
would die and the neighborhood itself would turn self-destruc-
tive. A number of people had begun to resent the jeopardy in
which the house officers were placing them and so one of them
replied to Mr. Toby, "You *stupid*, man? Whatchou *want?*
Make these fools *rich?* Man, they're *fuckin'* with us."

It was the first time house officers on the line had heard an
objection from their patients.

Michelle McCabe's piece in the afternoon *Post* did not help
at all.

Yesterday I took a second walking tour of the floors of
Back Bay Metropolitan Hospital. It wasn't much different from the tour I took before the house officers went
out . . .

Unless you spend a lot of time on a floor as an
observer, you can't be aware of how infrequently doctors
are actually there at bedside attendance. Most of the time
the nurses are alone. As they are now.

Much of what I read in the press and see on television
insists that it's the patients who are alone.

Mrs. Heidi Armstrong is typical of the patient reaction
I encountered on the floors.

I found Mrs. Armstrong on Surgery Six, where she is
recovering from bilateral amputation of her lower legs.
She had a portable television set and she told me she had
been watching coverage of the HOs' job action.

"It's unfair. What's being said about conditions since
the doctors left. I don't feel my case is being compromised. My case is not being compromised. All the usual
day-to-day care is being done as usual because the nurses
are here. God bless the nurses."

Selma Pushkin read the piece and said to Elin, "It doesn't
do the HOs any good at all."

"What she wrote is true and it screws them."

"They're in trouble. I wonder if they realize it."

"Selma, they're partway down a greased tube and slipping
fast."

Jan Fox, invigorated by a little late afternoon vodka and her
terror at expulsion from the hospital, went up to the phone
booth on Med Four and reported to Lynn Keating. She had
nothing real to report, so she simply made it up.

"Lynn, it's bad here. It's being well covered, but it's bad.
I mean, the nurses *could* be taking care of us, but they're not."

"How so?"

"Patients are being left alone—abandoned, unattended. So
far no one has died, *thank God*. There're not enough nurses
to take care of everyone. Some patients are being favored
over others. For instance, Dom Volante gets all the attention
on the third floor. Someone's going to die, I think. Unless the
nurses start being fair."

*   *   *

Day was concluding a late afternoon conference with Dorothea Kullgren.

"All right," Dorothea said, "you're running tight everywhere. I understand that. Still, we're managing."

"With a lot of double shifts. That can't go on indefinitely. People get tired."

"What about you? Carrying that baby around must be getting tiring these days."

"It is. I promised Jimbo as soon as the HOs come back I'll take my maternity leave." She skipped back to the original subject. "The serious danger is with the ICUs. I can't emphasize that enough. It's a scary situation, Dorothea."

"I agree."

"I have two people I can take off floors to work on a unit *under supervision*. But I have only one nurse who's unit-qualified to supervise if I need her."

"Who?"

"Nan Lassitter. If a head nurse or charge nurse is out, I can bring Nan in. But I haven't got any reserves beyond her."

One other ICU charge nurse was away from her usual duties for a week of update training. A second was on personal leave and a third was in another hospital as a patient after emergency abdominal surgery. In normal times a house officer would have filled in.

103

AUDREY WAS VERY tired after the Nurse Practice Committee meeting but a little rejuvenated by the prospect of making dinner for Tim and Jason and being alone with the two of them in her own place. She stopped and bought a bottle of wine and then bought some flowers as well.

She entered her apartment smiling. She smiled even more when she saw that Tim had brought flowers for her and placed them in a vase. Then she saw that Tim was in an odd, *protective* posture near Jason and in the same instant she looked to the other side of the room and saw the doc getting up from her couch. She said in a voice she could hardly hear herself, it was so controlled, "Please leave. And give me back my keys."

"Your friends and I were just getting acquainted."

"Arthur, this is unforgivable."

"I need some time with you, Audrey."

"Just go."

"I won't intrude for long. I really am quite . . . needful of a few minutes alone with you, Audrey."

Oh shit, Audrey thought, what do you say to a man who pulls dependency on you?

You say, *Fuck off,* she thought, knowing she would not say it in front of Jason.

"Arthur, you're being an ass."

"It's humiliating to be here like this." His head did not move, but his eyes glanced to Tim and back.

"Then spare yourself, please, Arthur. I really don't want you here."

"Things don't change that quickly. I remember—"

"I'm not interested in what you remember. Neither are my friends."

Tim said, "I don't think Jason is interested in this. I think I'll take him out for a walk."

"No," Audrey said. "I don't want that. That's not the way it's going to be. If I asked you, Tim, do you think you could help Dr. Truell out the door?"

Tim was a foot taller than Arthur Truell and thicker.

"Why is everyone ganging up on me?" the doc said. "First you. Then my wife. Is it my age?"

"Your age has nothing to do with it."

"Sarah's left me, but it's you I want to be with. Surely there's something left, something good between us. You're not the sort of person to store so much bad feeling—"

"I don't feel bad toward you at all, Arthur. With you being here, I discover you don't get to me anymore. Not in a good way, not in a bad way. I wasn't so sure that was true. So thanks for coming, but I'd like to see you go now."

The doc looked at Tim. "What do you do?"

"I'm a nurse."

The surgeon said, "This is just incomprehensible." He

said it as if he were addressing listeners who were not in the
room. "All right." He started toward the door.

"Arthur, my keys."

"Oh, yes. As I won't have any further use for them." He
took out a leather folder in which a series of keys lay precisely aligned one after the other. He disengaged two bright
keys, returned the folder to his pocket, and then held them
out to Tim. "Changing of the guard, hand over the equipment
and all of that—"

Audrey took the keys from the doc's hand. "Who—if
anyone—gets my keys, Arthur, is a decision for me, not you."

"You're really not my old Audrey."

"I don't think so."

"That's a real loss."

"Not for me."

"Nice meeting you, Nurse," he said to Tim.

"Yeah. Same here. Seeya 'round the old OR."

"I'm sort of glad that happened," Audrey said. "I'm sorry
you and Jason were here. But it's sort of like taking off a
bandage and seeing that everything's all right."

"Did it hurt taking the bandage off?"

"Not at all."

They were sitting at the table and drinking the last of the
wine.

"I'm gettin' sleepy, Dad," Jason said. He was lying on the
floor doing a maze.

"We'll go in a minute, Jase."

"I was so tired after the meeting." Audrey smiled at both
her guests. "You guys really fixed me up."

"How about we make dinner for you tomorrow night?"

"Day asked me to do a double again. I told her okay if
she'd *guarantee* me Friday off."

"Did she?"

"Yes."

"Great."

"Yeah. Your star winess." She paused. "Jason—

"He knows all about it."

"Yeah," Jason said. "Friday they decide who gets me.
Again. Dad, I'm sleepy."

"Okay," Tim said, getting up. "Let me help Audrey clean
up."

"No. You get Jason home to bed." She stood and stacked some plates and smiled again. "As Coralee would say, I ain't gentry." She stopped. "You know, you got it pretty good, Holbrook."

"I know. Great dinner, great broad—"

"I mean professionally. Coralee's doing a double tonight, I'm doing a double tomorrow, you *never* do a double."

"The *stress* of working on a unit, don't you know. Can't do doubles. Might fuck up."

"The strike really doesn't mean anything to you up there, does it?"

"Yeah, it means something. I'm kinda split, I realized today. I agree with what they're trying to do. But part of me is pissed off at them for going out. I guess I believe they shouldn't have gone out.'

104

SELMA, ELIN AND Molly had all worked well on into the evening, but instead of going home afterward, they went to an address given them by Scotty McGettigan. It turned out to be Anita Rounds's apartment. Scotty and Mozart were there as well as several other house officers. They looked tired and dismayed. Coffee cups and soda cans and a couple of bottles of beer stood about the small living room, and though the windows were open there was an odor of sweat.

"Get you something?" Anita said.

"A beer," Molly said.

"Coffee," Elin said.

"Nothing," Selma said. "Let's get to it. What is it?"

"We need the support of the nurses," Scotty said.

"That's up to the individual nurse."

"We need NSA's support," Anita said.

"We're getting clobbered all around," Scotty said. "The press, City Hall, Management, the public outside the neighborhood—"

"And now the neighborhood people are starting to get edgy about us," Mozart said.

"We're getting nowhere at all," a house officer said. "We can see we're going to get nowhere at all."

"It's only the second day," Molly said.

"Things are getting dangerous," Scotty said. "For all of us. Nurses included."

"You'll have to diagram that one," Selma said.

Anita said, "Scotty has word from inside City Hall. There really *is* a faction there that's pushing to shut down the hospital entirely."

"I don't want to be responsible for that," Scotty said.

"It hasn't come to that," Anita said. "*If* it comes to that."

"Bennett Chessoff would not allow that to happen," Selma said.

"Then why won't he negotiate with us?" No one answered Scotty.

"They sure are jerking you around," Elin said.

"I think you've got it just about right," Scotty said.

"This interim order," Selma said. "I haven't seen it. It's a threat?"

"According to our counsel, it's a pretty good one. It says go back to work. It orders compliance. Noncompliance will result in subpoenas. Work or jail."

"Well, what is it?"

"We polled our members." Scotty sat with his head down, his hands between his legs. "We don't comply."

Molly was surprised by the silence. After several seconds she said, "Charles Street Jail isn't fun, you guys. In case you've never talked to someone who's been there."

"We don't comply," Scotty said, looking up.

"We're in a hopeless situation," another HO said. "We just can't achieve anything this way. But we can't go back."

"Why not?" Molly said.

"We're committed to this."

"We thought we'd have time to make our case," Scotty said. "We didn't think the reaction would be so fast, so negative. We thought they'd negotiate before they sent us to jail. We made a lot of false assumptions."

"They'll have you jailed first," Selma said to Scotty. "You and Anita and Mozart. Then the other officers. That's the way it works."

"I know. After that the court won't be so selective."

Anita said, "We need NSA's help. We need you to go out with us."

Selma did not even pause. "No way. We have legal obligations. We have a contract."

"Talk it over with your exec committee."

"I agree with Selma," Elin said. "We're not organized for agitation. NSA is simply an instrument for the protection of its membership."

Scotty spoke angrily. "How about letting it be an instrument for the protection of the patients?"

Molly said, "We'd just fragment over something like this. We'd end up without any Nursing Services Alliance at all."

"You may end up without any hospital at all."

"I think that's far-fetched," Molly said. "But a fast road to that end would be for us to go out, too. The hospital would have to shut down for sure. Then the fight would be to ever get it opened again."

"Look at Med Five," Selma said. "Closed down one Memorial Day weekend when there was skeletal staffing. Four years later and it's still closed."

"All right," Scotty said. "It figured we couldn't expect anything from you."

"Yeah," another HO said, "it figured you'd look out for your own ass first."

105

WHEN VIOLA ARRIVED on Children's Seven at ten forty-five, she was apprehensive. Her anxiety had no focus and she determined that it was simply a function of her fatigue. The night lighting on the floor, which used to augment her feelings of the protection in which the children slept, now appeared ominous, a culture for the sort of accident that had killed Natalie Briggs.

There was a new patient on the floor. "Mahalia Dodd," the charge nurse said. "Eight years old. Late afternoon admission through the ER. Tight asthmatic. She's stabilized on an aminophylline drip along with a schedule of chest PT."

Viola visited the child with the charge nurse and examined her herself before moving on to the children she already knew.

Finally she went in to check on Jamaal. Nancy had taken over, but the evening vent nurse was still there. "The visit was in about three times this afternoon," the evening nurse said. "Not only that, some of our guys snuck in off the line to see him."

"Why is that?" Viola said, her anxiety finding a focus. Then she saw that Nancy was grinning as she checked through the equipment and readings.

"Well, he's still restless, he's still running that fever off and on. But what's perplexing everyone is, they think Jamaal's lungs are showing signs of some positive development."

It was nothing Viola had ever considered as a possibility. She and the evening nurse looked at Jamaal. "I almost can't leave him," the evening nurse said. "Like I'll break the spell."

"That was nice work with Alice and the scurvy, Vi," Nancy said.

"You've been a busy lady today," the evening nurse said. "I want you to know, it gave me a great deal of personal satisfaction the way you told that bitch Bader off."

"We're not supposed to do that sort of thing," Viola said.

"Oh, I didn't say it was professionally correct. I just said it gave me a hell of a lot of satisfaction."

It was near two o'clock, the anniversary hour of Natalie's death. Viola got up from the station, pulled by apprehension.

She saw the stillness of Mahalia Dodd's body.

She saw Natalie Briggs come back from her secret trip to the playground and then go away again.

Viola moved with a swiftness that strained her muscles.

Mahalia Dodd *had a pulse*. But Viola could hear no air moving in the child's chest. The bronchial tree was in muscle spasm, intense broncho spasm. Maybe the aminophylline was doing it but she didn't have the opportunity to consult with *anyone* and the child was in a mode where something had to be done immediately, even though her life could go to further risk. Viola knew—*thought* she knew—what a physician's order would be. Start an aerosol therapy *immediately*. Allupent. Make sure the pulse isn't too high, not too much aminophylline on board—the toxic levels of the theophylline family could activate the cardiac system, make the heart very tacky, dangerous to fool with. The pulse was acceptable, she needed to check for nausea, but there was no way of doing that, and Viola had the medicine locker open and the Allupent in her hand and she went to Mahalia and stuck the medication right into the in-line nebulizer, right into the oxygen system maintaining the child, jammed the Allupent right into the respiratory tree, went to the station and called for a pedi HO stat off the picket line, and went back to Mahalia's bedside and found the little girl's body moving with voluntary respiration.

106

THE ER NIGHT security guard thought he saw a figure in the darkness of Psych Two. From outside the room he switched on the light, illuminating a young woman, motionless, with light brown skin, eyes fixed somewhere that wasn't in the room, maybe not even on the planet, eyes not shocked by the sudden light.

"What you doin', girl? What you doin' in here?"

"Waitin'."

"Waitin' on what?"

"Waitin' on my friend."

"What friend?"

"Fixin'-t'be-uh-doctuh. Gonna fix my ovaries."

"A doctor told you to wait here?"

"No doctuh. Snake Lady."

The guard picked up the telephone and called the psych nurse. But the young woman walked past him. He watched her walk down the corridor and briefly described the situation to the psych nurse.

"Stay with her," the nurse said.

The young woman had turned the corner and, as quick as he was, the guard could not find her.

107

WEDNESDAY.

Lynn Keating's column began on the front page of the *Eagle* again.

Back Bay Metropolitan Hospital is, as anyone who has ever had the misfortune to be there knows, a joke.

In fact, it's lots of jokes, none of them funny, though some of them are pretty deadly by the time the story's told.

The biggest current jokes, I mean real boffos, are those courageous young men and women, the house officers, who have willfully gone out on strike in order to make a bad story worse.

This story was in the worst taste to begin with. I mean, the whole facility ought to have been abandoned as soon as medicine turned the corner of the twentieth century.

Which leads to the thought that if the HOs succeed in shutting down the hospital—a real possibility—perhaps we taxpayers ought to applaud them.

Still, one wonders, even as one regards with awe their personal and professional bravery, if these valiant physicians, many of whom will soon be in private practice, will tolerate job actions in their own offices, strikes at the hospitals where they will be full staff members.

Will these self-sacrificing Dr. Kildares, who are out to get their own paychecks enlarged by us taxpayers, will they, after leaving BBMH, support equality of pay for their own offices, hospital workers, and junior physicians? (Hah.) For nurses? (Hah, hah.)

I told you it was a bad story.

One can only take comfort in the conclusion of a similar story, that of the air traffic controllers, another self-aggrandizing gang that put its own avarice miles ahead of the public good and the public trust.

Such a conclusion is a satisfying prospect.

A letter followed the column:

To the Editor:
    The medical community is a responsible one. The very
long days and nights required of interns and residents are
meant to instill self-discipline and exacting standards
under the meanest of conditions. The regimen is a proven
one. But somehow in the case of the BBMH house
officers it has not worked. The hospital did not fail and
the regimen did not fail. It is the ethical, professional,
and personal standards of this group of mollycoddles and
malcontents that failed. The organization that left the
patients and went out on the street ought to be flushed
down the sewer. In the meantime, while the HOs parade
outside the hospital with their signs of self-proclaimed
righteousness, some few of us who still remember the
stern lessons of our own days of internship and residency
and who honor the dicta of our profession are inside the
hospital and we are holding the fort.
                                        Lucius Schoonoler, M.D.
    (*Editor's Note.* Dr. Schoonoler is a senior visiting physi-
cian at BBMH.)

In the *Post*, Michelle McCabe wrote:

Nothing has changed. The house officer job action is
ineffective.
    Granted, the procedure the house officers have chosen
is radical and open to legitimate criticism.
    Still, their actions are taken out of deep concern for
the hospital and its patients, a concern that much of the
city does not share.
    This concern, and the willingness to stand by it as
individuals in the face of public and judicial opposition,
is rapidly leading the house officers to a tragedy.
    On Friday or Saturday they will begin going to jail.
    Scotty McGettigan reaffirmed last night that the house
officers will not comply with the LRC's order to return
to their regular duties.
    The house officers will be subpoenaed this afternoon
to appear before the Massachusetts Supreme Judicial Court
on Friday to show cause why they ought not to be jailed

for noncompliance. Thursday has been granted them as a day of grace in which to comply.

"We have to stay out and we are agreed to stay out," Dr. McGettigan stated. "Otherwise it will be years before house officers ever again attempt effective change at Back Bay Met. By then the hospital will be in extremis."

Driving in to work, Nan had her radio tuned to an all-news station to see what was going on with the HOs. She was familiar with all the characters and it was sort of fun hearing their voices—Scotty's, Bennett's, Selma's, Dorothea's, and others'—on the radio. She was in great spirits anyway and it made her feel a little like a celebrity herself because she knew all these people. She was joshing herself about her presumption to celebrity when she heard her old buddy from the OR, Trevor Davis, state the minority HO opinion of the job action.

"Well, frst of all, I wouldn't call it a job action. My colleagues are engaged in a strike, an illegal strike. They're arbitrarily endangering people's lives. There's a community out there we're charged with serving. Some of us are still fulfilling that mission. It's a matter of being honor-bound. I'd say my colleagues have grown deficient in their sense of honor. It's a matter of character."

Nan grinned. Old Trevor Davis was such a straight arrow he was amusing. Even his passes were so crude they made her smile. If Monk McGuire, the great Baltimore pitcher, was egocentric and inept, old Trevor Davis was out there in a league by himself. Nan rather liked him for struggling against his helplessness.

The spring air buoyed her. Even though she was buckled into her seat belt, she had the sensation of her body's bobbing and flirting on waves of springtime.

She was off the unit, she was glad to go to work and not be on strike, and she had a vacation of sorts coming up in a few hours—a party tonight and tomorrow off, something she had arranged weeks before. Her nursing school roommate, an "old family" sort, was back from her honeymoon in Europe and her family was giving a party for the couple at a North Shore country club.

She wouldn't be back to work till she filled in for Tim on the unit on Friday as charge nurse. She didn't even mind going back to the unit, not for one shift. And so that Tim would have a chance to keep his son.

She saw the buildings of the hospital in the distance as she
turned off the Mass. Pike and glided down the exit ramp and
turned onto Tremaine Avenue, and even the progressively
decrepit surroundings did not dismay or frighten her. She left
the window down for the fresh air that had penetrated even
this God-forgotten neighborhood and she stopped at red lights
and she was not aware of her uncustomary behavior, but only
of her joy in life. Med Seven wasn't heaven, but she loved
going there.

A block from the hospital she was surprised to see all the
white dresses and other whites across the street from the
hospital—some fifty nurses waiting on the other side of
Tremaine. It was ten minutes before seven.

108

JAN FOUND HER flowers irresistible. The hour made no difference, they were throwing her out the next day. She would
have a going home party, see herself off. Bon voyage. She
took a flower out of a narrow-necked vase and poured some
of the liquid from the vase into her breakfast tea. Chanda, her
roommate, saw it as craziness. But craziness was what Chanda
expected from Jan.

Jan sipped her tea, then smiled at Chanda and said, "Did
you ever wonder what makes paper flowers grow?"

Day had been through her master sheets and phoned everyone
who might be able to help her out. Finally she made the one
call she dreaded making to get it over with before rounds. She
dialed her own number—Jimbo would not have left for work
yet. She knew what Jimbo's attitude would be and she was
angry at him before she even finished dialing.

"Jimbo, I've got to do a double today."

He said nothing for a few seconds. Then, *"Got to."*

"Everyone has to fill in while the HOs are out. Me
included."

Again he was silent for a few seconds. "I can't put up with
this anymore."

"Look, Jimbo, look at it this way. I'm already in a hospital if the baby starts coming."

"You're so self-centered, you think you're so *important* there, *indispensable*—"

"Jimbo, you're making me angry—"

"You're only days away from delivery—"

"More like weeks."

"Two? Three? If you don't care about me, care for the baby."

"Caring is what I do all day long!"

"Not enough. Not for the people near you."

"All right. I've told you I'm staying over here. Anything else?"

"Nothing."

Day kept the receiver to her ear, hoping there would be something else, but there was simply a click.

The hospital had been admitting only a limited number of new patients, but on Wednesday, the third day of the strike, the economics of the city turned against Back Bay Met and other hospitals began referring people back to their own neighborhood's primary medical facility. The other institutions did not want a lot of welfare patients. Nonpaying patients tended to ruin the economic climate of the other institutions.

Mr. Wu was one such patient. He was sent to Med Three for observation—general malaise of recent origin, nothing indicative, no constellation of signs and symptoms, maybe all he needed was rest, and there was a list of conjectures, everything from mononucleosis to chronic appendicitis. An hour after he arrived on the floor he was sweating and crying out, and Audrey couldn't even get him to indicate what part of his body was giving him pain. He was running a temp and his pulse and blood pressure were up.

Audrey called for an HO and then dialed Special Services and said, "I've got a Chinese gentleman here—he's complaining, he's in pain, but I haven't got the slightest idea what he's saying . . . *Yes he's talking in Chinese. Yes we need a translator.*"

"Better come quick," the aide said to Audrey.

The aide took her to Mrs. Gehl. The elderly woman was semiconscious and choking. Audrey had Mrs. Gehl's history in her mind and she reviewed it swiftly and made a diagnosis all in the instant—Mrs. Gehl was choking on thick internal secretions she couldn't clear. It had happened before. Now she was turning gray in front of Audrey.

Audrey ran down the corridor and got a suction bottle. She heard laughter from Jan's room as she passed.

Back in Mrs. Gehl's room, she moved an IV pole and the bedside table trying to get to the outlet. She placed the suction bottle on the wall and tested it, but it didn't work. She ran for another one. Hooked up, the indicator read LOW suction, the needle almost stationary below the MED and HIGH readings. Audrey pulled down on the ball to check the seal at the top. But there was no time to troubleshoot the bottle. Mrs. Gehl was getting some relief. Audrey left her with the aide and called down for a portable suction machine, stat. The response was excellent. Audrey got Mrs. Gehl cleaned out and wondered what the cost had been to her heart. She was surprised again when two full-capability suction bottles arrived minutes later. Back Bay Met could almost be counted on for inconsistency.

But not quite. They were short a medical worker and Day had no replacement.

Dr. Geier himself met Audrey at the station. "I'm seeing Mr. Wu. The man is in pain. But I'm not getting anywhere."

"I called for a translator. They said they'd have to send out."

"Jesus Christ," Dr. Geier said. He looked very tired. "Send out for a Chinese translator. That's a bad joke. Where's Dr. Schoonoler?"

"I have no idea. He has a very full schedule outside."

Dr. Geier chuckled. "Left him time to write a letter."

"I saw it. How long is this going to go on?"

"I have no idea. The HOs are not making me privy to their plans. I only know what I read in the papers."

"Dr. Geier, I think we ought to have someone else on this floor. Someone who's more available. Dr. Schoonoler . . . has all those other responsibilities."

"Dr. Auerbach thinks he can come back tomorrow. Have you got someone to stay with Mr. Wu while I take some calls?"

Mr. Wu's symptoms subsided as abruptly as they had occurred, and when Dr. Geier left the floor Mr. Wu was reading a Chinese newspaper the translator had been carrying.

The translator, who had been brought in from the kitchen of a nearby Chinese restaurant, said, "Mr. Wu say he aw white. No go be sick now."

"What was wrong?" Audrey said.

"Not doctor." The man shrugged.

"I mean, what hurt?"

"Mr. Wu not say. Very private person." The translator looked embarrassed.

"You have an idea?" Audrey said.

"Not nice to say to lady."

"Think of me as a nurse."

"I think Mr. Wu's balls hurt."

Audrey turned to Mr. Wu with the translator. The general embarrassment proved to be contagious even to Audrey and, as desperately as it was needed, humor was not introduced for relief.

Audrey called Dr. Geier. "Mr. Wu is a bachelor. Yesterday he discovered Japanese technology and rented a VCR and a library of porno films. He spent the entire night watching them. His personal code would not allow him to masturbate. That may explain why one of the notes says he was walking funny when he came into the ER."

What was not funny was the amount of simple housework that was building up because they did not have a worker.

Coralee said, "Something funny's going on in Jan's room. I mean *funny* funny. Folks in there are laughin' their heads off."

"One thing we do not DC on this floor is laughter."

"I had no intention," Coralee said, dialing out. "You know my daughter Dale?"

"She's in college, right?"

"She's home this week . . . Dale, Momma. You come in and help out here. Pour water, make beds, like that . . . I *know* you got plans. What are you, still in bed? . . . Course you're in bed. That's where I'd be, too, I was nineteen years old and stayed out all night. You come in here and help out, you can have the car all day Saturday." Coralee listened and said to Audrey, "We got *help* comin' in. *College*-educated help."

Chanda was amazed, partly because of the amazing liquid in which Jan's paper flowers grew. She was sick, but she'd never felt this well in her whole life. The other part was being friends with two famous people—Dom Volante, who of course she knew, and Jan Fox, who she'd never heard of but Dom said was famous, too.

All her good friends, new good friends, gathered right here in her room, hers and Jan's. Dom put his arm around her and there was a flash of light, and Mr. Shaughnessy, who claimed he'd smelled booze from street level, handed her a picture and Chanda looked at it and nearly wept, it was as if she were on a record jacket with Dom Volante, though Dom kept saying he hadn't existed for a while.

Ralph Malamet felt as if he'd been on instruments for several days and had suddenly broken out into clear sunshine, refueled too when the indicators were flashing red and screaming E, and what did he happen into but a crazy lady in charge of a KC-135A loaded with vodka and offloading it as fast as anyone could drink it. He was itching with sexuality again. Chanda was pretty and well shaped and he was excited by her nearness. But she acted so young. Then there was that Debby who came in in the afternoon, looked like her underwear couldn't quite contain her, seemed like she didn't want it to.

Percy Stevens said to Jan, "Yer a fine lady. Last time I felt this good . . . I can't remember."

"Take a little wine for thy stomach's sake," Jan said, pouring from a vase into a small paper cup.

"Christ, why didn't the doctors think of this?" Percy said.

"No imagination," Jan said and went around refilling other cups, cups that had delivered water to accompany medication.

"I can see a new day," Dom said.

Jan filled his cup. "See several. See a whole fuckin' century."

"I can dig it, I can dig it."

"Sure you can," Jan said. "Man's been usin' a shovel long as I've known him. Tossed so much shit, can't even smell it anymore." She smiled at everyone.

Betty looked at them all and sipped. She had happened in. Took a drink. Knew it would be disastrous. It was. Took another. Got tired, uncomfortable, achy like brief parentheses between the bouts of real pain, like heartbeats of discomfort in the midst of the torment. She was beginning to feel nausea, and that was almost comfortable. Nausea had a normalcy to it, a familiarity. It wasn't deadly.

"Let's drink to Jan," Jan said. "Goin' home to die. Goin' home to die tomorrow."

"Bullshit," Dom said.

"Really am."

"You don't know what dyin' is," Percy said.

"Spent my life dyin'."

"Spent your life killin' y'self," Dom said.

"Lot you know," Jan said.

"Hold on to life," Percy said. "You got the chance. I don't."

"What for?"

"What for?"

"You got people care for you. You got people you care 'bout. No one cares for me."

"What're you doin'?" Dom said. "Tryin' t'suck blood, Jan? What the fuck." He looked away.

Jan took a flower out of a vase and tipped the vase into her mouth. "Isn't this fun?" she said. "Aren't we all having a most glorious time?"

Dom held out his cup. Jan filled it, then filled her own cup. They knocked paper cups together.

"Sure feels good," Percy said, holding out his cup. "I'd sorta like to die this way."

"They don't let you," Jan said. "They send you home first."

Audrey stood in the doorway.

Jan said to her, "Did you ever wonder what makes paper flowers grow?" She giggled.

Then Jan looked at Audrey and began to cry. *"Oh God, God, God!"* She stuck the vase into her mouth and emptied it.

The party dispersed and Coralee followed up on Malamet and Betty and Dom in their own rooms. Chanda was snoring in her bed, no great damage apparent, and Jan was crying and crying. Her signs were such that when she went to sleep, Audrey had no reason for concern.

The early afternoon grew swiftly gray and then darkened with storm. Audrey turned on the evening lighting. The darkness outside was eerily like night.

Debby came in an hour and a half early. Her yellow slicker

and boots gleamed with water and dripped on the floor inside
the station. The rain tattooed loudly against the window, and
when Audrey looked she could not see the tenements a block
away until they were suddenly and starkly backlit by lightning.

Debby hung up her slicker and took off her boots. "The
HOs are getting soaked," she said.

"In more ways than one," Audrey said.

"You'd think they'd know enough to come in out of the
rain," Coralee said.

Debby sat on a stool and bent over and started getting into
her white shoes.

"Good of you to come in early," Audrey said. "We're
short again."

Then they heard Jan screaming in terror and Chanda was
running to them in her nightgown. *"She's bleeding, bleeding
bad, she's bleeding all over!"*

The three nurses went to Jan instantly.

She was vomiting blood over the side of the bed onto the
floor. She had vomited blood onto the sheets and the front of
her nightgown. Between retchings she screamed at her body's
production. Audrey held Jan's head, her legs and shoes getting spattered. The bedclothes were partially pulled away and
there was more blood in the bed and the stink of feces. There
was the sound of liquid escaping under pressure and the stink
was intensified. Debby made a retching sound of her own.
Coralee had the bedclothes down and Jan's nightgown pulled
up. "It's a bloody diarrhea," she said.

The process slowed and Jan whimpered. "We've got you,
Jan, we've got you," Audrey said, and to Coralee, "I want
to start an IV, Ringer's lactate, stat blood call, two units at
least, type and cross match, an NG tube, iced saline lavage.
Debby, give me a blood pressure. Coralee, let's get a stat
CBC for blood loss, call an HO, I'll draw the blood. Debby, I
want you to wash her down and get the bed changed—"

"It's eighty over fifty," Debby said.

"O-two," Audrey called after Coralee.

"Gotcha."

They got the bed and the patient stripped and Coralee
returned with a syringe and Audrey drew blood for the complete blood count as Debby, with some gagging, began to
wash Jan, with Coralee setting the IV needle and hanging the
plasma substitute.

"Let's get her in a Trendelenburg," and Audrey and Debby shifted Jan and adjusted the bed so that Jan's head was lower than her feet.

Coralee attached the line to the adapter on the needle in Jan's arm and checked and said, "It's running."

Audrey handed Coralee the syringe. "Have the aide take this down."

But the aide was standing in the doorway. "Miz Gehl's feelin' sick."

"I'll get it," Coralee said.

"Okay, I'll get the other stuff."

"This will be a little uncomfortable till I get it set, Jan, but it's going to stop that bleeding inside you." Audrey had iced the nasogastric tube to stiffen it and now she inserted it through the nostril. Jan pulled back involuntarily and broke out in a new sweat. "It's okay, Jan, it's okay, just hang in there with me," Audrey said, manipulating the tube in a semicircular motion and depending it down through the throat and—*Ah, here's the tricky part*— bypassing the trachea. Jan coughed and pushed at Audrey and Audrey withdrew the tube slightly and turned it and edged it around, then she was by the trachea and through the esophagus and into the stomach. Jan looked at her imploringly. "You're doing great, Jan." Audrey took up a large syringe and placed the open end in an iced liquid, depressed the plastic bulb, and drew liquid into the syringe. "This is a saline solution, Jan. I'm going to squirt it down the tube and let it wash out your stomach and then I'm going to draw it out again. You'll just have a chilly, filling-up sensation. The cold and the salt should stop the bleeding."

Coralee came back with oxygen and set the NG tube through a hole in the mask. Audrey pumped and flushed for ten minutes.

"She's okay," Debby said. "A hundred and twenty over sixty."

"You stay with her. We repeat this in twenty minutes."

Audrey went out and called down for a monitor. "Don't *hassle* me, okay? My patient needs a monitor."

"We just sent you one. How many you want?"

"What do you mean, you just sent me one?"

Coralee put her hand up. "I already called down for one. I

figured you'd want it. I also called Housekeeping. For a cleanup.''

Audrey explained and hung up.

A messenger appeared at the station. "One of you ladies call for blood?''

The HO and Dr. Geier appeared at the same time. They seemed to be ignoring each other's presence. Audrey had already lavaged Jan a second time. "I drew up a little blood. Nothing like the first time. The third time should do it.''

"I think so," Dr. Geier said. "How did she get the booze?''

"An unknown admirer.''

"The admirer should be shot," the HO said.

"I concur with my colleague," Dr. Geier said.

The chief and the HO then agreed that Jan was in satisfactory condition. Housekeeping had finished swabbing out the room by the time the monitor was attached.

Audrey said to Debby, "I think you and I could use a change of clothes. The other patients wouldn't let us near them like this—the smell alone.''

The darkness outside was still severe and the rain was still spilling down the windowglass and contorting the flashes of lightning.

109

THE HOSTAGE SITUATION on the ER developed imperceptibly.

First there was the drunk.

The rain suddenly stopped, but the sky remained dark. The air was warm and heavy. The lights in the courtyard were on, the cobblestones wet and shiny.

From the window of the psych office, Trina saw a patrol car turn in. She went back to her paperwork.

There was screaming and crying from the courtyard. A stocky woman in a short-sleeved dress was fleeing two policemen, running away from the hospital. The woman fell and then the three of them were standing, the men trying to subdue the woman's violent and powerful protest. In spite of her size, she shook the men, but their combined physical strength overcame hers and, while she still struggled against them, they moved her toward the ER.

"I think we'll be seeing her," Trina said to Hal and got up.

The woman's dress was smudged and wet from her fall and she was sobbing loudly, but she was not struggling anymore. She stood by the triage desk, one officer still restraining her while the other talked to the triage nurse, who indicated Trina. "She's the one you wanna talk to."

Trina went to him. "What's her name?"

"Cathleen Monahan."

Trina walked over to the woman and touched her shoulder lightly. "Slow down, honey. Take it easy, Cathleen." The woman, still sobbing, managed to look at Trina and show surprise. "Cathleen, just slow it down . . . Please." The sobbing continued, but less violently.

Trina went back to the first officer, who said, "I didn't want to throw her in the drunk tank. She lives just a coupla blocks away. I figure she's so *goddamn* angry, maybe it's not just booze, maybe it's a psychiatric problem, maybe she's out of medication she's supposed to be on."

"That's merciful of you, Officer."

"Yeah, well. She's got this little kid at home. I figured I'd try here first, try her out on a psych nurse."

"What happened?"

"She was throwing things down from the third floor. That's where she lives, third floor. Threw down a tricycle, bunch of other toys. Screamin', drunk. Neighbors called her in. She was in the hallway throwin' the things out."

"How did she act when you got there?"

"Quiet enough. Like she accepted it. Till we drove in here."

The triage nurse said, "Personal questions upset her."

"Any psych history?"

"Says not. Nothin' in Records, except her little boy gets seen over in the pedi walk-in. Just the usual stuff for a four-year-old."

"No Trauma X?"

"None."

Trina said to the officer, "What about the child?"

"Locked himself in the apartment. She scared him pretty good, but nothing physical. Neighbor's got the kid now. Cathleen's sister's on the way over. The neighbor says the sister takes care of the kid a lot, they got full trust in her . . . Whadya say? Wanna take Cathleen or want us to?"

"I'll take her."

"Got to tell you one thing," the officer said, rubbing his ribs. "She hits like Rocky Marciano."

Trina said to the triage nurse, "Get me a couple of security folks to keep her company for a little while." She went back to the woman. The sobbing was softer but continuous. "Cathleen, hi. I'm Trina. I'm a nurse. We want you to be safe. You need to slow it down a little bit." Trina took out a handkerchief. "Here you go, babe, let me wipe your face. This is the pits, huh?"

"There's nothin' nobody can do," the woman said in gasps. Trina heard a brogue even through the gasps and sobs.

"I know you feel real, real bad. But it's not that bad. To start with, you just need to sleep this off."

"I'm here on something I decided for myself."

"What's that?"

"I won't say. But it's a terrible thing."

"What is, Cathleen?"

"I won't say."

Reynold and the red-haired, boyish-faced security guard moved to either side of Cathleen. When the city officer took his hands off her and moved back, the two guards took her lightly from each side.

She did not seem to notice.

"Will you walk with me?" Trina said.

"Where?"

"Where you can lie down. You need to sleep this off."

"You get this nigger's hands off me. The mick's, too. I can tell. He's a dirty mick like me."

Trina nodded at the guards. They released Cathleen and followed behind with Hal. Cathleen walked beside Trina and stumbled every few feet. Trina helped her keep her balance. "Have you been drinking a little bit?"

"A little bit." She sobbed again.

"I want you to sober up."

"I am sober."

Trina stopped and faced the woman. Cathleen, though

already gray, was, she guessed, in her early thirties. "I know a sober person when I see one. I know a sad, unsober person, too."

"What kind of a nurse are you?"

"I'm a nurse who talks to people."

Cathleen turned to the two guards and laughed. "Fuckin' crazy job is that? Talkin' t'people. I'd like to get paid, *talkin'* t'people." She turned back to Trina and started walking again. "Talk to me, *talk to me*."

"I want you to slow down and sleep it off a bit and then we'll talk. You been throwing up?"

Cathleen shook her head.

Because there were five of them, Trina took her group into Psych Two, the larger of the two psych rooms. Cathleen looked around. The room was so plain there was nothing in it for her to react to.

Trina helped her lie down on a litter. She said, "Alcohol. Okay. Did you take anything else?" Cathleen nodded. "Today?"

"I took aspirin."

"How much aspirin did you take?"

"I took twenty or maybe thirty aspirin." She began to sob again.

"We'll have to pump your stomach."

"I took, I only took eight or nine."

"When?"

"I'm a born-again Christian, you know?"

"Cathleen, when did you take the aspirin?"

"Maybe I didn't. I had a religious experience. I need the healing hand, the magic. All I need is magic."

"I don't do magic . . . What's my name?"

"Did you tell me?" She looked concerned—perhaps some beginning sobriety.

"Aspirin, Cathleen. How many today? I need the truth."

Cathleen looked at Hal. "Who is this? With the goggles. Starin' at me. *Who is this?*"

"This is Hal Levy. He's a medical student. He's accompanying me."

Cathleen regarded Hal. "Shalom," she said.

"Cathleen," Trina said. "In case of emergency, who do we notify?"

"Me."

The boyish-faced guard smiled.

"Who is this fuckin' creep?" Cathleen said. *"Who are they?"*

"They're security guards."

"They're men, they're pricks, they'll do a poor girl! Get them out, *please!"*

"I've got to have someone in here with you, Cathleen. Would you be more comfortable with a woman?"

"Oh yes, please."

"You behave?"

"Oh yes."

"Reynold, see if we've got a woman standby available." Reynold went to the phone outside the door. "Now, Cathleen, I asked you about who to get in touch with. I understand you have a sister."

"Bitch."

"She's taking care of your little boy."

"Like I always took care of her. Protected her." Cathleen put her head on her arms and cried, but then turned her head sideways to look at Trina while she cried.

Trina said, "Do you have any health insurance?"

"I'm a baby." She closed her eyes. They remained closed, her breathing loud and regular.

110

HAL FOLLOWED TRINA out to a cabinet where she got a blood kit. She locked the cabinet and Hal said, "Why did you ask her about health insurance?"

"Not for money. For medical records."

When they returned to Psych Two, Ginny was waiting outside the room. "You called for a female standby?"

"Yes. You up to it, Ginny?"

"Don't needle me, Trina."

Trina half offered the blood kit. "This is for the patient, not you."

"You're not funny."

"Okay. Can I have confidence in you, Ginny?"

"I do my job, Trina. I'm the only lady standby you got just now. You want me or not?"

Trina explained about Cathleen. Then she let the other two standbys go. Ginny looked untroubled. "Drunks are no problem for me," she said.

Cathleen awoke with a startle reaction. Trina put her hand on Cathleen's forehead. "There, there . . . This is Ginny. She's going to stay with you for a few minutes while I'm away. But first I'm going to take some blood from your arm."

"What for? *What for?*"

"This is just for a blood test. You keep your arm straight, okay?"

"You *don't* take blood. You don't even know why I'm here."

"You tell me, Cathleen. Why you're here." She rubbed Cathleen's arm with alcohol. Cathleen turned her head away. "Hold still, babe," she said, and held Cathleen's skin taut over the vein with the index and middle fingers of one hand while she inserted the vacutainer needle with the other. Then she quickly placed the blood tube into the vacutainer and watched the tube fill. "You're doin' great . . . super . . ." She withdrew the needle and Hal swabbed the puncture with alcohol for her and held the gauze in place. "Hope that wasn't too bad, Cathleen," Trina said. "You were real good. I appreciate that." She peeled a Band Aid and stretched it over the little needle mark.

She took the blood to an acute side desk and called down to the lab. "Alcohol for sure. I don't think anything else. But I'm telling myself not to rule out PCP." She went back to Cathleen.

Cathleen said, "I *know* what's wrong with me!"

"What?"

"Got locked outa my own apartment. So fuckin' mad I called the police and here I am in the hospital."

"They said you were throwing things out of a window."

"Them's goddamn lies"

"Cathleen, try taking it easy for a while, huh? Now, about your family, your son and your sister—"

"No family. I live alone."

"Something about toys, Cathleen. You were throwing toys—"

"*I live alone!*" She sobbed violently again.

"You have a four-year-old son—"

"I have a mother named Jeanie." She began singing. "*I dream of Jeanie with the light brown hair . . .*" Then, softly, she cried and sang another song. "*I'll take you home again, Cathleen . . .*"

Trina said, "I think Cathleen's going to entertain us for a while." She took Hal and went out to the triage desk. "Did the cops give you a telephone number for Cathleen Monahan?" she said to the nurse.

"Yup." The nurse found it and wrote it down for Trina. "The other number belongs to the neighbor."

"Trina was about to go to the psych office to call Cathleen's sister when a sharp voice said over the PA, '*Psych Nurse to Psych Two stat, Psych Nurse to—*" and Trina was running.

At the other end of the dimly lit corridor outside the psych rooms, Cathleen stood in a partial crouch facing Ginny.

The corridor was silent, and Trina was aware of rain sluicing down the big window at her side. She spoke quietly and moved forward as she spoke. "Cathleen. I asked you not to leave the room."

"Fuck you!"

"Cathleen, you have to stay here."

"No, I don't. Fuck you! *No and I don't want anyone fuckin' me!*" she screamed as Ginny made a swift move forward. Cathleen hit her in the cheek and spat in her face as Ginny grappled and then pinioned Cathleen. "*No, don't hit me!*" she screamed at the guard.

"*Not going to hit you,*" Ginny said, straining.

"Let me go! Fuck you all! Let me go!"

Trina said, "You slow down, we'll let you go."

Suddenly Cathleen's voice was small and imploring. "Don't hurt me."

"No one's going to hurt you."

They went back into the psych room. Cathleen's body had lost all its tension and Ginny was partially supporting her. Cathleen seemed almost relieved.

"I can't believe you hit her," Trina said.

Cathleen began weeping. Her tears and the sounds that accompanied them were rapid.

"Please lie down, Cathleen. On your stomach. We're going to tuck you in for the night."

Cathleen lay down on the litter as she w̲.
because I'm a poor mick.''

"This is a hospital, Cathleen. There are rules of b̲.

Trina got out the leather restraints from the cabin̲.
said to Ginny, "Wrist and ankle." She placed her han̲
Cathleen's back and massaged it as Ginny attached and an-
chored the restraints. Trina said, "These are to keep you from
hurting yourself. No more running." When Cathleen was
secured, Trina said, "I'll be right back," and left the room.
When she returned she held out a small paper cup of water
and two pills. "These are to help you slow down, Cathleen."

"I don't want to be hypnotized."

"You're in the hospital and we're not going to hurt you.
You're in Back Bay Metropolitan Hospital and," Trina said
gently, "you can't go around hurting people."

Cathleen's hands and arms and head were just free enough
so that she could take the pills and give herself the water.

"That's good," Trina said and took the cup.

Cathleen moved her head toward a wrist restraint. "They
did this to me before."

"This happened to you before?"

"No." She was silent, closed her eyes, then opened them
and stared at Trina. "Where is this place? What is this
place?"

"You're in the hospital."

"No, I'm not in the hospital." She turned her head away.
Her body was still.

Trina said to Ginny, "You took a pretty good hit there. It's
bruising up real nice. I'll get someone else in."

"No. I'm stickin'."

"I'll get you some ice."

"I'll be okay." Cathleen began to moan. "Ah, shut up,"
Ginny said.

Hal followed Trina into the corridor. "On second thought,"
Trina said, "I'd like you to stay in there. While I call the
sister."

"Why stay?"

"A leavening influence. I don't know what went on between those two, what set Cathleen off."

"She doesn't want a man in there with her."

"She doesn't want a man *guard* in there with her."

*　　*　　*

Trina went to the psych office to call the sister and the neighbor.

Hal went back into Psych Two. Cathleen was sleeping. Ginny had gotten herself a newspaper from somewhere and was seated by the door, reading. Hal took the chair that was kept for a second guard. Ginny said nothing to him. He heard Cathleen's deep, regular breathing and the lashes of rain against the big window outside the door.

There was a stillness in the room and Hal settled into it gratefully. And then he became aware of a silent figure in the doorway and looked up. Even Ginny wasn't aware of the young woman standing so close to her, Olivia, dripping from the torrent outside.

Olivia said, "Why you all in my place?" She shifted her head and almost focused on Hal. "Why you bring folks here?" she said quietly.

Ginny rose from her chair slowly, as if she had become aware of a deadly snake at her side. She stepped away, turning toward Olivia, one step and then another. She stopped, her eyes fixed on Olivia's.

Hal was getting up, and what he saw happen frightened him in some way that he did not understand. Olivia looked back at Ginny. Her eyes *focused* on Ginny's eyes.

Hal heard Trina saying to him once, *If I leave you alone with a patient and you get uneasy, get out, your body is telling you something.*

He was extremely uneasy. He could feel his heart rate accelerating. But there was nothing real to this flood of apprehension. He would not act on it. He would not be a fool.

The two women were fixed on each other, some sort of eye contact that was like a contest. Then Hal saw Ginny bend, as if she were bowing to Olivia. More peculiarly, she seemed to be adjusting her pants leg as Olivia took a step forward.

Then Ginny rose from her bow and she had a gun in her hand and she was pointing it at Olivia, her finger inside the trigger guard, her finger bent on the trigger—

And Hal thought again of Trina.

Trina would talk to Ginny and talk the gun away from Ginny.

Trina would see as Hal saw that there was no time for that. Trina would make sure no one got hurt by the gun.

He swung down on Ginny's arm, squeez~
hands. She cried out. The gun fell to the floor. ~
the motionless Olivia struck down and retrieved t~
held it at them.

The eyes went unfocused again. She went to the doo~ and
closed it. She moved around the room slowly as if in some
routine of housekeeping. She stopped at the door again, the
four of them now closed off together, and she said in Hal's
direction, looking beyond his head, "Gots to fix me now."

111

NAN BARELY HAD time to bathe and dress. The air was so wet
and heavy and warm she decided on her long, low-cut summer dress, bikini pants, and no bra. She felt marvelously free
and hoped she didn't fall out. Still, the secret nudity and the
reassuring enclosure of the warm air gave her feelings of
luxury and unassailable safety. She knew she was going to
have a good time at her former roommate's reception and she
was only a little concerned that she probably wouldn't know
anyone there. She didn't even know the couple who was
going to give her a ride to and from the North Shore country
club. But she was ebullient as she dressed and scented herself. She had washed her hair the night before. She had the
next day off. Getting off the unit had released her back to
life, back to the possibility of having fun.

When the telephone rang, she thought it would be the
people who were giving her the ride. But it was Oren Tolman.

"I've been thinking about you all day," he said.

"That's nice. That makes me feel good."

He was silent and Nan thought he was waiting for her to
speak for some reason. "Not so good," he finally said.

"Why?"

"Because it's unreasonable."

"Thinking about me is unreasonable?"

"Because you're going out tonight."

"Oh . . . Yeah. I guess that's a little unreasonable."

"I know."

He was silent again. Nan said, "I'm a little flattered, though."

"Okay . . . Well . . . See you Saturday."

"Yes."

"Okay, then."

"Oren?"

"Yes?"

"You have no right to be concerned about the time I don't spend with you. You know that."

"Yes, I know it."

"But it's sweet of you. I'm glad you could talk to me about it."

"Yeah. I'm not asking you to stay home." He laughed. "Just feel sorry for me. And guilty."

Nan laughed, too. "Sure."

"I hope you have a great time. I'm sorry I called."

"I'm glad we'll be together Saturday."

112

THE RAIN HAD stopped and the sky had lightened to gray. Far to the west Audrey could see a clear and sunlit horizon, broken here and there by the black silhouettes of buildings. But it was the roof of the hospital's laundry that had taken her attention.

The laundry was two stories high and stood on the other side of a grassy area about half a block from the Old Building. Two men had climbed out onto the roof from some sort of service hatch. She had never seen anyone on the roof before. The men wore caps and some sort of uniform. One carried a rifle with a large scope on it. The other carried binoculars. They went to the rooftop wall and knelt there. They took turns with the binoculars, looking down at what Audrey judged to be the first floor, the back of the ER, where there was a corridor and two examination rooms and the two psych rooms. Then the man with the rifle swung his weapon over the wall and scanned the area through the scope, moved his position, looked through the scope again, and held the

rifle steady. Then he slid behind the wall. Au⌐
the back of his cap. He was sitting with his back
wall. The other man was talking on a walkie-talkie.
aside and returned to his study of the downstairs w⌐ ⌐s
binoculars.

Audrey called Security. The voice was unfamiliar. "Police
exercise," she was told. "Try not to make a thing out of it,
huh? No one else has even noticed."

"It doesn't look like an *exercise*."

"Lady, don't go upsetting people. We got a lot of work
down here. Trust me, huh? Don't make waves."

She looked out the window again. The man with the binoculars was still in place.

Elin came to the station. "I'm ready when you are." For
rounds.

"We have to wait for Dr. Schoonoler. He's in with Mr.
Stevens. He's been in there a good long time."

"All right. I'll have a look at the charts."

The floor was presently overrun with staff—Elin and herself and Dr. Schoonoler. Coralee had not left yet, Debby was
in with a patient, an LPN was with them. Day O'Meara and
Molly Chang were both in with Mrs. Gehl readying her for
her new accommodations.

Then there was the shrill, insistent signal of a monitor
declaring a cardiac arrest.

The line display on the monitor in the corridor looked like a
profile of jelly shaking, a chaotic line. Jan Fox's heart was
not doing anything.

The stupid, stupid bitch, Audrey thought. *Jan had done it
to herself. Made sure she wouldn't go home*. She was cyanotic. Debby had begun CPR.

Audrey ran to the station to call the code, but Coralee was
already hanging up. "They've got another one, we're on our
own."

At least they had Day, Audrey thought, wrestling the defib
machine around as Coralee pushed the cart forward. Day
could run this sort of thing if Dr. Schoonoler would let her.

Dr. Schoonoler had not even entered the room. He stood
outside the doorway looking in. *Hadn't seen an arrest in
thirty years. If he'd just stay out of the way.*

Coralee tried to get by him, but the cart seemed to impel him into the room.

Molly had knelt on the bed by Jan and was counting out her strokes for Debby's mouth-to-mouth: ''. . . two one-thousand . . . three one-thousand . . .'' and Audrey pulled Debby back and said, ''EKG, suction and O-two,'' and she took Debby's place. Jan's skin was pale blue, the feel of it cool and moist to Audrey's fingers and lips. Elin was on the floor getting the defib machine plugged in, Coralee had opened the doors of the cart, and Dr. Schoonoler was standing with his back against the wall, one hand grasping the rail of the cart. Day stood where the CCU resident would have stood. Her voice was quiet, but rapid and penetrating. ''Okay, folks, first line drugs. Doctor, you want bicarb, epinephrine, and calcium chloride, right?'' Coralee passed the drugs without waiting for the doctor's order and Elin was on her feet, piggybacking them into Jan's IV.

''Zero zero,'' Audrey said, reporting blood pressure.

Debby was at her side with the oxygen and ambu mask. ''Hold it down good, get a good seal,'' Molly said, sweat flinging from her face. The LPN had the EKG pushed into the room and Audrey went to hook it up as Debby placed the mask over Jan's mouth and nose and Elin threw away swabs and got the CVP line in, saw blood pump, and plugged the IV into the central line. ''Zero zero,'' Debby said.

The EKG showed a wavy line of fibrillation. Day was gooping the paddles. ''We need to defib, can we go?'' she said to Dr. Schoonoler and did not wait for an answer. ''One hundred,'' she said to Audrey. ''Clear the bed, everyone back—is the EKG unplugged?''

''Yes.''

Molly's beeper sounded. She ignored it.

Day placed the paddles. Her pregnancy got between her and the bed and she had to lean to keep clear. ''Everyone back, I'm going to shock her—*hit it.*''

Jan's body went into spasm, but it was an artificial expression. The body remained inert.

Molly ambued oxygen and Debby said, ''Zero zero,'' and Audrey read the EKG and said, ''Nothing.''

''Two hundred,'' Day said.

''I think—'' Dr. Schoonoler began.

''Two hundred,'' Day said. ''Clear the bed, EKG—''

"Unplugged."

"I'm placing the paddles, get back—*hit it!*"

Audrey depressed the button. The body went into spasm, became inert again. *"Breathe, goddamn you!"* Audrey said.

Debby had her hand inside Jan's thigh. "I've got a pulse, I can hear—"

"Dopamine drip," Day said. "Two hundred milligrams and five hundred." Coralee extracted it and Elin piggybacked it into the long line.

There were some seconds of silence. "V tach," Audrey said.

"One-fifty over—"

Day was looking at the EKG readout. "Lidocaine, four milligrams a minute," and Coralee delivered it as Elin drew blood gas and Debby and Molly resuscitated. Day squeezed Jan's fingernails and they pinked up.

Molly said, "She's breathing on her own." Her beeper sounded again. She ignored it.

"Rate's one-fifty."

"Wait on the lidocaine."

Elin handed off the blood gas to the LPN.

Day watched the EKG readout. "Looking better."

Dr. Schoonoler took out a handkerchief and wiped his face, but his other hand remained on the cart.

In the silence people heard their own heartbeats, felt the throb.

"One hundred over fifty," Debby said.

"Jesus sweet Christ," Day said softly. "I think we're holding on to her." She found the paddles still in her hands. She replaced them on the defib machine.

"I didn't authorize any of it," Dr. Schoonoler said.

Was it an apology or an abdication of responsibility? Audrey thought. Jan could still die. Audrey found herself furious at Jan. But she watched Jan's rhythm coolly and reported to the others.

"Let's get her cleaned up," Day said. "Prep her for transfer to a unit."

Audrey saw that Day's hands were shaking. Then she realized she was trembling herself. And so was everyone else.

"Monitor. O-two running. Lidocaine drip," Day said.

Audrey began to clean the jelly off her patient with alcohol and wipes. Jan's eyes opened and Audrey felt like hugging her. Jan saw all the people around her bed. "What happened?"

"You missed a couple of heartbeats," Audrey said. "You're okay now."

"You keep cleaning me up."

"I wish to hell *you'd* clean up your act, Jan."

"You were all *terrific*, terrific," Debby said at the station. "I never knew I could do that."   •

"Do what?"

"Hang in."

Day put down the receiver. "CCU's filled. She's to go up to the ICU. I'd give a whole lot for a failure of will power right now. I'd *so* like a cigarette."

Both Dr. Geier and Scotty McGettigan had come to the floor. Both were sweaty and slow-eyed with tiredness. They spent some time in with Jan and then came out to the station.

Molly's beeper pulsed aloud again. She picked up the phone and dialed Page.

"Pretty good," Dr. Geier said. "Pretty damn good."

"Likewise," Scotty said.

Day looked at him and said, "Any chance of you guys' coming back?"

Scotty's reply was not to Day but to Dr. Geier. "None."

Molly was hearing that, as senior psych nurse on duty, she had an emergency in the ER and was to say nothing to anyone about it.

113

MOLLY WAS SURPRISED and concerned by the number of police in the ER. Her identification was checked even though Sergeant Cleveland was there to certify her. Then she was directed to a conference room on the acute side. There were surgical teams of eight members each grouped outside the two trauma rooms, HOs in their standard complement. Three men and a woman in dark fatigues and boots and body armor stood together, equipment pouched and strapped about them. The woman and one of the men had holstered sidearms. The third man cradled an assault rifle in one arm and the fourth had an automatic weapon. Molly was horrified. *This is a hospital.*

The man with the sidearm looked at the trauma teams and said, "Christ, isn't this the place? Gonna get yourself shot up, I guess this is the place to do it." Then he said to the teams, "Me and my people do our job right, you people are just goin' t'be *bored to tears* for lack of work."

There were blueprints on the conference table. The hospital's chief engineer was reviewing them with another man in fatigues, a Lieutenant Kincaid from the Bureau of Special Operations, the SWAT unit commander. He was saying to a sergeant, "Get on to Municipal Buildings for engineering plans, duplications or not. Get on to Public Works for sewer, water—whatever they have on the hospital's underground."

Molly learned that it had been forty-five minutes since Olivia had closed herself into Psych Two with three hostages and had fired a shot at Reynold when he had checked to see why the door was closed.

Molly remained outside the gathering at the table, sorting out people and conversations. Kincaid seemed to be carrying on individual conversations with everyone—Bennett, Trina, the engineer, the sergeant, a black woman in slacks and a shirt, others. "As soon as we shut the generator down, you go," he said to the black woman.

"I want to talk to her from outside the door."

"I don't want you in the corridor. Period. You use a hailer and stay clear."

"She's got the door shut."

"She'll hear."

"I know, but I'd like a more personal approach," the woman said.

"She's right," Trina said. "If she's going to negotiate with Olivia—"

"We'll do it my way," Kincaid said. His voice was calm. He was quick and calm, Molly thought.

"I don't think you know what you're dealing with," Trina said.

My Trina, Molly thought. Goes where even fools dare not.

"I'll tell you a story about that later," Kincaid said. "We're going to have lots of time."

"I think not. She's already warned us the Snake Lady can kill."

"I'm dealing with Olivia, not the Snake Lady."

"Not yet. But when you do—"

"I hear you. But we're going to take it nice and slow. It works. It's simply a time-waiting sequence. We let her exhaust herself physically and mentally—"

"So the Snake Lady can take over?"

"Patience. Patience is the word. Let her believe she's in control. In the meantime we control her total environment."

"Except where it matters," Trina said. "In the room itself."

"We have more control over that than Olivia knows. In a few minutes we'll have an eye and an ear in the air-conditioning outlet. Tiny thing. We can see and hear everything in the room, she doesn't know it's there. The area in which she can be active has been reduced to that one room. We control the areas on every side of that room and above and below it. The best that can happen is that the hostages do nothing. In the meantime, Olivia is going to feel more and more trapped and confined."

"So are the hostages," Molly said.

"So is the Snake Lady," Trina said.

Kincaid looked at Molly and so did Bennett. Molly said, "I suggest you pay attention to Trina. I'll go with her on this."

"I want to go in, Molly."

"No way," Kincaid said. He turned to Bennett and the engineer. "We're hanging lights from the second-story windows. We're erecting lights from the laundry and the Old Hospital." Molly appreciated the way in which Kincaid had manipulated the conversation. He was probably a helluva negotiator himself. He was negotiating with everyone at once. "We've got the corridor outside the psych rooms rigged with lighting already and it's on. If she takes a look outside the room, she's going to be minimally aware of day and night."

"The generator," Trina said. "I asked you about that. All that noise is going to scare her."

"All that noise is going to cover up what we're doing."

"It's going to *scare* her. It *is* scaring her."

"I have never met anyone," Kincaid said slowly, "who is clairvoyant, psychiatrically trained or not. The less so if trained." He returned his attention to Bennett. "The noise of the generator is allowing some important work to be done. Two jobs. We have a marksman and a spotter on the roof of the laundry. We're cutting out the window in front of the door to psych Two. The marksman will have unobstructed shooting if the door to Psych Two opens. Second, we have a machine in Psych One that's cutting away the wall between the two rooms. In a big circle. When it's finished, what we'll have left in there is about five coats of paint in Psych Two and the paper surface of the Sheetrock. That's where we place the apprehension team—"

"Excuse me," Molly said, "I appreciate all the trouble you've gone to, but—"

"You've always got the fucking *worst* sense of humor," Bennett said.

"But I'm very concerned about the Snake Lady. I think this is a psychiatric situation and—"

"It *is* a psychiatric situation," Kincaid said. "It is *more* a police situation. Can we get some coffee?" Bennett picked up a phone. Brilliant, Kincaid, Molly thought. Kincaid turned back to Molly. "I don't doubt you can treat her the best in the world for what ails her. When she doesn't have a gun. But she has a gun. I deal with people who aren't sitting around in a friendly therapeutic conversation. I deal with people who are sitting around with guns and hostages and a strong desire to blow someone's brains out, even their own."

"That's why I want to go in," Trina said. "I think she'll give me the gun."

"Now how the hell do you know that?"

"Self-confidence," Trina said.

"I'll tell you a story about self-confidence. A similar situation. Mental patient. Had a nurse hostage. His goddamn girlfriend snuck him a three fifty-seven magnum somehow, big sonofabitch, you know?"

Trina just looked at Kincaid.

"Shrink knew the patient real well. Not like you. Spent a lot of time with this guy. So I let him talk to him. The shrink was doin' a real good job quietin' the guy down, takin' him down step by step, and finally, well, he asked the patient if now wasn't a good time for him to come in and the patient would give him the gun and then they'd all see what they could do to get the patient feelin' better."

"I don't think I want to hear this," Trina said. "I think I've heard it before."

"Then hear it again. Let it add to your perspective. The

shrink left the protection of the SWAT unit. The patient was sitting in a chair, the nurse on the floor in front of him, sitting there with the pistol against the back of her head, and the shrink walks in for the patient to hand him the gun—and you know what? The sonofabitch takes the gun away from the back of the nurse's head and blows the shrink's head clean off. Almost clean off.''

"Oh shit," Trina said quietly.

"Yes. There were brains everywhere. Shards of bones.''

"What about the nurse?''

"We killed that sonofabitch before he could lower his arm.''

"That's what you mean by a police situation," Trina said.

Kincaid went on. "The nurse has not been able to function on a normal level since. Mother of two. Anxiety neurosis or something. Everything in the world scares the shit out of her.''

Trina pursed her lips, then said, "I understand.''

"What we do is very time-consuming. Might take two or three days. Might. Then everyone comes out alive. You know what? I didn't want to blow that patient's life away. He was just a poor sonofabitch in trouble every way he looked, same as all of us. But he didn't have clue A what to do about it. The doctor thought he had clues A through Z. I don't. I don't pretend to understand that woman in there. But I understand the mechanics of getting her and her hostages out of there alive.''

Trina said, "It's the Snake Lady who's not going to be patient.''

114

THE NEGOTIATORS NAME was Nell Dudley and Trina said to her, "When Olivia starts talking about the Snake Lady, that's a danger signal. I'd stay away from the Snake Lady if I could.''

Donald Kay, the hospital's public relations officer, came in to Bennett. "We've got all kinds of media outside and the mayor wants you on the phone.''

"All right, I'll talk to the mayor," Bennett said, getting up. "Then you and I will prepare a statement." He touched Molly's shoulder as he walked by. "Sorry about your sense of humor."

"Me too."

There was the sound of whimpering. "We've got audio and visual," a tech officer said. Bennett turned to see.

Kincaid had turned to a small television screen and sound monitor. The tech officer sat at the monitor and controlled the sensitivity of the listening device.

"Oh sweet Jesus . . . Oh Mary . . . Oh Mary mother of God . . ."

"That's Cathleen," Trina said. "The one on the table."

The images of the four figures were odd, distorted.

"Fisheye," Kincaid said. "About the size of a marble at the end of a tube. It's not hanging into the room, so there's some obstruction, of course. Those blurry lines are the grid of the air-conditioning cover. The motion is caused by the movement of air through the duct. The ear is highly sensitive. We can pitch it to hear individuals whispering or even breathing."

"She's got the door tethered from inside," Nell said.

Bennett came back to the table. "The mayor," Kay said.

But Bennett spoke to Kincaid. "Why not introduce gas through the air-conditioning duct. Something that would knock her out."

"Gas is a chemical compound. You don't get rid of chemicals just by wishing them away. They could float through the hospital. They could become established here. I don't want to fuck up the environment." He looked at Kay. "You got any word on the rest of the hospital?"

"We have a visit on every floor now. For the duration. We're telling people we're having a problem with a psych patient but it's confined to the back of the ER. We're not being specific about the problem. That's not going to hold up too long. Some of our people have already seen your people on top of the laundry. Now you've got all those lights on, too." He and Bennett left.

Trina was studying the little screen. "Lieutenant, you see how the people are placed. There's Olivia on one side of the room near the door, the hostages in the middle of the room. The apprehension team has the hostages between themselves and Olivia."

"That can't be helped. We can't go through the other walls. We may be able to distract her from the door. Maybe she'll move."

"If I went in there, I could move the hostages out of the way."

"Rule number one, two, and three is, you never give another hostage. We bargain with other things. She's going to want water, toilet facilities. We'll see what we can get in exchange. Nell'll give her a little water to begin with and then a lot. All she wants to drink. We play on a sexual differentiation. Women are humiliated urinating in front of someone else. It takes them down. Men don't mind so much."

Molly said, "She's a schiz, Lieutenant. It's not going to make a damn bit of difference to her."

"Lieutenant, this is not your classic hostage situation," Trina said.

"You're an expert?"

"I know more about Olivia than you do. What makes it atypical is, I'll bet you there's nothing Olivia wants. You can't bargain with her."

"We'll try."

"I wish you the best of luck. You can try offering her a hysterectomy." She explained to Nell. "But I don't think that's going to work."

"Why not?"

"The Snake Lady doesn't want a hysterectomy. All the Snake Lady wants to do is kill. It's the Snake Lady who's in charge, and she's getting stronger and stronger."

"You're being clairvoyant again."

"No, Lieutenant, I'm being observant. Look at her posture. What does it remind you of?"

Molly answered. "Coiled, defensive, head raised, ready to attack. A snake."

Nell Dudley stood in the corner at the end of the corridor with a hailer in her hand. The apprehension team was in position in Psych One. The spotter studied the door to Psych Two from the roof of the laundry. Support personnel were in place inside and outside the hospital.

Nell spoke quietly into the hailer. Her voice carried into Psych Two and from there to the voice monitor in the conference room.

"Olivia, my name is Nell Dudley. I'm a thirty-two-year-old black lady, a member of the police department, and I'm unarmed and I want to talk to you and see to it that you don't get hurt and no one in there with you gets hurt. Now, Olivia, can you hear me?"

There was silence.

Nell heard Kincaid's voice in her earplug. *"I don't see any response, but we read you five-by."*

Nell said, "Olivia, what we need to do is get talking together. We'll take all the time you want. Just you and me. There's no rush. There's going to be some things you need, some things you want. Maybe I can get them for you."

Olivia's voice came through the door. "Nothin' I need, nothin' I want."

"You don't have any food or water or toilet facilities. Sooner or later you're going to want them. Those are things I can provide."

Silence.

"I can get you those things, Olivia, but we have to talk."

Silence.

"I understand you may need a hysterectomy."

"Snake Lady say don't talk to you."

"Your ovaries cause you a lot of pain, don't they? Your ovaries hurt you a lot—"

"You shuts up out there," Olivia said mildly. "Gonna hurts people in here."

"You don't want to do that, Olivia—"

"Back off," Nell heard Kincaid say.

"I'm going away for a few minutes, Olivia. But you call out if you want me."

"We've got a subconscious ally in there," Kincaid said. "We've got to reach her."

"You're reaching the Snake Lady," Trina said.

"Most hostage-takers, there's a subconscious ally of ours in them. The ally wants them to try to help them save themselves."

Trina watched the screen as she spoke. "You've got a situation here that's more advanced than you know. Look at the two of them, Olivia and Ginny. They recognize each other. Two Snake Ladies. Look at the postures, look at the body language. They each recognize violence in the other, *crazy* violence. Those postures aren't just defensive.''

Molly said, "Listen to what Trina's telling you, Lieutenant. There's a little dance going on there. Those two are ready to kill.''

"Olivia won't stop if she starts," Trina said. "They're going to trigger each other real soon. The thing to do is get Ginny out of there. That's going to defuse a lot of what's going on in Olivia. Give Nell time to talk to her.''

"Sure," Kincaid said. "Why don't we just wish Olivia out of there instead? We haven't got anything to offer for Ginny.''

Olivia screamed out words suddenly. "Snake Lady wants the *talking* nurse.''

Trina said to Kincaid, "That sound like your ally? I'm not kidding. She's giving us a chance.''

"To do what?''

"For me to talk to her.''

Kincaid thought. He said to Nell, "Any objection?''

"No.''

"You stay with Nell. At the end of the corridor.''

Cathleen's whimpering continued in the background. *"Oh Mary and Jesus, get me out of here . . . Oh God in heaven, please . . .''*

115

"THIS FAR FROM your mouth," Nell said to Trina, showing her how and where to hold the hailer. "You raise your voice maybe one level above normal. Speak clearly.''

This isn't going to work, Trina thought. She's not going to hear the talking nurse, she's going to hear a police-sounding voice, riot control. She keyed the hailer and said, "Olivia, this is Trina, the talking nurse. Do you hear me, Olivia?''

There was silence and Nell relayed information from her earplug. "You're coming through fine. But there's no reaction.''

"Olivia, it's Trina. You asked to talk to me. I'm the nurse you spoke to about a hysterectomy.''

Silence. Trina could hear city sounds from outside the

window that had been cut away down the corridor outside Psych Two.

"She's like a statue," Nell said.

"Where's her visual attention?"

An officer with a handheld communicator sent the question. Nell said, "She's looking more or less at Ginny. The weapon's aimed at Ginny."

Trina spoke into the hailer. "Olivia, if you can hear me, just let me know you can hear me. Can you hear me?" Silence. Trina said to Nell, "She gave me one access but I hate to use it. She said the Snake Lady wants to talk to me." Trina raised the hailer. "Olivia, you said the Snake Lady wants to talk to me."

Silence. "She's raised the weapon and extended it toward Ginny."

"No," Trina said to Nell. "She didn't say that. She said the Snake Lady *wants* the talking nurse." She handed the hailer to Nell.

Of the team on the roof of the laundry, it was the spotter who had the most fatiguing portion of the duty. His responsibility was constructed that way. The marksman's vision would become blurry if he spent five minutes looking through his scope. The spotter did the looking for him.

The spotter said, "Oh, shit."

"What?"

"Looks like a nurse. Outside the room."

"Oh fuck," the shooter said. "Fuck, fuck, fuck," he said, looking through the scope of his rifle. A thousand feet away he could have performed surgery by puncture at any chosen spot on Trina's body. "My fuckin' line of fire," the marksman said. "She's fuckin' up my line of fire."

"She's not supposed to be there," they heard through their earplugs. *"We're asking her to come back."*

"The fuckin' idiot," the marksman said. He looked through his scope briefly again. He turned with his back against the wall and broke the target areas into acceptable and unacceptable circles of fire, positioning and repositioning the nurse's body in a screening in his mind in which everyone, even in the room, which he had studied, was seen through his scope and he could stop and start the action like an all-seeing cameraman. As he watched, he closed his eyes. "Wake me when it's over," the marksman said.

"I always do."

"Tell them to get her the fuck out of my line of fire."

Trina crouched by the door in the hope that her voice would carry to Olivia with some intimacy.

"Olivia, it's Trina. I'm right outside the door. I'm alone. I want to talk with you. Work things out. I want you to get out safe and sound."

Trina got no response from the room, but she was aware of Nell's instructing her to come back, though in her own voice, not with the hailer.

Trina said, "Olivia, isn't there anything you want?"

"Not me."

It was a response. "What does the Snake Lady want?"

"Snake Lady wants the talkin' nurse."

Trina spoke slowly. "Olivia, I'll come in and stay with you. But I've got to have something back, Olivia. Some kind of trade."

"Like what?"

"You show your good will, I'll show mine. Let Ginny come out and I'll come in." There was silence. "Did you hear me?"

"Snake Lady says, gets no people. *People belongs to the Snake Lady*."

"Olivia, you got any friends? Besides the Snake Lady?"

"Snake Lady not my friend."

"Oh. I thought she was."

"She jes tell me what to do."

"Ask her if I can come in and take Ginny's place."

"She wants you to come in."

"Good. And Ginny can go?"

"No."

"How about Cathleen or Hal?"

"That her name? *Pee-ewe-ee*."

"What about Cathleen?"

"She done peed and took a shit both. It sure do stink in here."

"Let her go, Olivia. Let her go and the smell'll go away. She's just going to keep crappin' up the place. She's going to make the air bad."

"I think on it." She laughed. "Yes, it sure do stink. You come here to the Snake Lady?"

Trina heard Nell's voice. *"Lieutenant says no."*

Trina spoke softly behind her to the closed door. "You get a patient out, a psych nurse in. Everyone's better off. I'll stay with you, Olivia, if you let Cathleen go. Just send her out."

"You come in first."

"The door's shut."

Trina waited a long time. Then the door opened the width of a body. Hal had opened it. His eyes went to the floor of the corridor. He could dive out to safety. He saw it. Trina hesitated, to give him the chance. It was not her decision. He remained in the room. The doctor was staying with the patient. Trina went in.

The stench was terrible. Ginny gagged quietly. She looked at Trina with hatred. Hal's eyes were as always enormous behind his glasses and staring. Cathleen lay restrained to the table on her stomach, her dress soiled around her thighs and buttocks.

Olivia was blank-eyed and smiling, her face shining damp.

Trina said, "Olivia, I'm going to remove Cathleen's restraints. Then I'll help her to the door." Going to Cathleen, Trina pushed Hal against the side wall by the door. If he stayed there he would be out of the way of the apprehension team coming in from the other end of the room. Ginny was right between Olivia and the team's entry. Trina believed she could do the work that would make the team's entry unnecessary. No one would get shot, no one would die.

"It's okay, babe," she said to Cathleen. "I'm going to get these off you—"

"Oh my, oh my . . . you angel . . . angel, angel . . ." Cathleen was weeping and shaking.

"Just take it slow, Cathleen."

"Oh thank God Almighty . . . . Oh Jesus . . ."

"You'll be out soon, babe."

Olivia said, "Snake Lady waitin'."

"Okay, Cathleen, up you come, just slide off the side of the table, I know you're a little stiff, I'll help, I've got you—"

"Oh, God, let me live, please . . ."

"We're just going to walk over to the door. I'm going to open it for her, all right, Olivia?" Olivia said nothing. "Cathleen, I'm just going to open the door wide enough for you to get out." Ginny looked at the door. Trina prepared herself to shove Cathleen out if Ginny moved. Olivia's arm and gun extended toward Ginny. Hal watched—the boyish medical student pursuing his studies, though this, of course, was not part of the curriculum. Trina guided Cathleen to the door. The smell of sweat was as strong as that of feces and urine. If I can just get her out the door, Trina thought.

"I'm going to open the door, Cathleen. You walk out. Keep walking." She said to Olivia, "I'm closing the door as soon as she's out."

The tethers hung loose. Trina opened the door partway, afraid there would be people with guns and visored helmets outside, but the corridor was empty, and Trina pushed Cathleen out and pulled the door closed.

Olivia smiled. "Snake Lady waitin'."

"I don't see her," Trina said.

Donald Kay had not been able to contain the story. The mayor agreed to make a statement at City Hall.

"Yes, we have a hostage situation at Back Bay Metropolitan Hospital," the mayor said. "It is confined to one remote room in the rear of the hospital and the situation has been absolutely and totally isolated. Now if you want to panic the patients there, you'll put that news out."

One of the television news directors on a conference line said, "This isn't going to last long, Mr. Mayor."

"God, let's hope it doesn't."

"I mean, before it breaks."

116

ON MED THREE Audrey had figured out that there was a hostage situation or one or more escapees trapped down below. She could think of no other reason for the rifleman on the roof of the laundry. Then Dr. Schoonoler came back to the floor in the early evening and surprised Audrey by saying that he was staying, maybe overnight, maybe even longer. He would be on immediate call somewhere in the hospital. He confirmed Audrey's theory about what was happening downstairs. He looked nervous and Audrey thought it was the incipient violence below them. He would not make eye contact with her and she thought he was distracted, preoccupied with the situation. She was wrong.

Audrey had her own preoccupation and it was very uncomfortable, a pervasive sense of loss and sorrow, and it came from Jan's arrest.

But, from the same origin, Debby was overflowing with excitement. It had been growing within her, as Audrey's sorrow had, and finally there were words for it, as yet Audrey had none. "It wasn't pandemonium," Debby said. "It *wasn't* pandemonium. I *helped*. I helped save Jan's life."

They were at the station and Audrey saw Dr. Schoonoler looking at Debby and then averting his eyes.

"I was *good*," Debby said.

"Yes, you were," Audrey said. "It feels good, doesn't it?" Then why do I feel so lousy? "Captain Malamet needs his nitro patch changed."

"Okay." Debby left the station.

Dr. Schoonoler replaced a chart and took out another. He was going through all the charts. He stood while he did it. He spoke to Audrey without looking at her. "Any other candidates for arrest on the floor?" He had placed one chart aside.

"None immediate," Audrey said. "No one I have any suspicion about, Doctor." She looked at the chart he had set aside.

He saw her look and said, "Something I want to talk to you about."

"All right."

He tapped his fingers on the counter. "You were all good, you know. You were all excellent. The way you saved that woman's life."

"Thank you."

He looked away. "I was helpless. She would have died if I'd had to tell people what to do. I can't get over that."

He *looked* helpless, Audrey thought. Bereft of his professional self-respect.

"I didn't know what to do."

"You've been away from that sort of thing a long time."

"It was my responsibility."

"I don't know why, but I feel lousy about Jan Fox too."
She had no idea why she told Dr. Schoonoler.

He picked up the chart he had set aside. "This is what I want to talk to you about. Percy Stevens."

"Yes?" Audrey was unprepared, apprehensive. Dr. Schoonoler had been looking for candidates for arrest.

"Once a patient's been assigned to Medicine here, it's a nursing decision what bed he gets."

"Yes. Usually."

"I've been reviewing Stevens with a colleague on New Wing Five."

"The Gold Coast."

"I'm aware of the attitude of much of the nursing staff toward New Wing Five."

"We feel every patient deserves the same level of care."

"That's not how society works. That's not how medicine works."

"Excuse me, Dr. Schoonoler. That's *exactly* how we work here, the nurses and the HOs."

"However you feel about it, the reality is, your patient would be better served on New Wing Five."

"Is that a promise or a point of view?"

"It's an informed opinion. A highly respected one. Not my own, Audrey, if you're wondering. There's been remarkable progress in the treatment of oatcell CA recently. Positive results. One of the leading men in the field is on the staff of New Wing Five. Dr. Quinlan. I would like to arrange Stevens' transfer to New Wing Five."

Audrey realized that she was not only protective of Mr. Stevens but had become possessive. "Couldn't he see Mr. Stevens on this floor?"

"He brings some of his own patients to New Wing Five. That's where he'd treat this patient."

"I think that would be fine. *Wonderful.*"

Dr. Schoonoler gave Audrey a very direct look. "I'm sorry to take him from you. I know you have a lot of emotional investment in him."

"That's sensitive of you, Dr. Schoonoler. I appreciate it."

"I was forgetting about such things until this afternoon. Nurses being adjuncts, you see. But I would have lost that woman."

"Thank you. You just did something for me."

Provided a link for Audrey within herself between her despondence and Jan's near-death. Audrey had no, one to contact. No kin to share the near-death with, no kin with whom to celebrate the marvel of Jan's survival. She had to keep all that inside herself and it was as if she had *lost* Jan—as, in a way, she had, and as, in a way, she would be losing Mr. Stevens. They would no longer be within her protection—as if her protection could ward off death.

All that was inside herself and she hadn't known it. She understood a little and she felt a little better.

She could tell Tim, she realized. Jan had been transferred up to Tim's unit after Tim had gone home. Sort of family. If there was a chance later, she would call Tim and tell him about Jan.

Debby was back at the station and her face was set in anger. "I was in there and Captain Malamet . . . expressed loneliness."

"You sympathized with him."

"Yes. He said he'd made it with lots of stews." She stopped.

"But never made it with a nurse?"

"Yes."

"He was probably lying. To gain your sympathy."

"He expressed various ways I could express my sympathy. He was explicit. I'm not going to go back in there."

"I know you don't *want* to go back in there. That's understandable. But you are going to go back in there. First *I'm* going to go back in there."

But before she got to Malamet, she heard Percy Stevens calling from his room. *"Excuse me. Miss Rosenfeld. Audrey."*

Maybe it was the medication or the chemotherapy or both, but Mr. Stevens looked very pale, his ruddiness gone, his hair stringy and unkempt, his face, Audrey suddenly thought, as if he were a prisoner, not a patient.

"I want you to answer somethin'. It's been a lot on my mind."

"Go ahead, Percy."

"I apologize for askin' it."

"Just go ahead. I'm not going to run out on you."

He looked down. "That's jes it, don'tya see? When I firs' come in, got people 'round this bed all the day and half the night, it seemed like. Now no one comes in. Hardly. Hardly ever."

"Well, Percy, you know the house officers are out."

"Oh, yeah. I know about that. I don't mean like that. I mean like, Miss Wafford—Coralee—and Debby? And the others that used to come in and out? They'd bandy some words with me. And you. You, too."

"We've been very busy, Percy."

"Is it me? Because I'm dying? Is that why no one comes inta see me anymore?"

"Percy, I don't think—"

"Sometimes I hear people go by, chattin' in the hall, they don't stop in. I think, it's because they're afraid of catchin' dyin' from me."

"Maybe you're right, Percy. Maybe I could have stopped in more often. Maybe we all could have. I'm ashamed. I'm worse than ashamed. Because maybe you're right."

"Now, Audrey, don't take on."

She went over and stood close by the side of the bed. "If you're brave enough to face dying, the rest of us damn well ought to show as much courage as . . . as we should." She took his hands in hers. "I thought I was treating you the same as everyone else, but maybe I haven't been." Death still frightens me, she wanted to say. It scares the shit out of me. I don't approve of it. It kicks up shit in me I can't handle sometimes. Except by turning my back on it. Maybe that's what I did to you, she wanted to say, and I will not do that anymore.

She sat on the side of the bed. "If I've been neglecting you, it's because you're someone I personally like a whole damn lot, and that happens sometimes. That's a bad reason, but it's a big, big reason—if I've been neglecting you. Because I care about you and your wife and your boys so *bloody* much."

"You ain't been *neglectin'* me, I dint say that." Then he was quiet and she sat by him for a few minutes and did not speak again because she saw he was going to sleep.

117

"IT'S ALWAYS NICE to have a nurse around," Trevor Davis said to Nan. "Let me introduce you to my friends."

Nan had not felt like such a wallflower since some long-ago middle school dance. She knew no one at the party except the former roommate herself and the couple, whom she had just met, who had driven her out to the club. She was delighted to find Trevor, a colleague from her days on the ER, someone she *knew*.

"Paul Squires. You may not know his pretty face, but you know his pretty voice."

Squires smiled at her nicely, Nan thought. She had no idea what to make of the allusion to his voice.

"And Ron Casey. Be careful of Case, he went wrong. Moneyman. Stockbroker."

She did not like Casey. His eyes slithered across her. But his voice pretended it hadn't happened. His voice was all manners and polite pleasure. The three of them had been roommates of the groom at Harvard. They were three or four years older than Nan.

There were two women about Nan's age, Josie and Donna. Whatever their age, there was a lot of schoolgirl sexual innuendo and flirtatious laughter in their byplay with the men. Nan was outside of it and glad to be. The bride and the groom and these five had all been at Country Day together before college and Nan was outside that, too. The conversation had a great deal of reference to which Nan was not connected. Trevor Davis, whom the others called Trees, was her only link.

She sipped her wine. They were out on the terrace. Waiters and waitresses passed canapés. It was a warm early evening, still light, and a long way away was the sea, but Nan could smell it and it excited her.

Josie and Donna were called away by some mutual relative and Nan found herself alone with Trevor and the other two. They stood around her, maybe a little too close, but there were a lot of people on the terrace, and she sensed the physical attraction of the three of them to her and felt ambivalent about it. It felt awfully good and it made her a little uneasy as well.

After talk about a public mistake of some sort that Squires had made, Trevor said to her, "You have no idea who this fellow is, do you?"

"Sorry," Nan said.

"Number two–rated afternoon radio show in the entire market," Trevor said.

"DJ," Squires said. He was so tentative Nan couldn't imagine it was so.

"He comes alive on the air," Trevor said. "It's amazing. Medical science is baffled."

"When are you on?"

"Two to five."

"I'm at work most of that time. Or going home."

"I'll send you a tape."

"Really?"

"Really."

Nan grinned. "That would be fun."

"I might call you after. See how you like it."

Donna and Josie came back, and the conversation tended to exclude Nan once again. They were talking about a castle, Slade's Castle. Nan had heard of it. It was a legend around Boston and Nan had never been sure that it really existed.

"We could go out there later," Trevor said.

"*Slade's Castle?*" Donna said. "Really?"

"I have the loan of it. Actually, I'm taking care of it."

"That's not too shabby," Josie said.

"How come you're taking care of it?" Donna said.

"My Uncle Augustus. It's his."

"Is it really a castle?" Donna said.

"Every inch of it. Copied from a real one in Germany."

Josie said, "Who's this Uncle Augustus? How come I've never heard of him?"

"Black sheep. Recluse—when he's home. Actually, he's not an uncle at all. He's an elderly cousin a few times removed. The important thing is, right now he's removed to Europe and I'm sitting the castle for him. C'mon back with me. If this breaks up early enough."

Squires said, "Everybody has to work tomorrow, Trees. Except you, being out on strike."

Trevor laughed. "It's not a strike. Don't you read the PR releases?"

"Well, what is it, then?"

"It's a laugh. Or as my old friend Lynn Keating wrote, it's a joke." He looked tenderly at Nan. "At least the nurses have the good sense to stay in."

Donna said, "That's not bad going, Trees. Slade's Castle."

Trevor said, "Shall we go then? After? Have a party?" He turned to Nan. "Come along with us?"

"Maybe. Where is it?"

"Over near Concord."

"I'd need a ride home."

"No problem. You'll like this place, I know."

"How do you know?"

"We know what's important to nurses," he said.

"Bad, Trees, *bad*," Donna said.

They were asked by a waiter to go in to dinner. Trevor placed his hand on Nan's waist. "I didn't know you were going to be here, but I've arranged for you to sit at our table."

Nan was relieved and thankful. She would not have to sit at a table of strangers.

118

THE HOSTAGE STORY broke on a suburban radio station, which cited "unconfirmed reports from reliable sources." Once the story was out one place it was everywhere.

The anxiety level on the floors rose appreciably, and Bennett and Dr. Geier and Dorothea Kullgren debated whether adding security personnel to the floors would help reduce the anxiety or intensify it. The debate was rendered moot when Scotty McGettigan came in and volunteered one senior house officer per floor to help calm patients until the situation was resolved.

Bennett rejected the offer. The HOs were to come back

full-time or not at all. Dr. Geier accepted the offer and maintained that it was a medical decision that had to be made, not a legal or administrative decision. Bennett sidestepped that by authorizing funds over budget to bring in flexies and agency nurses. Dr. Geier agreed. "If you can get them in fast enough. If they'll come in at all."

"Our flexies will come in," Dorothea said.

Scotty's anger at Bennett was absolute. "You've got us down, you've got us by the throat. You won't let go for even a few hours."

"No."

In her office, Day had a call from Jimbo. "You know what's going on in there?" he said.

"Yes."

"I want you to get out."

"I'm on duty, Jimbo. I'm nowhere near the trouble. Nothing's going to take me there."

"What if it comes to you?"

"It won't."

"You can't stay in there, Day."

"I helped save a life by being here."

He was silent and when he spoke his voice was small. "There's nothing I can do." He hung up.

Trina said, "I wish you'd give me the gun, Olivia. You're going to hurt yourself with it. Or one of us. Do you want to hurt yourself?"

"Through talkin'."

"What do you want to do?"

"Sit here. See my mind gets clear. Or decides to kill you. The Snake Lady."

"Do you want to hurt me?"

"I just wanta do what gots to be done. Don't know what that is."

"Give me the gun."

"Don't belong to you."

"Don't belong to you either, Olivia."

"That right. Belong to the Snake Lady."

"Tell me about the Snake Lady, Olivia."

"Tell you 'bout the Snake Lady? Girl, I look at you, you daid from the Snake Lady."

*   *   *

Kincaid was in a fury and had been since Trina had gone into Psych Two almost four hours before. It was a cool, dark, controlled fury, Molly saw. The predictability he relied upon had been interfered with. He had lost some of his own superintendence of the situation and it had gone into the room with Trina.

Molly understood that she herself, being Back Bay Met rather than Mobile Ops, was in disfavor and was tolerated in the command post only because she could help Kincaid understand what Trina was doing.

Trina alternated her attention between Olivia and Ginny. Molly said, "The Snake Lady is the turmoil in Olivia. Olivia doesn't know what to do with that turmoil. Trina keeps trying to find a safe access to it so she can help Olivia deal with it. At the same time, she's got to keep Ginny in control of her anxiety. Ginny's anxiety is like gasoline and a match. The second that anxiety turns to terror, it'll be blind terror. Consequences won't matter. You're lucky Trina's in there. I don't want her in there any more than you do. But the reason you haven't had a tragedy in there is because of Trina."

"Olivia, I know this must be a pretty bad day for you. I know you must be feeling bad."

Olivia suddenly laughed, but her face remained blank.

"I'd like you to let me take you to a doctor. So you don't feel so bad all the time. I'd like to see you get some help with that. I'd like to see you have some nice days for yourself."

"Only way that gonna happen, *daid*."

Oh Christ, Trina thought, have I got a suicide on my hands here? "Where'd you get that idea?"

"Snake Lady tol' me."

"I don't know much about this Snake Lady. You mention her a lot, but you don't tell me about her."

"You shuts up 'bout the Snake Lady."

"I know her name," Trina said.

"You shuts your mouth, girl. Don't be sayin' any names or I kills you, I swear."

"*Why is she doing that?*" Kincaid said. "*She said to stay away from the Snake Lady.*"

"*That was when Nell was outside. Trina's in there with the Snake Lady. It's what's open. It's what's available.*"

Hal said, "I wish you'd let me have the gun, Olivia. We'd all be safer."

She said nothing but pointed the gun at him.

Ginny moved slightly.

"That's okay, Ginny," Trina said quickly. "I know you're scared. That's natural. Let's just be patient till Olivia feels better. You hungry, Ginny? Boy, I'm starved."

"I'm thirsty," Hal said.

"He's picking up on Trina," Molly said. *"He can be a help."*

"If he doesn't screw up."

"Olivia," Trina said, "aren't you hungry, too? Thirsty?"

"Flyin'."

"What?"

Olivia began to hum.

"That's a pretty tune," Trina said. "What is it?"

Olivia stopped singing.

"If we could get some food in, would that be all right? And something to drink?"

"Gonna put *poison* in it."

"No poison. You won't have to eat and drink, Olivia. We will."

"Poleez Lady!"

Nell's voice responded immediately. "Yes, Olivia, this is Nell."

"You cuts the 'lectricity, I gots 'lectricity in my body, in my eyes, you know that, girl?"

"We're not going to turn the lights out on you, Olivia."

"How I know that?"

"We don't work that way. We just want you to take it easy. We want you to come out safe."

"Huh!"

"It's true, Olivia," Trina said. "Everyone wants you to be safe."

Ginny began to tremble and weep. Trina went to her and placed her arm around her. "It's okay, Ginny. We just have to wait this out. It's all going to be okay." She tried to ease Ginny to the wall opposite Hal but, in spite of the trembling, Ginny's body was rigid in its place.

The gun flicked back to Ginny and Trina. Trina had never had a gun pointed at her before. How easily it could go off.

She was looking into its barrel, the blind mouth of a snake open in strike. "Olivia, please—"

"Move off! Quick."

"Yes." Trina moved away from Ginny.

The gun remained on Ginny. "Don't you go touch that girl again."

"All right, Olivia."

Olivia began to hum.

"What's the humming mean?" Kincaid said.

"I don't know. She could be calming herself. But . . . My association is, bees swarming. That's not a clinical observation. That's subjective."

They listened to Trina trying to break through it.

Hal said, "Can I sing with you, Olivia?"

Olivia laughed. The humming stopped.

Kincaid said, "So far it's going our way. No action."

"You want to keep this up for two or three days?" Molly said.

"If we can. We're reasonably sure of a successful conclusion then. Everyone out safe. If we can keep a state of no action for two or three days."

"If *Trina* can keep a state of no action for two or three days. That's asking for a lot of stamina, physical and mental."

"She placed herself in there. Nell will keep trying to negotiate. The apprehension team is twelve feet and less than two seconds from Olivia."

Molly studied the screen. "Ginny won't make it through two or three days."

119

"IT'S NOT EVEN eleven yet," Trevor said. "Plenty of time. Put on some music, have a couple of drinks, lounge around in the fourteenth century."

"Sounds good to me," Casey, the stockbroker, said.

The castle, Nan had learned from Trevor at dinner, had been built around the turn of the century by an import mogul named Slade, who had had every stone cut from the same palatinate quarry as the original castle and then had had every stone borne across the Atlantic by steamship. Slade was Uncle Augustus' father.

"That would really be something—seeing the inside of Slade's Castle. Right?" Casey said, looking at Josie and Donna.

Donna said to him, "I have been to places with you at night and they are not the memories I cherish." But she laughed.

Negotiations got under way and continued, and as Nan listened to the flirtation and indirection, she realized that the five of them had probably been carrying on these exact same negotiations on different subjects since they had all been in kindergarten together.

The couple who had driven Nan to the club was ready to leave.

"One of us will get you home," Trevor said.

Nan thought about it quickly. She did not want to go out to the castle without the other two women and she wouldn't. But Trevor was a colleague, she'd worked with him, and it *would* be fun to go to the castle if everyone went. "Okay," Nan said. She thanked the couple.

Trevor drove Nan in his open sports car. The night was fair and warm. They were on Route 128 for a while and then on Route 2 toward Concord. Then they turned onto a two-lane blacktop that crossed residential streets and ran on into the night until there were no more street lamps, only telephone poles and fields and the black ridge of forest off in the distance. The road narrowed and became bumpy with unsettled frost heaves. Trees of forested land crowded the road now and obstructed the moonlight. There were only the beams of the car's headlights probing the darkness and the little pieces of illumination in the dashboard.

Trevor had slowed for the bumps and now he slowed again and turned off onto a dirt road. Abruptly the beams shone on a weather-tarnished steel crossarm barring further approach by vehicle. Stone walls, overgrown with vines, rose eight or ten feet on each side of the crossarm. Trevor reached below the dash and pressed a button. The crossarm rose slowly. They drove through. Trevor left the arm raised. Nan felt a smooth hard surface beneath the car now. Then they were out of the wooded area and out of the black darkness.

Nan saw smooth expanses of lawn, gray in the moonlight, tall, thick, hardwood trees standing singly here and there, and up ahead a black shape with turrets, some slits of light on one side of the ground floor.

Trevor parked to the side. They walked around to the front of the building, to an archway with huge, carved wooden doors within. The moon was so bright, the castle cast a shadow on its lawn. Incongruously, a kettle grill had been left outside, a cheap, folding lounger next to it.

Inside the entrance the floor was of stone. Nan followed Trevor into the main room. Light was provided by Tiffany lamps on a scattering of tables. There were Oriental rugs, a huge fireplace, a boar's head and a bear's head above the mantel, wood in place for a fire. Unlit candelabra on the walls. Tapestries. Leather chairs with wooden arms that became animal heads where the hands would rest. Two button-tufted sofas with scrolled and ornamented woodwork. Brown velvet cloths were draped on the tables and were nearly covered by Oriental jade and porcelain and glass boxes displaying replicas of medieval warriors.

Trevor turned off the lights with a hidden switch. When her eyes had adjusted, Nan saw that moonlight fell through the slit windows and made pale rectangles on the rugs. Trevor lit the wood in the fireplace and then the candelabra around the walls. He went away and returned with an enameled urn that contained ice and set it on a massive chest. He opened a door to the chest, to an abundance of bottles and glasses. Nan accepted a glass of wine. She couldn't tell what Trevor was drinking. She stood in the middle of the room, unsure of where to sit. Now she found the room chilly and went over to stand by the fire as it grew. There were the sounds of tambourines and wind instruments, recorders maybe, all around her. The music was coming from speakers hidden about the room.

Trevor came over and took her hand and led her to a sofa. He sat next to her, very near. "Nice to have you here."

"Thank you. It's a fascinating place."

"Anyone serious in your life?"

So abrupt, Nan thought. She took a sip of wine. She quickly thought that for some reason, some vague feeling of ominousness that might only be the room, the place, it was important to keep her personal life to herself. "Just me. I'm serious."

"I heard you turned down Monk McGuire."

"No big deal. He made a pass. A stupid one."

"That must be a thrill. Turning a man on like that and then turning him down."

"There's no thrill to it. It's a nuisance."

Nan heard noises from the hallway. *"Hey, Trees, where the hell are you?"* Casey.

"C'mon, Trees, we can't see a damned thing." Squires.

"In here. Can you follow my voice?"

"Yeah, yeah. Light would be a lot better." The two of them came into the room.

"Booze over there," Trevor said.

Nan waited, expecting the women to come in. Perhaps they had driven over separately.

Trevor got up and talked to Casey by the fireplace. Squires sat in a chair. The two by the fireplace had their heads bowed toward each other. Nan could not hear what they were saying. They looked like football players in a huddle. No, with their silhouettes fluctuating with the dance of the flames behind them, they looked like clerics.

Nan said, "Where're Donna and Josie?"

Casey looked over at her. "Oh, they decided not to come," he said.

120

THEY WERE NINE hours plus into the hostage situation. The hostages had found it necessary to urinate. Olivia had no observable bodily functions. Kincaid had Nell at work again. He wanted to give Trina some rest and he hoped that Nell might get lucky and start some trading.

They heard Nell's voice by transmission from her place at the end of the corridor near Psych Two. "Olivia, let me get you something to drink. You must be gettin' powerful thirsty, chile. Just figure out somethin' to give me back, will you?"

"Snake Lady say no."

Molly looked at her notes and said to Kincaid, "These references to the Snake Lady. They bunch up sometimes. The Snake Lady is the death commander. She's in charge of death."

They heard Olivia's voice. "Did I kill someone?"

And Nell's, "No, chile, you haven't killed anyone. You're still a *good* chile. Let me do somethin' for you, you do somethin' for me, we get you outa this safe."

Olivia began singing, "I seen the mornin' light ashinin'. . . ." She had a beautiful, clear voice and there was emotion in it. *"I see the starlight comin' down . . . starlight shinin' in the blue—"*

Ginny screamed, *"Stop it!"*

"The mornin' light is blue and bright—"

"Stop that!"

Molly said to Kincaid, "This is what Trina was scared of."

Trina's voice came over. "Ginny, honey, let's let Olivia have her song. Maybe it makes her feel better. I know it upsets you. But we want Olivia to feel better. You understand that."

On the screen they saw Ginny take a step backward. They heard Olivia continue to sing.

Kincaid said, "Do you know the song?"

"No," Molly said. "I think she's making it up. But I can't be sure."

Olivia continued her singing. *"I see the asshole in the sky . . . I see the sweet bye-an'-bye . . . I see the Snake Lady gots her wings to fly . . ."* She stopped and then called out, "Hi, Snake Lady!" Then she started singing again, rapidly. *"Snake Lady fly so high . . . Starlight shinin' in the blue, I see the mornin' light ashinin;, asshole got me in the sky, gettin' to, gettin' to, gettin' to that sweet by-'n'-bye—"*

"*Oh God!*" A whimper from Ginny.

Molly said, "Ginny guesses."

"Guesses what?" Kincaid said.

"That hole in the sky. The bye-and-bye. Death."

Kincaid spoke to the apprehension team in Psych One. "Be ready in there."

The team leader's voice came back, "We're ready."

Olivia continued to sing. Kincaid said, "She's speeding up instead of slowing down."

"The Snake Lady's hovering," Molly said. "Hovering."

Trina's voice came back to them. "That's a pretty song. You sing real pretty, Olivia."

Molly spoke to the screen softly. "That's it, Trina, keep it going, keep it going, then ease Olivia down."

Kincaid hit the table with his fist. "You know what the *fuckup* here is?"

"It's not my nurse."

"That bitch in there doesn't *want* anything. We can't trade, we can't negotiate, we can't *do* anything." He looked at Molly. She didn't say, I already told you that hours ago. He said, "We can't do anything short of going in." He drummed on the table. "And waiting."

Molly studied the screen, listened to Olivia's song. "I don't know if the singing is meant to keep the Snake Lady at a distance or to invite her into the room." She paused. "I just don't know. But I think the Snake Lady's getting in her attack position."

"Can you tell me when she's going to strike?"

"I'll try."

Outside there were gurneys at each of the three entrances to the corridor off Psych Two. They had been rigged for IVs and for hanging blood.

121

NAN FELT UNEASY. But she had no reason for that, she thought. She was here with Trevor Davis. She was his guest. She felt a little more comfortable. They had worked together. They were colleagues. In a while he would drive her home. Still, she was uncomfortable that the two other women hadn't come along.

The music was changed to rock and turned up. Casey's and Squires' glasses were empty already, the ice clinking in them. Casey picked up Nan's empty glass. She was about to say no, but it was just another glass of wine. It would warm her, take away the dull chill and her feeling of uneasiness. The feeling was inappropriate.

Casey returned with Nan's wine. His fingers brushed hers as he handed her the glass.

The fire had grown tall. It hissed and crackled, extending its warmth and illumination into the room. Nan felt easier. She drank some wine and thought that, after all, she was really all right. The familiar music made the place and her situation less disquieting.

Casey had finished half his drink. He shook the ice cubes in the glass. They made a rapid, clinking tattoo. He finished the drink. He looked at Nan and smiled and casually told a raunchy story.

Squires said, "That's a little crude, Case."

Casey said, "It's okay with Nan. She's a nurse. She's seen everything. I'll bet you've *done* everything, too, right, Nan?"

"No. You're not right."

There were refills again. Nan put her hand over her glass when Casey reached for it. She had drunk little of it. The others seemed to be drinking hurriedly, as if they had to leave soon. That was all right with Nan. She was getting sleepy.

Squires was talking about his station's play list. He was talking to her, Nan realized. "God help me, I love the stuff I'm playing. Half the time I've got to get up and move." He stopped, looked embarrassed, and then said to Nan, "Dance with me?"

She was touched by his embarrassment, his tentativeness. "Sure," Nan said. She let him take her hand and raise her from the sofa.

She danced with Squires for a while, their bodies in concert but not touching. It was pleasant. What she needed was this motion and activity. Trevor took the DJ's place and Nan saw that Casey was watching her. Trevor was not as good a dancer as Squires, but that was okay, it was Nan's own motion, her feeling of herself moving, that she was enjoying. And then she was dancing with the stockbroker and as gross as his attitude had been, he made Nan laugh with the way he moved his body and what he said to her. He was a very, very good dancer and his mimicry of a variety of dances was funny. She was perspiring a little and laughing and then she was back with Squires, less frenetic, a slower style, and she paused long enough to drink half a glass of wine, the way she would have refreshed herself with water. It began to be a good time and she was glad she had come.

"I told you so," Trevor said. "I told you you'd have a good time," and he drew Nan close to him in a sort of friendly embrace, danced that way for a moment, and then let her loose and Casey in his turn made her laugh again. Her glass was filled and she drank a little more, feeling both tired and stimulated now as she sometimes did when she accompanied friends who ran.

The record was changed, the mood changed, the vibrations got slower, but that was good too because Nan was ready for a slower pace. At that much slower beat and softer music, it did not seem inappropriate for the DJ to dance with her in his arms. He had his jacket off and was sweating. The other fellows had their jackets off, too. Trevor danced with her in the same slow style, his embrace less friendly, more . . . *romantic*, Nan thought, though she was not romantically inclined toward him. She did not actually recognize the mode she had entered and the danger around her until she was dancing with the stockbroker, his arms around her waist and his hands loosely clasped at the small of her back. Then she felt his hands separate and move down her buttocks in a quick, smooth stroke and then she felt the palms of his hands and the open fingers clasping her against him and the erection he was rubbing against her body. She pushed and slapped and jumped back and hit something hard immediately behind her—a body, she realized, Trevor Davis'—because the stockbroker was still right in front of her and Paul Squires was across the room getting a drink. Trevor *held* her, held her from behind, and then he *held* her with his hands enclosing her breasts. She tried to kick. Her feet were bare. She had taken off her shoes. *Could they have seen that as an act of invitation?* She tried to twist, to bend her body to force release, but the stockbroker held her in front at the waist and against him and now he was exerting all his strength and he had pinioned her arms as well and she was not able, even in the desperate strength that had sometimes come to her in an arrest situation on the unit, to break away. She felt and heard the zipper at the back of her dress torn down.

"She's not wearing a bra," Trevor said in a clinical manner, as if Nan were insensible. "This ought to be interesting. Turn her around," and they wrestled her until she was facing Trevor but still pinioned by the stockbroker. Trevor pulled her dress down to her waist. "Come look at this," he said. "This'll get your cock saluting."

The disc jockey's voice was soft, anxious. "I think I'm cutting out."

Trevor said, "We're in an interdependent situation here, Squires. No one's cutting out. We're all going to have a good time together, just like I said."

The DJ came over and looked at her breasts. For an instant he looked at Nan's eyes. Then he went back to the other side of the room.

Nan wondered why she wasn't screaming. *Stay, stay with yourself,* she thought. *There's still a chance at control.*

"Come back here," Trevor said to the DJ. "You're already a participant."

"You haven't done anything yet, Paul," Nan said.

Trevor touched her breasts. Paul Squires stood beside him. Trevor took Squires' hands in his own and guided the palms against Nan's breasts. "Now you're a participant," Trevor said.

Nan looked at Squires and said, "You could help me."

Trevor knelt and just as she tried to kick him he held her ankles. He said to Squires, "Pull her dress down."

Squires stared at her, the part of her body he could see, the part he could not. Then he pulled her dress down and her panties with it. Nan knew she was lost when her only possible ally had begun to help rape her. She felt the stockbroker's hands on her breasts and realized she had stopped struggling.

She found that, now that she was nude, she was able to step away and face them. It was quite like their conversational group on the terrace of the country club except for her nudity. She placed her arms across her breasts. She was still in control, at least of herself. She said the simplest and most sensible thing she could think of. "No, I don't want to have sex."

Trevor Davis said, "Like the advertisement says, 'We know what's important to nurses.'" He was getting undressed.

122

OLIVIA WAS STILL singing, but not so much, just the odd line
here and there, and Trina thought, If I can just help her to get
all the way down.

Nell's voice came in from the corridor. "Gettin' on late,
Olivia, honey. Real late. Couldn't you use somethin' to eat?"

*"Minnight skies real fine . . . Black skies gonna hurt . . .
You like that song, too, Pig Lady?"*

"Good song," Trina said before Nell could reply. "Sounds
like you had yourself some fun at night sometimes. Sounds like
you had a whole lot of trouble and pain out of it, too."

"Stays apart. That's what I does."

Molly said to Kincaid, "She's literally talking about some
split she sees in herself."

"She's that smart?"

"Oh shit, Lieutenant, being crazy has nothing to do with
intelligence, you know that."

They heard Nell's voice from the end of the corridor.
"How'd you like some sandwiches in there? Chicken? Ribs?
Burger? Pizza?"

And Olivia's voice from Psych Two. "Get the fuck away,
Pig Lady!"

Molly spoke to Kincaid softly. "Tell Nell to leave it to
Trina."

Kincaid keyed his mike. "Nell. Let the nurse do the talking till I say otherwise."

Olivia's voice became rapid again. Her singing was clear
and undistorted, but rushed.

Kincaid said, "The speed she's at, it sounds like drugs."

"No," Molly said. "If it's drugs, Trina'd let us know by
now. Trina hasn't seen any sign of drugs."

The singing went on rapidly.

Trina said, "You want to come down, don't you, Olivia?
You're wearing yourself out."

The singing stopped. "Sure am tired. You right about that.
Snake Lady gettin' real tired too."

"Does that mean the Snake Lady wants to rest?"

"Don't know. She don't say."

"Well, let's talk about you for a minute, think about you for a minute. That okay?"

"Oh, sure. Gots to do that. Been waitin' on it."

"Good. Olivia, you don't want to die."

"No."

"No, you don't want to die."

"Thas right."

"You can give me the gun and we can go outside and I'll help take care of you."

Silence. Then, "You really do that?"

"I swear."

"Fixin'-t'be-uh-doctuh. You gonna helps take care of me?"

"Whatever I can do for you, Olivia."

"I gots to give you the gun, though."

Trina said, "I think that would be a good idea. So you don't hurt yourself. Or us. You don't want to die." Silence. "You don't have to give me the gun. You could put it on the floor."

"Snake Lady say no."

"I'll *kill* the fuckin' Snake Lady, stamp on her head, you dumb black bitch, nigger, nigger—" Olivia turned the gun more exactly on Ginny and smiled and listened. Ginny did not move. She did not seem to see Olivia. She said the same words again. Hal went to place his hands on Ginny's shoulders.

Olivia nodded. "Snake Lady say, I don't like these people. I don't wants them. Snake Lady say—

Molly said, *"Send your people."*

Kincaid transmitted, "Go!"

Trina heard sounds of cracking and ripping behind her, a sharp explosion of sound, and she looked even though she knew what it must be and saw two helmeted, visored figures, handguns extended, two others behind them and someone else behind those two, heard an amplified, dehumanized voice saying, *"Down! down! down!,"* the wall between the two psych rooms torn open, and Trina looked to see Olivia's response and saw her fire, heard that separate explosion almost simultaneous with the first, and saw at the same instant a lens of Hal's glasses shatter and blow apart, the shot snapping his head backward and producing an enormous amount

of blood as he fell. Trina pulled Ginny to the floor behind the
bolted-down gurney and Olivia fired two shots where they
had been standing but not at where they were. Then the first
two members of the apprehension team immobilized Olivia
and the fifth figure, a psychiatric HO, followed and rendered
Olivia unconscious with an injection, and the third and fourth
members of the team, the shotgun and automatic weapon,
grabbed Ginny and then Trina and immobilized them with
restraints. Trina screamed at them, but it was because the
apprehension team did not know what the hostages' reactions
would be.

123

NAN SAID, *"Please. Please.* Don't do this to me and I won't
tell anyone you tried to.''

Trevor was undressing and Nan started to back away,
having no idea where she might go, and they got hold of her
and she struggled and for two or three seconds she thought
she was going to escape, get outside, run, hide.

When they got her on the floor what she felt was rage, not
tearfulness at all. A voice inside her head was talking to her,
observing her, instructing her. She felt fury. The voice said,
*They're dehumanizing you. You've got to stay alive. You've
got to have enough sense to stay alive.*

Otherwise they'll kill me when they're through?

Bargain with them. See if you can bargain with them.

Nan cried out in *fury*, not even at her physical pain. Fury at
the realization that she was powerless. She had been striking
with one hand, but her whole upper body was pinned now by
the stockbroker. She smelled cinnamon from his mouth. Oh,
the sonofabitch gave himself *breath spray* for this. Oh, the
sonofabitch. The stockbroker had both her arms pinned with
one hand. She could not have imagined that possible before.
He was at her breasts with his mouth, his free hand between
her legs. She had limited use of her legs. The DJ was sitting
on them. It was terribly painful. Terribly. Still, her cry was
from her fury, her powerlessness.

Trevor Davis stood over her without any clothes on.

She looked up at him, her eyes at his eyes. *"Why are you doing this to me? Why are you doing this?"*

Then it came—looking at Trevor's eyes, feeling the others on her body—a scream of rage and terror and pain that became sobbing and weeping and she tried to concentrate on that, the sobbing and intermittent weeping, and she tried to reestablish control, at least of herself.

She became aware that Trevor was kneeling beside her, a scalpel in his hand. He said to her, "Look at it." He turned it ever so much, enough for the light to strike on and off the blade. Like signals from a lighthouse, Nan thought and, *what craziness*. His. "Stop crying," he said. "Be careful. Don't move."

Nan was aware that she had stopped crying. She did not know how.

Trevor lay the blade of the scalpel flat against the tip of her nose. "Don't move," he said gently.

She did not move. She was terrified her head would start from the very terror within it.

So far, so good, the voice inside said, reminding her so much of herself when she was reassuring a patient during a painful or uncomfortable procedure. *You're doing okay. You can keep doing okay*.

Trevor touched the tip of her nose with the point of the blade. It might even have broken the skin, the feeling was so sharp. She didn't know.

"Steadiest hands in the hospital," Trevor said to the others. "Look at that. No blood."

"Jesus, Trees," Squires said.

"I want you to lie very still, Nan." The edge of the scalpel was just away from touching, some fraction of distance. "The others are going to release you, Nan. But you're going to remain still. You and I are going to remain exactly as we are. Squires," he said, looking at Nan with a gentle smile, the scalpel poised, "get up. Get your bod stripped."

Nan felt the DJ get off her legs.

The surgical hand slid down across her lips, her breasts, to her abdomen, the scalpel elevated just a fraction from her flesh. It remained on her abdomen. "Case, my boy, let her go, now be careful, don't *jiggle* her." He smiled at Nan. Nan remained still as the stockbroker released her. She was aware of his getting up and undressing nearby.

She did not move. Trevor straddled her, his genitals against her abdomen. He continued to hold the scalpel in his hand. "Good," he said. "Think you can be a good girl, Nan?" She nodded.

Trevor said, "Case, put this someplace safe." He handed the scalpel to the stockbroker. "No more foolishness, Nan. No more resistance. We're all here for a good time. Don't you agree?"

Now, the voice inside said, the one with all that distance and objectivity. Nan said, "All right. Maybe we can work something out. Something that's agreeable to me that you'll like."

"I'll entertain suggestions. If they're stimulating enough."

"I won't do sex inside me. I'll use my hand. I can be really good with my hand. You'll love it, I'll—"

"Not stimulating enough, Nan. I just want to fuck you, Nan."

Gently he separated her legs and she realized, looking up at him looking down at her, that what he was entering her with, what he had extended into her, was naked malice, hatred, and that made her sob and weep again and watch herself from a distance and talk to herself inside and keep track of what was going on. It was all right to sob and weep. Trevor Davis seemed to like that.

The stockbroker tried to use her mouth. He even hit her. Nan kept her head turned away. Trevor laughed.

Nan lay still for the DJ. So they wouldn't kill her afterward. So they would feel safe. Nan used her hand. She spoke to the DJ and to all three of them at once, not seeing any of them. "It's all right, it's all right," the voice in her head directing the voice that was speaking and directing her hand so they wouldn't kill her afterward because she would tell what had happened. "I didn't want to at first, but it was okay after it got started, it was fun, it was just a surprise, all three of you . . ." The DJ ejaculated against her thigh.

After a while she stood up. Trevor and the stockbroker were dressed. They were drinking beer out of cans and whispering. The DJ was pulling his pants on. She asked for the bathroom and Trevor took her there and she asked him to bring her clothes. The stockbroker remained at the door, a guard. Trevor returned with her clothes. She closed the door and began to clean herself off with a hand towel and then realized that might be a mistake, an evidentiary mistake. Her hand clenched the towel and then dropped it on the floor. Nan sat on the toilet lid and held herself and wept.

124

HAL WAS IN the OR with the trauma team. Trina and Ginny had been taken to the acute side for examination.

Kincaid and the psychiatric HO discussed Olivia. The HO said, "It doesn't meet the court's basic requirements. I did *not* interview her. She had no opportunity to respond to psychiatric examination."

"What I'm saying is, Doctor," Kincaid said, "the department is prepared to turn her over to the Department of Mental Health. For treatment and observation until DMH thinks she's in shape to be charged and stand trial."

"That would be the humane route."

"We need your say-so, your professional statement that she's in need of psychiatric care. Of course, we might get complaints later, if you understand what I mean."

"Legal complaints?"

"Incarcerated the prisoner like they do in the Soviet Union. No charges, no trial. Stick'em in a psychiatric institution."

"So called."

"Well, Doctor?"

"She needs psychiatric care. There's no doubt of that. I'll order it."

"You got a convenient institution?"

"Mass. Mental."

"Okay, do the paperwork. You get to ride with her, too."

"Your guys put their lives on the line," Molly said. "I'd think you'd want Olivia in the slammer as fast as you could drive her there."

Kincaid looked at Molly and nodded very slowly. "We fucked up tonight. You see all that shit on TV, the movies.

SWAT units. Trained killers. Our job is to save lives. Including the hostage-taker's. We fucked up tonight.''

"No," Molly said, "I don't think so. You had my very best nurse in there with Olivia. No reflection on your negotiators, Lieutenant, but Trina Frankian, if she can't establish a crisis intervention, maybe one couldn't be established. To use an old psychiatric expression, maybe it just wasn't in the cards.''

"I'd like to find out how Levy's doing."

"We can listen in. There's a mike over the table."

"We have a bullet hole in . . . No bullet hole out . . . There's considerable facial distortion . . . Swelling and matting of blood.''

After a long pause the voice said, *"Initial work reveals destruction of soft tissue and bone.''*

Molly picked up a telephone, got an outside line, and dialed Elin.

"It's the parietal. Splintered to hell and gone . . . Hematoma just inside the bone and just outside the dura.''

"Elin, Molly. We've had an accident here . . . Yes, the hostage situation. Hal Levy was in there. He took a bullet in the head. The trauma team's working on him now.''

Elin did not ask what the chances were.

After a few minutes outside the trauma room, Kincaid said, "I'd like to see how your nurse is doing."

"I can tell you how Trina's doing without even seeing her. She'll be acting like nothing happened. Real cool."

She was with a psychiatric HO named Judd. "I'm fine, I'm fine," she said. "I just want to go home."

"You're remarkable," Judd said.

"I told you I was fine." She looked at Molly. "Ginny's sedated. They've got her in bed."

"I'd like you to go to Mass. General," Molly said.

"What about Hal?''

"They're working on him."

"He's alive?"

"Yes."

"My *God*. Olivia?"

"Mass. Mental."

"Then I guess I'll go home."

"I'd like you to go to Mass. General, Trina. Just for overnight, anyway."

"All I want, *Mother*, is to go home to my own little beddy and go sleepy-bye so when the next lunatic walks in tomorrow afternoon I'll be rested up enough to deal with him. Or her."

"I can't order you to the General, Trina. But I can order a temporary leave of absence. Starting now. Want to think about it?"

Trina looked at Molly angrily and sat down on the examination table.

Molly left the room with Judd. Outside and down the corridor, Molly said, "I don't want to leave her alone for long. I want someone with her as long as she's here."

"She's remarkable," Judd said again.

"She's probably in shock."

"It doesn't show."

"I know her. I know she is."

"Molly, I've never seen anyone with fewer symptoms of shock. Given what she just went through."

"Send her to the General."

"What for?"

"For some caring attention. Rest. Doctors and facilities if she gets upset.

"I have no basis on which to order her anywhere."

Molly looked at her watch. It had been half an hour since the apprehension team had brought Trina out. "I give her about an hour before she loses it," Molly said. "Maybe less."

When Hal had been in the OR for almost an hour, Elin arrived. In pants and a jersey she looked like a sloppy matron in from the A&P.

"We're chasing another bleeder . . . There're bone fragments to pick out."

Molly sat with Elin and reviewed Hal's status as they listened to the voice from the OR. Elin interrupted with questions. Molly described what had happened in Psych Two. Elin merely nodded and stared at the closed door to the OR.

After a while Elin said, "Bone fragments to pick out. It's tedious and it's time-consuming. An operative nuisance." Then she folded her hands in her lap.

A rumpled and weary Bennett Chessoff joined them. He said hello and sat apart from the two women. They had established their own circle of privacy. He already had his report on Hal Levy. It had been brought to him from the OR.

"Brain injury," Elin said to Molly. "Is he . . . *Are we going to get the same person back?*"

It was not a question Molly could answer and Elin knew that.

Trina lost it about then. She felt trembly and chilly.

Molly came in a few minutes later and had the nurse who'd been staying with Trina leave.

"It's goddamn demeaning having someone babysit me."

"You look a little shaky."

"I *am* shaky. You'd be too."

"I'd be worse. But I'd probably have let it out sooner."

"Oh, it's coming out."

"What?"

"I feel panicky all of a sudden. I feel scared to death for Hal, and guilty. It's crazy—I feel guilty about Olivia. I feel like I could help her." She was speaking rapidly and she looked directly at Molly and said, "Is it me or the nature of my work that attracts violence?"

Judd was standing in the doorway. "I think Molly's right, Trina. I think you ought to spend a little R and R at the General."

"How long?"

"Let's get you down there, give you a couple of nights' rest, then see."

"We'll talk it over? After a *night's* rest."

"Think we'd forget you? Let you go down the psych chute and leave you there?"

Trina said, "Now I know how the patients feel about that."

"The knowledge will be useful in your work," Molly said.

Trina was trembling more pronouncedly, but she smiled.

Judd said, "In the parlance, Trina, I'd like to offer you some medication."

"What?"

"Haldol."

"I haven't gone bonkers, Judd. I'm coherent. I'm rational."

"Sure. And you're in a panic."

"Not Haldol. I do not assess myself as requiring Haldol."

Judd said, "You're hardly in a position to do the evaluation. I would *like* to inject you with a little Haldol and accompany you on a terrifically relaxed ride to the General."

"No Haldol."

"Valium?"

"How much?"

"You're so composed, Haldol is so terrifically too strong for you, how about ten milligrams?"

Trina nodded. "That's reasonable."

"They'll decide on their own medication at the General. You won't negotiate there."

"Don't be sure."

Molly laughed, relaxing a little, her back in pain from prolonged tension, the tiredness welling through her as she relaxed that little bit. "Don't be sure," she said to Judd.

Trina said, "Orally, not by injection."

"I guess you will goddamn well negotiate," Judd said. "You don't quit. Okay, orally."

Trina began sobbing and the trembling became shaking. "I didn't negotiate so goddamn well tonight, did I?"

Molly went back to the trauma rooms.

Her body reacted with a rush of despair. The doors to Hal Levy's trauma room were open. Elin sat bent entirely over her arms, her back moving in irregular little spasms. The neurosurgeon and the head ER nurse stood by her. The neurosurgeon was talking softly.

Bennett came over to Molly. She said, "I know."

Elin refused Molly's company. She put on her raincoat. "I'm going home," she said. She drove through the spring night aware of the traffic signals, aware of the familiar street-by-street route back home, and aware of Hal sitting beside her as she drove him to the country inn for dinner on Charles's money.

Molly said to Bennett, "I'll accept an invitation if it's offered."

They went to Bennett's apartment. In their weariness and sorrow, they had little to say to each other. But as Molly undressed to shower, she had the feeling that the silence was part of an accepted closeness with each other, no distance in it at all.

Bennett brought her a Scotch and she drank all of it. After
she had showered she lay in his bed and waited, listening to
the oscillating sounds of the water against his body, the
shower curtain, the tile and bath. She let the sounds fill her
mind.

When he was in bed and the light out, Molly tucked herself
against him, her cheek against his shoulder, and she did not
realize she was crying until she felt her tears on his skin as
well as her own. She found that she was holding Bennett very
tightly in her need, so tightly that it was almost as if she
would inflict pain. And she realized that she had begun to
love him, and along with the love and the fear of loss like
Elin's, she resented Bennett right now, resented him very
much for not feeling as deeply or as freely as she did. She
resented him for not crying, for remaining aloof, for containing his emotions when she herself was so needy.

125

NAN WAS TERRIFIED to leave the bathroom. Didn't they have to
kill her now? She forced herself to go out before they came
after her.

They were standing in the main room. *The rape room*, the
voice inside said. The music had been turned off, the candles
snuffed, the electric lighting turned back on. Nan could see
the cold light of dawn in the slit windows. The voice inside
told her what to do, what to say. *Take Trevor's hand.* She
did. She said, "It was good. You got me excited. You were
right. You made me feel good." She looked at each of them.
"I feel good now." She felt control returning.

"I've got to go," the stockbroker said. He stopped suddenly and turned at Nan. *"But how the Christ do I know
you're not going to charge me with rape?"*

"Because she invited this," Trevor said easily. "She joined
us here alone of her own volition. She danced with each of
us. She pushed her body against each of us. We agree on
that, don't we?"

The stockbroker said, "Yes." Squires looked down and nodded.

"That's all they'd have to hear in court. Our mutually corroborative testimony. We'll work out the details. Over drinks. Play some squash first." Trevor looked at Nan. "Also, she's a nurse. Everyone knows about nurses."

The stockbroker said, "Christ, Trees, it's *my life*. I'm not sure."

"I am," Trevor said.

It's Trevor's arrogance that believes you and believes that, Nan's voice told her. *He believes he can have his own way whenever he wants it. Casey's the one you've got to win right now. Squires is too ashamed to do anything.*

Nan took Casey's hand with her free hand, holding hands now with both Trevor and the stockbroker, and she felt faint and nauseated, but she had the control she needed and she said, "I'd be too *ashamed*. My mother and father . . . What happened here . . . is a secret. Don't you talk about it." She looked at each of them again. "Please. And I won't talk about it. The last thing I want is for anyone to know."

Outside there were the three cars. She did not want to ride with Trevor. Casey would not want her in his car.

Squires stood by his own car and said, "Can I do anything for you?"

"You can take me home."

"Thank God," Trevor said. "I just don't have the energy right now for that. The chivalrous male delivering his date home." He waved at his friends. "Well, good night, guys. Or good morning. *Ciao,*" he said and went back to the castle.

She did not give Squires her home address. She needed safety, security. The hospital was where she *had* to go. But she did not dare let him know that. She gave Squires the address of a small apartment house on Beacon Street where a friend of hers lived.

She was becoming numb in mind and body. There was the city way ahead in the gray morning light. She remembered the drive in with Molly Chang. When *she* had been driving, when *she* had been in control.

They had taken *her own self* away from her. She was bereft

and furious. The violent emotions and the numbness overtook her alternately.

They were coming in from the other side of the city, so she could not see the hospital. It was blocked by the profile of downtown Boston.

The drive in with Squires was silent until he said, "I'm sorry the way things happened, the way it turned out." They were on Beacon Street.

"That's it," she said, pointing to her friend's apartment house. She got out of the car as if the apartment house were her own.

The night man was sweeping in front of the open doors. "Morning," he said to Nan, recognizing her.

She was on the driver's side of the car, between the car and the curb, and she heard Squires say, "Call on me. For anything."

He sounded miserable and that gave Nan a feeling of pleasure along with her hatred. "What?" she said.

"Call on me."

"Rape," she heard herself whisper.

"What?" she heard him say as she kept walking.

"Rape," she said, still in a whisper. She wanted to scream it. But it would only come out as a whisper.

126

THE HOSTAGE STORY ran on the front pages of both the *Post* and the *Eagle*. So too did the bylined commentary. Keating's piece began:

> The house officers will start going to jail tomorrow or the next day. Let's not applaud the arrogance that the HOs cynically parade as courage. Going to jail is not an act of courage on the part of a malefactor. Going to jail is what the malefactor deserves.
>
> Also, let's not feel any misguided sympathy for the HOs. Jail is where they belong.
>
> They are responsible for the death last night of a

26-year-old third-year medical student named Hal Levy.
He was inside helping to take care of the patients whom
the HOs have abandoned. The HOs were outside, on
strike, walking a tidy picket line and trying to coerce the
taxpayers of this city into paying them more money.

In the same incident, the HOs are responsible for the
emotional destruction of an experienced and highly respected psychiatric nurse. The nurse has been institutionalized. for how long, no one knows.

When the court ushers the HOs off to prison, let's
wish them bon voyage and good riddance. Let's save our
sympathies for the people who are doing the HOs' work
for them. One of them is dead, another may be permanently impaired emotionally.

Michelle McCabe wrote:
Back Bay Metropolitan Hospital continues to provide
skilled and praiseworthy care for its patients despite the
general absence of house officers from its floors and
clinics.

The nurses are the key, as they are the key to any
hospital. You cannot run without them.

To be a house officer is to be in a very difficult
position. House officers are learners passing through.
They provide an enormous amount of service. But they
are passing through. Nurses stay on.

There are two kinds of nurses at Back Bay Met. The
Old Guard revels in hardship and is the spine of the
hospital. The younger nurses are inclined to be more
militant and more outwardly sympathetic to the house
officers.

There are serious inadequacies at BBMH and the house
officers are calling attention to them. The inadequacies
can be remedied, but only with money. The city budget
has been reduced. There is less money for every municipal service.

It is, however, still possible for the HOs to gain their
objectives. A nursing walkout or the threat of one would
strike terror into the heart of City Hall.

Placing BBMH's patients in other facilities, providing
them with walk-in care elsewhere, would be far more
costly than meeting the HOs' patient issue demands. The

salary dispute is another matter entirely and one in which
the nurses at BBMH have no concern as they do in the
functional status of a heart monitor or in the availability
of medicine.

Doctors and nurses are not like other members of the
professional work force. Doctors and nurses have a different sort of obligation. Part of the obligation is the
obligation not to strike.

But yesterday, after the HOs were issued summonses,
there was talk among the nurses (particularly the younger
ones) of joining the house officers if the patient issues
are not resolved. There was much more talk of that sort
among the nurses than could have been anticipated.

A nursing walkout at BBMH is a possibility, but not
one that appears likely even if the HOs start going to jail.

The potential for a nursing walkout at BBMH is there.
But it is awaiting a catalyst and there may be none.

127

NAN STARED AT the tiny fisheye in her friend's apartment door.
So much safety and security. Except that there was no safety
or security, Nan now understood.

The door opened. *"My God, Nan."*

Her friend was in a robe, drab from sleep. Her roommate
stood some feet back and held herself tightly when she saw
Nan.

Nan could hardly hear her own voice. "They raped me."
She felt tears in streams on her face. She heard herself
sobbing, again from a distance. Her friend looked at her as if
she could not comprehend what Nan had said, so she repeated
it, the enormity of it such that she could not comprehend it
any longer herself. "They raped me."

The friend's roommate stepped back.

Her friend gave Nan tea, got dressed, and called a cab to
take them to Back Bay Met. Now it was so easy to be numb.
Even to her friend who was helping her.

*   *   *

Across Tremaine from the hospital there were more nurses waiting than there had been the previous two days. They waited informally, singly or in groups, not lined up. It was ten minutes before seven. At five of seven they would cross the avenue.

Trina was asleep in her room at the General. She slept because of her ordeal and because of some medication and because it was her time in the twenty-four-hour cycle to sleep. She was in a double. Her roommate had been awake even at the hour Trina had come in and they had talked briefly. Her roommate was another nurse and she was awake now at seven in the morning because it would normally have been her time to go on duty and because she was awaiting test results that would tell her whether her condition was benign and she could go on living after minor surgery or whether she would have to go through an ordeal of chemo and radiation and might, anyway, die in a few months. The bed assignment was not accidental. It was thought the two nurses might support each other. The young nurse who was awake found herself sweating and wishing that Trina would wake up, too.

There were no cabs available. Between seven and eight-thirty it appeared they had all been hired. Nan's friend wanted to tell a cab company that it was an emergency. Nan would not let her. Her friend wanted to call the police or an ambulance, but Nan would not let her. There was a stillness to her friend's apartment. Nan had a feeling of not being. She was glad of the excuse to let the feeling go on and on.

It was interrupted when a driver called up from the lobby. The driver showed something that might have been revulsion when he saw Nan. She was wearing a long dress and leaning a little on her friend and her face looked like nothing the driver ever wanted to see again. It wasn't the bruise, it was the expression on the woman's face.

When they got to Back Bay Met, Nan led the way to the ER and spoke to the triage nurse and then sat in one of the orange chairs for people who were waiting. The daytime psych nurse came out to her immediately, but Nan refused to speak to her. "I won't talk to anyone except Trina," Nan said.

Nan's friend explained to the psych nurse. Nan sat almost

as if she were content, as she had been in her friend's apartment. The friend told the psych nurse what she could.

The psych nurse called over to Molly Chang and then had her paged. When Molly showed up, the psych nurse thought she looked as if she'd been on a bender, a real downer.

"Get me Trina, please," Nan said to Molly in a small voice. "Please? Trina? I don't want to talk to you—or her," she said, looking at the psych nurse.

"You've had a real bad time. Christ, Nan, we've got to start helping you." Molly forced Nan up from the chair and then sat her in a wheelchair. Nan did not resist. Molly rolled her to a vacant medical examination room. It was the same one Trina had been in six or seven hours before. Molly still saw her there.

"I don't want to talk to anyone but Trina," Nan said and began to cry.

"I don't know if Trina can help just now," Molly said. "She's had . . . She's dealing with a problem herself."

"Trina," Nan said.

Molly called the General. The psychiatrist she got was surprisingly comfortable with letting her patient out of her bed and room. "She's up, she wants out, she wants to get going, back to work. I had a jet fighter pilot like that once."

"What did you treat him for?"

"Impatience. He saw everything before it happened. He couldn't wait for the opportunity to deal with it. He couldn't stand the interludes."

"Trina can stand the interludes."

"She'd rather be at work. She'll be most effective with herself in that environment."

"What about her patients?"

"You're talking about one patient. A personal request. I don't see any reason to deny it if Trina doesn't. But I want her back here after she sees the one patient."

"I don't even want her to do that," Molly said.

"Suit yourself. You made the call."

"Let her go," Molly said. "Someone needs her real bad."

128

THE GENERAL GAVE Trina clean white pants and a shirt and the psychiatrist had several telephone messages for her, calls that had not been allowed to go through. Trina went down to the lobby and out to the cab line. The safety and security of taking a cab to the hospital felt like an indulgence, a luxury to be relished. The driver was white, male, lanky-haired, clean-shaven, cleanly dressed, late twenties. Trina said, "Back Bay Metropolitan Hospital."

The driver pulled out and called in the destination to his dispatcher. Trina locked the doors and rolled the windows most of the way up.

"Little trouble out that way," the driver said, "or maybe you know?"

"Like what?"

"Strike. Labor action. Social unrest. Like that."

"Oh." Trina looked down at her messages.

"Lot of trouble out there last night. Jewish guy got killed by an African woman."

I'm going to practice massive denial, Trina said to herself. I'm going to pretend nothing's wrong.

"You're not interested?"

"I already heard."

The driver was silent. Trina went through her messages and smiled. A lot of friends had found out that she had been the nurse in the hostage situation and that she was at the General. The last message was from Nicholas Prudhomme, the assistant district attorney, and she smiled even more.

"You're a nurse," the driver said.

"Yes," Trina said, but she did not look in the driver's direction or meet his eyes in the rearview mirror.

"I was going to be a nutritionist," the driver said. Trina said nothing. "But they wanted me to study things I didn't want to study. So I dropped out."

It would be another fifteen minutes to the hospital and the

driver was quiet for a while. "So then I started writing pornographic books."

Uh-oh, Trina thought. And she evaluated escape techniques along the route to the hospital and memorized the driver's number.

"Yeah. A guy paid me a hundred bucks apiece for 'em. Knocked 'em out in two, three days. Guy printed 'em on real cheap paper. I never saw 'em. I don't even know where he sold them. Bein' as you're a nurse and all, I bet you could've helped me a lot with those books, like—"

"I don't want to discuss this."

"Oh. I beg your pardon. I thought it might interest you."

"It doesn't."

"Bein' about sex and all."

Trina did not reply.

"You're right not to talk to me about it. And I do beg your pardon. See, I've changed. I'm different now. I'm a born-again Christian."

Oh boy, Trina thought. She could not deny her uneasiness now. And they were out in the ghetto area, still ten minutes from the hospital and following side streets.

The driver said, "You're no doubt familiar with Route One-twenty-eight. Of course you are. One of the great military-industrial complexes in the world. I follow everything I can about the military. This is Ground Zero. Right here. Boston."

Oh shit, this one is loose on the streets, doesn't even come to the hospital.

"Look, I'm a nurse on my way to work and I don't want to talk."

The driver stopped the cab. "Look. *I'm warning you*, lady. I'm being a friend. *God* said this is it. *Ground Zero*. Right here."

Oh God, and this is the luxury of safety and security.

"The apocalypse," the driver said, and he opened his door and got out.

There were some black guys on the corner, teenagers. Trina got out quickly and went over to them. "I'm a nurse and I need help. Getting to the hospital."

They looked at her silently. One of them glanced over at the cabdriver, then back at Trina. "Jes what you 'spect, lady. A lim-o-zeen?" He laughed and then the others laughed.

The cabdriver laughed. "Ground Zero. Just like I said.

You owe me five dollars and eighty cents. You want to stay here and find out what porno books are *really* all about, or you want to get back in my cab and get the hell outa here?''

Trina said very levelly to the cabdriver, ''Get out of here. These people will take care of me.''

The young man who had spoken looked at Trina and then at the driver, then walked over to the driver in a slouch, as if he were very tired. Trina wasn't sure she heard the exact words, but what she thought she heard from the young man was: ''How'd you like your balls cut off, white boy?''

The driver got into the cab and his tires burnt and screamed as he pulled away.

The young man came back. ''Don't mind walkin'?'' Trina shook her head. The young man said to the others, ''We gonna 'scort this lady to the hospittle.''

129

ONCE IN THE hospital, Trina had the extraordinary feeling that she had been on vacation for a long time. The intimately familiar surroundings looked slightly unaccustomed to her. She felt refreshed physically and tired mentally.

Molly was alone wlth Nan in the examination room. Initially the most significant presentation was a large bruise on Nan's upper cheek near her eye.

Trina said, ''Someone really hit you hard, huh?''

Nan nodded.

Molly said to Nan, ''I think I'll leave you and Trina alone. Is that all right?''

Nan nodded again. Trina tried to see her objectively, not as a friend. She appeared to be in control of herself. She explained that she had been raped by Trevor Davis and two others. ''I thought that couldn't happen with someone I know. Someone I *worked* with. You're writing all this down?''

''It's a medical history *and* a legal history.''

''Someone I *worked* with,'' Nan repeated. That was all she would say. Nothing about the circumstances. Just that she had been violated by someone she knew, someone she trusted.

Then Nan was silent, her trust gone, except about that one unbelievable factor in the violation.

Trina had to rebuild some trust. All right, that was partially still there, Nan had *asked* for Trina. But also Nan's trust in herself, this worthless, dirty thing.

Trina began with objective, neutral commentary. "We'll provide you with medical intervention. To take care of your body. The physical abuse. And there's the day-after pill."

Nan shook her head. She wiped away tears and listened.

"We'll also provide you with legal intervention."

Nan looked away.

"And we'll provide you with counseling."

"My God," Nan said. "I'm talking to a *rape victim counselor*. Because of *me*."

Trina let the implications of that phrase go by. It was a central issue that would be addressed later—the victim's belief that she was somehow responsible. Nan bent her head and cried, controlled crying. *"I don't want anyone else to know."*

"Nan, how can we help? . . . What sort of help would you like right now, Nan?" And then, "Do you want to talk, Nan?"

Nan nodded, wiped her face, but said nothing.

"Where were you, Nan? Who were you with?"

After several seconds she said, "At a party." She was hesitant at first, then spoke rapidly, and then she was done, having given Trina a superficial account, having avoided painful materials where she could.

Trina understood that. Now she needed to guide Nan to a recollection and recounting of specifics. "I know this is going to be difficult for you. I know it's going to be painful." Terror visibly changed Nan's muscular presentation. "What were the styles of the assaults?"

"Styles?"

"What kind of style did each perpetrator use? Vaginal? Oral? Anal?"

Nan shook her head. For seconds again she did not speak. Then, "Vaginal . . . the doctor. The stockbroker . . . he, he tried to, to use my mouth, but I kept turning my head away and I started to gag. He hit me"—she was talking rapidly again and shaking and crying—"and then he used me, vaginally. The other one. He came against my thigh. He apologized. Later." She bent over with tears.

Trina thought, Would someone like that, who had apologized, have enough guilt to testify against the others?

"I started him with my hand."

"Why was that?"

Nan would not answer.

What were the conversations—at the club, on the deck, in the house, prior to the assaults, during, after? Were there verbal threats, physical threats? Was she forced to drink or take pills, drugs? How active in struggling?

That was difficult for Nan to explain. As if she had not struggled enough. And it brought back further details of humiliation and violation because her struggling had failed.

"How did you cope, Nan? What did you think about?"

Nan thought and thought. Trina did not interrupt her. The crying came in brief eruptions now between periods of stillness.

"At first I kept telling myself, this isn't happening."

"Then?"

"Then I thought, I've got to observe everything. I began thinking about getting back at them, getting them in jail. I need evidence, I thought. It was like I went off and watched from a distance and also from inside my head, from behind my eyes. Sometimes with my eyes open to see what the room was like, to study it, to remember details, and sometimes with my eyes closed when I couldn't stand what was happening . . ."

Trina thought Nan was finished but she started again. "I really thought they were going to hurt me. I mean, I thought they'd hurt me if I didn't, I thought Trevor would really cut me and then have to kill me and then . . . when they were doing it, I thought they might kill me afterward. So I couldn't tell anyone what they'd done. So I lay still for the last one and that's why I helped him. That's when I told them it was all right. It wasn't bad. I hadn't wanted to at first, but it was okay with me now. That's when I told . . . *the doctor* it was good, he got me excited and made me feel good."

"Why did you say that to him?"

"Because he was the leader. I wanted him to feel safe. So they wouldn't think they had to kill me." Nan looked at the wall clock and Trina saw what was coming next, saw the need to make Nan feel protected. "He . . . *Trevor* will be back this afternoon. *He'll come after me, when he finds out I've seen a psych nurse.*" She stood up.

"We'll deal with Trevor Davis appropriately. The authorities will. We'll all see to it that you're safe. From all three of them. Want to sit down?"

Nan sat again. "I'm afraid they'll come back. I'm *terrified* they'll come back."

"They're not going to have access to you," Trina said. "We'll talk about how that's accomplished later . . . You're not married, Nan?"

"No."

"What about a boyfriend, a lover?"

Nan thought of Oren and she began to cry in sobs. She saw him looking at her. She had a quick feeling of despair and then anger at Oren. In her mind she tried to push the image of him away, but it remained. In her mind she averted her eyes, turned her head away from him. But there he was again, standing outside the flower shop, smiling at her. He threw her the bouquet of yellow flowers and she walked away from him while it was still in the air and fell somewhere behind her, in darkness. "Nobody," she said. She had quieted, but she was enfolded by an overwhelming sense of loss. "I don't know how . . . *people* will react to me. Now. I *hate* myself, I feel so *dirty*." She spoke to Trina in fury. "I want to *destroy* myself."

"Sure. That's normal, Nan. It's the perfectly natural feeling. Most people feel that way. Do you believe me?"

"Yes."

"Then don't do it. Okay?"

Nan's face hardened. "Yeah. Sure. Okay."

"That would be really dumb, Nan. That's the very best thing you could do to help those shits out."

Nan smiled very slightly.

"Now we need to get you examined."

"By a doctor."

"I know that's got a real bad association for you right now, but—"

"They all know me here."

"You've got to be looked at. There may be physical damage that requires attention. The examination is also to preserve evidence. That's the first step in the legal process to protect you."

Nan's body had drawn in on itself, almost in a sitting womb position.

Trina called over to GYN. "I have a woman here who's been sexually assaulted. Do you think we could get a woman doctor over here? A woman from GYN?" Trina hung up and then had a feeling of oppression, reality crowding in on her, as if the walls of the room were collapsing toward her. She saw the walls of the room for the first time. She said to Nan, "You know what? I was a patient in this same room last night."

The walls receded, returned to their proper stationary dimensions.

130

PERCY STEVENS HAD been moved to the Gold Coast and Audrey had a deep feeling of loss, as if her patient had been sent away to die, as Mr. Emerson had been sent away from the ICU to die.

Audrey laughed, or thought she did, because Mr. Emerson had been sent to Med Three and Percy Stevens, *from* Med Three to the Gold Coast. Coralee did not see or hear any laughter. She saw her partner slumped and tired and it was only ten-thirty in the morning.

Audrey looked up at Coralee. Her eyes were wet, but there were no tears, Coralee saw. "I feel weepy," Audrey said. "No goddamn good reason. Angry at the patients." She pressed a handkerchief to her eyes.

"Too many doubles," Coralee said.

"I'm doing a double today so I can appear for Tim tomorrow."

"Let up after that. I'm doing my share of doubles, but not every day."

"I could have screamed at Captain Malamet. Because he called me for a glass of water."

"When was that?"

"A few minutes ago."

"Did you scream at him?"

"No. I smiled at him and took him a pitcher of water.

Remember Barnitska? I'm getting like her.. Malignant bitch syndrome.''

"You've got a ways to go."

"Quick to temper. Barnitska resigned. She told me, if you love this work enough and you're good enough at it, you've got to quit."

Coralee placed her hand on Audrey's and held it for several seconds before she spoke. "I left this place, this profession, once. I said it was because of having children and needing to be home with them. And a lot of that was true. But it was also because I wanted out. I couldn't take—" she looked around—"*this* anymore. What we could do, what we couldn't do, what we weren't allowed to do, what we didn't have the time to do—the problems with supplies and equipment and facilities—"

"Like the HOs."

"They'll be leaving soon. It really doesn't make a big difference to them, the senior ones. They can afford what they're doing. They don't know that, of course. Maybe some of them will even go to jail before they give up and come back."

"Why did you come back?"

"I could give you a lot of reasons." Coralee considered them. "Kids pretty grown up. Need for more family income. Opportunity to come back. Pride in my skills. *Caring*. Mostly *caring*. The need for me here. And one more thing. I came back because I thought I could take it now."

The two women were silent. Coralee raised Audrey's hand and pressed it against her own cheek. "When I left I knew I *couldn't* take it. Not any longer. That's really why I left." Abruptly she released Audrey's hand.

Audrey looked up. She spoke softly. "I don't want to take it anymore."

"But you are."

"I don't know for how long."

131

DR. MILDRED ISAACS had gray hair and clear eyes. She said to
Nan, "I'd like to move you to a table with stirrups."

"Please? Can we stay here?"

Trina said, "I think Nan feels comfortable here." The
GYN table in the ER had only curtains around it.

Dr. Isaacs nodded and explained the general course the
examination would take. She had brought a rape kit.

Trina listened and then reviewed the history she had taken
from Nan.

Nan had had no control. Now she felt powerless and
helpless and hopeless and Trina understood that. Put control
back into her, Trina thought, a sense of control. Some hope
for herself. Some sense that she's not worthless.

Dr. Isaacs said, "I need to take a sexual history of the
assault, Nan."

"Again? I just—" Suddenly she looked around the little
room as if she had just discovered herself there. "Can anyone
hear?"

"This is all private here, Nan," Trina said. "No one can
hear."

Nan gave the account again, but abbreviated the physical
details. Once more she began hesitantly and then her voice
sped as she had to become specific and when the crying
returned she controlled it. She described Trevor separating
her legs.

She stopped at that. *I just want to fuck you, Nan.* And he
had *done* it. He had *done* it. Nan felt again the horror, the
revulsion, but what stilled her now was the *incomprehension*.

After a moment she heard herself speaking again, but it
was as if her mind had separated from her body, gone away
somewhere, and listened from a distance. "This just doesn't
fit in my life. I mean, nothing like it ever happened before.
Nothing that could make me say, Well, it's possible."

"I understand," Dr. Isaacs said. Trina was silent. Dr.
Isaacs' task was the primary one now. "Were you pene-

trated?'' Nan nodded. ''Did he ejaculate?'' Nan nodded. ''Inside you?'' Nan nodded. ''Why do you think that?''

Trina replied slowly. ''His rhythm changed . . . And he wasn't . . . hard inside me. Then he just lay on me. Like I was a mattress. *He got sweat all over my body.*''

When Nan finished, Dr. Isaacs said, ''Nan, I'm going to ask you to go over some of the physical aspects of the assault again. This has to do with what our medical response is going to be, to physical damage to your body. Were you hit?''

Nan touched her cheek. Blood beneath the flesh had discolored the skin. Dr. Isaacs examined the area and asked Nan about headache, ringing in her ears. She asked Nan about her teeth—did any of them feel loose? ''Were you bitten?'' Nan shook her head. ''Struck?''

''I just told you the stockbroker hit me.''

''Struck with something?''

''No.'' Then she remembered the scalpel and told about it again.

As the physical examination continued, Nan's manner changed subtly. Her body lost some of its rigidity, her voice became less strained. The physical examination sometimes could be comforting—someone helping, something being done. Something *can* be done. Trina knew the thought process.

Dr. Isaacs dabbed antiseptic on Nan's nose. Then she picked up a smooth white cardboard box. Nan looked at it with fascination that it was meant for her. So many labels on it, the wide tape guarding its security. Dr. Isaacs broke the seal and opened it. Nan saw slides and instructions and other paraphernalia. Dr. Isaacs opened another sealed package from inside the rape kit and drew on white surgical gloves. There was the slight perfume of talcum powder. Dr. Isaacs proceeded and described what she was doing and why. She began with external examination and collection.

When she got to Nan's thigh she said, ''Nan, don't touch, but indicate for me the area of exterior ejaculation.'' Nan indicated.

''I'm going to check for seminal fluid with a litmus.'' Dr. Isaacs wet the area with a four-by-four gauze. She opened an envelope and showed Nan the litmus paper. ''Acidphosphatase. I'm going to press it against the area where the ejaculation hit. The paper should turn purple.''

Nan tensed quite visibly. Trina touched her shoulder lightly. "What is it?"

"What if it doesn't turn purple?"

"What do you mean?"

"What if I'm crazy? What if it never happened?"

Trina left her hand on Nan's shoulder.

"There," Dr. Isaacs said to Nan, showing her the paper, "isn't that a fine shade of purple?"

Nan began to laugh. "Isn't that a fine baby? Dr. Isaacs, you look like you're holding up the new baby for the mother to see."

She laughed and cried together, but Trina felt and saw Nan's body relax and heard that the soft crying was free, no longer controlled.

"Now I'm going to do an internal, Nan. I'm going to check for the presence of sperm with a wet mount. I'm going to take fluid from back of the cervix." She said to Trina, "Since we don't have stirrups, I need you to hold Nan's feet apart." Dr. Isaacs inserted a speculum and Nan's body reacted in a jerk. "I'm sorry. Did that hurt?"

"No. Yes. A little. But it was something else."

"Yes. I understand. You've had a terrible intrusion and your body wants to resist another one." She worked quickly with swabs and a slide, placed saline over the secretion she had gathered and a coverslip over the slide. The slide would be examined under a microscope later.

When Nan was alone with Trina again, she said, "What's going to happen, Trina? What am I going to do? What are you going to do? What's Dr. Isaacs going to do?"

"I'm going to write up a consult note. What you told me in your own words—and what I observed. Dr. Isaacs will prepare an expert witness report. Now the question is, are you going to pursue this legally?"

"What would I have to do?"

"Call the police. A detective will interview you."

"A female detective? Can you get a female detective?"

"I'll ask. But it's unlikely. The people they send, though, the detective or street man, they're usually sensitive. They'll take your statement. You don't have to worry."

"But I already gave you a statement."

"I'm not the police."

"Can't you hand my statement over to the police? What I told you?"

"They don't want my report. They want a statement directly from you.

132

PAUL SQUIRES COULD not abide being alone with himself. In his apartment he talked aloud to himself to dispel the voice in his mind, the whisper that said *Rape . . . rape.* Sometimes it was Nan's voice he heard, sometimes his own. Guilt made him tremble and hug himself. He could not physically contain it. He threw up, vomited out all the guilt and remorse. His muscles ached from tension. He drank straight vodka. After a while it calmed him. And then suddenly he was sweaty and trembly again, felt stifled by his presence with himself in his apartment, and went out.

Lynn Keating had an early luncheon date at Fritz Moriarty's, but she did not follow the maître d' to her table. Her attention had been caught by Paul Squires. He was sitting at the end of the bar with the man with whom Lynn was to have lunch, an executive of a public relations firm. The man was in debt to Lynn for favors she had done the man's clients in her column.

The man saw Lynn but made no gesture acknowledging her presence. That was a signal in itself, but Lynn was already alert because of Squires' appearance. He was unshaven and in rough physical condition. Lynn knew him to be a straight arrow and so his condition interested her. He appeared to be drunk. Lynn knew he was supposed to be on the air in two hours.

Squires finished his Bloody Mary and waved at the barman, who came over and said, "Sorry, Mr. Squires, the way you're putting them down, give yourself a rest, huh?" The barman walked away. The PR man pushed his own Bloody Mary over to Squires. "You need it, I can see that." He did not look at Lynn, though she had come over to a few feet away.

Squires held on to the PR man's Bloody Mary. He said to the PR man, "I didn't want to do it . . . *Christ, I didn't even want to be there . . .*"

The PR man's eyes went to Lynn for an instant, only an instant, and she saw the slightest inclination of the man's head gesturing her away. She went to her table and ordered a salad and a glass of white wine. Before she finished her lunch, the PR man came over. Squires remained at the bar, his shoulders slumped, his head bent. The waiter placed a Bloody Mary in front of the PR man. He touched Lynn's glass with his and drank and smiled at Lynn. "Well," he said, "it's quite a story."

Lynn listened. Then she asked for the story again, and this time she made notes. When she was satisfied with her groundwork, she placed her notes in her shoulder bag and went over to Squires at the bar. She stood beside him and placed a hand gently on his shoulder and spoke to him soothingly. She was patient and finally, later, she was able to get the story from Squires himself by offering him forgiveness, something he could not give himself.

133

IN THE COURSE of the interviews and the sometimes unavoidable brutality of the questioning, Trina was astonished by Nan's stamina. The more resistance her body showed to the verbal examinations by strangers, the more reserves Nan seemed to find. She sat straighter and her replies held less and less affect, to the point of almost no emotional content at all.

The first interview was with a male detective and occurred at about the time Lynn Keating was entering Fritz Moriarty's.

Nan gave an objective report to the detective. Dr. Isaacs, as a medical expert, established that a rape had occurred and that even with the concurrent psychological trauma, Nan's account could be relied upon. Trina certified that the details of Nan's account had remained consistent.

The fourth interview, with an assistant district attorney called in by Trina and the detective, occurred about an hour later while the detective was obtaining warrants from a judge for the arrests of Trevor Davis, Ronald Casey, and Paul Squires.

Nan was outraged when she learned she couldn't have an attorney of her own choice, someone from whom she could expect sympathy, even empathy, perhaps a woman.

The ADA said, "It's a crime against the state."

"It's a crime against *me*."

Nan detested the ADA. When she smelled his cinnamon breath spray, she almost lost control of herself—the man's breath spray, his careful appearance, his manner and age, so very nearly those of the stockbroker.

Trina distrusted the man because he was more suspicious of Nan than professionally dubious.

He said, "I don't know how many interviews I've conducted on this sort of allegation, but very few of them prove to have a basis for going to court finally. It's a matter, we discover along the line, of people getting what they advertise for."

Nan looked at Trina. She spoke evenly. "I don't want this man. I don't want him around me."

The ADA said, "Obviously I'm not the attorney you chose. But I'm the attorney you got. You can consult anyone you want. And bring that person along. If we go to trial."

Trina said, "Warrants for arrest are being obtained now."

"I'm aware of that. It doesn't mean this will ever get to trial." He looked at Nan and seemed to take pleasure in the challenge when he said, "If it goes to trial, you'll probably have to go to court at least three times—plus continuances."

"All right."

"It'll be an ordeal, I guarantee it."

"All right."

Nan and the ADA stared at each other. "Okay," he said, removing a yellow legal pad from an immaculate soft leather case, "go ahead, let me hear your story."

Nan told it for the fourth time and exercised great control over her anger.

The ADA interrupted. "You'd been drinking. You went to this place alone with these guys."

"I didn't know I was going to be alone."

"Nurses are known for their pliancy," the ADA said thoughtfully. "I guess it's the profession, all that body contact all day long."

Trina said, "I thoroughly object to your manner and attitude and—"

"Why? Because of what I said about nurses? Forget it, Nurse. Everyone knows it. It's bound to be alluded to by the defense. Go ahead," he said to Nan. "Let me hear the rest of it." He sighed.

Trina said, "You're supposed to be this woman's advocate."

"I'm nothing yet. She's got to convince me. Go ahead."

Nan went on, still in control. When she had finished, the ADA questioned her. When Trina objected to the unnecessary brutality and innuendo of his questions, the ADA said, "It's nothing worse than what she'll have to go through in court. If it gets there. You still want to go that route.

"Yes," Nan said.

"These fellows," the ADA said. "The beginning of their professional careers. A surgeon about to go into private practice. Imagine the lives he'll save. And you want him professionally dead. A young, successful stockbroker. A young, immensely successful radio personality. And you want to ruin their careers, their lives. Isn't that just a little bit vindictive?"

Trina kept her own control. It had occurred to her that the ADA was being intentionally brutal in order to establish the veracity of Nan's report and her willingness to undergo the ordeal of prosecution. Perhaps, after this inquisition, he would display his sympathy, his professional concern and allegiance. Trina just hadn't seen this method employed before.

There were tears on Nan's cheeks. " *You're* going to represent me in court?"

"I'm going to represent the state. That's my job, lady."

"That's it," Trina said, standing. "I'll see you out."

"I haven't concluded."

"Yes you have. Just what interests you in this line of work?" She picked up the phone, dialed Security, and said, "Trina, ER twenty-three, unwanted visitor."

The ADA shrugged and got up. He replaced the legal pad in the leather case and zipped it shut. He said to Trina, "May I see you a moment outside?"

Trina noted that he did not say good-bye to Nan. She hoped that outside he would explain himself and the manner of his interview would turn out to have served some purpose for Nan.

When Trina came back in, Nan had stopped crying. Trina

said, "You know what that sonofabitch just tried to do? He tried to make a date with me."

Trina took Nan to the psych office, where the telephone allowed her to dial outside the hospital. Nan went to the cot and sat and then lay down and was asleep even as Trina dialed Nicholas Prudhomme at the district attorney's office. She explained about Nan and the conduct of the ADA.

"That's appalling," Prudhomme said. "Let me talk to some people here, call you back in a few minutes. What about you? I called the General this morning."

"I know. That was sweet of you. I'm fine. Getting tired." She paused and said, "I get a little shaky now and then." It was a disclosure of more intimacy than Trina felt justified in making to this man.

134

TREVOR DAVIS was apprehended at Slade's Castle. He was in his pajamas and had been sleeping. He dressed and was taken into Boston, where he was charged. Ron Casey was arrested at about the same time, a little after two, when he returned to his office from lunching with a client. He was immaculate in a three-piece summer suit. Paul Squires was not arrested because he couldn't be found—not at home, not at the station. No one at the station had any idea where he was. He had called in sick. He was at the *Eagle* just then and he *was* sick, sick to his stomach and sick of himself. Davis and Casey were taken to Police Headquarters on Berkeley Street and then immediately to court, where, accompanied by attorneys, they were arraigned and finally released on bail under their own recognizance.

Nicholas Prudhomme got back to Trina. "I've spoken to the district attorney. He is regretful and concerned. He's asked me to take over the case. I would suppose that Miss Lassitter isn't up to another interview today?"

"She needs rest now."

"I can understand that." Trina felt a rush of warmth for the man. "How about tomorrow morning, here?"

"She's sleeping now, but I'll say yes for her."

"Perhaps you'd come in then, too, Trina. I'd like to talk to you about my colleague's conduct. Also, it might be supportive to Miss Lassitter to have you present."

"That's very sensitive of you. How long have you been in rape work?"

"Too long. I've been trying to get out of it, but I have a good conviction rate."

"We'll see you tomorrow morning."

"As a matter of fact, I was hoping before. Strictly personal. I'd like to bring you dinner and a bottle of wine. For the now and then shakiness."

Trina felt suddenly cheered. "I'm supposed to go back to the General. But I don't think I will. I think I'll call in sick." She gave Nicholas her address.

They set a time and then he said, "I think you should know, Lynn Keating's been making inquiries about this case. She seems to have a lot of information."

"She didn't get it here."

"No, I didn't think so."

Lynn Keating finished both a front-page news piece and a commentary in time for an unscheduled two o'clock press run. The editor, the managing editor, and the *Eagle*'s counsel interviewed Paul Squires on their own and, when they were satisfied, they looked over Keating's copy and cleared it. By that time Keating had managed to get corroboration from sources in both the police department and the district attorney's office that the essentials of her story were correct. There were no names in her copy and no attributed quotes. The source that was Paul Squires was not referred to as a participant but as an informant.

Copies would be on the street around four.

135

BETTY BOWEN had become so fragile so quickly, Audrey thought. Her skin appeared to have become translucent overnight. Audrey felt helpless and knew she was. She wanted to move Betty—to Brigham and Women's, the BI, the General—"anywhere there's a full staff to take care of you."

"I'm comfortable here," Betty said. She spoke with her eyes closed, her body partially raised in bed. "This is where I want to be . . . You made me a promise, remember?"

"Yes."

"No further support."

"I remember, Betty."

Her face relaxed a little. "This is where I want to be."

At the station Audrey had a call from Day. "Could you take a patient post electric shock? Coming off a unit."

Audrey was astounded at her reply. "Do I have a choice?"

"Look, I'll be honest. The patient is still medically unstable. But he doesn't have to be on the unit."

Audrey said, again entirely surprised at herself, "I don't want to take the patient. I'm *sorry*."

"Audrey, that's a fair decision on your part. There's no reason to move the patient this afternoon."

"I don't think I have the staff." It's the same staff you've had, Audrey replied to herself. I think it's wearing thin, the first Audrey said.

"I'll suggest another medical unit. I don't have any problem with your reason."

"I'll take him if you can't find anywhere else."

"There are a couple of beds in other places. Catch you later."

Audrey was displeased with herself. Whatever extra effort it might have required, she could have accepted the patient.

136

A PRESSROOM WORKER at the *Eagle*, whose life had been saved by the docs and nurses at Back Bay Met after an automobile accident, recognized the gravity of the special edition to the house officers' job action. He lifted two bundles of the first run and took a cab to the hospital and gave the bundles to the picketing HOs, then returned to work.

Within minutes, the picket line was broken, the pickets and other ARI members dispersing like defeated runners, apathetic after their exertion.

The special *Eagle* flew a banner headline: HO ACCUSED IN NURSE RAPE

Keating's commentary paralleled the news piece she had done.

THERE IS NO EXCUSE

. . . Here is a senior house officer who has allegedly raped a Back Bay Metropolitan Hospital nurse, one of his own, a colleague with whom he worked, and not only that, he assisted and encouraged and accommodated two friends of his in also raping the same tragically assaulted nurse.

It ought to be obvious from this and other events that these young, striking doctors do indeed believe in their own ends, if you get what I mean. Look at the house officer who organized the rape, so to speak.

As a woman I am horror-struck. That a man of medicine, one of the most revered members of society, could do this to a woman. But I ought not to be surprised, ought I? Not when this doctor's colleagues are refusing to treat their own patients as a means to benefiting their own finances.

In the three and a half days of their strike, the HOs have been accomplices in the murder of a patient (Albert Cornelius), the murder of a medical student (Hal Levy), the emotional destruction of a psychiatric nurse, the terrorization of a female security guard, the harassment of patients and of the public in general, and now the rape of one of the hospital's own nurses.

House officers do not arrive at a hospital on their own whim. They apply for appointment, are screened and selected. There must be something terribly wrong with the evaluation procedures, both medical and moral, at BBMH. The chiefs and administrators must be held accountable for the unprincipled people they have chosen for their medical staff.

There is no excuse.

The moral responsibility of the City of Boston is to shut down Back Bay Metropolitan Hospital entirely.

Within a few minutes, copies of the newspaper were circulating inside the hospital.

Then the strike is over, Bennett thought after he had read a copy. The HOs would be helpless now before public reaction. One of them had committed rape.

He went to his window and looked down. The picket line had been partially reestablished. But the HOs on the street were mainly engaged in small groups of conversation.

The HOs would have to meet this evening, of course. But faced with a rape committed by one of their own and with orders to prison for some of them tomorrow morning, Bennett foresaw a call from Scotty McGettigan in a few hours and then a meeting to review the details of the HOs' return to work the following day.

What a loss, Bennett thought. What a waste of effort.

He called Molly to say that he would be at his apartment all evening.

When Selma was able to leave her floor for the day at three-thirty, she went to Molly's office for the privacy they could have there. Molly had not explained why they needed to meet nor why they needed to meet privately. When Selma came in, Molly handed her the *Eagle*.

Selma read and then reread. She lay the paper carefully on Molly's desk. "Is it true?"

"One of our nurses has been raped. She came here for help. Trina's been with her most of the day. The nurse has made statements to a detective and to an assistant district attorney. She named Trevor Davis and two others as the rapists.''

Selma exhaled slowly. Then she sat motionless for several seconds. "Who is the nurse?"

"That's confidential."

"I know."

Molly picked up the phone and called Trina. When she replaced the receiver she said, "It's not public, but it's no longer private, either. Nan Lassitter."

"My God," Selma said quietly. She sat very still again. "Trevor Davis?"

"Yes."

"It was almost a minute before Selma spoke again. "I don't think a meeting of the executive committee is appropriate for this."

"I agree."

"I think it ought to be a meeting of the entire membership. As many as we can get together and as soon as possible."

"I think eight o'clock would be the earliest and the latest we could get most people together."

"Let's get to work on it." She stopped and rubbed her forehead and closed her eyes. "How is Nan?"

"She's being gutsy. And she's terrified. And outraged and exhausted."

"Will we get the whole person back?"

"Never the whole person. Almost never. A lot depends on what happens to her after this. What kind of personal support she gets. What kind of support she gets from society. It's a long, long process. She's got to learn trust all over again. A lot of people get in the way of that."

Selma sighed, nodded, opened her eyes. "Trina?"

"Trina is a bulldog. Trina hangs on no matter what."

They began the process of convening an emergency meeting of the membership of the Nursing Services Alliance.

Trina called the General and explained to the psychiatrist that she would not be coming back that evening.

"You need follow-up, Trina. Not only for your own good, but for the patients you see."

"I understand that. I'm going to the district attorney's

office tomorrow morning. I hope to be back at work in the afternoon—''

"No. You see me first.''

"I'll come in next week in the morning.''

"Sorry. Molly Chang isn't giving you any choice. Tomorrow at one?''

"Okay. I'll be there.'' Trina hung up and looked at Nan. Nan slept sweatily, her body shaken briefly now and then by the images in her mind. Her voice made terse sounds of protest, fury, and pain. Trina let her sleep through the ordeal. Nan had refused Trina permission to call family members or friends who might come in and take her home with them. When Nan awoke, Trina would attempt to arrange it once more.

She called Nicholas Prudhomme and canceled their evening together. "A nurses' meeting,'' she said. "I don't know what it's about. I suppose it has to do with the house officers' being out.'' He did not suggest an alternate date and that disappointed her. "How about sometime this weekend?'' she said.

"I think that would be fine.''

"We'll check tomorrow.''

Trina made a call to locate some clean clothes for Nan, just as someone had done for her at the General.

Molly and Selma used separate telephones to alert the executive committee and start the telephone tree through NSA's secretary.

Elin was on Selma's list, and because it was the one call she did not want to make, she made it first. "How are you, El?'' There was a long pause. "Did I wake you, El?''

"No. I slept this afternoon, but I'm up now.''

"How do you feel?''

"A little groggy. I took some Dalmane so I could rest.''

"I mean about Hal.''

"*So* full of grief,'' Elin said and wept. Selma heard her sniffle and blow her nose. "Empty, too. So empty. How can you know someone so briefly and lose so much inside yourself?''

"Want some company tonight, El? I could—''

"I called Hal's parents before. They didn't know what to make of me.''

"There's a meeting here at eight. But I could come out afterward.''

"When I called them I felt guilty. Like I'd taken him from them. Like I'd caused it."

"You had nothing to do with it."

"I know that. His father's coming up. To make arrangements. To take the body back. I offered to meet him. To help with whatever has to be done. He said it was private. Between him and his son."

"They probably have no idea who you are, what your relationship was—"

"His mother said Hal had mentioned me. On the phone. She said I should come to the service."

"There. He must have had good things to say about you."

"I can't go. I'm ashamed. When they see how old I am. *Isn't that crazy?*"

"At thirty-three that's crazy."

"I can't help it."

"You offered to meet Hal's father."

"I felt obligated. I really didn't want to. And I *did* want to. To touch his family." She wept briefly. "If you're looking for sense, Selma, you called the wrong party."

"Actually, I'm calling you as a member of the exec." Selma explained what had happened and why an immediate meeting of the NSA membership was imperative. "I had to notify you, but that doesn't mean you have to come."

"I want to come."

Nan awoke a little after five. She cried out and sat up fiercely, her hands raised in clenched fists. She was not really awake, Trina found. It was a few minutes before they could talk. Trina was able to tell her that Davis and Casey had been arraigned. She also told Nan about the newspaper report. "You can look at it later."

"I want to see it now." Trina gave it to her and Nan read it. "It's hard to believe. From an objective point of view, it's hard to believe. That three people like that would rape someone." She looked at Trina imploringly. "It's going to be hard for a jury to believe, isn't it? They'll be like that district attorney."

"You have a new one. Someone I trust a great deal." Trina explained.

"What about the third one? What about Squires?"

"They looked for him. After the newspaper came out some

detectives went to the *Eagle*. The people there said they didn't know where he was.'' She picked up a piece of paper. ''Stated intentions are to turn himself in after consultation with his attorney.''

''All three of them are free.''

''Yes.''

''I wish I could die.''

''We went through that, Nan. You've got to live. The person who'll come through all this will thank you for living.''

''It's hard to believe.''

Trina took Nan to a shower and stayed with her while she washed and dressed. It was difficult for Nan to undress, difficult for her to surrender herself to the vulnerability of the shower, difficult for her to leave the numbing and cleansing of the water.

When she was dressed, Nan said, ''I'm okay to go home now.''

''I wish you'd let me call someone. A member of your family? A friend? Someone to be with you.''

''Being alone is going to be best.''

But when they got to the ER doors into the New Wing waiting room, Nan suddenly said, ''I can't.''

''What?''

''I thought I could go home. I can't.'' Trina heard Nan's panic. ''I can't, I can't.'' She started to cry. ''I thought I could. I can't even do that.''

Trina wanted to say *Come home with me. I've got a couch, I'll take care of you.* It was something she had to fight often—her deep urge to be a friend. And remind herself that she was a nurse and could not be a friend or else she would have to spend all her time being a friend.

''Who can I call for you?'' Trina said.

Nan thought of her friend on Beacon Street. Then she recalled the roommate's earlier revulsion toward her. ''I've got a cousin in Wellesley,'' she said. ''I'll call her.'' She paused and then began weeping. ''The trouble is . . . she's *married*.''

A little after seven, as the evening sky was beginning to turn gray, Paul Squires and his attorney went into Boston Police Headquarters. Squires, now bathed and shaven, wore a dark blue suit and a conservative tie. His attorney identified himself and his client to the sergeant behind the reception desk and said, "Mr. Squires is here of his own volition in response to inquiries made about him this afternoon by officers from this department."

On Med Three, Audrey was going to the station to check in a temporary relief nurse and collect a wheelchair that Transportation was supposed to be sending up. Day had arranged for the relief nurse as a favor to Betty Bowen. Betty had asked that she might go to this extraordinary nurses' meeting and that Audrey have enough time to go, too, and take her.

Chanda was out of bed, in the corridor, giggling. She showed Audrey a Polaroid of herself and Dom. "Dom's gonna visit me, come to the rest'rant, jes visit me right in the kitchen. Show them folks. Jes like Cind'rella."

Dom stood in the doorway to his room. "Old hospital buddies got to stick together." The Polaroid showed Chanda and Dom in their johnnies standing in front of a bed. "A Mr. Shaughnessy took it," Dom said.

"I didn't know he made rounds," Audrey said.

"He thought he was on the psych floor, he said."

Audrey took a step closer to Dom. "Did he know who you are? Mr. Shaughnessy?"

"Oh, yeah. He took some extra pictures, asked me to sign them."

"You did?"

"Yeah."

"You're a long way back, Dom."

"I guess. Not far enough. But company helps." He smiled at Chanda. "And you," he said to Audrey. "Everyone. How's Jan?"

"Not so good, but stable. She screwed up all kinds of systems. She wants you to visit her."

"Can I?"

"I'll call up tomorrow. Oh, no, I won't be in tomorrow. Ask Coralee."

At the station the relief nurse gave Audrey a beeper. "In case we need you back here."

"I'll just be gone about half an hour."

"Day said give it as long as Betty wants. Up to an hour."

A transportation worker delivered the wheelchair and helped Audrey get Betty into it. While they were waiting for the elevator, he said, 'Guy over on the Gold Coast? Got transferred to Med Eleven this after.'' A floor that did not exist.

"Who Was that?" Audrey said, startled and troubled.

"Dunno."

Percy Stevens. Audrey knew it was Percy Stevens. She knew it had been her responsibility to keep him on the floor and take care of him herself.

When Molly heard what Trina was going to do, she became angry. "You should be back at the General. You shouldn't even be coming to the meeting tonight."

"There's time before the meeting."

"Enough is enough, Trina. Go home."

"I'm going to see Ginny."

"For what? Don't answer. The question is facetious."

"Your tone of voice is not facetious."

"You're going to see Ginny to see if you can help."

"Yes."

"That's my Trina. Never quits."

Trina shrugged. "Don't make fun of me."

"We'll skip over the compulsive aspects."

"I said, don't make fun of me."

"I'm not making fun of you—that's why we'll skip over the compulsive aspects—"

"I hear you, Molly."

"—but let's remember that Ginny is responsible for Hal's death."

"I remember," Trina said quietly. "But I can't help Hal, can I?"

There was still late sunlight in the room at Mass. Mental where Ginny was sitting in a straight-backed chair, her hands clasped in her lap. There were more comfortable chairs in the room, and a couch and tables, but Ginny had selected a chair alone by itself against a wall. If Trina had not looked at the chart with Ginny's psychiatrist, she would have suspected that Ginny was heavily sedated. But she wasn't.

There was only one other person in the room. A man standing with his back to the room, looking out a window.

"Hello, Ginny," Trina said.

The eyes flicked to Trina and then away. "What do you want?"

"I came to see how you're doing." Ginny made no reply. "How're you doing?"

"What do you want?"

Trina sat on the arm of a club chair and faced Ginny over its back. "How's it going for you?"

"What do you want?"

Trina wanted to say You wouldn't let me help you before, please let me help you now. "I just thought I'd stop in, say hello. They taking care of you? Anything you want?"

"What do you want?"

"It's Trina, Ginny."

"What do you want?"

The man turned from the window. He took a step toward Trina and Ginny from the other side of the room, then stopped. "I'm her brother. John. John Shiffland. That's all she says, 'What do you want?' I been here off and on all day, mosta last night. That's all she says now. Last night, before they knocked her out, least she was talkin' okay. Now I don't know what these bastardsa done to her."

He came over and tugged at Trina's short sleeve and drew her a few feet away from Ginny. He whispered, but in the silence of the room he might as well have talked in a normal voice. "You're the nurse was with her?"

"Yes."

"Jeez. They really got her. It's one year mandatory, carryin' without, y'know?"

"I don't think—"

"I know, I know. I got a lawyer. He says there's ways."

"In her condition, I don't think—"

"I know, I know. But a brother's got a right to worry, right?"

"Yes."

"Jeez, there's no tellin' how it could come out. I mean, an innocent person could get sent off."

Trina's ears alerted her. "What are you talking about? *Who* are you talking about?"

The psychiatrist was standing in the doorway. "Enough?" he said. He nodded at Ginny and spoke cheerfully. "I don't think she's hearing what she doesn't want to hear. And that's just about everything."

Trina said, "I think last night just precipitated. It was all
there before. Most of it, anyway."

"You get no argument from me," the psychiatrist said.

Trina turned back to Ginny. Oh, Ginny, why didn't you let
me help you? Why didn't you let me find help for you?

137

THE SUDDEN EIGHT O'CLOCK meeting meant that a number of
husbands had to remain home with infants and children instead of participating in league baseball and softball games.
Some husbands were irritated and some were supportive. The
wives and lovers of NSA's few male members were just as
divided. PTA meetings were missed, dates were broken,
classes cut, and graduate theses remained wherever they had
been left the night before. By early evening it was already
understood that the meeting had been impelled by the rape of
Nan Lassitter by a house officer. In what way impelled was
not generally understood. But a Back Bay Metropolitan nurse
could not turn on a radio or a television or pick up a newspaper
without seeing her hospital and her staff examined and mal-
treated. Though Nan Lassitter's name was never mentioned,
Trevor Davis' always was. He had become emblematic of the
hospital.

The nurses met in a 150-seat amphitheater in the New
Wing. There were 372 full-time and flexie members of NSA.
The seats were filled, and people sat in the aisles and stood
against the walls. Some members had to work and others had
not been able to come or could not be contacted. Selma
judged that almost two thirds of the membership had made it.
Facing them from the podium, she was surprised to feel
fright, fright at her subject. The atmosphere was crowded,
animated, and sweaty. At five after eight, Selma turned on
the microphone and asked for quiet.

She began, "The stories you've been hearing today are
essentially true. One of our members was raped last night by
Trevor Davis and two others—"

"What's her *condition*, Selma?"

"The nurse was traumatized and physically abused in several ways. She's been released to the care of a relative and we need have no discussion of her or the rape—"

"Why the fuck not?" a young nurse said angrily.

The fright leapt up within Selma again. She had been afraid the meeting would be volatile. She had not thought it would be so quick to combust. "Because it's not central."

"Sure it is, Selma," Diana Vezzina said. Her voice was sweet or sarcastic, Selma thought. "That's why this meeting's been called."

The little bitch understood completely, Selma realized. And she was going to keep the meeting aflame. Selma had a vision of Diana, who had organized the slowdown, standing at the microphone in a few years, the head of NSA. Why am I calling her bitch because she's so quick to understand? Good Lord, if *I'm* ready to call someone bitch, what about the rest of them?

Her hands, Selma noticed, which had been resting flat upon the lectern, had curled into fists. When she spoke, she was careful to keep her voice even. "Dr. Davis has been arraigned. The charge is aggravated rape. Davis is a fourth-year surgical resident." Selma paused. "In case it's escaped anyone's understanding, the house officer walkout is finished." Her voice became hard. "Kaput. Hopeless. The house officers have been stigmatized by Davis—maybe beyond repair. The city already perceived them as greedy, self-interested, and ethically corrupt. That view is now extended to the hospital itself.

"From here on in, the house officers have nowhere to go except jail. No one is going to show them the slightest favor—"

"*Good.*"

"*Breaks my heart.*"

Selma went on. "Their condition is not poor or critical, it's terminal. Okay, the question is, the reason for this meeting is, do we want to do anything about that?"

"For those bastards?"

There was considerable vocal dissonance. Selma let it expend itself. "I imagine that most of us agree with the HOs' objectives in patient care issues. Some of us don't agree with the manner in which they attempted to gain those objectives."

"You got it!"

"Whether we approve of the method or not, the HOs went out for all of us. If they win, we all win. If they lose, well, nothing's changed. It's business as usual and we've all learned to cope with that—"

"You want us to go out, Selma?"

"I did not say—"

"Not in so many words," Midge Kelly said.

"I am trying, as best I can," Selma said with discernible patience, "to place this matter in perspective. There are two aspects. There's an opportunity here to change things by giving the HOs our support. Since they've already started this thing. Or we can let their effort go down the drain. But because of last night, *we've got to decide right now*. That's what this meeting is about."

"Sounds like you've already decided, Selma. *Without us.*"

"I haven't decided a bloody thing."

"Sure, Selma."

"Let her talk!" Elin said angrily.

"I just want to get this damn meeting over with," a nurse said. "I've got an infant and a husband at home, so shut up, huh?"

But the interruption, the discord, grew. Selma could not only hear it but, standing above it, she could see the activity of it—heads in motion, arms and hands gesticulating, figures standing briefly here and there to call to each other or to be heard by all the others, and none of the sounds breaking free of all the other sounds. Only Day O'Meara, in the front row, was still and silent. Selma wondered if Day ought to be there, whether she was Management's—Bennett's—eyes and ears.

Audrey was standing behind Betty's wheelchair at the side of the open area by the podium. In the crowd of voices that tumbled down on her she thought she heard someone say, "God made rounds on the Gold Coast an hour ago." She looked up, but could not see who had spoken. Several rows back she saw Tim, talking rapidly with Trina Frankian and Viola Chambers. Audrey's heart beat in fear and sorrow as she thought of Percy Stevens.

Selma spoke loudly into the microphone. "Molly Chang's going to give you some information before we open this up for discussion."

"What discussion? Nurses don't strike, right?"

"C'mon! Let's hear Molly."

"You won't hear Molly, you'll hear Bennett."

"What's that supposed to mean?"

"C'mon, lady, aren't you paying attention?"

Molly heard laughter as she took her place at the podium. She faced it down with silence until there was silence in return. Then she spoke quietly and deliberately. "I spent the latter part of this afternoon with our counsel and I want to give you a summary of what she said. If you decide to take action, she will be with us at our next meeting—"

"Action? What action?"

"Who's got the action? Molly's got the action—"

"For every action, there's a reaction, let's keep that in mind—"

"I know you're all feeling disoriented." Molly spoke calmly. "So let's settle down till we get this sorted out." She looked around the room until there was silence again. Her hand rested on a sheaf of notes she had made. "Okay. The action to be considered is a labor action, a *sympathy* labor action, to demonstrate support for the house officers' objectives on patient care issues. Like having meds on hand when we need them. Like being fully staffed instead of being skeletally staffed most of the time." Molly thumbed the corner of her notes but did not look down. "NSA is a clearly recognized union. We have more legal rights than the HOs. We also have more responsibilities." She glanced around the room now. "The court has determined that the house officers are involved in a concerted action in violation of the law. Fines will start tomorrow and the state can begin to jail ARI's members . . . If we decided to go out—"

"Molly?"

"Questions later—"

"This one needs to be answered *now*." Elin stood up.

"All right, Elin."

"When you talk about 'going out,' you're actually talking about a strike, aren't you?"

"We want to avoid that word. Avoid it *assiduously* is how counsel put it. We are here to discuss a sympathy labor action. Any other characterization would tend to misrepresent—"

"I hear the legal nuances, Molly. But we're talking about a strike." Elin sat down.

Molly looked at Day for an instant and then back at the others. "If you decided to go out, we'd give Management a ten-day notice of our intention.'' She looked at Day as she said, ''Management could counter with a series of legal moves.'' Again she looked back to the others. ''Or Management could simply accept NSA's intention of going out and negotiate. It might also take the same position it has with the HOs and refuse to negotiate at all. There are a number of legal obstacles Management might exhaust to prevent NSA from going out.'' Now Molly looked directly at Day and Day looked directly back at her. ''NSA could ignore the obstacles and face the consequences, as ARI has, or we could simply wait until the obstacles are exhausted.'' Molly stopped, then said, ''Excuse me, I've got to interrupt myself.'' She looked at Day again. ''Day, I'm unclear about your presence. You're Management.''

Day stood. ''Molly, my job description is managerial. That's accurate. A supervisory position. But my contract is a nurse's. The same as yours. If anyone wants to fight me about that,'' she said, turning to the rows of nurses behind her, ''we can put on boxing gloves.''

''That's unfair, Day,'' Coralee said. ''It would be two against one.'' There was some laughter.

''Okay,'' Molly said. ''I guess boxing gloves won't be necessary. What I've told you so far has been mild. Here's the rough stuff. It's illegal for us to strike. We risk all the penalties of the courts. Even so, there's the possibility of arbitration or a court-ordered change.

''We can take our contract with the City of Boston and enter a motion to compel and enforce. We would ask the court to require the city and Management to live up to every agreement in our contract. If the court did so and Management complied, that would eliminate about fifty percent of our misery. But it wouldn't repair or replace EKGs or monitors or wheelchairs and so on.

''Going out is a drastic and polarizing action. Management and NSA—and the individuals on both sides—we'll be angry at each other for months and years to come. Frankly, I'm a little chicken about it.''

''But there is no question we can go out.''

Molly looked at Diana Vezzina. ''Yes, there is no question we can shut the hospital down. It is likely that we can force Management to negotiate with us and the HOs on patient care

issues *if you should decide that that's what you want to do*. I
want to repeat—''

''Molly?''

''Okay, Audrey.''

''What's to prevent the hospital from getting replacements
in for us?''

''Nothing. In two senses of the word. There's nothing to
prevent it and, if we believe Management and City Hall,
there's no money to do it. Also, I can't see an entire hospital
staffed by agency nurses—''

''Just wait.''

''Why don't we all join an agency?''

''I've been thinking about it long enough.''

''All right, I want to get back to point number one. It's
illegal for us to strike. But our counsel would argue that
Management has consistently voided our contract, therefore
we can't be held to a contract that doesn't exist.'' Molly held
the notes just off the lectern and waggled them slightly.
''Regularly and recurrently voided our contract. Not enough
nurses on station. Unreliable facilities and support. We can
go out simply to make Management crew up the station to
contractual obligations—''

*''Sure we can go out, Molly. And they can leave us out,
too.''*

''We would need to put a strike fund together. We would
need to agree on and set the *methodology* of the action—''

''Molly, you said *strike*,'' Trina said.

''You see, you can't be careful enough. That would really
have to be worked on, by everyone . . . Well, our lawyers
would handle their lawyers. Side against side. But you would
have to be prepared for a bad time, a real bad time. Eventually some of us, even all of us, might have to go to jail. If it
goes that far.''

Diana Vezzina said, ''Realistically, Molly, can you see the
great City of Boston sending the good women in white to
jail?''

''Two weeks ago, Diana, could you have imagined Scotty
McGettigan being sent to Charles Street Jail?'' There was
silence. ''As far as the court is concerned, each member of
NSA who participated would share the same professional
liability.''

138

SELMA TOOK Molly's place. "What we have to decide is, with the walkout about to be smashed, and maybe ARI along with it—do we support ARI and its objectives? Do we say to Lynn Keating and the rest of Boston, Trevor Davis is *not* a typical house officer, we will not let you make ARI in his image? Or do we say nothing?" Selma waited before she went on.

"Ladies and gents, colleagues, we've got a lot to chew over here. The patients' rights. The patients' needs. The HOs' objectives. *Our* needs, *our* rights. I know I'm your elected senior officer and part of my duty is to advise, but no, not on this. I will not *presume* to advise what is in our best interests. I don't know. Please give us all the benefit of your discussion." She returned the microphone to Molly.

Audrey leaned forward to look at Betty. Her head had slumped down and to the side and her eyes were closed. But the fingers of her right hand moved in a delicate drumming on her knee and her breathing did not suggest sleep.

One of the younger nurses had stood. Molly recognized her. Her voice was quiet but firm. "We ought to desert this place. We ought to get the patients out and reduce it to rubble."

As some applause began, Molly said, "That's not practical."

"Of course not," the young nurse said. "You're not just in with Management, you're sleeping with it."

Selma took the microphone and spoke sharply. "We are concerned with our professional lives here, not personal."

"Excuse me. I thought that *was* professional." The nurse sat down.

Margaret Gaines, the pediatric head nurse, was standing. "I've worked in this hospital thirty-two years. I know there are a lot of things here need correcting. I just don't see that going out, *abandoning* the patients, is going to help. I would like to say that I'll support the decision here whatever it is. But I damn well *can't* say that. And I won't." She sat and then rose again immediately. "You all know Jamaal. Who are you going to turn *Jamaal* over to?"

Three nurses were standing now and Molly pointed to Midge Kelly, Day's opposite on the surgical side. "I'm sick and tired of not having enough nurses for the surgical floors. Sometimes I have to pull nurses off the floors for the ORs. I'm *bitter* that Management doesn't live up to its agreement about staffing. I'm exhausted from having to find people *every day* to fill slots that ought to be routinely filled. I'm against going out. I'll support the HOs, but not by going out."

Liz Swanzey got up suddenly and did not wait to be recognized. "Maybe we *ought* to go out. But it's not *right*. It's not fair to the patients."

Betty had whispered to Audrey and Audrey wheeled her to the side of the podium. Audrey looked up at Molly and said, "Her voice is weak, she needs the microphone." Molly carefully placed the microphone in Betty's fragile hands, but as light as it was, her arms could not keep it—or themselves—elevated, so Audrey held the microphone.

Betty spoke slowly and lucidly, but even with the amplification, her voice had the quality of a whisper. "I'm a patient here now, of course . . . But I'm still a dues-paying member of NSA . . . Not an active one . . . but I've got a few years even on Margaret . . . in service here . . . In my day we *never* would have thought of striking. It just wasn't our right . . . When it came to that, when we saw that things were *so* bad, we . . . some of us, too many of us . . . nurses would leave the profession entirely first . . . I don't approve of nurses striking. It's just not in me . . . But I'm so very glad that nurses have gotten to the point where we can influence conditions of patient care . . ." She nodded at Audrey and Audrey handed the microphone back to Molly.

"That says a lot of nothing," a young nurse said.

"Maybe you weren't listening," an older nurse said.

Audrey leaned down to Betty and said, "I'll take you back now."

"No. I want to hear more. Maybe you have something to say."

"I do. But I don't want to say it." Audrey moved Betty back to the side.

Diana Vezzina was standing and waiting. Molly nodded to

her. "Betty Bowen is one of the nurses who go back to the forties and fifties, one of the nurses who made this place a legend, one of the best teaching hospitals in the country." Diana wiped some hair back from her forehead. "She's one of the reasons an internship or a residency here is still considered a prize. It's the work she did here, the tradition she and the others established. That's why I'm here and a lot of others. *But I'm fed up.* The patients aren't getting the care they deserve. Ms. Bowen said she's glad we have some influence now. I say use it. Not with boxing gloves. With a baseball bat. *Or let's forget we're nurses.*"

"You already have," Margaret Gaines called at her.

Molly said, "Theresa."

The nurse pursed her lips. Her arms were crossed as if she were holding herself together and she spoke rapidly. "You haven't talked about money, no one's talked about money. I don't mean a strike fund, I mean *money.* What we live on. Enough money to live on. I live on my paycheck. And my husband's. We have three children. We hardly have any savings. Being noble and striking for the HOs is a great idea maybe"—she looked at Diana—"if you're single. But for someone like me, it stinks." She looked around. "There's a lot more like me here, in a similar situation. *Why don't you speak up?*" She sat down suddenly.

"It's a good point," Molly said. "It's a point that's got to be considered."

Several nurses were standing. One of them said, "I knew this was coming. I'd like to support the HOs, but I can't afford to go out."

Another said, "It's the same with me. I'd have to be a strikebreaker or I'd have to quit and get a job someplace else."

A third nurse said, "You vote a strike, you vote me out of this hospital. I can't afford it."

"All right," Molly said, looking around, "anyone else on this?"

"Theresa's right. A lot more of us could say the same thing."

"Anyone want to?" Molly said. No one spoke.

Viola Chambers got up hesitantly. "It's not about money," she said.

"Go ahead, Vi."

Viola looked about at the other nurses. "I'm responsible for Children's Seven at night. I've thought about all this real hard. I'm all for the HOs. But there's no way I'm going to leave the children." Viola sat again and there was applause.

Tim was seated next to her and stood as she was sitting. When there was quiet he said, "I've been asked to speak for the critical care nurses." Audrey heard an intensity in his voice that she had heard only in association with the way Valerie had treated him in regard to his time with Jason. "We won't leave our patients either. But if intensive care patients are triaged out, if there's no patient left to care for on a unit, as soon as that happens the critical care nurses on that unit will go out in support of the HOs . . . if NSA decides to go out."

Trina, on the other side of Tim, got up when he finished. "With all this talk about whether or not to go out, there's a problem here that's not being addressed. It's important to separate the issues—the ones we support and the ones we don't want to get involved in, like the HOs' salaries. That needs to be clarified."

"*What about my salary—the one I'll lose if we go out?*"

"*Frankly, I don't give a damn about the HOs' salaries—*"

"*Neither do I, but the patient care issues—*"

"*The Patient care issues are something else.*"

Selma had the microphone. "Okay, let's look at the house officers' issues. Which ones are legitimate nursing and patient care concerns and which ones aren't?"

Audrey kept looking at her watch. Her hour off the floor had passed by several minutes. But now that she was at the meeting she wanted to speak before she left. If only they would get through with the nitpicking, the dissatisfaction with words, the *semantics*. She finally decided to interrupt.

She got Selma's attention and got recognized. "I've got to leave, that's why I'm changing the subject. But I want to say what I think before I go. I think it would be all wrong for us to leave work, to leave our patients. We know conditions here are bad. We know they've got to be changed. But like Viola said, we've got to take care of our patients."

As Audrey rolled Betty to a ramp and exit, she heard the arguments become excited again.

Selma listened and made notes. Molly listened carefully to the mood. The meeting began to exhaust itself. Statements became redundant. Molly covered the microphone and said to Selma, "I think they've heard each other out."

Selma nodded and stepped back to the microphone. She said, "Up here in the leadership spot, I get the feeling that *everyone* wants to put the whole decision off. Maybe forever."

There was some applause, but, Molly observed, fatigue and confusion about obligation and responsibility quickly resulted in silence.

Coralee got up slowly, as if she might be preparing to leave. But she faced the podium. "I'm another nurse worked here full-time or flexie goin' back twenty years. Now about goin' out. In all that time, I haven't seen much change. What change there's been, some of it—the new technology, the new meds—that's been wonderful. But most of the change has been for the worse. Every year, every month, every day, there's been more deterioration—of what we have and what we can do for our patients." She stopped. "This is hard to say. But I say *yes*. Maybe we should go out. Maybe it's a good idea to try to change things. I don't want to leave any patient. But I'm thinking about it as *radical surgery*."

There was some conversation after that, though it was quiet and general and no one stood up.

Selma asked for silence. "I think we're ready to take a voice vote about our inclination at this point. This isn't a final vote. Under our rules, we'd have to prepare proxies for members unable to be present at the final vote. I—"

"When would that be, Selma?"

"Well, it's Thursday evening . . . Saturday morning, ten o'clock . . . I put it to you this way," and Selma wrote her own words down as she spoke. "Shall we or shall we not place a recommendation to the general membership . . . of refusal to continue work . . . under the present conditions of . . . regular and recurrent violations on the part of the City of Boston . . . . of the contract between the City of Boston and the Nursing Services Alliance of Back Bay Metropolitan Hospital?"

"Would you read all that back, Selma?" There was laughter.

Selma read it back. "If we vote such a recommendation, a strategy committee will have to be formed and prepare for Saturday morning. If we don't vote the recommendation— well then, we've thrashed it out, we can all go home, get some sleep, be at it again tomorrow as if nothing's happened."

There was some applause for that.

Day stood up. There was silence. She said, "You all know me. You know my prejudices. Stay on the job no matter what." She looked around the room, having to turn completely around in order to do so. "By now you probably all know who was raped last night. I'm not going to use her name. I just want to say I think we have to back her. I think it's the most important action any of us can take now. We have to reject Davis. We have to support ARI and this hospital. We cannot let our own nurse be used to destroy what the HOs are trying to do."

139

BETTY WAS SLACK in her wheelchair. Sleeping, Audrey thought. But when she was moved from the chair to her bed, Audrey realized that Betty was comatose. She took signs. Automatically she called for assistance and began offering it. It was when she was establishing supplemental O_2 that she recognized she ought not, had promised Betty not.

But she could not give it up or interrupt herself in ordering other procedures. She clasped the oxygen mask to Betty's mouth as if she were in arrest. Then Audrey found herself in arrest, unable to proceed, unable to withdraw.

She was entirely aware when Dr. Schoonoler took over, and she went back to work with her other patients, patrolling them aggressively in spite of the hour, as if it were day and they were all awake and consciously in need.

When Dr. Schoonoler came out of Betty's room, he went to the telephone at the station. Audrey listened to his conversation with Dr. Geier and then put her hand on Dr. Schoonoler's hand, the hand that held the receiver to his ear. "Excuse me, Mert," Dr. Schoonoler said, lowering the receiver.

"I promised her she could go this way."

"It's not up to you."

"She was afraid that it would metastasize to the brain. She was sure it would. I promised her that if she became comatose . . . I promised her I'd be her voice and do the best I could . . . that she didn't get any support. That's what she wanted from this hospital.''

Dr. Schoonoler briefly held the telephone to his breast. Then, ''Mert, we've got to talk about this one.''

"Jesus, Tim," Day said, catching up with him outside the amphitheater and breathing heavily, ''this a *fast break?*''

''I got to get home to Jase.'' He looked at Day and stopped. ''Slow down there, Day.'' He looked at her belly. ''You look like you got a full court press goin' in there. Sit, c'mon, sit.''

''I'm okay. Winded. Chasin' you, anybody but a fool'd be winded.''

''Just take it easy. Shouldn't you be home now?''

''Fuck it, yes. Maybe. Now listen to me, Timothy. I didn't chase you sixteen miles to talk about me. We've got a very serious problem.''

Day leaned against the wall and closed her eyes in pleasure at the support behind her. She opened her eyes and the pleasure was gone. ''We can't keep your unit open tomorrow unless you're there.''

"Shit's sake, Day." He looked at her with an anger that frightened her. ''No one's irreplaceable.''

Day spoke in her quiet voice. ''I know what tomorrow is. For you. I'll just tell you how it is. Here. We can't keep the unit open unless we have a head nurse. Nan was supposed to be there for you. There's no one else. We haven't got a visit who will take it. I asked. I pushed it as hard as I could.''

''That's hard to understand. My life, my boy's—''

''They all have their own schedules. Not going to play nurse at their level of expertise.''

''An HO?''

''Scotty says absolutely not. If they're going to start going to jail tomorrow, there's going to be no further assistance to this hospital. None whatsoever. Starting at seven tomorrow. He says if they have to go to jail it's going to be earned.''

''Day.''

''I'm sorry, Tim. It's your choice, I'll give you a few minutes, but you've got to let me know now.''

''What will you do with my patients? If I don't come in? If you close the unit?''

"They'll be sent to floors."

"You can't put those patients on floors."

"That's where they'd have to go. It's a matter of staffing and protocol. The unit can't stay open without a qualified head nurse or charge nurse. But it's okay for the same patients to be placed on floors. It's crazy, but that's the way it is."

"They'll die, a couple of them. Jan Fox—"

"If someone dies on a floor, it won't be because of wrongful performance on the part of the hospital. If someone dies on an intensive care unit that is improperly staffed, that's criminal negligence."

When Molly went outside, there was a notable change in the house officers' picket line. A number of women in white had joined the line.

On Med Three, Mert Geier sat down with Audrey and Lucius Schoonoler behind the closed door of the small conference room. They each had a mug of instant coffee before them on the pink Formica table. There were crumbs left over from someone's sandwich. Audrey related the details of Betty's instructions about her care.

"It's a family decision," Dr. Geier said "Has anyone been in touch with the family?"

"The husband is dead. There's a grown daughter somewhere, married with children. But Betty said she's not to be contacted till afterward. I have no address for her, anyway. I just have Betty's attorney's name and number."

"We should contact the attorney."

"I did. I spoke to him at home a little while ago. Everything Betty said to me, she'd said to him. He has it in writing as well. Betty came in here fully prepared never to leave. I said, 'We should be in touch with the daughter, with the family.' He said, 'You're her family. All of you at Back Bay Met. Betty's counting on you.'"

Dr. Geier said, "Luke?"

"I pass. It's not my sort of medicine. I was taught to keep people alive."

Dr. Geier said, "It will have to be reviewed by committee. In the meantime I'll write orders for maintenance."

"Does everything have to be reviewed by committee?"

Audrey said. "Does everything have to be decided at meetings? Betty made a decision about herself."

"We don't know if she has the right to make that decision," Dr. Geier said.

"She has the right to make that request," Audrey said.
"She has the right to have that request honored."

"It has to go before committee. What are her chances for
life?"

"She doesn't want the little extra life you can give her. She
doesn't want the pain."

Molly went to Bennett's. She carried within her a sexual
excitement, a hunger, that she recognized as driven and antagonistic, an overwhelming impulse that she had no intent of
countering with her mind. It was Bennett's aloofness that
pricked her, his reserve and control, his remove from the
turmoil. She had in mind to rape him, to see his strength
confounded, feel it diminish her subject.

She saw that he had recently shaved and put on clean
clothes. "Going out?" she said.

"I am prepared to accept Cornwallis' surrender as soon as
the telephone rings. I'll have to go out then."

"You don't sound happy about it."

He didn't reply. "Drink?" Molly took off her dress. She
was fascinated and thrilled again by his instant wonder. Her
body made her a goddess. He was as astounded as a primitive
by lightning. He was so much a man that the recurrence did
not reduce the effect. She stood in front of him and he
reached behind her to undo her bra. She felt his fingertips in a
very slight tremble. When they were bare he cupped her
breasts and then bent and licked and sucked them. She smoothed
the hair on the back of his head and watched him. He stood to
kiss her and Molly turned and walked into the bedroom. She
undressed and lay on the bed and watched Bennett undress. It
was as if he were a little unfamiliar with his own clothes. He
looked over at her, lying in the light of the single lamp, then
came over to lie against her, his leg between her legs, his
mouth settling to hers, his hand on her belly and in her hair
and then between her legs, and she twisted away from his
hand and his mouth and from beneath him.

Molly manipulated Bennett onto his back. She kissed his
lips, played with his tongue, licked at his nipples, moved

down with her mouth, felt his abdominal muscles tense as she brushed the skin with her lips and tongue, her hand moving up the inside of his thigh. The musculature of his body seemed to implode around his penis. She stroked it with her fingers, her tongue, teased whatever it pleased her to tease, played with his balls, the slight scent of urine, of sweat, and then she took him in her mouth, tasting him, drawing all that strength even harder, feeling the pulse of him, and insisting on slowness, her rhythm, not the fast male thrusting. She stopped, held him in her hand, and looked up at him, smiling, and thought she saw in his face the recognition of submission, of dependence . . . acknowledgment.

She went on to finish then, accepting his rhythm. *I feel like every woman in the world when I do this.* Until he destroyed himself in her mouth. *Ohhhh,* she heard in her ears and felt with her hand on his abdomen.

He pulled her to him before she could suck away any more of him, diminish him any further, and she kissed him with lips wet with his own spent force.

"Christ, Molly. Jesus Christ."

After a moment he reached down to bring her to orgasm. She took his hand away. He had no idea how deeply he had satisfied her. Molly was no longer angry. She was content. She was glad and peaceful when Bennett wanted to take her in his arms and hold her as she slipped into sleep. *All this power. Ours. We have so much power,* she thought. *Every woman in the world.*

When she was alone at the station—Dr. Schoonoler and Dr. Geier were off the floor, Debby was in with a patient, their med student off on an errand—Audrey picked up the telephone and called the charge nurse on the Gold Coast. "You had a death this afternoon?"

"Early this evening."

"Who?"

It was not a name Audrey knew. It was not Percy Stevens. She had a little surge of jubilation, a thrill of renewed energy, a feeling of freedom—and then there was *nothing,* a flatness like the lines of the Harvard criteria. She found the telephone still in her hand and pressed against her breast. She placed it in its cradle. She felt the deep, unaccountable despair of someone who herself has just been very near death and has escaped.

*   *   *

The telephone startled Molly and she awoke with fright. What were her dreams, what were the climbing emotions that had been surprised and sent to hiding, leaving her shaky?

Bennett sat on the edge of the bed, his hairy back to her, the crack of his ass halfway buried in the bed by his weight, making his ass look small, almost childlike, beneath the man above it. He was bent to the telephone, the prime executive in conference and no doubt about it, in spite of his nakedness. Molly smiled, the instant of fright and shakiness gone. She reached out and drew little finger patterns on Bennett's side and lower back. He reached around, grasped her hand into stillness, then let it go. He was talking to someone about ten days. Molly sat up, entirely alert.

Bennett put the phone down. He remained with his back to her. The clock showed that it had only been about twenty minutes since they had reached their odd accord and slept.

Bennett turned to her, grinning. He cocked a leg on the bed so he could face her. The seeking and thrusting part drooped, withdrawn, its head down in embarrassment or sleep. That did not seem to bother him. He was all pride and masculinity, which was only natural after the pleasure she had given him. But he was *supercharged*. Molly saw that.

He said, "You people voted to go out. You voted to recommend that to your membership." He kissed her and Molly pushed him away hard and moved apart.

She looked up suddenly, but not at Bennett. It was as if something had caught her attention in the corner of the room, up where the ceiling met the intersection of the walls. "You son of a bitch," Molly said. She said each word distinctly and in a voice that was almost a whisper.

She got up from the bed. She went into the living room, picking up clothing as she went. When Bennett came in, barefoot but wearing slacks and a shirt hanging down outside, Molly was dressed. She glanced at him, but just barely, and then she walked around the room, pausing but not stopping, her arms folded and her hands in fists. It was as if she were bent on taking some rapid inventory of the contents of the room. She circled the room once, twice, a third time. Then she stopped, as if tired, spent from exertion. Her head was slightly bowed. She looked up, this time at Bennett and from across the room. "You bastard," she said. Her voice was pitched at a normal level.

She went to the door. Bennett followed her suddenly and held an open palm against the door and leant his weight against it so that Molly couldn't open it.

Molly faced her body at his. "You're fucking around with people's lives, you know that, Bennett? I *mean* that. People actually *die* because of people like you fucking around."

When Bennett spoke, Molly heard his anger plainly, heard the control that constricted his voice. "*You* wanted to have an impact on the system. I'm *having* an impact on the system."

"No. *You're* having an impact on the *patients.*"

"I'm trying to help them."

"No, you're the hospital, I remember your saying. You have a confusion of identities, Bennett. You're so wrapped up in your own manipulations. You're trying to help yourself. To all the goodies you can get. And if you fail and the hospital goes, no big deal, you'll be a hero downtown to some—gave those arrogant, elitist bastards what they deserve, what? and closed the hospital at the same time, good riddance and let's set old Bennett up in another nifty job, look what the sonofabitch has done for us at Back Bay Met." Molly reached up and took Bennett's hand off the door and opened it and said, "What Back Bay Met?" and went out into the corridor and pushed the button for the elevator. Bennett closed the door.

Warren Gates had been Tim's champion since the beginning of the custody struggle for Jason. Warren had always been objective in continued defeat and maintained empathy with Tim throughout. Tim recognized it as an exhausting intellectual and emotional commitment on Warren's part. But now his voice was not only cool, it was hostile. "The hearing is extraordinary, it's peremptory, and it's at your demand. But you're not going to be there."

"I told you. The patients. I—"

"Your Honor, my client the nurse can't be here to seek his son's protection because he's at work being a nurse. Judge Harrelson's going to fuck you, Tim. You're giving him every excuse."

"Taking care of people's lives—"

"Judge Harrelson didn't see it that way before, he's not going to see it that way now."

"Warren . . . *Christ* . . . Oh *shit* . . ."

"I hear ya, man. You've got to be there."

"I can't. I wouldn't be in this fucking trouble if I could be some goddamn simple soul who didn't care. Sometimes I wish I were brain-damaged, I—"

"I'm going to try to draw the judge's attention to the circumstances at Back Bay Met. I'm going to ask him for a continuance."

"Do you think you'll get it?"

"I don't think so. You asked for the hearing. It was scheduled to answer your complaint, Tim—"

"And Valerie's."

"You've got the psychiatrist we got for Jason scheduled, his teacher, someone from the Department of Social Services, your friend Audrey, their witnesses—"

"*What* witnesses? Witnesses to what?"

"I have no idea. I thought you could tell me. When you see them in court . . . A lot of people, Tim. You can't tell Judge Harrelson, Go ahead, start without me."

"I'm sick, Warren. I'm doing what I have to do, it's not what I *want* to do. I'm having a crazy thought. It's like those three shits fucked me too when they raped Nan."

"Don't forget the house officers' going out on you. Tim, I'll do the best I can for you. I'm afraid you're at the mercy of the court, though. And Flynn is certinly going to push the court to deal severely with your absence. I'll call you."

On Children's Seven, Jamaal was again extremely restless. Nancy, his vent nurse, asked Viola to get the visit. There was the unexplained fever. That, at least, accounted for the rest-lessness. But the fever responded only slightly and temporar-ily to medication. An ice blanket was effective, but the variations in temperature were produced too rapidly no matter how carefully it was adjusted. The unexplained weight gain continued. But what was most amazing was the continuing ability of Jamaal's lungs to function for minutes at a time without the assistance of the vent.

The visit had been sleeping somewhere in the hospital and he was rumpled and unshaven. He said, "I've got this and my daytime practice. I forgot what it was like to be a house officer." He examined Jamaal and reviewed the charts.

"It's the restlessness," Nancy said. "Sometimes he's thrashing."

"I don't want to give him anything more to control that. Not with the positive signs we're getting. I could fine-tune some of the medication, I suppose, but I don't really want to do that. I want to leave him alone." He looked at Nancy. "Unless you have something specific in mind."

"No. I see it the way you do. I'm concerned about the thrashing."

"I don't want to address that till we know more about it."

140

TRINA AWOKE shivering. She had heard a voice in pain, a crying out. She listened to the silence in her room. Her own voice? Her face was wet, her pillowcase was wet. She felt herself crying. Hal Levy had been so close in the dream, so near, his kind, studious eyes caring for her, and then she understood that he was dead and there were snakes trying to kill her, slithering across the floor from Olivia.

Trina lay still, though her body was shaking. Grief, despondency . . . no, *depression*. She wanted to call Nicholas Prudhomme. She wanted to be *close* to someone. But it was after three in the morning. The very, oh so very, needful child in her wanted to call Nick for his comfort, his protection . . . Daddy, Mommy.

Trina sat up and turned on the light. The *adult* could use some tender loving care too, she thought. Shut up, kid, she said to her pain and need, the big person's making the decision. No calling Nick.

She sat up for a few minutes and listened to the two voices in her head, one patient, the other therapist. Together they worked on it, didn't work it all out, but reduced it. Trina got herself a dry pillowcase. She had a little night left, a little sleep left, and she could rest even if sleep wouldn't return. She felt secure with herself. She was glad she was going to have the benefit of the shrink at the General.

* * *

Toward dawn Audrey awoke feeling weepy but without tears.
She was furious at Betty Bowen as well. She had been
dreaming about speaking for Betty, arguing that no additional
support be given to continue Betty's life. She had been putting
Betty's case, but to herself she was putting Betty to death.
She was furious at Betty for making her death's advocate.

Audrey looked at the clock. Five-ten. Just when the music
would have begun to get her out of bed. But the clock-radio
was silent.

She remembered then. She had the day off. She was going
to court as a witness for Tim. Ten days from tomorrow she
would not have to go to work either. It felt so good she did
not feel weepy anymore or angry at Betty. She had two more
hours to sleep. But she could not fall asleep. Finally she got
up, too uneasy to remain in bed.

Molly arrived very early, but instead of going into the hospital, she went across the street. She stood there alone. Tremaine
Avenue was empty—no cars, no pedestrians. The morning
was warm, but Molly felt chilly and vulnerable. There was a
gray sky and low gray clouds that did not seem to move. It
was almost six-thirty.

Molly wondered if Bennett was up there in his perch
looking down, waiting to count heads, waiting to see what the
will of the nurses might be this morning—as Molly was—and
what it might bode for the strike vote scheduled for the next
morning.

Job action, Molly thought, *job action, job action*. Not
strike. Labor action, sympathy—

"Waiting for the troops?" Selma said.

Molly turned to her. "Yes." Both of them wore white
dresses. Selma carried a raincoat over her arm.

"I thought I'd have a look, too," Selma said. She looked
up and down the avenue as Molly had. "It's strange like this.
Nothing at all."

"Not even the HOs. I thought they were picketing twenty-
four hours."

"I think they've got the hearing on their minds. Or getting
some rest. Some of them may be going to jail today."

"I hope not."

"Some of us may have to go, too. Next week. Depending
on what this morning brings. And the vote tomorrow."

"We'll know about the vote tomorrow in a few minutes."

"That's what I figured, too."

There was a silence that was unusual for both of them until Molly said, "I feel lonely out here."

"Don't worry. There'll be others along." But Selma held her arms to herself anyway.

"It's being apart from that," Molly said, inclining her head toward the hospital. "Out here away from it. Separate. I feel like it's shutting me out."

"You can walk across the street anytime."

"I know that."

"Feels like walking out on your family?"

"Yes, that's it exactly. Doing my job for me, Selma?"

"Since you're not doing it for yourself." Selma looked down and rubbed the sole of her white shoe against the pavement. "I feel the same way. I recognize the symptoms."

Molly nodded. Then she caught herself glancing up at the glass exterior of Bennett's office.

Selma looked up, too. "No fun, huh?" Selma said.

"None."

At twenty of seven other nurses began arriving, Day among the first.

"You could have slept a little later," Selma said.

"I always get here at this time."

"If you're not crossing the street, you could have slept a little later."

"I'm not crossing the street. I always get here at this time."

Selma nodded.

"Morning," Coralee said. She looked at Day. "I'll save you time. The answer is no, yes, maybe."

"What's the question?" Day said.

"It's after you look at your master sheets. Will I do a double?"

It was a quarter of seven. Some of the nurses stood in groups now. Others lined up along the curb, Audrey one of them. She felt removed from the nurses she stood with. She was a temporary now, not one of them.

"Uh-oh," Midge Kelly said. "Unwanted visitor." Molly and Selma turned to look. "Lynn Keating is among us."

"She's got a tape recorder in that shoulder bag," Molly said. "The mike is that pin she's wearing."

Keating came over and spoke to Molly. "Bennett Chessoff's a sonofabitch, don't you think?" She smiled and waited. Molly smiled back at her and said nothing. "Don't you think?" Keating said to Selma. Selma walked away. "*Ah*," Keating said, and made her way to Diana Vezzina. "Now that things are going the way you wanted, you must feel good. This was all really your idea, wasn't it?"

"My colleagues will reach a decision tomorrow. I'll do what they decide."

"Of course, if one of you could get off alone with a house officer again, that would cinch it, wouldn't it?"

Diana looked at Lynn Keating and then hit her on the side of the face with her fist. Keating was struck backward against another nurse and waved her arms and moved her feet to keep her balance. When she had herself still again she smoothed her skirt and said, "That's a criminal offense." Diana shrugged and turned toward the hospital.

There were enough nurses now so that they jostled each other at the curb as they waited. Foot police had taken positions on the other side of the street. Two cruisers drew up in front of the hospital.

Selma was making her way back to Molly. She was surprised to find Margaret Gaines waiting with the others. Margaret said, "I'm not saying I'll strike. But I'll wait here till the others go over."

Selma went on to Molly. "You don't have to feel so down. You haven't left yet."

"Yes, I have."

"Really?"

"Inside me I have."

Molly found Liz Swanzey next to her. Liz grinned. "I didn't think people would stand together like this. Not till after the vote, anyway."

"This is the vote," Molly said.

Bennett had been watching from his office as the nurses began assembling. No nurse entered the hospital, no nurse crossed the street. By five of seven there was a band of white from corner to corner opposite the hospital. The band was fringed and irregular near the storefronts, straight and unmoving at curbside. From above there was a physical stillness to the assembly that seemed unnatural. Bennett saw policemen consulting with each other, then a cruiser drew up and another one. The officers remained inside the cruisers while a sergeant came over, ducked down, and spoke to each pair in turn. At three minutes before seven, the band of white broke and the nurses began crossing the avenue. From Bennett's office it looked like a flood of white water in slow motion.

Word had gotten around on the floors. The nurses had to deal with an unaccustomed reaction in this hospital: patient hostility. Among the elderly there were feelings of despair and despondency. Everywhere there were accusations of abandonment and falseness. Some of Viola's children cried. Leaving Pedi if the nurses went out would be like the loss of home, of parent, of protection. Some of the elderly on Selma's floor cried as well. But common to all the patients was anger at the nurses. There had been anxiety when the house officers went out. Now the nurses quickly understood that they were being seen by the patients as malevolent.

141

PROMPTLY AT nine-thirty the Massachusetts Supreme Judicial Court, Judge Gardner McIninch presiding, solicited testimony as to whether or not the Back Bay Metropolitan Hospital house officers had complied with its order and returned to work. Counsel for the house officers renewed argument that it had never been demonstrated that the house officers *had* left work. Judge McIninch dismissed the argument and found ARI as a legal entity and each of its individual members in contempt of court. He instituted fines.

McGettigan, Rounds, Wills, and some other ARI officers stood before him as he said, ''This court is not without understanding of the reasons for the action you have taken. We are not without understanding that you will need to consult with your membership at this juncture. I am advised that Back Bay Metropolitan Hospital has sufficient physician staffing for this weekend because of the presence of its attending physicians. I wish to be informed reliably on Sun-

day, before twelve-thirty in the afternoon, that each of you
and the entire membership of your association has returned to
work by Sunday noon." He paused. "Or Monday morning it
is going to be the unpleasant obligation of this court to start
sending each of you and your colleagues in this matter to
prison. I hope someone has advised you of the conditions you
may expect to encounter if you choose to take the road of
incarceration."

142

ALL PARTIES INTERESTED in the matter of *Holbrook v. Holbrook*
were summoned to the courtroom before Judge Andrew
Harrelson a few minutes before ten. All parties save Timothy
Holbrook were present.

"ICU Five, Tim."

"Tim, it's Warren."

"Yeah, Warren, go ahead."

"How are things on the unit? I need a few minutes."

"Things are quiet. What is it, Warren? It doesn't sound
good."

"It's not good. I want you to hear what the judge said.
Then we'll talk."

"Go ahead."

"You were the only one who wasn't here. Harrelson called
Flynn and me into chambers. His mood was very negative,
Tim. He said he's sick and tired of these cases coming back
to court after the judge has issued an order. He said it's
always the dissatisfied parties who drag their children through
the muck and mire."

Tim felt a chill around his body. He had had to expect this
response from Judge Harrelson, but he was not prepared for
it.

"The judge said he's going to put an end to this one. He
said he's going to dismiss this case with prejudice and rule
that there shall be no further challenge to custody unless an
independent agency substantiates actual harm to the child—"

"But *there*, DSS, the Fifty-one-A—"

"Hold on till I've finished. I pointed out to the judge that the court can't cut off rights to challenge, that custody issues are expected to be ongoing in front of the court at any time.

"He said, 'Your client dragged this one back here. Then he doesn't have the decency to appear. It's a purely frivolous action on his part—' "

"Didn't you tell him about the hospital, the unit, the situation?"

"Tim, I'm trying to *inform* my client. Now listen. The judge said, 'Mr. Holbrook's absence signifies to me that he is fearful of the allegations brought by Mrs. Holbrook.'

"Tim, the judge is giving serious consideration to Flynn's motion to grant an uncontested hearing on the issue of visitation. If he did that, he would rule entirely on the basis of Valerie's pleading."

"Oh Christ."

"You knew the possibility. We discussed it—"

"I thought you could get a continuance, I didn't think . . . Deep down I didn't think it could get real, not with the situation we have here, not with people's lives—"

"Tim, listen. I reminded the judge of his test—substantiation of harm from an independent agency. I said we would present as expert witness an assessment person from the Department of Social Services. I asked him please not to dismiss or rule until he'd heard that testimony. Flynn said if the father couldn't bother to attend the hearing, why bother? Harrelson agreed with Flynn on that.

"What we have now, Tim, is this. You present yourself in court to Judge Harrelson at four o'clock this afternoon. Not a moment later. No excuses. You can't afford to get run down by a car, you can't afford to become the victim of an act of God. I mean that. Harrelson has no patience with you. He had very little before and he has none now. I just want you to understand that thoroughly. That's why I've gone into all this detail."

"I understand."

"He's letting the assessment person be heard and that's all you can expect of him. He can cut it off there if he wants to, if he decides that harm to Jason isn't demonstrated. He can cut it off there because of your failure to appear this morning. As far as he's concerned, he's doing you a favor hearing the one witness."

0

143

NICHOLAS PRUDHOMME'S manner with Nan was entirely different from that of the assistant district attorney the day before.
He was concerned and sympathetic. When it was necessary to
call into question or challenge details of Nan's narrative, he
did so without innuendo and derision.

He sat at his desk with a legal pad in front of him and made
careful notes, page after page, with a fountain pen. Nan
found that and his solemn regard for what she told him deeply
reassuring. His manner took away some of her feelings of
hopelessness and helplessness. The specificity of some of his
questions when he interrupted gave her encouragement that
had the potency of an antidepressive drug.

"But Casey was scared that you'd charge him with rape.
He actually said that?"

"Yes."

Prudhomme wrote it down carefully, black ink on the
yellow paper.

Trina sat to the side without comment. Nick's jacket hung
on a wire hanger on a clothestree. She was charmed again
that he wore suspenders.

When he was finished, Nicholas said, "Thank you, Nan. I
know talking to me has been an ordeal for you. We ought to
have more women on this staff. We certainly ought to have
women available for other women." He gently shook the
yellow pages together against the desktop and set them down.
"Your memory for detail is invaluable. Your honesty is
extraordinary. You'll be a fine witness."

"Just a witness," Nan said. "As if it didn't happen to
me."

Nicholas sighed. "Legal terminology is not always sensitive to its subject. That you're the victim, as well as a
witness, I have no doubt. But it's up to the court to decide
that you're the victim, and of what, and to what extent.
That's what the trial will be about. In the meantime you're a
witness. Until the crime has been established."

"Is there a doubt?" Nan asked. She felt that her voice hardly got out of her body.

"There is always a doubt about any alleged crime. That's why we have courts. We just don't know a better way."

"You . . . have reservations," Nan said. "I could tell. When you were making notes."

"Reservations about what?"

"When I got to the part about Squires. And after that." Nan looked at the ADA directly.

"I said your observation was keen. It is." He glanced at Trina.

"You'd rather not tell me about it," Nan said, "but I insist. Don't look to Trina. *I'm* your client."

Nicholas nodded. His expression was mournful. "It might turn out to be tough to get a conviction. Due . . . because you assisted the last of your attackers. And you told them it was okay, good, and so on. I know why you did it. I will do my utmost to demonstrate your reasons, your *thinking*, in court. We'll back it up with psychiatric testimony. But because of everything you did to ensure your survival, it might be difficult to get a conviction. Because it could be made to appear that you assisted them and then thanked them for a good time. That, of course, is the appearance. It's not what happened. But that's what the defense will make it out to be."

"Is it . . . isn't anyone going to . . . is this just going to happen to me?" Suddenly Nan said, "It's a whole male world! *Men* did it to me, a *man's* telling me he can't do anything about it, *men* are going to decide about it and forget about it, *and it happened to me!*"

Nan sat still, her eyes closed, and cried. Her control was more horrifying than her anguish. She would not respond to Trina. Abruptly the control imposed itself over all the other emotions and Nan stopped crying. She sat straight and looked at Nicholas.

He looked back at Nan and spoke to her as if there had been no emotional interruption. "If this radio fellow, Squires, if he'll cooperate, justice will be done."

Trina said, "It sounds like he feels so guilty, so eager to expiate—"

"Sure. Then he lives with the guilt awhile and it starts diminishing. He talks to his pals. All of a sudden it comes to Squires—*they* got raped, the three of *them* got raped. Enticed.

Invited. That's when the insurance Nan got herself to save her life turns against her." He sat back and looked at Nan and spoke to her softly. "It's easy to become a lost soul in this system, very easy for a rape victim. I do not want you to become a lost soul, Nan. I *personally* do not want to see that happen. I will do my utmost to see that that does not happen."

144

SELMA WAS ABLE to leave Med Seven a little after three-thirty. She called ahead to Molly and they met in Molly's office in the New Wing and then went up to Bennett's office. There was no waiting. Bennett's executive secretary took them in immediately.

The office, like the Gold Coast, seemed to belong to another hospital entirely.

Bennett said, "You know Howard Sylvus."

"You asked for an informal meeting, Bennett," Molly said. "*Informal* does not suggest the presence of Management's counsel."

"I want Howard to have an accurate perception of our exchange."

"Then keep accurate notes, Bennett. As you can see, we are not accompanied by counsel. We have no intent of meeting with Management's counsel without our own. If you'll permit me a personal observation, Bennett, this is a shitty maneuver on your part."

"Molly, I plead innocent. I just thought it would be in everyone's interests if Howard heard what's going on at the same time I do."

"That's why you didn't suggest we bring our own counsel? To hear you at the same time we—"

"Howard isn't even going to say—"

"That's right. He's not going to be here or we're not going to be here."

Bennett looked at Molly and said, "Lady keeps threatening to leave. One place or another."

"Bennett, Howard's presence is just another one of your

acts of manipulation. Don't you know your manipulation is about to shut this hospital down?''

"That's what we're here to discuss."

"Without Howard Sylvus," Selma said.

"I'm sorry, Howard," Bennett said.

"I'll wait outside," Sylvus said.

"No offense," Molly said.

"None taken," Sylvus said. He left and closed the door.

"I'd say you handled that very well," Bennett said to Molly.

"It's not for you to say."

"It bodes well for a legal career."

"Ahem," Selma said, drawing the word out. "If I may remind all those present? We are here as employee and Management. I think it's cute the way you two go at your differences," she said without smiling, "but I'm too tired for entertainment. Get to it, Bennett, please, whatever it is."

"Sit down?" Molly and Selma sat on the white couch, Bennett in a chair at one end. "I'm informed NSA intends to go out."

"That has not been concluded formally yet," Selma said. "There are bylaws that have to be satisfied, a meeting with sufficient notice, proxies delivered—"

"Yes, yes. You're holding the ceremony tomorrow morning. At ten A.M."

"We hardly need be here, do we?" Molly said.

"Your executive committee is drawing up a list of grievances and a recommendation to strike. That needs to be ratified by your membership. I should like to know the nature of the grievances."

"You mean that the mayor would like to know the nature of the grievances," Molly said.

"It would not surprise me if he had an interest."

"Bennett, you met with him this morning. Then you asked for this meeting. You called from City Hall."

"How did you know that?" He was genuinely curious.

"The mayor is getting edgy," Molly said. "I suppose you didn't tell him that you want him that way."

Bennett said to Selma, "There are a lot of people down in City Hall who want to close this place down. If the nurses go out, they may do it. I'd just like to know what the issues are. Yes, the mayor would like to know. It's a shambles for everyone if this hospital gets closed."

"Essentially patient issues. The same as the HOs'. Some
exempted, some restricted, some added. The ones that belong
to nurses, those are the issues."

"You're legally forbidden to strike. Your contract specifies
it. Your members ratified that contract. You can be fined, go
to jail, the same as the HOs, if you strike."

"No," Molly said. "The contract between NSA and the
City of Boston is null and void and went up in smoke about
an hour after it was signed. It was never honored by
Management."

"Molly, that's an allegation that's not going to give a
strike any sanction."

Molly was glad to see that Bennett was taking notes. "I'll give
you one example. Short-staffing. Regularly and recurrently."

Bennett smiled. "That is part of the tradition of the hospital."

Molly did not smile. "When one side breaches a contract,
the other side does not have to perform. That is one of the
remedies of contracts, Bennett. Contracts are bilateral. Both
parties have to perform. If either party refuses to perform, the
other party may also refuse to perform. As you say, the
Management of this hospital has a tradition of not performing. The Nursing Services Alliance is not going to strike. It's
not even going to get involved in a sympathy labor action—
though, of course, we all thought that was the course NSA
intended to take. No, indeed, Director. There is no contract
between NSA and the City of Boston. NSA is simply going to
exercise its right of anticipatory repudiation."

145

NAN WAS AFRAID to return to her own apartment. But she was
too uncomfortable staying with her cousin and her cousin's
husband. She did not want to be with anyone. It was difficult
to be with herself, but it was excruciating being with others.

A taxi took her to her building. She fumbled with the
money for the driver, fumbled with her keys, and dropped
them when she was outside her own door. She felt that the
apartment was vulnerable, that she would be vulnerable in

there, that *the others*, Davis and his friends, might come for her there, might already be there.

But when she opened the door there was silence and stillness. She was afraid to close the door behind herself, afraid to leave it open. She checked her room, the closet, the kitchen and bath. Then she closed the door. She took two steps away from the door and then stood unmoving.

When the telephone rang she had not moved for several minutes. She raised the phone to her ear but said nothing.

"Nan? *Nan?*"

It was Oren. She had nothing to say to him. She wished he hadn't called. She was angry at him for some reason.

"Nan. Nan, please. It's me, Oren . . . Nan, that *is* you, isn't it?"

Nan found herself shaking her head, *No*.

"Nan, please just tell me it's you, that I'm talking to *you*."

"Yes."

"I know what happened. I'm here for you. I'm here to help. I just want you to know I want to help."

Nan was shaking her head, *No*, again.

"Nan, I've been trying you and trying you. I'm at work now. But I'll leave. Can I come over?"

"No, please don't."

"Nan, I want to help. *Please* let me come over."

"No. No. Please, please don't." She carefully set the receiver down. She felt oddly unburdened.

146

ELIN'S GRIEF would not leave her alone, not even for a few minutes' sleep, though she was desperately tired. She was glad to go back to the hospital, glad of anything with which to occupy herself. And so she went to the hospital, though she did not have to, during the afternoon. For once she welcomed all the paperwork that was waiting in her office.

But when she got to the hospital, she did not go to her office. She saw Trevor Davis waiting for an elevator in the lobby of the New Wing and she went over and stood with the other people waiting. The elevator was large enough and deep enough to accommodate two gurneys. Ten or twelve people got on with Elin, Trevor among them. Trevor ignored Elin. There were no other medical people. When the elevator came to its first stop, Elin flipped the emergency stop toggle before the doors could open.

"Excuse me," Elin said, facing the other passengers. "I'm a nurse on the staff here and I'd like to point out a pathological curiosity to you." Elin had no idea why she was doing what she was doing. But she knew it would be satisfying. "We have a celebrity with us. The fellow in back." People turned their heads. "Trevor Davis. The noted rapist. How's that, Trevor? Not the noted doctor, not the noted surgeon— the noted rapist." Elin smiled at her audience, the briefest smile, and then her face returned to the deepest sadness. Had it not been for that sadness, she might have frightened the other passengers.

"We're in a hospital," she said. "I may be keeping some of you from appointments. Forgive me." She opened the door. There were others outside waiting for the elevator, including two physicians and a lab technician in white. Three of the women in the elevator got off, but then remained outside and watched.

Elin flipped the toggle switch to Stop again.

"I have to go up to the director's office," Trevor said. "I have to collect my records."

"The noted rapist. It won't be *Dr*. Davis much longer. I really don't think so, Trevor. No status, Trevor. I think you've always enjoyed people's pain. But now you won't have a license for it, will you, Trevor."

The other passengers had drawn away from him. There was room for him to walk away. But Elin seemed to have pinned him with her eyes. "I see you're angry, Trevor. Furious. But I have a consoling thought for you. Maybe you haven't lost everything after all, Trevor. Maybe they'll let you be an orderly in prison—do you think so?"

Elin switched the emergency toggle so that the elevator would run as she got off.

147

TIM GOT TO COURT at twenty minutes before four, immediately after the shift change. Warren Gates took him to a small consultation room and closed the door. He placed his attaché case on the table and sat down.

"I know how you feel toward Judge Harrelson, but I want you to be unfailingly correct with him."

"I will be."

"There is to be no sign of rancor toward Valerie or her attorney. Your conduct is to be exemplary. The conduct of a father who would be a fit role model for a boy."

"I understand."

"When you take the stand, I want you to apologize to Judge Harrelson for your absence this morning. I think you can include Valerie and her attorney and the other witnesses in that apology. I want you to explain that there was a critical need for you at the hospital. If necessary I will establish the nature of your professional expertise. But that will be later. First you apologize, then you explain, then you thank His Honor for rescheduling the hearing."

"All right."

"Remember, you've broken this man's order. He doesn't like you for that one bit, quite aside from his aversion to males who are nurses and litigants who don't show up for their hearings. We have two objectives here, and I now don't know which one ought to take precedence. One is to transfer custody from Valerie to you. The other is to protect the visitation rights you already have. Judge Harrelson could rewrite the original decree entirely in Valerie's favor. He could take away all your visitation rights. He could even issue a restraining order preventing you from visiting Jason at school. He could cut you off."

"I never get used to it. It's always unbelievable. That I could lose Jason—"

"If you'd believed a little more, you would've been here this morning. This judge has already taken Jason away from

you about ninety percent." He stood up. "We'll get in there
a few minutes early. Oh, I forgot. Valerie's motion that you
be found in contempt. It also asks that you be 'chastised
accordingly.' That could mean a slap on the wrist. Or it could
mean a fine or a jail term or both. So there's yet a third
objective. Keeping you out of jail."

"The first two take precedence."

"If he sends you to jail, that's not going to matter a fig.
He's a narrow old bastard, as you know. You haven't just
found fault with Valerie, you've besmirched motherhood in
its entirety." Warren looked at Tim. "Don't be hopeful,
Tim. I thought things were going to look better than they do
now. Our position of concern for Jason got undercut by your
going to the hospital this morning. It doesn't matter too much
what we say. You know that from the last time. Judge
Harrelson can hear hours and hours of testimony, and when
it's all over and he hands down the decree, it's as if he hadn't
heard a word from our side."

148

OUTSIDE THE COURTROOM, Tim nodded to the psychiatrist and to
the woman from the Department of Social Services. He put
his hand on Audrey's shoulder and squeezed gently. They all
went in.

Valerie and her lawyer were already seated at a table facing
the bench. Tim and Warren took seats at the other table.
Tim's witnesses took places in the spectator seating area. The
doorman from Valerie's building was seated behind Valerie
and Flynn. Valerie looked over at Tim and said, "Nice of
you to bother to come."

They waited till a few minutes after four and then the
bailiff entered. Before he could say "All rise," Valerie stood
and shouted at Tim, *"Why did you take my child?"* Judge
Harrelson was just entering.

The other people in the courtroom got to their feet. Judge
Harrelson seated himself with no acknowledgment. The bailiff said, "You may be seated." He announced the names and

numbers that identified the case. Judge Harrelson looked at Tim.
The judge was physically narrow. His white hair was trimmed
close in a crew cut. His face was dark from outdoor activity
and his eyes were steady and, Tim thought, condemnatory.

"Mr. Gates," Harrelson said, "in regard to the allegations
made by Mrs. Holbrook, is there any argument?"

Warren rose. "Your Honor, for purposes of expediting the
hearing, we'll stipulate that, generally, the allegations are
substantially accurate. Mr. Holbrook removed Jason Holbrook
from Mrs. Holbrook's apartment at around three-thirty in the
morning of Saturday last. Mr. Holbrook has retained the
minor child in his custody since that time."

"Very well. We'll hear the assessment person from DSS.
It is understood that the hearing may be concluded after that
testimony."

"Yes, Your Honor." Warren sat down.

The investigative social worker's Fifty-one-A was entered
into evidence, then she was questioned about her background,
her methods, her interviews, and the thoroughness and fair-
ness of her procedures in so short a time. The social worker
reported repeated neglect "so as to endanger the child" on
the part of Mrs. Holbrook.

Flynn said, "Can you offer the court any instances of
actual harm befalling the child?"

"No. There is a strong likelihood."

"But no actual harm."

"Psychological harm."

"But no physical harm."

Flynn turned to Warren. "You may inquire."

As Warren proceeded, Tim felt discontented. Whether or
not the hearing even continued depended upon the assessment
person's testimony, and all Warren was doing was having her
repeat testimony she had already given: instances of neglect
that jeopardized the safety of the child.

Finally Warren broke from that line. "No doubt there is
significant psychological injury to a child left alone repeat-
edly in such circumstances—"

"Objection," Flynn said, rising. "The witness is not competent to make a psychological assessment of Jason."

"Sustained."

Warren said, "If it please the court, we are prepared to
offer expert testimony as to the extent of psychological injury

done the child. We will need the opportunity of presenting our expert witness.''

"Have you finished with this witness, Mr. Gates?''

"Yes, Your Honor.''

"Mr. Flynn?''

Flynn re-elicited the testimony that there was no evidence of physical harm done to Jason. "Thank you,'' Flynn said to the witness.

"You may step down,'' the judge said.

Warren wrote for Tim: *This is it. This is where he decides whether to let this go on. Or dismiss us.*

Flynn rose to his feet. His tone suggested that he was bored and that the judge must be bored as well. "Your Honor, I submit that after the thorough investigation by the Department of Social Services, nothing of substance has been offered here that would conceivably indicate that harm has been done to the child by his own mother.'' He paused and looked at Tim. "I submit that the only matters of merit remaining before the court are Mrs. Holbrook's motions to modify the original decree and to find Mr. Holbrook in contempt.'' His concluding tone suggested compassion for the judge in his travail.

Judge Harrelson nodded. "Thank you, Mr. Flynn.'' He looked down at the material before him. At the motions to modify and for contempt, Tim thought. *How can he take Jason away from me? Take him away completely?*

"Mr. Flynn,'' the judge said, looking up at the attorney, "I'd like to satisfy myself in regard to Mrs. Holbrook's behavior last Friday night and Saturday morning. If there's no objection, I'd like her sworn now.''

"No objection, Your Honor.''

He looked at Warren. Warren stood up partway and said, "None.''

Valerie took the stand and stated that it had been her intention to return home by ten that evening, eleven at the very, very latest, but that a series of obstacles and misfortunes had occurred. A watch that wasn't working properly. A cab company that just didn't answer the phone, another cab company that promised to send a cab and after an hour it still hadn't come and she discovered it hadn't even been dispatched. A third cab company whose driver was drunk or on drugs so she had gotten out and walked back to her friend's place. But she was locked out there for twenty minutes or half an hour before she could rouse him. And so on. She smiled at the judge as she recounted the outlandish occurrences that had prevented her from getting home to Jason at ten o'clock. Her smile at the judge said, *You understand*. The judge nodded.

"When I got home and discovered that my child had been *kidnapped*—"

"Objection."

"I'll allow it."

"When I discovered my little boy had been *kidnapped*—" She placed her head in her hands. "It was the worst moment of my life." She looked up. "I was in despair. I was terrified." She looked at the judge. "My little boy taken away by a man whose moral posture in society . . ." She looked at Tim. "I mean, his morality is open to speculation." She looked back at the judge. "I was terrified."

"You may inquire," Flynn said.

"Thank you," Warren said, getting up. "I'm pleased that this little symphony of despair has reached its coda."

"Objection."

"Sustained. Mr. Gates, you will refrain from characterizing the witness' testimony. At this time, certainly."

"I find the chain of events that you say prevented you from returning to Jason at a decent hour, Mrs. Holbrook, I find that chain of events extremely unlikely. It's the stuff of old radio sitcoms."

"Objection."

"Mr. Gates, I will not ask you again."

"Very well, Your Honor. Mrs. Holbrook, you went out at about what time?"

"I was called for at seven."

"Your friend had a car?"

"We rode with other people."

"So, commencing at seven-thirty, you left Jason alone and unprotected while you went out on a date from which you did not return until nearly four A.M."

"He wasn't unprotected. The apartment has locks. It's a good apartment building. Jason is a grownup boy. He's mature. He can take care of himself. I've taught him to be self-reliant."

"You just referred to Jason as 'my *little* boy.' He's six years old, I believe."

"Nearly seven."

"A *mature* six, Mrs. Holbrook?" Valerie looked at the judge but he said nothing. Warren went on. "Mrs. Holbrook, when you were unable to return home at ten o'clock, at eleven, twelve, one, two, three in the morning, why did you not call Jason?"

"Oh, but I did."

"It is my understanding, Mrs. Holbrook, that Jason received no telephone call from you that night at all."

"Objection. Counsel is not testifying."

Judge Harrelson said, "I don't want to bring the child into court. I'll hear it. For now. I am aware of the bias."

"Mrs. Holbrook, Jason has told me—"

"Objection."

"I'll hear it. For now."

"I assure you that Jason will tell this court if he is asked to do so that he received no communication from you that evening, that night, or in the black hours of the morning when he was so terribly frightened. And alone."

"I *tried* to call him. But the line was busy. Always busy. I think he left the phone off the hook . . . I found a receiver off the hook when I got home . . . Maybe he tried to call one of his little friends."

"This is strange, Mrs. Holbrook. We will present eyewitness testimony from three people that the telephone receiver was in its cradle when Mr. Holbrook, Jason, and the doorman left your apartment. Would you like to reconsider your testimony?"

"The line was busy. Whenever I called. The receiver was off the hook when I got home."

"Well now, Mrs. Holbrook, you found it impossible to reach your son."

"Yes."

"Didn't it occur to you to call a neighbor?"

"Well . . ."

"Didn't it occur to you to call a neighbor?"

"I think I tried. A couple of times. I guess they were out."

"Till three-thirty in the morning?"

"I don't know. I don't keep track of them."

"The gentleman sitting in the third row behind your counsel's table. He is the doorman who was on duty at your apartment building that night. Isn't that so?"

"Yes. He is. He was. He's here to say that Tim Holbrook took Jason from my apartment."

"He is also here under subpoena. Mrs. Holbrook, when you were unable to reach Jason by telephone or get in touch with neighbors, did it not occur to you to call the doorman? Have him look in on Jason? Reassure Jason? See that he was all right? Safe?"

"I don't have a number for the doorman."

"I would think it would be important, when you leave your child alone at night, to have the telephone number of the building where you have left him."

Valerie's attorney did not call the doorman.

Warren presented Tim. Then he called the doorman himself. Then the psychiatrist who had interviewed Jason and Tim.

"Did you call Mrs. Holbrook and identify yourself and your work and offer her the opportunity of meeting with you?"

"I did. I offered her several opportunities. I offered her the opportunity of selecting her own time."

"And?"

"She declined to meet with me."

"You have an associate."

"Dr. Elaine Hamlish. She has a Ph.D. in clinical psychology and fourteen years of experience. She also spent a considerable amount of time with Jason. Her report runs some twenty pages."

Warren picked it up from the table. "Is this Dr. Hamlish's report?" He handed it to the psychiatrist.

"It is."

"I'd like to enter it, Your Honor."

It was marked and entered. Judge Harrelson looked annoyed. The psychiatrist's testimony took forty minutes. The stenographer was on overtime. The bailiff was on overtime. The court was in extended session, nearing six o'clock. Tim Was uncomfortably aware that it was because he had failed to appear in the morning.

At the conclusion of the psychiatrist's testimony, Judge Harrelson said, "I am not much impressed with psychiatric gibberish. But where psychiatric testimony addresses itself to fact rather than theory and speculation, the facts cannot be ignored. Dr. Thundstrom has testified that Jason is upset, that

he feels himself to be uncared for in the domicile of his
mother . . .'' He looked at his notes and then peered at his
courtroom with suspicion and perhaps anger. ''Testified that
Jason has demonstrated a clear preference for having his
home with his male parent.''

Flynn rose. ''Your Honor, we know no such thing.''

The judge looked at Valerie's attorney and said, ''I am
summarizing Dr. Thundstrom's testimony.''

''Thank you, Your Honor.''

''The Department of Social Services, in testimony given
here together with the Fifty-one-A entered with this court, *has*
established that there have been periods of parental neglect on
the part of Mrs. Holbrook.

''Be that so, nevertheless, this court is not infallible and, I
hope, harbors no pretension of infallibility. The court may
err. Be that so, it has been the policy of this court to err—*if*
an error is to be made—it has been the policy of this court to
err on the conservative side, on the side of custom and
tradition.

''Counsel may approach the bench.''

The two lawyers rose and went to the judge. They stood
before and beneath him and he leaned forward and they
whispered.

The judge got up. The bailiff said, ''All rise,'' and the
judge left the courtroom through the door beside the bench.

Warren came back to Tim and began stuffing his notes and
documents into his attaché case. ''C'mon. The judge is going
to hear the rest of this in chambers.''

''What does that mean?''

''It means the judge wants to know a considerable amount
about your private life.'' He went to the bar between the
spectators' area and the court. ''Audrey? Going to need you
inside.'' He said to Tim quietly, ''What's going to happen
next is outrageous. Keep your cool.''

149

IT WAS GROTESQUELY familial, Tim thought. The old judge, the fucking family arbiter. The former wife. The mistress, lover. The two professional adversaries, the uncles, who sometimes even referred to each other as "brother."

The judge sat behind his desk, still looking stern in his robes. "Well, Mr. Holbrook, you've managed to put together a case. And yet. As I found necessary to observe when you last appeared before me, Mr. Holbrook, your occupation is clearly an unusual one for a male. Would you agree to that?"

"It's becoming less so."

"Society still regards it as unusual. Would you agree to that?"

"Yes."

"It's as if you had a change of life on the occasion of the birth of your son. That aspect troubles me. Would you agree to that? A change of life at that time?"

"I discovered what was most important to me, Your Honor. What my values are.

"Jason is most important to me. After that, I want to take care of people. I want to be helping, not just working at a job the way I was before."

"Yet you found it necessary to put your occupation before your son this morning."

"I hoped I'd explained that inside, Your Honor. It was an obligation to my patients. A professional obligation. Two of my patients are in critical condition. The best of them are in poor condition. I'm the head nurse on that unit."

The judge looked away. "It would be . . . inappropriate . . . for the court to question you on . . . intimate matters about which neither counsel has inquired. Still, homosexuality is socially recognized as having a detrimental effect. I am thinking, in this case, of the effect upon children. Of the role model. There is, too, the possibility of sexual abuse."

Tim found himself ready to go and strike the judge. *"Keep your cool,"* he heard Warren cautioning him in his mind.

"It is therefore, no matter how painful to all concerned, including this court . . . It is therefore *incumbent* upon this court to inquire after the presence, possible presence, of immoral conduct." He looked at Tim. "And so I am compelled to ask questions of a personal nature. Mr. Holbrook, are you now engaged in a sexual liaison with anyone?"

"Yes, Your Honor."

"Male or female?"

"Female."

"Have you ever been engaged in a homosexual liaison?"

"No, Your Honor." Tim received a glance from Warren. He kept his cool.

"Your . . . lovemate," the judge said. "Is she present in chambers?"

"Yes, Your Honor."

The judge looked annoyed. "Would you *identify* her, please? By *name*.

Audrey thought that Harrelson was being humiliating to Tim and especially to herself.

"Miss Rosenfeld," Tim said. "Audrey Rosenfeld."

Judge Harrelson swung his chair to look at Audrey. "Again I am compelled to ask a question of a personal nature. Miss Rosenfeld, do you have sexual intercourse with Mr. Holbrook?"

"Yes."

"Does he acquit himself as a man?"

"Yes." Then she repeated, *"Yes."*

"Thank you." He looked over toward a window. He continued to gaze at the window as he said, "I am reminded of the day of John Kennedy's assassination. I was conducting a jury trial. It had been going on for some days. There were multiple litigants and three insurance companies involved as well as counsel and assistant counsel to everyone. I learned of the President's death just as the jurors were returning from lunch. The jurors, the litigants, the witnesses—everyone had heard of the assassination. Some people were not ashamed to cry.

He shifted his gaze to Tim. "In such circumstances it occurred to me to recess for the weekend. It was a Friday . . . as today is. There were only two to three more hours in which to work. The jurors would be preoccupied with our national loss—how could they pay proper attention to testimony?

"My decision was that in spite of our grief, we must attend

to our work. Our democratic system had been grossly violated by the assassination. It was our duty to keep the system intact. It was my decision that the judicial system, to the extent that it was in my stewardship, the judicial system must not recess, must not pause.''

He looked at Tim very hard. Tim thought he saw the point. He had taken it upon himself to interrupt the judicial system, a progress to which the judge had given no pause even for the death of John Kennedy. Tim felt himself lose all emotion, he had closed off his ability to respond.

The judge continued to regard Tim. "There are moments in our lives, Mr. Holbrook, when it is *incumbent* upon us to preserve the *order* of things, the *necessary* order of things, no matter what our personal exigency. You made such a choice this morning when you failed to appear before this court. In the necessary order of things, I can think of nothing that takes precedence over the preservation of life.''

Harrelson cocked his head and folded his hands. "I have had grave suspicions about you and your choice of career. Those suspicions have not gone unexpressed. But you have relieved me greatly, Mr. Holbrook, of my troubledness. I kept the trial going on that Friday, you went to your patients today. I have no doubt as to your integrity and professionalism. Neither was easily come by, I can appreciate, by either you or by myself.''

Valerie stood suddenly. *"Judge* Harrelson—''

"I have heard you, Mrs. Holbrook. Now you will hear me." He looked at the attorneys. "Since this matter begs of and requires an immediate response from the court, an order will be entered along the following lines.'' He stopped. "The DSS assessment person recommended that custody be expedited to the father. That situation is already in effect.''

Both attorneys agreed.

"For a trial period of six months, the minor child Jason shall be transferred to the custody of Mr. Holbrook.''

Tim listened with a mixture of exultation and released anguish.

"The social worker is to continue to monitor the child's well-being. I'll have a report from the psychiatrist at that time, too. Visitation with the child's mother shall be on a daily basis, three Saturdays a month, I think, and Wednesday afternoons from school release time until seven.'' He looked

at Valerie. "Returned by seven on each of these occasions.
There is to be no overnight visitation. If Mr. Holbrook decides to provide you with the opportunity of additional visitation, that shall be at his discretion.

"The entire dispensation shall be reviewed by this court in
six months' time. I am entering it on the calendar today.
Gentlemen," he said to the attorneys, "you may place it on
your own calendars."

The judge began writing.

"What about contempt of court?" Valerie said.

The judge continued to write.

150

NAN HAD DIFFICULTY following the street directions through
Jamaica Plain that she had received over the telephone. The
area was green, affluent, the houses set back at the reaches of
driveways, no one on the sidewalks to help with directions.

Finally she drove up a smooth black driveway to a parking
circle. The house was of red brick and separated from its
neighbors by hedges nearly as tall as trees. An expensive
sedan and station wagon were parked near the house. In the
center of the circle, a sweating, white-haired gardener worked
in a large round area setting out both vegetables and flowers.
Nan recognized green peppers and marigolds, zinnias and
tomatoes, waiting in flats.

She turned off the engine and began to tremble. There was
a terrifying flood of adrenaline and her heart went tachy in
panic. She was flushed wth heat from the panic and she sat
still, trying to think and wish the panic away. It was a few
minutes past six.

The gardener stood up and came over. If Nan had been in
sufficient control, she would have driven away. He was a
large man and unshaven. His hands were dirty, the knees of
his khaki pants were wet with dirt, his shirt was dark with
sweat at the chest and armpits. He spoke to Nan with a quiet
regard that surprised her. "Are you looking for Dr. Start?"

"Yes."

He spoke solemnly. "I'm the shrink. We spoke on the phone. Dr. Krantz's referral?"

"Yes. Nan Lassitter." She did not move to open the door. He did not ask her to get out.

He looked back toward the circle. "I have a friend who says that gardening is his shrink. The trouble is, he's obsessive about it." He turned and stood with his hands in his pockets. "I don't mind talking out here if you want. I'd rather take some history inside, but . . ." He shrugged. He rubbed the stubble on his face and said, "When I moved here a couple of years ago, I stopped keeping myself like a doctor in an office. I don't shave every day. Funny thing is, I discovered, a lot of patients are relaxed by it. The doc's just a gardener."

Nan smiled slightly.

He looked at her directly and said, "You're in a panic. You wanted a woman doctor and Myrtle Krantz wasn't available and she recommended me. It's understandable that you would feel more secure working with a woman. Are you interested in gardening? Would you like to help plant? Chat while I do? Come into the office? It's an act of courage for you to come to see a man. An act of tremendous trust." He stopped.

Nan said, "I wish you would keep talking."

"All right. But I need some help from you."

"I still feel panicky . . . but not terrified. It was good of you to make time for me. The end of the day, the end of the week. I know what that means."

"I imagine what you most want to do is hide."

Nan bowed her head and silent tears flowed down her face.

151

NICHOLAS PRUDHOMME'S apartment was small, and It was still sunny at seven. One side of the living room was a clutter—a long worktable with books and papers stacked about. By contrast, neatness and order were pronouncedly evident near the television set, where there was a video cassette player and shelves of films.

Trina left Nick cooking. She carried a glass of wine with her and had a good look at the rest of the apartment. The bathroom was clean, the bedroom had the smell and look of recent vacuuming, clean sheets and pillowcases were drawn tight, wrinkleless, on the bed. For me? Trina thought. She smiled. Now she knew, sort of, what areas of Nick's life were ordered and presentable to her and what were his alone, ordered in some arcane way or a clutter. She resisted her inclination to look in his medicine chest for a profile of his doubts and needs and practicality.

Tim was both charged and exhausted. In his apartment Audrey was cooking for him and Jason. He sat with Jason and tried to sort out with him all the changes there would be in his life, things that might be unexpected in the changes from Valerie's world to Tim's. Jason stared so fixedly at Tim that he became fearful. He wasn't doing this right, helping Jason through the transition. "I guess I'm trying to tell you too much at once," Tim finally said.

Jason said, "This is where I want to be, Dad. With you." Then he leaned over and put his arms around his father.

Audrey was uneasy, almost tearful again, whether from happiness or sorrow she did not know. She washed and dried pots and pans and utensils as she used them. Tim and Jason were talking a few feet away from her, but it was another room and might have been another country. She was alone in the kitchen and the fear and sorrow were that her life with Tim was over. He had Jason. There was not that void for her to help fill anymore. She was not so needed and she recognized it.

She had wanted to leave Tim alone with Jason this evening. They were a family establishing itself, coming together after separations she knew she could not begin to understand.

She stopped. She had forgotten what she was cooking. Broccoli. That was the next thing. Jason adored it.

Audrey wiped her hair away from her brow, feeling the mixture of sorrow for herself and happiness for all three of them.

Tim stood in the doorway to the kitchen with his hand on Jason's shoulder.

"We've been talking," Tim said. "We sort of wish you'd stick with us. We both do."

Jason looked at Audrey, and she realized he expected her to say something. But she did not know what to say. She did not know what commitment she was being asked to make.

Trina was asleep by nine o'clock. She was asleep on Nick's couch, a Spencer Tracy–Katharine Hepburn comedy playing from a cassette, unfinished espresso and cognac on the coffee table beside her. She didn't know it, but she snored. Nick woke her when the movie was over.

"I just want to sleep," Trina said.

"Okay. Do you want to sleep here or do you want me to take you home?"

"I just want to sleep."

She closed her eyes and hunked herself together in the narrowness of the couch. Nick went to get a blanket to cover her. Then, instead of putting the blanket over her, he picked her up and carried her into his bedroom and placed her in his bed.

Trina awoke partway. "I should go home."

"Just sleep."

She closed her eyes again. She mumbled, "I shouldn't take your bed."

"Just sleep."

"All right."

Nick went back to the kitchen and cleaned up. He thought about watching television, a movie. Central in the clutter on his worktable were the photocopies of all his material on Nan Lassitter. He got himself more espresso and sat down with the photocopies and a fresh pad of paper.

152

BENNETT WAS ALREADY in the mayor's office when Selma arrived, summoned by telephone immediately after the Saturday morning nurses' meeting. Indeed, Bennett already had a copy of NSA's executive committee memorandum to the membership and was reviewing it with the mayor. The memorandum had been handed out less than two hours before at the meeting. Selma said, "How did you come by that?"

"My secretary stood at the doorway until she was handed one. Really, it speeds things along for us, Selma, now that we know what you want. We also know that the vote was three-seventeen to forty-five to go out, ten absent or abstaining."

"It was very strong to go out. We're together on this. You'll get formal notification of intent this afternoon. Ten-day notification."

The mayor said, "Selma, I really hope that can be avoided."

"I'll give you the sense of what was ratified," Selma said. "The City is to be informed that the nurses at Back Bay Metropolitan Hospital will leave duty after the daytime shift a week from Tuesday no matter what orders, sanctions, or penalties are imposed upon us in an attempt to prevent us from taking this action."

She looked at the mayor and Bennett. "We want to make certain you understand we're going out. We want to impress that on you. So that you and the City understand that as of three in the afternoon of that Tuesday, the patients are the City's responsibility. You either have to provide replacements for us or move the patients out. But we won't be there."

"Unless the City settles with you," Bennett said.

"That is a possibility much to be desired."

"The issues for which you seek redress," Bennett said, "are remarkably like most of the HOs' patient care issues."

"Not a coincidence. Nurses are by profession patient advocates." Selma turned to the mayor. "Shawn, my executive committee is a pretty savvy group.

"I don't doubt it, Selma."

"One of our members made an interesting observation. The members of NSA could prove to be the vanguard of other city unions. The other unions could all try to pick up something from this. Out of sympathy for us, of course. Cash in on what we expect to be public sympathy for us."

"Noted, Selma. And acknowledged."

Selma went on. "We had a cost analysis done. If Back Bay Met is shut down, it will cost the City approximately three dollars to treat patients at other facilities for every dollar it now spends at Back Bay Met."

"Actually, the figure is closer to three dollars and eighty cents," Bennett said. He placed the memorandum on the mayor's desk. "I've recommended to the mayor—and I will recommend to the council this afternoon—that emergency funding be provided and that the substance of these grievances be redressed. In turn, that would resolve most of the house officers' patient issues.''

"So quickly done?" Selma said.

The mayor tapped the pages on his desk. ''Bennett is surprisingly agreeable to this catalogue. Of course, he's not dealing with his own money anymore. I have to pry it loose. In any event, the City simply can't afford to have Back Bay Met shut down. That's economic reality.''

Bennett picked up the memorandum again. ''I want to go over this with you, Selma. I want to see what's absolute, what's negotiable, and what can be dropped.''

"Everything in there is covered by our contract with the City.''

"The cover is stretched in some places.''

"I'll go through it with you. What about the HOs? Aside from the patient issues.''

"The salary dispute will depend upon permanent funding. I don't know what may be provided. I'm not prepared to discuss other demands of theirs with you.''

The mayor said, ''A woman is raped and a hospital is served as a result. It defies my sense of consequence.''

"But not your sense of politics,'' Bennett said.

"Nor yours. Neither the nurses nor the house officers asked for this Medical Five floor to be reopened.''

"You did that?" Selma said to Bennett.

"Oh, Bennett hasn't missed an opportunity. It's almost as if he were getting his own way. Not the nurses, not the house officers, but Bennett.''

"Nonsense,'' Bennett said. ''The nurses have been the key. If the nurses didn't want it to happen this way, it wouldn't happen this way. Med Five is just part of an overall situation that requires correction.''

153

AUDREY WENT OUT to a Chinese restaurant with Tim and Jason. It was strangely difficult for Audrey. It was their celebration dinner—Tim's and Jason's—and she knew that because of Tim she was necessary to it, but she felt distanced from Tim. Tim's and Jason's joy in each other and their new circumstance was almost exclusive. It was as if only by talking about it and making plans could they ensure its reality.

Audrey felt like a little girl in the second grade, excluded from something the other kids were doing. *C'mon,* she said to herself, *you're a little bit older than Jason. Act it.* Her head would, but her emotions wouldn't. She wanted to be a part of what was going on between them. *You are,* she said, *and you aren't. You can never be an equal partner in that relationship.* Audrey was annoyed at herself, that her feelings were not on a level with the maturity of her thinking.

Her fortune cookie read, "You have good friends who will take care of you."

Jason would not read his. "It won't come true if I do."

Tim rolled his in a ball and placed it in an ashtray. "Whatever it says, it's already come true."

Audrey said, "May I?"

"Go ahead."

She unrolled and flattened the little strip of paper. She began to laugh. "It says, 'You have good friends who will take care of you.' "

Outside the restaurant Tim held Audrey and said, "This is the happiest time in my life." His arms closed her against him and he kissed her, and when he released her there was Jason with his arms raised toward her.

Tim and Jason walked home and Audrey drove home. She and Tim had to work the next day, but because it was Sunday, Tim had friends who would be home with their own children and who would have Jason over while Tim was at work. After work they were having a barbecue for Tim and Jason. Tim had asked Audrey to come along.

Still, driving home, Audrey felt a little anxious and more than a little despondent. It occurred to her then that a lot of these uncomfortable emotions might not be related to Tim and Jason at all.

Her telephone was ringing as she got to her door but stopped before she had the door open. It was a quarter to nine. Sometimes Tim called her to say good night. She got ready for bed and waited for the phone to ring again, but it did not. She got a book of art reproductions and turned on her bedside radio and leafed through the book and waited. She was ready to try to go to sleep when the phone finally rang again.

"Audrey, it's Debby. I thought you'd want me to call you. Betty Bowen died around eight o'clock. Everyone thinks it was peaceful."

Despondency raced through Audrey. She asked some necessary questions. After she hung up she went and got her datebook from her bag. A piece of paper was stuck to it. *You have good friends who will take care of you.*

Was I a good friend to Betty?

She looked up Betty's lawyer's number and called him so that he could call the daughter. Then Audrey sat still for several minutes before she got herself to dial Elin. Two losses in three days for Elin.

As Elin listened, Audrey had no suggestion of how Elin was responding. When she had no more to say there was silence. "Elin?"

"Will you hold on for a minute?" Audrey heard the receiver being placed on a table. She heard sounds of something being opened and closed. Then Elin was back. "You and I and Betty are a line—do you remember that? Three head nurses, one after the other, on Med Three."

"I know."

"Betty wrote me a letter last week. To be opened if she became comatose. She asked me to back you up if you needed it. About not offering additional support. You were a good friend, a good nurse to her, Audrey. I'm thankful to you for that. The letter goes on, some stuff about her and me, but then she starts writing about nursing, the profession, all her years in it. There's one thing she writes that I want you to

542   *Richard Frede*

hear. She says, 'In spite of the tribulations of the profession. In spite of the fact that these tribulations continue, we *are* successful at what we do.' ''

At four in the morning Selma Pushkin's telephone rang. Her husband answered it. "It's Bennett Chessoff," he said.

Selma took the phone. "What in God's name—"

"I need you and Molly and Elin here as soon as possible."

"Where's here?"

"My office. Call yourselves cabs. The City will pay for it."

At four in the morning Audrey awoke frightened and tearful. Again.

It was a kind of hell, waking at four in the morning and knowing that she was useless and had been useless and would be useless, and being chilly even though the night was warm, chilly with unspecified fear and hopelessness. She knew she would not get back to sleep no matter how tired she was and no matter how much she needed sleep. And she knew that no one could help her, not even herself—especially not herself, she was so alone.

There were all the losses—Betty, Mr. Emerson, Mr. Hines, the others—going back so many, many years, it seemed. They had all crowded into her dream and their shouting had awakened her. She could have screamed aloud, but she could not permit that, and so the scream stayed inside her, writhing to get out. The pain was so strong she began to cry.

In ten days the nurses would walk out. She wouldn't have to go to work. That gave her the only will she had at four in the morning to go to work that day. She was against the walkout, but she no longer wanted to be a nurse.

154

BENNETT HAD discarded his tie and jacket and opened his shirt, but his shirtsleeves remained buttoned. He must have shaved, Molly thought, gone off and used an electric razor sometime during the negotiations. Only his eyes appeared tired.

Scotty and Mozart had stubble on their faces. Their short-sleeved shirts had sweat stains. Their eyes, and Anita Rounds's, looked better than Bennett's. They were used to these hours.

Howard Sylvus sat apart as if he were no longer a participant but a spectator.

It was a little after five. The three nurses looked as if they had dressed rapidly in whatever was closest to hand. They each had an extra uniform at the hospital.

Molly saw that there was a calmness to Elin, or a resignation, that had not been there even that morning.

"What we have here," Bennett said, drawing coffee from a large electric maker, "is a standstill." He set out coffee before the three nurses and creamer and sugar. "ARI finds the proposed new contract unacceptable."

Anita said, "No sonar EKG. No CAT scan. No seat on the Director's Council."

"I've told them, you can have this, this, and this, you cannot have that, that, and that."

"We need the seat on the Director's Council," Scotty said.

"I can't grant that. I have specific instructions. The City will not countenance it."

"Our membership is willing to continue our action over it," Scotty said. "I recommended that we do so and they're backing me on it."

Selma said, "Why is the seat so important to you?"

"It's our protection for the future. For house officers in the future. So that the conditions we've had to work in for years, the deterioration . . . So that can't possibly go ignored and unrectified again. We'll stay out on that. The seat."

Bennett nodded. He looked at his watch. "Judge McIninch said he'd jail the three of you tomorrow morning."

"We'll go," Scotty said.

Bennett turned to Selma and Molly and Elin. "Actually, they've won an awful lot. City and Management will jointly stipulate compliance with the *regular and recurrently* clause. That goes for both the HOs and the nurses. There will be sufficient nurse staffing and ancillary personnel so that you will not have to function regularly and recurrently in capacities other than those of house officers and nurses."

"What about floor clerks?" Anita said.

"I'm sorry, Anita, no. You'll still have to do your own paperwork."

"That's the trouble. It's not *my* paperwork."

"Excuse me," Molly said. "Why are we here? Selma and Elin and I? What was so urgent?"

"I'd hate to see our house officers go to jail," Bennett said. "It would give the place a bad reputation." He sat down on his couch and spread his long arms out on its back. "As I said earlier today, quoting Michelle McCabe, you nurses are the key. Without your support the HOs are helpless. We'll simply have a replacement staff in here in a few weeks—"

"But the HOs have our support," Selma said.

"A new contract with significant concessions has been offered to the house officers. I got you in here to review it. NSA's leadership, ARI's leadership. You can discuss the new contract."

"He's trying to get you to call off your walkout," Scotty said.

"He's trying to get you to dump us," Mozart said.

"And he's right," Anita said. "Without your support, anything further we do is useless. Even going to jail."

Bennett picked up some typewritten pages from the coffee table. "This is the memorandum of the proposed new contract with the house officers. Your own issues are addressed throughout. I'd just like you to go through it, determine for yourselves if the house officers have any legitimate reasons to remain on strike. Will you do that?"

"Divide and conquer," Anita said.

"Negotiate and unite," Bennett said.

"Leave us alone for a while," Selma said. "The three of us."

155

WHEN THEY HAD each finished reading the proposed contract, they compared their notes.

"There's an increased staff all around," Selma said. "Aides, messengers, transport workers—even nurses."

"Increased staff of technicians," Elin said. "Funds for a

full-time hematology lab. Reequipment and expansion of the present unit. Scavenger systems in the ORs. And new autoclaves."

"Functional on-call rooms. Phones to be installed. Fresh bedding stocked in the closets," Molly said. They continued.

"Quite an accomplishment," Elin said.

"It's our doing," Molly said. "How come they got a ten percent increase in salary and we could only get seven?"

"We didn't go on strike," Selma said.

"Let's see what they're holding out for. It can't just be the seat on the Director's Council," Elin said.

"One-to-one nursing ratio on the ICUs," Scotty said. "More security staff, a patient care fund, the seat on the Director's Council."

"No one-to-one on the ICUs," Bennett said. "Even the nurses didn't ask for that."

Scotty looked at Selma, who said to Bennett, "It's desirable. But not critical."

Bennett said to the ARI group, "One-to-two has proven reliable. No one has ever been harmed by that staff ratio."

Anita said, "Sometimes that staff ratio hasn't been there. You've had to close beds."

"That will not happen with the increase in the nursing staff."

"Security?" Mozart said. "People *have* been harmed by insufficient security."

"We believe that problem can be addressed through a program of regular retraining and through restructuring the present security procedures. At any rate, there will be no increase in the security staff. The new funds the City is providing are for medical expenses only."

"That includes a salary increase of *ten* percent, I see," Selma said to Bennett.

"I thought you might want to discuss that."

"Parenthetically. The City told every city union, including NSA, that all increases were going to be rigidly held at seven percent."

"And so they have been."

"Except this one."

"I suggested to the mayor and to the council that ARI be given a seven percent increase. And that's what's been done.

546   Richard Frede

However, I pointed out that house officers work nights as
well as days. Because they work nights they could be given
an additional three percent differential paid monthly. That
comes to ten percent. Nurses are paid on an eight-hour basis.
When you work longer, you're compensated.''

"Part of the time," Selma said.

"The patient care fund," Anita said. "That's a medical
expense.''

"I forget that one," Elin said.

"Money to be administered by the house officers," Mozart
said. "For materials and equipment the hospital isn't providing that we feel the patients need.''

"There is no money in this budget for a patient care fund,"
Bennett said.

Scotty's voice was antagonistic. "We've brought up four
issues for discussion and you've ruled out three of them, just
ruled them out.''

"That is not my intention," Bennett said. "Really, you
don't seem to appreciate what I managed to do for you at City
Hall.''

Bennett was clearly irritated, Molly saw. It was not his
style. She wondered if the show of irritation was intentional.

Howard Sylvus spoke from his chair away from the others.
"I've been thinking about this one. May I make a suggestion?"

"Please," Bennett said.

"The following to be entered in the contract. Patient care
fund. Provision will be made for such a fund subject to
appropriations and availability.''

Bennett thought it over. "That's agreeable to me.''

But Mozart was irritated. "The way that's worded, it
grants us something we'll never get. Due to the qualifying
phrase.''

"I think," Bennett said, "it guarantees the possibility for
you.''

"It is not dismissed," Sylvus said. "It becomes part of the
contract. You only have to show availability.''

"All right," Scotty said. "We compromise on that. We
accept. Though God knows what we're accepting is nothing.
Now let's get to the seat on the Director's Council.''

"I have no choice but to be intransigent on that," Bennett
said. "The City will not allow it.''

Scotty looked at Anita and Mozart. He turned back to

Bennett. "I would like to tell you and the City what you can do—"

Molly said quickly, "It's a physical impossibility. You're a physician, you know that."

Scotty turned his anger on Molly. "You'd know more about the director and his abilities than I would."

"I don't think that was appropriate," Elin said.

"I'm sorry," Scotty said to Elin.

Anita stood up. "That's it, then."

Scotty stood and Mozart followed. "That's it," Scotty said.

Selma said, "Just hold on. We have a stake in this, too."

"Yes you do," Scotty said.

"Then let's have a few minutes alone together again."

Along with the CAT scan, the sonar EKG, the floor clerks, and the four other issues they had just discussed, there were several other items that Bennett, representing the City or himself, had turned down. "There might be tradeoffs in some of them," Selma said.

Elin looked straight at Molly. "Is Bennett playing games?"

"You just defended me. Now you're invading my privacy."

"I'm asking you as our psych expert."

"As your psych expert, I think he's being straight. I think Scotty's being straight, too. But you can aim at something so long that you get blurry. I learned that from the SWAT commander."

"Meaning?"

"Scotty and Anita and Mozart have thought about this so long, they've worked so hard, they're blurry from staring at it. They're dedicated, single-minded, and a little fanatic about the objective. The seat on the Director's Council. It's as if nothing else they went out for existed. And it's Bennett's turf."

"How badly do they want it?" Selma said. "Badly enough to go to jail?"

"Yes. They think they've filled otherwise. They think Bennett will have to give in. Sometime."

"Will he?" Selma said.

"It's not Bennett," Molly said. "It's the City. I believe him on that. The City has decided not to give in on it."

* * *

Alone for the moment in Bennett's office, Selma looked down at her colleagues waiting across Tremaine. She looked at her watch. Ten before seven. She picked up Bennett's phone and dialed the station on Med Seven. "Hi, Lenore, Selma. I'm delayed. Can you cover? . . . No, I don't know how long. I figure a couple of hours at most . . . No, Nan won't be in. Chambers is coming over from Pedi . . . Okay, thanks." Selma hung up, and as she looked down across the avenue the straight line of white along the curb broke and individual white uniforms began crossing the gray concourse. She heard people entering the room behind her. When the last of the nurses had come over and the avenue was vacant of pedestrians again, Selma turned back toward the room. Molly had seated Scotty, Anita, and Mozart on one side of Bennett's conference table and Selma took her seat between Elin and Molly on the other side. Bennett and Sylvus had not been asked to the meeting.

"I don't see how you're going to resolve this," Scotty said.

"I'm not going to resolve it," Selma said. "I'm going to give you the benefit of the discussion we've just had."

Anita said, "God save us from any more talking. I hope they put me in solitary."

Molly spoke evenly. "You've never been in prison."

Anita looked at Molly angrily. Selma interjected herself. She pushed the pages of the proposed contract across the table to Scotty. "You know that's a good contract. It benefits everyone. You, patients, nurses, the hospital, everyone. Speaking for myself, I can't recommend to our membership that we go out—not when you've been offered so much and turned it down. Molly?"

"I agree . . . Look, you guys, my opinion is, you've gotten so deep into this you're just being stubborn now."

"It's fair," Elin said. "The contract is entirely fair."

"It's meaningless," Scotty said. "Unless we want to get regularly and recurrently fucked again. We need that seat on the Director's Council. For protection. Your protection, too. You can see that."

Selma said, "Let me repeat something I said to the mayor earlier today. Excuse me, I mean yesterday. A nurse is, I think, *by duty* a patient advocate. That's why we voted to go out in support of you. Now the patient care issues have all been satisfied. I'm afraid you're back on your own on this seat thing."

The three nurses left.

In the outer office Bennett sat hunched on a radiator, eating a doughnut and dribbling crumbs on the carpet. He wiped his mouth. "What's going on in there?"

"I wouldn't be at liberty to say," Selma said, "even if I knew."

156

BY ELEVEN O'CLOCK most of the members of ARI were gathered on the grassy area behind the New Wing.

The ARI officers had gotten cleaned up and put on fresh clothes for their appearance before the minicam crews and the photographers. Bennett had been back to his apartment for a shower and a shave and a clean suit, his third in twenty-four hours.

Scotty McGettigan had a microphone and a public address system. He read the terms that City and Management had offered. He grinned and said that the ARI executive council had agreed to accept the terms.

The nurses on the floors learned of the change in the ARI situation when, through open windows, they saw the gathering below and then heard an abrupt and continuing cheer.

Down below the house officers were clapping and hugging and cheering. Bennett, standing to Scotty's side, was careful not to smile.

The house officers met with reporters and said they had won the world.

After that, Bennett made his own statement. "I want to thank the house officers for their reasonableness and willingness to negotiate. Concessions were made on both sides. The contract that has been approved is a constructive one.

"I should also like to thank the nurses, our nurses, for their care of the patients and for their patient care during this trying period. For the past several days our nurses *have been* Back

Bay Metropolitan Hospital.'' He paused for attention. ''Finally, I should like to thank our nurses for their participation in the dispute and their contribution to the deliberations.''

There were no nurses at the gathering. They were at work or away from the hospital on their own time.

157

WHEN, on Med Three, Audrey heard the cheering, she immediately recognized what it meant. She smiled. But only a few seconds later she felt profound sadness and anxiety again. She felt so terribly weak that she had to force her body down the corridor to the conference room. She shut the door and was alone.

She sat and put her head down on her arms on the table. She felt her body shake intermittently as if she were sobbing, but she knew she was not.

She was against the nurses' strike, but she had come to work because she had believed they would be striking in nine days and then she would be through all this for a while, perhaps rest and get to feeling stronger, perhaps not come back at all. But until the strike she would hang in because of her patients.

Now there would be no strike, no relief, and whatever decision she made about her career, her profession, she would have to make by herself—without the assistance of an enforced interruption.

She got up and found that her body was still weak. She went to the station and called Day and made an appointment for immediately after work.

Bennett located Molly in her office. He stood inside with the door closed. ''I'm going home to sleep,'' he said.

''Some of us need to sleep, too. But we have to work.''

''That's the difference between labor and management. Working tomorrow?''

''No.''

''I'm giving myself the day off. I'd like to spend it with you.''

"I don't know that I trust you, Bennett. Oh, I like you well enough, there's all kinds of attraction. But I don't know that I trust you. All that manipulation."

"We all manipulate each other—or try to. All the time. You know who told me that?"

"I think I did. I know I did."

"Then don't be so surprised. ARI tried to manipulate the City. In the end, NSA manipulated ARI."

"In the beginning, *you* manipulated ARI. You manipulated ARI into their walkout."

"I sped the process up. Maybe by a couple of years. It was time. The hospital needed it. And someone like Scotty doesn't head up ARI every year. We could have dinner in tonight. Or stay at your place."

"On the surface you're a good fellow to be with, Bennett. Most of the time, anyway. But my trust is seriously impaired." She sat back behind her desk. *"For Christ's sake,* Bennett! You fucked around with ARI, you fucked around with the hospital, with the patients, the mayor, the council, you fucked around with the City of Boston. And no one saw it.

"You did."

"Late. And only because of personal intimacy."

'Yes. Because I wasn't hiding it from you. I didn't draw you a battle plan either, granted. But I never manipulated you. NSA's second ranking member. I never misdirected you. I never did any of the things I could have done to try to influence NSA through you. I never elicited information from you. I didn't even ask you how that first strike vote went. That would have been natural for anyone else close to you. But I was scrupulous not to."

"I realized it and I appreciated it." He stood leaning against the wall behind him. Molly sat tipped back behind her desk. "I'm uneasy, Bennett. Maybe it will go away, maybe it won't."

"You can be suspicious of me—when you're representing NSA. Selma has been for years."

"Selma doesn't sleep with you."

"Molly, I'm tired."

"I am, too."

"I've got nothing else to say on my behalf."

Molly tipped forward, put her arms on her desk. "I'll tell you what I would like."

"All right."

"You fucking well better not tell me the City of Boston has instructed you not to."

"I think I can promise that."

"I want you to pick me up after work and drive me home so I can get some clothes. Then I want to drive to the Cape and find a place to stay. I want to walk on the beach tomorrow. I want to walk barefoot and feel the water and the sand. I want to smell the air, too."

"You have a rich fantasy life."

"You have no idea."

"I've been up a long time, Molly. I'm not going to have any time to sleep if I pick you up in two hours."

"You pick me up and I'll drive."

After a few minutes of each, Nan's emotions could not tolerate either sound or silence. She was home in her apartment and alone. She could not stand to be with people, either. She turned on the radio, tried different stations, different music, turned it off, sat in silence or went about, turned the radio on again, tried other stations, other music. She could not tolerate the sort of music or beat that she had heard at the Castle. Even the all-music formats were filled with romantic associations that reversed themselves and became unendurable. Silence was initially calming, then her heart would be tachy again and she would feel nausea from the rapidity, the adrenaline, and the images that stalked her mind. The images violated her by their presence, afterimages left by the three rapists, and there was nothing she could do about them.

The bastards were still *doing it* to her, but now they were raping her mind.

Dr. Start said none of this had to be. Not always. First a healing process had to take place.

She could not stand living with her anxiety.

Those three bastards still tortured her.

She thought of Dr. Start, Nicholas Prudhomme, Trina. First it helped, then it didn't help at all. They weren't helping her at all. She wasn't worth helping. They were pretending. She was enraged at them. No one *cared* about her.

See how alone I am? No one cares.

She felt sick from anxiety, tachycardia, the afterimages,

the three bastards stalking through her mind, and she could do nothing about them.

I cannot stand living this way.

She went to the bathroom, opened the medicine chest. There was the Librium Dr. Start had given her. Five-milligram capsules. Puny. Take one, two, or three up to four times a day. Slow the heartbeat, soothe the nerves, as they used to say. Some of her pharmacology had been idle for so long it was no longer precise. Nan couldn't remember the lethal dosage per pound of body weight for Librium. On the ICU she was used to dealing with Valium suicide attempts.

Her mind became practical. The practicality was soothing. Dr. Start would not have given her enough Librium for a lethal overdose. She looked over her stock of meds. There was Valium and Dalmane and Thorazine and others. Collected over the years and rarely used. Not even from month to month. Enough there to take her out, Nan saw.

It was a satisfying thought. Start and Prudhomme and Trina would realize how they'd abandoned her . . . *No! Davis and Casey and Squires would be the ones who would be satisfied!*

She opened the brownish plastic cylinder and poured the contents into her palm. Little yellow and pale blue capsules. She picked around her palm. Her fingers made her think of the beak of a slow chicken groundfeeding. She placed all but four capsules in the cylinder, returned the cylinder to the chest, and swallowed the other four.

She went to her bedroom and turned on the radio and lay down. She got part of the hourly newscast and heard Bennett Chessoff's voice. *". . . I should like to thank our nurses for their participation in the dispute and their contribution to the deliberations . . ."* Nan heard the applause and shouting. She could even recognize the voices of some house officers. She understood that the strike was over and that the nurses would not be going out.

She had to go back to work. To escape the panic. To escape the afterimages. To be *doing, caring,* forgetting about herself. She called Selma.

"I'm dubious," Selma said. "I'm glad to hear you, Nan, the way you sound."

"Let me try, Selma."

"Look, I've got the floor staffed for tomorrow. Amazing as that may seem."

"Let me come in anyway. Let me show you."

"I'd be awfully happy, Nan. I'd be so happy if you can hack it. You come in and try it. I've got an agency nurse coming in in your place. You'll supervise her, break her in. We'll see how you get on back here. It hasn't changed yet." Selma's voice softened. "I'm concerned about you and the rest of the staff. That's going to be hard for you."

"Yes. I know."

158

AUDREY FOUND Day restless, uncomfortable, often glancing at her watch, but attentive nonetheless. They talked about the walkout for a few minutes and about Day's recommendation that NSA go out. Then Audrey said, "I'm here to resign."

Day showed no surprise. "Anything specific?"

"Everything."

Day nodded "People dying. Laundry late. No one gives a fuck."

"That's about it."

"Whether you stay or go, you ought to talk to a shrink. What people like to ignore around here is, they're dealing with their own insides. Along with the patients, of course. About half the time they're dealing with their own insides inadequately. So they quit. It's a great loss. A lot of the best ones quit, resign." Day stood up behind her desk and massaged her lower back. "I don't want to see you go, Audrey. You're one of our best, one of our very best. You care." She sat down again.

Day looked oddly concentrated, Audrey thought. She was concerned by Day's care for her and touched. But she said, "When can I leave?"

Day smiled at Audrey. Audrey studied Day. There was something familiar about her posture and breathing. Audrey recognized it just as Day said, 'You'll have to excuse me now, I think I'm going to have a baby." She looked at her watch again. "Two minutes apart. Time to go to the hospital."

*   *   *

Dom sat on the side of his bed, alone in the room with Trina. "I've been here ten days. It's going to be bad leaving, bad."

"I know."

"I'm back together with myself."

"Yes."

"It hurts like a sonofabitch."

"I know it does, Dom."

"I've got to start all over again."

"It may be the most courageous thing you'll ever do."

"You hung in there with that crazy woman with the gun."

"I was doing my job. You don't have that opportunity. You've got to make it for yourself. That's tough, Dom. When you want to work and you've got to struggle for a job."

"Maybe I'll find another kind of work. I can dig ditches, fill in holes, spread tar, rake gravel . . ."

"Disappear again?"

"Is that disappearing again?"

"I don't know. After you've raked enough gravel, what do you do next? Try to find more or curl up inside yourself?"

Dom Volante put his head down. "I'd like to sing. I'd like to record. I don't mind singin' in clubs, the little joints. I'm embarrassed about askin', but I'd be glad to do it."

"What about an agent?"

"No one I could call."

"C'mon, Dom, don't *shit* me."

Dom looked up sharply. "It's been a *long* time, Trina. It's been three years."

"I can turn on the radio and hear you anytime."

"Not *anytime*."

"You gonna back out again, Dom?"

"No." He hung his head. "But what's the use? I struggle, they laugh. No one wants me."

"Where have I heard that before?"

Dom looked at Trina angrily. Then he said softly, "From me."

"Maybe it's your decision. Why do they play your records?"

"People make money off them. Not me anymore. People do."

"Records don't play themselves. People do." Trina stood up. "I'm on your side. The people who listen, I guess they are, too. I wish you were on your side."

Dom looked at Trina directly. "What you don't understand, Trina, is that's old stuff, they like it, but they don't like anything I can do now. Even the same thing. Lip syncs make more money with my records than me live.''

"That's hard to believe."

"It's true."

"When you leave here tomorrow, you going to rake gravel, disappear—what?''

"I'm going to have an overnight transformation into Caruso.''

"I'd prefer Volante. Caruso is scratchy. Jan Fox is coming down tomorrow. She's getting bumped from the intensive care unit. She'll be down about ten, I guess. I hope you'll stick around. She's very concerned about seeing you.''

"This isn't love," Molly had said, "it's tension."

"Oh Christ, what therapy," Bennett had said.

And then they had slept in Molly's bed till it was twilight and Molly had gotten them up to drive to the Cape. Bennett was too tired to stop and eat at a restaurant. Molly drove and then stopped and picked up delicatessen sandwiches and beer and a bottle of Scotch.

She drove with all the windows open. The night air was smooth and warm. Down near Plymouth, where Route 3 sidled within view of the ocean, the air had a primal smell, salty and invigorating and a little fetid. It was in darkness, anyway. A lighthouse whipped around in the darkness. It was way, way off.

She drove with great contentment. The night sea air of decay and resurgence invigorated her. She spoke to Bennett even though he was asleep in the passenger seat next to her, his large frame adapted like melted plastic to the bucket seat of his small sedan.

"It's temporary relief," Molly said. "In spite of all your efforts, it's only temporary relief, dear Bennett. You've got the hospital back to where it ought to have been four, five, *six* years ago. I looked at that budget. It can't even be maintained at that level.''

To her surprise, Bennett spoke. "You're right."

"I don't want to be depressing, but it's just going to start decaying again.''

"It is already," Bennett said. He was awake and glum.

"As soon as the new level is implemented, it's going to decay and regress.''

"Yes."

Molly looked for a sign that would show her she was near the bridge over the canal. "I suspect you're already plotting some new plot," she said.

"I hope so," he said. His continued glumness surprised her. "I hope so, but right now I'm tired, Molly." She thought he had gone back to sleep, but after a moment he said, "When the good fight has to be fought again—I mean *all out*—maybe the good guys will have a new attorney to help out. The one who said she wanted to have an impact on the system."

159

IT WAS FIVE-THIRTY in the morning. The air was scented, beginning to warm already. Nan pulled on full-length white pantyhose instead of the knee-length white stockings she normally would have worn as the weather turned warm. She stepped into her white, drawless shoes and then stretched herself into her white dress. She closed it and pulled it into place. She went into the bathroom and quickly combed her hair back into place with her fingers. Then she took two Librium. She put four more in her pocket.

Downstairs the street was quiet, the sky dark overhead, beginning to lighten and blue up in the distance over Boston.

Nan wanted to get to work so early that she would not run into any of the people who would be changing shifts, not even the very early ones. She checked to see that her doors were locked, the windows up. The air was warmer still and her skin was hot and prickly from anxiety, but she left her own window open only an inch and a half. She didn't think a hand could reach in through that space.

She was on the Mass. Pike in a minute. She was a good driver, but she was not comfortable with herself driving anymore. She had betrayed herself once ("No," Dr. Start had said, "you were betrayed by others"), she might again at any moment. She simply didn't trust herself with herself. The reason she was going to work. One reason. The other was to be useful. If the patients didn't reject her. If the doctors didn't reject her. Oh Jesus, the house officers. They caused her the greatest anxiety. *Fear*. Trevor Davis' colleagues.

Nan found herself maneuvering out of the way of other traffic when there was no need to do so. A truck horn almost made her scream. She had pulled over in front of a huge truck, not even knowing it was there, just to get out of the way of some fast-approaching but distant headlights in her rearview mirror. She was trembling badly by the time she was back in her proper lane and out of the semi's way.

The Pike seemed loud with noise signaling danger, though there was much less traffic than the minor amount she encountered when, usually, she came in half an hour later. Far ahead were the buildings of downtown Boston against the lightening sky.

Soon, from high up on the Pike, Nan saw at another far distance the dominating buildings of the hospital, a gray, sullen presence in this light. A refuge, she hoped, at the same time that it made her terribly fearful.

Nan slowed and checked and then moved into the exit lane. The Tremaine Avenue exit was coming up. She could still drive past it. She wanted to. She rolled her window all the way up, checked the locks on the doors again.

She turned off the Pike, then was held by the red light at the bottom of the ramp. She was stopped but, thank God, not boxed in. The thought of driving home in slow-moving traffic on Tremaine—boxed in when it stopped and helpless—gave her a surge of panic. Her heartbeat and her vision softened and she felt that she might lose consciousness. The light changed. Her breathing changed ever so slightly. She realized she could turn left and away from the hospital and go home. A horn immediately behind her frightened her terribly again when she thought there was no more energy for renewed fright. She turned toward the hospital.

She did not see the change from grimy storefronts to tenements and spilled garbage and derelict buildings. She did not see the trees in full green leaf. She barely slowed for intersections at red lights. The back of her neck was rubbed sore by the collar of her dress because she was looking around so much. She drove on, heart beating, fingers trembling, body perspiring. A teenage boy ran across in front of her and stopped and held his hands out at her. She accelerated into the wrong side of the street and kept going.

She drove under the elevated trolley. Two blocks later she was in the courtyard of the Old Building. She parked and sat in the car. Her body was still again, but waves of near unconsciousness passed through her brain and receded, wave after wave. Fear made it worse, increased the debilitating frequency of the waves.

She sat in the car, eyes closed. She opened her window. After a while the tachycardia slowed and lost its depth. The process reversed. The less the fear of passing out, the slower the heart rate, the slower the ventilations, the less mechanism for hyperventilation and a hypoxic loss of consciousness.

Nan saw that the very early people were starting to come in for the day shift. She got out of the car. She was very tired. Just moving brought on a little wave of light-headedness and panic. But she went up to work.

Day's baby was a nine-pound, eight-ounce girl. Audrey had stayed at the hospital until Jimbo arrived. Then she had gone home and called Tim. "When Day heard the weight, she said, 'I told you she was going to be an elephant.' "

"How about you?"

"I'm not an elephant—last I checked."

"You were down when you went home last night."

"Yeah."

"You shouldn't be. I mean, not about us."

"You've got so much—" Audrey heard herself saying and stopped.

There was some silence and then Tim said, "I hear you. But you're part of it."

"I told Day I was resigning. That's when she said she was going to have the baby."

"Interesting way of inducing productive contractions."

"You know what you're doing, Tim. That's part of the so much you've got."

"Are you excluding me now?"

"No . . . No, no . . ."

"It sounds like you're excluding yourself. From me. From Jason. From work."

Audrey's mind jumped. "I felt a little different. After Day had the baby."

"Catharsis?"

"I just felt a little different. I'm tired now, Tim. I've got to go to bed."

"I wish I were with you."

"Me, too. We will be. I just need to rest. Day said we don't know how to take care of our insides. Do you understand what she was saying?"

"Yes."

"I didn't feel so alone when she said that. Maybe that was what made me feel different. Maybe it wasn't the baby."

But Audrey did not go to bed immediately. She stayed up and drank half a bottle of white wine. She thought about not being alone in the misery of her profession. She thought about what Day had said about the good ones, the caring ones, people who shared that misery. And the need to do something about it and that something *could* be done about it. The sense of shared misery comforted Audrey a little.

She thought about not being alone because of Tim. And Jason, too. She took along her glass of wine and went and got out the framed poem, "To Whom It May Concern," from beneath her underwear. She had taken it down and not put it back up since Tim had been calling.

> *Well, I got through New Year's Eve without you,*
> *again,*
> *whoever you are, you sonofabitch,*
> *who wasn't with me again this year*
> *. . . Who are you?*

Audrey smiled. Well, you sonofabitch, now I know who you are.

She placed the poem on the table beside her bed.

Audrey awoke a few minutes before her clock radio would have been getting her up with music. She lay in the stillness. She had rested thoroughly. She could not remember the last time.

Because of what Day had said she did not feel so isolated. Because of Tim she did not feel so alone. She was committed to go to work today, anyway.

Barnitska had said if you love nursing enough, if you're good enough at it, you're going to have to leave it. Coralee had left and come back. Betty Bowen had never left it until retirement. Margaret Gaines had not left it in thirty-two years and had said sometimes she didn't know how any children— her patients—survived.

Audrey dressed. Going to work was a matter of courage, really.

How long might courage carry me? As long as Betty? As long as Barnitska?

When Audrey got to work—earlier than anyone this day, she thought—she saw Nan Lassitter in her car, head back, eyes closed, forehead glistening. Audrey went over. "You all right, Nan?"

Nan opened her eyes but did not move her head. "People coming in to work already?"

"Not people. Just me."

"I'm okay. Be in in a minute." She closed her eyes. Audrey moved away. She knew what had happened to Nan and did not want to intrude.

Tim was able to sleep until seven. He had the day off. He made breakfast for himself and Jason and then took Jason to school. The school was in Valerie's neighborhood. It was only a few days until the end of the school year. Tim assumed they would not make Jason transfer into a whole new school situation with only a few days left. He sat down with the principal and explained the situation. The principal was understanding and amenable to Jason's staying. "If you hadn't come in, we wouldn't even have known."

Tim was embarrassed as he took out an envelope. "It's an interim court order. To prevent Mrs. Holbrook from taking Jason out of school."

"We have to deal with this sort of situation more often . . . more often than is good for anyone. I don't like it at all, Mr. Holbrook, but we know how to handle it."

Tim explained about his working hours. "I understand you have an after school program."

"Yes."

I'd like to enroll Jason in it."

"See Mrs. Lawrence outside. She'll take care of it."

Tim stood up. "Thank you." He held out his hand.

The principal did not extend his hand. "You've got an

unusual occupation, Mr. Holbrook. For a man. I don't know any male nurses.''

"We're not a bad sort," Tim said. He kept his hand outstretched. "It's not dirty, really."

160

THERE WERE HOUSE officers *inside* the hospital. The ER was fully staffed. When Audrey got to Med Three, some HOs were already there an hour before rounds, going over charts, seeing some patients, catching up. They had a lot of talking to do with her and Coralee and they delayed report until Audrey insisted upon taking it.

The night nurse said to her, "Message for you. You're to call the Gold Coast between seven forty-five and eight. A Dr. Quinlan wants to talk to you."

Percy Stevens' specialist. Audrey felt a little queasy and chilled. She ignored it. She looked at her watch and ignored her feelings.

She took report and kept at her work, but a mental clock ran accurately and relentlessly and preoccupied her. Every so often she checked it against her watch. At a quarter to eight she called the Gold Coast and asked for Dr. Quinlan. He took a few minutes to come to the phone.

"Tried to get you Friday," he said flatly.

"I was off."

"I know. Wanted to speak to you about Percy Stevens."

"Yes."

"Well, I know you have a concerned interest in him."

"Yes."

"I think you can allow yourself a measure of relief, a measure of hope. His prognosis is turning positive."

Dr. Quinlan explained, but the details of the clinical picture and their changes, although indicative to Audrey, were also like some rapidly read sports scores. She was thinking of Percy and his boys. He would be so happy to be able to go further with them. *I'll visit him*, Audrey thought. She felt remarkably well, as if her course had changed along With Percy's.

She put only partial faith in that. But it felt good and she felt some renewal of energy and enthusiasm for her work as well. Some.

On Med Seven, Nan found herself going about her work and the patients warily, as if she might be rebuked at any moment, as if she deserved to be.

Nan left the agency nurse with a patient and came out into the corridor to go to another patient. She stopped, startled. Scotty McGettigan was at the station. When he saw Nan he immediately came toward her.

Nan felt like fleeing. Intellectually she knew that flight was irrational, but emotionally she was impelled to flee. She did not move. Her heart raced, went tachy, her breath was short, a terrible OD of adrenaline constricting her chest, her vision beginning to blur.

Scotty stood facing her, but not close. "You don't look well."

Nan closed her eyes briefly. It made the feeling of faintness worse.

"Sit down."

There was a padded bench for visitors. Nan sat. Scotty sat beside her, but not too near. "What's going on?" he said.

"It's nothing. I know what it is."

"What is it?"

She felt easier sitting. She felt easier hearing her own voice. The rush inside her body slowed. "What do you want?"

"The HOs asked me to see you. I would have come to see you anyway, but this is official, too. A group message."

Nan looked up. She hadn't realized her head had been bowed. "What is it?" She was very afraid.

"We're sorry. All of us. As individuals. We're outraged. We want to do anything we can to help you.'

"Keep Trevor Davis away from me."

"We tried to make his suspension a condition of our return but Dr. Geier had already suspended him. We're all on your side, Nan."

"There hasn't even been a trial yet," Nan said. It was a vacant statement and she did not understand why she made it.

"Considering what he did, Davis made some imprudent remarks to two house officers. They've been in touch with Trina and she put them in touch with your district attorney."

Nan nodded. It was probably a good thing, and she recognized that intellectually, but she had no emotional response.

"I don't know if you can trust any of us or anyone at all just now, Nan. But to the extent that you can trust us, we're all there to help you if we can. The men as well as the women."

"I don't need anything from you."

"You may discover little things now and then. I don't know. It's not like a physical procedure where we could help you . . . Nan, I've worked with rape victims in the ER. I'm not unfamiliar with what you're going through. I know a little bit about what's happening inside you. Maybe you'll find a way of letting us help you." He stood up. "We all understand a little bit about what has to be happening inside you. That's what makes Davis *incomprehensible*. Almost incomprehensible."

"Almost."

"There's a part of every human being I suppose we'd like to excise. Even from ourselves."

After Scotty left, Nan stood up. Her hand slipped into her pocket. Her fingers felt the four capsules of Librium there. Her emotions were not beating inside her so terribly anymore. She didn't take the capsules.

When Jan was brought back to Med Three, Audrey said, "We've got a new room for you."

"What about Chanda?"

"Chanda was sent home. She just needs bed rest for a while."

"Did she say anything about me?"

"She said to say good-bye and she hopes you get well." Audrey and the transportation worker transferred Jan to her bed.

"Dom?" Jan said.

"Dom's going to come see you in a few minutes. As soon as I get you settled. You did remarkably well in intensive care, Jan, considering the job you did on yourself. You scared the hell out of me, you know that? I didn't think we were going to be able to bring you back."

"I trusted you all."

"What do you mean?"

"I knew no matter what I did here, you'd take care of me."

"And you wouldn't have to go home, right?" Jan didn't answer. "You wouldn't have to be alone." Jan still didn't reply. "We're going to get you well, Jan. I want you to resign yourself to that. Getting well. Then you're going to have to go home. Nobody gets to stay here. Let's start out with that understanding." Jan did not reply. "Jan, I want you to acknowledge what I just said."

"Nobody gets to stay here. I understand."

"Because I don't think you understood that after you were brought in.

"Yes," Jan said weakly.

"No booze. I'll draw blood every hour, if I have to, to make sure. Do you understand that?"

"Yes."

"Something that occurred to me, your chart confirms. Everything that happened to you recently has been a matter of self-abuse. You didn't take your meds, you did take alcohol. The GI bleed, the arrest—those were self-inflicted. I don't know why you feel that way about yourself, but I understand you do. Trina wants you to start work with a psychiatrist while you're here."

"Is it compulsory?"

"No one can force you. But you talk it over with the doctor. She'll be up to see you this afternoon. I said I don't know why you feel about yourself the way you do. I want you to know I missed you. I'm real glad to have you back."

"Now you say that. First you say as soon as I get well I've got to go."

"Standard hospital practice."

Jan looked around the room. "My flowers. My beautiful flowers. Are they in the old room? Does someone else have them? Did you throw them out?"

"I saved them for you, Jan."

When Dom came in, Jan said, "You're all dressed up."

"Well, I'm dressed, anyway." He wore the slacks and open shirt he had had on when he was brought in. "I'm being discharged." Jan looked startled. "I just hung around till they brought you down. How were the accommodations upstairs?"

"Where are you going?"

"L.A. That's where I know the most people."

"Are you going to . . . Are you going to try again?"

"Yes."

Jan looked and sounded angry. "You're abandoning me."

"No, Jan. I'm being discharged."

"You're going back to them."

"Back to who?"

"*Everyone*. You're *abandoning* me!"

"No—"

"Get out!"

"Jan, for chrissake—"

"*Get out!*"

Dom went to the station and tried to explain to Audrey what had happened. But the conversation had made so little sense to him, it was difficult for him to report it.

"That's Jan," Audrey said. "I think that's Jan. She rejects and forces herself into isolation. There's never enough for her, always too little."

"But she did it herself."

"I'm glad *you're* rejoining the world, Dom."

Audrey looked around the floor as if she could see through its walls. *My world*, she thought. She felt as if she were rejoining it after a long absence. Something very odd was happening and very quickly.

A transportation worker arrived with the wheelchair to take Dom downstairs. "It's damn silly," Dom said, "having to ride in a wheelchair." He waved his hand, brushing aside his own words. "I know, it's the rules." He shook hands with Audrey and the transportation worker wheeled him away. Amazingly, an elevator arrived within the minute and the corridor was empty.

Audrey was trying to deal with her own amazement. *My world*, she thought again. *It's horrid and sometimes I make it less horrid. Sometimes it's okay. My world. That's the way it is.*

She felt a part of it again and she could not explain it to herself. She did not think of Jan's return.

Audrey did think of Betty, of Betty's twenty-seven years on the floor, all the good work and hard work she had done in that time. *I've inherited the floor from Betty. To keep it going.* She had a sense of Betty's being with her, if only in her thoughts. Barnitska was there, too, working terribly hard, charged with intensity, fading, like paper curling and fading to smoke.

Audrey kept looking about the floor, rediscovering it and that she was part of it.

There was, of couse, everything that was wrong with it.

In her mind Betty said, *You're not helpless. You can do something about it. You always do.*

She found that Coralee was standing next to her. Audrey placed her arm around Coralee and hugged her tightly, shoulder against shoulder.

161

ON MED SEVEN lunch had been delivered and there were a few minutes of quiet. Selma was off the floor momentarily. Nan was having a container of coffee with the agency nurse. The agency nurse had proven to be a good and willing worker— and bright, quick to implement the instructions she was given. She was older, maybe even sixty, Nan thought. They were talking about the house officers' walkout.

"It was surprising," the nurse said. "The nurses here voting to support the HOs, voting to go out."

"I know," Nan said.

"You're the nurse who got raped, aren't you?" the nurse said.

Nan was all right until Selma got back on the floor. Then the anxiety became acute. She knew she was going to lose consciousness. Her body and mind were in a panic. Her heart was struggling powerfully—*too powerfully*—like something caged that would beat its way out. Her vision was blurring. Nan went to the nearest available bed, where a patient had been released that morning. The patient in the other bed was eating lunch. "Pretty good today," the patient said. Nan went to the other bed. Everything became white and pale like the overexposed color film she had once brought back from the Caribbean. She did not hear the patient scream as she collapsed.

She was lying on the floor, her eyes open and unblinking, when Selma knelt by her. Selma spoke to her. The eyes did not blink, the body was rigid.

* * *

Nan found herself staring up at Selma. She was lying on a bed. She could hear the patient in the other bed whimpering. The agency nurse was trying to comfort the other patient.

"Do you know your name?" Selma said.

"I'm oriented, Selma."

"What's your name?"

"I know what happened. I'm okay."

"What's your name?"

"Nan Lassitter.'"

"What day is it?"

"Monday. This is Med Seven. I had an anxiety attack. I'm okay, Selma."

"You gave me an anxiety attack."

Nan felt her heart still racing, her abdomen tight and slightly nauseated. Selma was wrapping the cuff of a blood pressure machine around her arm. Nan tried to sit up, but Selma forced her back. "Just lie still." Selma placed the stethoscope and pumped up the machine.

"What is it?" Nan said.

"One-seventy over one-ten." She took the pressure on the other side.

"What is it?"

"Same."

Two HOs came in, one with an oxygen cylinder, and placed the oxygen mask over her face. They took some history and examined her.

"It's not a rhythm that's going to take charge," the HO said to Nan.

They kept up the oxygen for fifteen minutes and watched her and took signs and talked to her. They moved her to another room. She had the room to herself. She wanted to get up. Selma brought her fifteen milligrams of Valium. After a while Nan's heart slowed and she rested. Then she slept, an awful, fitful sleep. When she awoke, Selma took signs and gave her another fifteen milligrams of Valium. "You're exhausted," Selma said. "In your head, in your body."

"It's anxiety."

"No kidding." Selma had a book.

Nan looked at her watch. "You're off."

Selma sat and opened her book. "I'm going to stay with you awhile. Pass out on me? People will think I overwork you."

* * *

Everything was pale. It was the light in the room, not her vision. Someone was outside talking with Selma. A man.

Dr. Start came in and turned on the overhead light. He wore a suit and tie and was freshly shaven. "Hello there," he said. He pulled a chair to the bedside and sat down. "How're you feeling?"

"Tired."

Selma came in with the BP machine and wrapped Nan's arm. She listened with the stethoscope and watched the column of mercury. She dropped the stethoscope and pulled the Velcro apart. "One-thirty over ninety."

"It went up when you came in," Nan said to Dr. Start. "I could feel it. My heart rate."

"Like this afternoon?"

"No. A little. That was intense."

"Describe it, Nan."

"I'm going home," Selma said.

"Thank you," Dr. Start said to her.

"Thanks for staying with me."

"It was an opportunity I could've done without."

Nan described what had happened. When she was through Dr. Start said, "I'd like to move you over to Beth Israel. I'd like you to get some professional rest for a few days. I'll see you there as well. What do you say?"

"Going to a hospital? I mean, as a patient?"

"You are a patient for the time being, Nan. I want you taken care of for a few days."

Nan looked down. "I wouldn't want . . . any male doctors. Interns, residents . . ."

"None of that. I have a colleague over there, Joan Cunningham. I've already spoken to her. She'll supervise your stay. I'll get in to see you about six each afternoon."

"I don't want to go. I'm afraid."

"I know. A new environment, unfamiliar. Anywhere is going to be a little scary to you right now, Nan. Even Med Seven. I have an idea the BI won't be so scary once you get there."

"All right."

"I'm going to the station and call over there. Why don't you get dressed?" He closed the door behind him.

* * *

When Dr. Start came back Nan was in her white dress. She looked at the bed and said, "I got out of it, I got dressed. And then I started to straighten the bed for the patient."

Dr. Start smiled. "Dr. Cunningham will meet you at Admitting over at the BI and I'll be along after you're settled."

"Aren't you going to take me over?"

"They'll run you over in a rig. What is it?"

"I'm scared. The rig. It's all closed in. The EMTs, paramedics, whatever—I'll be alone with them."

"You'll be riding with a female EMT. I saw to that. All right? Are you having that panicky feeling?"

"No. Yes. A little." She sat on the side of the bed. She realized that Dr. Start was studying her. "It's okay," she said.

"Are you feeling light-headed?"

"No."

"Transportation will be up with a wheelchair soon."

"You know how to get things done here."

He smiled. "Yes. You rely on the nurses. I did my internship here in fifty-three. That's the first thing I learned."

A uniformed nurse in a wheelchair, everyone staring at her. Nan couldn't endure the HOs' looking at her, not even other nurses. It was an effort of will to remain seated. Dr. Start was beside her. She remained seated.

I have to come back, Nan thought. *Pursue those animals. I will not give up. I will not let the legal system beat me down. I have to come back. I know what's happening. I'll be all right.*

Dr. Start accompanied her to the ambulance.

162

THE PROGRAM that was to rehabilitate Back Bay Metropolitan Hospital was a paper one. It began with signatures on a document. This caused the creation of a number of protocols. Eventually there were the most important pieces of paper: checks. The checks were transformed into increased staffing, sufficient and operative equipment, and even the reopening of

Med Five. But all of this took place after the senior members of ARI had moved on to private practice. In the meantime the rehabilitation proceeded invisibly, its only manifestation in the movement of paper from one office to another.

The week was ending, the week the house officers had come back. Both Audrey and Tim had Saturday and Sunday off. They were going to take Jason to a wild animal farm in New Hampshire and then drive to Maine and find a place on the coast to spend the afternoon and stay through Sunday.

Audrey went down the enclosed stairs from the elevated trolley to Tremaine Avenue. She was not alone this morning. Several other members of the staff had gotten off when she did.

In fact, it occurred to her, she was not alone at all. But she was not about to ascribe the diminished tension and despondency simply to the presence of Tim in her life. Not after the day after day and month after month of what she had been through. And she was not through it yet. She wasn't fooling herself about that.

It was midmorning and Captain Malamet was in a wheelchair, but dressed. "Going home?" Audrey said.

"Not exactly."

"Figure of speech," Audrey said.

"Mrs. Malamet has a negative attitude toward my coming home."

"What about your lady friend? Can you stay with her?"

"She invited me to. But I don't want to be taken care of. I feel old."

"You'll get over that. When you occupy yourself. You're going to have the cath done—"

"In a couple of weeks. At Mass. General."

"Good teams there."

The transportation worker stood behind the chair. Captain Malamet held out his hand. "Thanks for taking care of me. Thanks for caring."

Elin was finishing grand rounds. It was late morning. Some of the patients she had seen had been original patients of hers. They were doing well. A couple of them were going home. She reviewed some charts in her office, patients she had seen during the week. They were all doing well under her supervision. She thought of Betty. In spite of everything, Elin thought, we *are* successful at what we do.

The afternoon was hot and bright, the very sort of day Viola had imagined when she had thought of the wooden sailing ship becalmed in the South Seas, the hot white beaches, the green waters.

Viola was coming to work at quarter of three now. Margaret Gaines had made her the new charge nurse for the second shift on Children's Seven. She crossed the cobblestone courtyard of the Old Building to the doors of the wing that contained the pedi walk-in and the GYN, Maternity, and Children's floors.

A very silly looking man was holding a door open as a transportation worker rolled a lady in a wheelchair out. The lady held a baby in her arms and was accompanied by a couple of nurses. She was smiling. The man was so silly-looking because of *his* smile. His face could barely stretch enough to accommodate the dimensions of his smile.

Then Viola saw that the lady in the wheelchair was Day O'Meara and she realized that the man holding the door must be Jimbo.

Viola experienced an abrupt thrill, a sense of the vitality of the hospital, of its care, its readiness, the hope it offered.

But it was upstairs on Children's Seven that she experienced the hospital in its wholeness.

She stood in Jamaal's little room and watched him look up at her—little brown body, white diaper, white socks, baseball cap—and smile and breathe without a ventilator, fifteen and twenty minutes at a time now. The lungs were growing stronger, developing, and the weight gain and bone growth continued, and Jamaal was breathing without a ventilator.

Glossary

ADA	assistant district attorney
ARI	Association of Residents and Interns
BID	twice a day
BP	blood pressure
cath, cardiac cath	a procedure in which a catheter is introduced into chambers of the heart in order to measure pressures within and without
catheter	a slender, flexible tube that may be inserted into a vein or body cavity
CBC	complete blood count
CCU	cardiac care unit
C-Med	Communications-Medical; a communications system originating in the police department for ordering medical assistance by EMTs and paramedics throughout the city
code, "call the code"	signal a cardiac or respiratory arrest
CPR	cardiopulmonary resuscitation
crash cart	a large compartment of drawers on wheels containing medicines, instruments, and other supplies for countering an arrest
CVP	central venous pressure
defibrillator	a machine for producing electroshock in order to stimulate activity in an arrested heart or to establish a regular rhythm in a quivering heart
DC	discontinue
DIC	disseminating intravascular coagulation; failure of the blood's clotting mechanism

DNR   physician's order: do not resuscitate
DT   delirium tremens; a delirium accompanied by physical and mental distress that is a psychosis produced by alcohol poisoning; also used as a verb to describe someone experiencing the condition
DVT   deep vein thrombosis; blockage caused by a blood clot
EEG   electroencephalograph; a machine that records electrical activity in the brain
EKG   electrocardiograph, electrocardiogram; a machine that monitors and records electrical activity across the heart; the readout from such a machine
EMT   emergency medical technician
ER   emergency room
ETOH   literally, ethyl alcohol, but used to signal the presence of alcohol in a patient; "booze on board"
GI   gastrointestinal
HO   house officer; either an intern or a resident
ICU   intensive care unit
intubate   to introduce an endotrachial tube through the mouth or nostril and into the lungs in order to provide oxygen and respiration from a ventilator or into the stomach to empty its contents
IV   intravenous
IVAC   a company name used to identify its own product and similar products of other companies, specifically, a continuous infusion pump; a machine that regulates and delivers liquid medicines intravenously
LPN   licensed practical nurse; "elpan"
MAT   maternity, as in Maternity Floor
med   a medication or medicine
Med   a medical floor as opposed to surgical
MI   myocardial infarction; coronary thrombosis

mic.	microgram
neonatal	newborn; special reference to premature
NPO	nothing by mouth
NSA	Nursing Services Alliance
O_2	oxygen
OBGYN	obstetrics and gynecology
OR	operating room
paramedic	a medical technician more highly trained than an EMT and authorized to conduct more sophisticated therapies and procedures
PCP	a hallucinogenic drug; "angel dust"
pen	penicillin
piggyback	to add medication by introducing it into a line already delivering another medication
PO	by mouth
PRN	a physician's order: as needed; at the nurse's discretion
PT	as used here, physical therapy; "chest PT"
SICU	surgical intensive care unit
stat	immediately
SWAT	a police unit that employs special weapons and tactics
thrombosis	a clotting of blood; a complete or partial blockage of a blood vessel or chamber of the heart by a clot of blood
unit	short for a unit of blood ("a unit"); short for an ICU or SICU ("the unit")
vent, ventilator	a machine that provides oxygen and respiration by means of a tube extended into the lungs
VF	ventricular fibrillation; wild or uncontrolled contractions of either of the lower chambers of the heart

About the Author

Richard Frede is the author of more than ten novels
including the best-selling saga *The Interns*. He lives
in Peterborough, New Hampshire, with his two sons.